P9-EMH-604

Shirley

DISCARD

The Whisper of

PEACHTREE PUBLISHERS, LTD.

he River

Ferrol Sams

Published by
PEACHTREE PUBLISHERS LIMITED
494 Armour Circle, N. E., Atlanta, Georgia 30324
Copyright©1984 Ferrol Sams, Text
Copyright©1984 William D. Cawthorne, Art

Manufactured in the United States of America

First edition

"How Many Biscuits Can You Eat"
By John Bach
(c) Copyright 1938 by Duchess Music Corporation.
Rights Administered by MCA Music, A Division of MCA Inc.
New York, NY Copyright renewed.
Used by permission. All rights reserved.

Excerpts from "God's World" and sonnets
from COLLECTED POEMS, Harper & Row.
Copyright 1917, 1923, 1931, 1945, 1951,
1958 by Edna St. Vincent Millay and
Norma Millay Ellis.

"The Thousandth Man" copyright 1910 by
Rudyard Kipling, from RUDYARD KIPLING'S
VERSE, DEFINITIVE EDITION. Reprinted by
permission of the National Trust and Doubleday
& Company, Inc.

"Autumn Sonnet 24" from THE GREEN LEAF:
THE COLLECTED POEMS OF ROBERT NATHAN,
Alfred A. Knopf Inc. Copyright 1950 by
Robert Nathan. Reprinted by permission.

Excerpt from "Invictus" by William Ernest Henley
reprinted from ANTHOLOGY FOR THE ENJOYMENT
OF POETRY, Charles Scribner's Sons, 1939.

Library of Congress Cataloging in Publication Data

Sams, Ferrol, 1922-
    The whisper of the river.
      I. Title
PS3569.A46656W45 1984 813' .54 84-42777
ISBN 0-931948-60-6

To
Helen

Also by Ferrol Sams:

Run with the Horsemen

The Whisper of the River

it was wood and it was white, and it was balanced like a box on upturned native stones. Its back snuggled close into the brow of a little hill, and the front, because it was level and true, stood several steps above the ground. It had no underpinning; roaming dogs and wind could course freely under the floor and around the supporting pillars. The powdery soil beneath it was pocked with doodle craters, inviting depressions that were inviolate and undisturbed because they were never seen except by children already arrayed in Sunday finery.

The building stood in a grove of red oak and hickory nut trees, and the yard around it was hoed free of weeds and then swept clean with dogwood brooms. Its windows, tall and narrow, were filled with squares of handmade glass. The irregularity of each clear pane gave a slight prism to reflected light and produced a mirrored mosaic that was mismatched and undulating. The steeple had no ornamental frills but was proportioned well to the size of the building, and it housed an ancient iron bell that compensated in clanging volume for its lack of timbre and tone. It was a one-room building, but should anyone think it crude or spartan, let it be quickly known that this was the House of the Living God.

It had been erected before The War as soon as the scattered community of settlers had cleared their lands and built their homes. It was fashioned of offerings from its members — great oaken sills from virgin forests, knot-free boards sawed from the hearts of tall, straight pines, square nails from a merchant so fat he wheezed, and gallons of lead paint from a planter too old to work with his hands. That was in the dim, distant days before people in the area were prosperous enough to own slaves or hire carpenters. It was erected by the strain and sweat of farmers and their sons who had felled the forests of Brewton County, Georgia, and turned its fields to the face of the sun. Their hands were sure, their hearts were pure, and they built the church as a place of worship. It stood there forever after in witness that the prayer of their hands was good.

The cemetery behind it was a thicket of unmatching tombstones confined by wrought iron spears to prevent their spreading over into Mr. Horace Snead's cotton patch. The gravel walks were mossed over just enough to mute footfalls. Giant cedar trees, older than the church, shaded a corner outside the rusted fence and dropped their needles on mysterious graves that entombed long-forgotten slaves. Those mute mounds were marked with sea shells embedded in concrete but lacked any names. On a hot day, the pungent fragrance of the cedars mingled with the faint cat smell from ancient boxwoods in the MacLean lot and brought visions of dried spinsters who preserved in penury the house of their father and fed fresh warm milk to their pets. The graveyard at Peabody Baptist Church was the quietest place in the whole wide world.

Perusal of its dates and names manifested that God will provide and He will nurture His children. Everyone in Peabody slept there eventually, and folk for miles around knew their histories and their kin. The church had stood through The War, Reconstruction, the World War, and even now gave no sign of being conquered by the Depression. The graveyard was testimony to any sensitive person that farther along we'll know more about it; farther along we'll understand why.

There were probably some people who thought themselves indifferent to that church, but they all wanted it there. It gave a feeling of security and it guaranteed succession. Even the most outspoken cynic would have been uncomfortable and filled with foreboding had it vanished. It was needed right there, where it was, in the quietly supervising grove at the heart of Peabody, Georgia. The church was hope and assurance; it was challenge; it was judgment. It was also comfort and benediction. The area would have been desolate indeed without it.

* * * *

2

It was imperative that one be Saved. By the end of high school every member of any graduating class would have acclaimed this verity. The boy, of course, had known it forever. In his culture, life eternal was assured. It was a given. The only question was whether it would be spent in the fires of Hell or the blissful security of Heaven. Belief in the Lord Jesus Christ guaranteed one the bucolic freedom of the latter as opposed to the packed and crowded tortures of the former. Everyone believed. No one was fool enough to put any desire ahead of being Saved.

It was just as important to be Raised Right. The child who had been Raised Right was not only Saved but had spent a large part of his formative years in the House of the Lord. Attendance at piano recitals did not count, but everything else did. From Sunbeams through BYPU, from Sunday school to prayer meeting, from Those Attending Preaching to Those With Prepared Lessons, everything was counted. So was everybody. In the midst of all this scorekeeping, the concept of being saved by grace was a nebulous and adult bit of foolishness not to be contemplated with anything approaching the fervor accorded perfect attendance. A pin with added yearly bars swinging like a sandwich sign on an adolescent chest proclaimed indisputably to the world that its wearer had been Raised Right. A place called Nashville was the source of the Sunday school literature, but the more highly anointed preachers of the day came from a mystic place called Louisville. Elders may have thought that the seat of the Southern Baptist Convention was in Nashville, but to any Raised Right child, "Seminary at Louisville" had exactly the same ring as "Temple at Jerusalem." Methodists probably could be Saved, but there was a question whether any of them really had been Raised Right.

The boy from earliest memory had spent every Sunday morning bathed and slicked into his best clothes with the admonition not to get dirty before Sunday school. Raised Right children wore suits and neckties which produced a stiff-legged discomfort that lasted well into adulthood. These children also regarded Sunday afternoons as periods of tedium, since fishing, hunting, and attendance at movies were undeniable violations of the holiness of the Sabbath and consequently were forbidden. There was in addition the subliminal impression that one might go to Hell for failure to wash one's

3

hands before eating, and one certainly never forgot to say the blessing. Even the simplest of joys were tempered with piety. Guilt was established early as spicy seasoning for pleasure, and the boy's composure was preserved only by the conviction that God could not see under the covers and most likely not through wood.

His mother carried him to more church-related functions than most children dreamed existed, but it was not because he was her favorite child. He had three sisters with whom he furiously fussed and fought at every opportunity, and it was much easier for the mother to transport the solitary stimulus of all that friction than to dress three little girls and carry them. Besides, there was no telling what devilment that boy might get into when left unattended.

"Separate them, Vera," the grandmother pleaded. "For the Lord's sake, and for mine, separate them."

The boy at an early age, wide-eyed and attentive, sat through prayer meetings, missionary meetings, Bible study courses, Flint River district rallies, and county-wide WMU conferences. He listened with analytical attention to everything. He believed most of it. As soon as he could, he read the Bible daily and he prayed a lot. He knew that in the New Testament people were exhorted to pray unceasingly, a requirement he regarded as excessive, perhaps even a little ridiculous. He struggled manfully with it, however, and did the best he could. He prayed a whole lot.

While very young, he became convinced that he was smarter than Adam. He discovered that either he could fool the Lord or else the Lord was not really watching all the time. Otherwise, He would have been compelled to smite the boy both hip and thigh on several occasions. The boy was careful to explain things in little prayerful asides and felt that he was a very favored person in the eyes of the Lord. To get right down to it and tell the truth, the Lord was a little easier to fool than the boy's mother.

John Mortimer Folds probably saved the boy from being a preacher or maturing into "a life of full-time Christian Service," the latter being a confusing condition the boy thought reserved in all likelihood for people not quite good enough to be preachers. John

4

Mortimer was an older cousin. He lived in Atlanta and was brought every Sunday afternoon to visit the grandparents. Sometimes they came on Saturday and spent the night. Everyone knew that Atlanta was huge and wicked, full of movie theaters and other flesh pots. John Mortimer was regarded, consequently, as something of a parolee from Sodom and Gomorrah, protected only by family connections on his mother's side from the fire and brimstone that were sure to engulf, sooner or later, that sinful city of Atlanta. He swaggered around, spoke aggressively of things undreamt by his country cousins, and was an unsolicited but memorable mentor for the boy.

John Mortimer once herded a gaggle of younger cousins behind a large crepe myrtle bush and persuaded them all to drop their pants. The crowd spent an hilarious interlude skinning back their penises, arranging dried crowder peas around the glans, and then holding them in place with the replaced foreskin. The undisputed champion with the lumpiest result was John Mortimer. The boy tried to look up in the Bible whether or not the group had been sinning. He could find no reference whatever to crowder peas, and research into foreskins led him from Abraham to a long drawn-out dispute between Peter and Paul that was boring.

John Mortimer assured him they had done nothing wrong, and the boy decided there was no scriptural reference to it because it was apparent to anyone who could read that Jews were not equipped to play with crowder peas. His guilt had almost dissipated when he chanced to think at bedtime that just such activity might have precipitated that covenant between God and Abraham in the first place. He leaped in horror from his bed, knelt, and said his prayers for the second time that evening. He promised God that if he might be spared, he would never play with crowder peas again the longest day he lived. As added expiation, he vowed to abandon the Story Book Bible and read the Real Bible from beginning to end.

John Mortimer's aspiration to be the leader in his generation of cousins was impaired by his considerable reputation for mendacity. He was the son of a domineering mother who was overly ambitious for him and covertly contemptuous of her obstinate and phlegmatic mate. She unleashed on John Mortimer a great deal of her frustration as she strove to mold him to her will. Confusingly her will changed often, and her only begotten son was expected one month to be a scholar, the next a violinist, the next an orator, and so on. He lied to please her and he lied to placate her, and nothing unleashed her fury more than to catch him lying. She would beat him for lying and yell, "John Mortimer Folds, if you don't tell me the truth, I'm going to whip you to within an inch of your life."

When he complied and told her the truth, the whipping he then got would be worse than the one he had originally received for lying. He became inured to whippings, shrugging them off as part of his lot in life, and continued lying. Occasionally his baffled mother hung him by his clothes on the back of the kitchen door for an hour and whipped him if he kicked. Once she tied him in a sack with only his head protruding and suspended him from a hook in the ceiling, but still he needed whipping. It was in the days before old age pensions and the resultant rise to power of the self-perpetuating Welfare Department, and no one had ever heard of child abuse. There were frequent references by John Mortimer's mother to "Bring up a child in the way he should go." It was apparent to the cousins that being Raised Right was a more painful process for some than for others.

John Mortimer had told the boy there was no Santa Claus and unhappily had been proven correct by the passage of time; so he never became completely incredible. When he came down from Atlanta, however, and informed his younger, more innocent cousin in graphic gutter language how babies were made, he went too far. The boy called him a liar and with prim righteousness asserted that his parents would never do a vulgar thing like that. John Mortimer resented being called a liar by a squirt who came barely to his shoulder and persisted in his enlightening stance, even proclaiming that his mother had told him so. The boy defied him by answering, "I don't believe you; I'm going to ask your mother."

John Mortimer weakened his position by quickly retorting, "You come back here! She don't know nothing about it!"

The boy, bolstered by this reneging, proceeded to instruct John Mortimer that babies were sent through God by a process called conceiving, which was a purely feminine function. He went and got the Bible to prove it. "Just listen to this: 'And when the Lord saw that Leah was hated, He opened her womb; but Rachel was barren. And Leah conceived and bare a son, and she called his name Reuben; for,

6

she said, surely the Lord hath looked upon my affliction; now therefore my husband will love me. And she conceived again, and bare a son....' You see? The man doesn't have a thing to do with it."

John Mortimer, less precocious than his younger cousin, disliked to read and was intimidated by all books, especially the Bible. In the abandon of anger, however, he yelled, "Read on about all that going in unto and laying with! They don't come out and call it that, but they're talking about fucking right there in the Bible! You so smart, you don't even recognize it when you read about it!"

The boy read on, emphasizing the word *conceive* and stumbling through an attempt to explain the transitive and intransitive differences between *lie* and *lay*. His sure air of virtue goaded John Mortimer into shouting, "I don't care what you say! The only reason your mama and daddy had so many chillun is they're fucking every night! My folks only had me and that's cause they don't fuck as much as yours! Yaa, yaa, yaa!"

This so infuriated the boy that he passed the first lick. Whenever he and John Mortimer were alone, it was certain they would fight, and John Mortimer usually put a drubbing on him. This time it was different. John Mortimer's mother appeared in time to overhear her son's last statement and to be further scandalized by witnessing her puny nephew land a solid right to the jaw. It was the more impressive because the assailant still held an open Bible in his left hand. She snatched John Mortimer up, shook him until he was limber-necked, beat him with a wooden spoon, and washed his mouth out with Octagon soap. Redfaced but unspent, she turkey-trotted him to the smokehouse, sacked him up, and hung him from a rafter between the hams and middlings until, she said, it was time to go back to Atlanta.

The boy was awed by this avenging whirlwind sent from God and felt vindicated by all her explosive wrath. Never one to pass up opportunity, he casually settled himself beneath the holly tree that had been planted before The War on the day the grandmother was born. Taking care that he was in full view through the open smoke house door of the twirling, chagrined John Mortimer, he pretended to read the Bible for another half hour. As he theatrically turned a page in studious display, he thought, He's lying again. That may be the way common folks get babies, like cows and hogs do it. But not my mother and daddy. They go by the Bible.

There were several cousins present a few months later when the worldly John Mortimer propounded the rudimentary technique and sensual delights of onanism. Open-mouthed, with furtive glances at each other, they listened while the sophisticate from Atlanta blustered and bragged. He assured them that everybody in town was not only familiar with the procedure but habitually indulged in the pleasures thereof. He even described a social event among older boys, to which he had not yet been privy but which he anticipated, called a circle jerk. When one of the quieter cousins timidly demurred that this activity might be wrong, John Mortimer was indignant. "Wrong? What's wrong with it? It's your fist, ain't it? And your pecker! You're just scared, that's all."

Another small boy ventured to question the purpose of such solitary activity and was met with scorn. "Why? Why do you do it? Because it's fun, dammit! And to get the feeling."

When the cousin continued his quest for information, John Mortimer was beside himself. "What's the feeling? I ain't believing you asked that! The feeling grabs you right here and it's the goddamdest giant tickle you ever felt."

At this the boy intervened. He was on sure ground. "John Mortimer! Don't take the Lord's name in vain!"

"Oh, shit," responded John Mortimer in disgust. "Is it all right to say 'shit' in front of Your Majesty? Just grow up ignorant and see if I care. I don't know why I ever bother myself with you little country turds anyhow."

The boy called to the retreating back, "I'll pray for you, John Mortimer." He glanced at his younger cousins and set a good example before the Lord. "We'll all pray for you. Unceasingly."

Smug in the conviction that had John Mortimer's mother witnessed this exchange it probably would have earned for him an overnight sojourn in the smokehouse, the boy dismissed the affair as another example of exaggeration and lying. He had enough of both curiosity and prurience, however, to investigate. He took care to sequester himself for the event within the wooden walls of the privy, securely insulated against the scrutiny of God. It was a short-lived experiment, ludicrous and non-climactic. He was bored. There were better ways than this to spend an idle hour in the afternoon. He

8

fastened the metal buttons to his overalls and emerged from the privy to toss pebbles in the air and hit them with a broom handle. He knew all along that John Mortimer Folds had been lying. He stood in the sunshine, guiltless before the Lord.

The first time he had an orgasm the boy very nearly tumbled off the top plank of the barnyard fence. He was through with his Saturday chores, it was too early to milk, and he had just finished reading, with virtue and relief, the last chapter of the Book of Ezekiel. It was late March and the sun was shining, but such a wild wind was scouring across the farm that he was obliged to wear his mackinaw and his leather aviation helmet.

When he climbed the fence to check on the baby pigs, he discovered a secluded spot next to the barn wall that was out of the wind and deliciously warmed by the reflected sun. He rested snugly there, content in the idle joy of an undemanding moment. Perched eight feet above the ground, he listened to the rich soughing of the wind roaring over the barn, watched a sun-glinted buzzard scud in lean and stiffened control across the rapid sky, breathed the vaguely spicy, musty smell of dried horse manure, and became aware of an impelling erection.

Idly he unbuttoned his overalls and slowly began the puerile manipulation. He concentrated on interpreting his afternoon reading, assuming that the Lord would be so interested in his thoughts that He would ignore his hand. For long moments he pondered and played. He noted that the buzzard had wheeled in the opposite direction and now hung, much higher and almost stationary, facing the wind. The boy envied the bird. Of a sudden he became absolutely inundated with sensation. His toes curled upward against his shoes, his elbows and upper stomach tingled, and then irresistible force came tearing and shocking in overwhelming pulsations through his loins. His mind was already on Ezekiel, and he saw myriad golden wheels spinning within wheels, covered with eyes and surrounded by coals of fire. He thought he must have a lightning rod in his lap, but the lightning was coming from within him. His hat fell into the barn lot, and he clung dizzily to the plank with both hands until his body shuddered into immobility and relaxed.

"Good Lord! What in the world was that?" he cried aloud. He suddenly realized that he was out in the open, full under the gaze of Jehovah Himself and indeed in direct communication with Him. There was no way to hide this from the Lord. He was no smarter than Adam after all. His fig leaf had even slipped. He glanced around to be sure there had been no human witness to this sensual cataclysm. Only the buzzard was watching, and it appeared unbelievably disinterested, still intent on balance and glide. He was not surprised to note that the wind had stilled. That seemed fitting.

As he climbed down the fence and retrieved his cap from the attention of a curious pig, he identified again with Adam and his humiliating expulsion from the Garden. He thought of John Mortimer and decided that anyone who could dismiss the experience he had just undergone as a "giant tickle" was either insensate or inarticulate. He flapped his helmet against the fence to dislodge some dirt and bits of straw it had accumulated and hurried to the house. He wanted the protection of a roof over his head. The boy felt so guilty he was frightened.

In the safety of his own room, he decided not to pray. The better course, he thought, would be to ignore this incident and see if the Lord brought it up first. A little extra penance, however, might accumulate some virtue for him and certainly could not hurt anything. He opened his Bible and began trying to read for the second time that day, but he could not concentrate on Daniel. He kept thinking back to Ezekiel and was surrounded by the great, golden, whirling wheels with eyes and coals of fire. He realized that another erection had inflicted itself upon him and that he was contemplating repetition. He dropped in terror to his knees.

"Oh, Lord God of Hosts, look down in Thy infinite wisdom and have mercy on Thy poor humble servant. This is Porter Osborne, Jr., speaking to you, Lord, but I am still a little boy. Really. And if Thou just won't cast me into the Outer Darkness this time, I promise to be good in the future. And I most definitely will finish reading Thy Bible. Forgive me, Lord, and I thank Thee in advance. Amen."

Porter took refuge in the Baptist doctrine of "Once saved, always saved" and an incommensurate degree of comfort in the

10

admonition to forgive an erring brother seventy times seven. He later quit counting. He decided that he would not go to Hell for an act that immediately prior to its performance was so irresistible and immediately afterward so disgusting. There was no possibility, however, of his ever becoming a preacher or even considering full-time Christian service.

Porter worked hard on the farm, harder in his books, and by the age of fifteen had graduated from high school. As valedictorian, he had climbed to the top rung of the ladder of local opportunity. College was the next step and was taken for granted. He told his father that he would like to go to the University of Georgia. If that gentleman heard him, he gave no sign of it. He informed Porter that he was going to Willingham University. This was a school of four hundred students in a very old and cultured Georgia city. It was Baptist.

Most significant of all, his father had gone there. Although the father no longer attended church, no one ever doubted his devotion to Baptist principles, particularly the one that proclaimed Man to be the head of the house. Porter did not demur at the decree about Willingham, nor did he even feel rebellious. He had read about the Medes and the Persians, the laws of whom could not be changed, and he privately thought that his daddy was descended from both of them.

He spent his last summer at home working on the farm and preparing himself for a major change in his life. As the time actually approached when he could foresee giving up milking, he came to hate that chore and be impatient with it. He was so eager for the adventure of college and his establishment of a new and individual identity that he began to resent his parents and family. On the other hand, he was so timorous about change and so unsure about living all alone in a strange land removed from all things familiar that he clung to the family. It was a confusing and miserable summer.

As September neared and the cotton which he would not have to help pick this year began ripening, Porter gauged his standing. He was small but he was smart. He was not good-looking, but he had whatever it was that girls called personality. He was timid, but he never let anyone know it. He did not have a girlfriend, but he had been on a date. He was a disaster at sports, but boys seemed to like

11

him anyhow. He was genteel and consequently got along well with his elders. He had never been able to pick a hundred pounds of cotton a day, but the Negroes liked him regardless.

He had the loan of his grandfather's pocket watch and even the chain that went with it. He had new pants, all of them long, and two new pairs of shoes. He knew the Bible better than most of his peers, and there was not the slightest inkling of doubt that he was Saved. He was convinced that there was a special relationship between him and the Lord, manifested by the fact he usually was able to rectify his mistakes and even profit from them.

He believed unquestioningly in God the Creator but just as fervently in God the Manipulator and God the Great Intervener. He knew in his heart that the Lord had placed him on this earth at the opportune time in the ideal place and family to be perfectly instructed and totally enlightened. He was Baptist to the bone and the flower of his civilization. He was Porter Osborne, Jr., and he had been Raised Right.

Despite recurrent faint misgivings about leaving home, he assumed that, all things considered, he was ready for Willingham University. It never entered his consciousness that perhaps Willingham University might not be ready for him.

The family gathered to bid him bon voyage. Impatient to leave home and run his own life, Porter had some last-minute misgivings. The little sisters cried and told him to write, a truly touching tableau since two hours earlier they had been revengefully locked in furious alliance against him because of some cutting word he had uttered. The grandfather adjured him to be a man and to remember that he was an Osborne. Even the aunt, forgivingly forgetful, dabbed at her red-lidded glass eye and told him they would miss him. Her husband was pulling weeds in the garden, an activity he did not interrupt to say farewell. The grandmother held his face between two faintly palsied hands and told him not to forget who he was and that she was counting on him to make them all proud.

He approached his mother with an impersonal kiss and conflicting feelings. Over the summer she had become the focus of his eagerness to leave home. She had found innumerable tasks for him to do around the house and yard, "before," she said, "you leave for good." He began to feel that her sole function that summer was to annoy and irritate him. He felt so nagged and nattered, so constantly suppressed and directed, so badgered and harassed that he often wanted to scream, "Leave me alone!" Such rebelliousness, of course, would have produced upheaval in the secure order of things and was unthinkable. Instead, Porter had responded with exasperated sighs, patient and formal answers through gritted teeth, unwitnessed rolling of his eyes, and extreme feelings of guilt.

She put her hand on his shoulder and looked down into his eyes. Her own eyes were brimming over. "Oh, my son, I'm going to miss you. Walk with God and grow in grace. You're so young." As he twisted impatiently, she blew her nose and added in a brisker tone, "Don't forget. If you don't smoke before you're twenty-one, I've promised you a solid gold wristwatch."

Porter heard this promise with the long familiarity engendered by frequent repetition and was untouched by it. He had never had any desire to smoke. What moved him of a sudden was a feeling of remorse that he could ever have been ashamed of this lovely person who had done him nothing but good all his life. He hugged her tightly and kissed her, but he remained dry-eyed. "I'll see you Thanksgiving, Mother. Thanks for everything."

Porter Osborne, Jr., was going off to college and he was sophisticated. He could not bear to let anyone see how very precious this woman was to him. Big boys had to outgrow their mothers.

He stuck his head around the kitchen door and spoke to the black woman at the sink. "Good-bye, Matt. I'm gone. Look after everybody."

That personage answered him with exactly the same sentence she had used at some point in every encounter between them for the last ten years. Only the feeling ever changed. This time it was both insouciant and cautious, but at least it was free of wrath. It was not quite affectionate. "Behave yoself, Sambo."

The grandmother was already turning to go to her room for a brushful of snuff. She wheeled so abruptly that her shawl slipped from her shoulders. "Porter, come here!"

The aunt attentively replaced the shawl.

"You're going off to a new town and a new school and a new life. Not a soul down there knows you. Don't you let anyone hear that nickname everybody around here uses. You've got a perfectly good name, and you see to it that people call you 'Porter,' not 'Sambo.' You hear me?"

"Yes, ma'am, Memaw." It was unthinkable to respond otherwise. Even the father and the grandfather voiced only affirmation when this tiny tyrant spoke with asperity.

He hopped into the front seat of his father's Buick that Wes had washed and polished only that morning. Despite a flicker of cold fear way deep inside, he felt confident. After all, he was Porter Osborne, Jr. He was the last of his line, the bearer of the name, the hope of the future, and a light on the mountain. He was going off to college.

14

* * * *

Porter Osborne, Sr., drove his son to Willingham. The boy could not remember his father's ever carrying him anywhere before, except to a football game in Athens two years earlier. They had not been alone then. A man and his wife had gone to the game with them, and in spite of the contrived innocence of the arrangement, Porter was so conscious that the man's wife was his father's girlfriend that he had been ill at ease all day. In addition, they had a silver hip flask they kept replenishing and sharing, and they laughed loudly at things which weren't funny.

Huddled under a blanket on a wooden seat in a gray drizzle, periodically startled when adults all around him leaped to their feet and screamed, he was afraid that his father might get drunk in this sea of strangers and felt as tautly pulled as new-strung barbed wire. Aware that a junior in high school was supposed to know at least the rules about this game, even if he had never seen one before, ashamed to ask any questions, Porter had stared at the scrambling chaos called football in bewilderment but with a determined pretense of interest.

He developed a lump in his throat, an ache behind his eyes, and a despairing sense of inadequacy. He resigned himself to misery, shrugged at the renewed realization that he had failed to measure up, counted the hours before he would be home, and passively drifted to his father's lead. In the returning car he had feigned sleep. That way it was easier to ignore under the secrecy of nightfall where the nice lady kept putting her hand.

The trip to Willingham University, with only the two of them in the car, was an intensely emotional experience for Porter. His father was part of his trinity, and as a consequence of this enshrinement was more than human, a little distant, and to be obeyed regardless of sacrifice. Periods of intimacy between the two had been rare events, so colored by the son's awe of the father that when occasion compelled them and chance complied, they had been fleet

15

and unfulfilling.

Porter, Jr., had always blamed himself for any inadequacy in the relationship. His father was a busy and important man, responsible for no telling how many projects and how many people, brilliant and directive, popular and admired, and most extremely sought-after. In addition, he was tall and handsome and glittered like a prince. The boy knew that if he could rise to the challenge of this heroic figure, if he could excel enough to gain his notice, if he could develop his own potential, then he would walk in favor through the land and be cherished forevermore. He knew he might never do it, but he was determined to try. If he were good enough, his father would like him. He carried this feeling with him into the Buick, locked deep within his gut, even while he swaggered a little beneath his mantle of conscious achievement.

Porter Osborne, Sr., accustomed to snapping orders over his shoulder to an undersized and obedient son, approached the trip casually and competently. The son was sure that this noble figure was not riding to college with him because no one else was available, or to help him with his trunk, or because this was an enjoyable way to spend the morning. He waited to discover the purpose.

Into seventy-five miles and two hours, his father crammed fifteen years of advice, admonition, and occasional approbation. Porter was enthralled. This much individual attention, this much personal interest, this much obvious caring and acceptance filled him with hope and rewarded his dreams. It was a milestone of his life. He vowed silently that he would never forget a word. Of course, by the time they stopped for gas in Barnesville, he could not remember half of what he had heard on the dirt roads between home and Griffin. And when they went through Bolingbroke, he had forgotten much that had been expounded between Barnesville and Forsyth. He retained, however, a surprising volume of material, a great deal of which he fell back on later for consideration.

"Son, your daddy is not a rich man. My folks were wiped out by the War, and it was all your granddaddy could do to hold on to the house and some of the land. Your grandmother took in boarders and sold butter and eggs to help educate those of us who wanted an education. Pa would have helped, but he had all he could do to feed us and keep the taxes paid. When I got back from France, it looked for awhile like things would get better, but the boll weevil hit and then the Depression came, and cotton fell to five cents a pound. Lots of folks sold their farms for a dollar an acre, if they could find a buyer. I had my law degree and a little check coming in every month for being County School Superintendent, or I don't know whether I could have made it. Of course, we raised everything we ate, and your mother was good to sew, and I even managed to save a little cash and buy some more land every now and then."

Porter nodded his head sagely.

"But don't you ever think we're rich. We're not. I want you to hold up your head, but don't you ever think you can run with the playboys at college. Think twice before you spend any money unnecessarily."

Porter idly watched the diamond on his father's hand reflect light as the man plucked the dark green package of cigarettes with the red circle from his shirt pocket and shook one between his lips. The first two fingers were stained a rich walnut brown and the nails a deep yellow. Porter watched the exhaled smoke sucked out the open window and silently vowed that he would be a veritable legend of frugality.

"I've got a lot on me, son. Now, I want you to remember that. I've got that whole bunch of kinfolks to feed and nobody else helps support your grandparents at all. Not that I'm complaining. After all they've done for me, it's a privilege to do whatever I can for them. It's just that I've barely finished putting one child through college and now there's you and then your two little sisters are coming along, and it's going to have your old daddy stretched pretty thin."

"Gosh, Dad, I'll help all I can. I want you to know how grateful I am to you. The tuition and board come to four hundred and fifty dollars a year. They gave me an NYA scholarship for being first honor graduate. That'll be a hundred dollars. But that still leaves three hundred and fifty. When I find out what kind of NYA work I've got to do, maybe I can get another job."

"Well, now, boy, I don't mean things are quite that bad. I can swing it. I just don't want you to think it's easy for me. Here." He reached into his inside coat pocket and handed Porter a thin rectangular packet.

"What's this?"

"It's a checkbook, boy. What does it look like? It's on my account at the Farmers' and Merchants'. You write whatever you need — tuition, books, what have you. I've told Cranford Sims to clear it at the bank."

"Golly martin, Daddy, I've never written a check in my life."

"Well, I'm sure you know how. Just write a little note about what it's for in the lower left corner and then sign my name and put 'by Sambo' under it, and that's all there is to it."

"By Sambo?"

"Sure. That's what I've called you ever since you were born, isn't it? Porter Longstreet Osborne, Jr., is a lot to write. In fact, it's a lot to carry around."

"Yessir, but Memaw was sure up on her dewclaws about me not getting called anything but Porter at college. You heard her, didn't you?"

"Sure, but you don't have to go around telling anybody what to call you. You know, my experience has been that you better watch a guy who's gone all through life without a nickname. There's bound to be something wrong with him. He's usually lonely down inside and can't unbend and make close friends. Anyhow, you sign the checks that way."

"Yessir, I will. Gee whiz, I don't know what to say."

"Well, just relax and don't say anything. I want you to know this isn't a right that's being bestowed on you. It's a privilege, and it's yours as long as you respect it. The first time I catch you abusing it, I'll take it away from you."

The boy was stunned by the magnanimity of this act. He closed his eyes. The wind blew cool through his hair; the tires sang on the highway and gave rhythmic punctuating twangs as they crossed the concrete dividers. Porter's heart sang with the tires. He was laden with responsibility, but he was buoyed by trust. He predicted that he would spend less money than any freshman in the history of Willingham University.

"Sambo, it's a good faculty they've got at this college. A couple of them even taught me when I was there. The thing for you to do is

18

work hard and establish a reputation with them as a serious student. If you'll make it a point not ever to get behind in your work, I think you'll find that college is not too hard. Now, that means not putting anything ahead of your studies. Get your homework and assignments prepared before you go to a movie or the drug store or get in a bull session. First things first, you know. If a student makes the dean's list, his parents pretty well know he's working."

Porter cleared his throat and asked with some diffidence for definition. His father explained that since Willingham was on the quarter system, the dean's list would consist of a minimum of two A's and a B.

Porter smugly considered that A was the only acceptable grade for him. B's were tacky; anyone at all could make C's; D's were reserved for indolent louts; and an F was such an embarrassing calamity that one mentioned it only in whispers and kindly averted one's gaze from its recipient. He relaxed a little.

The man pushed against the steering wheel and rotated his shoulders to relieve driving strain. "You know, Sambo, you and I never have talked a whole lot about some things. You go along and just sort of take for granted that people who are close to you feel the same way you do. For instance, you look like your mother's people, but I've always known that your attitude toward life was more like mine. Inside you're an Osborne, no matter what you look like on the outside."

Porter considered this statement and decided that it was a compliment. "Thank you, sir."

"Now, there's one thing I want to caution you about. A lot of times they have pretty wild parties at college. Young boys can get wound up like clock springs; sometimes they just plain bust loose. That's understandable. But watch the liquor. There's some bad stuff being made around the country, and a man really needs to have a bootlegger he can trust. Some of that stuff will kill you and some of it will drive you wild. You've got bottled-in-bond available now, and it's a good idea to stick to that even if it does cost more. It's not that I've got anything against drinking." He lit a fresh Lucky Strike off the one he had just finished and tossed the butt out the window. "As young as you are, I think I'm going to offer you a proposition. Whenever you want to take your first drink, just let me know and

19

we'll sit down together and you can take it with me."

Porter had a kaleidoscopic recall of occasions when his father had imbibed alcohol. He heard his grandmother intoning, "Osborne men can't drink." He saw his mother's eyes, tear-shimmering and anguished. He had resolved years before that he would never, under any circumstances, ever take a drink of liquor. With diplomatic discretion, he avoided any semblance of confrontation. "I promise you if I ever take that first drink, it'll be with you, Daddy." He paused a moment and added, "Thank you, sir."

After a few miles of aimless conversation, Porter's attention was again captured. "Another thing we've never really talked about, Sambo, and that's women. Now, I don't know how much experience you've already had. I know parents tend to think their children are too young for things sometimes when they've already been doing them for years, but you have to be careful. There are some things you have to learn from experience unless you've got sense enough to listen to someone who's already had the experience."

"Yessir. Buckalew Tarpley had a few drinks one day last week and talked to me about this."

"He did? Well, Buck Tarpley's a great friend of mine and wouldn't steer you wrong. What'd he tell you?"

"Well, he said a man wants a lady in his parlor, a cook in his kitchen, and a whore in his bedroom, but he doesn't hardly ever find that combination.

"He said to treat a lady like a whore and a whore like a lady. He said always use a rubber with a whore because of disease, but that you could also catch it through kissing.

"He said a gentleman should never kiss a whore or shake hands with a nigger. Said he learned that from the British in their colonies while he was in the Merchant Marine.

"He said some men could have any woman they want and some men couldn't get any woman at all and had to buy them. I hate to say this out loud, but he said a man that won't fuck won't fight and vice versa. And a few more things like that.

"He told me a saying about why older women are fun: 'They don't yell, they don't swell, and they're grateful as hell.' He was feeling pretty good.

"Oh, yes, he recited a poem by Kipling about 'I learned about

20

women from her' and ended up by saying all women are sisters under the skin."

Porter regarded the radiator cap a moment and added, "It wasn't too well organized, but it was a pretty good talk. He said he'd been all around the world several times and he'd never seen any sense at all in buying something that was walking around free. Said if a man had good equipment and sense enough to keep his mouth shut at the right time, he'd have more than he could shake a stick at.

"He said the thing he approved of most about God, if there was a God, was that He'd fixed it so good-looking women fell in love with ugly men. But he was just about to take plumb drunk when he said that, 'cause he started laughing and singing, and we all know Buck Tarpley can't sing."

The father lit another cigarette and exhaled deeply. "Well, looks like he pretty well covered the waterfront. Buck's quite an unsung philosopher. Speaking of venereal disease, Sambo, did I ever tell you about Mr. Raymond Gardner?"

"No, sir," responded the boy, sitting more erect. The words *venereal disease* were usually voiced in a lowered tone and caused little prickles of shock.

"Well, I guess you don't remember Mr. Raymond Gardner. I think he died before you were born. But he was really a great person, a fine gentleman. Always wore a white shirt and spoke very precisely and grammatically. You never saw Mr. Raymond Gardner when he wasn't courteous and dignified, and he never had a hair out of place. Well, one of his hands got in trouble with syphilis or gonorrhea or whatever it is causes strictures up inside a man. You know, in his penis. Anyhow, this darkie got to where he couldn't pass his water good, had to strain and grunt, and then it wouldn't be anything but just a dribble. He went to see Mr. Raymond about it and asked him to take him to the doctor.

"Mr. Gardner was using Dr. Walden then, and he carried the darkie to him. John Walden is a good friend of mine, and he told me about it. He told Mr. Raymond he could fix it, but it was a little painful, and he'd have to help hold the man. Seems that doctors have a little metal tool they grease and stick up inside your penis when you've got strictures bad, and then they push a button and little knives open out like a little tiny umbrella all around the end of it, and then they jerk that back through you and it cuts the strictures loose.

"Dr. Walden said it was awful tight and he was having trouble getting in, and the darkie was hollering and Mr. Raymond Gardner was fanning him with his hat. Then when he popped those little knives open and jerked, the patient let out this loud scream and fainted. And Mr. Raymond Gardner, still using those formal tones of his and pronouncing every syllable, said, 'Doctor! The man is shitting,' and then he sort of slowly circled around and fainted himself. John Walden said that's the funniest thing he ever saw in his life."

Porter Osborne, Sr., glanced at his son, who was now studying the radiator cap as though it might be another Rosetta Stone. "The reason I'm telling you this is so you'll know something about venereal disease and can watch out for yourself."

Porter took a deep breath. He felt attacked, very much alone, and more than a little scared. He thought briefly of David and his slingshot. "Daddy, you don't have to worry about me. I've read the Bible about this, and what you're talking about is fornication. Of course, it hasn't been a problem yet, what with my size and all. In fact, if it'll make you feel better, I haven't even kissed a girl yet.

"But I've thought about this an awful lot, and the time to make up your mind about what you're going to do in case something happens is before it happens. Then all you have to do is grit your teeth and hang on. I'm good at that, at gritting my teeth and hanging on. I've spent my whole life gritting and hanging.

"So I've made up my mind that no matter how tempted I may get, I'm not going to be a fornicator. I'm a virgin and I'm going to stay one until I get married. It's only fair, because I sure want to marry a virgin."

The father moved in his seat and took a quick little breath. Daringly, Porter cut off rebuttal. "And after I do get married, I'm sure going to be faithful to my wife. The Bible has a lot more to say about adulterers than it does about fornicators, and it's a heap harder on them, too."

The father's lip tightened with annoyance, but his tone was so offhand that Porter wondered for a moment if his last sentence had been heard. "Let's stop and get some gas and take a leak. We're almost there. I'll set you up to a Coke."

Porter poured a nickel package of Planter's peanuts into his

22

Coca-Cola bottle. Waiting for his father to come out of the restroom, he chewed and drank rapidly, enjoying the fizzing sting in his nostrils and the resultant series of burps. He had never seen Willingham University, but he knew he was going to love it. He also knew that he was going to enjoy his college experience more than anyone else before in the history of the world.

In the unconscious arrogance of innocence, it never occurred to him how rigidly he had restricted his collegiate opportunities by all the resolutions he had just adopted.

Willingham University enjoyed a modest but secure academic reputation, so great that the children of the poor aspired to attend and so solid that those children of the rich who could not be educated more prestigiously elsewhere condescended to attend. It was entrenched for sustenance in the budget of the Georgia Baptist Convention. It was also heir to occasional windfalls from sons who had rededicated themselves after amassing fortunes and consequently felt moved to expiate with gifts any taint of Mammon they had accrued. Willingham — comfortable, unpretentious, and rooted in consecration — dutifully instructed its students while it placidly awaited the Second Coming. There was no doubt that it would last until then.

The University, already a hundred years old, had been founded by a Baptist preacher. One listened to the solemn recitation of his deeds and goals, perceived the rules he left behind him, and could believe that he had been close to a hundred himself. It was a Christian university dedicated to the Christian education of Christians, and this purpose still dominated the campus. It was there like dense fog shrouding low-lying land on still summer mornings — never a real hindrance to progress but frequently a nuisance to vision. It seemed to be heaviest around the Administration Building.

This building dominated the campus. In fact, regardless of progress and new building programs, the Administration Building was Willingham University. It was planted round with magnificent magnolias, so old and so big that they smelled faintly of must and imparted a little sadness as well as tranquility. It was ringed with walkways that were constantly moist and lined with soft and silent moss. The building rose in majesty and time-faded brick four stories in the midst of the trees, and then its two towers leaped in sun-splashed light above the foliage. It was a great monolithic mother, brooding in passive power over the architectural spawn which had grown up around it. That spawn had been sired by a progression of frenetic mates who never produced progeny approaching in dignity, experience, or function the qualities of their dam. Since all South-erners were personally aware of such occasional genetic embarrass-ments, the students ignored the appearance of some of the other buildings and revered the mother figure.

Immediately adjacent and in hovering range was the oldest child, the afflicted one, the Chapel, which had had its steeple burned off in infancy. Because of family economics, it had not yet been replaced, but it was still a proud and well-loved member of the family and nestled in the shadow of the great mother in dependency and contentment. Immediately beyond the Chapel was a much younger relative, not a child but rather a close cousin, a Baptist church which did not really belong to Willingham. It was ruled by a Board of Deacons from the town, although it was the church most of the students attended. These three buildings were the face of Willingham University. They sat near the street high on a bank above a tree-rimmed park and stared at the city in massive and solemn dignity — changeless, self-assured, and content.

Behind the skirts of the matriarch were arranged the other children. The Christianity Building obviously had been built during Reconstruction or some such impoverished time, as had the Chem-istry Building. Both of them showed the malnutritive effects of penny-pinching, although white pillars had been erected in front of the Chemistry Building in a gallant but futile effort to conceal penury behind frippery. There was even a scattering of concrete gingerbread under the eaves of the Christianity Building, but these embellishments emitted the same feeling as new bows in the hair of a girl with a ragged dress.

The Law Building was the reserved child, blending in under-statement into the architectural scene but aloof from any levity and unapproachable by rollicking undergraduates.

The Library looked like a flapper, raised in the twenties and conspicuous in limestone rather than crumbly red brick. One had

25

the impression that she had led a wild life before coming home to settle down, and despite the reverent hush required within, she had the rakish appearance of someone who did not quite belong. The Biology Building was the youngest child, crew-cut and flamboyant. Perched directly behind the Administration Building, it was boisterous and ebullient in bright red brick with new limestone trim. The pretense was maintained that it was collegiate Gothic, but it looked like an adolescent with brand-new saddle oxfords, the red rubber soles not frayed or the shiny tops yet soiled by use. Its presence and appearance accentuated the aura of tolerance and benevolence emanating from the protective old Administration Building, and one had the impression that it was placed where it was so that its mother could keep a watchful eye until it grew up.

This was the campus. There were outlying buildings to the rear and to the sides, but this quadrangle constituted the heart and viscera of Willingham University.

The father drove his son slowly down University Avenue. The street was paved with bricks worn down by generations of horses and then smoothed slick by twenty more years of rubber tires. The bricks had not yet been covered with the newer and more economical macadam; they produced a little rhythmic bumping and a sweetness of whine when the Osborne car went down the shaded street. They whispered of heritage and dignity; they cautioned against interlopers who had no sense of reverence. The antebellum houses, white-columned and faintly melancholy, presided over empty lawns in assurance that nothing had ever changed, and their vacant verandahs bespoke with understated pride that change was in poor taste. No children were to be seen anywhere on this street.

When the car emerged from tree-arched dapple into the bright sunlight of intersection, Mr. Osborne slowed even further. "There it is, Sambo."

Across the green of the park and rising from the embracing clutch of magnolias, the towers and spires of Willingham University floated white and majestic on their rose-brick pedestals. They beckoned like a citadel of civilization breaking abruptly above a verdant

26

jungle. Porter gasped. As they turned down the street directly at the base of the buildings, he looked up at the Administration Building and thought it quite the most majestic manifestation of man he had ever seen. The state Capitol in Atlanta was bigger, but it looked raw and sharp-edged in comparison.

"Look up, Sambo. See the round window just beneath the smaller tower? Well, that's my fraternity hall, and that's a replica of the fraternity pin done in stained glass and framed in that window. Ours was the only fraternity hall allowed in the Administration Building, and it takes up the whole top floor. The glass that makes the jewels around the pin is cut with facets just like real rubies and sapphires and diamonds, and they're four inches thick in the middle. The window doesn't open, but when it's lit from inside at night, it's the prettiest sight in all of Macon, especially when you're walking toward it from across the park."

Porter craned his neck and gazed through the car window, impressed and more than a little subdued. "Just what does a fraternity amount to, Daddy?"

His father drew a breath and spoke at patient length of groups of young men who were supposed to have much the same ideals, the same goals in life, who joined together to help each other uphold those ideals. He pointed out that there were many different fraternities, and while most folks thought they were just social clubs, that KA was not like that.

It was founded, he said, at Washington University, and Robert E. Lee was sort of a guardian angel while they were getting started. "You'll always find a picture of Lee in any KA house, and the KA's try to live up to his principles and maintain standards of the Old South. Why, our motto is 'God and the ladies.' I tell you what: When we get you unloaded and your trunk in your room, we'll just sort of drop around to the KA house and introduce ourselves. I promise you one thing sight unseen — you'll find a great group of fellows there. They're not just a bunch of playboys out to have a good time; KA's are real brothers banded together to help each other. That's part of our tradition."

Porter sat owl-eyed and silent, relegating fraternities with impersonal interest to the same mental shelf where he kept such activities as playing football, listening to radios, and bathing auto-

27

mobiles on Sunday. He was disinterested but looked politely as they turned a corner and his father pointed out the president's house and told him that he was sure to be invited to tea there. He felt that might be all right for fraternity boys, but he was going to be a serious student. Frittering away precious time drinking tea with the president of the University was not Porter's idea of getting a college education. After all, the president did not teach any classes or give any grades and consequently must function as a relatively unimportant figurehead.

One of the strongest teachers Porter had ever met was a maiden lady who had majored in home economics but was hired to teach mathematics. She qualified herself for this pursuit by poring over every book on the subject she could find and ended up as an expert in the field. She taught Porter that anything could be learned from books by a hard worker who would concentrate. Life for her held no nonsense and few frills. Porter had overheard her expound her philosophy of teaching to a younger, gentler woman who had been rosily impressed by college courses in Education. "All that stuff's tommy-rot. Pour it to them, I say, and then give em an exam, and if they don't pour it back, flunk em." Porter assumed that all college professors would have this attitude, and tea time with the president would be a distraction for dilettantes almost approaching decadence. He tolerantly said nothing to his father.

They progressed up the street between the back of the Library and the starkly skimped apartments for the faculty and on the corner of the next block turned into the parking area for the dormitory.

"There's your home for the next four years," his father said. "Luther Farmer and I had that corner room on the end down there our last two years. That's where we were living the night we stood the policeman on his head in the garbage bin down on Mulberry street. Had to run through every back alley in Macon and climb in the window, but we didn't get caught."

Porter uttered a respectful response but barely listened. He had heard all about Luther Farmer before. His father's extracurricular exploits in college had somehow the same aura of epic as Beowulf grappling with Grendel and then swimming five miles in full mail. It had never entered Porter's head to question the veracity of these accounts. It was just that in his extremely human state, he acknowledged a hero when he saw one, and there were some aspects of greatness to which caution forbade his aspiring.

Nottingham Hall was shaped like a boomerang, with its apex molded to the corner of the block and its flanges fixed in permanent balance between the elm trees which shaded it. Although it was three stories tall, it gave the impression of being as solid and squat as a Mayan temple. The front porch was actually an appendage but looked to be carved out like a cave from the bottom story. The banister around it was interrupted by brick pedestals that were topped in turn by fat limestone columns. Along the curve of the porch was a row of rocking chairs. The bricks were red, the columns had once been white, and the banisters and chairs were so deeply recessed and shadowed that the entrance to Nottingham Hall always seemed cool, albeit somewhat somber.

When the Osbornes carried their first armloads in, Porter, Sr., spoke so genially to the boys in the rocking chairs that one of them leaped up to hold the screen door open. Thanking him in courtly fashion, Mr. Osborne turned to Porter with tones that carried to the porch.

"You see, son, what I told you. It's just part of tradition that all Willingham men are courteous and helpful."

Porter was examining the inside of Nottingham Hall and made no reply.

The front door opened into a vestibule covered with ribbed rubber matting that extended to right and left down each hallway beneath high ceilings. The walls were fashioned of plaster as coarse and white as dirty gravel. The doors and trim were painted the same dark green of the banisters and chairs on the front porch. The dominant feature of the vestibule was the staircase; it seemed to begin almost as soon as one entered the door. As wide at the bottom as outstretched arms, it rose and narrowed to a landing and then split and reversed direction to attain the second floor. Its banisters, rails, and risers were painted brown, and the steps themselves were covered with the same rubber matting as the floors. The staircase invited, almost impelled, but the Osbornes turned right on the first floor. They passed the coin telephone, mounted in indulgence of students on the wall beside the archway, and proceeded all the way to the end of the hall. As they reached the last room on the right, they heard a noise and looked back up the corridor.

Two of the courteous and helpful gentlemen of Willingham had abandoned their rockers and were bearing between them Porter's trunk. It was a wooden footlocker bound in iron that had belonged to his father in the World War. "Capt. Porter Osborne, Co.K., 120th Infantry" was painted in black letters on the top and two sides. Now it held all of Porter, Jr.'s bed linens and clothes.

"Well, well, well! What a thoughtful thing to do! You men didn't need to bother yourselves with that trunk, but we are indebted to your graciousness and good manners. This is the room right here. Come on in and put it down somewhere. My son can arrange things later." Mr. Osborne opened the door and stepped in.

A young giant of a man leaped from a bed and stood with shoulders squared, hands clamped to his sides, and head thrown stiffly back. Porter's father extended his hand and began introductions with charm, casually implying that he was accustomed to such reception and accepted it as his due.

Porter observed the cavernous room with its four tall windows. He noted the three beds, three study tables with straight chairs, the lavatory mounted on the wall with an unframed mirror over it, the two commodious closets, and the high plastered walls. He turned his full attention to the figure in the center of the room who was shaking hands with the father.

"Robert F. Cater, sir. Atlanta. Everybody calls me Bob. Pleased to meet you, sir."

"Well, Cater, you're a fine figure of a young man. I'm sure you're as well-bred as your appearance indicates. Congratulate your parents for me. I'm Porter Osborne and this is Porter, Jr. I guess you fellows are going to be roommates, and I'm sure you'll get along famously."

Bob Cater was taller than the boy's father, weighed well over two hundred pounds, and obviously had to shave every day. He leaned down to shake hands with Porter, and the two boys stared at each other in amazement.

Porter was shy his sixteenth birthday by two weeks and was exactly sixty inches tall on the kitchen door at home ... with his shoes on. He looked up through round, gold-framed spectacles which were forever crooked on his face and studied this young Goliath.

Bob Cater had blue marbles for eyes and a round peg of a nose, which seemed to anchor his full cheeks while they fell like drapes around each side of a small mouth. He had a dimpled chin which protruded in more than a suspicion of underbite. His features were beneath, but not under, a rounded bulge of forehead and seemed to be as much in one plane as the face of a lugubrious and preternaturally aloof Pekingese.

"Pleased to meet you, young Osborne, or Porter, or whatever they call you."

Porter assessed the voice as kindly, but was there just a trace of patronizing condescension? His leg is bigger than my chest, Porter thought.

"Glad to meet you, and Porter will do just fine." The piping treble of his voice shrilled loudly in the room, and Porter felt the bigger boy's hand startle involuntarily. He clamped down with the grip of a veteran milker — surprising strength in so small a creature. "Unless you can think of something that suits both of us better," he added, smoothly repressing any open tone of defiance. This situation needed immediate solution.

"I think Porter's a great name," the bigger boy replied.

They stared at each other a moment. Bob's grip loosened first and Porter relaxed a little. The rather formidable stranger was obviously from an alien culture, but Porter liked him. There's even a chance, Porter thought, that I might make this big guy from Atlanta like me.

Mr. Osborne excused himself to find the restroom. Bob explained to Porter that he already had made up the bed that was first in line and that he really thought the second bed would be the next most preferable, since the third one was jammed right under the north windows and probably would be colder in the wintertime. He helped Porter make up the middle bed, hang his suit in the closet, and watched as Porter unpacked his trunk and arranged the clothes in his dresser drawers.

He chatted about Willingham, the dormitory rules, location of the dining hall and showers, when they could take their laundry out, and then told Porter that a third roommate had been assigned since they were in a corner room that was larger than the others.

31

Porter listened attentively. He glanced carelessly to be sure Bob was looking when he arranged toilet articles on the glass shelf above the lavatory. Porter had never shaved or developed any need for such a process, but for college he had purchased a Schick injector razor, a small wooden tub of Yardley's soap, and a shaving brush, the fibers of which were ringed and bushy like a raccoon's tail. Bob's shaving brush was so old and worn that it resembled a wet duck's tail.

"Better leave some room for that other fellow," Bob cautioned. "We wouldn't want him to think we're crowding him out just cause we got here first. I see by your trunk that your dad was an officer in the Army. My dad wasn't in the service, but I went to Riverview Military Academy and was a student officer there."

"You did?" Porter paused a moment and decided to ask it anyway. "Did you happen to know a boy named John Mortimer Folds?"

"Ole Foul-mouth Folds? Yeah, everybody knew him. He graduated last year. Made pretty good grades, but he was forever in trouble and walking the bull-ring to pay for it. He'd believe anything anybody told him, and the other guys would set him up for all sorts of things, and he could out-cuss anything you ever heard, even for a military school. Where'd you know him? Everybody said that whenever his mama got called to Col. Spencer's office about him, she yelled and hollered and put a whipping on him right there. Col. Spencer finally quit calling her, cause it embarrassed him to see ole Foul-mouth catch it like that."

"Yeah, that sounds like John Mortimer. He used to visit in Brewtonton a lot before he went to RMA, but he was a year ahead of me in school." Porter looked thoughtfully out the window. "It sounds like his mother, too."

Porter, Sr., appeared in the doorway and resumed control of conversation. "I thought I'd run by to see my fraternity house, Cater, and introduce my boy to the brothers there. Would you care to join us?"

"Yes, sir, Mr. Osborne, I'd like that. I'm all through here and don't have another thing to do. What fraternity did you belong to?"

"KA. Kappa Alpha Order. I was a member right here at Kappa Chapter, and it was the richest part of my college life. I was just saying a while ago that there are a lot of good fraternities here, but none of them

32

can top KA in serious respect for our Southern heritage and in loyalty of the brothers to each other. Come along, men."

As they trailed the man down the hall, Bob Cater nudged Porter, who noted that the bigger boy's elbow caught him just on the point of the shoulder. "This is really great. KA is one of the top three fraternities here, and I haven't met any of them yet. Your dad is swell to include me."

Porter was not interested, but it was apparent that his roommate was. Politeness compelled participation. "How many fraternities are there at Willingham?"

"Seven. Like I said, there's KA, Phi Delta Theta, and SAE. Then there's ATO, Kappa Sig, and ALT." He paused. "If you can't get in any of them, there's always Pike. They pledge what's left, and they've got a real duke's mixture of odd-balls and coal miners."

"I didn't know there were any coal miners around Willingham."

"There are now. Just wait'll you see our football team. The coach ships em in here on scholarships from Pennsylvania and Ohio on account of their muscles, and they're sumpin else. They're all Dagos or Hunkies or Polocks or something like that. Anyhow, they're all Catholic." He gestured up the staircase. "They put all of them on the third floor. Sometimes they get to cussing and yelling on the hall and get the preachers all upset."

"The preachers?"

"Yeah. They put all the ministerial students on the second floor, and sometimes they put in to convert the football players and that never works, and then the preachers report em to Mother Capulet for blasphemy."

"Who?"

"Miss Kate Capulet. She's our house mother. Lives on the second floor at the head of the stairs. Her husband was president before he died, and they've given her a job and a place to live. She and the preachers live on the second floor, the football players on the third, and then just us regular fellows on first."

As they climbed into the car, Porter said, "You sure know a lot about Willingham already."

"Well, I got here last night and haven't had anything to do except prowl around today. There's an ATO sophomore three doors

33

up the hall from us, and he's real friendly. Mr. Osborne, that two-story brick on the corner is the Phi Delt house; they're the ones with the money. That's SAE on the corner over yonder, and the KA house is just around this corner and on the left."

They parked at the end of the walk, and Porter followed along behind his father and roommate. The KA house was a modest, one-story frame building perched high off the ground and roofed with black tarpaper. It was underpinned with lattice work all around the front porch and reminded Porter vaguely of a big chicken coop. The most distinctive thing about the house was the gigantic fraternity pin, illumined from within, that hung on the wall beside the front door. It announced the function and purpose of this building and asserted that nothing else really mattered.

Two boys had come out of the front door when the auto-mobile stopped and were now halfway down the steps, obviously welcoming and friendly. One of them had lank brown hair, parted in the middle and greased immaculately backward. He looked slightly like a fox. The other one was a blond with round blue eyes and the carelessly erect carriage of a well-muscled athlete. At first glance he seemed buck-toothed, but a second look belied this impression. Instead, he had the longest, widest, whitest teeth Porter had ever seen ... and the most of them. There was an upper one incongruously missing on the left side. The gaping empty hole in the wall of white shrieked of its absence whenever the boy laughed or spoke. One felt it had been popped out in an expanding frenzy by its splayed and crowding neighbors. Porter felt that all of the unbeliev-able energy one sensed within this human was intensely gathered into his teeth, where it pulsed and glowed and crackled for release.

The foxy one spoke first and held out his hand in greeting. "Yes, sir. Welcome to KA. What can we do for you?"

The father grasped the proffered hand. "I'm Brother Porter Osborne, Kappa chapter, class of 'fourteen. This is my son, Porter, Jr., who is enrolling as a freshman, and Bob Cater, his roommate over at Nottingham Hall. I thought I'd bring them over to meet you fellows before I went back to Brewtonton."

"Yes, sir, Brother Osborne. We're awfully glad you did. I'm Brother Relaford Roundtree, but everybody everywhere calls me 'Slick.' "

34

And that's a real good idea, Porter thought. He glanced at Bob Cater and considered muttering this thought aloud to him, but Bob's mouth was slightly ajar like a caveman observing his first camp fire, so Porter remained silent.

"I'm rush chairman for the fellows this year, and I want you to come in and meet some more of the brothers. This is Brother Clarence Spangler here. He's a sophomore from Chipley and our Number IV this year. He's my roommate."

"Glad to meet you, Brother Spangler. What do they call you?"

Porter noticed that they exchanged a sort of four-handed greeting with their hands covering the right wrist of the other. He also noted that Clarence Spangler extended his right hand with the little finger flared and faintly crooked, like a missionary lady drinking tea. It obviously was not his leading hand, and Porter watched closely enough to realize that he was left-handed.

"Just Clarence, sir. Or Spangler. Some folks probably call me worse than that, but I've never had a nickname."

His voice and bugling laugh were dominant and aggressive enough to complement his energetic teeth. Porter felt gravely inexperienced as he shook hands with this urbane and self-assured pair. These were real college men. He was not at all certain he would make it.

In the living room, standing under a picture of Robert E. Lee in full white beard and gray uniform, Slick Roundtree was smoothly introducing everyone.

"Brother Osborne, I want you to meet our chapter advisor. This is Brother Theo Montagu from here in Macon. He's an architect and is the one who's drawn the plans for our new dormitory here at Willingham that's going to be built next year."

Theo Montagu was a short little man with a great thick chest which he kept pulled up under his chin in forced inspiration to make himself look taller. His appearance, consequently, was that of a passionate pigeon. It gave extra importance to anything he had to say. He had an aristocratic wafer of a nose that pinched his lip upward in a perpetually tight hint of disdain. When he spoke, one thought at first he had a lisp, but closer attention indicated that an unusually high palate caused uncontrollable and slight currents of whisper in his speech. He made little clattering sounds which added a faintly mechanical effect. Although Theo was sartorially splendid almost to the point of foppishness, Porter was reminded, when he heard him talk, of a duck trying to eat corn, drink water, and quack at the same time.

"Mr. Osborne, I'm very glad to meet you." Four hands met again in what Porter by now realized was some secret grip used by KA's to prove each other's identity. Porter for a fleeting moment felt unexplainably like Huckleberry Finn, but these lordly cavaliers were so gravely serious he did not pursue the impression.

The two adults were involved in the ritual of assessment men use to get acquainted instead of asking bluntly about bank accounts, credits, and debits. Within minutes Theo had spoken of a job he was doing for Georgia Tech, referred to a well-known banker by his first name, and mentioned ever so casually that he had just built himself a house in Ingleside. His tone implied that this was real estate somewhere between Palm Beach and Valhalla.

Mr. Osborne in response had identified himself as an attorney, a county school superintendent, and a farmer. He played the true farmer's role by complaining that crops were poor this year and that the weather had been terrible and he wasn't going to make anything at all. He then implied in beautiful deprecation that he didn't farm to make money anyhow. It was a yoke he shouldered to ensure livelihood for the faithful retainers surrounding him and to keep his ancestral acres open and arable for the comfort of his aged parents. Porter thought his tone hinted of liveried servants, rolling lawns with peacocks, and teams of blooded mares. He held himself a little straighter and hoped none of the boys present had read *Aeneas Africanus*.

His father shook out his cigarettes and offered them around. Clarence and Slick accepted, but Theo preferred his own, extracting it from a thin silver case and tapping it gently before lighting it.

"Brother Osborne, I probably spend as much time on KA matters as I do on my job. My wife thinks so, anyhow. Of course, she loves KA almost as much as I do, and she's planning a big party at our home the end of rush week for our new pledges. I sure hope your son will be there. It's great for the order to have old blood in it. I wish I had some boys to be true KA's. Maybe my little girls will grow up and marry in the Order."

"Well, the chapter is fortunate to have an advisor like you, Theo, and I'm sure you'll do well in rush this year. I've got to be going, so I think I'll just leave these two boys here and run on. They can walk back to the dormitory."

Mr. Osborne shook hands all around in cordial farewell, and Porter was glad to see they all had returned to a normal two-handed grasp. He followed his father down the steps. At the curb, they stopped and looked at each other. Porter had a surging desire to jump in the car and go back to Brewtonton and all that was familiar to him. He gazed steadily into his father's eyes and held out his hand.

Bravely he spoke. "Good-bye, Daddy. Thanks for everything."

"Good-bye, Sambo. Have a good time, but write home as often as you can. Let me know if you need anything."

Porter watched his father crank the car, waved a forlorn farewell, and turned back up the steps.

"Sambo?" said Bob Cater.

"Sambo?" thundered Clarence Spangler.

"Oh, that's my nickname. My dad's always called me that."

"Well, he sure is a fine fellow," said Spangler. "You're lucky as hell to have a father like that. I've never met anybody more impressive."

Porter watched the empty tooth socket move in and out of view as Clarence's muscular lips worked at controlling his booming voice. He did not trust himself to respond.

"Where's your bathroom?" he asked.

Coming out a little later, he heard a sibilant clattering around the corner. "I don't care about that. We can't help it. He's a legacy and you be nice to him. What I want is for you to get busy and get us a rec on that big one. Cater. We want him. I tell you, we've got to have a good year, Slick. We don't have but three seniors, four juniors, and two sophomores besides you and Clarence. I love you boys to death, but I'm tired of paying rent on this house all by myself."

Porter spent the evening nesting his room and visiting with Bob Cater. He learned that Bob was an only child, planned to major

37

in accounting, and had heard that Macon was full of beautiful women. He was a pleasant boy who laughed easily, and Porter was comfortable with him. When they prepared for bed, Porter noticed that Bob wore pajamas; so he put his on, too. He picked up his Bible and silence descended on the room.

He thought of the day, of the distance he had come in such a short space, and of the strange new world in which he found himself. He remembered something in the last verse of Malachi and turned to it.

> And he shall turn the heart of the fathers to the chil-
> dren, and the heart of the children to their fathers,
> lest I come and smite the earth with a curse.

He thought of the interchange he had experienced with his father on this day.

"Bob, do you reckon my daddy took all that time with me today just so he and I would be closer together? You know, like it says here in the Bible, have our hearts turned to each other?"

Bob was already on his side, his massive back proclaiming sleep-seeking privacy. He raised his head from the pillow briefly but did not look around. "I think your dad brought you to Willingham just so he could hand-deliver you to the KA's. Turn off the light, Sambo."

38

Porter was loosely under the aegis of the towering and lumbering Bob Cater for the next two days as they took English placement tests, registered for classes, and paid tuition and fees for the first quarter. Bob affably introduced the two of them to any unidentified classmate who paused long enough to look interested. Bob had laughed at Porter's anecdotes, admired his wit, and acknowledged his intelligence to the extent that the younger boy felt almost relaxed in this company of peers. It never occurred to him that in more ways than one he was an anachronism at Willingham University.

He instinctively knew that his desire for acceptance here was so intense that rejection would be a form of annihilation. He longed so tremulously for these new people to like him that he would do anything it took to join their ranks — anything, that is, except let down his guard and be himself. He presented an exterior so polished by loquacious impertinence that it was as deflective of wounds as a warrior's shield. Only his eyes pleaded, "Do you like me, children?"

If Porter had known about his eyes, he would have worn dark glasses. The only thing he knew was that very few people ever met his gaze for more than a few seconds before averting their own, as if from some inner embarrassment. His daddy had taught him always to look someone straight in the eye when talking, and he assumed that other people just did not have as attentive a father as he.

It was a cheerful, bustling process, this getting registered for classes. The line was a slow one, and the waiting freshmen moved lazily in and out of chattering groups. Bob Cater never failed to introduce him as "Sambo."

IV

39

Upon finally reaching the registration table, Porter discovered he had done well on his placement tests and had been put in Dr. Minor's class for English 11. Since he already had completed two years of French, he was assigned to Dr. Huber for three quarters of intermediate French to satisfy the school's foreign language requirement. He chose Biology as his third course, having been advised by the helpful and ever positive Clarence Spangler that this was the best selection for a pre-med student from a small school.

When he produced his father's checkbook and wrote a check for the quarter's fees, he dutifully signed it "by Sambo." This caused a little flurry among the clerks and secretaries, and the check was passed all the way up to the registrar himself for inspection. While the line waited, that pock-marked, chain-smoking World War veteran, pragmatic rock awash in a sea of intelligentsia, growled, "He ain't goin' anywhere; take it. What a name! Is he white?"

By the time he had registered for his first classes at Willingham University, Porter Longstreet Osborne, Jr., through no effort of his own, was recognized universally by sight and name. He was "Sambo." He never told his grandmother about his nickname getting out at college.

Bob Cater and Slick Roundtree boastfully claimed that the best-looking women in the world walked down Peachtree Street in Atlanta, Georgia. Porter asserted that if this were true, it was because a busload of girls from Miller High School in Macon had arrived. He was fascinated by these girls, and they were as plentiful on the Willingham campus as the grackles that feasted in the sugarberry trees. They all wore skirts and blouses, a uniform of sorts. The blouse was invariably white with a little round collar. The skirts hung exactly one inch below the knee and were full and flared. There might have been some difference in quality of fabric according to individual affluence, but this was a nice distinction apparent only to other females and completely missed by obtuse boys. Every girl from Miller wore exactly the same hairdo — shoulder-length and slightly curled on the ends in a bouncing swirl. A thick central tress was pulled straight back from the forehead and secured just beyond the

40

crown of the head by a clamp, comb, or piece of ribbon. Very red lipstick drawn heavily to the outline of choice was customary, and saddle shoes with socks completed the uniform.

Adding to the charm of the girls was their irrepressible vivacity. They all smiled brilliantly through the thick bright lipstick, chattered incessantly, and often flipped a hand inconsequentially backward through their tossing tresses. They moved as constantly and cheerfully as a carousel. They shrieked and gave a little push on the shoulder to any male who said anything daring or the least bit interesting, their wordless cries, rolling eyes, and pouting postures replacing most effectively any concern for intelligent conversation.

Slick said these girls couldn't hold a candle to Atlanta Pinks, although he worried that the proposed merger of Washington Seminary with NAPS might needlessly intellectualize a previously delightful natural resource. Porter had been all over Atlanta, from Rich's to Davison-Paxon's, from the Peachtree Arcade to S&W, from Terminal Station to Cotton Jim's and Kress's, and he had never before seen any girls like those from Miller High.

All the out-of-town girls who lived at Mrs. Garrison's boarding house in lieu of a dormitory took one look at the local bevy of beauties and aped their hairdos and make-up; so Porter regarded this as the "look" of Willingham women. He was so entranced by them that he could never thereafter regard Slick Roundtree as any arbiter of taste. Slick was a good boy, but he had no perception of quality or appreciation of beauty. His taste was all in his mouth.

In the thronging display of beauty and personality on registration day, one girl repeatedly drew his attention. She was obviously from Miller because all the other girls seemed to know her and she shrieked one or two decibels higher than the others whenever she spied someone she had not greeted that day. In addition, she wore the uniform. Her blouse, however, strained at its buttons and her skirt did not flare. Rather, it hung low in front and it was suspended high in the back by the pull of her massive buttocks.

The backs of her knees constituted an invasion of privacy. One did not want to see them but could not refrain from looking. Each had a thick white column of flesh down the sides and a wide expanse of tissue in between. Just above the knees, little veins had already broken and disappeared up the thighs as unsightly purple

41

estuaries. Thick rolls around her chest kept her arms at a slightly swaggering tilt, and her great torso and belly pressed down so irresistibly that she was knock-kneed under the weight. Her legs stuck out in an everting angle of balance. Her features were mired in flesh.

Even her ear lobes were puffy and protruded embarrassingly at the angle of her jaws, and her head seemed to rest on the rounded shoulders without benefit of a neck. Her mouth, however, was a slash of scarlet, and her hair was pulled back in the stylish sweep and tied with a scarlet ribbon in valiant rejection of the fact that it was too wispy and thin to reach much below her ears. She smiled incessantly and chattered a lot, and her eyes moved quicker than a telegraph key. Porter sensed a desperation in her glance that made him uncomfortable. He made it a point to include her in some of his own conversational sorties.

Her name was Eunice Yeomans, but everyone called her "Tiny." It was a nickname that bespoke acquiescence to the role of reluctant buffoon. Her goals had been narrowed to achievements associated with intelligence and personality, and Porter heard other students refer to her several times as a good ole girl. He felt that behind her smiling facade there had to be weeping for some of the glances she caused and some of the gibes she pretended were funny. Her reactions were predictable, however, and her attitudes assured. Everyone knew that fat people were jolly.

Porter noted that she called all the girls she knew by their last names, thereby implying a camaraderie that exceeded reality. He wished that he would quit running into her.

"Hi there, Swygert. Good to see ya. Where ya been keepin' yaself all summer? Still drivin' all the men crazee? Way to go, baby!"

She was addressing the lovely Sybil Swygert, whom Porter also had noticed several times. She was so close to being a platinum blonde that only the most rigid of purists would have quibbled over shades or tones. She had a daintily bulging forehead and a smile as constant, wide and toothy as that of a death's head. In addition, she had very long legs and what had to be the most beautiful body in the whole wide world. Her cool blue gaze swept Sambo indifferently and her smile never faltered.

"Hello, Tiny."

42

"Listen, gal, I hear you made first group of English with me and that you're taking Biology and French, just like old times. We got perzackly the same schedule. We'll show that Dr. Huber with his Ph.D. from Paris how Miss Stratton teaches French at Miller. Show those smart ROTC Lanier boys something, too, won't we kid? Look beautiful, act dumb, study hard, and cut their feet out from under them before they know where the grades even start. Do it right, babee."

She would have nudged Sybil with an overlapped elbow, but the latter apparently had not heard what she said and pivoted on one saddle oxford in a twirl of skirt and missed the contact. She looked over Porter's head to the boy behind him.

"Hi, David! Haven't seen you since graduation week. You have a good summer? I'm so used to sleeping late I've got to get back in the groove."

Unbelievably, not more than two feet from Porter's face, she stretched her shoulders and upraised elbows back and arched her beautiful bosom forward and upward in the relaxing gratification of a tremendous yawn. If Porter had realized his mouth was hanging open he would have closed it, but he could not have stopped staring if his life had depended on it. It was of no consequence because it was obvious that Sybil Swygert did not see him. He wondered how a girl could yawn and smile at the same time.

Later in the dim wood-panelled Co-op, the freshmen were milling around with their lists of required textbooks, comparing prices of new ones as opposed to the second-hand ones being hawked by upperclassmen. He had a reverence for books that was almost mystical. They were more than friends. A brand-new, un-opened book that belonged to him alone was something of a private kingdom, replete with maturing adventure and responsibility, and it bestowed power and authority on its owner. One could feed on books. Any relationship this important deserved to start out pristine and inviolate.

Porter examined the merchandise and decided to splurge and buy all new books. He assured himself that he would skimp on something else. He felt that the extra dollars involved would not prohibit his little sisters being sent to college four years hence nor take food from the mouths of his kin, but he still experienced a little guilt about his pledge of frugality.

He wrote a check, scrawled "for books" on it, and signed it "by Sambo." Ignoring the raised eyebrows and muttered comments behind the book counter, he carried his load of crisp, tight volumes to a corner. For precious moments he was oblivious to time and place. His English book, *Principles of Composition and Rhetoric*, was bound with black covers and a contrasting dusty-pink spine. He thought it the smartest looking book he had ever seen. When he riffled the pages, they made a snapping whisper and emitted a smell as crisp and clean as fresh starch under a hot iron. A glance at the contents assured him that this would be new material. He thrilled to the challenge. "I'm going to like English," he said aloud.

"That's what you think," sounded a familiar voice above his right ear.

He looked up and around to see Eunice Yeomans pouring Coca-Cola over two scoops of ice cream in a large paper cup. Her smile flickered bright and dim like a neon advertisement and was just about as personal.

"Just wait till Dr. Fred Minor gets through with you. It's two themes every week in his class. One every weekend, and then one that you have to write in class every Wednesday. This goes on for six solid months. And he grades every one of them. Every now and then he'll read one out loud because it's so bad it demonstrates what you ought not to do. If you make one comma fault it's an F, and if you make three comma faults you have to repeat the course in a lower section. He never gives A's and he never smiles. One comma fault! And you think you're gonna like English?" She tried to flip her hand backward through her hair but barely created a wispy stir.

"But, Eunice, I plan to study hard. I never said it would be easy. In fact, I like to study. I never made anything but A in English in my life."

"In all your life? And just how long has that been, honey lamb? An A at home and an A at college are two different things. Just how many folks in that little town you came from?"

Porter felt a twinge of defensiveness. "Right at eight hundred, counting the nigras, but I didn't live in town. And there were only thirty-eight in my graduating class. What's that got to do with it?"

"Law me, I can't believe you asked that question." She ladled a spoon of fizzing mush into her smile. "Do you realize there are as many people in my high school as there are in your entire home town? And that they are all girls? There are just as many boys as that over at Lanier High. And these are two of the best high schools in the state. You think you gonna go up against that sort of competition and *like* it? You lucky you even got placed in the top section."

"Well, now, Eunice, I don't know so much about that. It depends on how you define luck. Being from a little town doesn't make you mentally retarded, and living on a farm sure teaches you how to work. Our school may have been small, but we had some of the best teachers in the state. I can't afford to let them down."

She threw back her head and laughed. Her entire attitude bespoke rollicking condescension. "Well, they sure got their hopes riding on a mighty puny horse. How much do you weigh anyhow?"

He could hear his grandfather saying, "It ain't the dog in the fight, son. It's the fight in the dog." He reared back.

"Ninety-five pounds, Eunice. How much do you weigh?"

Her eyes settled on his briefly. "None of your business, buster. And let me tell you something else. All my friends call me Tiny."

He relaxed into a laugh. "OK, Tiny, I get your message. We'll be friends. Us freaks need to stick together anyhow."

She gave a gasp. Her eyes blazed, and then for just a moment, he saw the hurt lurking around like a kicked dog. "We will *not* be friends. What do I need with a midget and a hick?"

He felt a rush of contrition. "Gosh, Tiny, please don't get upset. I was only kidding. I thought *you* were. I wouldn't hurt your feelings for anything in the world."

He tried to catch her eyes with his own. He reached and grasped her upper arm. The flesh was a little bumpy and abnormally cool, its capillaries strained thin through at least four insulating inches. It reminded him of the belly of a fresh-scraped hog. He gave a little pat, and a jiggling wave went all the way to her elbow. "Really, Tiny, I like you. You've got a pretty face."

"That does it! That's the most insulting thing people ever say, and they're always stupid enough to think it's a compliment!"

She leaned forward and looked him full in the eyes. He noted that her lashes were thick and stuck almost straight down. Her eye was as baleful as a boar's. "Take your stinking, prepubescent farmboy hands off me, and don't you ever touch me again, you hear? And quit lookin' at me with those hungry hound-dog eyes! I don't give a goddamn what happens to you!"

"Please don't take the Lord's name in vain," he said instinctively. He stumbled backward into someone and looked up into the face of Sybil. It was unsmiling, solemn with a lovely maturity.

She squeezed his shoulder and whispered, "I'll take it, Sambo."

She snapped her fingers, suddenly smiled like a skeleton and swung around so that her hair and skirt twirled. "Tiny, ole gal! Where you been? I've been looking all over for you. You got a car today? How about giving me a lift down to Chichester's on the way home?"

Porter watched Tiny's smile reappear in a flash. She rolled a hip and made her own skirt flounce. "Yeah, Swygert. Let's go, gal. I got no car but I'll walk over with you. I'm starvin'. Let's get a cherry Coke and some peanut butter crackers."

Porter mustered what dignity he could and looked around to see if there were any other witnesses to his evisceration. He felt as though his pants were down and his entrails were trailing the floor. Fortunately, the Co-op was a confusing swarm of little groups, all of them completely oblivious to him. No one but Sybil Swygert had witnessed his humiliation. He took a deep breath and raised his chin. His gut slid into place, the wound snapped briskly shut, and his pants were miraculously in order. No blood was visible. He still ached in the pit of his stomach and there was a fist-sized lump in his throat, but at least his shaming was secret.

He searched for Bob Cater. "Hey, big boy. Where you been? I'm headed up the hill to the room to put up my books and get ready for supper. You about ready to go?"

"Sure. I was just coming to get you and I got myself introduced to the cutest little gal you ever saw. Her name's Billi. You spell it with an 'i,' and she comes to right here on me. She and I got acquainted buying used books. We found some good buys. I got a third-hand English book for just a dollar. The covers are almost off, but you can still read it, and somebody has even already underlined the important things. I tell you, I sure don't believe in spending money on new books if you can find used ones."

46

Porter took a little extra step to match his roommate's stride. "I met Billi this morning. Her real name is Mary Jane. She's from Miller High School. You still think they're not up to the Atlanta Pinks?"

"OK, you got me. This one is. She's about the cutest, cuddliest little thing I ever ran across. I'll admit these Miller girls are friendlier and have more personality than the ones from Atlanta, but I can't go back on the Pinks. You stand on Peachtree Street at the corner of Cain and they go by in droves. They're the prettiest things you ever saw. These chew more gum than the Pinks do, too." He looked around self-consciously and then added with a little forced laugh, "I tell you one thing, though. Even Roundtree cusses the Atlanta Pinks for being a bunch of prickteases, and I sure don't think that applies to these Macon girls."

"What's a pricktease?"

"Are you serious? That's when a girl leads you on and lets you do a few things and then when you get all excited and, you know, get just a terrible hard-on, laughs at you and makes you take her home. You never heard of a pricktease?"

Porter gave another little skip and cleared his throat. "No. I don't think we have any of those in Brewtonton."

"Ah, sure you do. There's 'bliged to be some of them everywhere. You just don't know much about women yet."

Porter considered this statement for only a moment before abandoning any defensiveness. It was true, and truth must be faced. Perhaps, however, he was not as alone in this condition as the conversation implied. "Tell me, are you still a virgin, Bob?"

"Yep, but it's a pitiful condition and I sure don't intend to stay one any longer than I can possibly help."

"Well, I do. The Bible teaches it's wrong to do that before you're married."

"You just happen to be a little bit better Baptist than I am. The Bible says you'll be forgiven for your sins, too. All you got to do is believe, and I already believe. And I don't think losing your cherry is so big a sin it won't be forgiven."

"Bob! That's sacriligious! I don't think God will let you plan sin and forgiveness all in one package ahead of time. Besides, these are all nice girls at Willingham. I don't know how you are going to manage."

47

"There's ways."

Porter looked up at his roommate looming above him. "Well, I sure don't know what they are. But then to tell you the truth, I haven't even kissed a girl yet. I searched the scriptures about that, and I can't find anything at all about not smooching. That's what I'd like to do."

"Yeah. But who with? It doesn't matter who you screw, but you sure don't want to smooch anybody who isn't pretty and cute. To be real honest with you, I've never kissed anybody yet either, what with going to that military school and all."

Porter felt mollified by this admission. Cater was all right. "Well, maybe you're not supposed to smooch anybody unless you're in love with them."

"Aw, that's crazy. How you goan tell you in love if you don't catch a little woo first? Anyhow, I want to know what kind of hold you got over women."

"What do you mean?"

Bob Cater looked at him with a mischievous twinkle. "I looked across the Co-op one time and you were all bunched up in a corner with that Tiny. You know, she's a pretty good ole gal. Has a jolly personality. If she just didn't weigh about two hundred pounds too much. She was smiling and flirting with you. Then the next time I looked, that Sybil Swygert has her arm around your shoulder and is plumb huggin' you, and she's built like a Petty girl. Boy, you got something I don't know about."

Porter felt his gut tighten and begin aching. He made no reply.

"I tell you, Sambo, women are funny. I saw Sybil and Tiny leave the Co-op together. I've noticed that a lot of times when you've got a goddess like Sybil who's a real raving beauty that she pals around with the most unattractive girl she can find. I've never quite figured that out, unless it's because she thinks an ugly girl makes her look even prettier."

"Or else the other pretty girls are too jealous to be friends with her. You're wrong about Sybil. She's not stuck on her looks."

Bob hunched his shoulders forward and actually leered. "Maybe not, but she sure does a lot of yawning and stretching, and she doesn't do it when there's nothing but other girls around."

48

"I don't care, I think Sybil is a great person. But you're right about Tiny. She's a good ole girl, even if she does get a little fractious at times. Tell me. What exactly is a comma fault?"

"Lord, I don't know. You're the scholar. I've got the middle section of English, and I hear it's not too hard. You going to the KA house tonight?"

"I guess not. I hadn't thought anything about it."

"You ought to go, Sambo. I ran into Slick and Clarence at the Co-op. In fact, Billi bought a biology book from Clarence. They want us to come by the house after supper tonight. It's not a real party or anything. We're going to have cookies and Cokes, but they told me to be sure and bring you in case they didn't run into you themselves. They just want some of the freshmen to meet all the brothers and have a little bull session. Rush doesn't really start until next week. I told them we'd both be there."

"Classes start tomorrow. You don't think we should stay in the dorm and get ready?"

"Come on, Sambo! We don't even have any assignments yet. What would you do to get ready? Oh, I almost forgot. You got a letter. When I checked to see if I had any mail, I asked for yours. I didn't get any, but you did." He opened a book and handed Porter a thick envelope.

He recognized his mother's writing and felt a pleasant rush of anticipation. They were at the room and he put the letter in his pocket as he reached for his key. The door, however, was unlocked. The three beds in the room were covered with books, clothes, and toilet articles. The chair to one of the study tables had been pulled out and turned around and a figure sat on it, holding a white enameled walking cane, giving the vague impression of an enthroned monarch. As Bob and Porter stopped on the threshold, this apparition rose and stood patiently waiting.

"My name's Tom Christian," he said.

Spellbound, Porter stared and stared. The newcomer looked to be a grown man of at least twenty-five years. His hair was not the familiar white of Anglo-Saxon toddlers but was of almost transparent sheen, possessed of inner light. His bright pink scalp shone through in shocking accent at the part. All of his skin was a vivid pink, so bright that his eyebrows and the hairs on the back of his hands showed in startling contrast. His nose was thin and raw and his teeth were yellowed and prominently bucked, requiring purpose to close his lips.

His eyes were his dominant feature, however. The sockets, deep and shadowed, imparted a feeling of intensity and mystery. The irises shimmered and gave off reflected light that was sometimes violet, sometimes almost pink. They were bedded in thick, completely white lashes like those of a pet rabbit. The eyes, never in their existence having focused on anything or brought information to the controlling brain, wandered in aimless drift anywhere they wanted. They were in constant motion, now rolling, now sliding, now jerking back to some ill-defined starting point to begin all over their idle trek in fruitless orbit. Lacking witness of animation in others and consequently having no model to imitate, Tom Christian's face was almost expressionless, subject to occasional involuntary grimaces that were the result of no discernible stimuli and which were usually inappropriate.

Porter stole a look at Bob Cater, whose small mouth was agape, making him look more than ever like an attentive Pekingese. He flicked a glance to meet Porter's and recovered himself.

"Glad to meet you, Tom. I'm Bob Cater and this is Sambo Osborne. You must be our other roommate." Tom extended his hand in the direction of the voice and Bob took it. When he released it Porter stepped forward and grasped it firmly. He did not trust himself to speak. He felt so guilty at the moment for possessing perfect vision that he could have wept in atonement. His own good fortune thus far at escaping the punishment of an affliction had to be a delay in the divine delivery system rather than a manifestation of flawed judgment. For a moment he cowered naked in the garden and besought mercy instead of justice.

"I'm glad to meet you fellows. I hadn't tried to put up any of my things until you came because I couldn't tell exactly what space you'd already taken over."

"That's fine!" boomed Bob Cater. "We'll get you straightened out in no time. This is your bed over here under the windows. You'll get good breezes across here in the hot weather and can enjoy the birds in the trees outside. Sambo will help me and we'll make it up for you. You and Sambo can share that closet over there. I've got so

50

much stuff you might be a little crowded trying to share one with me." At this smooth rationalization, Porter jerked his head up and looked at Bob but did not catch his eye.

"There's a study table at the foot of your bed, against the wall right next to Sambo's. You can put your toothbrush and things out on the shelf above the lavatory there. Put them on this end. Sambo is in the middle with everything else; he might as well be in the middle with his toilet articles. Where are you from?"

"I guess you could say I'm from Macon. I was born and raised in south Georgia, out from Blackshear, but I've been here at the Academy so long I consider Macon my home." Tom's voice was almost devoid of expression and flat as the muscles of his face. His fingers were moving like ten busy people arranging toothbrush, razor, comb, and hairbrush on the shelf, the surface of which he carefully felt and explored.

Porter was mitering a sheet on Tom's bed. He straightened and spoke for the first time. "What's the Academy?"

Tom whirled toward his voice in immediate reaction. "Who's the girl? I didn't hear anybody else come in here."

Bob Cater gave an involuntary mirthful snort and then quickly stifled it as he looked at Porter's face.

"I'm not a girl." He tried to put all indignation out of his piping reply. "I guess I could prove it to you, but you'll have to take my word for it. I just wanted to know what the Academy was. And everybody in the world doesn't have to speak bass."

Bob Cater laughed and Tom Christian followed suit. As Porter watched his mouth open in a grimace of strong yellow teeth, heard the overly sibilant huff of laughing breath, and saw again the undirected wandering of the useless eyes, he was filled with contrition. "I'm just sixteen years old this month and my voice hasn't quite finished changing yet. That's probably what confused you."

Tom made an effort and tugged his upper lip over his teeth — for all the world, Porter thought, like old man Waddell Harrell pulling the sweater over his bulging belly button. It was as temporary a result. "Well, I'm not usually that dumb. But I pride myself on always knowing how many people are in a room and exactly where they are, and you really fooled me there for a minute."

Bob Cater, stiff and a little self-conscious, interposed, "What

51

he was talking about was the Georgia Academy for the Blind, Sambo. That's a place here in Macon where blind people come from all over the state to study and learn how to live and get along like regular folks. Isn't that right, Tom?"

"That's a rather simplistic description, but if it suits you, it's all right with me. But let me tell you something, Cater. You can quit yelling at me when you speak. If we're going to room together, you need to realize that I'm just blind, not deaf. I comprehend a normal tone of voice.... What in the world is that?"

A low growl seemed to shake the room and then rapidly wailed into an ear-splitting, painful scream that killed any effort at conversation. It was the summons to supper and was easily audible a mile away. It came from a siren mounted in the kitchen window so that it faced directly into the back windows of Nottingham Hall. It was sounded three times a day to announce that the dining hall doors were open. Strident, harsh, and overwhelming, the noise should have congealed gastric juices and curbed appetites, but it had no such effect on healthy Baptist males. Rather, it created an almost unbelievable pandemonium.

When the siren began, the rooms emptied. Everybody ran to meals. Preachers abandoned any pretense at dignity and tried to storm off the second floor before the football players streaming down from third trammelled them on the stairs. When the deafening shriek of the siren inundated the halls, it washed over masses of hungry, determined boys, who crammed the entrance to the dining hall like cattle overriding each other in a loading chute. Any student possessing enough detachment to walk leisurely down the hall during the galvanic stimulus of the Nottingham siren had to be a senior and was probably also an English major who had just finished a course on Dr. Johnson.

Porter waited until the summoning scream subsided and explained it to Tom. He then offered to escort him to the dining hall. Bob had bolted at the first growl. Tom took his walking cane in one hand, gripped Porter's arm lightly with the other, and they proceeded down the rubber matting of the hallway with Tom tapping the cane on the unmatted margin of the floor until he touched the baseboard and then back again. He held his head in an attentively listening position as they walked and assured Porter that he would need no help on his return trip. Porter felt virtuous and assured Tom that he was happy to help in any way he could.

He sat at the table with Tom and tried not to watch him eat. The blind man handled his fork well, but before each bite he used the tenderly probing fingers of his left hand to identify the position and type of food on his plate. In addition, he used a rigid forefinger to clean his gums on several occasions. Porter ate little and was glad when the meal was over. On the way back, Tom wanted to go to the toilet, and Porter left him there after his assurance that it would be no problem for him to return to the room by himself. When he opened the door, Bob Cater swung around from the mirror.

"You're a nobler soul than I am. That Tom Christian is a son of a bitch."

"Bob! You mustn't say that. He's blind."

"OK then, he's a blind son of a bitch. We worked our butts off fixing his bed, putting away his things, and hanging up his clothes, and he never even thanked us for it. Then that business of pretending he thought you were a girl. He was just putting on, trying to get your goat. And the idea of jumping on me for talking too loud to him! I don't have to speak to his royal blindness again at all. Look at the desk! He's got his old typewriter on yours and some of his overflow books on mine, and before you know it he'll crowd us out of here like that camel getting his nose warm in the tent."

"Well, Bob, maybe we should look on this as a challenge. Maybe it's like we learned in Sunday school — it's an opportunity to help somebody who is not as fortunate as we are."

"That sounds good when you're in Sunday school, but I didn't come to college to wet-nurse some ungrateful freak. I've got myself to think about."

"Maybe you're having trouble because you're an only child. You know, not being used to living with other people and having to share things."

Bob drew himself up. "That's got nothing to do with it. I get sick and tired of people acting like you're abandoned if you don't have a half dozen brothers and sisters swarming around you and contending for breathing space. 'Only child' hasn't got a goddamn thing to do with Tom Christian."

"Please don't take the Lord's name in vain, Bob."

53

"I'm sorry, Sambo. I know how you feel about that and you're right, too. But you're wrong about Tom. All you're looking at is his blindness. You're not seeing what sort of person he is. You know, a lot of folks are like that about old people. They think just because somebody gets old, they're automatically a great person and deserve to be respected. I learned this from listening to guys talk about their grandparents and what not. Well, I started watching when I was just a shaver at how mean my grandmother was to her husband and all her children. The older she got, the meaner she got. If you're a nice person when you're young, you'll be a nice old person. And the same thing applies if you're blind." The faint tapping of the questing cane became audible. "Hush," said Bob. "We don't want him to hear us talking about him."

Porter looked at his roommate. "If I were as big as you, I wouldn't care what anybody heard me say. Why do you care?"

"Because I want everybody at Willingham to like me, even the sons of bitches." He paused and met Porter's look with candor. "And because I'm really a nice person. And because I've been lonesome all my life. You coming to the KA house?"

"No, I don't think so. I've got some other things I'd rather do. Tell em I said thanks anyway."

As Bob left the room and Tom entered it, Porter seated himself to study. He looked with possessive pride at his books. Deliberately he reached for *Principles of Composition and Rhetoric*. Turning to the index, he looked up "comma," made a note of every page reference to it, and began reading. He felt the letter from his mother in his pocket occasionally and promised himself the reading of it just as soon as he learned everything Jensen knew about commas.

Tom puttered around the room, memorizing its geography, bumping gently into furniture, locating closet doors and windows, and muttering to himself. When he went to the lavatory to brush his teeth, Porter watched in revulsion as he fingered every toothbrush on the washstand like an exploring raccoon before finally selecting his own. They engaged in occasional desultory conversation, but primarily Porter concentrated on commas.

Finally he was finished to his satisfaction. He pushed back his chair and extracted his mother's letter. It was in a prestamped three-cent envelope with George Washington embossed in white profile on a purple oval. The handwriting was flowing and beautifully distinctive. He glanced across the room at Tom and decided that he wanted more than just visual privacy for the reading of this letter. "Excuse me, Tom. I think I'll take a little walk around campus. Is there anything I can help you with before I leave?"

"Help me with? No. I was expecting to go out with a friend myself, but it looks like he's not going to show up."

When Porter stepped into the hallway, it was quiet and deserted. Daylight still shone through the open window at the end, and he wedged himself on the sill and began reading.

Dearest boy of mine,

It is not quite time for supper and I thought I'd drop you a line. Memaw and Pa Jim are on the front porch rocking, Uncle Bung is in the swing on the back porch, and Auntie and Comp are in the garden picking the dried pole beans for seed. You know those beans have been in the family for a hundred years and your daddy doesn't want to be the one to lose them. The little girls are around the radio listening to that Ovaltine show about Little Orphan Annie, and Jimps is somewhere with her nose in a book.

Wes is milking your cows and I'm waiting for him to bring in the milk for me to strain it. Your daddy has hired him to bring in stovewood and milk the cows since you've gone off to college, but it's not going to be the same. Already he gets about two quarts less than you were bringing in, and I fear he is not stripping old Stell properly. You know, she won't give her milk down for just anybody. Also, I worry about his being careful with the milk and not cleaning the cows good. You were always so conscientious that I'm spoiled.

I'm enclosing a dollar bill for you. I sold some butter. I know Daddy has provided for you, but I'll send a little extra along when I can lay my hands on it for you to spend on "foolishness" — picture shows, milkshakes, etc. I know you are going to work hard and make good grades, but there is more to college than just books, and I want you to relax occasionally and have fun.

You've only been gone one day and already we miss you so badly we can hardly stand it. Daddy says you have a nice room and a fine roommate, and that the boys in his old fraternity are being nice to you. I know that you will be happy there. Well, I hear Wes coming in the back door. Take care of yourself, and remember that you're constantly in the heart and prayers of your loving

Mother

His eyes blurred with tears and he felt a choking in his throat. He would have wept but he heard a noise. Another blind boy was tapping his way down the hall. Apparently the echoes told him where he was, for he stopped directly in front of their door and called, "Tom?"

Tom Christian answered, "Come on in. It's not locked. I was about to give you out. Just a minute and I'll be ready." Porter heard the murmur of their voices for awhile and then they both emerged from the room. Tom was still talking.

"Yes, I think I've about got things arranged to my satisfaction. My roommates are obnoxious, but no worse than I expected. One of them is a great big lummox from Atlanta who's not too bright, but he's a real milquetoast and I've already got his number. The other one is a Christ-bitten little turd from way out in the country. He's just a child, and I can't imagine how he thinks he's going to make it at college. His voice hasn't even changed yet. When you meet him, pretend you think he's a girl talking. That really tears him up."

Porter huddled in disbelief as the two friends walked arm in arm down the hall, canes pecking away in unison, comfortable in the community of shared experience. He went back in the room, prepared for bed, and knelt to say his prayers. Slipping between the sheets, he reached under the pillow and touched his mother's letter. He thought of the farm and his family. He added a postscript to his prayer. "Lord, I don't want you to think I've got anything against fat folks and blind folks. They're the ones who don't like me."

A wave of homesickness bore down on him with irresistible

force and he sobbed until he hiccupped. Finally, peaceful from sheer exhaustion, slipping into sleep, his memory stirred him. "What does he mean, Christ-bitten? I spect You and I better tend to him, Lord. Mother's right. There sure is a lot more to college than books."

He opened his swollen eyelids so that contact with the Almighty would be less intense. "That white-headed, pink-skinned son of a bitch," he said.

When he finally slept, he dreamed that Tom Christian was milking Eunice Yeomans. When her milk wouldn't come down, he kicked her in the side. Wes was sagaciously standing in the stable door, shaking his head and advising that she needed more cotton-seed meal and better stripping.

V

The real college experience began in earnest on the following day. Classes started. English met at eight o'clock, and all of Dr. Minor's students were in place when that fabled professor opened the door from his inner office and walked into the classroom. He was heavy-jowled and dark-eyed, his front teeth worn and colored from long friendship with a pipe. His dignity was unassailable and his presence inspired awe. He called the roll in a controlled, emotionless voice, looking in memorizing identification at each respondent. Then he handed out a mimeographed sheaf of instructions and assignments — a calendar of events in English 11 from the first day through the final examination in December. There was a ponderous finality to seeing those dates written out that made Porter quail. Summer was indeed over.

Dr. Minor's gaze went all around the room. Porter met it directly, as was his custom, but it slid past him impersonally to another row of students. When Dr. Minor was looking at someone on the other side of the room, he spoke. "Mr. Osborne, tell us everything you've ever learned about the comma."

Porter's heart lurched in his chest like a startled rabbit, and then very calmly and in explicit and accurate detail, he recited everything he had read the night before.

Dr. Minor's eyes were glued to his. When the recitation was finished, he spoke to the class without breaking eye contact with Porter. "I would call attention to the class that there are two things very remarkable about this recitation. One is the exhaustive and specific information presented with such perfection. The other, and of the two this is the more remarkable, is the total absence of any misinformation. It is in the latter that one finds the revolting comma fault. Tell me, Mr. Osborne, where did you go to school?"

"At Brewton County High School, Dr. Minor. It's a very small school, and there were only about thirty students in my class."

He took a deep breath and looked earnestly at Dr. Minor through the little round gold-rimmed spectacles sitting crookedly on his freckled face, their sparkle somewhat marred by a smear of butter left from a careless breakfast. Then he took the plunge. "We had very good teachers, though, sir. In fact, I was one of the poorer English students."

He deliberately closed one eye in a broad wink at the dignified professor. Dr. Minor's gaze did not flicker, but his voice became a little more thoughtful. "Indeed, Mr. Osborne. I hope you do well here."

"I certainly intend to, Dr. Minor. I'm a hard worker."

He lowered his eyes demurely. His heart was racing, his triumph tempered by the audacity of the lie he had told. If God has a sense of humor, surely Dr. Minor does, he comforted himself. At any rate, the gamble was sweetened by the knowledge that Eunice Yeomans was sitting on his right and had heard every word clearly. He could hear her breathing stertorously through her thickened pharynx but did not venture a look in her direction. He wondered what she was thinking now of prepubescent country boys.

In Biology class, there were more than twice as many students as there were in Dr. Minor's English. The head of the department was a septuagenarian who, Porter felt, would have been well advised to have retired forty years earlier. He had helpers who worked for him, older students who received part of their tuition for being at the beck and call of this high priest of Biology at Willingham. These boys were lab instructors but never gave lectures in the formal classes. This was Professor Hansford's prerogative, and he guarded it with the jealousy of an impotent old dog half-snoozing in a fenced back yard.

He was white-haired, red-faced, fat, and smiled frequently, thereby displaying the smallest, whitest, most flawlessly even teeth ever to have been fashioned free of charge by trainees at the State Prison Farm. A watch chain was looped through a buttonhole in his vest, hanging in two festooning swags from the tucked-up and protruding abdomen. From one loop dangled a Woodmen of the World insignia, from the other the twinkling key of an insignificant national educational fraternity, the sole requirement of membership in which centered around perseverance in the teaching profession until one grew old.

Professor Hansford at one time must have been a very able teacher, for he enjoyed a good reputation among the alumni. Porter Osborne's father was included in this group and had told his son on their ride to college that Professor Hansford had taught him in 1913 and really knew his subject matter. The current upperclassmen agreed with this assessment, but they all grumbled that he had succumbed in later life to a passion for conservation and spent more class time discussing soil erosion and game management than he did in presenting Biology lectures.

Clarence Spangler had made an A in the course and said that Professor Hansford took his examinations strictly from the book, and that the only students in trouble were the ones who relied on their classroom notes to study. It was the only A Clarence had made his freshman year, and he talked frequently of biology to the freshmen who came to the KA House.

The professor had a nickname. He was called "Bo-cat" Hansford and had been labeled thus for decades. No one was exactly clear about the appellation, nor when or why it had been bestowed, and no one knew if the professor was aware of it. Porter noted that he was extremely Miller-susceptible and wondered if there were a connection. When the Miller High girls began twirling, bouncing, and smiling around him in the halls before class, his grinning, white-thatched head pivoted independently of the overstuffed body like a great horned owl regarding a field of frolicking mice. Sybil Swygert sat on the front row, and when she grew sleepy and yawned, Bo-cat's upper plate slipped, causing him to slur a few words and swallow before regaining his red-faced composure. He had been heard to tell his lab instructors, "Just because there's snow on the roof doesn't mean there's no fire in the furnace."

Porter thought Bo-cat was a fitting nickname, but he was

careful to refer to him as 'Fessor Hansford. He secretly predicted that Sybil was sure to make an A, but he did not confide this to Bob Cater; he was still a little defensive of Sybil around Bob. He examined the Biology book and realized he had two entire quarters to memorize it. He privately wagered that he also would make an A. All he had to do was stay on the good side of the professor, keep his mouth shut, and do his memory work.

During the first class, 'Fessor Hansford spoke desultorily and vaguely of the purpose of the course, relegating twenty minutes to the student head of the laboratory and his instructions about lab supplies. Then with an avuncular twinkle, he glanced around the room and settled on Henry Bean. Henry was a freshman from Macon, a neatly tonsured boy of medium height with small, tight features, a humorously cynical eye, and a mouth that barely escaped looking like a rat trap because of deep dimples at each corner. Porter had encountered him several times in the last two days and had been impressed by his intelligence and his mature disregard of superficialities.

"You look like a fine young man. Perhaps you could tell us how many eggs a wild turkey lays."

All eyes turned to Henry. He reddened a little, lifted his chin, and spoke with precision that was almost a snap.

"I dare say it is one at a time."

Professor Hansford's smile faded and his blue eyes turned flat as agate within their fleshy folds. A titter came from somewhere in the back of the classroom.

"What is your name, young man?"

"Henry Bean, sir, and I'm a pre-med student interested in Biology and not conservation."

"All right, Henry Bean. I'll remember you and we'll try to see that you get all the Biology you can handle. Miss Swygert, maybe you are a little more concerned about the natural resources of our state. Would you care to speculate on the wild turkey hen?"

"Oh, 'Fessor Hansford, I sure don't know. I didn't even know we had wild turkeys in Georgia anymore. Tell us about it."

Porter's admiration for Henry Bean soared and he timidly congratulated him after class. He would have liked to emulate him, his independent attitude and his cavalier approach, but he was afraid to stray too far from the sycophants who enjoyed 'Fessor Hansford's favor. He also admired Sybil Swygert.

When one left the Biology Building with its waxed linoleum floors and the flat odor of new concrete intermingled with nostril-stinging formaldehyde, there was a journey of eighty linear yards and one hundred years backward in time to the rear of the Administration Building. Entering this venerable edifice always imparted a little awe, a little awareness of forgotten generations of earlier students, a mildly sobering sense of the responsibility demanded by continuity, and a subliminal feeling of pride that something could have endured this long completely unchanged.

The first floor was given over to classrooms, Education on one side of the stairwell, Psychology on the other. On the second, or main floor, the northern end of the building housed the offices of the registrar and the business manager. On the southern end of this floor, the sunny, comfortable part of the building, the president's office occupied the eastern exposure, bathed by morning sun and shaded by magnolias. Across the hall was the dean's office. In the afternoons it got hot as a blister, but the dean was never heard to complain in public. He had tenure, but he also had pride. It was beneath him to notice such nit-picking irritants as creature comforts.

The stairs leading from second to third floor were wide and curving. Their risers were solid and gave forth a gratifying thump, a booming echo through the cavernous halls, but the steps themselves emitted groans and squeaks when trod by mounting feet. This combination of sounds identified that particular stairwell and made it unique. On the third floor were the offices and classrooms of the History, French, and Spanish departments. There was also a locked meeting room of the ADPi sorority. Next to the history classroom was a commodious office which the head of the department had transformed into a one-room apartment with a bed, washstand, and electric hot plate. He was retired from the British Army and had permanent residence in that one room of the Administration Building. His classroom always smelled of tea, oatmeal, and ginger, for he cooked in his room. He bathed and used the toilet down the hall.

At the very end of the hallway on third floor was a securely locked door. It was the entrance to a boxed-in stairway that led to the mysterious level of the fourth floor, controlled in its entirety by the KA fraternity and utilized by them only for formal meetings and initiation ceremonies. Since the sole approach to the main tower of the building was through this locked and hidden stairwell, no small degree of importance rested on the KA official who controlled the keys to this suite. Porter learned very early that this was the exclusive responsibility of the treasurer of the fraternity, an office designated by the secretive, clannish KA's as Number VI. A really dedicated KA could pronounce it with a nuance of inflection that projected the Roman numeral.

The French classroom had windows all the way to the floor, the windows themselves being of a height greater than most ceilings. The desks for the students were one-piece affairs, the very first ones in the world, Porter imagined. They had a book compartment under the seat and an armrest and desk attached above. They were fashioned of oak and polished shiny by generations of rubbing buttocks, backs, and elbows. Strained by use, as loose and comfortable as any cane-bottomed relic in country kitchens around Georgia, they tottered and listed under the weight of students.

Dr. Huber gave the illusion that he was a monochromatic statement saying, "Life is gray." Certainly his clothing, hair, eyes, and even his skin were varying shades of that color, and his voice heightened the effect. It was full but soft, clear but muted, audible but devoid of resonance. It reminded one of fog in which sound travels differently than it does in the brightness of sunshine, and one constantly wanted to clear Dr. Huber's throat for him. He had the habit of accenting speech or emphasizing questions by unconsciously opening his eyes wide, so that an encircling limbus shone momentarily white around the gray iris.

Porter had once seen a mockingbird running through grass on rapid, dainty legs suddenly stop, stretch its wings deliberately to full extension, and then sweep them upward before settling them slowly back in place to start the cycle all over again. He had been fascinated by the repetitive run, stop, stretch, and relax of the bird and had watched it for an imprinting quarter-hour until a roaming dog sent the bird, scolding, to a blossoming branch of privet hedge.

He had asked Wes about it and had been assured that this "wan't nuthin but dat ole bird scarin up hoppergrasses out'n the weeds so he could eat em." Porter had watched the phenomenon again, had not seen the bird feed at all during the process, and realized that Wes was wrong. He finally had decided that this was a preening declaration on the part of the bird that gray and white were also important in the Lord's palette for a summer garden. He immediately associated Dr. Huber with the mockingbird — a wintry man with a hint of summer only in his eyes.

"*Mesdames et Messieurs, bonjour. Je vous souhaite la bienvenue à votre première classe de français ici à l'Université Willingham. Je me présente: Monsieur Huber. Je vais être votre professeur pour ces six mois. Quand j'appellerai votre nom, répondez poliment, s'il vous plaît. Je compte évidemment sur votre bonne prononciation. Même mauvaise, je l'écouterai avec intérêt.*"

Porter Osborne, Jr.'s heart plummetted below his belly button and stayed there. He could feel it thumping like a trapped animal. It was one of the blackest moments of his life. This gray and distant ghost of a man with his Ph.D. from the University of Paris, the last vestige of humanity purged from him by overeducation, zealous and gravely dedicated, would be his downfall. He had understood only the first word of Dr. Huber's little speech and had been hopelessly lost thereafter in the flow and rhythm of strange sounds. He was looking an F squarely in the face. He experienced terror as real as if his life had been threatened. What if this goes on for two whole quarters? This will be the first F I ever made in my life, Porter thought. He might as well be speaking a foreign language. For a split second, he missed the humor of such thinking.

"*Monsieur Sage Anderson.*"

"*Anderson ici, Monsieur le professeur,*" snapped back the boy from Lanier High School, sounding comfortably bilingual.

Porter felt cowed and wormy, like a mangy puppy quivering and cringing in a corner. Desperately following the progression of the roll call, he nearly missed his own name because of Dr. Huber's pronunciation.

"*Monsieur Porter Osborne, Jr.*"

He recovered after a pause in which two students looked in obvious expectation directly at him.

"*Osborne ici, Monsieur le professeur,*" Porter bleated in frantic imitation of Sage Anderson. His voice cracked. Tiny Yeomans, ensconced in the chair directly in front of him, gave the faintest of titters. Dr. Huber's eyes swung to Porter's face, flared briefly, and moved on.

"*Mademoiselle Clarice Parker,*" the soft voice continued without expressiveness.

Porter's ordeal was temporarily over, and he took a relaxing breath.

After the roll call, Dr. Huber continued to speak to the class in French. Occasionally he would turn to a table beside him and lift up a book for the group's inspection, obviously illustrating some point of his mysterious peroration. Porter noted that the other students were taking notes; so he opened his own notebook and began making periodic entries. Feigning attention and concentration, which were the ultimate in deception, he wrote "Help me, Lord" over and over. He wrote "Where are You now, our Heavenly Father?" and he wrote in English. Finally Dr. Huber selected a thin volume from the stack beside him and walked over to Tiny's desk. Porter noted that the title on the cover of the book was *Le Secret de l'étang noir* and dutifully made a note of it just below "Thy humble servant needs Thee, Lord."

Dr. Huber spoke for several minutes in his soft, foggy monotone and then handed the book to Tiny. The only words intelligible to Porter were "Mademoiselle Yeomans." Tiny accepted the book and calmly began reading aloud. She read and read and read. Porter understood not one word but noted that she gargled her R's and that Dr. Huber was nodding approvingly. He also noted that her bottom was bulging like a sack of meal through the space between the seat and the first rung of the back of her chair. He longed to kick it. Finally she stopped and returned the book to the professor.

"*Très bien. Et maintenant, nous allons voir si quelqu'un veut bien avoir l'obligeance de faire une explication de ce passage. Voulez-vous bien, Monsieur Osborne?*"

The mockingbird spread its wings. Porter's ears roared. The only word he had understood was his name, but all eyes were upon him. The very air in the room was expectant. A vision of Wes appeared before him. He saw his black friend when he had received instructions from the father too complex and too rapid for immediate comprehension. Impulsively, Porter reached one finger up and scratched his head like a jack-a-napes. His eyes met those of Dr. Huber. In exaggerated Negro dialect, he spoke.

"Say which?"

There was a moment of complete silence and stillness. Dr. Huber's expression did not change. Of a sudden, Tiny Yeoman's head went down on her desk and she gave a loud snort of laughter. The rest of the students followed suit with an explosion of delighted hilarity. In the uproar Dr. Huber's gaze never faltered. Porter Osborne, Jr., had more sense than to allow his own eyes even to flicker. It was almost a form of ophthalmic Indian wrestling.

Tiny, taking a hiccupping breath which almost strangled her, completely out of control of herself, broke wind so loudly that the entire class stopped laughing. There was the same shocked and startled silence, the same interchange of glances that a shotgun blast at the front of the room would have produced. Dr. Huber swept the class with a coldly formal look, and the hush held. Tranquility would have been maintained if it had not been for the humiliated Tiny herself. She turned her head and raised it from the encircling cushion of her elbow. In bell-like tones and with perfect accent, she broke the spell.

"*Excusez-moi, s'il vous plaît,*" she said.

Sage Anderson led the revolt. With a howl, he slapped his thigh and guffawed one time after the other. The Miller girls and the rest of the boys followed his lead. They threw back their heads and laughed and laughed until the sounds shook the wavy old window panes. Only Porter Osborne, Jr., and Dr. Huber did not laugh. Porter kept his eyes glued to the professor with a solemn expression of exaggerated innocence upon which he felt his very life depended. The professor's eyes shifted first, and he drummed on the wide-planked floor with a booming heel. The laughter subsided.

"*Mesdemoiselles! Messieurs!* Ladies and gentlemen! *Vous exag-gérez! Arrêtez tout de suite ce chahut! Maintenant, c'est fini! A demain, à la même heure. Sortez, s'il vous plaît.*" He swung toward Porter Osborne, Jr., and opened his mouth to speak, but Porter was there before him.

"May I see you after class, Dr. Huber?" he said.

A few minutes later, as the descending footsteps of his fellow students reverberated in hollow echo through the old building, Porter faced the dignified mien of his teacher.

66

"Dr. Huber, I think I'm in serious trouble in your class. I come from a very small school in a very poor county, and we didn't have the best teachers in the world. I can read and write French fairly well, but I never in my life heard it spoken before. Do you think I should change to another class or something?"

"Mr. Osborne, do you mean to tell me that you had two years of high school French and never had drills in phonics?"

Porter swallowed and looked sincerely through his grimy glasses at Dr. Huber. "What are phonics, sir?"

Dr. Huber widened his eyes. "Are you serious, Mr. Osborne?"

"Dr. Huber, I haven't laughed since I got to Willingham. I'm serious as a hog on ice."

"Indeed. It's been years since I heard that expression."

He turned to the window and looked out over the tops of the magnolia trees with his hands clasped behind him. Porter did not move. Presently the teacher turned. With no trace of passion in his voice, he spoke. "Mr. Osborne, it is totally degenerate to consider that a student could complete an intermediate course in the French language at a university of the excellence which this one possesses without a command of the spoken as well as the written word."

"Yes, sir. I certainly see your point, sir. I'm a hard worker and a serious student and I'll do anything you tell me to do, sir. The only thing is when you talk like you did this morning, I don't even understand what you're telling me to do."

"Ah, yes."

The man turned again to the window. Porter stood motionless and breathed as quietly as possible.

"Mr. Osborne, I do not believe in the exchange of personal confidences between teacher and student. I am of the opinion that any familiarity between the two breaches the academic discipline which is essential to a studious climate. Formality and politeness engender mutual respect. In the words of one of the modern poets, 'Good fences make good neighbors.' In my years at Willingham University, this precept has served me well. Today is the first time in my memory that any raucous outburst has ever occurred in my classroom. I am tempted to believe this is because of your presence and your personality, but judicious consideration forces me to admit that this is teleological reasoning."

In reply to Porter's quizzical intake of breath, he continued. "That is reasoning which rests ultimately on the premise of '*Post hoc, ergo propter hoc.*' That is not French, Mr. Osborne, that is Latin, and you may look it up later for your edification."

"I don't need to look that up, Dr. Huber. Doesn't it mean 'After this, therefore because of this'? I was pretty good in Latin, but I didn't have but three years of it."

"Indeed. Well, that's a fairly accurate translation. But we digress, Mr. Osborne. The point I was about to make is that I have a very definite feeling I should advise you to drop this course and enroll in Dr. Lobo's class in Spanish for beginners. You might be very good for that lady, who for years has engaged, in my opinion, in excessive familiarity with her students. I am not, however, totally devoid of a certain empathy for what apparently is your situation."

He paused and actually cleared his throat and then continued with no improvement whatever in timbre. "You see, Mr. Osborne, I was born, more years ago than I care to confide, in the small hamlet of Hahira, Georgia. I was sent at a very early age to boarding school in a condition of preparedness, both academic and emotional, which one can in all charity only call inadequate. I encountered some of the problems which seem to be surrounding you. I had not thought of them for years until your appearance in my classroom this morning. My approach to the solution of problems was somewhat different from yours, and I became what some people along the way have called overly studious and others have rudely labeled shy and withdrawn.

"My energies, Mr. Osborne, have been dedicated to scholarship. I have had no wife, no children, and only a few quite carefully selected friends. Although my life has not been a lonely experience and to me has been a satisfying progression of orderly and expected events, I rather think it would be difficult for you to quell enough of a certain ebullience you possess to fall comfortably into a similar pattern. No, I would not recommend this for you."

He turned again to the window. Porter looked at the hands clasped behind his back, gray and soft and devoid of calluses. He wanted to move but felt that to do so would break some sort of spell. The distant wail of the siren sounded for lunch at Nottingham Hall, and he envisioned the stampede that must be occurring right now.

Still he waited, motionless. Finally Dr. Huber turned.

He looked at Porter, and the mockingbird briefly spread its wings. "Mr. Osborne, I believe that you can master the French language or at least make a passing grade in this course. Although I have not heard it since my childhood, your inflection and pronunciation in Negro dialect were linguistically beyond reproach this morning. The comparison of situations and responses thereto which was inherent in your terse question was thought-provoking and possessive of an almost exquisite universality. Although you used only two words, you painted an entire canvas across my memory. I do not fault the students for laughing. One does not have to be ponderously wordy to evoke eloquent thoughts and images, Mr. Osborne, and to this point, I call the book of Job to your attention.

"Again, I wander. What I am saying is that a person who can master one foreign dialect can perfect himself in another. You are no stranger to phonetics except in formal definition thereof. I suggest that you get someone to help you practice correct French pronunciation. You will have to work hard, but I believe you can do it. That way you may not fail my course."

"Gee, Dr. Huber, that's wonderful. Will you be able to help me outside of class?"

"Me, Mr. Osborne? Me? Certainly not. I am recurrently surprised at the brash presumption of American youth. My time is filled with serious study to the total exclusion of any such elementary activity. No, not I, Mr. Osborne. I would suggest rather some fellow student who is amiable and has a better grasp of the subject than yourself. Miss Yeomans, for instance. She has quite an excellent accent and obviously a penchant for the tongue. She probably would be receptive to the idea of helping you."

"Tiny Yeomans? I don't think she likes me, Dr. Huber."

"Likes you? Likes you, Mr. Osborne? What has that to do with the learning process? I suggest that you make it a point to ingratiate yourself with the young lady. She has an excellent grasp of what you need to learn and probably more time to share it than some of her sisters of, shall we say, more fortunate physiognomy."

"Yes sir, I see what you mean. I think I'll just ask her about it. After all, the worst she can do is say no."

"One more thing, Mr. Osborne. I shall make it a point this

69

first quarter to speak enough English in class for you to understand easily the instructions and directions for study. In return, I shall expect — nay, I shall demand — that you curb a certain proclivity you appear to have for inciting insurrection."

"Anything you say, Dr. Huber. But I'm not sure I quite know what you mean there."

"I mean, Mr. Osborne, that until the day I die, I never intend to hear another fat mademoiselle poot in my class. You may go now."

The eyes widened, and the wings of the mockingbird stretched full for a long moment, but there was no hint of a smile around his lips.

Porter suppressed his own desire to laugh and turned to the door.

"Mr. Osborne, forgive a question of a personal nature. Is your mother living?"

"My mother? Oh, yes sir. Both my parents are living."

"Indeed. How interesting. When my mother died, her brothers sent me to boarding school. *Au revoir,* Mr. Osborne."

everything about the presentation of food at Nottingham Hall was designed to force a student to eat fast. The summoning siren engendered such excitement and everyone entered in such a rush that it seemed a letdown not to continue the hurried pace. The dietician, however, was a Christian lady, and she would not allow her student patrons to touch a morsel of the food waiting on the tables until a blessing had been said. There was a pause, then, at every meal after the boys had scrambled to their places, when Mrs. Raleigh tapped on a glass and honored some student by calling on him to say the blessing. Pandemonium erupted again after the "Amen" when the boys assaulted the serving dishes and spooned their plates full. They yelled if someone took a lion's portion; seconds were hard to come by under Mrs. Raleigh's frugal supervision.

Mrs. Raleigh was a widow of impoverished but genteel background who had three boys of college age, all of whom had managed to obtain athletic scholarships — one in football, one in basketball, and one in baseball. The powers at Willingham, who were experts at maintaining dignity and prestige on a shoestring and also well understood the Southern penchant of ignoring reality for the glory of pretense, had hired Mrs. Raleigh to supervise the cooks, the meals, the waiters, the purchasing, and the upkeep of the dining hall in general. They called her the dietician.

She had grown up on a farm in Worth County, one of two girls in the middle of eight brothers. She very early became an expert at gathering vegetables, curing meats, and cooking in large quantities. She was adept, under the tutelage of a mother who had no conception that Reconstruction was over, at making a little go a long way,

71

and she presented leftovers with persistence until they were devoured in desperation. She was also well trained in the art of controlling males in a ladylike fashion. When one is doling out the food to ravenous farmers, one has the whiphand and does not have to raise one's voice to get attention and cooperation. A reputation for sweetness and patience is preferable to one for shrewishness, especially as long as things are going to suit.

The mottos under which she was reared were, "Waste not, want not;" "Do unto others (her mother only rarely finished this verse);" "A penny saved is a penny made;" and "A soft answer turneth away wrath." By the time she had finished the tenth grade, she was so bone-weary of hungry boys, but so sweetly incapable of open acknowledgement of the fact, that she persuaded herself she was in love with Walter Lee Raleigh over on the next farm. Walter Lee was an inarticulate youth three years her senior, with muscular arms, a slow smile, and earnest eyes. Adding to his attraction was a reputation for being a very finicky eater. The first time he mentioned marriage, she pretended he was the one who had thought up the subject. She accepted him, arching her neck and bridling in a very ladylike way to accept a kiss upon her cheek.

Walter Lee Raleigh was a farm boy and knew very little of kissing, but this same farm background had made him proficient in animal husbandry, and he knew a great deal about mating. Within two years, he produced three sons from his bride's body without so much as a single comment about the process. Mrs. Raleigh named the oldest one Randy, because the euphony of Randy Raleigh appealed to her. She named the twins Rusty and Dusty in expedient haste, perceived that she was in peril of becoming surrounded again by famished boys, and vowed not to have any more children if she could possibly help it. She knew better than to suggest that Walter Lee participate in any form of birth control; he would have grunted that he needed all the plowhands he could get.

So, smiling and sighing, she mapped out such a program of activity for herself that she worked to the point of exhaustion every day before bedtime. This martyring ploy, accompanied by unusually heavy suppers for Walter Lee, lent her credence and produced a measure of somnolent relief in her husband when she murmured, "I'm too tired." She had listened carefully to the granny-woman who delivered Rusty and Dusty and managed, without his ever realizing he had been put on a schedule, to confine Walter Lee's sexual activity to evenings before and immediately after her period.

She curtailed early morning sex because of aesthetics rather than fear of pregnancy. She hated her mate's morning breath, felt self-consciously that her own smelled the same way, and, in addition, preferred to awaken in a leisurely fashion without such a frenzied animal activity. She solved the problem by appealing to an unsuspected streak of sensitivity in the phlegmatic Walter Lee. Badgered by his insistent fumblings, one morning she turned herself over on her back, flung an arm over her eyes and, completely unresponsive, muttered, "I'm too sleepy. Just help yourself." To Walter Lee, there was something degrading about relieving oneself on an inert body which could sleep through penetration by what he was secretly convinced must be just about the biggest ole pecker in all Worth County. After accepting a couple of these invitations, he avoided with resignation further such experiences, packed his throbbing penis into his overalls, and after a half-hour of energetic plowing was troubled no more by it until the following morning.

Walter Lee felt that this incompatibility was a pity, for his most magnificent erections invariably occurred at dawn after a period of restful slumber. He knew, however, that there were things about ladies that men were supposed to accept without any effort at understanding. His wife never had a headache in her life, but he assumed that she was the only delicate female in the world who ever murmured, "Not now. The children might hear us." Walter Lee Raleigh would have felt vaguely perverted if he had attempted to discuss sex with anyone, let alone his wife. They became known as the hardest working young couple anywhere around.

On their sixteenth wedding anniversary, the mules shied at a rattlesnake and ran away with the wagon. One of them stepped in a gopher hole, broke his leg, and threw Walter Lee out of the wagon and broke his neck. Mrs. Raleigh's brothers shot the mule and dragged him off into the piney woods for the buzzards and possums to attend. They buried Walter Lee in the country graveyard, beside a maiden aunt who had died with pneumonia, two spaces over from his mother's parents. It was a quiet and dignified funeral service in the bare little church. Mrs. Raleigh had told the preacher she wanted no personal references, and she told her boys and her family that she wanted no crying out loud when they went by the casket. After all, they were genteel. Everyone said that it was a sweet funeral, that Mrs. Raleigh was a very brave woman, and that the gnats were the worst that year they had ever seen.

When the preacher came by the house to console her, she clasped her three sons until he finished. Then she faced him with dry eyes and reassured him with a sentence she coined on the spot: "There is work to be done, and I am no stranger to suffering, Mr. Carver." She liked the saying so well that she adopted it as an additional motto to the ones her mother had implanted and used it frequently. Her years of habitual hard work served her well, and she managed to stay on the farm until her three boys got through high school.

By then her church had called a new preacher. He was a settled man who took his profession seriously and had enrolled in Willingham University in preparation for the ultimate in ministerial education — matriculation at the Baptist seminary in Louisville. He and his wife were most admiring of the plucky Widow Raleigh and supported her ambition for college educations for her sons. When an opening occurred in the dining hall at Willingham, the preacher apprised the business manager that a thrifty, hard-working Christian lady lived in the recesses of south Georgia who understood boys and was such an accomplished mistress of frugality that she could do with field peas and roasting ears what the Master had done with loaves and fishes. She was hired for an undisclosed salary, but everyone knew she enjoyed the fringe benefits of free housing, free meals, and free education for her sons. During the employment interview, the businss manager made up his mind when she arched her neck, looked him softly in the eye, and told him in tones of exaggerated refinement, "I am no stranger to suffering, Mr. Mullinax, and I know when there is work to be done."

Halfway through her first year at Willingham, her superior — a spinster with rimless glasses, marcelled white hair tightly bound in a white net, and eyes of flint to match her heart — had a stroke and died. Mr. Mullinax considered the problem for five minutes and elevated Mrs. Raleigh to the position of head dietician of Willingham University at a still undisclosed salary. Although it was less than her educated predecessor had extracted from Mr. Mullinax, it was still enough to enable Randy, Rusty, and Dusty Raleigh to join a fraternity. It was not Pike, either.

Mrs. Raleigh did a superb job and stayed so well within her budget that Mr. Mullinax won approval from his superiors for sagacity and shrewdness, two virtues not at all incompatible with Christianity when endowments and operating funds are low. She retained the siren and the head cook, a Negro male, but fired the second cook, who was a Negro woman.

Mrs. Raleigh, descendant of yeoman farmers of limited means as well as vision, had never been around any Negroes and knew them only by reputation. She was convinced, however, by decades of raised eyebrows, half-finished whispers, and knowing nods that all black women actually enjoyed sex, and she had suspicions that Bessie was no exception. Since Mrs. Raleigh wanted no contact at all with a female who looked on marital duty as pleasure, Bessie had to go. She was replaced by the first cook's brother-in-law, and the dining hall was run thereafter by one white lady, two black men, two student dishwashers, and twelve student waiters. Everyone involved was completely cognizant of the lady's supreme authority.

They served three meals a day to two hundred and fifty Baptist boys for six days out of the week. On Sunday, they served only breakfast and lunch and passed out for supper paper bags containing a sandwich, a banana, and a package of peanut butter crackers. This gave Mrs. Raleigh and her staff an opportunity to rest. If she ever regarded her bustling kitchen, considered the bowed and gobbling heads of ravenous boys, and felt that her life had come full cycle, she voiced the feeling to no one. Anybody could tell by looking at her that she was a hard worker and no stranger to suffering.

Porter had two choices on the day that Dr. Huber made him late for lunch. He could go to the Co-op and buy a milkshake and sandwich, or he could throw himself on the mercy of Mrs. Raleigh and beg for special dispensation in the form of a plate in the kitchen. The former would cost him twenty cents and would amount to throwing money away, since he thought he could arrange the latter.

Mrs. Raleigh should be a little on the defensive with him, he thought, and feel a bit apologetic, since she had twice accused him of being someone's little brother and demanded a visitor's ticket of him. He decided that he could enlarge the advantage he had.

"Mrs. Raleigh, I don't know if you remember me, but I'm a freshman student here. I know I'm late, but my French teacher held me after class. He thinks I'm too little to study French. Could you please, ma'am, let me have something to eat?"

"Of course I remember you." She twisted her head on her neck. "I pride myself on knowing all my boys and never forgetting a face. You're called Sambo and you room with Bob Cater. You brought that poor, pitiful blind boy in the first time he came to the dining hall. I noticed you being so nice to him. Leading him for all the world like a pitcher I seen of a little boy in the Bible. You're small of your age, but you've got a good heart. Do unto others, I always say."

Porter tried to look a little self-conscious but not self-righteous. It was a delicate balance which not just everyone could achieve.

"I'd like to help you out, but we've got strict rules about that." She was extremely self-righteous but not the least self-conscious. "The absolute latest you can get fed is to get to the table before they serve dessert. I don't want you to think it's just me. Mr. Mullinax has me on a very tight budget, and he says that if a student is late, he has to pay the same as a visitor's ticket. And that's twenty-five cents. A stitch in time saves a quarter around here.

"You can see that everybody is finished and gone except that big boy in the corner with the pretty yellow curly hair. His name is Quinton Pickett. He's a football player — gonna study law. Somebody told him it's bad for your health to eat fast, so he loads his plate up and chews every mouthful ten times. You can watch him counting. He's always the last to leave. A diller, a dollar, I say. Somebody told him about germs on doorknobs, too, and he'll wait long as he can, hoping somebody else will come along and open the door first after he's washed his hands. If anybody had been left eating besides Quinton, I might be able to make an exception for you, but I just don't see how I can."

Porter looked up at her. His eyes pled. "But Mrs. Raleigh, I don't have a quarter. My daddy's got a big family to educate and I'm on a short rein about money. If you could spare just a couple of crusts of bread with maybe a little butter between them, I could make out till suppertime. I'm really hungry, Mrs. Raleigh."

"Law, boy, don't say that. I can't stand to think about a boy being hungry, let alone hear him say it. Just this one time I'm going to fix you a plate, but don't you go telling that I did it free. I am no stranger to suffering, and I know what it is not to have a quarter. Besides, a penny saved. You'll have to eat in the kitchen while the boys clean the tables and mop the floors. Don't get in the way of my helpers, now, because there is work to be done. Boston, you come here. Take Sambo back and fix him a plate. He can eat at my desk."

She hurried away to supervise a student who was sweeping carelessly and leaving crumbs behind a table leg. Porter and Boston were left to survey each other. Porter saw a slightly rotund man in his late twenties or early thirties with a friendly smile that displayed an accenting space in the middle of his upper teeth. He was colored like a cup of coffee with just a touch of cream in it, and his white apron was spotted around the midline with stains of only the latest meal he had prepared. Boston was meticulously clean and a fastidious dresser. He had a sixth finger on his right hand — a small, quivering, jellylike member that looked boneless but had a little fingernail embellishing it.

"Boston? That's an unusual name. What's your last name?"

"Last name's Jones. What you mean to say is that's a funny name for a nigger, ain't it?"

So strong was his projection of well-being and so deep his reservoir of good humor that there was no feeling at all of antagonism in his question.

"Certainly not. I was taught not to use that word."

"Well, don't get prissy bout it with me. Jest you saying that tells me more'n you think about yo'self. Lessee now. Musta been raised around a heap of us if the subject come up enough for you to have to be taught. Spect yo pa be called Bossman a heapa times. Spect yo maw an maybe yo granmaw high bawn ladies if they go to the trouble to teach you that. None of yo women folks ever helt a hoe handle or done nothin more'n a little yard work. Prolly lay down an stretch out awhile after dinner ever day. Uh huh, boy. You quality, an you raised on a cotton farm somers tween here 'n Atlanta."

"Boston, how in the world you know all that?"

"Gotta watch, gotta listen in this ole world, boy. Lemme tell you somepin else. My full name's Boston Harbor Jones, an that is a crazy name for a nigger. Before you laugh, you tell me how come it ain't funny for a white chile ain't big as a bar of soap after a week's washing be named Sambo?"

They laughed simultaneously. Porter felt better than he had since arriving at Willingham. "Can I feel your finger, Boston Harbor Jones?" he said.

The plate Boston presented him was mounded up with potato salad, fried corn, string beans, and peas. Porter noted with relief that they were English peas; he never ate crowders. Two slices of bologna lay on top, and three rolls were pressed around the edge to keep the peas from rolling off.

"I know this more'n you'n eat. Don't fret about it. I jest like to tease Mrs. Raleigh ever now an then. She ain't never been around no colored much, and she bout half scared of us. Act like she think we some strange mix tween King Kong an Step'n'Fetchit. She talk sweet an kind all time out there in the dining hall, an then she holler when she git back here an talk to us. Bout oncet a day I try to do somepin dumb as she think I be so she won't get herself disappointed. Now you watch. I give you a five dollar bill if she don't look at yo plate and say, 'Waste not, want not.' You git to eatin an lemme help my brother-in-law git this ole kitchen clean up."

"What's his name? Your brother-in-law."

"His name Jesse. Jesse Lee Ponder." They looked at each other with delicious awareness and then spoke in unison.

"Now that's a good nigger name."

Their resultant roar of laughter attracted Mrs. Raleigh. "Boston! You get busy and help Jesse clean the kitchen. Why do you always have to wait for me to tell you before you do anything? Land sakes, look at that plate. That's enough food for three men to prime tobacco all day. One little boy can't possibly eat it all. I'd think even you had more judgment than that, Boston. Think of the thousands of Chinese children starving right at this moment. Waste not, want not, I always say."

Porter and Boston exchanged brief glances, but neither

smiled. Boston even managed to look crestfallen and chagrined.

"Boston, I declare, I just despair of ever learning how to teach you anything. I know a soft answer turneth away wrath, but you've got to learn to think. This isn't just waste, it's stupidity. If Sambo doesn't clean that plate, I'm going to charge you for two visitor's lunch tickets and have Mr. Mullinax take fifty cents out of your check when I turn the time in. Come on, now. There is work to be done."

Porter recognized a challenge and immediately involved himself. He looked around the kitchen door and across the dining hall at Quinton Pickett, who was still chewing deliberately while he sat in solitary splendor at a table upon which all the chairs were now upended except his own. He sat militarily erect with his left hand rigidly in his lap and unmoving. A waiter was mopping the floor around him and under the legs of his chair.

"Mrs. Raleigh, if it's not too much trouble, could I please, ma'am, have a glass of milk to wash this down?"

With gusto he attacked the plate of food, abandoning all pretense to any table manners he had ever learned. He was the embodiment of famished impatience. He wolfed and bolted food with head almost in his plate and with a frenzy that would have earned at least six adult reprimands at home. He observed from the corner of his eye that he had Mrs. Raleigh's attention. She watched disbelievingly as she scurried about her duties. He considered snapping and growling but decided that would be overacting. He sopped the plate clean with a morsel and popped it in his mouth with simulated relish. Mrs. Raleigh shook her head wearily as she left to rush the methodical Quinton Pickett. Boston sat down beside him.

"Hoo whee, Sambo, that was somepin else. You go through that plate of vittles like a dog, or at least one nem yankee football players. Me an Jesse bout to bust open not to laugh over there. Mrs. Raleigh be confuse all afternoon now, an liable to git a sick headache bout suppertime. Say she ain't never had no headaches in her whole life till she commence workin round me an Jesse. Cain't dock me no fi'ty cent now, an them Chinese chirren yet hungry, too. I glad you come to school here, but me'n you together sho goan have to watch not to git in no trouble."

The burp Porter emitted was the only sincere act he had performed in the last five minutes.

"What you talkin bout, Boston? I'm not planning on getting into any trouble. I came here to study. I'm a serious student." He paused. "I want to make the Dean's List, but that French is going to kill me."

Boston cocked his head to one side and rolled his eyes at Porter. "Uh huh. I ain't worry bout you an no Dean's List. Jest watch you operate already, I spect you'n fool yo way in French good as anywheres else. I know a special person when I see one. Ain't you never hear white folks say you cain't fool a small chile or yet a nigger? I feels thangs in my bones. Comes like a gift from havin this extra finger. Had one on the other hand, but Maw tied a string on it when I was a baby, an it dry up an drap off. Else I prolly have second sight an know everthing. You got a knowin in you, and I got a knowin in me, an it gonna be fun watchin you git a education. But don't tell me you ain't no troublemaker. I know you been settin here studyin that ole sireen."

Porter looked at the man uncomprehendingly. "The siren? Where is it? I never saw one in my life. I never even heard one before I came here, except in Atlanta one time when a fire truck went down Broad Street. This one's the loudest thing in the whole world. Where is it?"

"There it set, right over there in the window by the dishwasher. An there you set, wonderin how in the world you goan manage to crawl in that window some mornin bout two or three o'clock an set that ole sireen off an then run back to yo bed real quick fore anybody else git enough awake to git they clothes on, an then you set up in bed rubbin yo eyes and sayin, 'What's all that fuss about?' Oh, you ain't foolin me none. I saw it all in a flash when you et that last mouthful of peas."

Porter swallowed and countered in a scoffing tone. "Boston, you don't have any second sight. You just crazy."

The brown hand went up and the gelatinous finger quivered. "Little somepin somebody need to know bout that ole sireen, in case some dumb nigger forgit to fasten the catch on the window when we lockin up round here at night and somebody can climb in. The switch broke on it. It froze in ON position an ain't been fixed. You know bout a penny saved is a penny made, don't you? All somebody gotta do is plug in the electric cord on that ole sireen an fly way from there fore it git to growlin good. Fast runner be in bed fore it scream hard enough to wake anybody up."

"Why in the world would anyone want to do something like that?"

Boston continued as though he had noticed no interruption. "An you know ain't nobody but Mrs. Raleigh an Mr. Mullinax got keys to the dining hall, an it prolly take least half a nour one them git over here, unlock the door, turn on the lights, an disconnect that ole sireen. You imagine that thing screechin for half a nour? Hoo whee! Wake the dead!"

Porter interposed with determined emphasis. "Boston! I still want to know why anybody'd do that."

"Cause it need doin, that's why. Ain't been done, an it need doin. Fresh things up around here. Git folks' minds off theyselves, stir up the whole patch. Do unto others, Sambo, do unto others. Hit good for em. Good for ole Step'n'Fetchit an good for all them Shirley Temples' mamas. Shake em awake. Ain't nobody around here no stranger to sufferin no how, and this git they minds off they troubles. Bet that ole window git left unlock for at least a week to see do anybody think about that sireen some night when he have to git up to pee anyhow."

Porter looked at Boston as though truth had recently been revealed to him. "Boston Jones, did you ever read Uncle Remus?"

"Who? I don't read nothin much save the *Macon Telegraph*, a little bit of the Holy Bible, an my dream book."

"Dream book?"

"Yeah. Ever dream got a number. Dream bout somepin, look up the number, write it down for the man, an give it to him along with a nickel, an you might hit good. Lots more'n jest plain guess-work. Only trouble is I sleep so sound, I don't ever dream. You dream, Sambo?"

"Course I do. Every night. I thought everybody did. But I don't understand what you're talking about with the numbers."

Boston gave a sigh and spoke patiently. "Talkin bout the bug, Sambo. You ain't never heard of the bug? Fella make a heapa money when he hit. I been playin for a long time. The secret is to do it ever day, regular. Used to, I play a penny, but since I got this good job, I plays a nickel. You ain't got to hit but one time real good an you done got well."

"I never heard of such a thing. How do you know what the winning number is?"

"Last six numbers on the stock market report up there in New Yawk City ever night. You git four of em, you git a good hit. You git five right, you come home on the glory train. But you hit all six, you be so rich you have ever nigger in town jest wanna touch yo clothes. Trouble is, I needs me somebody what dream regular. I sleeps too sound. I goan stand over there at the door ever mornin an you come by an snap out what you dream about. OK? An I swear I give you halfa what I win. How bout it? You be my dream boy, Sambo?"

Porter shrugged his shoulders and tried to mask condescension. "Well, for Pete's sake. I don't mind telling what I dream about, but I don't think there's anything to it but superstition. This bug business sounds to me like some sort of gambling, but I don't see any harm in telling you my dreams."

"Atta boy, Sambo. You sho talkin white when you git off on thangs like superstition and gambling. You leave all that for me to worry bout. I gotta go. Hope all that dinner don't make you sick. You be bout et yo weight, an it sho was fun watchin you. I say, 'Waste not, want not.' You all right, Sambo, an you save me a half a dollar."

"Bye, Boston. I still think you read Uncle Remus. You sure got me feeling like a cross between Brer Rabbit and the little boy."

He walked out into the dining hall where the dietician was locking the door behind Quinton Pickett. "Mrs. Raleigh, you'll never know how much I appreciate this. You saved my life. You're the sweetest lady in the whole wide world."

"I'm glad you enjoyed it, Sambo. It's nice manners for you to come and tell me that. Now, I don't mean any harm, but we're going to have to work on those table manners of yours just a little bit. There has to be a happy balance somewhere between you and Quinton Pickett. I wouldn't hurt your feelings for anything in the world, but somebody needs to love you enough to tell you. Do unto others, I always say."

"Yes'm, I spect you're right about that. That's the best way to live. I appreciate your telling me about the table manners."

* * * *

In the Biology laboratory a little later, Porter forgot his abdominal distress. The lab instructor was a senior student, a balding, bespectacled, serious young man with a nasal twang and a shortness to his syllables that identified him as a yankee. He assigned desks in the laboratory and then passed out the dissecting equipment. Perfectly willing to be impressed by the glamour of advanced science, Porter felt vaguely let down when he inspected what his five-dollar lab fee had produced. There was a tawdry, imitation leather case that contained scissors, tweezers, two wooden sticks with long needles in the ends, two shiny metal chains terminating in sharp hooks, and a flimsy scalpel. There was a rubber-coated apron with areas of scaliness attesting previous use, and a pair of rubber gloves. There was a dime-store cake pan, discolored and darkened by repeated heating. It was filled to half its depth with a mixture of beeswax and paraffin, remelted in the pan after use the year before and now cooled to a hardened surface yet unmarred by dissecting needles and scalpels.

On a stool in a corner was an unlidded jar, reeking of formaldehyde and packed with fleshy cylinders twelve inches long and gently waving in submerged grayness. Porter watched attentively as the instructor demonstrated how to dissect an earthworm. From two tables behind him, he heard a familiar voice.

"There's no way in the world I will ever be able to touch those horrible, slimy, stinking things."

Eunice Yeomans had recovered her aplomb and was drawing attention to herself again. "I'm not kidding. I can't stand the sight, I can't stand the smell, and I can't bear even to imagine how one of those beastly things feel. Then on top of that, we gotta do grasshoppers, crayfish, and even frogs. What am I going to do?"

Porter realized that her wail was sincere. He eased around to the side of the distraught girl and spoke gently. "Move over Tiny. Let me do that for you."

With a few deft movements, as though he had been doing it all his life, he slit the earthworm from one end to the other and pinned the edges in everting display to the wax.

"Now all you have to do is poke around with your dissecting needles a little bit, and you don't have to touch it at all. Just be real quiet about it, and I'll help you with your dissection all quarter."

He cast a mischievous glance at her. "Us ole prepubescent farm boys don't mind handling varmints. We're used to it."

At the end of the laboratory session, Eunice approached him. "Thanks, Sambo. You saved my life. Come to the Co-op with me and I'll set you up to an ice cream Coke."

Porter became conscious of his belly again and almost gagged, but he accompanied her.

Walking across campus, Tiny continued. "You know, I guess maybe I misjudged you. There is more to you after all than just a loudmouthed smart aleck. That really was a kind thing for you to do."

"Aw, Tiny, that wasn't anything. Do unto others, you know."

"It was something, too. It was something very extra special. I can't help the way I feel about bugs and things, and most people think I'm putting on and kidding. There are some things I'll always feel like a little bitty girl about down inside no matter how big I look. And I guess I'm surprised that it was you who recognized that and acted like a grown man about it instead of the bigger boys in the class. Size sure isn't everything."

Porter uncontrollably felt his chest swell out a little. With nonchalance he proclaimed, "My granddaddy always says that it ain't the dog in the fight, it's the fight in the dog, Tiny."

"That's cute... Don't touch me! Don't you dare touch me! You didn't even wear gloves when you were handling those awful things and God knows what your hands smell like!"

"Gosh, Tiny, I wasn't going to touch you."

"Yes you were, too. I could see it in your eyes. You were fixing to pat me. I like you fine, Sambo, but just don't ever touch me."

"I promise, Tiny. No matter what happens, I won't ever touch you. But let me ask you something. Would you mind very much helping me with my French? You know, accent and pronunciation and stuff they call phonics? I'm going to help you with your dissections in Biology anyway, but I sure would appreciate it if you'd help me with French."

"Sure, I'll be glad to. No trouble, kiddo. Me and you and *la belle France, cinq jours par semaine.* First thing you gotta do is learn to trill your R's. Wait a minute. When did you decide you wanted me to help you?"

84

Porter drew a deep breath, considered for only a moment, and took the plunge. He looked Tiny squarely in the eye; her gaze never flickered or wandered beneath the stubby lashes. "Right after Dr. Huber and I decided I was going to flunk French if I didn't get some help. He's the one who suggested you. He admires you a lot and thinks you have a real flair for the language. I told him I didn't think you liked me much, and he said that's not important if you really want to learn something."

"Well, I declare. You really fooled me. The only thing is, I'm not sure which time. I can't decide whether you're an unusually perceptive and sensitive man hiding behind those little glasses or just another self-serving little shitass."

Porter jumped. He had never before heard such language from feminine lips. "Thou sayest."

"Thou sayest? Thou sayest? What the hell kind of talk is that? I swear, you're the dopiest little guy I ever saw. That sounds like Bible talk to me. What do you mean?"

"I mean, Tiny, that I can't make up your mind for you about me. Any way I tried to argue, it would look bad, so you're on your own. But listen to this. *Je comprends très bien tous les mots* Anglo-Saxon. Now. Would you mind repeating everything you just said in French?"

They looked at each other a moment, threw back their heads, and laughed in unison.

VII

declining Tiny's well-intended but nauseating offer of refreshment, Porter entered the Co-op and headed directly for the bank of mailboxes mounted in one of the paneled walls. A look through the glass window of his box revealed that he had mail, and he hastily twirled the combination lock to extract his treasure. He recognized the fat envelope with his mother's handwriting and ever so casually slipped it into his pocket, as if such a gesture might deny the importance of the missive not only to some onlooker but even to himself. He could hardly wait to read the letter, but communication with her had become such a personal experience that he did not want it interrupted by anyone. Besides, he felt that his feelings about his mother were too private to share and had nothing at all to do with the new personality he was presenting to Willingham. He carefully hid those feelings a layer or two above the recess he reserved for thoughts even God could not see.

The other object in the box was a pink card, wrinkled from repeated use and faintly greasy in a couple of spots. Its big black letters said CLAIM PACKAGE AT WINDOW. The package was also from his mother, but there was no way he could conceal that from anyone. It was incorporated in a limber pasteboard box which had been slipped into a brown paper sack, encircled with innumerable festooning loops of string, addressed, and launched in the mail as trustingly as little Moses in his boat on the Nile. That it had arrived in one piece was almost as miraculous as the recovery of Moses and made one feel that Miriam must have been watching nearby. The covering was blotched with grease, and he could see through two torn corners of the sack and a crack in the box that he had received a fried chicken, some biscuits, and a burnt caramel cake.

As he tried to balance the shifting load on top of his books, Bob Cater approached. "Hi, Sambo. What ya got there? A box from home already? Gosh, you're a lucky boy — and I'm lucky to be your roommate. Wait'll I check my mail and I'll help you tote it up the hill."

Walking along, Porter entrusted his books to Bob and carried the package himself, occasionally extending a finger to loop up another escaping piece of string. He spoke with nonchalance. "You know, Bob, my mother is the most totally female person in the world. If she runs into something she can't cook, sew, or kiss, she's at a complete loss what to do with it."

"What are you talking about?"

"Well, look at this package, for instance. She's cooked up a whole batch of chicken, baked a cake, and put in some graham biscuits, but she has absolutely no idea of the rigors of the United States mail. She tied it all up like she was going to hand-deliver it next door. How it got here in one piece is beyond me."

"Well, I guess I see what you mean, but didn't you tell me your mother has a car? Mine can't even drive. I'm just glad that food got here at all. I'm tired of Mrs. Raleigh's bologna and salami. When we going to open this box? I'm starving!"

Porter considered the lateness of his lunch and his persistent feeling of engorgement and told Cater that it might be midnight before he felt like eating again.

Bob eyed the box and ignored the remark. "There's a piece of chicken about to fall out now. You care if I rescue it and eat it?"

"Oh, no, go right ahead. But that's a wing. Better hold it up to the light and check for hairs."

"Check for what?"

"If Mother fixed that chicken, she singed it good after she picked it, and there won't be any of those hairs sticking up out of the little part of the wing. But if she let Matt fix it, you have to watch. Matt's careless with her singeing and sometimes a little sloppy about pinfeathers, too."

"Well, it sure tastes great. There's a drumstick that's gonna drop, too. I might as well rescue it. I saw you and ole Tiny headed down the hill while ago with your heads close together. She's not getting sweet on you, is she?"

"Not so you could tell it. It's just that we wound up having all our classes together, and we were talking about school. She's going to help me with French and I'm going to help her with Biology. I'll tell you one thing about Tiny, though." He swaggered a little. "She's sure no prickteaser."

Bob Cater assured him, "That's one thing I would never suspect her of. I really had a good day. Spanish under that Dr. Lobo is going to be fun. She jokes a lot with the class and has a cute personality. When we going to cut the cake?"

Porter instinctively clutched the box closer. The cake was a special, individualized expression of his mother's indulgence. She made each child's favorite cake on the appropriate birthday — banana for the older sister, amalgamation for the second daughter, and lemon cheese for the baby. Porter's burnt caramel was the most difficult to ice, and he had a sudden vision of his mother in the kitchen at home, patiently melting sugar in the black frying pan on the wood-burning stove, her face flushed and her dress wet across the shoulders with perspiration. This cake was an icon.

"Bob, I may save it until tomorrow. I know this sounds silly, but I may want to look at that cake awhile before I cut it. Have another piece of chicken."

"OK. Don't mind if I do. You're swell to share it. I'm glad you're my roommate. When you do get ready for the cake cutting, let me know. My mama doesn't bake cakes. I tell you what. If you're serious about not going to the dining hall, let's drop our books in the room and run by the KA house. You really do need to go over there and jolly around with the fellows a little. They're about to decide you're a bookworm."

Porter shifted his box and changed pace to adjust his stride to Bob's. He saw no point in going to the KA house. He did not think those boys really wanted him to be a KA, and in honesty felt that he was not at all certain he was cut out to be a fraternity man anyway. "Bob, have you ever heard of a legacy? I'm afraid I'm one."

"Of course you're one. But that's a compliment. All that means is that you're guaranteed a bid. The rest of us have to worry about it and maybe act nicer at times than we'd like to, but you guys whose fathers or uncles were fraternity men have got it made. You can just relax and know for sure and certain you're not going to get blackballed by some brother who doesn't like the way you comb your hair. I wish I was a legacy."

"I see your point, I guess, but I'd sure like to know somebody wanted me somewhere and wasn't just putting up with me because they had to. I guess I'll go for a few minutes, but I really do need to get back and study. Did you know that if you keep up every day and don't ever let yourself get behind, it actually doesn't take nearly as much time to study as if you're always having to catch up? When we get to the room, let me leave my cake over on your dresser if you don't care. Mine's next to Tom's, and he's liable to go feeling all over it to see what it is; but if I put it on yours, he's got no business at all prying around way over there."

"I know what you mean. I tell you, Sambo, we've got to figure out some way to get rid of that fellow. He gives me the creeps. He's revolting. I'm gonna start studying in the Library with Billi. I didn't come to college to get sick at my stomach in my own room."

The KA house had been transformed. It still had gray shingles covering the walls, but the brothers had been busy during the week and had painted the lattice work underneath the high front porch a brick red. Porter thought it now looked like a red and gray chicken house, but the illuminated sign on the front porch still gave it a certain air of elegance. He thought Bob Cater's welcome was much more cordial than his, although the boys in the living room made courteous effort at conversation with him. Clarence Spangler intimidated him by asking if he had heard from his father and then turning to the newly introduced group of boys and informing them with strident voice through sparkling teeth what a magnificent man Porter Osborne, Sr., was. Conversation was a little stilted and formal.

Clarence and Slick moved around the room paying special attention to each boy, inquiring about his classes or special interests. Slick seemed genuinely interested in Porter's classes, and Porter was tempted to confide his trepidation about French to him. Before he could do more than consider it, however, he was accosted by a tall, lanky town student humped at the shoulders in languid non-

89

chalance and dangling a cigarette from the corner of his mouth.

"Hey, boy. I been wanting to meet you all day. I'm in your French class, and that's the funniest thing I've ever seen the way you slicked under ole Huber's skin this morning. And what you did to that Tiny Yeomans! It was almost as though she farted on purpose, it was timed so right. And everything would have been OK if she'd just ignored it, but when she up and apologized out loud for it after it was all over, and that in French, it was more than I could stand. What'd ole Huber say to you?"

The recapitulation drew such a chorus of interested questions that Porter found himself the center of admiring but unwelcomed attention. There was no way he was going to reveal what had really transpired between him and Dr. Huber nor what his true feelings were about the incident. He smiled benignly and said nothing while the boys laughingly proposed their own premises, made their own deductions, and drew their own conclusions. The fact that all of them were based on only smidgins of truth bothered Porter not one bit. The legend being forged before his eyes was preferable to exposure. The real Porter Osborne was as naked, bug-eyed, and vulnerable as a newborn rat.

Presently Clarence yelled for everybody's attention, and the room quieted. "We want you fellows to help us with something. You're a great bunch this year, and I don't have to tell you that we really like every boy in this room and look on all of you as KA material. You know that or we wouldn't keep asking you back just for the pleasure of buddying around with you. What we want you to do is think if there's somebody in your class we're overlooking that would be a good prospect for rush. We're going to have a great year, and we don't want to leave somebody out that's such a good guy we'll be sorry later we didn't pledge him. Brother Slick Roundtree is going around the room now and make a list of guys you fellows think might be prospects."

A serious discussion followed, in which Porter participated no more than he would have in a recital of football scores. He sat quietly unnoticed in the corner of the dingy sofa which smelled faintly sour and strongly smoky. He felt alien but comfortable as he studied carefully the print of General Robert E. Lee astride Traveler. The KA's really are nice guys, he thought.

"Sambo, what about you? I understand you're getting well known in the freshman class. Can you think of anybody who would make a good KA and be a credit to the Order that we ought to ask around to the house and maybe put the rush on?"

"Well, Slick, there are a couple of guys I've met that I really like and who I think would be an asset to any group. One of them's a boy from Macon named Henry Bean. He's got a good sense of humor and is really intelligent."

Clarence's voice slashed through the room. His teeth looked electric. "Henry Bean? Come on! You're off your rocker, Osborne. That guy's got a bad attitude and is a downright smartass. I've already got the word from the Biology department that 'Fessor Hansford has him marked and is out to get him. Forget Henry Bean. I'd blackball him before he got through the door. He's a troublemaker."

Slick spoke blandly around the echoes. "You think of anybody else, Sambo?"

"Yes, I can. There's a real friendly guy on my floor who's always smiling and is nice to everybody. I've watched him around the dormitory and he's just one of those fellows who stands out in a crowd for being friendly and easy to get along with. He'd do anything to help anybody out, and I'm sure no other fraternity is rushing him. I think he'd probably like for you all to invite him around and I'm sure he'd make a good KA."

"What's his name?"

"Darnell Baskin, but his nickname's Bubba. He's from Eatonton."

"Wait a minute!" shouted Clarence Spangler in an interrupting bellow. "Hold the bus! What's this guy look like?"

"He's got dark hair and a cowlick in front and freckles and kind of smiling eyes and dimples when he grins."

"Yeah, that's who I thought you were talking about. You know what else he's got when he grins? A cracked gray tooth with a gold rim around it — right in the front. That's what. And what kind of shoes does he wear, Osborne? Tell em what kind of shoes he wears."

Porter tried to look Clarence in the eyes but found himself staring uncontrollably into the polished glitter of his incisors.

"I don't know what you mean. What do his shoes have to do

91

with it?"

"Aw, come on, Osborne. Quit playing dumb with me. This guy wears brogans, fellows, plain ole hillbilly, plow-boy, swamp-stomping brogans. And he wears em all the time. Everywhere. He'd make as good a KA as Li'l Abner or one of the Scragg brothers. If you could keep the hayseed out of his hair and the beggar lice picked off his corduroys, he would. There's no way any of us would let a guy with shoes like that even come in the KA house, let alone give him a bid. Why, the Phi Delta Thetas would laugh us off the campus.... Wait a minute."

He looked at Porter a long moment. Shattered light bounced from his smile, and fragmented echoes of his strident voice played in the corners of the room. "You know, you're beginning to get quite a reputation as a prankster, young Osborne. For a minute there you almost had me fooled. Fellows, Sambo's just pulling your legs and making a joke out of this whole thing. What a card, Osborne, what a card you are. You'd do anything for a laugh."

He slapped his thigh and his laughter boomed loud. Most of the freshmen joined him, and Porter tried to affect a knowing look as he studied the gaping black hole in the side of Clarence's smile. He felt that he was being challenged by an antagonist the likes of which he had not previously encountered. Of a sudden he recalled Mr. Seab Whitlock from Brewton County — amiable, levelheaded octogenarian who was the unquestioned political boss of Rareover district. Porter had overheard his counsel one election night when his father was exploding in fury about an individual who had betrayed them at the ballot box.

"Now, Mr. Osborne, stay calm. I've knowed a heap of son-bitches in my day, and I never yet seen one change for telling him he was one. Lay low and bide your time."

Porter smiled and rose from the sofa. Small talk erupted, and several boys made jocular remarks to him. Bob Cater told him that he and Deacon Chauncey had decided to go with Clarence and Slick to get a hamburger and take in Errol Flynn's latest movie and invited Porter to join them.

"Bob, I promised my dad I'd get my studying done every night before I did anything else. I'll go on to the room and get to work. Don't you stay out too late and get behind in your work this early in the year."

He welcomed the solitude of his walk back to the dormitory. In the distance an unhurried student sauntered into Nottingham Hall to clean up before supper time. A small dog trotted sideways down the sidewalk like an automobile in need of alignment, his tongue dripping saliva and his eyes disinterested and self-contented. A large gray cat sat on the Mullinax porch, one leg cocked straight in the air as it attended with energetic tongue a tedious point of hygiene at the base of its tail. It froze in caution as the little dog passed and then resumed its toilette in disdain of the boy walking up the street. Everything was so quiet that Porter could hear the crunch of the sugarberries beneath his feet. Glad to be alone and free of the demands of human companionship, he felt relaxed and peaceful. At home, it's time to milk, he thought. I bet Wes wishes he were at college. He fished his mother's letter from his pocket and read it as he walked very slowly and quietly down the hallway toward his room.

Dearest boy-of-mine,

This is just a note to let you know I'm thinking about you and loving you and missing you. Everybody does. Old Matt even said, 'Sho is quiet and lonesome 'round here without that Sambo.' She was here frying some chicken to send you while I made your caramel cake. I've already got it all wrapped and ready to go when the mailman runs. Hope it gets there all right. The girls have already left for school, the house is cleaned up, and I've got dinner on. The only thing left to do is churn, and I'll just fudge on that until I write you a little birthday note early enough so you'll be sure to get it.

Oh, son, it was a happy day sixteen years ago when Dr. Walden leaned over my bed and said, 'Mrs. Osborne, you have a fine baby boy.' You've been a joy to me all your life, and it's such a thrill to watch you growing into such a splendid young man. I know that God holds you in His hand as surely as I hold you in my heart. Oh, my son, I do love you so!

Happy birthday (next week),
Mother

93

P.S. Hope you enjoy the cake.

As he tried to swallow the lump in his throat, Porter opened the door to his room. With guilty abruptness, Tom Christian swung around from Bob Cater's dresser and faced him. He was clad only in his underwear, and his penis was visible like a pink and blue mouse in the nest of snow-white pubic hair showing through the gap in front. His eyes drifted aimlessly and uncontrollably in frantic movement beneath contracted white brows. His mouth was agape in concentrated grimace, and his teeth showed yellow against the pink and white.

Porter's box from home was uncovered, and there was a series of thumb-sized nicks in the beautiful caramel icing. They went all the way through to the cake beneath. A crumb of burnt caramel clung in the nasolabial fold around Tom Christian's contorted mouth, and the dresser top was littered with crumbs. Porter, mesmerized and breathless, felt he was observing a huge wharf rat, crouched and filthy and evil. If a great scaly tail had slithered across the dresser behind Tom Christian, he would have been repelled but not surprised.

"Who's there?" the great rodent demanded. "That you, Cater?"

He nervously stuck his right forefinger in a nostril and ferreted around. With his other hand he pushed the little mouse into the left leg of his drawers.

Porter slammed the door as hard as he could and tiptoed silently back up the hall, folding and pocketing his mother's letter on the way. Entering the restroom like a runner in slow motion, he leaned over one of the toilets and retched until he was exhausted. Finally he repaired to the window in search of cooling air. He wanted to cry as he felt the letter in his pocket but instead thought of a story his father had told him.

A woman had sworn out a warrant for rape, and the judge had instructed her to recount in detail how the crime had occurred.

"Well, Jedge, I was cookin supper an he come in my kitchen and try to grab me. I run through the house an he chase me plumb out on my front porch an jam me up against the banister an dat's

94

when he done it. Dat's when he rape me."

"Standing up?"

"Yassuh, Jedge, standin up."

"He raped you standing up? And you didn't resist?"

"Course I resisted, Jedge. When he hunch me, I hunch him back. You don't think I gwine jest stand there and let somebody push me off my own front porch, do you?"

Porter thought of this anecdote for the space of three hiccups, washed his face, and left the restroom with the stride of purpose. He stepped noisily down the length of the hall to his own door again. It was locked. He took his key, unlocked it, and swung the door open. Tom Christian, fully clothed, was sitting at his typewriter, fingers busy while his face vacantly pointed toward the ceiling. The lid was back on the box and no errant crumb marred the dresser top. The typing stilled.

"Hello, Osborne. Where you been?"

Porter kept his voice level and very, very impersonal. "Hello, Christian. Have you been typing all afternoon with the door locked?"

"Not all afternoon. Did you come in about half an hour ago?"

"Bob and I dropped our books off after lab, but that must have been about two hours ago now. We went to the KA house and Bob's gone on to a movie, but I came back to study."

"Well, somebody sneaked down the hall while I was here by myself and flung the door open and wouldn't answer me and then slammed the door shut and left. I thought it might have been you or Cater."

"It couldn't have been Bob because he was still at the KA house when I left. You knew me when I came in just then. How'd you do that?"

"Well, for God's sake, I *heard* you. I recognized your footsteps. I'm just blind, Osborne, not stupid. Whoever that other fellow was didn't make a sound, though, almost as though he was deliberately sneaking up on me. That's why I locked the door."

"Well, gosh, I don't blame you. That sounds almost like some-body was out to get you or something. I'd lock the door, too. You haven't done anything to make somebody mad, have you? Maybe somebody was just playing a prank on you. But that'd really have to

95

be a pretty low-down character to go around teasing a blind person."

"Goddammit, Osborne, when will you quit patronizing me? You act like being blind is all there is to me. I'm just like anybody else except for missing one of my five senses. The others are perfectly intact, and I probably use them more than you do in compensation. I'm like everybody else in more ways than I'm different from them, but all you do is concentrate on the difference. I'm getting goddamn tired of it. When are you going to overlook my blindness and treat me like everybody else?"

Porter took a deep breath. A round-eyed, soulful look was futile in this encounter. He would have to rely on his voice for guile. He stared at the roving translucent eyes and replied in a level tone, "Just about right now, Buster. How would you like a piece of fried chicken? Here's a wing."

"Why, thank you. You don't think Cater will mind? He has a cake in that box, too, a caramel cake that's out of this world. I'll just eat this before that horrible siren calls us to supper. God, how I hate that thing. It makes every nerve in my body scream."

Porter averted his gaze as Tom Christian devoured the chicken wing. It had several blue-black reminders that Matt had cleaned the chicken and had done so in inordinate haste.

"This is my box from home. You thought it was Bob's just because it was on his dresser. Now tell me, Tom, how'd you know it was there? You sure didn't hear it."

"Of course not. I felt it. It doesn't take a genius to identify chicken and cake when he feels it."

"I still don't understand. Why were you feeling over there? You don't feel everything in the room every time you come in, do you?"

"Hell, no. I *smelled* fried chicken, and it was easy as falling off a log to locate where it was."

"Gotcha. But now tell me this. How'd you know it's a caramel cake? You can't smell that in the middle of a batch of fried chicken."

"No, I pinched off just a little corner of the icing and tasted it."

Porter paused a moment and watched Tom Christian gnaw the end of a bone. He forced a faint note of admiration into his voice. "Well, you've accounted for taste, touch, smell, and hearing. That's four of the senses you're using great. I'm glad you crawled on me about not being able to see beyond your blindness. I needed that and it really opened my eyes. Tell me, have you ever heard of the Seab Whitlock maxim?"

"Hell, no, and I don't want to hear it. Cater is impressed with your store of useless information, but goddamned if I am."

"Well, it really doesn't matter. I just thought if you'd heard it, you'd understand better what I'm trying to do."

"Whatta you mean? What *are* you doing?"

"I'm trying to work things out so we'll all get along. Remember telling Bob what he was going to have to do if he was going to room with you? Well, that's a two-way street. There are some things you need to do to get along with us."

"Like what?"

"Well, for one thing, you know how I feel about using the Lord's name in vain, and yet you keep on doing it all the time. And you've got to quit this business of feeling everything in the room that doesn't belong to you. That's as much an invasion of our privacy as us reading your mail would be of yours. You know, we've all got to live together for nine solid months."

"Listen, Osborne, you're not dry behind the ears yet and Cater isn't much better. I'm a grown man and yall are children only just now beginning to learn what the world's all about. Get off my back, will you?"

"Tom, I hate to ignore anything as true as the Seab Whitlock law, but I keep hoping there are exceptions to his rule. Has it ever occurred to you that it's not just your eyes that are blind?"

"What the hell do you mean by that?"

"I mean, you're not missing just the sense of sight. It's not just physical vision you lack. I mean, you're also blind to other people's feelings. You can holler all you want to about me not seeing beyond your blindness, but you'd better not tell anybody else that. You'd better hide behind it hard as you can and use it to the hilt and exaggerate it so everybody's always conscious of it. You know why? A little while ago after you yelled at me, I started imagining you're not blind. I really started looking at you as a person who could see. And you know what? It was awful. If you had 20-20 vision, nobody would put up with you till the water got hot."

Tom Christian's purple eyes shifted ever more rapidly and aimlessly. His mouth contorted in a yellow-fanged snarl, although his face remained smooth. His voice quivered with rage. "You can't talk to me like that, you goddamn precocious little bastard!"

Porter was proud of himself for not having raised his own voice. He kept it evenly modulated and continued. "Oh, yes, I can. Seab Whitlock says it won't do any good, but at least I can say it. And you know something else? We've got a deacon at home who can cuss without using the Lord's name. I could tell you that you're a cud-chewing, base-on-balls, three-strikes-you're-out, revolting son of a bitch, but I'd be copying him; so I won't do it. I would like you to know, though, that it offends me for you to go around telling people that I'm a Christ-bitten turd."

"What are you talking about? I've only said that to one very close friend."

"And he talked, didn't he? How else would it have come back to me? Maybe you don't even have any friends you can trust, if they go around repeating private conversations."

Tom's eyebrows jerked together in uncontrollable squint, and his face flushed scarlet. "You shut your goddamn mouth! I can make things so unpleasant for you, you'll want to go home to Mama."

Porter calmly goaded him further. "To be perfectly honest, Tom, you did that the first time I met you. I'm way past that point now. But if you're threatening me, there's something else you need to know. Nobody's going to push me off my own front porch. Did you know I wear glasses, Tom? Well, I do. And I don't like them, either. You keep score. It'll be no-eyes and fo'-eyes. But don't forget, it's my front porch."

"I'm sick of you!" A familiar wailing became audible. "Christ, there's that goddamn siren! I'm going to supper — by myself. God, I hate that noise."

Porter watched as Tom Christian swung his cane and impatiently maneuvered out of the room and into the hall. He opened his English book and studied in furious concentration for thirty minutes. He was very calm. All he had left for the evening were French and Biology. He had plenty of time.

He filled the trash can two-thirds full of water, lugged it to the door, and borrowed a chair from the unlocked room of his neighbor across the hall. Standing on the chair, he heaved the heavy container of water atop the door and then tilted it to a delicate balance that kept the door slightly ajar and the trash can tipped in readiness. Replacing the chair, he walked down the hall, speaking to the early returnees from supper. He waited by the screen door to the front porch until he saw the familiar pink and white figure with erect back swinging its white cane and heading down the hall. He followed along some thirty feet behind, admiring the easy confidence with which his blind roommate walked behind the exploring and informing arc.

Just as the cane tip bumped the door jamb of their room, Porter called out, "Tom Christian! Wait for me."

"Whatta you want, Osborne?"

"Just wait for me, that's all. Don't you try to go in that room without me."

"I've told you I don't need you for anything! Mind your own goddamn business!"

Tom imperiously grabbed the knob, pushed the door open, and took one step forward. Three gallons of water emptied in one quick movement sounds like thirty and is enough to drench an elephant. The empty trash can banged into the room with metallic clatter. Tom Christian lost his balance and sat down in the puddle, his scant white hair clinging to his scalp and forehead like silvered snail tracks. His clothes were sopping wet.

"Gosh, Tom, I'm sorry. But you wouldn't listen. I put that can of water up there to help you. I thought maybe we'd catch whoever it was who busted in on you this afternoon. Why wouldn't you listen to me? Golly, you're a mess. Let me help you up. I wouldn't have had this happen for the world."

"Don't you touch me! I don't believe a word you're saying except that you put it up there. I can get up myself. Just hand me my goddamn cane. I dropped it somewhere."

Porter's voice was honeyed. "Yes, Tom, I know you did. I can see your cane. I can see your cane with my eyes. How it got way over there is a marvel. I'll be more than glad to get it for you because you'd never find it by yourself. I'll get it for you just as soon as you tell the Lord you're sorry for taking His name in vain. And, Tom, lower your voice. Remember what you told Bob Cater? I'm no deafer than you are. Neither is God. Now tell the Lord, Tom. Tell Him!"

There was a moment of silence in which only labored breathing could be heard. Then grudgingly through clenched teeth it came: "I'm sorry, Lord."

"Here it is, Tom. Here's your trusty cane. Now, if you're sure you don't need me, I'll run find a mop and clean up this mess. Golly, this worked like a charm. I just wish it had been that ole intruder we caught instead of you."

Tom Christian stood against the wall, cane loosely in one hand, the other wiping his chin and pushing wet hair off his forehead. "Osborne, I'll get you for this."

"Why, Tom? Why? But more than that, Tom, how? How do you think you'll get me? Don't forget I can see — in more ways than one. And don't forget that I don't feel sorry for you anymore because you're blind. You taught me that, Tom. I'm beyond your blindness now, and I see you for what you really are."

"I'll tell you one way I'll get you, you goddamn little runt! If you mess with me again, I'll knock your goddamn head off or punch your goddamn eyes out with my goddamn cane! You got that?"

"Tom, you'll never learn. You're yelling again. Remember, it's nine more months we have to live together. I don't know whether you'll be able to stand it that long. I gotta go get the mop."

By the time Porter had finished cleaning up the mess, Tom Christian was seated at his study table, fingers furiously busy with a thin tin case peppered with holes. He had inserted a long slip of heavy paper between the lids and was busily punching holes with an instrument that resembled an awl. It made, Porter thought, as infernal a noise as children playing with the metal crickets Buster Brown Shoes issued for advertising. He briefly considered going to the library to study, but he decided that would constitute a withdrawal from the battlefield and abandonment of his own front porch. Memorizing Biology was impractical at the moment. He seated himself at his own table and concentrated on transcribing a group of complicated sentences into French. Frequently he coughed, sniffed, bumped his table leg, or riffled the pages of a book. Before long, Tom Christian flounced out of his chair, grabbed a thick volume of Braille and his cane, and announced, "I'm going to the library! I can't imagine anybody being as noisy as you are!"

100

Porter suppressed the obvious retort and also the impulse to thumb his nose. In the silence that followed Tom's departure, he completed his French, including a reading assignment in *Le Secret de l'étang noir*, and had just finished Biology to his satisfaction when he heard a noisy entourage coming down the hall.

Clarence Spangler's voice dominated the clatter with a decibel level and timbre that, if too coarse to shatter crystal, was certainly capable of rattling windows. "Boy, Sambo, you shoulda gone with us. That was really a slick movie. Errol Flynn's the best thing in a fencing scene you ever saw. I wish they'd put him against Tyrone Power instead of Basil Rathbone sometime. Yall saw him when he jumped backwards up on that table, didn't you?"

Bob Cater chimed in. "Yeah, he was good, all right. But Rita Hayworth was better. She's got the prettiest titties in Hollywood. I'm in love with her."

"Prettier than Betty Grable? You're crazy," scoffed Slick.

"Well, just as pretty, and I think Betty's feebleminded. That keeps her titties from looking as good. I like intelligent women."

"Anyway, Sambo, ole Cater here said you got a box from home, and we decided we'd drop by and see if you'd eaten it all up. We had some hamburgers at the Krystal before the picture show, but they're long gone."

Porter surveyed the quartet for only a moment and opened his box from home. He winced when he saw the scalloped edges of the cake and was visited again with the spectre of Tom Christian in his underwear. "Help yourselves to some chicken, fellows. I'll get a knife to cut the cake. These are graham biscuits made from our own flour. They're better when they're buttered hot and you can eat em with a sliced tomato or ribbon cane syrup, but they're pretty good with cold fried chicken." He was feeling a little hunger again since emptying his stomach earlier. "Here, just let me have that pulley-bone from the bottom of the pile there. I don't like a piece with much skin on it."

"You know, Sambo," Clarence proclaimed around a jaw full of food, "you're turning out to be all right. I'll just be honest with you — the first time I saw you, I wondered about you. You know, I couldn't see how in the world a man like your father had ended up with a boy like you." He laughed loudly.

101

Porter gave him a nervous smile in reply.

"Yeah, man, you're all right. Ole Cater here tells us that you're dragging your feet a little about KA and think we've been nice to you just on account of your father. Slick and I wanted to drop by and tell you that's not the case. Ain't that right, Roundtree?"

"Sure is, Clarence. Sambo, we all think you're a fine little fellow and we want you to be in KA on account of yourself. We think you'll be a swell Brother and be a real credit to the Order. Specially if you're gonna keep getting boxes from home like this. Tell your mother this is the best food I ever ate."

Porter looked earnestly at the two upperclassmen, smooth and mature and urbane. He thought it unlikely he would ever be like them, but he longed to believe what they were saying.

Bob Cater spoke up. "Sambo, some of us were telling Slick and Clarence walking back from town how great you are and how you're well-liked in the freshman class, and we think it'd be a shame for you not to join a fraternity."

"That's right," Slick pursued. "KA has meant everything in the world to me. We really are Brothers, you know, and we should stick together and help each other out, no matter what comes up. It's a real privilege. We think we have a lot to offer you."

"I've never had a brother," Porter said slowly.

Bob Cater interrupted. "Sambo, have you ever thought that you might have a lot to offer the fraternity? For one thing, they have to maintain a minimum grade point average, and you're sure to help that. They don't want everybody to be just alike, you know."

"They don't? Well, I don't know whether I'm cut out to be a fraternity man. For one thing, fraternities are expensive, and I promised my daddy I'd be as frugal as I possibly could."

Clarence broke in with flashing noise. "For God's sake, Osborne, don't hand me that. Don't forget we've met your daddy. You're obliged to have as much money, if not more, than the rest of us. Hell, you even write your own checks. Nobody else does that."

"That's because I know which checks to write. If I ever abused that privilege, it would be a betrayal of trust. My father and I have an understanding about it."

"Well, anyway, we came by here to invite you to our special rush party. It's the big one of the season and we don't ask anybody except people we're sure to bid. It's going to be at Theo's out in Ingleside. He's got this antebellum mansion he built out there and it is some more place. His wife's gonna wear a hoop skirt and sing KA songs. She's a real KA rose. You'll love her."

Porter looked around, but no one was laughing. None of it sounded like fun to him, but he could not catch Bob Cater's eye. Theo's wife? Sing? He prudently said nothing.

"Now, I can remember when I was a freshman going through rush and how I felt. Let's look in your closet and see what you'll need to wear on that night. This your only suit? It's OK. It'll do fine. Now, let's look at your ties."

Porter regarded him expressionlessly. "Clarence, I'm fixing to cut the cake. How'd you like to have the first piece?"

"Gee whiz, that's a whopper. Thanks. What happened to the icing around the edges?"

"Maybe it fell off in the mail or something. I was laughing and telling Bob that my mother isn't the greatest in the world at wrapping packages."

After a quarter hour of frivolous and ribald superficialities, Clarence, Slick and Deacon made their farewells. Porter insisted that they take the remaining half of the cake with them, proclaiming that it was not one of his favorites and that he was a little nauseated anyway.

When they were alone, Bob Cater said, "You told me caramel was your favorite cake and that your mother sent it for your birthday. You didn't have to give it to Spangler and Roundtree. They really want you to pledge. It'd look bad if they had a legacy and he turned em down. I wish you hadn't given the cake away. Sometimes I have trouble figuring you out."

"Bob, sometimes I have trouble figuring myself out. We'll get another cake sometime. You'd better get your studying done before Tom Christian comes back from the library. I tried to study with him, and he makes more noise than you'd believe. He's got some sort of instrument that he clacks and punches a piece of paper in and then reads the holes with his fingers before he types em."

"Well, I'd sure tell him to quiet down if I was around when he was doing it. Especially after he got on to me about talking loud. Boy, ole Spangler would drive him crazy, wouldn't he?"

"Bob, there's this old man at home named Mr. Seab Whitlock who'd tell you in a hurry it wouldn't do a bit of good to tell him. I guess we just have to put up with it."

As Bob settled down to studying, Porter pulled his notebook toward him and began writing.

Dearest Mother,

Thank you for the cake. It got here in great shape and has to be the very best one you ever made. I have already cut it and shared it with some of my new friends, and they all pronounced it delicious and wanted seconds. I may save the rest of it for Sunday afternoon. The chicken and biscuits are great, too. I sure do appreciate them. Tell Matt thanks.

This has been a pretty hectic day around here. I have very good professors, especially the one in English. I think I will do all right in that and in Biology. I want you and Daddy to be braced for a bad grade in French, though. I have a good teacher, but he does not speak any English in class and not our kind out of class. I can read French and write it, though, and I promise I will work hard on it. I just want you to know that I may not pull it off.

They say the French have a word for everything, but that is not true. I have looked it up and the word those folks have is *nostalgie* and that does not begin to cover just plain old hound-dog homesick, and that's what I am. I miss all of you so much I can hardly stand it at times. I do not understand how anybody can be lonely in a crowd, but I can do it. Tell Daddy I go to the fraternity house when I have time, but that does not always help a whole lot. Some of the KA's came by our room tonight and were real nice to me, but I don't know yet whether I want to pledge or not. It might get in the way of my school work. Also, I am not completely sure they want me to pledge. They may just think they do. I will find out before I decide.

104

He paused and nibbled the end of his pen before beginning a new paragraph.

> Please look in my sleeping porch under the bottom shelf of that bookcase I built and mail me my work shoes — the ones I plow and milk in. You will find them right under *Tale of Two Cities* and *Anthony Adverse*. I need them right away because some of us are planning to do some hiking.
>
> You are right about there being more to college than books. I have made a lot of new friends already. Mrs. Raleigh is the dietician and she likes me. Mother Capulet lives in the dormitory and she has invited me to go to church with her on Sunday. She drives across town to Vineville Baptist and likes to have a student ride with her. Boston H. Jones is a colored man who works in the dining hall and he has sort of taken me under his wing and looks after me. I like him a lot. Sylvia Swygert is a Miller High girl who takes the same classes I do. She is very beautiful. There is another girl from Miller in all my classes, too. Her name is Eunice Yeomans, but people call her Tiny. She is very fastidious. I am going to help her with Biology and she is going to help me with French. I think we will probably wind up being friends.
>
> Tom Christian is the blind man I wrote you about who is our new roommate. He is having a little trouble getting adjusted to dormitory life and is probably going to move back to the Academy for the Blind very soon. We will miss him.
>
> Well, I must close and read my Bible and get ready for bed. Thanks again for the box and thanks for the sweet letter. Give Daddy and everybody else my love. Tell Wes I miss him.
>
> Love,
> Sambo

He sat a long moment staring at the wall and continued.

> Next morning
> You would not believe what happened last night.
> Someone broke in the dining hall and turned the siren
> on. This is the biggest and loudest siren in the world. It
> screeched for twenty minutes and woke everybody in the
> dormitory up. Mrs. Raleigh had to come and unlock the
> door and turn it off. It sure was exciting. College life is
> very interesting. Tom Christian does not like loud noises
> and he hates the siren in particular. It made him very
> nervous.

Porter folded the letter, sealed it in an envelope, and put it in his English book. He considered Bob Cater's back bowed in last-minute concentration over Beginner's Spanish and silently dressed for bed and climbed between the sheets. He opened his Bible and thumbed through the Old Testament. Tonight he wanted none of Jesus' adjurations to forgive one's enemies, turn the other cheek, or pray for those who despitefully use you. The Jews before the Messiah were oriented toward revenge, and he sought them out for inspiration and confirmation. He turned to Ecclesiastes. "Whatsoever thy hand findeth to do, do it with thy might; for there is no work, no device, nor knowledge, nor wisdom in the grave, whither thou goest." He flipped backward to Psalms. "It is vain for you to rise up early, to sit up late, to eat the bread of sorrows: for so he giveth his beloved sleep."

Thoughtfully he closed the Bible and said his prayers. He got out of bed, went to the lavatory mounted on the wall, picked up the heavy glass tumbler shaped like a small barrel, and drank two glasses of water. He remembered Boston Harbor Jones's voice: "Cause you had to get up to pee anyhow." He drank a third glass.

Fulfillment was pulse-racingly exquisite. He sped on silent feet back down the hall before the siren reached its full crescendo. As he jumped into bed and feigned sleep, it settled into a steady, unwavering scream that was nerve-shattering. He thought, Boston is right! That's a *sireen*. I'll never call it just a siren again.

Tom Christian was the first of the roommates to wake. "What's that goddamn noise?"

"Oh, Lord, what time is it, Sambo?"

106

"Uh, that's the sireen. It's not time for breakfast, is it?"

Lights were coming on in all the houses across the street. The dormitory was atremble with pounding feet and awash with shouts and curses that could be heard above the horrible whining shriek. Bob Cater opened the door and stepped into the hall. The noise of the siren doubled. Tom Christian buried his head under the covers and yelled, "Shut the goddamn door!" Porter went to the window.

He watched in disbelief as two police cars raced up the street and skidded to a stop at the front door. He saw neighbors from the lighted homes come across the street in assorted stages of dress and cluster around the police. He was reminded of a motto frequently inscribed in the autograph books that had been fashionable in Brewton High School four or five years before. He murmured it aloud as he watched barefooted students and Mother Capulet, who was wearing a long lavender housecoat, join the neighbors: "How far that little candle sheds its beam./ So shines a good deed in a naughty world."

Mr. Mullinax and Mrs. Raleigh arrived almost simultaneously. Porter noted that Mr. Mullinax had on bedroom slippers and a coat thrown over his BVD's, but Mrs. Raleigh was fully and properly dressed. She held both hands over her ears as she hurried up the sidewalk, a large ring of keys hanging from one hand and dancing accompaniment to her frantic steps.

Just when it seemed that auditory nerves had been permanently seared and that even peripheral flesh might be skinned and raw, quivering in responsive pain to the flagellating sound waves, the noise stopped. The transformation was as sudden and startling as being thrown from a horse. The silence sang for a long moment. Nottingham Hall hummed like a giant beehive, and Tom Christian could be heard whimpering from beneath his pillow.

A beaming Bob Cater returned. "Golly, what a ruckus! Why didn't you come, Sambo? I heard several people accusing you of doing it. Of course, I had to tell them it couldn't have been you because you've been in the room all night. Seems somebody pried open the window by the siren and came in that way and plugged it in. Mrs. Raleigh is fit to be tied. She keeps wringing her hands and crying. It's a shame to see somebody who's had as hard a time as she has get all that upset, but still it was a magnificent prank. You're

107

going to miss half of college if you don't quit staying in the room all the time!"

"Naw, I won't. I watched from the window. I get out plenty, believe me. Tell me, Bob, did Mrs. Raleigh say she was no stranger to suffering?"

"Now, how'd you know that? I'm fixing to turn out the light. Let's try to get some sleep. I can still hear that siren."

Tom Christian's voice was raised for the first time since the noise had stopped. "I'll hear it all my life. For God's sake, go to sleep."

Porter was fully dressed and wetting his hair preparatory to parting and combing it when Bob's alarm clock chattered the room awake next morning. Bob's satisfying, fresh-wakened yawns were interrupted by Tom Christian, groping in pink and white frustration around his bed.

"Where in the world is my goddamn cane? I always put it right here."

Bob Cater volunteered, "I don't see it anywhere, Christian."

"Well, maybe one of you kicked it under the bed last night when that goddamn racket started. I've hardly slept a wink since then. See if you can help me find it."

Porter looked at him cooly. "You made it pretty plain last night you didn't ever need or want my assistance. Maybe Bob will help you. I'm going to the dining hall before the siren starts."

"You kiss my ass, Osborne! Will you help me find my cane, Cater? I'm paralyzed without the thing. I can't bear the idea of hearing that goddamn siren again before every meal."

When Porter entered the dining hall on the first wave of hungry boys, Boston was waiting at the side. "Mawnin, Sambo. I hear tell yall had a heapa fuss round here bout three o'clock this mawnin. Hit wake you up?"

"Boston, I believe it woke the dead. I never did leave my room, but I could see the police from my window. Did you know they came?"

"Don't sprize me none. Always showin up either where they ain't wanted or ain't needed. What you dream about?"

"Let's see. I dreamed about wharf rats and fried chicken."

Boston was busily writing in a fertilizer booklet with a stubby pencil that obviously had been trimmed with a knife.

"And I dreamed about killing a lot of birds with one stone."

"Hoo whee, Sambo, slow up a little. Dat's already rats, chickens, birds, and rocks. You a good dreamer sho nuff. I git some good numbers from all these."

"And I dreamed about hands with six fingers on them, and one time I dreamed I was wetting the bed. But I didn't."

"Lawdy mussy, that's a heapa dreamin. Lemme get my book and check all these numbers out. Behave yoself, Sambo."

It was after the blessing had been said that Porter saw Bob Cater leading Tom Christian into the dining room. Without his cane, Tom was clinging with both hands to Bob's elbow and sliding his feet along the floor in cringing dependence. Bob seated him at another table and joined Porter.

"I'm glad to be rid of him for a minute. He's about to go crazy because he can't find his cane. Pass the oatmeal and sugar. He keeps jabbering and cussing the siren, too. I didn't dare let him know how funny I think it was."

Mrs. Raleigh tapped on a water pitcher until all the students became quiet. "You all know what happened here last night. In fact, I saw most of you at 3:30 this morning when I came over. Now, I want you to know that I consider all of you my boys and I love each and every one of you. We are Christians together and working toward the kingdom. I have reason to believe that one of you boys got to pranking last night, though, and turned on the siren. Now, I want you to know that although I'm a little hurt about it, I'm not mad. I have boys of my own, you know. I am used to hard work and certainly no stranger to suffering."

She paused for a moment and her neck arched enough to tilt her head to the other side. She was the picture of gentility.

"I want whoever did this to step forward like a gentleman and own up to it. I have talked to Mr. Mullinax and you will receive no punishment from either him or I if you confess like a man and take suspicion off your fellow students. Now, won't you step forward, whoever did it? Like a man?"

The dining hall was as quiet as a church. Although Porter was conscious of heads turning at random and eyes darting from one fleeting contact to another, he steadfastly gazed solemnly at Mrs. Raleigh.

"Very well, then. I want this explained to me. Does anyone recognize this?" She held up a white walking cane.

There was a little gasp and everyone looked at Tom Christian, who was addressing a sweet roll with the same concentration as a dog licking its own genitals. Mrs. Raleigh walked over to him, extended the cane, and placed one of his hands on it. His eyes spun in an uncontrollable frenzy.

"It's my cane! It's my cane! Thank you."

Mrs. Raleigh tilted her head and spoke demurely but incisively. "Tom, could you explain to us why this walking stick was found under the edge of the dishwasher a few minutes ago? Not three feet from the siren?"

There was a hushed moment. Tom grasped the cane and rose confidently to his feet. Sightless, he could not identify anyone's position. He pointed his cane to the heavens, and his voice rose hysterically.

"Yes, I can explain it. I can't prove it, but I can explain it. Don't ask me how because I can't tell you, but I know as sure as I'm standing here that goddamn Porter Osborne did it!"

Mrs. Raleigh's head jerked upright on a rounded neck, and her voice cracked like a whip. "Tom Christian, don't you dare take the Lord's name in vain! You're a disgrace to your last name! Sit down!"

She walked over to Porter's table. He rose as she approached and looked soulfully and sadly into her eyes.

"Porter."

"Yes'm?"

"Can you tell us how Tom Christian's cane got under the dishwasher?"

Porter's chin quivered. He looked earnestly up into Mrs. Raleigh's eyes.

"Mrs. Raleigh, it cuts me to the quick that you would even raise the question. What kind of a boy do you think I am?"

Then ever so slowly and steadily his eyes filled with tears. So did Mrs. Raleigh's. Her gaze wavered first.

110

"Forgive me, Porter."

As Porter turned to resume his seat, he saw the kitchen help watching, attentive and rapt. He thought Boston Harbor Jones possessed the quickest and slickest wink he had ever seen.

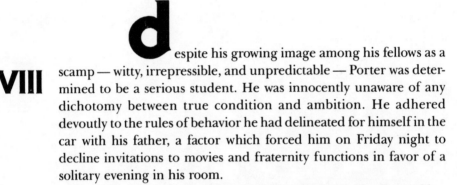 **d**espite his growing image among his fellows as a scamp — witty, irrepressible, and unpredictable — Porter was determined to be a serious student. He was innocently unaware of any dichotomy between true condition and ambition. He adhered devoutly to the rules of behavior he had delineated for himself in the car with his father, a factor which forced him on Friday night to decline invitations to movies and fraternity functions in favor of a solitary evening in his room.

It was the quietest time he had yet experienced in the creaking old dormitory, and he used it efficiently to prepare his assignments for Monday. He even wrote his theme for the weekend, a momentous first occasion that caused him considerable concern. He tried to be attentive to all of Dr. Minor's instructions:

> Choose a subject about which you have some knowledge.
> Narrow your subject to your own experience.
> Do not use contractions in formal writing.
> Do not make a comma fault; such an error ensures an F.
> Above all, write about something you know.
> Use only black ink.
> Avoid redundancy.

Dr. Minor had given the class a list of subjects from which to choose: Art, Roads, Ships, Theaters, Clothes.

Porter balanced his new Parker fountain pen for long moments between caressing fingers and regarded its gleaming gold point. Perhaps it had lovely words and magic phrases stored tightly within its pink cylinder just waiting the proper touch to line them out on pristine paper in contrasting blackness. He sighed. Perhaps it didn't. He cautioned himself; perhaps it did not. Hesitantly he wrote "Roads" at the top of a page. But what did he personally know of roads? After a moment he wrote "Dirt Roads." Is that subject narrow enough? What did he know about all dirt roads everywhere? He modified his title to "Dirt Roads in Brewton County, Georgia." Certainly his own experience encompassed that subject. He considered what he might have to say about the subject. Was the subject itself redundant? Finally he selected a new sheet of paper. "Winter Roads in Brewton County."

He abandoned himself to the rush of recall and visualization, writing busily in fulfilling spurts, pausing for long periods to consider structure and content, totally absorbed in mastering a new challenge. When done he searched carefully through his theme for misspelled words, errors of punctuation, comma faults, contractions, or other sins of composition. At last he read it through. He liked it. He felt drained and relaxed, not fatigued but deeply self-satisfied.

"That didn't even sound like I wrote it," he mused aloud. "I like this theme business."

When he went down the long hall to take his shower, the dormitory was still apparently devoid of life other than his own. With no one around, he relaxed while taking his bath. The toilets in the old building were so plumbed that if a commode was flushed while someone was bathing, there was a temporary but immediate loss of cold water in the shower. This produced a sudden scalding torrent from under which a soapy student would spring with angry shrieks. Some of the football players, mostly a lusty lot, thought it hilarious to roam through the bathrooms at peak periods of use and flush the toilets deliberately, swaggering with delight at the uproar left in the wake of such stinging activity. It was pleasant to relax in the shower and not be constantly on guard to leap out at the first hiccup of lowered water pressure.

Back in his room he read the Bible, prayed openly on his knees in the solitude, and lay in bed reviewing his first week in college. He considered the great mass of academic information that brooded and hovered over him in ponderous threat, waiting patiently to be nibbled and ingested but threatening to smother him

113

in terrible avalanche if he made one wrong move or snapped a twig. He felt tiny and alone.

He thought of the hordes of students on campus and in the dining hall, all of them strangers who must be learned and appeased as individuals and among whom he must walk with the semblance of ease and confidence. He felt tired. Surely Macon must be one of the largest and loneliest cities on earth and Willingham University unassailably sophisticated and lofty.

He thought of the fraternities on campus and for the first time considered KA as a small and friendly haven, a home away from home, a protective band of brothers who supported each other in the large and bewildering maze of university life. Perhaps they really did like him; perhaps he could find there a safe and useful niche. He felt wistful and yearning.

He thought of his home, the grandparents who scolded him occasionally but nevertheless were a familiar constant, the aunt and uncle who gave him grudging respect if not open affection, the mother who adored and constantly supervised him. How could he possibly have resented that heavenly creature? He thought of his dogs, Big Boy and Spot, of their slavish and unquestioning acceptance of him. He closed his eyes and howled aloud in the high-ceilinged dormitory room. Alone and abandoned, cut off from his past, afraid of his future, homesick to the bone, he utilized the luxury of solitude by succumbing to his misery and wallowing in self-pity. He cried himself to sleep again, but this time with no compulsion to do it quietly.

As he dressed for breakfast next morning, conversation with Bob Cater was uninspired but comfortable. "I didn't hear you come in last night. Did you have a good time?"

"Boy, did I! I went by the fraternity house and about six of us went downtown later to a movie. Brother Hudson had his daddy's car and gave us all a ride, but we had to walk back."

"Gosh, that's the second movie you've seen this week. You sure have a lot of spending money."

"Aw, come on. It doesn't cost but a quarter to get in at the Ritz or the Capitol and thirty-five cents at the Bibb. That's not a lot of money."

Porter was indignant. "It is, too. On top of that you're always going to the Krystal for hamburgers and to Chichester's drugstore for Cokes. At this rate you'll go through a fortune before the year's over."

"Cokes cost a nickel, and you've got to do something while you're jollying around in the drugstore. How much have you spent this week?"

"Not one thin dime. I promised my dad I was not going to throw money away, and I haven't. You know what Mrs. Raleigh says: 'A penny made is a penny saved.' "

Bob Cater laughed with exasperation. "I ain't believing you, Sambo. You're supposed to have fun at college. What'd you do last night? Stay in and study the whole time?"

"Yep. And I'm through. I've even finished my English theme. The only thing I have to do is copy it over in black ink and make it neat."

"Well, you are ahead. Now you can go to the KA house tonight without worrying about anything. They're having a bunch of girls over to play records and drink Cokes. You're supposed to go. Where's Christian?"

Porter shrugged his shoulders with simulated indifference. "I don't know. He doesn't speak to me at all anymore, and I like it that way. I guess he went out with some of his friends from the Academy."

"That's a depressing thought. What do you reckon blind folks do for fun? Get together and tune pianos? I thought I'd die last night when we went to bed and he put that cane under the covers with him and slept with it all night long."

"Bob, you ought to be ashamed of yourself. You're still hung up on the blind business. You're supposed to regard Tom as an eccentric person who sleeps with walking canes and just happens not to be able to see. Come on, let's get to the dining room door before the siren goes off."

"Let's go. And don't you wake me up in the morning. I understand they don't blow the siren on Sunday, and I sure want to sleep late."

At breakfast Porter ate his grits and scrambled eggs and

waved sweetly to Mrs. Raleigh. When he left, Boston followed him to the door. He reached a hand into his apron pocket and surreptitiously folded a five dollar bill into Porter's palm.

"Sambo, I ain't believing you. You the best dreamer I ever seen. I bet so big the man didn't wanta pay off. Made twenty dollar an fi'ty cent. You somepin else! I was goan give you ten dollars, but I come up on a pair black and white wing tips and this all I got left."

"Boston, I can't take your money. You keep this five dollars. I never heard of such a thing. That was just coincidence. I didn't have anything to do with it. Here, take it back. I don't want it."

"You crazy, Sambo. Everbody want money, but hit's all right with me do I got a dream boy what's crazy to boot. Be sure an let me know Monday morning what you dream about."

"I had some stemwinders last night. You want to hear about them?"

"Naw, the bug shut down on Sariday an Sunday. I won't even see the man till Monday. I much obliged to you for this five dollars. I just mought have to go windin tonight. Reckon hit time to blow the sireen again?"

"Naw, Boston. I don't think so. It's too soon. Besides, it looks like everything shuts down here on the weekends. I've already heard that everybody sleeps late on Sunday cause they don't blow the sireen for breakfast."

"That's right. Everybody but the Christians and the preachers. They up early as usual. Got to go bout they business on Sunday too. You sure it ain't time to blow again?"

"Oh, why not? You gonna leave the window open again?"

"Naw. This time I leave the catch off the Yale lock on the door. Nobody spect that. Then when you leave you spring the catch an nobody figure out how in the big, bright, blue-eyed, ever-lovin world anybody got in here to blow that awful sireen, but somepin wild is loose in the land. Oh, boy!"

"Boston, you're terrible. But so am I. I'll see you tomorrow."

"Sambo, one thing. Don't you put no walking stick under that dishwasher again. I bout crap in my pants when you fool Mrs. Raleigh bout that, but you can't do hit twicet."

"I'm sure I don't know what you're talking about, Boston Harbor Jones. You certainly have an active imagination."

116

"Uh huh. You, too. Take one to know one. See you later, dream boy."

Porter spent part of the morning cleaning his room and washing socks. The dirty clothes were carried to the University laundry every Monday morning with a careful list and gathered up again in a clean, nondescript bundle every Thursday, but upperclassmen had warned the freshmen that socks were either so mangled or shrunk in the process that it behooved all but the most unfastidious of students to wash their own in their rooms.

The morning passed fairly rapidly with good-natured visiting back and forth on the hall. After lunch Bob Cater and a trio of other freshmen departed for a tennis match, and Porter was left to his own devices. Alone in the room, he felt a lump developing in his throat and a resurgence of the feelings which had thrown him into tears the night before. He bolted down the hall for the outdoors, as ashamed of his secretive weeping as he would have been of thumb-sucking or other childish sins.

On the porch he remembered his rat cap and returned to the room for it. It was tight-fitting and orange with a short bill and the letter W on the front in black. They were sold for seventy-five cents at the Co-op, and the school made a huge profit on them. Threats of dire punishment had been issued for any freshman caught without one on his head at any time he or she was outdoors. This was about the only type of hazing allowed at Willingham University, and most of the freshmen and upperclassmen accepted it with good humor and outward tolerance. Porter, despite thinking that the caps made the freshmen all look like Donald Duck's nephews, took the entire affair seriously. He was too small to hazard an encounter with a sophomore bent on exacting chores for infractions.

He wandered down the hill toward the Co-op, watched the tennis players for awhile, marveled at the intricacies of this civilized sport unknown to him in Brewton County, and made his way aimlessly toward the quadrangle by way of a dirt path between the Biology and Chemistry buildings. The day was bright and still with just barely enough crispness to cause sound to carry and to remind one that fall was approaching even in this mild mid-Georgia climate. He studied the large camellia japonica bushes around the Administration Building, gently squeezing the fat bloom buds, curious about these plants which did not grow at home.

Rounding the front of the Chapel building, headed back toward the dormitory, he noted a group of boys clustered around the steps of the Library, closed now for the weekend. Their piping voices stilled as he approached, and they observed him carefully. He felt like a strange dog wandering into a neighborhood pack, stiff-legged and wary, pausing to be sniffed and examined.

He spoke first, trying to convey nonchalant superiority.

The tallest boy in the group, thin as a reed, freckled and tousle-haired, replied, "Hello, yourself. Where you from?"

"I'm from Brewtonton, Georgia, up close to Atlanta. You ever hear of it?"

"Naw. Who you visiting around here and what you doing with that Willingham cap?"

"I'm not visiting. I go to Willingham and this is my rat cap."

"You mean you in college here? How old are you?"

"I'm sixteen, but I'm small for my age. I'm a freshman all right."

"You sure are little. I'm just thirteen and I'm taller than you. My daddy teaches at Willingham."

"He does? What's your name?"

"I'm Bill Kruger, Jr. My dad teaches Physics. That's Johnny, my little brother, over there. This is Joe Twilley, and that's Bob Culpepper. Their daddies teach here, too. That's Scotty over there. He's from South Carolina and he's visiting his granddaddy here at Willingham. What's your name?"

"My name's Porter, but nearly everybody calls me Sambo. What are yall doing?"

"We're playing fox and hounds. It's fun on Saturday and Sunday when all the buildings are empty and nobody's around. You wanta play?"

"Sure. I got nothing else to do."

His eyes were drawn to a boy sitting on the bottom step, a little apart from the others. The body was stocky and balloonlike, giving the impression that it moved as a unit without benefit of joints. The back was abnormally straight, ending in a massive neck and bullet-shaped head, small and prognathous. The mouth was too small to contain the large tongue, which looked to Porter as thick as a flannel

118

cake and protruded not only to the front but curled up the sides as well. He made audible snuffling noises when he breathed. The nose was flattened with a broad bridge, and the little eyes, brown and feral, were set wide apart and were markedly slanted. Porter stared so hard that he felt self-conscious. He stuck out his hand.

"Hi. My name's Sambo. What's yours?"

"My name Wichard. I wike your cap." His hand was stubby and thick, and the muscles were flabby.

"Richard keeps the base for us while we're running," Bill volunteered. "Come on, Sambo, me and you'll be the fox first."

Porter looked at the long quadrangle, breathed in the sunny air, and threw all his cares aside. Reaching down, he took off his shoes and socks, rolled his trousers halfway up his skinny legs, and turned to Richard. "Do you mind watching my shoes for me while we play? I won't be gone long. Let's go, Bill."

He stuffed his rat cap in his hip pocket and trotted across campus, breeze deliciously parting his hair and mowed grass sensuous beneath his summer-toughened feet.

"What's wrong with Richard, Bill?" he asked. It was a bold question and he knew it, but he asked it as tenderly as he could. Years before in Brewton County, there had been a lady named Mrs. Della Kincaid who had an afflicted child. Hubie Kincaid was never seen in public except at revival meetings. He never came to Sunday School, but he was carried to every revival meeting conducted at Peabody Baptist Church. Consequently, twice a day for an entire week in August, he stood upright in a church pew and drooled while his mother sang hymns and listened to sermons. His head was no bigger than a good man's fist, but his face looked normal size and his nose, inherited from some distant Roman progenitor, was even bigger than average. He was tiny and thin, and it seemed improbable that his rope-like neck could support even that small a head. Something was wrong with Hubie's eyes, too, so that he had to tilt his little head backwards and look down the sides of his nose to see. He looked for all the world like a scrawny, molting chicken turning his head from side to side, perched in the church pew as if on a roost, trying to decide if it were a good day to fly to the ground.

Hubie was a wonderful teaching aid to the children of Peabody Baptist Church. He was the stimulus for all of them to be

119

admonished at an early age, "Don't point. Don't stare in public." They were all immediately obedient, since Hubie spent the entire sermon time staring at them and pointing, and the inference was clear that if they stared and pointed they might look like him. The children of Peabody grew up with exquisite manners on these two points, but they also carried with them an unspoken shame and sense of guilt about mental retardation. All of it centered around the church, for there was the unvoiced conviction that Hubie's condition was punishment for some sin, coupled with a private sense of relief that Jehovah's awful eye had not been directed everywhere it should, and one had escaped again under a celestial Mr. McGregor's fence. There was always the feeling of "Thank God, that isn't me."

"Usually," Bill replied, "I say, 'None of ya business,' but you're different. You were nice to Richard and treated him like somebody. He's a Mongolian idiot."

"I never saw one before."

"Lots of folks keep em fastened up at home, but Richard likes us and likes to get outdoors. He's my cousin from Fort Valley and he's a year older than me, but he doesn't ever go to school. His mother had an operation and my mama has been keeping Richard. He's going home tomorrow. You must be awful smart to be in college as little as you are."

"I am," Porter replied comfortably. How could he explain to this boy, this child, that he was enjoying running barefooted across campus with him and his fellows more than anything he'd done at college so far? He was their physical equal and reveled in that sensation. They loped around the lower end of the Administration Building under the old magnolia trees. "Where we gonna hide? The hounds oughta be coming any minute."

"Don't worry. They'll never find us. We're gonna hole up in Dr. Highsmith's toilet."

They circled around to the north end of the building under the rusting fire escape, and Bill quickly raised one of the tall slim windows with the handmade panes and climbed inside. The boys flattened themselves against the wall to either side, and Porter studied the tiny cubicle in which he found himself. The floor space was roughly three by six feet, and the shadowy recess of the ceiling was twelve feet above his head and seemed to be formed of the underside of a narrow spiral stair. The light up there was too dim to see clearly. To his left was a lavatory mounted on the wall with only a hole where the hot water faucet belonged. There was a green, yellow-tinged stain etched like a giant teardrop on the porcelain beneath the cold water faucet. On top reposed a curled wafer of soap marbled by black lines delineating the cracks that had dried into it after infrequent use. Opposite the lavatory, mounted on a rounded brick wall, was a commode with the flush box high overhead. Porter gazed around him and whispered coarsely across the window to Bill, "Who's Dr. Highsmith?"

"Aw, he's just a teacher at Willingham. Teaches Education or Sociology or something strange like that. Education, I guess. My dad says it's the most misnamed course in the catalog. Nobody gets educated taking it. Says anybody can make an A in it if they don't mind being bored to death. Don't worry about Dr. Highsmith; he's not ever here on Saturday. Besides, you can smell his pipe a mile off if he is coming."

"This is the strangest room I ever saw. Makes you think of a dungeon if it wasn't for the window."

"You think so? This ain't nothing. See that little wooden panel behind the toilet? You pull that out and you're in the bottom of the tower. That really looks like a dungeon."

"The bottom of the tower?"

"Yeah, it's a brick shaft with iron rungs on the side that go all the way to the top."

"Golly, have you ever climbed it?"

"Not on your life. It's about a hundred miles to the top, and those old rungs, some of em are so loose they rattle when you touch em. I wouldn't climb up there for a thousand dollars. Yonder go the hounds around the Chapel. Come on, let's circle behind em and let em chase us again. Next time we lose em we'll hide in the Biology basement."

For more than an hour Porter raced over the campus with his new friends in blissful reversion to a more carefree period. He forgot college, fraternities, studies, girls, French, and all responsibility. He ran as a child, unself-conscious and happily aware of only the immediate moment. He even forgot Brewton County. Finally he ran apart from Bill and doubled back to the Administration Building. Alone in

Dr. Highsmith's toilet, timorous but excited, the only sound his thudding heart, he removed the panel behind the commode and stepped into the base of the smaller of the two towers adorning the building.

It was a perfect cylinder that soared through four stories and then projected another two stories in freedom above the roof. Light in the tower was filtered down from the open end of the shaft above and was uncertain and as precious as anything in Chillon. As his eyes adjusted, he finally discerned the outline of a ladder, iron rungs mounted across one curve of the tower, bare rods embedded between ancient bricks. Bill was correct. The lower one did rattle loosely in one's hand. The second one, however, was firm.

Tentatively, he began to climb, carefully testing each rung before he entrusted his weight to it. Not all were loose, but enough of them answered his touch with a rattling spray of dislodged mortar crumbs to make him very cautious. About thirty feet up the shaft, one rung was missing entirely and he thought his journey ended, but by stretching he could reach the next one above and pull himself on up.

The light grew steadily brighter as he ascended, and somewhere more than halfway up he found another small doorway in the wall of the shaft. Creeping through it he found himself in another restroom, this one stacked with boxes and draped with cobwebs like Spanish moss, the grimy porcelain fixtures obviously unused for years. He cautiously opened the bathroom door and discovered a bare room with four windows, a table, and a forlorn grouping of folding chairs. On the table was an envelope addressed to "Miss Anne Nolan, President ADPi, Willingham University, Macon, Georgia." He realized with pleasure that he was on the fourth floor of the Administration Building, for he had heard that one of the sororities had a meeting room there.

Exploring his surroundings on tiptoe, he saw the old metal fire escape just outside the toilet, its terminal platform an easier approach to the tower, albeit a more conspicuous one. Resuming his adventure, he returned to the grimy restroom, gingerly leaned over four stories of free fall in the shaft, and grasped an iron rung in the opposite wall. Swiftly he clambered the rest of the way to the top and burst into glorious sunshine and fresh air. There was nowhere to stand except on the top rung, but he was quite securely anchored by clasping his elbows over the edge of the parapet.

All of Willingham lay below him. The tennis players looked like tiny puppets, and the occasional car on the street beyond them crawled along as inconsequential as a toy. To the west he observed the oval of the football stadium, came closer in and defined the fraternity houses, the laundry, Nottingham Hall, and all the buildings of the quadrangle. From somewhere he heard the distant voices of his new friends, still involved in their chasing and hiding. Everything seemed compacted and telescoped, even the trees with their spreading crowns far below him. Porter had never been this high before in his life, and the experience was exhilarating. He thought maybe he was going to be able to conquer college after all. Peaceful and relaxed, he daydreamed for half an hour. Then he swiftly climbed back to the bottom, slipped unseen through Dr. Highsmith's window, and walked across to the Library to reclaim his shoes.

Little Richard sat where he had been left, a wet spot in his crotch attesting how long that had been. His face was so red and swollen that his eyes were almost obscured. Mucus streamed from his nose and slobber from his protruding tongue as he softly moaned and sobbed, his shoulders squared and his hands hanging loosely at his sides, relaxed in misery and abandoned to sorrow.

Porter reached for his shoes, embarrassed but concerned. "Don't cry, Richard."

He might as well have not spoken. The crooning and blubbering continued. With a shrug, Porter started on his way and then turned back. "Why are you crying, Richard?"

The sobbing ceased, the small eyes focused, and the thickened voice asserted, "I want my mama!"

Porter dropped his shoes and, oblivious to anyone else, sat down by the child and pulled the small head over to his shoulder. His own eyes filled. "Cry all you want to, Richard. I want mine, too."

They sat for long moments, and finally Richard straightened, gave a shuddering sigh, sniffed wetly, and said, "Can I have you cap?"

Porter rose, picked up his shoes, considered the seventy-five cents involved, and refused. "I have to keep my cap. I'll get in trouble if I'm caught without it. Don't worry, Richard; you're going to see your mother tomorrow." He hastened to the dormitory without looking back.

A car was parked as near the front steps as possible, the back seat filled with clothes and books, a familiar typewriter and Braille case wedged to one side. Tom Christian was moving! His rat cap gleamed orange atop the pile of clothing. Not a soul was in sight. Porter reached in, snatched the freshman cap, and ran as fast as he could back to the Library. Richard still sat ponderous and patient but crying no more. Without a word, Porter placed the cap atop Richard's head, waited briefly to see an approving smile crinkle the eyes and curl the mouth, and walked around the Library. From behind a pyracantha bush he watched the car, driven by a young woman with braided hair, acne, and no makeup, leave the dormitory. Beside her sat his departing roommate, brightly pastel, unknowing and unseeing.

"Bye-bye, Tom," he murmured.

He thought of his favorite movie, *A Tale of Two Cities,* with Elizabeth Allen and Ronald Coleman, and added aloud with pseudo-British accent, "It's a far, far better thing you do than you have ever done. Bye-bye, Tom."

He entered the dormitory with a lightened heart, confident that his own front porch was still secure.

The education of Porter Osborne continued more rapidly than he had anticipated.

IX

"What's a Mongolian idiot?" he asked Bob Cater. He received an account of monsters in Atlanta who were confined behind fence to their front yards, since they were prone to rape young girls or assault people in Frankensteinian rage during moments of passion.

"What's a French kiss?" he asked at the KA house during a discussion that tended to be a little intimate and in which the phrase was mentioned. Clarence Spangler and Slick Roundtree laughed while they explained it and then discovered that Porter had never been kissed at all. Their delight was boundless. In the presence of hilarious onlookers, they persuaded a dimpled dumpling of a girl to raise him from the ranks of the ignorant for the glory of old KA. That was not all she raised.

She wore a cashmere sweater, thick red lipstick, and looked a little like Winnie Winkle's friend, Patsy. She was in the Miller High uniform, although Porter knew that she was a sophomore who lived in the girls' boarding house. He was about as tall as she and felt enveloped in a sweet-smelling haze. He was not prepared for the softness of her lips, followed by the tender tightening of the muscles underneath. His head whirling, he lost for a moment awareness of spectators and involuntarily clasped her close. At this manifestation of aggression, the co-ed pushed him away. She laughed like a coquette as she broke the embrace and moved off, the contact having meant nothing to her.

Porter stood in silence with pleading heart, smeared mouth, and the left leg of his drawers straining against the most instantaneous erection he had ever experienced. As his fellows hooted in thigh-slapping humor, he thanked God for baggy pants with pleats down the front. He tried to go along with the joke but could not force himself to smile. Thinking back to one of his conversations with Bob Cater, he decided that he must have just encountered an Atlanta Pink.

A senior girl, pinned to a KA brother who had graduated the previous year, was present at the party as a show of feminine force and to help rush the freshman boys. She and Porter had earlier carried on a bantering conversation replete with brittle humor and repartee. Now she tapped him on the shoulder.

"If you're really interested in pursuing this educational process, meet me Monday at four in the Histology lab. No need for a child from the hinterlands to be taught something this important by anyone but the best."

He turned and looked into her mocking blue eyes. "Are you earnest?"

"No, I'm Mary Martha, but you be there and I'll really teach you something. You'll have to remember, though, no hands!" She looked so compellingly into his eyes that Porter ignored her bantering tone and felt like Ulysses struggling at the mast while his deafened followers rowed him away from temptation. The bonds broke.

"I'll be there," he vowed. Of a sudden he felt that fraternity life was the only way to exist at college. How could he have doubted?

That night he drank only one glass of water at bedtime, and the siren did not sound until four o'clock in the morning. He barely made it into the room before Bob Cater arose from his bed. This time Porter joined him in the hall — clad in the striped bathrobe discarded by one of his aunts and thriftily altered by his mother to an approximate fit for him. Doors slammed, boys yelled, the siren screamed, and if possible the pandemonium was more riotous than before. Certainly it was lengthier. Mrs. Raleigh was spending the night with a maiden cousin on Pio Nono Avenue; so Mr. Mullinax was summoned to unlock the door and turn off the siren. It took him only a moment to find his pipe and light it, but he could not

126

remember to save his life where he had put his keys.

The football players and city boys, only a few hours in bed after late Saturday night socializing, had anticipated sleeping late on Sunday, and they tended to be angry. The preachers and farm boys, accustomed to early bedtime and daylight hours, viewed the entire episode with hilarity. The noise lasted so long and at such a pitch that everyone pressed hands over ears in an effort to salvage hearing and relieve pain. By the time Mr. Mullinax arrived, puffing smoke in little balls like a laboring locomotive, Mother Capulet had become so proficient at lipreading that she was scolding the football players for cursing.

At breakfast Porter approached Mrs. Raleigh before she could accost him. "We missed you this morning, Mrs. Raleigh. I hope you had a good time at your cousin's house. The rest of us sure became acquainted with suffering while we waited for Mr. Mullinax."

He looked around and lowered his voice. "I want you to know that I am one person who does not believe for a minute that Rusty and Dusty snitched your keys and turned the sireen on while you were gone. People will say anything, won't they?"

Boston Jones was at Mrs. Raleigh's elbow and was as careful as Porter to prevent their glances crossing.

Later that morning he learned some more religion, about which he already knew a great deal less than he thought he did. Mrs. Capulet had invited him to accompany her to Vineville Baptist, and he dutifully appeared on the front porch a little ahead of the appointed time, clad in his suit, Bible under his arm. While waiting he watched the other boys stream out of the dormitory in their Sunday best, most of them headed for Tatnall Square Baptist Church on the corner of the campus. The high rate of attendance was not surprising. After all, Willingham was a Baptist school, and at least ninety percent of its students belonged to Baptist churches and had come from Baptist homes. Attending church on Sunday was such an ingrained habit that absence from morning worship instilled guilt that could be expiated only by going to evening services and following up with prayer meeting on Wednesday night. The more

127

devout even suffered guilt about missing Sunday school.

Porter felt very pious and protected as he rocked and waited. He thought of the muscular, hairy football players snoring away in their dens upstairs, grateful for a day away from their demanding schedule. They were nearly all yankee Roman Catholics and had strange accents and stranger names. Porter dismissed them smugly. Everyone who had been Raised Right knew that sooner or later Catholics would wind up in the haunts of Hell anyhow. There was no way a scrawny Southerner like himself could accept responsibility for these huge and formidable foreigners. He felt that in all honesty he was doing well to save himself.

When Mrs. Capulet appeared, Porter rose and extended a hand to help her down the steps. This morning she affected a little color in her wardrobe and wore a lavender dress. It was after the first of September; so the gloves were black, as were the shoes and hat. It was a distraction to Porter that Mrs. Capulet always wore sheer black stockings. Since her legs were as shapely as those of any co-ed, this custom contrasted sharply with her unplucked, unpainted face that was surmounted by two thin braids of hair pinned rigidly into the semblance of a black and white cap.

She accepted Porter's hand and came down the steps a little sideways, peering carefully through her bifocal, rimless spectacles. When he accompanied her to the driver's side of her car and held the door for her, she beamed at him. Driving out to Vineville (and Porter thought she drove the same way she came down the steps), she rewarded him.

"You're a regular little gentleman, Porter."

"Thank you, ma'am."

"You remind me of your father."

Porter made no reply but stiffened in sudden wariness.

"You didn't know I knew your father?"

"No'm."

"Oh, yes. He was very polite and much sought after by the girls. Dr. Capulet was alive then, and Porter Osborne used to come to our house for tea. He was quite the gallant young gentleman. Of course, he was full of life, too. I used to tell Dr. Capulet — I was quite a bit younger than he — that Porter Osborne was not a bad boy, he was just mischeevious. And you're Porter Osborne, Jr. Are you the

128

only child?"

"No'm. I have three sisters."

"I see. But you're the only boy. Well, I know your father is proud of you. Who was your mother?"

"She was a Gilstrap from Bartow County."

"Yes. Well, Porter, I'd like for you to drop by my rooms about four this afternoon for tea. Sunday afternoons get pretty long for freshmen. Especially during the first quarter."

"Yes'm. I'd like that."

"Now. I want you to enjoy church this morning. You know, every boy needs a church family away from home. It's sort of an anchor when the winds blow. If you want to transfer your letter this morning, you could ride with me every Sunday. We have lots of Willingham boys at Vineville for the four years they're in college. You think about it."

"Yes'm, I will."

He wondered if Mrs. Capulet's mother had been a Hodnett. The Hodnetts had been a family in Brewton County noted for the gentility and grace of its women. For one spanning generation, the family had produced only women and was now defunct, but the name lingered as the ultimate symbol of ladylike refinement.

He had never in his life seen such a church as Vineville Baptist. It had a lofty ceiling, crystal chandeliers, and soaring windows filled with rich stained glass. A thick red carpet silenced footsteps so totally that only the squeak of a shoe, pulled out and polished for Sunday worship, betrayed the progress of a worshipper down the aisle. The pews had gracefully curving backs and a long cushion down each seat. Behind the pulpit there was a velvet curtain parted just enough to show a mural of Christ in the water with a dove above his head. These people did not even have to go outside to be baptized. Porter was dumbfounded with reverence.

They seated themselves behind two fat ladies in time for Mrs. Capulet to tug off her gloves finger by finger before the opening hymn was sung. Porter decided that the buffeting music which swelled through the church must be from a pipe organ. He had heard of them before but had never seen one. He thought the rows of sharp-pointed pipes with a beveled hole cut precisely in each one looked like the teeth of a not particularly friendly giant, or else a strange gate closing the entrance to a supernatural cave, and would have been more attractive covered over with something. The instrument was being played by a man instead of a woman, and he was so active that Porter watched him instead of the chorister. He had never seen such gyrations; the man was as busy with his feet as with his hands, constantly bending and bowing and shifting his buttocks on the seat. Porter knew all the hymns by heart but noted that these people in town sang none of the fast ones.

The collection plates were solid brass, very heavy, and lined with felt. As he put in a nickel and passed the plate to Mrs. Capulet, Porter virtuously reminded himself, and thereby the Lord, that except for the checks for tuition and books, this was the only money he had spent since arriving at college. He had avoided Coca-Colas, movies, and hamburgers, and he thought with piety that it was both appropriate and significant that his only cash outlay was occurring in the House of the Lord.

When the preacher got up and grasped the pulpit on each side, it was obvious that he was a little too well-fed. His shirt was heavily starched and the collar tight. His hair was carefully arranged with comb tracks apparent on both sides, and his tender jowls were as carefully shaven as any hog prepared for butchering. He had an accent and a delivery, however, that acknowledged no superior. Porter knew that he sat in the presence of a preacher who had made it all the way through the seminary at Louisville and maybe even had gone to Yale or somewhere. He was impressed.

The text was from Second Kings, the story of Elisha curing Naaman's leprosy and thereby leading Naaman to belief in God. The sermon revolved around Naaman's predicament of feeling one way in his heart and having to appear another way in public. Through contortions of logic, the preacher thus exhorted all visitors or temporary residents of the city to join his church and continue to worship the one true God while away from home. Porter was moved. Certainly this was a foreign land. Certainly he needed the strong hand of God to guide him through the maze in which he now found himself.

The invitational hymn was "Just As I Am," but the music had never sounded like this before. Four boys from Willingham walked down the aisle during the first stanza and shook the preacher's plump hand. Feeling a little nudge from Mrs. Capulet's elbow, Porter half rose himself. Instantly he had a vision of his home church, bare-floored, bare-windowed, with uncompromisingly straight-backed benches. He could hear the thump and whine of the untuned piano. He knew that the present opulence in which he found himself could not be pleasing to the stern Jehovah who presided in the spare and echoing church-house in Peabody, Georgia, and provided only gas-mantle lamps to light His worshippers at night. He wondered if he would be betraying not only God but his own heritage if he succumbed to the sensuous call before him now.

He had been fascinated all through the sermon by the lady on the pew in front of him. She wore across her shoulders a series of little animals fastened to each other in butt-biting daisy chain, their feet and tails dangling in limp display, their sharp little teeth exposed in fierce grimace, their beady eyes glittering in permanent malevolence. He had not been able to identify the animals but presumed they were worn for ornament only and that they must be unbelievably expensive. He looked one of them squarely in its glass eye and thought that the string of mean little creatures probably cost more than the entire Lottie Moon offering at Peabody. If anybody wore that thing to church at home, Cuddin Alice probably would beat it with a stick, and for sure and certain Miss Maggie Mae would pray out loud for its owner. They were devil dogs. They were an omen to him in this foreign land.

He felt that the sinewy arm of the one true God was laid momentarily across his shoulder in comforting approbation for recognizing that he was really in the house of Rimmon and that these misguided worshippers were off the narrow way and missing the gate that is strait. They were, therefore, of little consequence in The Kingdom. He sank back in his seat.

While the choir sang a strung-out series of amens and everyone in the congregation was supposed to have his head still bowed and eyes closed at least in pretense of prayer, the portly, tastefully-tailored preacher made silent and rapid pilgrimage to the door of the church. Porter could have marked his passage by the smell of

Yardley's aftershave even had he not been peeking.

He resented the preacher's monopoly of the exit. It caused a hopeless bottleneck of sycophants within the church while the preacher took time to beam and shake each worshipper's hand. Porter regarded this activity as an unfeeling adult impediment to Sunday dinner. Anyone with a grain of sense should know that twelve o'clock was time to eat and that healthy people were ravenous. This was no gesture of hospitality. This was ostentatious boasting that Vineville Baptist was "friendly." This was additional opportunity for the preacher to preen before the faithful and also a last chance for mildly judgmental gibes at the not-so-faithful.

"Good to see you this morning, Mrs. Williams. We missed you at prayer meeting Wednesday night....

"Thank you, Mrs. Blount. I'm glad you enjoyed it. My wife says you weren't at the last two WMU meetings. Hope there's nothing wrong at home....

"Good morning, Mrs. Krenson. Tell your husband we missed him this morning....

"Hello, Mrs. Capulet. Who have you brought with you this morning? You're a student at Willingham, little man? Well, well, well. I'm sorry you didn't join our church family with the other Willingham boys this morning. A little shy, maybe? We'll expect you next Sunday."

Porter interrupted him. "I'm like that fellow when Paul got through with him, Preacher — 'Almost thou persuadest me.' But not quite."

He looked him earnestly in the eye and silently vowed, If I ever get out of here and get some food in my belly, you'll never see me again, you fat sapsucker. I say amen, amen, and a-a-a-men.

Dinner in Nottingham Hall was quieter and more decorous than usual, due in part to all the recent churchgoers still being clad in their Sunday suits. Even comments about the siren were heard mostly from the boys who had skipped church and tried to go back to bed.

After the meal Mrs. Raleigh presided at the door over heavily

laden aluminum trays piled high with paper bags. Each contained an apple or orange, a banana, a package of peanut butter crackers, and a package of sweet crackers. The assortment constituted Sunday night supper, and Mrs. Raleigh passed them out to the departing students with sweet smiles and salutations and smirking gestures of graciousness. Porter knew her real purpose was to be absolutely sure that no student got more than one sack, but he returned the smile with the same degree of sweetness. Mrs. Raleigh was a very important person at Willingham.

In his room, Porter undressed and painstakingly rewrote his theme for the morrow, careful of neatness and penmanship. He had not the faintest idea where his roommate might be. Restless and bored, he presently pulled on a pair of corduroys and wandered aimlessly over the campus. None of his playmates from the previous day was in sight. He wondered if little Richard was back in Fort Valley with his mama. He wondered what his own family was doing at the moment and quickly forced his thoughts away from home as he felt a tightening in his throat and a threatening fullness behind his eyes.

He gazed upward at the spires of the Administration Building, looked around for confirmation that no one was in sight, and rapidly scaled the fire escape to its termination on the fourth floor. It was only a matter of minutes to enter the well of the tower from the hole behind the ADPi commode. The moment of leaning across four stories of gaping black emptiness to grasp the ladder rungs was exhilarating enough to clear his mind of all other thoughts. Clambering swiftly to the top, he clamped his elbows over the parapet and surveyed the scene below him. It was a study in serenity. Only in Tatnall Square Park was there any activity. The muted voices of playing children floated to the tower and accentuated his detachment. He spent a long time in contemplation, pensive and alone.

Brewtonton was far away but so was Willingham. He tried to sort out his problems and assess them. He felt confident about English and Biology. It was only when he considered French and fraternities that he experienced a pulling sensation in his stomach and a prickle in the back of his neck. After a while, he prayed, not neglecting to express gratitude for Tiny Yeomans and Boston Harbor Jones. He searched his heart and added a postscript for Bob Cater. Although Mary Martha crossed his mind, he was careful not to mention her to the Lord.

As four o'clock approached, he climbed down from the tower, feeling sad but peaceful when he dropped from the fire escape. In the liriope beside the walkway, he sensed a wary movement and watched a box terrapin stealthily retract feet and head into its brightly-patterned shell. He squatted down and studied the creature. Only the tip of the nose appeared in the wrinkles of flesh between the folded front feet. He waited patiently. As slowly as the minute hand on a clock, the head gradually appeared. Striped with orange and black, skin stretched taut over bone, it looked like a mummy with a fierce overbite. The eyes glittered red rather than gray, and Porter classified the animal as male. He picked him up and marveled at the sudden protective snap of the hinged carapace that hid all evidence of life and produced an immediate chunk of armor, impenetrable and wondrously wrought. Porter decided to carry the inanimate object along. No need to waste a perfectly good terrapin.

He hid it behind his back as Mrs. Capulet greeted him, and when she turned to get her china after seating him, it was childishly easy to place the secretively withdrawn terrapin beneath the loveseat. It was completely hidden behind the decorative flounce, and Porter felt so secure from detection that he did not even bother to look innocent.

For a few minutes he was intimidated. He had never imbibed hot tea in his life, let alone been exposed to such fragile china and lacy wisps of crisply laundered napkins. The sugar bowl was stacked full of little blocks, and a pair of silver tongs lay alongside. Porter had read about lump sugar but had never seen it before. His hostess increased in stature. Her mother must have been a Hodnett. As she remarked that the teapot and china had belonged to Dr. Capulet's grandmother and had been brought over from England, Porter felt loutish and ill at ease. He remembered his mother's returning once from a UDC meeting, which was about the most proper event a person could attend in Brewtonton; she was bubbling with irrepressible mirth as she regaled the aunt and grandmother.

"Yall would not have believed Saphronia Woolsey. She was already having trouble balancing her cup and plate, and when Mrs. Blalock asked her if she preferred cream or lemon in her tea, she said, 'I think I'll have a little of both.' Then of course it curdled and

Saphronia sat there, game to the end, and drank it down. I thought Mattie Lena Redwine would burst trying to keep from laughing." Porter recalled Miss Saphronia with fondness and identified with her gaucherie as he realized that he had no background for drinking tea.

"I'll have two lumps, please. No cream. You certainly have beautiful furniture, Mrs. Capulet."

"Why, thank you for noticing, Porter. All of them are old Capulet family pieces. The apartment is a little crowded, but I just had to hang on to these when I gave the rest of it away to Dr. Capulet's nieces. That little secretary is seventeenth century and these chairs are original Chippendales."

Porter had not the faintest idea what a Chippendale was and felt even more out of his element. He identified this time with the terrapin, wondering if it felt impressed. Mrs. Capulet was looming every moment as a personage to be taken seriously in the hierarchy at Willingham.

"Yes, sir, I believe you're just like your father, although he was a little older and considerably larger than you when he came to Willingham. He played football, you know."

"Yes'm, I've heard."

"Well, those were the days. They didn't wear all those pads and harnesses then, and the football players were gentlemen and were shaped like Christians. They didn't waddle around the halls with their legs and arms stuck out, murdering the King's English in horrid northern accents like those we have today. And we won, Porter, back then we won! Do you know that one time Willingham played Army and beat them?"

"Yes'm, I've heard about it."

He held his breath as the terrapin thrust out its legs and craned its head around on extended neck, methodically inquisitive and exploring.

"Oh, that was glorious. Now we have these huge, chunky creatures from Pennsylvania and Ohio and we can't even beat Furman or Wake Forest. Of course, the boys were bad to celebrate. I remember one time your father tied a calf into the Morris chair of the top ministerial student. We never let him find out that we knew who did it. Are you as mischeevious as your father, Porter?"

"Oh, no ma'am. I'm a serious student."

The terrapin was lumbering silently across the carpet, perilously close to Mrs. Capulet's feet, but disappeared undetected beneath the little seventeenth century secretary. Porter relaxed.

"Porter, are you sure you won't have another cup? How did you get into the dining hall this morning to turn on the siren?"

"Who? Me? Why, Mrs. Capulet...."

"Don't compound the matter by lying, Porter. And don't attempt to manipulate me as you did Mrs. Raleigh this morning. Oh, yes, I overheard you in the dining hall. All the ladies in Macon are not simple country lasses who mouth platitudes and use past misfortunes as tools. You see, I was having a little insomnia and was heating some warm milk when I first heard the siren this time. I opened my door wide enough to see a very small boy in a peculiar orange-striped dressing gown racing barefoot down your end of the hall. Then later when we were all trying to keep from going half deaf while Mr. Mullinax fumbled around with that silly pipe of his, I had a chance to notice you. Tell me, did your dressing gown formerly belong to your mother?"

"No, ma'am. Her oldest sister gave it to her and she cut it down for me when I started to college." He wished with desperation that he could retrieve the terrapin, which by now was wedged into a completely inaccessible corner beneath the secretary. He felt the terrapin was safer than he.

"Well, she neglected to move the buttons from the left side to the right. If she had, you couldn't tell it had ever belonged to a woman. It's quite a distinctive bathrobe, Porter, and your mother is very ingenious and thrifty."

"Mrs. Capulet, there's a poem our preacher claims is agnostic but I like it:

> In the fell clutch of circumstance
> I have not winced nor cried aloud.
> Under the bludgeonings of chance
> My head is bloody, but unbowed.

I think I can safely promise you that the siren will be quiet from now on."

"Oh, nonsense, Porter, that siren doesn't bother me. I haven't slept well since Dr. Capulet died anyhow, and I rather enjoy the excitement. Occasionally. I just wanted you to know that I am neither blind nor dense, and I shall be watching you very closely. If you are able to deceive me, you can feel secure about the other faculty members, but for me there will forever be an aura of suspicion about you. Heightened, I might add, by that look of innocence you affect with such accomplishment. It reeks of long practice. For as experienced an observer of boys as myself, it's just a little overdone.

"One more thing: Your preacher probably objected to the line, 'I thank whatever gods may be.' Most of them are very insecure about even the slightest attack on their dogma. Are you sure you won't have another cup of tea?"

"No, ma'am. But I certainly have enjoyed it. I had no idea tea could be so interesting."

"Porter. Before you leave, have you met Professor Twilley?"

"No, ma'am. He teaches English, doesn't he? I have Dr. Minor."

"Yes. But he is also chairman of the discipline committee. I don't want to say that Professor Twilley is devoid of a sense of humor, but I will say that it is so wry and unusual that most people miss it altogether. I have known him since he was a student here, and I have seen him smile on occasion, but I have never seen him laugh. When I say that he is chairman of the discipline committee, I am really saying that he *is* the discipline committee, for it is the passion of his life. The other members do nothing but echo his opinions. He is a dedicated but detached man. The only thing he loves more than justice is punishment."

Porter wiggled on the edge of his seat. If he possibly could he was going to remove that terrapin.

"You wonder why I tell you this. Students who appear before Professor Twilley in his disciplinary capacity receive very short shrift. I put up with intolerable activity occasionally because of the consequences if I should report it. He will send even a star football player home so quickly if he is caught drinking that the poor boy would be mining coal again before he got to Bolingbroke."

The light glittered from her quivering spectacles. "He is extremely severe in punishing vandalism. I am sure that you would never be guilty of anything more than mischeevious pranking, but

137

be aware of Professor Twilley when you feel too impulsive. I would prefer that you never appear before his committee, but if you can't fool me, you might not be able to fool him. There is more to college education than just books, Porter."

"That's what my mother says, Mrs. Capulet, but I don't think she means the same thing you do."

"I think I shall call you Sambo. You don't mind, do you?"

"No, ma'am. My grandmother wouldn't like it, but she's a hundred miles away. I sure have enjoyed it, Mrs. Capulet, and I thank you for everything ... if you know what I mean."

He dared not venture, under this lady's eye, even a surreptitious glance to find the terrapin. The beast was on its own, and so, Porter felt, was he. At the door, he impulsively turned.

"How did you find out about Daddy putting the calf in the chair, Mrs. Capulet?"

"One of his fellow students told us. In strictest confidence. You see, the calf was in the room for several hours and absolutely wrecked it, what with that chair tied to its back. And other things."

"Was Professor Twilley the student who told?"

"I told you he abhorred vandalism. Come again, Sambo."

Porter went straight to his room, so concentrating on new levels of awareness that he failed to notice or speak to several boys on the way. After a while he opened *Webster's New Collegiate Dictionary* and looked up *dogma* and then *vandalism*. They meant what he thought, but a fellow could not be too careful. Thoughtfully he looked up *mischievous*. It was pronounced the way he thought, but Hodnetts could be forgiven minor peccadillos. Mrs. Capulet certainly was an interesting lady. Forewarned, he thought, is sure enough forearmed.

He finally wearied of contemplation and cast around for something to do with the tail end of Sunday afternoon. Bob Cater was still unaccounted for, and the rolled-up mattress and bare springs in the corner confirmed the permanence of Tom Christian's departure. He was so alone that he dared not think of home. Forlornly he picked up his supper sack and sat down by the window. He pretended that he was in a chic bistro overlooking the Champs Elysee as he munched on his peanut butter crackers and gazed out at the deserted street.

He selected the apple for his second course and ate it slowly as he became a recently bereaved young English lord being served a light supper in the dressing room of his London flat. He got up and procured a glass of water. *Just a touch more claret, Jeeves, and see what's on the wireless.* He turned on Bob Cater's radio. *Not too loud, Jeeves. Her Ladyship never liked to disturb the children at this time of day.*

When he opened the sweet crackers, hard little plaques with cream filling between them, he was transported to Venice — an expatriate advising his lovely but slightly retarded young wife not to have her head turned by that dashing Italian Count. *Have another of these delightful pastries, dear, and reconsider your position. He may have looks and sophistication, but I have the future and I own the land. What would the folks back home think?* He peeled the banana and became Lord Greystoke, relaxing in a loin cloth on the deck of an elaborate tree house while he watched Tantor and Cheetah disport themselves below and longed for Jane and Boy to return from a visit to her mother. Finished with the dispiriting meal, he flung the banana skin across the room toward the metal trash can and peered into the empty sack. Disconsolately he blew it up and popped it like a balloon between his hands.

He became conscious of the radio and a sweetly crooning voice:

> "Home, home on the range,
> Where the deer and the antelope play...."

He listened pensively and sadness swelled within him.

> "Where seldom is heard a discouraging word,
> And the skies are not cloudy all day."

He flicked it off abruptly, swallowed hard, and admonished himself that it was too early to cry.

Bob Cater returned, undressed, put on his bathrobe, and began studying Spanish and trying to write his English theme.

Periodically he would laugh and make a remark. Twice he increased the volume on his radio. "Lord, I hate Sunday afternoons. Always have, but they're worse here than anywhere. Lonesomest time in the world. Drive you crazy."

Porter turned away from consideration of that observation and busied himself with reading. He picked up the cellophane from his crackers, an apple core, and the banana skin while Bob Cater studied with the furious diligence affected by dilatory students who panic at the approach of previously ignored deadlines.

"You writing that theme first time in ink, Bob?"

"I'm writing it the only time in ink. I'm not an English major."

"Oh."

"You get all your work done ahead of time, and it makes me nervous to try to catch up."

"I'm sorry if it bothers you. I've been trying to be quiet."

"Gosh, that's all right. I can't study anyhow when it's too quiet. That's why I have to have a radio."

"Oh. Well, I'm going to bed. Good night."

After he said his prayers and was drifting off to sleep, he thought that despite the inherent melancholy of Sunday afternoons, this was the first time he had not cried himself to sleep. He certainly was maturing.

He dreamed that Cater and Slick were walking across campus in Army uniforms. They took off their shoes and began playing fox and hounds with Porter and the faculty children. Mary Martha stood watching and shouting for them to stop. As Porter scurried for Dr. Highsmith's bathroom to climb the tower, he tarried in the toilet, realizing that he had to void. The commode was freshly cleaned and shiny white. Porter resisted his urge. Something was wrong. Somehow he knew that it would be disastrous to urinate in Dr. Highsmith's commode. He heard water trickling urgently in the lavatory behind him. Slowly he unbuttoned his breeches. He heard Mrs. Capulet's voice from inside the tower. "That's far enough. I would advise you not to do that. Yet." Defiantly he pointed his penis downward and splashed into the water with all the force his bladder could muster.

He awoke immediately with his bed sopping wet. Anger changed rapidly to chagrin that soon became dismay. He was so ashamed of himself he could hardly bear it. What would Bob Cater say? Would he tell the KA's? Would Mrs. Capulet find out and tell Professor Twilley? Was this a shipping offense? Was there something bad wrong with him? There must be. He wanted to weep.

Craftiness prevailed. He decided that he could delay going to breakfast when Bob went, substitute Tom Christian's abandoned mattress for his defiled one, put on clean linens, and no one need ever know about it. It just might work. The mattress was getting cold and beginning to chafe. He squirmed to a dry spot and shrugged.

As he drifted off to sleep again, he recalled the way Willingham had looked from the top of the tower. With any sort of luck this was still his front porch. Please, God.

dr. Huber gave back the test papers and rocked
on black-shod feet before the class. The big red D nauseated Porter
and confirmed his worst fears. He looked inside his folded paper
with trepidation but hope. The red markings and scribbles scattered
over and under his own script proved the diligence of Dr. Huber in
correcting papers. He could not for the life of him see how he would
manage to survive this course.

X

He peeked over Tiny Yeoman's shoulder. The only red mark
on her paper was a gleaming cursive A; his despair was accented by
envy. The familiar lump appeared in his throat. He fought it back.
He would survive. He would pay closer attention, work harder, ask
more questions, prove to Dr. Huber that he was a dedicated student.
If Tiny could do it, he could do it. He would not be conquered by
French. He desperately did not want anyone at home or college to
know he had made a D.

The soft gray voice of Dr. Huber settled like a blanket over the
room, and even the squeaky desks were stilled. *"Mesdemoiselles et
messieurs.* Ladies and young gentlemen. I wish to make a departure
from my usual time-tested method of teaching intermediate French.
Les petits papiers, the little tests you are holding, have convinced me.
As you know, this was a classroom exercise in which I gave you the
questions and instructions in French and you wrote your answers
similarly. This *is* a class in French; I assume you are learning English
elsewhere. However, the harvest I gleaned was a bitter one. Since my
own methods have not changed in something approaching a score of
years, I am led to the assumption that either the University has this
year scoured the back woods of the state for students of the lowest

142

mentality it could find, or else this particular class has been victimized by high school teachers with only a perfunctory interest in
the subject and also an appalling lack of ability to share their meager
grasp of it." He paused and the mockingbird flared its wings. The
room was hushed.

"I say without fear of contradiction, since none shall hear
these words but you and none of this group is in position currently to
voice the slightest demurrer to anything I say, that except for one or
two gratifying and redeeming exceptions, there sits before me the
most poorly prepared class that has ever been visited on me.

"My burden is not only onerous; it has, after a weekend of
consideration, become a real challenge. I shall not be conquered. I
refuse to turn in failing grades for over a third of this class and
thereby acknowledge in the files of the registrar my own ineptitude
as a teacher. You will learn French! You will learn it if it half kills all of
us. I shall change my style and speak in English for this first quarter.
You, in turn, will dedicate yourselves to the eventual goal of not
requiring English instruction in learning this most beautiful of all
tongues. You will study, you will apply yourselves, you will *work*.

"We shall go back a few steps and review some basic concepts
which you have neglected. If at any time you do not understand
something, do not be ashamed to ask questions. You shall learn
French."

Porter's heart sang with the realization that he was not alone
in his misery. In fact, he ventured to believe his ears and think that
some more unfortunate students had even made F. His spirits lightened to the extent that he fancied he had probably made a high D.
What a teacher this was. With half a chance and this much help, why
should he fear? He gazed raptly at Dr. Huber and prepared to
inscribe every word in his notebook.

"Today we consider some of the more frequently used irregular verbs which are so very important in the French language. *Voir,
aller, être, avoir* — to see, to go, to be, to have. There are others of
importance, of course, but these make a nice beginning."

Toward the end of the hour, furiously scribbling, Porter had a
minor distraction in that he noticed Tiny Yeomans was tapping her
front teeth idly with her pencil, so obviously familiar with the material that she disdained even the pretense of taking notes.

"And now, young people, it behooves me to caution you about the practical usage of a certain verb form. I refer to the present tense, second person singular of *aller*. *Tu vas*, literally, means *you go*, and one would ordinarily expect this to be reserved for the so-called 'familiar' address — small children, intimate friends, members of one's family, and so on. Not so. In France one says *va-t-en* to animals only. If the dog or cat or chicken is where it should not be, one says to it, *Va-t-en*, which means, 'Get out of here.' This is permissible.

"One never uses this phrase in addressing a human being, except in the very rare instance when one has occasion to view a fellow human with both loathing and contempt, at which time these are the emotions that this little phrase carries with quite deadly precision to any discerning ear in France. In fact, if delivered in a scathing and withering tone, this word is a most formidable weapon indeed in that most civilized, and consequently class-conscious, of all countries, *la belle France*. It is more effective than a well-directed kick."

Dr. Huber paused and drew himself more erect. His tone changed slightly but so significantly that Porter put down his own pencil and stared with attention at his professor.

"I recall once on a little side street in Montmartre when I had occasion to use this phrase both appropriately and effectively. I was strolling slowly along, my hands behind my back, enjoying the sights and the sounds, when I was accosted, young ladies and gentlemen, by a pimp. You can imagine my shock. As soon as I comprehended the creature's message, I pointed my finger in his face and with supreme scorn I said in such a loud voice that it stopped passersby in their tracks, '*Va-t-en! Va-t-en, sale bête!*' I tell you, young people, he slunk away like the cur that he was."

Porter's hand leaped upward.

"Yes, Mr. Osborne? You have a question?"

"Yes, sir, Dr. Huber. What's a pimp?"

The eyes flared white in the silence, and Dr. Huber swallowed visibly. Tiny Yeomans was motionless. "Are you serious, Mr. Osborne?"

"Yes, sir."

The hush was somehow ominous, and Porter felt apprehensive. Now he heard the faintest of gasps from Tiny. After a moment

Dr. Huber responded in an expressionless voice. "A pimp, Mr. Osborne, is carrion. He thrives on human misery. He is a person, in a word, who procures customers for harlots. You do know what a harlot is, do you not, Mr. Osborne? A pimp brings men to the harlot and then pockets exorbitant amounts of her revenue."

Porter felt his cheeks flaming hot and squirmed like a worm on a hook, the focus of all the eyes in the universe. In his embarrassment, he awaited the thunder of ridicule. It never came. He winced as he thought that Tiny might once more lose control of her sphincters. Total silence prevailed.

"And now, young ladies and young gentlemen, in the brief time remaining to us, we shall consider a few characteristics of the verb *d'être.*"

At the end of the hour, Porter clutched his books defensively to his chest, looked steadily at the wide plank flooring, and tried to escape the classroom without notice.

"Mr. Osborne."

"Dr. Huber, could I possibly see you a few minutes in your office?"

"I was preparing to extend exactly that invitation, Mr. Osborne, but I fancy we shall both fare better on a full stomach. Go eat your lunch and be here at precisely 1:30. I have fifteen minutes then that I can devote to you."

At exactly 1:25 Porter deposited his Biology lab manual on the floor outside the office, lest Dr. Huber take offense at being reminded of the world of science. He rapped on the solid oaken door. Dr. Huber's office adjoined his classroom and was as sparsely furnished as it could be and still be called an office. Its owner sat upright on a straight wooden chair before a bare pine table, grading papers. As the tall door swung ponderously open and Porter peered around the corner, Dr. Huber removed his glasses and tucked them into his coat pocket.

"Come in, Mr. Osborne. You may have a seat."

"Excuse me, Dr. Huber. I didn't realize you hadn't finished your dinner."

"Oh, but I have, Mr. Osborne." He slipped a watch from his pocket with two fingers and a thumb and glanced at it. "Exactly twenty-two minutes ago."

Porter stared at the square of white linen tucked into the neck of Dr. Huber's shirt. It cascaded, he thought, in amplitude enough to protect one from a banquet, but he said nothing.

"Oh, you mean this." The voice was controlled and a little whispery. "This is my handkerchief, Mr. Osborne, not a napkin." He removed it and put it in his pocket.

"Oh."

"You see, when one grades a great number of papers, as I do, one's neck is constantly flexed, so much so that frequently the chin almost touches the chest. Now, there are oils, Mr. Osborne, secreted by the skin of even the most hygenic of men, and I discovered years ago that prolonged pressure of the chin produces on the knot of one's necktie a greasy area that is distressingly noticeable in otherwise immaculate attire." He leaned forward with an air of confidentiality, obviously unaccustomed to such intimately personal revelation.

"I resolved long ago, Mr. Osborne, not to become careless or slovenly as I grew older, and I developed as a young man the habit of putting my handkerchief around my neck when I grade papers. It is automatic, and it is successful. I do not have even one greasy tie, and some of them are twenty years old or better."

Porter spoke with what he hoped was an admiring tone. "I declare."

"Now, Mr. Osborne. Relax. Tell me, why did you request this audience?"

"Well, Dr. Huber, I guess the main reason was to apologize for that question this morning. I didn't want you to think I was a smart-aleck or anything. I sure didn't mean to embarrass you."

"Me, Mr. Osborne? Me? Whatever gave you the idea I was embarrassed? I was not the one with hanging head and reddened face. Any doubt I may have had concerning the sincerity of your question was certainly dispelled by your abject demeanor. I felt that you of a sudden had acquired more knowledge than you were prepared to assimilate in so public a place. My heart quite went out to you, in a manner of speaking. You are forgiven. What else can I do for you?"

Porter took a deep breath. "Dr. Huber, do you really think it's any use?"

146

"Be more precise, Mr. Osborne."

"Can I pass French? I'm working with Miss Yeomans and I'm studying as hard as I can, but this is the worst grade I ever made in my whole life and it makes me wonder if I'm even going to make it through college at all. I feel awful."

"Mr. Osborne, you are being overly dramatic, a trait I find a not uncommon one of youth. Your 'whole life' does not yet encompass either a significant amount of time or, I suspect, any great range of experience. You are suffering from panic because your vanity is bruised. Excellence in the provinces often proves to be lackluster mediocrity in the capital. You are not the worst student in the class if that is of any cheer to you. You are, in turn, far from the best, and I fancy that is what dismays you. Work, Mr. Osborne. Apply yourself. Study with Miss Yeomans. Try to think in French. Yes, you can pass French. I shall be disappointed if you do not excel with more than just a passing grade."

"Thanks, Dr. Huber. I'll try harder."

"Now, Mr. Osborne. About the college career. The entire college experience. The making of a man, so to speak. *Je ne sais pas.* Forgive me. I do not know. You are so young and, to be perfectly honest, you are so callow, so unformed. And yet there is something about you I have never seen before — a drive, a spark, a toughness of spirit, a completely unpredictable gift for doing the most outrageously unexpected things." The eyes protruded and showed white for emphasis. "I cannot sit here, Mr. Osborne, and with perfect candor reassure you by saying with a disinterested 'Tut, tut' that of course you will make it through college. There are pitfalls along the way. There are perils; indeed, it is a veritable maze you have entered. It will be miraculous if you finish, but miracles are most entertaining to watch. I am reminded of a little story, Mr. Osborne, if you will indulge me."

Another covert glance at his pocket watch followed. "We have approximately six minutes left. Yes. *Quand Louis Quatorze était Roi de France* ... I forget. Forgive me. When Louis XIV was King, he one day in formal judgment sentenced one of his courtiers to life imprisonment for some crime against his throne — treason perhaps. That part escapes my memory but it is not vital to the story. Now, King Louis had a pet donkey which he carried with him everywhere, and the little animal stood by the throne that day, caparisoned most richly in white satin suit and red velvet shoes, with a gold circlet around its ears and a garland of flowers around its neck.

"The condemned man spoke up and said, 'Sire, you are my lord, and your will is my will, but it is a pity that you incarcerate me at this point in my life. For I have discovered and developed a great talent which could amuse and enrich your entire court. I have learned, most painstakingly, to converse with animals, and if only I had twelve months with it, I could teach yon ass to speak.' The King considered the man and questioned him further and finally told him, 'I do not believe you, but we shall see. I grant you the twelve months, for which time you will live in my palace and teach in my stable. If you succeed, you will be rewarded beyond your wildest dreams; but if you fail, you will die by the most horrible tortures my executioners can devise.'

"As they were leaving the courtroom, the man's friend remonstrated with the courtier. 'You are a fool. You have exchanged a life of at least security in prison for a certain and horrible death. Whatever possessed you?' And the courtier responded, 'My friend, I have gained twelve months of freedom. In twelve months the King may die. Or the ass may die. Or I may die. Or ... the ass may speak.' "

Dr. Huber rose, walked to the window, and stood looking out with his hands behind his back. "Mr. Osborne, I was standing here on Saturday taking a respite from my labors when I witnessed the incredible and astonishing sight of you gamboling barefoot across this campus with a bevy of children, kicking up your heels and cavorting like a young colt in a spring meadow after confinement all winter in the barn. I heard your voice, unmistakable and easily recognizable, some while later as you called to one of your confederates from within the tower just adjacent to my classroom wall over there.

"Then I heard something I have not heard before in all the years I have been at Willingham University. I heard someone actually climbing to the top of that tower. I assumed it to be you. I was both fearful and incredulous as I listened to the rattle of those ancient rungs in loosened bricks, and I prepared myself to summon someone to retrieve your body. Later, all effort at concentration on my project futile by now, I observed you across yonder in the act of purloining from one of your peers the ridiculous headgear you new students are forced to affect, and then clapping it, Mr. Osborne, upon the head of *ce petit misérable,* the unfortunate nephew of Mrs. Kruger."

Porter sat in careful silence. Dr. Huber cleared his throat softly in a detached fashion. "Then this morning I was trapped into a conversation with one of my more tedious colleagues, a man so passionately immersed in his own field of English literature that he in his ignorance reviles by indifference any subject taught by his better-prepared colleagues on the faculty. He has the beastly habit of addressing me by my surname without a courtesy title, a trait so personally offensive that I have difficulty after such annoying salutation maintaining my own academic detachment and objectivity toward him.

"I am always most careful to address him as *Mister* and *Professor,* a formality which I can assure you keeps him at a not insignificant distance, since he has never bothered to possess himself of any postgraduate degree except a Master's, and that was a most modest endeavor accomplished right here at Willingham. Indeed, he is boastful that he has never left Willingham since his matriculation as a freshman some thirty years ago. Boastful, Mr. Osborne, of his insularity and provincialism. Can you imagine?

"He dared at a faculty meeting once to say, 'Huber, I see no reason for an intelligent and literate man to endure the personal discomfort of travel to France when he can sit in his own study and read of it in McCauley and Dickens.'

"At any rate, our paths crossed in front of the library as we both paused to lift our hats and speak to Mrs. Capulet. This man's only interest outside English literature lies in his activity as chairman of the discipline committee. I sometimes feel that he regards this campus as his personal fiefdom and views the students passing through with the coldly searching eyes of the Grand Inquisitor of Spain seeking heretics, or else with the hotly rapacious gleam of an old hawk in a hayloft of young pigeons.

"This morning he inquired politely enough about Mrs. Capulet's health and well-being, a formality covered with such beautiful succinctness by the phrase *comment ça va,* a small refinement of course totally unknown to him. Then, Mr. Osborne, he mentioned

149

your name to the good lady and I was so intrigued that I tarried awhile.

"He said that he had observed on Saturday afternoon from the window of his apartment a young boy standing on the back lawn of the Library, holding his shoes in his hand and obviously talking to himself while he waved at an automobile transporting a blind man down the street. This so piqued his curiosity that he established your identity by questioning his young son, a lad in my opinion so overly indulged that he is fated to a life of sloth, already exhibiting a distressing tendency toward corpulence in one so young.

"The professor inquired of Mrs. Capulet if you comported yourself well in the dormitory, and she gave you a very good name, her exact words being, 'like a lamb,' a feminine exaggeration which is nonetheless communicative. He then mentioned the fact that the dining hall siren had been vandalized twice already and that he has suspicions that any college student who would appear on campus with his feet unshod might possibly be eccentric enough to engage also in other erratic behavior not expressly forbidden by formal decree, an oversight resulting from no one in authority ever heretofore even considering such activity.

"Mrs. Capulet assured him that you were an unlikely candidate for such suspicion, that you attended church with her, that you were a young gentleman in every sense of the word, and that you already had the reputation of being a serious student. Whereupon he turned to me and said, 'Huber, do you know this boy?' I replied with dignity, 'Professor, the young man whose integrity you impugn is in my intermediate French class and has already demonstrated an intense desire to learn, manifesting at the same time an ability to influence others that is rare in one so young.' Then I looked him straight in the eye and said, 'Professor, the French have a proverb which might serve you well: *A tout comprendre, c'est tout pardonner.*'

"Then that absolute vulgarian of an Anglophile, who could not trill an R if his salvation depended on it, answered with coarse burlesque unworthy of the most loutish of posturing sophomores. 'Mercy buckets, Huber' he said, thereby insulting an entire race as well as a beautiful tongue. I bowed very formally to him in cold silence, murmured *'Au 'voir'* to Mrs. Capulet, and betook myself from his presence."

150

He turned again toward the window. "When one considers all the possibilities, Mr. Osborne, it is indeed fascinating to project whether or not you will finish college. I am bemused by the little anecdote I have recounted to you. Perhaps the ass *may* speak. This is an absolutely enchanting premise.

"You will be late for your Biology laboratory, a rote activity I am sure you accomplish with all ease and excellence. It is a subject unworthy of your powers, but *à chacun son gout.* Do not forget, as I have already told you, you will learn French. If the ass does speak, it will most certainly be bilingual."

Porter rose and spoke daringly. "*Au revoir, Monsieur le professeur. Je vous remercie beaucoup pour votre temps et pour votre attention.*" He turned for the door.

"One moment. Tell me, Mr. Osborne, are you very homesick?"

"Me, Doctor Huber? Me? Homesick? Whatever gave you that idea?"

"Years ago it was a considerable detriment to my adjustment, and I wondered if you might not have similar problems."

"Maybe times have changed. *Je n'ai pas la nostalgie.* Good-bye, now."

As he glanced back from the doorway, Dr. Huber was tucking his handkerchief into the neck of his shirt and reaching for the stack of folded papers.

Porter ran down the curving flights of stairs to the first floor. Dear Lord, he thought as he jumped completely over the last two steps, with all these folks watching me and some of them even watching over me, I guess I could tell You to take a little rest. But I won't. You keep on looking after me, Lord; I mean, I've got to be a good boy around this place. But Lord, Thou lookest on the heart of man and You know what a job You've got.

That was the last time he spoke to God all day. He refrained from even thinking about his upcoming rendezvous with Mary Martha.

In Biology he finished his own grasshopper and then helped

Tiny Yeomans with hers.

"How'd you make out with Dr. Huber? I think you're really coming on with your pronunciation."

"Oh, pretty good, I guess. Now watch ... this is head, thorax, and abdomen. All this hard part here is carapace. Gimme your scissors and I'll take it off for you. These are the biggest grasshoppers I ever saw. I wonder where they came from. I don't know how I'm going to do in French, Tiny, but Dr. Huber says I'm going to learn it. I hope he knows something I don't. You know, he's sort of strange."

"Strange?" exploded Henry Bean from the opposite side of Tiny's lab desk. "He's downright peculiar."

"Oh, Henry, I don't know about that. You and Sambo are too critical. I think Dr. Huber's sort of a lamb, really."

"Well, I wish the old Francophile would come into the twentieth century. I get sick and tired of the way he glorifies the French as though they're superior to everybody. And the language isn't all that great anymore, either. It may still be important in some diplomatic circles, but it's fast being replaced by English. If the Frogs don't quit looking down their noses at the rest of the world, they're going to lose their hat and fanny. The Germans are fixing to eat em alive again, and the French act as though everything's going to be all right because they're so civilized. The guy who said, 'If we can't learn from the past we're doomed to repeat it,' didn't mean every twenty years, for Pete's sake."

"Well, Dr. Huber can't help that. He sure can't do anything about Hitler."

"Oh, I know that! It's just that I resent all this smugness about accent and whatnot. He acts like you've belched at the table if somebody doesn't get just exactly the right intonation on a phrase." He cut his eyes at Tiny and added, "In fact, he'd probably handle that better; he does have a certain amount of sang-froid."

Porter wanted no explosion, of any sort, from Tiny and hastily interposed. "Well, I certainly think he's sincere; he's sure devoted his whole life to learning and teaching French. It's almost as though he's done that because he didn't want to be bothered with anything else."

"Oh, I'm not saying he isn't a good teacher. I'm just down on

152

the French and their superficial snobbery. We had one visit Lanier High School last spring and speak to our French class. He said 'zis' and 'zat' and called Mr. Hughes 'M'sieur Eee-gey' and then turned around and looked pained when one of our boys said 'France' instead of 'Frawnce.' I mean, if they're going to take our words and put French accents to them, why are we so vulgar when we Anglicize their words that we adopt? Why shouldn't we say 'souffel' instead of 'su-flay?' I'll bet that little chicken on the scouring powder that's pronounced 'bonn ammy' drives em crazy."

"Be back in a minute, fellows. Let me go ask Sybil Swygert if she can give me a ride home. You gonna clean out my pan for me, Porter? *Vous êtes très gentil.* That's speaking French, not Anglicizing it, and you better not let old Henry here get you off the track."

"Chevrolet coupay, Yeomans, and au reservoir," responded Henry Bean. "Go for the high A, girl, you can do it. But don't forget old Osborne. The worms and grasshoppers and frogs don't speak French."

As they left, Bubba Eaton sauntered by. "I been listening to yall. You oughta talk to my uncle . He's in the Merchant Marine and he come home one summer when I was fourteen. He'd been all over the world and was telling me about it. He used to laugh and say,

> The French they are a funny race.
> They fight with their feet and fuck with their face.

That's baad, ain't it?"

He moved on, and Porter turned with puzzlement to Henry. "What's he mean by that?"

"Are you serious, Osborne? By God, you are. Well, I understand that the French are very prone to kick and use other unfair blows when they're fighting."

"Oh. Well, what about that second line?"

"You'll have to figure that out for yourself. I'm too busy to explain it to you."

"You're not doing a blame thing."

"I am too. I'm planning my career. I'm going to graduate from this school with a good solid B average, go to med school, and then specialize in psychiatry. If you still want to ask that question

153

then, drop by in about ten years. But I warn you, it'll cost your ass."

Professor Hansford waddled over, beaming and wheezing, and laid an avuncular arm on each boy's shoulder. "How are things going, lads?"

"Just fine, 'Fessor Hansford, just fine. Would you like to see my preliminary dissection drawings? I mean, we're really learning a lot of Biology this afternoon." Porter tried to establish himself with Henry Bean as a fellow cynic by deliberately winking at him. "Henry and I were just discussing some of the finer points of the progenital tube. I mean to tell you that Eunice Yeomans is a good student. She really knows her material, but she has an allergy to formaldahyde even if she wears gloves, so Henry and I've been helping her with just the mechanical part of her dissection."

There was a little pat from the massive hand. "That's fine, boys, that's fine. Bean, I want a word with you about the importance of cover crops in preventing soil erosion."

Henry answered, "That's too bad Professor. I was just explaining to Osborne how busy I am this afternoon and I've about run out of time. Now, Bubba Eaton over there would probably be fascinated to hear about it. I understand his father has a plantation of well over two thousand acres, and that's a lot of soil to have erosion on. I think he's even seen a wild turkey. You know, I live in an apartment and my father works in the mill."

Later the boys waved good-bye to Tiny and headed out the door. "Why'd you tell 'Fessor Hansford that about Bubba? His daddy sharecrops fifty acres in south Georgia, and Bubba is real ashamed of it. He told me he didn't want anybody to know it. That's kind of mean, isn't it?"

"Naw, it wasn't mean. It was just a lie and it was a good lie. If you lie *up* about somebody, you may confuse things but you don't hurt people. Besides, we'll call it propaganda. Look what the Germans are doing with that, and everything they're saying is a bunch of lies."

"Golly, Henry, I never met anybody like you before. How'd you like to go around to the fraternity house with me?"

"How'd you like to go to a communist cell meeting with me? I wouldn't be caught dead at a fraternity house, Osborne. My father couldn't get me but to one Boy Scout meeting, and I even balked and

154

got out of the Baptist Church when I was fourteen. As far as I'm concerned, group stupidity is not a spectator sport, and it makes me itch when imbeciles organize to the point they take themselves seriously. Intelligence is the only attribute man has that's worth a damn, and fraternities constitute an adolescent insult to it. Thanks, anyway."

"Are you really a communist, Henry? Or were you kidding me? I never saw one before."

"Oh, God! I can't take you seriously, Osborne. You're not real. I went to a couple of meetings once, but that's a group worse than fraternities and Baptists rolled together. If you're going to believe everything people tell you, it's going to be real fun watching you get through college. See you around."

Porter walked expectantly up the deserted stairs to second floor, which accommodated the smaller, more advanced laboratories. He heard Clarence Spangler's voice echoing from the Comparative Anatomy lab on his right. With studied propriety he pushed open the door to the small cubicle across the hall that housed the Histology lab. Mary Martha perched atop a high stool, wearing a long white laboratory coat and peering into a microscope. Two boxes of slides were open on her left, and a sheaf of drawing paper with colored pencils lay on her right. When she looked up from her microscope, Porter was conscious anew of how lovely her eyes looked, all bright blue and twinkling, the lashes a thick frame of black.

"Well, Sambo, what brings you here to the rarified atmosphere of advanced science?"

"I thought I had an appointment with a beautiful sorceress who was going to change me from an ignorant country lout into a charming man of the world."

"And just who has such astonishing magical powers as that?"

"Well, the little god Nqua does, for one."

"What in the world are you talking about? You've left me on that one."

"You know. When the kangaroo got his tail. He went to the little god Nqua and said, 'Make me popular and most widely sought-after. Make me different from all other animals by four o'clock this afternoon.' I'm a little bit early, but it's almost four o'clock."

"What did the god do?"

"Well, I think that's where the comparison ends. He called up Yellow Dog Dingo and chased Old Man Kangaroo all over Australia until he grew great hind legs and a long strong tail."

"Now I remember. I remember Dingo. 'Grinning like a coal scuttle, grinning like a horse collar.' You're quoting from a children's story by Kipling. I hadn't thought of that in years. What in the world made you think of it?"

"I guess it was another line about Old Man Kangaroo. 'He was grey and he was wooly and his pride was inordinate.' I feel kind of stuck-up that a girl who's a real lady would go to the trouble to help me like this."

"Like what?"

"Well, Mary Martha, you did tell me to meet you here and you'd teach me how to kiss."

"Lord, boy, I thought we were just joking. What makes you think you need to learn?"

"Cause I don't know how. The other night was the very first time I'd ever kissed a girl, and you saw how everybody laughed at me."

"You're really serious, aren't you? Most people learn without any formal instruction. People were laughing because it was a ridiculous and comical situation. It wasn't any kind of bear baiting. Haven't you ever had a date?"

"Sure, I've had dates. But only with nice girls. And nice girls in my little town won't kiss any boys unless they're from another town, because it might get out on them and ruin their reputations."

"Well, that's probably the way we felt when we were in the eighth grade, but this is college, for pity's sake."

"I know it, and what if some of the fraternity boys get me a hot date and then I don't even know what to do with her? I tell you, Mary Martha, I need you."

"This is like helping your mother clean house — it's easier to do it than talk her out of it. Lock the door and come here."

"If we lock the door and somebody tries to get in, it might look real suspicious. Why don't we sit on the floor behind the sink there and spill a few of your slides, and then if we hear the door open, I'm just down there helping you pick up your slides."

Mary Martha laughed and sat with folded legs at the desig-

nated spot. "Well, you sure don't need any help at conniving....
Now.... Don't shut your eyes so soon.... Always turn your head so
your noses don't bump.... You really ought to take off your glasses....
That's not bad at all.... You're getting better all the time. Just do what
comes naturally."

Porter's heart was thumping fast, and he was giddy with both
pleasure and disbelief.

"OK.... You're making real progress now.... See, there's really
nothing to it at all. I tell you what. If you think she's really a fast girl,
open your mouth a little and stick your tongue in. Just a little way....
Slow, slow.... I believe you're going to make an A in Smooching 101."

Porter was immersed in rapture. He felt that he was dreaming. "That's just because I've got such a wonderful teacher. Let's be
sure I've got the fast-girl kiss down right. It's fun."

A few moments later Mary Martha drew back and delivered a
roundhouse slap that jerked Porter's head around. "What do you
think you're doing? Keep away from that KA pin! I told you, no
hands! This is a class in smooching, not petting. Boy, you don't need
any teaching; you need a governor!"

"Excuse me, Mary Martha. I guess I got carried away. You told
me to do what came naturally. I certainly didn't mean to offend you.
Especially after you've been such an angel to me. Can you forgive
me?"

Mary Martha scrambled to her feet and twisted her skirt
straight. "Oh, get out of here. This is the craziest caper I ever got into
in my life."

"Well, I really appreciate it. Same time next week?"

"What?"

"I'm really enjoying the lecture series on Smooching 101, but
it is a lab course too, isn't it?"

"You're the craziest kid I ever saw. We'll think about it, but I'm
not promising anything."

"I just thought of something."

"What?"

"What happens if they get me a date and she's not as good as
my teacher?"

"You just have to bear it and be brave. It's better to have loved
and lost than never to have loved at all. Nothing ventured, nothing

gained, you know."

"You sound a little bit like Mrs. Raleigh, except that you're still a stranger to suffering."

"What are you talking about now?"

He turned at the door. "I just thought of something else."

"What?"

"Next time you could take the pin off."

He left the Biology Building feeling ten years older than when he had entered it. He almost swaggered. Looking over at the Administration Building, he sought out the window to Dr. Huber's office and muttered, "I'll say the ass may speak."

A few days later he received from home the shoes he had requested — massive, clumsy things designed for the feet of laborers. On him they looked unwieldy because his thin legs stuck out of them without touching. He laced and tied the brogans one hook down from the top and wore them to the KA house to a Coke party. The effect was even better than he had anticipated. The girls at first made a concerted effort to ignore the shoes, but there were gratifying glances and fulfilling whispers. E.V. Derrick appeared and put things right.

"That's the funniest thing I ever saw! Looks like two churns with the dashers sticking out of em. Osborne, you're a mess."

"He's a damn character. You should have been in French class when he asked ole Huber what a pimp was. You coulda heard a pin drop. And Osborne didn't even crack a smile."

"Yeah? Well, you shoulda been in English class when we got our themes back. Ole Osborne made the only A and got his name called out loud. First time anybody ever made an A on the first theme turned in to Dr. Minor. He's gonna help our grade point average."

"Osborne, where'd you get those shoes? You know they're not really yours."

Porter laughed and bantered and waited for Clarence Spangler. He got an unexpected reaction.

"Laugh, fellows, cause it's funny. But looks like we better get used to those shoes. Remember ole Bubba Eaton? I made fun of him, but I'm gonna have to back down about him. 'Fessor Hansford wants me to be lab instructor next year I think, and so I take up a little extra time talking to him. You know. After all, what's a fellow supposed to do to get ahead? Anyhow, he was telling me to be nice to Bubba. Turns out his daddy is one of the richest farmers in south Georgia and 'Fessor Hansford wants to get one of his plantations in his soil erosion program.

"I guess Bubba just wore those shoes cause he likes em. Ha, ha, like you can get the boy out of the country but you can't get the country out of the boy. I asked him to drop by tonight, but he told me he'd already promised to go to another fraternity party. I checked, and ain't nobody but the Phi Delts having a function tonight besides us. If the Phi Delts want him, we sure as hell do, too. Yall work on him. We might still have a chance."

Later he told Porter, "You're not fooling me. Those shoes weren't in your closet when I checked the other night. You sent for them just to rub my nose in it, didn't you? OK, I can take a joke. But let me tell you one thing. You'd better not even think about wearing them to our formal rush party at Theo's. That'd be carrying a joke too far."

Porter looked at him innocently. "You mean when they're going to wear hoop skirts and sing? I wouldn't think of it. These are more or less leisure shoes for us country boys." He added sincerely, "Don't feel bad about Bubba, Clarence. You can't win em all. And you were sure right about another one of my good friends."

"Who's that?"

"Henry Bean. I've decided he's definitely not fraternity material. You sure wouldn't want him in KA."

When Porter went home from school the first
time, he was a little apprehensive about traveling. He had never
before been on a Greyhound bus, and he was gratified by the
nonchalance with which he bought his ticket and the aplomb he
exhibited while waiting in the crowded bus station. One would have
thought, he fancied, that he had been doing this all his life.
Willingham University and Mary Martha had wrought worldly
changes in him. He did not dwell on the fact that he was going home
on the very first weekend that Willingham permitted it. He dis-
regarded his farewell pledge to his mother of returning at Thanksgiving. That had been a hundred years ago.

He walked outside and studied the great machines pulling in
and out with hiss and sigh or waiting in their appointed bays with
pulsating patience and noxious snorts. When it was time to board his
bus, he stood in line with ticket in hand and felt that he was entering
the bowels of Behemoth. Truly this was a marvelous age in which he
lived.

He seated himself next to a window and wondered why the
people who ran the buses did not make the colored people get on
first instead of waiting until all the white passengers were seated.
After all, their designated place was the rear of the bus. When they
came out of their waiting room at the terminal and dragged their
shopping bags and paper sacks down the aisle in the center of the
bus, it was an unsettling activity that could have been avoided if they
had been seated before the white people came aboard. It was not that
he questioned the propriety of the designated seating, a fact of life
which he took for granted, but he was interested in increasing the

efficiency of the operation. He made a mental note to comment idly about this situation sometime to Henry Bean. He suspected that Henry would be complimentary of his powers of observation. It never occurred to him that the people in question had paid exactly the same amount of money as he for the privilege of travel.

The woman who shared his seat ran a practiced hand beneath her buttocks to smooth her dress before she sat down next to him. She used no makeup and wore a brown voile dress with a wide collar that extended over her shoulders to form rudimentary sleeves. She was holding in her bulging, ungirdled lap a puffy, blond baby who was obviously her grandchild. Its hair was snarled and sticky, and a smear of dried mucus across one rosy cheek bespoke indifference to nasal hygiene. The woman ducked her head to avoid a bulging reticule protruding from the arm of a black woman sidling down the aisle.

"Don't they staink!" she said to Porter.

For some reason, Porter thought back to his encounter that morning at breakfast with Boston Jones. "Hoo whee, Sambo. I got fifteen dollar offa that last dream. We got the world licked, boy. You sure dream a heap about water, though, you know it? Wanta make the sireen blow tonight?"

"Naw, I'm going home soon as I get out of lab. What makes people homesick, Boston?"

"Lawd, don't ask me. I don't know nothin bout no homesick; I ain't never been to college. I don't know what cause it and I don't know what cure it. Heapa folks has it, though, and hit seem like the nicest boys the ones what get it worst. We tend to the sireen when you get back."

"Well, Boston, I sorta promised somebody that sireen was gonna be quiet at night."

"Uh huh. I spect I know who that was, too. Mrs. Capulet don't care do the sireen blow."

"How do you know who I'm talking about?"

"She come get me yesterday afternoon when I was peeling taters. Tell Mrs. Raleigh she need me for an errand. Hit turn out somebody done slip a monstrous big ole turkle in her room and she don't know nothing about it until she hear somepin bumping under her bed in the middle of the night. Scared her half outta her wits, she say, hear somepin bump under her bed in the dark. She done hem him up between some boxes, but she ain't bout to touch him. Say she started to make you come get him but decided she'd let you keep on wondering what happen to him. Say that keep you on the anxious seat and prolly be good for you.

"She bust out laughing and say, 'Boston, that boy is a mess. Don't you let him get caught in his pranks, more especially next time he blow that sireen. I wanta watch him get through Willingham and see do he turn out all right.' I rare back and say, 'Why, Mrs. Capulet, what make you think that little bitty tad do something like that?' and she say, 'That pernt is not under discussion, my good man. I not blind and I not stupid, and I see you two with your heads together. Don't you let Sambo get in no bad trouble. Tell Mrs. Raleigh you moved a sofa for me.' And she gimme a quarter and sent me packing with that ole turkle. You want him back?"

"Heavens, no. I never want to see him again. Boston, I wish you could come home with me."

"Hoo whee, Sambo. You dreaming. Say I go home with you. Where I gonna sleep? Where I gonna eat? I can eat in the kitchen, prolly behind the stove. I bet you got a woodbox there make a fine seat. But ain't no white folks alive gonna bed me down; they be ruint for life. So you have to fix me up with a colored friend, and his wife get all cited bout having a stranger in the house and put clean white sheets on the feather bed and mop the floor and stew around a plumb sight. Then in the middle the night she feel bliged to check out the lonesome sojourner in there twixt her clean white sheets. Ain't no woman alive kin resist a sojourner, specially one from way off. So she come in there to check on me and we wind up together twixt them clean white sheets.

"Hoo whee! I kin smell em now. Smell like sunshine and fresh air and a hot flat iron. And then just about the time I git in the short rows with my hostess, here come her husband busting in mad as the devil and I have to cut him with my knife and I cut him too deep and he die. And then the sheriff ain't got no way to keep from locking me up and you paw hafta get me outta jail and he mad as hell at me for killing his best hand and all the cotton ain't picked yet, and he mad as hell at you, too. I can hear him now: 'Ain't spent my good money for you to go bringing no sorry six-fingered nigger home from college with you.' And then you have to argue with you paw to keep him from whipping me and you both.

"Time we do all that, ain't no way we get back here by Monday morning and you flunk outta college and I get fired by Mrs. Raleigh. I can hear her now, say me and my sorry laying out done give her a splittin headache. Naw, Sambo, I better not go home with you. I thank you for the invite, though."

"Boston, I still say you've got the wildest imagination I..." As the hand with the extra finger came up in arresting salute, they both spoke in unison. "Take one to know one."

It had been a delight. Now his neighbor on the bus shifted the baby to her other thigh. Porter regarded its dirty fingernails and the black beading around its pasty neck. The woman spoke again and nudged him with an elbow. "I said, don't they staink, sonny."

Porter thought of Boston Harbor Jones and pretended he was Dr. Huber. He drew a deep breath, looked her straight in the eye, and spoke as rapidly as he could. *"Je ne parle pas anglais. Je parle seulement française, et quand je parle, je ne parle jamais avec les femmes avec les grosses hanches et les poitrimes le plus grande."*

"Huh? What kinda talk is that?"

"Aussi, je ne parle jamais à une femme qui porte un enfant très sale avec lui. Il faut que j'étude maintenant. Ferme la bouche." He selected *Le Secret de l'étang noir* from his stack of books and opened it. He thought of Tiny Yeomans, again of Dr. Huber, and spoke once more to his neighbor. *"Va-t-en, sale bête,"* he said softly.

"Well, I do declare!"

As the bus turned into Cherry Street, she lurched across the aisle into a vacant seat and plopped down beside a man of greater girth than her own. Having raised her voice to overcome the roar of acceleration, she was easily audible when the motor settled down into a rhythmic rumble. "Who'da thought that wormy little kid was a dad-blame furriner? Don't that beat all? I'd be better off with them." She jerked her head toward the back of the bus. "Steady the baby just a second, mister, while I get my snuff out'n this old ragbag of a pocketbook. I ain't going but just up the road a piece. To Forsyth. Where you headed?"

Locked into his role of lingual isolation, Porter spent the rest of the trip trying to study. Every time the bus made a stop, however, and then geared again into purring progression, his excitement grew. He was going home. He could hear the heavy tires singing on the pavement, and his heart was in tune with them. He leaned his head against the rough, white antimacassar covering the green wales of his seat and stared out the window. The telephone poles flipped by in rapid accent to the rolling wheels. After all the horrible, wonderful, comic, tragic, good, bad things that had happened to him, he was going home.

Arrival at the bus station on the main street of Griffin was as exhilarating to him as any conqueror's return. His mother's old black Chevrolet was angled in at the curb, and his two younger sisters were in the back seat. He saw their faces impatiently scanning the windows of his bus, and when they spied him they abandoned any semblance of reserve and began waving energetically. In fact, the sisters stood in the car with their torsos out of the rear windows and waved with a fervor ridiculous for two young ladies in their early teens who were already permitted to wear stockings on Sundays. Porter felt not the slightest twinge of embarrassment.

As soon as the bus hissed to a stop, he grabbed his father's Gladstone bag and ran to the car. The bag was a leather relic of some pre-Depression spurt of prosperity and was the only decent piece of luggage in the family. His older sister had used it throughout four years of college, and now it had been entrusted to him. The grandeur of this benevolence was offset by the pragmatic realization that nobody else in the family was going anywhere for four years, and leather is a very enduring material. He hurled the bag into the back seat, leaped into the front, and, completely oblivious to the possible wonderment of passersby, repeatedly hugged and kissed his mother and sisters.

"Son, you're looking wonderful. I believe they're feeding you, but you need a haircut."

"Tell me about your roommate. Is he cute? Why didn't you bring him home with you?"

"What are the girls at Willingham wearing? Sally had twelve puppies and no two of them look alike. They've already got their eyes

164

open, but you have to crawl up under the smokehouse to see them."

Porter was exhilarated by his welcome. When they crossed the river, he was so jubilant that he exclaimed aloud, "Good old Brewton County! If you'll stop the car, Mother, I'll kiss my native soil."

His little sisters were mightily impressed with that statement. Indeed, they hung on his every word and so generally evinced admiration and respect that he in turn was overcome with affection for them. He wondered what had become of the old feelings of envy and annoyance. These were absolutely delightful people. They had really changed a lot in a very short time.

His reception at home was similarly adulating. The grandparents hailed him like a prodigal, and even his aunt, bygones smothered in sentimentality, embraced him warmly and told him how much they had missed him. Her husband, reserved product of a less demonstrative upbringing, shook hands and said, "Hello, Sambo." The tone was level and devoid of feeling and implied that although absence might be enough to make other hearts grow fonder, his own was still controlled by wary memory and he would await some evidence of change. Porter felt that at best he was still on trial.

The uncle's lack of enthusiasm was more than offset by the behavior of the dogs. Spot and Big Boy went into convulsions of pleasure at sight of him, grinning and leaping and wagging their tails so vigorously they imperiled their own balance and nearly knocked Porter off his feet. There is no welcome more open and unselfish than that of a dog at the return of a beloved master. Even Sally, exclusive property of the youngest sister, crawled from under the smokehouse, eyes a trifle sheepish and dugs dragging the ground, to hail him with pawing and sneezing and energetic convolutions of her tailless behind. Porter Longstreet Osborne, Jr., was home. The fields of conflict were far removed. This was his sanctuary.

He dutifully inspected and admired the new hen house and the gleaming wire fence around it. It was the fulfillment of long years of yearning on his mother's part. No more chickens scratching and fluffing in flower beds, no more roosting flocks in the chinaberry tree. No more chicken mess deposited in random mine fields around the swept yard to squash unexpectedly between the bare toes of careless children.

The guineas could not be confined by the fence, since they could fly better than chickens. They were not the nuisance, however, that the more domesticated fowl constituted. They roosted in the holly tree, their droppings neatly arranged in precise spires and cones, and no one ever walked barefoot under a holly tree anyhow because of the thorny leaves. Also, they tended to forage further afield and ignore the flower beds around the house, their stream-lined metallic-colored bodies darting in single file along fences or open pasture like tiny units of armor mounted on prissy stilts.

In addition, they had a proclivity for dusting themselves in the big road and had such a defensive sense of territory that an occasional passing automobile indifferently kept their census at a manageable level. The chicken yard was impressive, and Porter marveled that progress had come to Brewton County in his brief absence. Perhaps he *would* invite his roommate home with him some weekend.

That night after family devotions, the singing and praying done, he visited awhile with the grandparents, kissed his mother good night, and settled down at the dining table with his books. He planned to study until his father came home and then have a long, bedtime visit with him. He finished French and Biology and completed the first draft of his theme for English. By one o'clock he could no longer fight off sleep and went upstairs to bed thinking that Brewton County had not changed all that much.

Saturday morning early he went with Wes to the cow pen. He had volunteered the night before to do the milking himself, but his mother had informed him Wes was receiving a dollar in cash and three gallons of buttermilk each week for tending the three cows, and that so handsome a recompense certainly required no relief. She mused that of course she could subtract fourteen cents from the dollar for that week and give it to Porter but she hardly thought it worth the effort. Porter agreed. He was dismayed to discover the stalls had not been shoveled clean since he left but did not chide Wes about it. He well knew that a man did a better job when he was working for himself.

He spent the rest of the day exploring every cranny of the farm, delighting in the warm rush of security at sight of familiar landmarks. In the chaos of upheaval in his own life, the land was reassuringly changeless. It was an Indian Summer day, and the air was full-bodied and thrilling. He smelled muscadines and browning leaves and just a hint of wood smoke from an earlier cooking fire. The earth was brooding and patiently silent, all the usual noises stilled except for the keening of hidden insects so tiny one wondered if their song might not be only the ringing of one's own ears.

The cotton fields were checkered in black and white, all leaves fallen, the bare stalks of harvested plants in spare contrast to the billowing white richness of the ungleaned rows. Everyone was busy. So urgent was the need to get all the cotton picked before rain set in that one's view of the workers seemed to be only of rounded backs, punctuated occasionally by a briefly erect figure stretching for a moment the tortured muscles of unchanging position. Saturday afternoon leisure was not an option during cotton-picking time.

Some things, however, took precedence over work. Beatrice sat on her front porch in a kitchen chair bottomed with white oak splits, her wooly hair unbraided into a bizarre aureole around her small face. Both her earlobes were skewered with broom straws. On Sundays all the black women wore gold hoops in their ears, but during the work-a-day week these would have been hazards in the cotton fields, and the hoops were replaced by straws or toothpicks to keep the holes patent. White girls and white women did not have pierced ears unless they were very old or very loose, but it was mandatory among the blacks.

Beatrice's mother stood over her plying a fine-toothed comb through the rank forest of hair in extraction of even the finest particle of lint. The girl held a bottle of Vaseline with its blue and white label in her hands and maintained her head in such careful position that only her eyes moved. Her mother separated the hair into sections with the geometric sureness of a surveyor dividing a tract of land and then parcelled each of these into three hanks. Combing Vaseline into the hair, she expertly fashioned plaits of an evenness and uniformity that bespoke decades of practice and chastened the great bush into gleaming, glistening coils that tightened skin and implied demureness. There was something about this transforming toilette that had always seemed to Porter too personal to be performed on the front porch in front of God and everybody.

167

He averted his gaze to the frizzy chickens around the door-step. They were kept, he had been told confidentially, to scratch out mo-jos from under the steps and thereby prevent anyone from putting a spell on any of the occupants. They were weird fowl, their feathers growing forward instead of backward, giving the appearance that they were constantly in the presence of a high tail wind or had just emerged from a threshing machine. Porter wondered idly if Beatrice could help them with that jar of Vaseline, and then he tried unsuccessfully to imagine Boston Harbor Jones at his side. His new-found friend definitely would not fit into this bucolic scene. It never occurred to him to compare the Miller girls at Willingham with Beatrice in Brewton County. He was much more comfortable with contrasts than with similarities.

"Evening, Matt. Evening, Beatrice. Yall through with your cotton?"

"Hidy, Sambo. Caught up enough the menfolks do without us an hour or two. Gotta get Beatrice ready for church tomorrow. Sprised to see you. Thought you wadn't coming home till Thanksgiving. You done with school already?"

"Naw, just thought I better get home and check on everybody. College lasts four years. I've just started."

"Uh huh. You better git to eating. You pore as a garter snake. Ain't grown a dab since you left here. Keep yo head still, gal, and hold that grease up here where I'n git at it."

"I'm eating all the time, Matt. The food's not good as yours, but there's lots of it. College sure is hard. And different. The books take a lot of time, but then there are lots of strange people from strange places. And you have to room with people you never saw the likes of. And you have to study hard every night so you won't get behind, and everybody else is spending more money than you are."

Beatrice, her neck still bent under the coiffing fingers of her mother, spoke from near her chest. "I wish I could go to collitch."

Matt released her head and stepped back. "Collitch? I say collitch! Gal, you done finish the sebenth and learnt all Miss Willie Grooms know already. You write a good hand and you read all the time now. Here me taking all this trouble to get you pretty for that boy at church tomorrow and keeping you out the cotton field to do it, and I can't even read. You mighty big-ike! You think you better'n yo

168

maw?"

"Beatrice, you wouldn't like college. I'm sure you'd get homesick."

Beatrice raised her head and looked levelly at Porter, her neck as straight as a queen's. Half of her hair was groomed to perfection with new braids centered in contoured little garden plots. The other half was still untamed in the bushy frenzy of unplaited defiance. Porter was a little embarrassed to look but could not avert his gaze.

"Homesick? Homesick for what? What around here to make you homesick?" she demanded.

"Gal, you hush yo mouth fo I slap it shut. Gimme that grease and hold still, or I'll put you in that field so fast it make yo head swim. Good to see you, Sambo. Bye, now."

That night at supper, Porter rediscovered how annoying petty habits can be when people live together. The grandfather poured coffee from cup to saucer for cooling and then drank it noisily from the saucer. The uncle still made audible chewing sounds and swallowed so that he could be heard across the table.

After Porter had cleaned his plate, his mother began. "Son, won't you have some more sweet potatoes? How about some biscuits and gravy? Come on, just a little bit more? Here, there's not enough of this okra left to fool with putting up; finish it for me. Would you like some of these warmed-over butterbeans from night before last? I just worry about you not eating enough."

Next morning he listened to the Sunday School superintendent stumble through his scripture reading and winced when he sounded the *w* in *sword*. He winced even harder when Miss Maggie Mae Harris rose to pray. She was notorious, not only for issuing news bulletins to the Lord, but also for calling names and getting very personal with her public prayers. When a new minister had come to serve the church and Miss Maggie Mae had favored another candidate, she had risen on the newcomer's maiden Sunday and prayed aloud, "O Heavenly Father, if it be not Thy will that this man serve our church, and I personally think that it ain't, then we pray Thee, Almighty Lord, place obstacles in his path."

169

She had leered at Porter this morning with dingy dentures, her breath snuff-tainted, and he feared the worst. Now she delivered. "We hold up to Thee our college freshman home for the weekend from that great Baptist school in Macon. Bless little Porter Osborne, Father. Keep him from harm and hold him ever close to Thee as he studies hard to make good grades so he will be a worthy worker in Thy vineyard and Thy fields which are even now white unto the harvest. Let him enjoy, Father, where he is at, but keep him ever mindful of where he is from and do not let him get to thinking too much of his little self. For we ask all these things in the blessed name of Thy sweet and holy Son, Jesus Christ. Amen."

Porter thought of the opulence of Vineville Baptist, thanked God this was not a preaching Sunday at Peabody, and wondered fleetingly if he had made an error in choice.

After Sunday School, true to family custom, the *Atlanta Constitution* lay in inviting Sabbath fatness on the back seat of the car. The mailman did not run on Sundays, but he lived next door to the church and through years of neighborliness had received the Osborne paper at his house and deposited it in their automobile on his way to worship. There was a firm family rule that no one could open that paper and extract the enticingly colored comic pages until it was delivered at home to the uncle. Intact.

The uncle paid for the Sunday paper and it was his. He wanted no messy children wrinkling the front page or the sports section before he perused them. The three-mile trip home on Sunday morning with the temptation of the unread paper was tantalizing and tension-building.

When the uncle removed his favorite portions that morning, he handed the rest of the paper back to the second sister in much the same way one grants a yearning dog a long-watched morsel. Within minutes, the three siblings were fussing loudly over the funny papers. When Porter realized what he was doing, he withdrew in disgust to another room. He could not believe a college man had reverted so quickly to such infantile behavior. He was ashamed of being annoyed with his little sisters and crestfallen at the shrill melee in which he had just participated.

The door opened and the two girls, teetering like fledglings on their unaccustomed Sunday heels, silk stockings wrinkled on unfilled calves, not yet women but already ladies, solemnly offered the two sheets of comics.

"We want you to read them first. We can read them after you go back to school."

He pulled each one of them to him and hugged her roughly, not trusting himself to speak. Then he charged outdoors and cavorted with Spot and Big Boy until his mother rang the dinner bell.

He felt much more mature through Sunday dinner, relished the traditional pot roast, rice, gravy, string beans, and homemade biscuits. He noted with approval that his mother still dressed the table with her best linen, china, and silver. There was a comfortable sameness to the rituals of Sunday that was solid as bedrock and made him feel secure.

After dinner his father retired to the south veranda with the newspaper and sat in a rocker with his feet propped against one of the columns, relaxed in the fall sunshine, thick smoke from his postprandial cigarette crawling and weaving through stained fingers. Porter pulled up another rocking chair and seated himself quietly with an air of camaraderie properly suffused with diffidence.

"Well, Sambo, how's college?"

"Just fine, Daddy. I'm studying hard and I'm keeping up like you told me. I had to write a couple of checks for tuition and books, but other than that I haven't had to spend much money yet. I really appreciate you carrying me down there that day, busy as you are."

"I enjoyed it. Are the KA's rushing you?"

"Yessir. So are the SAE's and the Pikes. Clarence and Slick say the Pikes have sidewalk rush."

"What's that?"

"They grab anybody going down the sidewalk who doesn't fight back and slap a pledge pin on him. Clarence swears that last year they pledged a guy who didn't even go to Willingham and were three weeks finding it out. But Clarence exaggerates a lot."

"Well, I hope you pledge KA. That is, if you like the fellows. I thought they were a good bunch of boys."

"Oh, yessir. They're fine. I like the chicken yard. Mother sure is proud of it."

"Yes, I believe you're right. I was glad to do it for her. She's been wanting one for a long time. Sambo, I've been thinking about it and I believe I'm going to buy a tractor."

Porter considered the relative costs of chicken yards and tractors. "You are?"

"It can break up more ground in one day than four men with mules can in a week."

Porter rocked a few times and then asked, "What'll happen to the nigras and the mules?"

His father flipped his cigarette out into the yard. "There'll be plenty for them to do. We may be able to get rid of a few of the mules. You don't have to feed a tractor when it's raining or if it's sitting in the shed. I know you're going to say the hands will tear it up, but I'm not going to let anybody but Wes run it. He's pretty good with machinery."

Porter had no prickle of foresight that the culture of his region, basically unchanged for one hundred years, was on the verge of disappearance. He changed the subject.

"Daddy, do you remember Mrs. Capulet?"

"Kate Capulet? I reckon I do. She was the wife of the acting president when I was at Willingham. A finer gentleman never lived than old Dr. Capulet. Where'd you run into his wife?"

"She's the house mother in the dormitory. She's been real nice to me, and she remembers you. Said she and Dr. Capulet thought a lot of you."

"Well, I'll swear. Please give her my very best regards when you see her, and tell her that I remember her and her husband with the greatest admiration and respect." He extracted a fresh cigarette without removing the package from his shirt pocket. "To tell you the truth, Sambo, I kept trying to figure out some way to frig Kate Capulet. She had the prettiest ankles in Macon, and her husband was at least twenty years older than she was. You know he couldn't have satisfied her."

Porter quickly changed the subject again. "Do you remember 'Fessor Twilley?"

"Hiram Augustus Twilley! I reckon I do. One-eyed farm boy from Screven County. He was a good student but didn't mix much. Thought fraternities were the rabbit warrens of hell. He didn't play sports on account of his eye, I guess, but he did a lot of running and calisthenics. Said he could keep his body in good shape without letting it get pounded into beefsteak by somebody else. Where'd you run into him?"

"Oh, I haven't met him yet. I just know that he teaches English; some of my friends have him. They're bout half scared of him."

"The only thing that kept him from being plumb pompous was a big streak of meanness in him. He was obsessed with the Book of Amos. Luther Farmer tried to get old Hiram A. to drink some wine one night by reading him what Paul said about thy stomach's sake and thine own infirmities. The rest of us got pretty high, but Twilley wouldn't even take a sip. Just sat there watching us and saying, 'Let justice roll down like a river.'

"Luther got a little nervous about the third time he said it and finally told him if there was ever any hint of us getting reported, that justice wasn't the only thing that was going to roll like a river, because he would personally beat the piss out of him. We never saw much of Twilley after that. I always liked him, but he was a lonesome sort of fellow. Kept to himself."

"How'd he lose his eye?"

"Nobody ever knew for sure. Didn't get close enough to him either to ask or be told. Luther Farmer always said it had offended Twilley and he had plucked it out. You don't notice or comment on someone's affliction, Sambo. How's your blind roommate doing?"

"Tom Christian? Well, he sort of decided dormitory life was too loud and boisterous for him and moved back to the Academy for the Blind. He still comes to classes, but I don't have any with him. I've sure enjoyed talking to you, Dad. I'd better go get my things together so I'll get to the bus on time."

"You haven't written me a letter since you've been to college. They're all addressed to your mother. If you ever need to write me confidentially, just address it to P.O. Box 16 in Brewtonton and I'll get it in town with my office mail."

"Yes, sir. Thank you."

Porter had endured about all the camaraderie he could stand. He left the porch with as much diffidence as he had approached it.

His mother was busy at the back porch table packing a box of food for him to take back to school. She brought out a red tin box in which peppermint candy from the previous Christmas had been packed. "I thought I'd send Mrs. Capulet some of my butter. She's been so nice to you."

The butter was packed in fresh-churned softness into the wooden mold to produce a measured pound. It hardened under refrigeration into perfectly sculptured symmetry and was adorned on its top with an exquisitely detailed sheaf of wheat. The unmeasured remnants from a churning were always patted by hand into ovals and decorated by diagonally crossing lines with the butter paddle, but they were saved for home consumption.

She wrapped the butter carefully in waxed paper and then extracted three treasured ice cubes from the tray in the kerosene refrigerator. She placed them in the bottom of the candy tin and deposited the butter on top of them before tightly closing the lid on the can. She then taped an envelope addressed to Mrs. Capulet on top of the lid.

"There. I think that'll keep it fresh until you get there. You know, son, I do wish your daddy would get us a new refrigerator now that we have electricity. I'm so tired of this stinking old kerosene thing I don't know what to do."

Porter made mental estimates of the combined cost of a refrigerator and a chicken yard balanced against that of a tractor. He silently predicted that the tractor would appear before the refrigerator but said nothing. He was accustomed to the jousting between his parents, the sublimated thrusts and parries, but had long since decided that this was an activity properly confined only to its participants. He was very adept at feigning both ignorance and indifference.

On the bus he ignored the gentleman sitting next to him and carefully removed the envelope from the top of the red tin.

Dear Mrs. Capulet,
    Thank you from the bottom of my heart for being so nice to my precious boy. He is so young and so innocent, and you have no idea how it lightens my heart to

174

know that he has found a true lady like you who loves him in somewhat the same fashion I do. The butter is a small token of my esteem and respect for you.

Yours truly,
Vera G. Osborne

Porter crumpled the note into a tight ball and thrust it into his pocket. Realizing that his seatmate was studying him intently, albeit askance, he gave him a broad wink and a conspiratorial leer. "It's all a fellow can do sometimes to keep his women folks separated."

He leaned his forehead against the bus window and pretended to be studying the landscape while he remembered the weekend. When the lump began appearing in his throat, he assured himself that beyond any shadow of a doubt, absolutely and positively, the best place in the world for him to be was in college. Perhaps.

XII

On Saturday night before pledge Sunday, the KA fraternity had its long awaited, exciting, slightly intimidating gala — the final rush party at Brother Theo's house in Ingleside. So intense was the anticipation, so privileged the invitations, so inviolate the sanctity of this gracious home at the very heart of Kappa Alpha Order, that no freshman had the temerity to attend if he had any intention of pledging anything else.

Porter had a troubled scene with Clarence and Slick late in the week when they were making their rounds to be sure that everyone who was going to attend Brother Theo's party was indeed going to follow through with membership. He did not reiterate his insecurity about legacy this time but let his misgivings surface in the form of concern about finances. He pointed out that pledge dues were two dollars a month, initiation fee with pin was thirty-five dollars, and then dues after initiation were five dollars a month. This, he informed the upperclassmen, did not fit into the family budget, since his father was planning to buy a new tractor and his mother wanted a new refrigerator. It behooved him to be unselfish and deny all but imperative expenditures because he was only one unit in a family that relied completely on the father's resources. It all sounded so sincere and so logical that he convinced himself and became adamant that, despite his love for the group, he must nobly reject KA because of duty and prior loyalties. He probably was not destined to be a fraternity man, he said.

Clarence and Slick heard him out and wasted no more time arguing with him. Instead, they put in a long distance call to Porter Longstreet Osborne, Sr., and that night Porter was called from his studies to the pay telephone at the end of the hall. Long distance was not only expensive, it was an extremely complicated process in his community. It involved a trip to town to reach a telephone and all manner of inconvenience, and Porter was immediately impressed. Furthermore, when he discovered from an inquisitive operator with a nasal twang that this was a person-to-person call, he was almost overcome. Long distance was intimidating enough, but person-to-person could render an adolescent tongue-tied with self-importance.

"Sambo, what's this I hear about your not joining a fraternity?"

Porter lamely repeated the reasoning he had advanced to the boys, his histrionics weakened by sputtering and the knowledge that his theatrical range in the presence of his father was rigidly restricted by that man's knowledge of unadorned truth.

"Well, don't worry about that. You go ahead and join KA, and I'll pay all your expenses. Just use my checkbook like you do for tuition."

Porter's heart swelled with love and appreciation.

"I really want you to join the fraternity. To tell you the truth, son, I think it'll be good for you."

After a subservient farewell, his heart shrunk to normal again, Porter regarded the granular plaster wall for a moment and studied the painted column on which the telephone was mounted, its surface messily inscribed with numbers the football players could not remember long enough to call. He slowly replaced the heavy black receiver on its hook. His tone was almost dreamy and certainly held a note of wistfulness. "I sure as hell hope so."

Dressing for the party, he considered his work shoes and the contrast they would afford his suit and tie but discarded the idea. He had already done that. Repetition was the forerunner of monotony and he knew it. He needed some unexpected gambit to keep people from knowing how overwhelmed he was by the grandeur of this party and how socially inept he felt. He needed to enhance the embryonic reputation he was establishing for carefree irreverence.

He recalled a trick he had learned from a Boy Scout magazine and fancied that perhaps these city folks might never have heard of it. He knocked on Mrs. Capulet's door and asked if he might borrow a needle and some thread. He selected a spool of fine green silk and promised to return it on the morrow, congratulating himself anew that he had delivered her butter without his mother's note. He carefully inserted the needle into the thread for protection and placed it in the pocket of his coat. He was prepared but not committed.

Back in the room, Bob Cater was stooping with bent knees before the mirror, carefully parting his hair. "Are you ready? Do I look all right? Wouldn't it be terrible after all this if we didn't get bids tomorrow? Here. Brush my shoulders to be sure I've got all the dandruff off. Let's go."

Porter had never visited such a place as Theo Montagu's white-columned, recently-built house way out in Ingleside. Every light was on, both upstairs and down, and the front door was wide open in beckoning welcome that he thought was an extravagant disregard for the peril of flies. Then he noted the absence of any outbuildings or livestock and realized that flies were not a problem in the lives of these city folk. He was impressed beyond belief. He could not imagine anyone in this place saying, "Shut the door or you'll let the flies in," and it immediately became more of a movie set than a house. Theo was dressed in a tuxedo, the first one Porter had ever seen, and it made his barrel-chested strut even more noticeable. He was preening and prancing at the front door by the side of his wife, positively twinkling with pride.

His lady was diminutive to begin with, some half a head shorter than Theo and as fine-boned as an elegant finch. She was appareled to appear even tinier. She wore a genuine hoop skirt, yards and yards of pale blue satin that surrounded her in a perfect circle. From the center of it her small waist rose to a tightly fitted bodice that proved even little people could be grown women. Her swanlike neck was accented by a cameo resting in the notch at its base, fastened on a velvet ribbon just a shade darker than her dress. Her eyes were the same blue. Her hair was swept back to fall in a cascade of golden curls from the crown of her head. Every detail was perfect. Porter thought that it would take a Phi Delta Theta to notice that she had a tendency to be horse-faced and that her teeth were crooked and a trifle too long.

He watched her intently as he waited to be welcomed. He was bedazzled by his surroundings and enchanted by the appearance of his hostess. Mary Martha, attired in a full-skirted evening gown, in mode with a cameo around her neck, sidled by him and whispered, "Close your mouth. Feathers don't make the bird. You look real country gaping like that. She's just a plain, everyday, walking around woman who squats to pee like the rest of us."

Porter jumped like a startled rabbit. The mystique of the Old South always hung heavily around any KA function to the extent that any sensitive student automatically capitalized the two words and uttered them with appropriate reverence. Certainly Old South was so thick in the air this night that it could be spread with a butter knife. That was no way for a lady of the Old South who was actually pinned to a Knight of Kappa Alpha to be talking, but before he could gather his wits to remonstrate, Mary Martha had strolled off, her face as innocent as a babe's.

The clucking and clattering were more noticeable in Theo's voice tonight. There was the hint of a lisp. "Darling, this is Porter Osborne, Jr. — Porter Longstreet Osborne, Jr. — but everybody calls him Sambo. Sambo, this is my wife, Jo Beth. She was named after two queens, Josephine and Elizabeth, but she was Jo Beth up at Hollins and she's been Jo Beth, queen of my heart, ever since I saw her."

Porter had a stronger sense of social survival than to bleat "What's Hollins?" He could find out about that later. He bowed from the waist. "I'm honored to meet you, Miss Jo Beth. Theo and all the Brothers talk about you all the time, but none of them had prepared me for how perfectly you grace this house."

"Law, Theo, he's every bit as cute as you told me he was. Drop the 'Miss,' Sambo. All Theo's boys call me Jo Beth, and I love every one of them as much as he does. You're going to make a wonderful KA!"

Porter tried not to smirk as he moved aside for her to greet another guest. He was not a total newcomer to Old South himself.

Later in the evening, as had been promised, Jo Beth sang. She planted herself in front of the mantelpiece, clasped her hands formally in front of her, tilted her chin upward, cleared her throat

179

twice, and sang without accompaniment. Porter was in a corner trying not to brush against any of the fine furniture or step too hard on the thick rug. He was glad he had not worn his brogans. On the wall across from him hung an oil portrait of Jo Beth and her two small daughters. The artist had softened her face into a perfect oval and her teeth did not show, but one could tell in an instant who it was supposed to be. Porter was impressed anew.

His own family was blessed with an in-law who had "talent," and two of her paintings were framed and hung in the parlor at home. The aunt referred to them as "original oils" with a tone that imparted luster to the whole family and made the children feel vaguely elegant. They were copies of early covers of *The Youth's Companion*. One was an Indian man with a misshapen thigh and a twisted foot, shading with a grotesque hand his fiercely white eye as he searched a desert horizon. The other was a preoccupied Indian maid in perpetual peril of slipping off an overhanging rock into a forest pool as she strained to touch the water with her bare toe. For the last four years, Porter had been convinced that beneath her romantic garments her thickened body proclaimed that she must be about five months pregnant and that her handicapped husband, or lover as the case might be, was trying desperately to find his way from the other side of the mantel before she delivered. He had not, of course, voiced his fantasies about such revered relics to anyone. Family loyalty was a cardinal virtue and did not tolerate irreverence for shrines. A Southern parlor was nothing if not a shrine. He felt overwhelmed by the grandeur of the one in which he now found himself, and the portrait accentuated the feeling.

When he heard the first phrase from Jo Beth's throat, he realized that he was in the presence of something which his mother would have admiringly called a "trained voice." It was constantly tremulant in a fashion that he and his sisters had managed to attain only by singing in an empty two-horse wagon when the mules were trotting. If he thought there was a whiney thinness on high notes or an occasional unpleasant rasp, Porter attributed it to his own lack of ear. Everyone else was raptly attentive. Eventually there came the climax of the recital.

180

She has two dreamy eyes of blue,
A smile beyond compare,
Two ruby lips to kiss you with,
And a wealth of golden hair.

She's the sweetest girl in all the world,
The fairest flower that grows,
She's my sunny Southern sweetheart,
She's my Kappa Alpha Rose.

Porter thought she was singing of herself but applauded as vigorously as his fellows, then joined them in rousing, off-key performances of "In eighteen hundred and sixty-five at Washington and Lee" and "It's a grand old gang and together we'll hang." He had not felt so securely enfolded in a group since he left the Sunbeams. Fraternity life was going to be great.

Mary Martha came up to him later. "How's my innocent country boy tonight? I haven't noticed you snowing any of these sweet young things, but at least you've quit gawking."

"I've had only one lesson and I'm still a little unsure of myself. I'm hoping to improve my technique with my lab instructor Monday afternoon."

"Well, I don't know. Young people are getting to be a bit of a bore to a mature woman like me. I may be there and I may not."

Porter resolved to relieve Mary Martha's boredom immediately. He locked himself in the bathroom, took off his coat, and threaded the needle he had borrowed. He then put the spool back in the coat pocket and ran the thread through the pocket, up the inside and out the front of the coat. When he dressed again, there was a tantalizing three-inch fragment of green silk thread shining just to the outside of his left lapel against the dark gray fabric of his suit. If Mary Martha could resist trying to remove it, she was a more disinterested and aloof female than he thought. He found her in a group talking to Jo Beth. So much the better. She would not soon forget this evening.

He strolled up to the group, presented his left profile to Mary Martha, and spoke to his hostess. "Jo Beth, this is a wonderful party. I've heard about your singing and you certainly lived up to your reputation. They ought to have you in *Gone with the Wind* instead of that girl from England."

Jo Beth fluttered her eyes and paraphrased Scarlett. "Fiddle-dee-dee, Porter Osborne, how you do run on." She spoke again before Mary Martha had a chance to take the bait. "I declare, you've picked up a thread there."

She gave a little rectifying yank, the spool wheeled freely in his pocket, and three feet of thread came floating through the air. Uncomprehendingly, she pulled again. And again. Girls squeaked. Puddles of green thread lay on the carpet, and Porter stood transfixed in the faux pas of his career while Jo Beth looked in bewilderment at the thread in her hand. As the girls began laughing, she finally glared at Porter in awareness, lifted the edge of her skirt, and moved away with what dignity she could muster.

Mary Martha leaned over and bit the thread off cleanly. "That was wonderful! Where'd you learn a prank like that? You are one more amazing country boy. You'd better go apologize, but I don't really know for what. She's mad as an old wet hen. See you Monday."

Porter moved automatically to her bidding. Jo Beth was talking to Theo, her voice shriller and louder than she usually permitted. "I don't care what you say; it was not funny! All those girls laughed at me right in my own house. And I've worked my fingers to the bone being nice to these snot-nosed adolescents you pull in from God knows where for years. I tell you he's trouble. He may be brilliant, but he's malicious. Do we have to pledge the little bastard? He'll wreck the chapter."

"He already has his bid, and he's got an impressive old man. Don't talk so loud, honey. He really got your goat. You don't want anybody to know you're mad about a harmless, childish prank."

Jo Beth drew herself up. Her voice sank two octaves to a lovely contralto, and control was obvious. "I'll have you know I'm not mad. I'm just hurt."

Porter veered sharply and disappeared. In the face of that danger signal, masculine prudence dictated a low profile.

On Sunday afternoon eight of the dormitory freshmen, bids

182

securely in their pockets, deliberately waited an hour past pledge time and then marched in unison down the street past the Pike and the Phi Delta Theta houses, turned the corner and, to the cheers of the punctual town freshmen and the Brothers assembled, climbed the steps and pledged themselves to Kappa Alpha Order. The delay was the inspiration of Deacon Chauncey, a quiet freshman from Laurens County who had stayed out of high school and worked a year before coming to Willingham. He consequently seemed more mature than his peers, possessed persuasive charm, and was firmly of the opinion that Clarence Spangler and Slick Roundtree could stand a bit of apprehension at the end of a hectic rush season. Porter Longstreet Osborne, Jr., who got the undeserved credit for formulating the plan, was squarely in the middle of the group. He wore his brogans. Hurrah for the Old South, Southern chivalry, Brotherhood, Womanhood, God, and Country. But hurrah for Bubba Eaton, too. He shook the hand of the president in affirmation of allegiance. For better or for worse, he was in the fold. Contrary to later rumors, the picture of Robert E. Lee did not come crashing off the wall.

The next few weeks were sweet and were spent bonding the group of pledges together. They even enjoyed the mild periods of hazing by the upperclassmen, most of them manifestations of prankish humor rather than degrading intimidations. E.V. Derrick had pledged KA, and his room adjacent to the dining hall soon became a gathering place for the brothers as well as for the other pledges. They congregated there before supper so that they would be first in the door when the siren sounded. Supper at Willingham that year soon began to look like a KA social function, since the first ten or fifteen boys in the door invariably belonged to that fraternity.

E.V. had a roommate from Pennsylvania who was on football scholarship and completely new to the South. He was a smiling, affable fellow named Antek Bartolome Sylvestre Muscovoski, and E.V. soon renamed him "Ole Boy." Porter assumed on hearing the nickname that E.V. was trying to establish friendship on a basis of acceptance. He never paused to think how puzzled the newcomer from Pennsylvania might be by the gaggle of adolescents who gathered in his room every evening, all of them voluble about the virtues of Old South.

Muscovoski handled his college adjustment in his own way. He smiled a lot, studied hard, and at the end of his second quarter started dating Miller girls, changed his name to Bart Moore and pledged SAE. E.V. Derrick had given Porter the private name of "Sonny Boy," and was fond of saying, "Sonny Boy, ain't cha proud of Ole Boy? Came South and turned human."

One afternoon Porter wandered into their room early. E.V. and Ole Boy were both studying because they planned to go to a movie that night. Porter quietly began reading the school paper while he waited for the pack of KA's who would appear nearer the supper hour. He heard a metallic snap from within E.V.'s closet, a faint rattle of wood, and an even fainter squeak. E.V. leaped out of his chair.

"Got another one, Ole Boy! Hey, look at how lucky we are. Don't even have to change the cheese. Caught him right across his neck and broke it. Here, Sonny Boy, I'm going to give him to you."

"Throw that thing away. What do you think I want with a dead mouse?"

"Well, I thought you might have something interesting to do with him. He's a fine young mouse, and it's a shame not to use him for something. Waste not, want not, you know."

"You sound like Mrs. Raleigh."

"No, I don't, for I am a stranger to suffering. But that's what you could do with the mouse. You could put it in one of the water pitchers at supper. Mrs. Raleigh hasn't prayed for all of us in several days now."

"I'm not about to do that. No telling what would happen to me if I got caught at that. You put it in a water pitcher if you want it in one."

"But, Sonny Boy, you wouldn't get caught. Nobody but you and Ole Boy and I even know there is a mouse, and you're so slick and quick nobody'd ever see you. And I sure can't do it."

Porter glanced at him with skepticism. "Why not?"

"Because I'm a coward. I don't have the nerve you've got. I'm shy."

184

Porter looked at the bigger boy and gleefully capitulated. "Gimme the mouse. But don't tell a soul! I already get blamed for things I don't even do."

E.V. exchanged secretive but supportive looks with Porter during the pre-supper soiree and the jostling press of entry into the dining room.

The scramble of students and the last whimper of the siren stilled simultaneously. The boys of Willingham stood behind their chairs like trained dogs eyeing the prepared food greedily but waiting the releasing word of the master before attacking it. Mrs. Raleigh tapped on a glass. "I'm going to ask Preacher Hampton to return thanks tonight."

Preacher Hampton stood at the head of the table where Porter had selected his own seat that evening, two chairs down from the end. He was as gaunt and taut as a dried mummy, skin pulled in shiny tightness over bony cheeks and hands. He was at least thirty-five years old and had the look about him that he had preached for fifty. After all those years of ordination, why he and his little country church had decided that college and then the Mecca of Seminary at Louisville should be his destiny was a question no one pondered too seriously. It had to be Divine Calling.

Of all the ministerial students at Willingham, Preacher Hampton was obviously the most dedicated lieutenant of the Lord. He was never seen without a suit, his tie unrumpled beneath his vest. He never raised his voice, and his smile was an impersonal glow of detached tolerance that bespoke absorption with deeper, more spiritual considerations. So universal was the respect he commanded on campus, so unassailable his aura of righteousness and dignity, that everyone called him "Preacher Hampton." He even walked through the football players without attracting gibes, and most of them did not realize he had a first name until the student annual came out in the spring.

When Mrs. Raleigh called on him for the blessing, he did not bow his head. He gripped his chair back tightly, threw his head backward, and pointed his chin toward the ceiling. His closed eyes were at the bottom of sockets so deep that his gold-rimmed glasses resembled covers on small sarcophagi. With unquestioned authority and impeccable roundness of tone, he uttered three syllables with such ponderous reverence that every student's eyes automatically closed.

"Let us pray."

It was simple for Porter to lean forward during the absorption of this group ritual and drop the velvety, limp little body into the water pitcher. It sat directly in front of Preacher Hampton's plate. Porter did it early and he did it quickly. No one saw him. The prayer was of some substance and a great deal of fervor. Some of the less reverent students were even fidgeting before it was done. It was such a good prayer that when its author finally said "Amen," he earned chorusing amens of support from nearly all the other ministerial students in the dining hall.

He seated himself trying not to look self-conscious at having done a job well. Flushed as a zealot, pious as a nun, he reached for the water pitcher and his glass. The other boys at the table were busy with the distribution of mashed potatoes and gravy, but Porter watched with covert attention as Preacher Hampton poured himself a glass of water.

The mouse, thoroughly soaked by now, its darkened fur standing up in little prickles of wetness, rolled to the edge of the wide lip of the pitcher and hung there, its tiny buck teeth gleaming. As the preacher's glass filled, the mouse divided the flow into two streams but still lay on the lip of the pitcher in sodden inertia. Porter realized that he would not be able to let this man drink a glass of water that had been poured around a dead mouse. He feared drawing attention to himself, but there would be no choice.

Just as he drew a breath of resolve, Preacher Hampton, his glass filled, tilted the pitcher back upright. The slight jerky motion was enough to dislodge the mouse, and it fell with a heavy, audible plop into the glass, splashing ice water over Preacher Hampton's hand. That man of God peered in wonderment for only a split second and then slammed himself and his chair back from the table with a crash that drew all eyes.

In unaffected south Georgia accent, Preacher Hampton yelled at the top of his voice, "Good Godamighty! What the hell is that?"

Amid the delighted pandemonium that ensued, Porter sat conscience-stricken and crestfallen. All the other students were

186

laughing and pointing and jostling, but Porter was sad. He had been responsible for the downfall of one of God's servants. And downfall it was. Preacher Hampton had taken the Lord's name in vain. The expletive about hell could have been excused, but taking the Lord's name in vain was as severe proof of shallow consecration as wearing the mark of Cain. He was defrocked. If the good man's pants had dropped in public, exposing baggy drawers and knobby knees, Porter could not have been more embarrassed for him.

Preacher Hampton, in an effort to cover his gaffe and rescue what fragments of grace might be left him in the eyes of these boys who had been Raised Right, assumed a posture of righteous indignation. The mouse in the drinking water was an insult. It was unsanitary; it was filthy; it denoted sloth in the dining hall; it was indicative of the nasty personal habits of the waiters; it surely would lead to pestilence and death. It was inexcusable and unforgivable, and the Georgia Baptist Ministerial Association certainly would hear of this.

Mrs. Raleigh wept.

Several of the law students, crafty by nature and suspicious by training, were grouped around the hypochondriacal Quinton Pickett. It was obvious that every loose bowel movement in the law school for the next six months would be blamed on this evening.

Mrs. Raleigh wrung her hands.

Jolly Boy Czonkowski, muscle-bound and hairy, transplanted in uninhibited freedom to the Southland from Ohio in the name of football, leaped forward and plucked the mouse from the glass. Holding it aloft by its tail, he bellowed into the hubbub, "Shut up, youse guys! Forget da priest. Nuttin happened to him! Lookit da poor mousie. He's da one got drownded! You Southern boys got no soul. Dis mouse is da one what suffered. Poor little t'ing." He lowered it to his lips and kissed it with tenderness.

Mrs. Raleigh screamed and struck Jolly Boy on the back of the head with her flyswatter. She closed her eyes and screamed again. The dining hall quieted. Jolly Boy shrugged his massive shoulders and, with his little finger curled daintily, dropped the mouse back into Preacher Hampton's glass, resumed his seat, and ate a mouthful of potatoes.

Mrs. Raleigh belatedly tapped for attention. "Now, boys, con-

187

trol yourselves. This is very serious. I want you to know that these pitchers are taken up from the tables after every meal, washed, and turned bottom upards on that rack right over there. Then each waiter takes his pitcher down and fills it fresh when he sets the table next time. There is no way a mouse got in that pitcher by hisself. Spilt milk does not run uphill. I know two plus two when it hits me in the face. The fine Christian boys on my staff are not to blame for this."

She paused and her voice approached the quality of righteousness manifested by Preacher Hampton's. "Somebody *put* that mouse in that pitcher!"

She arched her neck. "Now, young men. I want you to remember the Golden Rule. Our Savior said, 'Do unto others,' and I'm sure that none of you want my waiter boys to get blamed for this. Just step up like a man and confess who did it and we'll all forgive you and clear the good name of my waiters. They're suffering over this, young people. They're suffering. Oh, do unto them as you would have them do unto you if they had the chance."

E.V. Derrick's hand shot up from across the dining room.

"Yes, E.V. Do you know something about this?"

"Yes'm."

"Did you put that mouse in the water pitcher?"

"No, ma'am."

"Do you know who did?"

"Yes, ma'am."

"Who was it?"

"Sambo did it."

There was a shocked silence. Even if this were true, no one could believe that E.V. Derrick would be perfidious enough to tell. All eyes turned to Porter, who was open-mouthed, drained of blood, and praying to be taken up. In the silence, E.V. suddenly bent over and started laughing. He laughed so loudly that he brayed and cried. He slapped a thigh and pointed a finger at Porter and laughed some more. A few students joined him with nervous titters, but most of the dining hall regarded him with quizzical silence.

Ole Boy Moscovoski hastened forward, took E.V. by an arm, and led him from the dining hall. As they left, Ole Boy looked back over his shoulder at Mrs. Raleigh and made a circular motion with his forefinger around his temple. He shrugged a shoulder, and his black eyes flashed.

Mrs. Raleigh tapped again on a glass. "All right, young men, that's not something to laugh at. It's pitiful. I'm sorry that happened, Porter. Now, who *really* put that mouse in the pitcher?"

At the end of first quarter, Porter was a seasoned student and ready for final examinations. The little blue books dispensed by each professor before he wrote questions on the blackboard were a novelty to him and seemed extravagant largesse on the part of the school. He felt that each student should have furnished his own paper. Then tuition might not have been so high.

He had studied as hard as any human could before each examination, grateful in the throbbingly silent dormitory that he was reviewing material rather than confronting it for the first time. He watched his friends engage in a torture called cramming and felt thankful for all the movies he had missed. As an extra precaution, he rose early every morning during exam week, sneaked into his closet, pulled the door shut, fell on his knees, and prayed earnestly to his Father which is in Heaven. He always ended his prayer with, "Nevertheless, Father, not my will but Thine be done," taking care to insert prior to that placating phrase supplications so detailed and precise that God could not possibly miss knowing what Porter thought he needed.

He even prayed about Dr. Huber and the subjunctive mood of *avoir*. Since that man miraculously made no reference to the subject on the examination, it was obvious to Porter that Jehovah was a benign and lofty confederate in the process of higher education.

When the grades were mailed out three days after Christmas vacation began, Porter had A's in English and Biology and a B in French. He had made the Dean's List!

It all went to prove that if a boy were Raised Right, worked hard, prayed a lot, and loved the Lord, he would be successful. The seed of the Anglo-Saxon work ethic had long since sprouted and grown in Porter's soul, but inclusion on the Dean's List was fertilizer that made it flourish so vigorously he never got over it.

XIII

Winter quarter at college began smoothly. Porter was taking the same subjects, albeit in progressive difficulty, that he had during the fall quarter, and there was none of the frenzy of registration. He knew by now every student on campus, and furthermore every student on campus knew him. He still felt young and insecure at times, but he also felt very much at home at Willingham University. His eyes, except on rare occasions, no longer unguardedly beseeched, "Do you like me?" Rather, he had trained them to be impersonal mirrors whenever he was shocked or surprised. He fancied that he had matured more in three months than any other boy at Willingham. He was probably right.

Another metamorphosis now separated him even further from his revered origins: He was initiated into his fraternity. Ordinarily a freshman was not approved for initiation until he had maintained a C average for at least two quarters. Porter and David Blanton had made the Dean's List, however, and their qualification was jubilantly assured. In addition, the chapter needed the money. Sonny Ralston was a sophomore pledge, left over from the previous year, who finally had managed to accumulate his grade requirements, and the brothers were desperate to gather him safely into the fold of Kappa Alpha Order. After all, he could not take freshman Christianity or Education 101 again, and there was no assurance that he had not now reached the absolute zenith of his academic career. If Sonny was ever to be a KA, now was the time.

The three of them were herded to the fourth floor of the Administration Building on the second Wednesday night in January. At last Porter was admitted through the locked door, up the walled-in stairs to the private domain of Kappa Alpha Order. The hall was cavernous and dimly lit by one large, clear light bulb with a flickering incandescent filament and a sharp tip, denoting it was handblown. Porter decided that it must have been among at least the first dozen Edison had produced. The rooms to each side were dark and yawning caves with bare brick walls and foreshortened windows that sat at floor level and made one conscious that this suite was snuggled immediately beneath the roof.

A small gas heater, crafted in rococo iron and fragile tiles of unglazed porcelain, hissed in a valiant effort to conquer the chill. One smelled the dust of its burning and realized how rarely it was used. On the walls, framed in elaborate and tarnished Victorian gilt, hung at least a half dozen life-sized pictures of zealous Kappa Alphas. Their beards, haircuts, and clothing bespoke their spots in time; their rigidly formal poses and stern expressions recalled the solemn earnestness of the photographer who had attempted to immortalize them. The aloofness of these nebulous predecessors was enhanced by the dimming glass in which they were framed, its surface clouded by the flyspeck and skim of dusty decades. The presence of the pictures confirmed reverence for tradition, but their uncleansed condition implied that the current Knights of Kappa Alpha were too caught up in the vigorous surges of youth to concern themselves with washing the faces of ancestors.

Waiting in this elongated antechamber for the return of their shepherd, Porter gave a little shiver. He watched a curl of cat fur lazing along the baseboard on some unsuspected current and calculated his preparation for this evening. In Brewtonton he had been initiated into Beta Club and Future Farmers of America with little fanfare and no emotional disruption. Sonny and David had belonged to high school fraternities and had chatted casually of the experience during passage up the stairs tonight. Porter did not understand his growing apprehension now and would have questioned them had he dared break the ban of silence imposed when their guide departed. When Sonny caught his eye and silently mouthed, "What's keeping them so long?", Porter virtuously lowered his lids and pretended not even to see such a violation of orders.

Suddenly Clarence Spangler appeared in the hall. He for once was neither talking nor smiling. The absence of the white slash of teeth gave his face a surreal, almost ghostly cast, and his uncharacteristic silence was portentous. Air blowing through his nostrils was the only sound that Clarence made, and Porter involuntarily shuddered in acknowledgment of a force great enough to quell such a reservoir of obstreperous energy. Clarence grasped him by the arm and in very formal tones uttered an obviously memorized assurance that no harm would befall him so long as he followed instructions. Porter lowered his eyes to accept a blindfold and noted the everyday brown and white saddle oxfords protruding beneath Spangler's floor-length robe. They seemed a jarring note, a contradiction of mood, a small hint of hypocrisy. The sight did nothing to reassure Porter.

By the time Clarence led him in darkness the length of the hall, he was trembling as if chilled and had to clench his teeth to prevent their chattering audibly. They stopped and made an awkward right face. Air whistled somewhere in the tunnels of Spangler's nose, and Porter heard a faint whisper of fabric as his arm was raised. He knocked on a door, slowly and ritualistically, and silence was violated forevermore. There came a shouted challenge from the other side of the door, loud reply from Spangler, louder acknowledgment from the sentry, and unbelievably but unmistakably the sound-shattering rattle of what must have been a sword crashing back into its scabbard. A warm draft could be felt as the door opened, but there was no comfort in it. Porter Longstreet Osborne, Jr., was scared half out of his wits.

In the ritual of initiation, the voices of his older fraternity brothers were so formal and so grand that he barely recognized them. There was a Sunday stiffness to their speech that fitted well the lofty ideals and the formal phrases they mouthed. Porter attended carefully what they were saying and felt young and unworthy. When the blindfold was removed and he knelt in candleshine, he comforted himself by thinking that if the boys he had met so far were worthy to be KA's, then no less was he. He prayed a little and pondered the gulf between aspiration and fulfillment.

He was constantly aware of the round window fixed in the wall behind the presiding triumvirate. Beginning at the floor and six feet in diameter, it was completely filled with a stained-glass replica of the KA fraternity pin. The jewels surrounding the pin were at least three or four inches thick and were faceted like real gems. Every color of the rainbow was there, and it glittered and winked in the light from street lamps below with iridescent beauty, very old and very rich.

Even older and just as rich, the ritual of Kappa Alpha Order thrilled his soul and permeated his mind. By the end of the ceremony he was so awed, so filled with idealism, so saturated with nebulous aspirations, that he gazed with love on all his brothers. Tears were running unnoticed and unchecked down his face. He would have embraced Satan himself as the respository of salvation had he been a Kappa Alpha brother. He floated down the stairs of the old Administration Building that night new born and shining, warm and secure in the midst of a group that no outside force could penetrate nor unsuspected evil ever tarnish. Porter was a Knight of Kappa Alpha Order.

From his new eminence he sought several days later to enlighten Henry Bean.

"For God's sake, Osborne, don't drip that treacle under my nose like a Boy Scout. You're in and you can't help it now, and I'm prepared to overlook it, but I still think the only ninnies on campus sillier that the KA's are the Phi Diddly Poo Poos. Wake up and smell the coffee, boy."

Porter was so offended that for at least two weeks he discussed only Biology with Henry Bean and that in the most formal and serious of tones and always in the presence of Eunice Yeomans.

A few weeks later he and Bob Cater were studying quietly in their room when Brother Slick Roundtree visited them unexpectedly, his hair smoothly immaculate but in an obviously excited condition.

"Where's Spangler? You fellows seen Clarence? He ain't in our room."

"We haven't seen him since supper," said Porter. "Maybe he's over at the house. What's the matter?"

"I'll tell you what's the matter. I was coming across Tatnall Square Park and got approached by a damn queer, that's what!"

"How you know he was queer?"

"Cause he asked me if I had a match and I told him 'No,' and then he propositioned me."

Bob Cater snickered. "Well, you didn't let him have it, did you?"

"Hell, no! You know better'n that. I looked him in the eye and I said, 'If you don't get the hell outta here, I'm going to bust you in the nose,' and I would have, too. He ran off in the bushes. I want to get Spangler to go back over there and help me run him slap outta the park. Spangler was state Golden Gloves champion in high school, you know, and I'm a little leery of going after that guy in the dark all by myself. See you later."

"Hah! I don't believe a word of that," Bob Cater laughed when the door closed.

"What's Golden Gloves?" asked Porter.

"It's a contest for boxing put on in the high schools across the state. It's sponsored by the YMCA, I think, and supposed to develop good character and sportsmanship as well as encourage boxing." He caught the question forming on Porter's lips. "YMCA is the Young Men's Christian Association. I mean, there's a lot you don't know for someone who made the Dean's List."

"Well, they don't have Golden Gloves or YMCA in Brewton-ton. Where would I have learned that? Why don't you believe Slick?"

"Cause he wouldn't threaten to punch anybody in the nose. Some guy probably coughed behind him in the park and he ran like a rabbit and made that tale up to get back at Spangler for not going to town with him. Hell, Roundtree's as jumpy as an old maid and scared of his own shadow. If a queer really propositioned him, he'd probably faint."

E.V. Derrick and Deacon Chauncey looked around the open door. "Who's queer?"

"Nobody. Slick Roundtree just came through here with a wild tale about getting propositioned in the park and how brave he was and all, and I was telling Sambo I bet ole Roundtree'd be scared half to death if it really happened."

"Yeah," said E.V. "Roundtree doesn't impress you as being a very stout fellow if somebody got to crowding him."

"Right," agreed Deacon. "And on top of that, he's a little fast and loose with the truth sometimes. Why don't one of you proposition him and back him down?"

"Nothing doing," replied Bob Cater. "He might believe me, and then where'd I be? I wouldn't want even the suspicion of that to get out on me."

194

"Well," offered E.V., "you could do it right here and all the rest of us could hide in the closet and listen. That'd be fun! Then you could just walk over and open the closet door and there we'd be. Boy, that'd shock him."

"Naw, I can't do that. I haven't been initiated yet and a pledge could get in plenty of trouble pulling that on a brother. I might even get thrown out of the fraternity or something."

All eyes turned to Porter.

"Sonny Boy," proclaimed E.V., "you're elected. You've already been initiated and you're just as much a KA as Slick Roundtree. Besides, you're good at acting and can pull it off."

"How about rephrasing that, Derrick," said Deacon Chauncey.

Amid the general laughter, Porter was surrounded and persuaded to be the decoy while the other boys waited in the blind. They decided to perpetrate their hoax early the following evening right after supper.

"Wait a minute," said Porter. "Just what does a queer do?"

"Whatta you mean, what do they do, Sonny Boy? We don't really want you to go through with this, you know."

"Fool! I mean *how* do they do? How do they act? What do they look like? Yall have me all set up to proposition Slick and I don't even know how to go about it. I can't ask him for a match. Neither one of us smokes. Just what is a queer, anyhow?"

"Aw, come on, Sambo, you ain't from that far out in the country. You know what a queer is."

"Well, we don't have any in Brewton County, so how would I know? I heard Rooster Holcomb telling about folks like that one day at school when we were eating lunch, but nobody at home ever saw one. Rooster called them pricksuckers."

"They call em homos in La Grange," E.V. contributed.

"They call em goot-gobblers in Dublin," said Deacon.

"I don't care what you call em," said Porter. "Have you ever seen one?"

"We got one in Dublin," volunteered Deacon. "He's about fifty years old, rich as hell, kind of puffy fat, and drives a big Packard automobile. Everybody acts like he ain't one because they're crazy about his mama, but my brother told me not to ever get in that car

195

with him. Said he'd gobble my goot for sure."

"Who's gonna gobble a goot?" sounded a voice from the doorway. The new arrival was fortunately also a KA pledge, Lamar Hargrove from Waycross, Georgia — self-contained and apparently mature because he was always solemn. The conspirators hastened to inform him of their plans and invite him to share a closet the next evening.

"What do you know about queers?" asked Porter.

"Well, I know they have this uncontrollable urge every now and then to go out and suck somebody off, maybe like on the full moon or something, and they don't like girls but they walk and talk like them. *Pansy* is another word for them."

"Naw it's not. That just means sissified. Pansies don't always suck."

"Do they have queer girls?"

"Are you kidding? Of course not. Girls haven't got anything to do anything to each other with. Besides, if one ever had any inclination that way, a good stiff peter would cure her in a hurry."

"Well, there was kinda one at RMA," said Bob Cater, "except I never felt like he'd have been one if things had been different. He was a puny little fellow with real bad acne and thick glasses that were like he was looking at you through a fish bowl. His mama had been born in Alabama somewhere, but she got divorced and married this rich man in Chicago and they sent this kid to RMA to make a man out of him. He was good in his books, but all the boarding students picked on him all the time, and a bunch of them started making him go in the shower after lights out and suck em off. One night one of them told him he'd beat him up if he didn't swallow it, and the kid threw up all night and got to crying in class the next day. He went plumb to the head of the school and told him he couldn't stand it anymore and wanted to go home. But his mama was in Europe and Colonel Spencer didn't have anywhere to send him until spring; so the kid had to stay there almost three months with everybody knowing about him. Colonel Spencer sent two boys back to Cuba, one to Venezuela, and two to Mississippi before dark, though. I mean, he didn't mess around."

"I'm getting a little sick at my stomach," said Porter. "I don't think this'll be a very funny thing to do to Roundtree after all."

196

"Sure it will, Sonny Boy. You know ole Slick needs somebody to take the wind out of his sails."

"Well, I don't know. Maybe I'll ask Boston Jones in the dining hall about it before I decide to do it."

"No, you can't do that."

"Why not?"

"Well, first of all, I don't think we ought to let anybody outside the fraternity hear anything at all about this. It's just sort of a joke to get back at Slick for lording it over the pledges. It's not the sort of thing you'd want anybody outside KA to know about. Besides, Boston is colored and won't know anything anyhow."

"You're crazy. Boston's smart as hell and knows a lot more about a heap of things than any of us."

"Well, he won't about this. Everybody knows they don't have nigger queers."

"Oh. I didn't know that."

"There's a whole lot you don't know, Sonny Boy."

"Well, look who's talking. Everybody knows all about these folks and only two of you have ever even see one. What makes you so sure there is such a thing? I can't imagine anybody doing that of his own free will. Maybe queers are just a myth. Boy, Roundtree really is stupid if he falls for this."

Cornered by peer pressure, bolstered by belonging, Porter was also irresistably drawn to a prank the likes of which he had never before heard. The next night he went back to the kitchen after supper and told Slick Roundtree that as soon as the evening dishes were washed, he needed to see him on a matter of the utmost urgency in the privacy of his room. When Slick demurred and mentioned pressing assignments, Porter solemnly assured him that this matter would not take long and that the future of Kappa Alpha Order depended upon it.

When Slick knocked on the door later, Porter was at his table with only his study lamp lit.

"Where's Cater?"

"He's gone to a movie. I tried to talk him out of it till he pulls his grades up, but every now and then he just has to go."

"Well, what's all this business about the fraternity? I really am in a big hurry. I hope you freshmen are thinking about who to vote for for president next year. We're not supposed to do any politicking in KA, but I know I can mention this to you in private, and besides, this really isn't politicking. Have you heard it mentioned?"

"Well, all us new boys are probably going to vote for Brother Skip Brannon. We all think he's a great guy and he's sure the smartest Brother in that class."

"Skip Brannon? Oh, my Lord! No! I'm glad I brought it up and mentioned it to you in time. Spangler wants to nominate me. Skip will never do."

"Why not?"

"Well, he just doesn't have the class you need to be president of KA. Look at him. He's hardly got any chin at all, and on top of that he tells everybody he doesn't have but one nut."

"What does he have to *do* to be president of KA?"

"Aw, now, Brother Osborne, quit being smart. You know it just wouldn't sound right to say that the Number I of KA didn't have all his balls. I can hear the jokes in Pan-Hellenic now."

Porter thought he heard the faintest of whispers from the closet. "Well, I'm sure you must have two, and that brings us around to what I wanted to talk to you about. I'm in deep trouble, Slick, and I know how much you love KA, and that's why I came to you first."

"Whatta you talking about?"

"Well, I don't know any way to tell you this but just to haul off and tell you. I'm a queer. You know, a homo, a goot-gobbler."

"Aw, Sambo, you're crazy. You aren't queer."

"Yes, I am, too. You think I'd be telling you so if I wasn't?"

"No, I can't even believe you're telling me that anyhow. Why are you telling me?"

"Well, I've been doing pretty good about it since I got to Willingham, what with studying hard and all, but it's coming up on full of the moon and I've just got to have it. I can't wait any longer. And I thought it'd be a whole lot better if I kept it in the fraternity."

"Oh, my God, yes! Whatever you do, don't let this get out. I just can't believe it."

"Well, I wish it weren't true."

"Does your daddy know about it?"

"No."

"Why don't you tell him?"

198

Porter thought fleetingly that Slick ought to do well in Law. He certainly could ask the questions. "I don't want him to know."

"Whatta you think he would do?"

Porter paused only a moment and felt a little respite of virtue by being able to answer at least one question honestly. "I think he'd beat my butt."

"Well, if you don't want your daddy to know, let's ask Brother Theo. Maybe he's had some experience with this sort of thing and can help you get over it."

"But, Slick, that's not what I want. What I want is some sexual relief and I want it right now. You know Brother Montagu wouldn't let me have it, and besides, he's too old. And on top of that he's married."

"Well, what do you want?"

"That's what I'm trying to tell you, Slick. I want you. You don't want me to go to a Phi Delta Theta to help me out, do you?"

Slick looked steadily at Porter for a moment and his face began flushing into the roots of his hair. Porter felt a little twinge of guilt over the entire situation as he realized that Roundtree finally believed him.

"Come on, Slick, let me have it and I'll work real hard to get you elected Number I."

The room was deathly still. Tension was almost electric. Finally Slick Roundtree drew a deep breath. "Sambo, I feel real sorry for you. Honest I do. I feel sorry for your daddy, too. You're already in KA and I'll stand by you, but there's no way I can do what you're asking me to do tonight."

"Why not, Slick?"

"Because I just can't. Why to tell you the truth, it hurts my conscience now every time I beat my dog."

The closet door slammed almost off its hinges as five gleefully shouting, finger-pointing boys tumbled into the room, riotously delighted at the success of their project and at Slick's self-denouement. It took several minutes for Roundtree to rise from bewilderment through incredulity, anger, and embarrassment to the level of simulated amusement. His laughter was halfhearted and his glances at Porter venomous until one of the pledges slapped him on the back and hilariously suggested that they all should get back in the closet and pull the same trick on Spangler. Porter, flushed with congratulations for his histrionics, was easily persuaded to go to Spangler's room and lure him to the baited field.

When they entered Porter's room, Clarence boomed in heartiness, "OK, Brother Osborne, out with it. What kinda crap you got on your mind?"

Porter widened his eyes lugubriously and told him. It was evident that Spangler did not share either the objective attitude or the legal inquisitiveness of Roundtree. With eyes flashing as much as his teeth, he yelled, "I knew it! I knew there was something wrong with you the first time I ever laid eyes on you! God knows this never crossed my mind, though! Especially not with a father like you've got. He ought to kick your ass! Why didn't you tell us before we initiated you? God, this is awful! Maybe you can transfer to another school. Why did you wait until you were a Brother? Oh, goddamn!"

"Don't take the Lord's name in vain, Clarence. I know it's terrible, and I keep thinking maybe I'll get over it, but the moon's getting full and the urge is stronger than I am. You've just got to let me have it tonight, or I'll be forced to go to the Phi Delta Thetas."

Spangler drew himself up, thrust his chin out, and proclaimed in ringing piety, "You'll just have to go to the Thetas. I'm prouder of my sex life than anything about me!"

Unable to contain himself any longer, Slick Roundtree led the howling, laughing eruption from the closet. Clarence was too much the good sport not to laugh with the others as soon as comprehension settled in, but while Roundtree pointed out with choking glee the fallacy of pride in a non-existent entity, because everyone knew that Spangler still had his cherry, Clarence looked over at Porter. "Someday I'm going to beat your ass," he said. Porter laughed.

Bob Cater was the one who mollified Spangler by telling him that Roundtree had preceded him in this farce and had confessed before the witness of a full closet to childish activity that all college men vowed to be only in their past.

The charade rapidly became a two-closet endeavor as another victim was selected and gulled, and then another and another, each being added to the unsuspected audience after his own starring role was ended. Their only failure was Pledge Brother Frank Anderson from Griffin, who alone in the freshman class still wore his rat cap two months after they were no longer required. He simply refused to accept the premise. "Don't be ridiculous, Sambo," he repeated over and over. "Don't be ridiculous." The closet finally erupted from lack of oxygen, but the mirth was missing.

"I tell you what'd be funny," Porter heard Deacon Chauncey say, "and that's for the closet to be empty next time Sambo puts on his act. How'd he ever explain that? Talk about being up the creek!"

The idea of such an event sobered Porter, who already had grown weary of the hoax. "Well, that winds it up, fellows. I can't think of any more KA's in the dormitory."

"Wait a minute. What about Brother Skip Brannon? He's working at the Library and gets off duty in ten or fifteen minutes. Run over there, Sonny Boy, and tell Brother Brannon you've got to see him in private about something terribly important to KA and bring him on over here to talk to him before he goes to his room."

Slick Roundtree spoke up. "Skip Brannon? Hey, Clarence, Sambo tells me that he and his buddies are thinking about voting for him for Number I next year."

"What? Not that jerk! That'd be the worst thing that could possibly happen to the fraternity. Look, fellows, we were hoping you'd elect Slick next year and then me the year after."

"What's wrong with Skip?" demanded Deacon. "We sure don't think he's a jerk. All us freshmen like him."

"Yeah, Clarence," contributed Porter, "and what about the rule of no politicking in KA because we're all brothers together?"

"Aw, shut up and forget that. Just go get Brannon."

Porter left the room and headed for the Library. When he returned with his prey and they seated themselves, Porter was so conscious of the expectant horde of humanity in the closets that he wondered how Skip could be unaware of it. He soon discovered that Brother Brannon could ask as many questions as Slick. In fact, Porter was taxed to the limit of his inventiveness to answer some of them without contradicting himself.

Of a sudden he remembered Deacon Chauncey's idea of infusing new humor into the prank and became apprehensive that the closets were empty. What would he do?

"Well, I'm not condemning you, you understand, but if you've been queer all this time, Brother Osborne, how have you been gratifying this appetite while you've been at Willingham?"

"Well, Skip, I'm not supposed to tell, but the fact is Spangler and Roundtree have been letting me have it."

"They have? My Lord, this is awful! Why don't you go to them this time?"

"Well, I did, but they said I've worn both of them out and they're too tired. In fact, Roundtree had just finished beating his dog and didn't even want to think about it."

"Gosh, you're real thick with those two, aren't you?" Skip rose and paced a few feet with hands behind his back. He stopped and looked across at Porter. His face reddened and when he spoke his voice was unusually husky.

"I tell you what you do, Sambo. You ask Clarence and Slick one last time. If they turn you down again, come back to me and I'll help you out."

For one apocalyptic moment, Porter had time to hope that the closets were indeed empty. Then the horde was upon them. They formed a semicircle around Skip and brayed and crouched and pointed their fingers and jumped up and down. No one said any-thing, but the deriding laughter made unendurable cacophany. Skip Brannon's face turned white as chalk. Roundtree and Spangler were in the forefront, pointing and laughing and slapping their thighs. Skip gave a weak smile, turned his eyes toward Porter with a look that struck to the heart, and collapsed on one of the beds with his forearm over his eyes. He lay supine for several moments while the laughter swelled and Clarence's voice was heard above all the rest, taunting, accusing.

Suddenly Skip bolted from the bed, desperately thrust pledges aside, and reached the lavatory mounted on the opposite wall in time to project a torrent of vomit into it. The room stilled. Skip Brannon hung over the lavatory, his back to all of them, his broad shoulders heaving, retching his guts out.

Clarence Spangler broke the silence. He pointed to Brannon with a Jeremiad gesture. "Look at that, men. Look close. That's what you freshmen wanted for president of KA."

Porter stepped forward. "Shut up! This isn't funny anymore! All of you get out of here!"

The brothers in the bond silently trouped out the door. Porter turned toward the figure bent over the basin.

Without straightening, Skip Brannon turned his head sideways and looked at him. His nose and eyes were streaming and his voice was weakened from straining.

"You get out of here, too."

XIV   **T**oward the end of winter quarter, Porter came in from Biology lab to a surprise. On the unused bed in his room, the pillow lay with no covering other than its blue and white striped tick. The bed itself was recently made, with two blankets but no sheet. Two pairs of shoes were under the bed and a battered leather trunk at the end of it. Unannounced and unforeseen, a new roommate had moved in on him and Bob Cater. Porter looked around with misgivings. He and Bob were getting along well and enjoying the luxury of extra space in the big corner room since Tom Christian had left. A third occupant might be a cramping intruder. He hoped this interloper was a nice guy.

His eye caught an unfamiliar object on Bob's dresser. It was a five-by-seven photograph mounted in a pasteboard frame that folded back on itself for display. Porter picked it up. The photographer's name was stamped on the back, the address Scranton, Pennsylvania. He studied the picture. It was a posed study from the shoulders up of a grinning young man dressed in cap and gown, the tassel from the mortarboard hanging over his right ear, neat knot of necktie showing above the gown. Porter gazed at it with curiosity and some disbelief. The eyebrows were thick and dark in an uninterrupted line with no break at all above the nose. The hairline was a scant two to three centimeters above the brows and formed a widow's peak more pronounced than that of the cap. Porter shook his head and took a ruler from the desk drawer.

This must be the older brother of their new roommate, he surmised, and this must be a photograph of him at college graduation, since he is obviously much older than any student at

204

Willingham. He projected further that the subject came from poor parents and had worked his way through college and that it had taken him forever. Also, he must have been killed just last fall in an automobile wreck, which would explain his younger brother arriving this late at Willingham and further would explain why the grief-stricken young man was displaying the photograph so prominently. It was not, Porter thought, an object one would show except from the depths of bereaved love or a blind and fanatical sense of family loyalty. He felt that the subject could model either for Millet's "The Gleaners" or for Edwin Markham's "The Man with the Hoe." He sighed and began studying French.

Bob Cater arrived from chemistry lab. "Hello, Sambo, you already in the books? I've got to get out and play a little tennis before I start. I'll never make the Dean's List anyhow."

"Bob, we've got a new roommate."

"What? Well, so we have. I heard they were bringing in a new bunch of football scholarships from Ohio and Pennsylvania to beef up the team for spring practice. I guess we must have drawn one of them."

"Well, I sure hate it. It's been nice having all this room for just the two of us. It's going to be crowded."

"Aw, no, Sambo. Don't look at it like that. We'll enjoy meeting somebody new. Is that his picture on the dresser?"

"Well, I would certainly hope not. Who ever heard of going off to college with your own picture in a cap and gown? That guy in the picture has got to be a lot older than we are. I figured maybe it was an older brother who had graduated from college and the whole family was proud of him."

"Naw, that can't be right. This is just a plain cap and gown. When you graduate from college, you get a hood to wear around your neck. This is a high school graduation picture. Hasn't he got a big chin?"

"I measured it with a ruler. From the hairline to the upper lip is exactly the same distance as from the upper lip to the point of the chin. I can't decide, though, whether that's altogether due to the chin being abnormally long or maybe partly to the forehead being abnormally short. That picture looks a little like Neanderthal man with clothes on."

205

"Well, I'll bet you five dollars it's our new roommate. This ought to be interesting. Let's see if we can find his name."

"It's not on his trunk. I looked."

Bob Cater opened a drawer and took out a bundle of letters in blue envelopes, all tied compactly with a ribbon.

"Don't read somebody else's mail, Bob! That's awful!"

"I'm not. I've been raised better than that. I'm just looking for a name. Ah, here we are: Mr. Michael J-u-r-k-i-e-d-y-k. Jerky-dick? Jerky-dick? My Lord, Sambo, we've got a new roommate named Mike Jerky-dick."

"I'm not believing that. Let me see that envelope. You're right, but there must be some other way to pronounce it. If it was Jerky-dike, there should be a terminal *e* to make that *y* sound like a long *i*. I just can't imagine anybody having a name like Jerky-dick. They'll laugh him off the campus every time roll is called."

"You're right, it does sound funny. I bet Brother Roundtree will want to pledge him. I can't wait to introduce them. Hey, ole Beat-my-dog Slick, I want you to meet Michael Jerky-dick."

From the doorway came an indignant bellow. "Jeesus Christ! What da fuck youse t'ink ya doin a'ready yet?"

Both boys jumped around. Arms akimbo and legs spraddled by muscle mass, the newcomer was impressive indeed. He wore only a pair of shorts and a T-shirt and obviously had been exercising heavily, for he was dripping with perspiration. His neck seemed larger than his head and the towel slung around it only made the neck look shorter. He was so hairy that Porter thought of a teddy bear stuffed into doll clothes. The face was definitely that of the photograph with the added accent above the left eyebrow of a large mole which the photographer had obliterated.

"Gimme dem letters, cocksucker! Dey from my girlfriend, see? Don't youse never let me see ya fucking around wit my mail no more, see? Jesus Christ!"

He snatched the packet from Bob Cater, slung it down on the dresser top, and jabbed Bob in the chest with one finger. Although Bob was a good head taller than his attacker, he backed away.

"Anudder t'ing, cocksucker. Da name's You-*kay*-dk. Got dat? You-*kay*-dk. Me'n my brudder done cleaned out a whole neigh-borhood in Pennsylvania teaching Irish cocksuckers how to talk right, for Chrissake, and I'n handle dis li'l backwater place by myself. Youse got it now? You-kay-dk. I gotta go shit."

After he slammed the door, there was a long moment of contemplative silence.

"Brother Osborne, I think you're wrong. Nobody's gonna laugh at him when the roll is called. Not more than once, anyhow."

Porter let his breath out. "Bob, what's a cocksucker? I mean, I can tell what he thinks it is, but what I'm talking about, I guess, is a matter of terminology. Where I come from, a cock is a woman's thing — you know, a synonym for pussy. And I'm sure the same thing is true in Atlanta; I have a cousin from there and that's what he says."

"Hey, you're right, Sambo. The only person I ever heard say 'cock' for 'peter' was a nasty-mouthed cadet at RMA and he was a yankee."

"Was he from Pennsylvania?"

"By golly, he was! From Allentown."

"Well, maybe it's just a local idiom. I'd love to ask Dr. Minor about it, but he'd probably look at me hard and give me an F and I'd have a stroke. It's such an ugly term, though, that I'm relieved it's confined just to a pocket in Pennsylvania. I'm glad that a word that horrible, let alone that inaccurate, won't ever get accepted into the language. I say, 'cocksucker.' Why didn't you get mad and push him back when he called you that?"

"Why should I get mad? I ain't one. And he was mad enough for both of us. Besides, if I had pushed him back we might have got in a fight, and you get expelled for that in a hurry."

"If I were your size, I wouldn't take anything off anybody. I don't see how you stay so calm all the time."

"Look, Sambo, when you're my size there are all sorts of reasons not to fight. First of all, somebody might get bad hurt if I tangle with a guy big as I am, and there's just no way to fight anybody smaller than you are."

"Not even when they're being obnoxious and pushing you around and just asking for it?"

"Especially then. Anybody littler'n you are who's ready to fight is probably mad enough to kill. And you ain't that mad. And then you get in a fight. OK? And then he whips your ass. OK? And there you are. Not only have you got your ass beat, but everybody's on his side cause he's the littlest and they all laugh at *you*. You can't win. I've been big all my life and I learned a long time ago not to get in fights. Why didn't you jump on him for saying 'Jesus Christ?' You're always on people for taking the Lord's name in vain."

"Well, for Pete's sake, it's not the same thing at all. The Bible says, 'Thou shalt not take the name of the Lord, thy God, in vain,' and that's talking about the Father. It doesn't say that about the Son. Besides, you never hear anybody but yankees saying 'Jesus Christ,' and they say it all the time over and over. Somehow it just sounds cheap and common instead of blasphemous. Nobody around here pays any attention to the way yankees talk. Most of them are Catholics and going to hell anyhow. You sure don't hear any Baptists hollering 'Jesus Christ' as a swear word. It's sort of like a double negative; it's ignorant and you just ignore it. It's yankee-talk, like 'cocksucker.' "

"I'm sure glad you got me all straightened out. At any rate, it's going to be a real experience having..." he looked carefully around, "ole Jerky-dick as a roommate."

"He can't possibly be as bad as Tom Christian, and it'll probably be very broadening for us to have the opportunity to discuss things in a calm and informal setting with somebody from up north. Of course, I know ahead of time that his opinions are invalid because they're so colored by yankee arrogance and bias, but it'll be interesting to hear them all the same. I like to keep an open mind."

"Yeah. It sounds as open as a scared oyster. And I've been in on some of those informal discussions of yours. You're a sight, Sambo, but I don't believe anybody ever considered calling you calm. Let me know and I'll arrange to study in the Library when you discuss the Civil War with ole Jerky-dick."

Bellowing in outrage, a hairy fury leaped through the doorway, spun Bob Cater around, and flung him supine across the bed. "Aw right, cocksucker! Youse ast for it and, Jesus Christ, youse about to get it! If you don't say You-kay-dk real quick three times in a fucking row, I'm going to tear a hole in ya flabby belly and string ya fucking guts around ya goddamn neck. Then I'm going to rip ya goddamn nuts off and stuff 'em in ya fucking ears. Say it, cocksucker, say it! You-kay-dk!"

The avenger stood over the bed in trembling rage, hands on

208

his hips, jaw thrust out in such exaggerated underbite that his breath squeezed through distorted pharynx in tortured snorts.

Porter stepped in front of him. "Michael, calm down! Bob doesn't mean any harm and he apologizes. We both apologize. It's not right to make fun of a man's name, and we've both had better raising than that. We can say You-kay-dk. Hear that? You-kay-dk, You-kay-dk, You-kay-dk. I like that name. It sounds sort of like little summer night noises in the trees. You-kay-dk, You-kay-dk, You-kay-dk. It was the spelling that was throwing us off. Relax, Michael."

"OK, OK, OK, a'ready yet." He stepped back, the breathing slowed, and the arms dropped as nearly straight as they could. "Youse a good kid. What's ya name?"

"My name is Porter Longstreet Osborne, Jr., but people call me Sambo."

"Jesus Christ! You poor kid! Not around me, dey won't! I knock some cocksucker's block off for you, for Chrissake."

"You don't understand, Michael. That's my nickname and I'm used to it and don't mind it at all."

"Yeah, yeah, OK, gotcha. Everybody calls me Mick. Nobody calls me Michael but my mudder."

"Well, this is Bob Cater. We've been rooming together since the first of school, and we're glad to have you with us."

"Yeah, please ta meetcher, big fellow. Got a little hot dere, but we get along fine now. I come down on scholarship for spring practice. Ole Mick gonna beef up ya goddamn football team, for Chrissake."

"Michael, there's one thing. We don't allow the Lord's name to be taken in vain in this room."

"You don't what? Christ, I never will learn to unnerstan youse guys. All of youse talk like ya had a mouth full of shit."

"We do not permit blasphemy in this room. Specifically, please do not say 'goddamn.' "

"Jesus Christ! I never said 'goddamn.' "

"You certainly did. You said 'goddamn neck,' 'goddamn nuts,' and 'goddamn football team.' "

"Well, for Chrissake, what are you? Some kind of goddamn preacher?"

"No, I'm just a country boy who has been Raised Right. And

we do not put up with the Lord's name being taken in vain. It's one of the Commandments."

"My old man worked in Birmingham for six monts one time before he got on at da mines up home and married my old lady. When he found out I was coming to Georgia, he told me it would be a strange place, but mosta da people would be friendly. He said da only t'ing I really had to watch out for was if one of em tole me he was 'just a country boy.'

"He said, 'Mick, if one nem Rebs tells you he's just a country boy, watch out. Dat's da fellow what'll smile while he cuts ya t'roat and youse won't even know it's cut till youse try to move ya fucking head.' You don't look so tough to me. Whatcha plan to do if I don't talk to suitcha, country boy?"

"I'm not sure. The last one that didn't is blind and has dropped out of school."

"You t'reatening me! Jesus Christ! Dis l'il turd's t'reatening old Mick! Listen, baby boy, I could bench press ya little body wit one hand a hunner times and never even raise a sweat. You t'reatening old Mick?"

"No, I'm not threatening anybody, Michael. I'm just telling you the truth. I always tell the truth. In one form or another. I tell you something else. I'm not scared of you. You could beat my butt before the water got hot, but you won't."

"To hell youse say. What makes ya t'ink so?"

"Because it's so easy to do. I've got friends on the football team who'd whip you just for the fun of it if you hit a little runt like me. And if you really beat me up you'd be so ashamed you couldn't take it and you'd pack your trunk and go home and never get a college education and your mother and all your cousins and aunts would cry and try not to let everybody else know how humiliated they were and your girlfriend wouldn't write any more letters because you were such a coward to beat up a boy that much littler than you."

"Shut up, for Chrissake! Shut up! Youse make me dizzy. I ain't even laid a finger on ya and youse aready got me inna coal mine ona night shift resta my life! You know somet'ing, kid? You're crazy!"

"I'm not crazy. I'm just on my own front porch and I don't aim to be pushed off."

"Now what da fuck does dat mean, for Chrissake?"

210

"It means I'm not scared of you. You've got a belly like a scrub board and hands like ice tongs. You've got the biggest legs, arms, and neck, the longest chin, and the shortest forehead I've ever seen in my life, but I'm not scared of you, Michael. You're not going to say 'goddamn' in this room."

"And what if I do? Youse gonna call me Jerky-dick, huh? To get even wit me, huh?"

"No. A promise is a promise and I already told you Bob and I aren't going to make fun of your name, no matter what you do. As Mrs. Raleigh would say, 'Two rights won't make it wrong.' Besides which my granddaddy says, 'A man's word is as good as his bond,' and I'm not going to break my word just for you. No, I'll find some other way to stop you."

"Know somet'ing, kid? Youse ain't big enough to be in high school and ya got de crookedest little dirty eyeglasses I ever seen and de rattiest little sharp face and I could smash ya like a fucking roach, and yet youse standing up to me while da big boy over dere keeps his goddamn kisser shut — I mean his fucking kisser shut. Course, I ain't quite sure yet what youse standing up about, but youse stand- ing. You aw right with old Mick, for Chrissake. Besides, I like whatcha said about little night noises."

"Thank you, Michael. I think you do know what I'm standing up for, and it's not just a matter of semantics, either."

"Jesus Christ! Don't bring da fucking Jews into it, for Chrissake! I can't stand dem cocksuckers. I leave ya in a hurry over dem."

"I'm not talking about Jews, Michael; I'm talking about words. But while we're on the subject, the Jews are God's chosen people. It says so over and over right in the Bible. You must be Catholic."

"Ya fucking straight I'm Cat'olic. What's wrong wit dat, for Chrissake?"

"Nothing at all. It's just that I've heard Catholics aren't allowed to read the Bible and only know what they're told about it; so I'm going to let the Pope worry about you saying 'Jesus Christ.' Jehovah and I are going to work on your 'goddamns.' It is to be hoped that your coarser epithets will disappear as you become acclimated, especially since they are misnomers and physically inaccurate anyhow. My English professor says that swearing is an indication of an inadequate vocabulary and an admission of lazy mentation."

"Jesus Christ! Listen to him! Jesus, look at me! I can't believe I'm standing here in dis place hearing all dis crap. For Chrissake! Here I come south to get a education and I wind up in a loony bin full of Baptists and a fucking baby genius talk like a school teacher for a roommate. Jesus Christ!"

"Michael, my mother says there's a lot more to a college education than just books, and I...."

The siren began to growl and prepared to shriek.

"What da fuck is that?"

"That," said Bob Cater, "is the dinner bell. Pull a pair of pants on over your shorts real quick and go eat with us."

"Dinner bell? Christ, what a noise! Come to t'ink of it, dough, it does make ya hungry to hear it."

"How," asked Porter, "would you like to hear it some morning at two o'clock? It could be arranged."

As the threesome made its way up the hallway, Bob Cater looked down at Porter. "You know something, Sambo? Your mother is right."

Michael Jurkiedyk, ebullient scion of immigrant parents, was a cultural shock to Porter Osborne, Jr., and contributed a great deal to his sense of growing away from home and family. Within days Michael pledged Pi Kappa Alpha and thereafter trouped frequently through the room with swarthy, swaggering buddies who spoke in strange gutterals that required concentration for Porter to identify as English. Bob Cater abandoned any pretense at adjustment to the newcomer and again forsook the room for study in the Library. He also renewed his old movie habit despite Porter's concern that his grades might not improve enough for initiation.

"I can't help it. I can't stand to listen to him. I have to sleep there and watch him get up in the morning, but I don't have to be there and watch him go to bed at night. I tell you, Sambo, it's almost more than I can stand to see that hairy body slide between those

212

blankets. I never saw anybody who slept plumb nekkid before, and I thought everybody used sheets on their bed. I don't care how often he showers, it looks nasty. It makes me itch all over for thirty minutes just to watch him get in the bed. He hasn't changed those blankets since he's been here, and you know it's just going to be a matter of time before he gets crabs or itch or mange. Or something."

Porter, more rooted to place and more conscious of territorial responsibilities, refused to abandon his front porch and maintained residence through both invasion and occupation. He had not been homesick since Christmas; the Dean's List had cured that, he fancied. Now he stopped reading his Bible nightly and said his prayers only after he was in bed under privacy of darkness. Religion and devotion were two things he had no desire to explain to Mick Jurkiedyk. Interchange with that self-assured person was occasionally illuminating but rarely edifying. Porter discovered to his chagrin that Mick had little knowledge of and no interest in the event regarded locally as the most important occurrence in America.

"Whatcha mean, War Between da States? For Chrissake, youse talking about da fucking Civil War? Jesus Christ! My old man wasn't even in dis country till 1920, and I don't know nuttin about it. It didn't amount to a fart in a windstorm nohow, and youse Sout'ners gotcha fucking head in da sand about it. I tell ya dem Spades ain't wort' fighting over, for Chrissake. Hanging around working for less than white people and putting some of us outta work, for Chrissake. Dey oughta send em all back to Africa. Dey worse'n da fucking kikes."

"What's a kike, Michael?"

"Jesus Christ, boy! A kike's a Jew."

"Why don't you just say Jew, then?"

"Because a kike's worse'n just a plain fucking Jew. A kike's a Jew what's got in ya way and trying to climb over ya shoulders to get his own Christ-killing ass ahead. Always t'inking about money and rob ya blind for a fucking penny."

"We don't have them in the South."

"Youse shitting me, for Chrissake. Dey everywhere."

"Not in Brewtonton, Georgia. We only have Mr. Rosenbloom, and he most definitely is not a kike. Everybody loves him. And we don't have any Catholics, either. And there are some questions I've been dying to ask a real live Catholic. For instance, what is the historical origin of the Rosary? I'm serious."

"Whatcha mean, historical origin? Youse always worrying about history, for Chrissake, always asking questions. Jesus Christ, youse ask more questions anybody I ever seen before."

"I mean, how did the use of the Rosary get started? And when? And really, I guess, why? I never talked to a Catholic before."

"Well, lay me down and turn me over, I don't know dem dates and reasons. Ya ain't supposed to know all dat crap. Ya just supposed to have fait' and believe. Dat's enough." An expression of craftiness tightened his brows. "As for da Rosary, if we didn't have it, what da fuck ya t'ink we do wit all da Hail Marys and Our Fadders? Huh? Where would we put em? Answer me dat, smartass. Where you t'ink da world would be witout Hail Mary and Our Fadder?"

"I don't mean to be a smart aleck, Michael. I still want to know *why.*"

"I tell ya why, punk. I tell ya why. I tell ya once and for all and don't youse bodder me no more about it. It's just our way, dat's why. It's just our way. Unnerstand? Now shut up, for Chrissake, before old Mick forgets how little ya are and beats ya ass anyhow. Cat'lics! Rosary! Dumb fucking questions! How'd I get into dis, anyhow? Jeesus Christ!"

If Michael Jurkiedyk caused Bob Cater to absent himself from his own room, he forged an unexpected bond of friendship between Porter and E.V Derrick, based on shared experiences and community of burden. A rivalry of sorts even developed between them over who owned the most yankee of yankees for a roommate. Chances for comparison were frequent. The KA's still congregated in E.V.'s room before supper time and could observe Ole Boy at will, and E.V. made excursions to Porter's room where he endured increasingly briefer exposures to Mick. E.V.'s judicious comments evoked Porter's admiration by the tone of mature detachment with which they were delivered but caused him to giggle by the obvious subjective passion of their content.

"Sonny Boy, I'll grant that you can understand what mine says easier than yours, but does yours stink?"

"E.V., yours is so civilized he has sheets and a pillowcase. Does

214

yours sleep in pajamas? Or at least his underwear?"

"Sonny Boy, I know yours talks nastier and strings those words together more interestingly than mine does, but can you smell his feet the whole time you're trying to study?"

"E.V., mine pledged Pike in forty-eight hours, and yours held out for SAE, but yours is changing his name from Moscovoski to Moore and mine is teaching everybody in Macon to say You-kay-dk. And before it's over, all Willingham may be saying cocksucker, too."

"Sonny Boy, the average citizen back in LaGrange or Brewtonton just doesn't understand yankees. The other night it was warm and we were studying in our underwear. I'm used to armpits and feet, but I swear to you for two hours I smelled asshole."

"E.V., yesterday morning before the breakfast siren went off, Michael waked us up hollering, 'I can't stand it! I can't stand it! I gotta slipped disc! I gotta slipped disc!' Bob Cater sat up straight in bed and says, 'What's the matter, Mick? Your back hurting?' And Michael jumps out of bed, buck-nekkid and hairy as a bear, with this tremendous hard on and commenced beating the foot of Bob's bed with it. Sounded like Gene Krupa on the drums and looked like an oak club. And he yells, 'My back's all right, for Chrissake! I just gotta slip dis in somebody!' Bob told me later, 'Sambo, that does it. He's got to go.' "

"Why, Sonny Boy? Does he stink?"

"Like you said, E.V. Nobody at home understands yankees."

Sometime during fall and winter quarters while he was engrossed in academics and his strange new surroundings, so gradually that Porter was unaware of it until confronted with the actuality, a strange and awe-inspiring biological process occurred. Porter Osborne's penis grew. He did not gain weight and his height did not increase an inch, but all of a sudden, it seemed to him, his genitalia were grown up. He likened it to the birth of Pallas Athena, springing full-grown from the brain of a sleeping Zeus, and tended to regard it as an entity separate and apart from himself. Indeed, it behaved that way, springing up in awe-inspiring magnificence at the most unpredictable times. It was a great inconvenience.

Porter thanked God anew for baggy pants and was glad that Sybil Swygert had no way of knowing the transformation her yawns in Biology class now produced in her little friend. He continued sporadic smooching lessons with Mary Martha but was very careful about full-length embraces. In his tutoring sessions with Eunice Yeomans, he was blissfully free of this new distraction and was still able to concentrate on accent and irregular verbs.

He regarded his new acquisition with pride but also a measure of chagrin. He had long aspired to this condition, had even prayed over it, but had never anticipated such glory. He felt that he was in the predicament old man Root Stinchcomb ascribed to his collie dog which chased cars: "Ef you catch it, 'y God, whatcha gonna do with it?" A natural resource of this unexpected richness surely entailed some measure of responsibility. Porter was bewildered and chided Jehovah, "Lord, I meant I wanted to grow all over. This is ridiculous. I'm not complaining; please understand that, and if You're testing me or rebuking me for not trusting Thee, I can live with it. But please, Lord, let the rest of me grow up to it."

This great change was a secret one, a process of inviolable personal privacy. Southern boys who were Raised Right did not prance around naked before their roommates, and they turned their backs in modesty when disrobing. In the event that nudity was unavoidable, one carefully averted one's gaze to avoid any semblance of interest in another's crotch. Genital comparisons were made with only the most furtive of side glances.

Mick Jurkiedyk, as manifested by his own exhibitionism, was encumbered by no such taboo. One evening when Porter was donning his bathrobe for a trip to the shower, he turned from the closet with the garment half open and happened to catch his new roommate's eye. With a whoop Jurkiedyk leaped in front of him, crouched, and pointed his finger.

"Jesus Christ! Holy Mary, Mother of God! Lookit dat t'ing! Christ, kid, dat's da biggest cock I ever see! Ya ever step on da fucking t'ing?"

With priggish embarrassment, Porter clutched the robe tightly closed and fled down the hall to the shower. Minutes later he felt the slight hiccup in water pressure that signified someone had flushed a toilet and he leaped backward to avoid being scalded. A hairy simian arm encircled his waist and snatched him from the shower stall.

"Gotcha!" yelled Mick. He spun Porter around, lathered and dripping wet, to face two of his cronies recently roused from their rooms. "See? What I tell ya? Eit'er youse ever see a cock dat big before?"

"Christ, Mick, I ain't believing dat if I ain't see it wit mine own eyes. It's almost to his knees, for Chrissakes! Go on, kid, let it git hard!"

Porter struggled futilely in Jurkiedyk's grasp and realized to his horror that this treacherous new member of his body with a life and a will of its own was slowly responding to the exhortation. He yelled and kicked. Jurkiedyk laughed and lifted him from the floor, the activity causing such flopping and swinging that the onlookers were gleeful.

"Blessed Virgin, lookit da head on it! Youse need a license to carry dat t'ing around, kid. Dat's a goddamn dangerous weapon."

With a bellow, Mick lowered Porter to the floor, leaned over his shoulder with his free arm, and poked a stiff and violent fore-finger into his friend's chest. "Watch ya fucking nasty mouth, cock-sucker. Don't take da Lord's name in vain in front my roomie, unnerstand?"

"Whassa matter, ape-shit? You da one brought us down here. I ain't done nuttin."

"My friend got delicate ears. Big cock but delicate ears, unnerstan? Say anyt'ing youse want in front him save 'goddamn,' got it? Jesus Christ, youse want him to t'ink we a bunch of fucking heat'ens?"

The bathroom door swung open and Tindall Barfield came in, one hand already unbuttoning his fly, and headed for the urinal. Tindall was a senior from Alabama, a good but lazy student, and a football player as misshapen by weight-lifting as any of his comrades. He stopped and surveyed the activity. "What the hell are you guys doing? Turn that kid loose, Jurkiedyk."

"Christ, Tindall, we just checking out his cock. It must be da biggest one at Willingham, for Chrissake. Lookit da t'ing! Ya ever see anyt'ing like it?"

217

Tindall slipped a wink at Porter and slowly drawled, "Waaal, 'cept for that ugly knot on the end, my paw's got a hoss-mule puts me in mind of it a little bit."

"Well, Jesus Christ, ain't it da biggest one you ever see?"

"Naw. It's bout average for Georgia. Run a little bigger when you cross the Chattahoochee and get in Alabama."

"Youse shitting me. Barfield, youse shitting me, for Chrissake."

"Don't ever believe that, yankee-boy." He looked over one shoulder from the urinal as he flipped himself dry and added loftily, "You fellows are just victims of perception distortion. The Alabama gals got a saying: 'Big man, big dick; little man, all dick.' Yall got a lot to learn down here in the South just to catch up. Now get outta here and let my little friend finish washing."

A few days later Porter was walking to the Co-op with his fellow sufferer and yankee owner. "Has yours ever made fun of your privates? I tell you, E.V., I've finally come around to Bob Cater's view. He's got to go."

"Now, Sonny Boy, you mustn't be so touchy. He still doesn't stink, does he?"

Mick Jurkiedyk was not easy to uproot. Porter prepared for him a waste can of water over the door. Mick sputtered and spat, laughed with delight, and thereafter devoted a large portion of his time to perpetrating the same prank on acquaintances all over the dormitory. After a week, no one in Nottingham Hall would enter a room without looking upward first.

The uninhibited Mick, impatient because one of the ministerial students saw his trap and was successfully avoiding it, gave the student a push through the door anyway. The water soaked the hapless victim, and Jurkiedyk and his friends laughed loudly in the hallway. This particular south Georgia preacher was more of an adherent to the militant philosophy of Charlemagne, baptizing reluctant Franks at the point of a sword, than he was to the docile counsel of turning the other cheek. In addition, he had plowboy, guano-hefting muscles and had never learned "Sooey." He stripped to his underwear, refilled the trash can, and doused the fully-clothed football players as they scrambled in disbelief for the haven of the third floor. It was the clarion call to action, the release of tensions that had been months abuilding.

Within minutes third floor was pitted against second floor — football players against preachers, jocks against scholars — in a wild and unrestrained outburst that approached lunacy. Mincing, introverted ministerial students who had moved in mouselike self-deprecation all year under the blustering gibes of fanatically athletic extroverts joined the foray in a frenzy. They became veritable lions now that water was the weapon instead of fists. Everyone shouted. Trash cans clattered. Someone hooked up hoses, and water came cascading down the staircase to first floor in as irresistible a torrent as a waterfall in the north Georgia mountains.

Mrs. Capulet barricaded herself in her room, from which haven she summoned the police after she first carefully chinked her door to prevent flooding of her apartment. The police stood at the front door of the dormitory unwilling either to get their uniforms wet or to accept anonymity by doffing them. The hullabaloo lasted for almost two hours and ended when the participants were exhausted. Everyone swept water until two o'clock the next morning, good humored and emotionally drained. It became known as The Great Water Battle of '39 and escaped official comment from the discipline committee.

Following a discussion of the physiological peculiarity that things taste stronger and worse when one is sleeping, Porter prepared a mixture of Ipana toothpaste, Listerine, quinine, and red pepper and one night injected a teaspoonful into the sleeping Jurkiedyk's snoring maw. The resulting pandemonium was memorable and awakened students three rooms away. "Jesus, Joseph, and Mary! Good Christamighty! Save me, Jesus! I been poisoned! For Chrissake, I been poisoned! Oh, shit! I catch da cocksucker did it I smash his skull like a fucking eggshell!"

Bob Cater shook with mirth in his bed and feigned sleep. Porter soothed the tortured man and apologized for leaving the

219

door unlocked, thus inadvertently affording entry to some skulking prank-player.

A few nights later, Porter arranged to retire first and leaped out of his bed fuming and fussing and pretending to be victimized by itching powder. Mick had never seen such a commodity and voiced dire and explicit threats about what he would do if anyone ever treated him thus. He crawled, naked and muttering, between his blankets that had been liberally treated with the irritant Bob Cater had purchased at a trick novelty shop. Porter thought it looked like peach fuzz and probably was not worth the dime it had cost. The three lay in darkness for long moments while two of them wondered if the substance was not working, perhaps, they said later, because it couldn't get through all those hairs.

Suddenly there was a roar that deafened them. Blankets went flying across the room, there was bumping, thumping, and crashing of furniture, and Jurkiedyk — a furious, howling hairball — hurled himself down the hall toward the showers, scratching and clawing. The bellowed supplications to his Catholic pantheon awakened all the Baptist boys on the floor and brought Mrs. Capulet to the foot of the stairs in reprimanding dignity. While Porter explained to her the misfortune that had befallen both him and Michael, each tried to ignore the shrieks and shameful curses that were only partially muffled by the sound of the shower and by the closed bathroom door.

He coaxed Mrs. Capulet into returning to her apartment before the nude Jurkiedyk emerged from his ablutions and visually embarrassed them both, but he had no illusions about her insight when she turned at the stair landing. "I hope Professor Twilley hears nothing of this."

Porter gave up. He even developed a guarded affection for Michael Jurkiedyk, tempered by the same tolerance one exhibits toward an awkward dog with perpetually wet muzzle and fresh meat odor to lolling tongue. He stopped discussing him with E.V. Derrick and became so numbed by repetition that he no longer winced at the accent and vocabulary.

* * * *

When Michael moved out, Porter's role in the decision was only peripheral and certainly accidental.

Following his unmasking in the shower, it had become a fad among the football players to apprehend Porter when he was bathing and vie with each other in making prurient and exaggerated comments. Although these jokes were good-natured, they embarrassed Porter to the extent that he began waiting until everyone else in the dormitory was asleep before he took his daily bath. One night, freshly scrubbed and tied securely in his bathrobe, he heard voices as he came out of the bathroom. One was louder than acceptable for the hour, obviously northern and just as obviously slurred with liquor. Porter stuck his head around the post supporting the telephone.

On the landing stood Mrs. Capulet, primly attired in her lavender floor-length robe, her glasses discarded for the night. She was a perfect symbol of righteous authority. "What in the world can you be thinking of? You know it's against the rules to have intoxicants on campus and certainly in this dormitory."

Facing her on the step, swaying wide-legged for balance, was Tom Czernig, a frequent companion of Mick's and one of the trio who had tormented Porter. "Whatcha talking about, lady? Jesus Christ, I got no 'toscants. See here? My pockets all empty." He stuck a hand into each side of his tight-fitting trousers at peril of losing his balance on the stairs and pulled the pockets out. Several pennies, three dimes, and a quarter fell out and rolled down the steps. The pockets reminded Porter of ears accenting the massive thighs.

"You know very well what I mean, young man, Tom Whatever-you-call-it. You are drunk, and that is not only reprehensible, it's a shipping offense."

"Aw, sweet lady, ole Tom's not drunk. Just little happy, fer Chrissake. Happy and homesick, dat's ole Czernig. And horny. How dat sound, huh? Homesick, happy, and horny. Where ya Southern hospitality allus hear about, huh?"

"Young man, if you don't march straight up these stairs and get in your bed immediately, I'm going to call the superintendent."

"Aw, don't do dat. Might make ole Czernig mad, fer Chrissake." He mounted the last step and stood on the landing, towering over Mrs. Capulet and looking down at her. She retreated until her back was against the wall, and Tom lumbered closer to her.

"Gotta better idea. Youse good looking ole broad fer ya age. Good looking pins on ya, too. I see em when youse go to church ever Sunday and t'ink to myself, Dem damn fine pins on dat dame."

"I'm not sure what you're saying, young man, but you had better obey me! This instant! You go to bed!"

"I gotta better idea." He was leaning against the wall with Mrs. Capulet effectively penned between his forearms. "Youse got somet'ing I could use, and ole Tom's got somet'ing you'd love. Let's both go to bed. In your apartment dere."

"Young man, this is preposterous! Move on now and do as you're told. Immediately!"

"Aw, c'mon. I promise you'll love it. Ole Tom do a good job. Bet youse ain't had any lot longer'n me and you'll love it, I promise."

"Thomas Czernig, stop it! I have never in my life been so outraged! The very idea!" Unaccountably and to Porter's great consternation, her voice broke and she began crying. She bowed her head. "I'll have you and the rest of the world to know, young man, that my heart is buried in a grave in Birmingham."

The tears did it. Porter sped up the stairs on silent bare feet and hurled his hundred pounds squarely into the back of Tom Czernig's hyperextended knees. The leaning figure toppled instantly, crashed backward, and rolled thumping and bumping down the stairs to the first floor. Porter gazed downward in disbelief. The prostrate body looked crumpled and vulnerable. Mrs. Capulet wiped her eyes and nose. Porter turned to her.

"I'm sorry he talked to you like that, Mother Capulet. Go on to bed and I'll tend to him." As she turned and lifted the hem of her robe to mount the steps to second floor, he added, "I do hope Professor Twilley hears nothing of this."

He flew down the steps and managed to heave the unconscious Tom Czernig over on his back. He was breathing regularly and not bleeding but gave no response to slaps on his face. Porter ran down the hallway, jerked the blanket off Mick Jurkiedyk, and shook him awake with trembling hands. "Michael, get up quick and come with me. Something terrible has happened to Tom Czernig."

As the two bounded back down the hall, Porter explained to his naked roommate, "I was coming out of the shower and heard this terrible racket and there was Tom, out cold. I think he must have come in drunk and fallen down the stairs."

Mick assessed the situation differently. "Jumping Jesus Christ! Lookit! He drinking all right, I smell it. Laying dere like he's sleeping wit his pockets wrong side out. But he ain't fell down no steps, kid! Lookit! Who pulls his fucking pockets out to fall down da stairs? Huh? And feel da fucking lump on his head dere. Naw, kid! And lookit da money scattered around here! Youse lived in da fucking sticks so long ya don't know nuttin, kid. Old Czernig been mugged! Somebody sapped him and stole his fucking roll. I catch da cocksucker did it, he dies! Wake up, Tom, you bastard, and tell old Mick who rolled ya."

Tom groaned and moved his head but offered no conversational response. Mick dropped to one knee and lifted his friend in a fireman's carry. "I put his ass in my bed tonight. I save climbing dem fucking stairs."

With the larger Czernig draped across his shoulders, he strode down the hall more smoothly than he had walked when unburdened. To Porter's astonished eyes, he did not even look naked anymore.

The following afternoon Porter walked in as Mick was closing his trunk. The blankets were off the bed and the photograph was off the dresser top.

"What's goin on, Michael?"

"I'm leaving, kid. Had it up to here wit dese fucking Baptists in dis cocksucking dormitory. Ain't safe for good northern guys. So many country boys in dis building, it's dangerous.

"Me'n Tom got a room wit a widow lady next door to da Pike house. Look after da yard and da fires in da winter time and she charge ten bucks a mont' for da two of us. Somebody gotta look after old Czernig and guess it'll be me.

"He's OK now. Got a headache bout to kill him but, Christamighty, dat could be from da liquor same as from da lick. Says he don't remember da cocksucker what sapped him. Tell da fucking trut' he don't remember much of nuttin. Said he t'ought maybe da fucking house mudder had somet'in to do wit it, but I ast ole lady Cap'let and she come out wit, 'My good man, I'm sure I don't know what you're talking about.' Anyhow, we moving out so we'n get some

223

peace and quiet."

"Gosh, Michael, I'm going to miss you."

"T'anks, kid, youse been good to me. I still ain't sure youse ain't in da middle some da t'ings happent to me, like da itching powder and da poison, but youse learnt me a lot about da Sout' and youse OK. Tell da big fella so long for Mick."

He started out the door with the trunk on one shoulder like a toy and turned. "Ya know, kid, save fer my mudder, youse da only person in da whole world ever call me Michael. Keep ya fucking nose clean."

That night Porter wrote a long letter home, an occurrence that was becoming increasingly infrequent.

Dear Dad,

Sorry not to have written sooner, but things have been a little hectic around here. Hope everything is fine at home and that everyone is well.

There are two things that I really want to thank you for and to say you were really wise about. One of them is encouraging me to join the fraternity. KA is great and it is an extra thrill to know that you and I share that as an added bond. I am sure KA will make me a better person.

The other thing is that I want to thank you for making me come to Willingham when I wanted to go to the University of Georgia. You were right. I would have been lost in a big state university without a concerned Christian atmosphere. I don't think I would have been happy at all in a bigger school where wilder things happen than here. I love Willingham and am sure it has all the challenge I can possibly meet.

Give everybody my love and keep some for yourself.

It looks like I'll make the Dean's List again.

Sambo

P.S. Do they have yankees at the U. of Ga.?

224

With the lights out, Porter considered the tranquility of Mick's empty mattress and the events that had led up to that great silence. He thought solemnly of some of the ramifications and implications of those events and decided that he wanted no personal contact with God this night. For the first time in his memory, he went to sleep without saying his prayers. He slept soundly.

XV

Pledge Brother Cloud Hollingsworth had a car, a vintage La Salle. He bought it second-hand, or third- or fourth-hand; he never knew for sure. He paid thirty-five dollars and it was his. The car had a crack in the muffler and a hole in the floorboard and filled with fumes after a quarter of a mile, but he bought it in the early spring and it was comfortable to ride with the windows open. Everyone in the fraternity was envious. Cloud was a town student who previously walked to school or rode the bus, but now he had an independence and an air of substance that few possessed. The KA's were proud of him.

The other town students had access to an automobile only on the infrequent occasions when a social event was prominent enough to justify borrowing the family vehicle. The only dormitory student who owned a car of his very own was Jimmy Dewberry, slick-haired, sharp-faced only child of a newly-prosperous merchant from Sylvania who was determined that his child would fare better than he had and would never lack for anything. The Phi Delta Thetas had taken one look at Jimmy's sparkling new red Ford convertible and pledged him without a recommendation.

Jimmy was an almost sullen boy who revved the motor of his car and spun gravel in the parking lot of Nottingham Hall but seldom volunteered any conversation. He did not need verbal skills. His car spoke for him. One frequently saw the unsmiling Jimmy with a car load of Phi Delts, laughing and yelling as they were transported all over Macon. On rainy days when he had to keep the top up and driving was not so pleasant, Jimmy seemed to brood and his fraternity brothers ignored him.

226

It was not until after midterms of winter quarter that he flunked out of Willingham. A non-fraternity ministerial student who happened down the hall helped him load his trunk into the convertible for his trip home. His fraternity brothers were nowhere to be seen. Theo Montagu said Jimmy Dewberry was going to be a classic illustration of shirtsleeves to shirtsleeves in three generations, but one could expect that of Phi Delta Thetas.

Cloud Hollingsworth used his car with more purpose, for Cloud was a responsible and seriously motivated person. Only once did Cloud let his automobile be used in any frivolous manifestation of the college experience. It was shortly after he had acquired the vehicle and just before fraternity initiation for the majority of the new pledges. Cloud was in the expansive mood of new ownership and dropped by the dormitory to share his good fortune with his incipient brothers. Everyone trooped out to the sidewalk to admire the old car and then returned to Porter's room to divide his latest box from home. For some reason the conversation of a sudden turned to prostitution. There was the usual plethora of opinions, few of them rooted in reality but all of them defended stubbornly as truth.

"Whores are all riddled with disease, and if you mess with them you have a slow and horrible death when you're an old man in your late forties or fifties."

"That's not true. Whores are cleaner than other women because they're licensed by the government and get inspected every night before they go to work. It only makes sense you're going to look after the machinery you make a living with."

"Whores are all fixed so they can't get pregnant."

"You're wrong about that. They get a lot of their new whores by recruiting daughters of the old ones."

"I know this guy in Covington; he's a real lady killer. He says whores don't enjoy screwing, it's just a job to them, but if you ever really hit the button on one she'll screw you half to death. He swears he had one fall in love with him cause he satisfied her, and she kept him all night and wouldn't let him pay a nickel."

"That's a lie. Whores always make you pay in advance. Now, don't tell me he was so good she gave the money back. Ain't you ever heard the expression 'Hard as a whore's heart?' "

"All whores don't make you pay in advance," Porter piped up.

227

"I know because I have this friend, an older man, who was in the Merchant Marine for years and years and went all over the world several times and knows everything. He told me about one of his shipmates one time, a Scotchman, who got through with this whore and asked her how much he owed her and she said, 'How much do you think it's worth?' He said, 'Do you think a quarter would be too much?' and she said, 'Hell, if it wasn't worth more than that I'd sew the damn thing up.' And the Scotchman said, 'Aye, and a stitch or two wouldn't hurt it, Miss.'"

Into the silence that followed this contribution, Porter spoke defensively. "Well, Buckalew Tarpley told me and he told it for the truth."

"For God's sake, Osborne, we're having a serious discussion. We're not telling jokes."

Porter subsided again into silence.

"There's a whole string of whorehouses right here in Macon, down on Oak Street."

"Really? I sure would like to see inside one."

"Well, why don't we just get ole Cloud to haul us down there tonight in his car? I sure wouldn't want to go by myself, but there's safety in numbers. Do you know where they are, Cloud?"

"Everybody in Macon knows where Oak Street is, and there's nothing much on it except whorehouses. The nicest one is supposed to be Lillian's."

"You ever been in one?"

"Hell, no, but I hear they're plush and fancy."

"Tell me, who knows how you're supposed to act after you get in one? I ain't talking about after you get in bed; I'm talking about before."

Deacon Chauncey had been doing some free-lance reading and volunteered, "Yall know what Lord Chesterfield wrote in a letter to his son? He advised against sexual intercourse at all. He said the pleasure is brief, the expense is unbearable, and the position is ridiculous."

Porter thought about Buckalew Tarpley's advice to treat a whore like a lady and also his admonition never to kiss one, but decided not to offer these helpful hints to his friends. He did not want any of them sneering at Buck Tarpley again. Apparently he was

228

not so well received as Lord Chesterfield.

"I know they got a jukebox in there and that it takes quarters instead of nickels."

"Yeah, and they charge three dollars to get your ashes hauled and ten dollars if you stay all night and fifteen dollars for Around the World."

"What on earth is Around the World?"

"She goes all over you with just the tip of her tongue. Runs it in and out real fast like a snake and touches you all over with it till you can't stand it anymore. Front and back."

"Gosh, I can see why she charges so much but I can't see why anybody'd want to fool with getting it done. It sure doesn't sound sanitary."

"This fellow told me about it said it was worth a week's pay. Said it makes your toes curl."

"Well, let's don't sit around all night talking about it. Let's get rolling while Brother Hollingsworth is in the notion to give us a ride in that new car. Come on, fellows. Kappa Alpha meets the harlots!"

"I've got some studying to do," said Porter.

"Hell you say, Sambo. You're going, too, if we have to drag you. This is a sociological investigation only, not a pleasure trip. You aren't going to lose your cherry tonight. Come on."

Porter carefully divested himself of his wallet and made sure that he had only twenty-five cents in his pocket. If he had no more than that, he could spend no more than that. Surely it was no sin to play a jukebox in a whorehouse. His presence there could be pardoned by the knowledge that Jesus Himself had been accused by His enemies of associating with harlots and publicans. Porter had not the faintest idea what a publican did for a living but felt that he would vastly prefer visiting one tonight in preference to the mission upon which they were presently embarked. He was unnaturally quiet on the trip downtown and felt even younger than his sixteen years. He would have died rather than suggest turning back.

Oak Street, despite the jocular mood of his fellows and their ribald enthusiasm and despite the grandeur of old water oaks in the yards, looked dilapidated to Porter. A row of houses stood precisely equidistant from the uneven sidewalk, the sameness of their facades confirming both haste and apathy in their builder. Each was mounted high on brick pillars and lacked any sort of underpinning or foundation planting. The resulting impression was of fragile crates perched temporarily on spindly supports until the flooding Ocmulgee River or some other irresistible force removed them from the resentful soil on which they sat.

One of the houses had a Coca-Cola sign in the front yard. A smiling Nehi girl painted on tin with a long thermometer at her side was nailed to the wall of the front porch. The windows were brightly lighted and covered with curtains so green they were phosphorescent. Worn ruts and dried hollows laced the grassless yard in witness of close parking to the porch during rainy spells.

Cloud bumped his car across the curb and the sidewalk and cut the motor. The group became very quiet.

"Now what do we do?"

"We go up those steps and knock on that door like we been doing it all our lives."

"Naw, this is far enough. Let's go back to the dormitory."

"You're chicken. Let's go."

Someone opened the door and the six boys piled out. It was too late for retreat. Not looking at each other, they climbed the steps with the reserve and dignity usually manifested at a house of mourning. As Deacon Chauncey raised his fist to knock, Porter became aware of the beating of his own heart.

Treat a whore like a lady, he desperately reminded himself. Treat a whore like a lady.

The door was possessed of no secret identifying slot such as Porter had imagined. It swung open like any ordinary front door at home, and a lady in an evening dress welcomed them inside. It was so commonplace that two of the boys reflexively wiped their feet before stepping over the threshold, although there was no doormat on the faded gray floor of the porch. Porter inspected the living room for evidence of opulence and sin. Neither was visible. A linoleum rug covered most of the floor, its flowered pattern worn away to dark brown spots in areas of heaviest travel. A drop cord hung from the center of the ceiling with a rose-colored paper shade softening the glare of the single light bulb. Against one wall stood a lighted nickelodeon, but except for this exotic object, the furnishings were unremarkable. Indeed, the two sofas and the chairs scattered around the room were soiled and weary enough to have been removed recently from the KA house. Lillian's overhead did not seem excessive.

"What you want?"

"I suspect you know what we want," responded Deacon. "A little lighthearted fun and entertainment."

Porter thought him the epitome of sophistication.

"OK, where you boys from? Lanier High? This ain't no high school initiation prank, is it? We're not busy right now, but we're too busy for that."

"Certainly not. We're all Willingham men. Tired of studying and looking for recreation."

She laughed. "Hey, girls, come on out. It's a bunch of horny Baptists with a basket full of cherries. Get on out here and pick every one of them. I mean I don't want you boys to let that jukebox get quiet till you leave here. Who's got a quarter?"

Billy Foot was a perpetually smiling town boy who always joked and looked with determination on the brighter side of every event. He leaped forward with a laugh and a quarter, and the room filled with loud jazz at the same time it filled with fancy women. They did not fit Porter's image of ladies of the night. Each wore a different colored evening dress, but their makeup produced the same scarlet and white masks affected by Miller girls, and they seemed to possess the same degree of animation and superficial will to please.

Billy Foot grabbed the one in orange around the waist. "Come on, baby, let's dance."

Everyone laughed with delighted relief and paired off in dancing couples. Porter had never danced a step in his life and, feeling more alien than ever, shrank unobtrusively into the corner beyond the boarded-up fireplace. He sat formally erect on one of the two straight chairs by a small table. His hands were clasped in his lap and were sweating.

"Hi Buster, aren't you lonesome? Want a little company?" She was the only one left and looked, Porter thought, no more than seventeen or eighteen years old. She was small and thin and dressed in a dark blue evening gown with straps across the shoulders and a plunging neckline. The straps exposed stringy arms with little granular bumps down the backs of them, and the neckline revealed

231

extremely small breasts with no evidence whatsoever of a brassiere. Porter gazed with determined concentration into her eyes.

"Oh, yes, ma'am. I'd love that. Please have a seat." He jumped up and held the other chair for her. Resuming his own seat, he could think of nothing to say.

"You wanta dance?"

"No, ma'am. I don't know how. Besides, I'm kind of tone-deaf and can't keep time to the music."

"Have you got a cigarette? I'm about to have a nicotine fit."

"No, ma'am. I don't smoke." He thought it vastly improper to mention his mother. "A certain person promised me a gold wrist-watch if I don't smoke until I'm twenty-one."

"Do tell. My name's Laverne. What's yours?"

"Porter. But my nickname's Sambo. That's what everybody calls me."

"Well, Sambo, you want something to drink? I'n git you a beer for a dollar."

"Oh, no, ma'am. I don't drink."

"Well, what about a Coke?"

"Oh, yes, ma'am, that'd be fine."

"They don't cost but a quarter."

"Twenty-five cents for a Co-Cola? I thought they were a nickel everywhere."

"Well, they're a quarter here. Miss Lillian has a lot of expense."

"Well, to tell you the truth, I just ate supper a while ago and I'm too full to drink anything. Would you mind putting this quarter in the nickelodeon for me? Pick out the song you want." He managed what he thought a generous wave of his hand.

As Laverne returned to their corner and he rose again to seat her, Porter noted with horror how everyone was dancing. He hastily averted his eyes from rolling, thrusting, rubbing pelvises and blurted, "Tell me, ma'am, are you from the city or the country?"

"What difference does that make?"

"Well, I thought if you're from the country and were raised on a farm like me, you might know about milking and be interested in hearing about an English theme I wrote not long ago. I don't mind telling you I made an A on it. It was about barnyard odors in the early morning and the professor read it in class. Have you ever milked a cow?"

"Milking? Me? I wouldn't think of getting close enough to a cow to even touch her. I was born in the middle of Nashville."

"Oh. Well, I've heard that's a very cultural city. Tell me, how do you feel about the two little princes in the Tower of London?"

"What?"

From the corner of a disbelieving eye, Porter glimpsed Bob Cater stooping in his dancing so that his partner's vigorously thrusting pelvis would more closely approximate his own. Even to a charitable eye, Cater was definitely hunching.

Porter spoke so rapidly he sounded breathless. "You know, the two little brothers who were murdered and interrupted the line of succession to the English throne. Shakespeare wrote a play about that, and he, I guess, influenced all the rest of history's attitude about it and presented King Richard III as the murderer."

He saw that E.V. Derrick was actually kissing his girl as they danced slower and slower, and he gave a little shudder at the terrible and unknown fate that awaited E.V. some months from now, but it was too late to warn him. Laverne placed a hand on Porter's thigh.

"King Richard was the little boys' uncle, as I'm sure you already know, and has gone down in history as the worst kind of villain."

Laverne's hand moved a little, very slowly. Upward. "Do tell."

"Well, I want you to know I ran across this article in the Library the other day while I was reading something for Dr. Minor; he's my English professor. It's very interesting and portrays Richard as a very kind and great man."

Laverne's hand moved again. "I bet you got a big 'un. Country boys always do."

Billy Foot had quit dancing and was snuggling on the sofa with the orange dress. Porter crossed his legs tightly and spoke even faster and more shrilly.

"This article, of course, is based on a lot of circumstantial evidence, but it leaves you with almost no doubt at all that Henry was the one who had the little princes murdered. He killed Richard on the field of battle, and with the little princes out of the way, this left him wide open to be king of England even if he was illegitimate. He started the Tudor line and was Queen Elizabeth's grandfather."

"Do tell. You don't say," said Laverne as she leaned out of her chair across Porter's chest.

All of a sudden Billy Foot jumped from the sofa, laughed exultantly, and yelled at the top of his voice, "Hot damn, fellows! I'm hard as rocks!"

The dancers stopped and everyone bent double with laughter. Even Laverne laughed. Porter ignored the merriment and took a deep breath. "Do you see how that changes all of the world's thinking about poor King Richard and even Henry Tudor? But not, of course, the poor little princes."

One of those unexplainable sudden lulls in sound occurred in the midst of the merrymaking, and everyone's eyes turned toward Porter's corner. "I also read an article by someone suggesting there never was a Shakespeare at all and that Sir Francis Bacon really wrote those plays. Under a pseudonym."

Laverne made a lunge and grabbed him in the crotch. "Goddammit, honey, you gonna fuck or not?"

Porter was halfway across the room with one leap and out the door so rapidly that he was on the sidewalk before the swell of raucous laughter overtook him. He ran and ran. Never mind that this was a strange part of town to him. Never mind that for all he knew every house for miles around might be swarming with whores or that the shadows through which he sped might be filled with knife-wielding villains or that some of the dogs that his wild flight startled into hysterical barking might overtake him. Never mind any of that. There was no fear to approach that engendered by Laverne's demands and his own unforeseen wish to fulfill them.

He ran so fast that the speed of his passage whipped tears from his eyes. Gasping for breath, choked by his own heartbeat, he thought of Lot's nameless wife and felt that for the first time in his life he understood why she had been fool enough to look back. He lowered his head and charged faster through the maze of foreign streets.

He came up behind a church that was a welcome landmark and slowed to a more tolerable pace when he finally emerged on College Street. Approaching Tatnall Square Park, he recalled Slick Roundtree's adventure therein and considered walking around instead of through it. He was tired, however, and longed for his room and his bed and the soap-stained smells of Nottingham Hall. Queers, he thought, could hold no fears for him this night, and he took the sanded path that was the shortest route to Nottingham.

He had finished his shower and was climbing into bed when his comrades returned, still gleeful and voluble. He defended himself. "I did not leave because I was afraid I'd have to do something. The very idea! I had used up all my money and was tired of watching the rest of you make fools of yourselves."

"Yall can say what you want about tonight, but I tell you one thing. Ole Billy's got a new nickname. From now on he's 'Hard-as-Rocks Foot.' That's the funniest thing I ever saw."

"Sonny Boy, why in the world did you ask yours if she could milk? That was pretty country for a fraternity man. And whoever heard of talking Shakespeare to a whore?"

"She was not mine! I just happened to be sitting there. Besides, what did you mean by kissing yours? Now you're liable to get one of those diseases and have little knives run up in you and jerked out and then you'll wish you hadn't laughed at me."

Next morning he dutifully gave Boston Harbor Jones a list of things about which he had dreamed.

"Humph. Womens, sand, and a well fulla water. There you go dreaming bout water again. We do good on this un, I bet. Where you go and what you do last night, Sambo?"

"Well, I studied awhile and then Cloud Hollingsworth gave some of us a ride downtown in his car and then I walked home."

"Uh huh. You giving good example how come they say when you get on the witness stand, 'Tell the trufe, the whole trufe, and nothing but the trufe.' You giving me the trufe and the nothing but, but you sure a long way from the whole trufe, boy. I got a cousin stay at our house. Ma raised her like she one her own chirren. Her real ma trashed away to Detroit when she was three. Name Viola.

"Viola got her a little job cleaning up and cooking supper one them lady houses down on Oak Street. Funny hours. Two till ten, but them kinda womens like to sleep all morning and don't want be woke up early. Ma say all right Viola work there cause the pay good. Long as she don't set foot out that kitchen after dark. Viola been raise right.

"Last night I setting up waiting for 'Moon River' come on the radio. Hear all these white boy talk about 'Moon River' all time and how they girlfriends like it and thought I oughta hear what it all about. Viola come in. Say, 'Boston, I believe to my soul I done met yo frien.' I talk about you at home a lot, Sambo, specially since yo dreams done bought the radio and a new cookstove for Ma.

"Viola say last evening Miss Lillian say, 'Girls, finish yo supper. Here come a load college boys up the walk. One of em look like just a chile and got the most pitiful little crookety eye-glasses you ever see. Won't be no tricks in this bunch, but we ain't busy and maybe one or two get so hot they come back next time by theyself. Remember, girls — nice manners, good business.'

"Viola say them little crookety eye-glasses rung a bell and she peek through the kitchen door. Everbody dancing but that little one who's sitting in the corner with Laverne like he at a missionary meeting. Bout that time she hear one them other boy say 'Sambo' something or other, and she know it have to be you cause the chances they being two white boy name Sambo in Macon, Georgia, bout as long as me winning all the way across on the bug. You was there, wasn't you, boy? You was in that fancy lady house last night."

Porter dropped his eyes in shame. "I was there, Boston, but I didn't do anything. Honest, I didn't. I got scared. Of a lot of things. And ran home. But I didn't do anything."

"I know you didn't. Neither nobody else do nothing. Viola say them boy laugh so hard you running outta there they leave the womens alone and don't put no money in the juke. Viola say Laverne sorta the fractious sort anyhow, and all sudden she grab up the fire poker and yell out, 'All you stingy little shitasses take yo hard little pricks and get hell outta here and don't come back less you horny enough and got the money to hump.' She little but she mean, and she swanging that fire poker and them boys clear out in a hurry. Don't hear no more laughing till they git to they car.

"Miss Lillian come running in the front room and grab Laverne by the hair and snatch her around and smack her real sharp on both jaws and say, 'Willie Mae Gooch, you crazy, gal? I done tole all yall good manners, good business, and here you go gittin impatient and act like a cheap little whore off the street don't do nothing but rent a room somewheres. I got good notion to send you straight back

236

to Ocilla, Georgia, where you raised. Also, how come you curse out and grab at that chile and talk nasty to him? Prolly scared he little pecker so far up in him it never come out no more.'

"And Laverne start crying and say, 'Oh, Miss Lillian, please don't torture me no more. Reason I grab up the fire poker and run them other boys outta here was they laughing so hard at Sambo and I already feeling bad bout treating him like that. He only boy in world ever talk to me about King of England and Shakespeare. In fact, he the only boy in world ever talk to me at all. All the rest of them just try to get in my britches quick as they kin. And out quick as they kin.'

"And Viola say Laverne keep crying and say, 'Oh, Miss Lillian, I think I falling in love. I longs to get that Sambo back in here and smooth him and stroke him and sleep with him all night long without charging him no money and hold him up tight between my breastes. Miss Lillian, ain't that love?' "

"Boson Harbor Jones, stop it! There goes your imagination again. You know perfectly well that girl said no such thing. Besides, you haven't seen her or you'd know she's got the least little titties in all of Macon, and even I know enough about girls to know they never refer to them unless they've got em."

"You right. I lying. You know it and I know it, but who else know it? Them other boys ain't got no way knowing it cause they ain't got no cousin work in a whorehouse. I thought I slip around and tell one two of em. Make em jealous and make you look better. Who was they?"

"Boston, you're awful. Just tell E.V. Derrick. He's enough."

"Hot zig! Ole Mouse-in-Water-Pitcher Derrick. You mighty right I tell him, Sambo. I tell him the trufe and the whole trufe and get him so confuse he wouldn't reckanize nothing but the trufe if it come tippy-tapping through the Liberry."

"Pour it to him, Boston. Nothing's too good for ole Derrick."

"I aim to. And, Sambo, you know I yo friend, don't you?"

"Boston, I certainly do."

"Well, boy, I wanna tell you one thing. You keep yo tail offa Oak Street."

"Boston, you don't need to worry. Wild horses couldn't drag me back down there. Besides, it says somewhere in the Bible that it's better to waste your seed in the sand than in the belly of a whore."

"Hoo whee, Sambo! Good thing you talk history with Laverne last night instead of the Bible."

"Well, thanks for everything, Boston. I gotta run. Lemme know what E.V. has to say."

"Sambo, just a minute. Laverne really did tell Miss Lillian that about Shakespeare and King of England. Viola right impress with you."

Initiation into the fraternity released in most boys previously concealed eccentricities of behavior. Such mildly rebellious assertion of individuality was manifested in E.V. Derrick by a non-conforming musical taste.

XVI

A good, solid fraternity man in 1939 liked swing and jazz and deviated neither to the right nor the left. People who liked classical music were regarded as effete. Although Tchaikovsky and Rachmaninoff were tolerated for having contributed themes for two popular songs, no one listened to the originals. An older fraternity man could nod approvingly when "Tonight We Love" came over the radio and murmur, "Ah, Concerto Number Two," but the run-of-the-mill Greek letter aficionado was content to pat his foot to "Begin the Beguine" or hum along with "When the Deep Purple Falls."

KA's were no less cultured in this respect than the Phi Delta Thetas and considerably ahead of the SAE's and ATO's. Their radios were always tuned to WMAZ, so orthodox a station that one assumed its license could have been revoked had the nasally whining lyrics of hillbilly music been sung on its airwaves. Hillbilly music was regarded as the most uncouth expression one's taste could manifest, and an adherent to it probably would wipe his nose on his sleeve and eat mashed potatoes with a spoon. *Country* was a term applied not to the music but to anyone crude and shallow enough to listen to it. All of it had exactly the same tune, Bob Cater said, and sounded as though a frightened cat had knocked over all the pans in someone's kitchen.

On the morning after E.V. Derrick's initiation, Ole Boy was startled out of a sunrise snooze by the strains of Roy Acuff singing,

239

"How many biscuits can you eat this morning?
How many biscuits can you eat this evening?
How many biscuits can you eat?
Forty-nine and a chunk of meat,
This morning, this evening, right now."

So shocking was this to the nervous system of a northern boy of Polish extraction, familiar with polkas but totally unsympathetic to the new wave of folk music coming from the mountains of Tennessee, that he voiced a mild remonstrance. "You lost ya fucking mind? Change that damn hillbilly station!"

The radio belonged to E.V., however, and E.V. had liberated himself. Even in the face of sterner, albeit more genteely phrased, concern from his fraternity brothers, he steadfastly refused to knuckle under to convention. E.V. liked good old mountain music played by the Hill-Bill-Billy Band, and his room was loud with it whenever he was in residence.

One day when they were walking to town, Porter undertook to counsel his older friend. His own musical education had consisted entirely of Baptist hymns, except for yearly attendance at piano recitals where he had been exposed to a repetitive handful of classical pieces played by nervous, fussily-dressed pubescent girls before fatuous parents. The radio in his home was used for news broadcasts, baseball games, and certain selected programs such as "Amos and Andy," "Fibber McGee and Molly," and "Little Orphan Annie." It certainly was not turned on for background music while one studied or worked. Porter had no particular aversion himself to hillbilly music, and he did not really care what music E.V. preferred; he simply decided to see if he would succeed with him when everyone else had failed.

"Why you wanta play that hillbilly stuff all the time? You know it upsets the Brothers, especially Slick and Clarence."

"Listen, Sonny Boy, I know more about music right now than they'll know for the rest of their lives. Don't I sing in the glee club and play the tuba in the marching band? They wouldn't know 'Ave Maria' from 'The Stars and Stripes Forever.' "

"Well, they think you make the whole fraternity look country."

"Country? Me? Look, Sonny Boy, my daddy's a doctor and a

240

specialist to boot. One of them's got a daddy works for the post office and the other one works for a cotton mill. They needn't worry about me being country. Hillbilly's not the only music I know. What's your favorite song?"

"Well, I guess it's 'Deep in a Dream.' "

E.V. threw back his head and sang in a truly melodious voice that caused a housewife sweeping her steps to turn and look at them.

> "I dim all the lights, and I stink in my chair.
> The smoke from my cigarette floats through the air.

And then the next verse goes,

> My cigarette burns me; I wake with a fart.
> My hand doesn't hurt, but there's pain in my heart.

That the one you talking about, Sonny Boy?"

Porter looked over his shoulder. It seemed to him there were more ladies in front yards than he had ever before seen along this route. "E.V., I think that lady heard you. You've ruined the song for me now, but don't sing so loud they can hear you."

"Ah, Sonny Boy, people don't listen to words. They just hear the tune." He looked across the street at a woman sweeping her doorstep and burst into song again.

> "Oh, take it in the mouth, Mrs. Murphy;
> It only weighs a quarter of a pound.
> It's got hairs round its neck like a turkey,
> And it spits when you shake it up and down."

Porter was so scandalized and so convinced the neighborhood would be affronted that he threw back his head and trilled as loudly as he could a song he had heard Uncle Bung sing.

> "Going up Crappie Creek, going on the run,
> Going up Crappie Creek to have a little fun.
> I'll roll my britches up around my knees,
> And I'll wade up Crappie Creek as far as I please."

E.V. stared at him without smiling and began his horrible song again. Before he could get into the second line, Porter drowned him out with,

> "Oh, little feet, be careful
> Where you take me to.
> Anything for Jesus
> Only let me do."

E.V. smiled benignly and spoke with amused tolerance. "Oh, you like religious songs, Sonny Boy? OK, how bout this one?

> I don't care if it rains or freezes;
> I am safe in the arms of Jesus.
> I am Jesus' little lamb.
> Yes, you doggone right I am.
> He will wash me white as snow.
> What a dirty little job for Jesus."

Porter glared at him in exasperation and raised his voice in off-key cancellation.

> "I washed my hands this morning
> So very clean and white,
> And gave them both to Jesus
> To work for him till night."

A lady smiled and waved at them. E.V. smiled and bowed and waved back. Then he sang,

> "Oh, the game was played on Sunday
> In Heaven's own back yard,
> With Jesus Christ at quarterback
> And Moses playing guard.
> The angels in the grandstand
> Oh, Lord how they did yell
> When Jesus made his touchdown

Against the boys from hell.
Oh, stay with God, pray with God.
Rock 'em, sock 'em, Jesus, block 'em!
Stay with God."

Porter had begun,

"On that bright and cloudless morning
When the dead in Christ shall rise
And the morning breaks eternal bright and fair...."

but he was so horrified at the content of E.V.'s latest song that he forgot the peril of being overheard by the ladies.

He feared that the Lord God of Hosts, Jehovah Himself, might happen to be paying attention to the sidewalks of Macon on this spring Saturday afternoon and be moved to clear them with a thunderbolt. He quickened his pace frantically and moved out in front of his partner. "E.V. Derrick, you should be ashamed! I know you were raised better than that! That's the most sacriligious thing I ever heard."

"Well, Sonny Boy, you caused it. I don't want you and the other KA's thinking I'm a hillbilly. I know part of one about Hi-ho, Cathuselem, the harlot of Jerusalem. It ain't the least bit country. If you won't walk so fast, I'll sing it for you."

As he turned a corner, almost running, Porter promised the Good Lord that if He would spare him just this one more time, he'd never ever walk to town again with E.V. Derrick. The Lord heard him and assented, for nothing untoward happened either to E.V. Derrick or to Porter, thus strengthening Porter's conviction that plea bargaining with the Almighty was patently efficacious and therefore worthwhile.

Henry Bean had other views. In the midst of a discussion one day in lab concerning Neville Chamberlain, Hitler, and the Balkans, Henry muttered in disgust that another world war was inevitable. He said that England was doomed unless it could find a leader who had

243

some balls and a less sissified first name. He further asserted that the first thing Roosevelt had done to preserve instead of destroy America was call for a full-scale military conscription. All Henry's listeners were entrenched in student deferment. They were more interested in an examination predicted for the next day or the coming weekend change in movie programs than in anything occurring half a world away. The conversation fizzled to death from indifference.

Walking with him to the Co-op through the opulent springtime that caresses Macon every year, earlier and more softly than anywhere else in the world, Porter sought to reassure his friend. "Henry, we're not going to get into war. They pray about it at chapel three times a week and every night at vespers. God will keep us out of war."

"Still believe in magic, don't you, Osborne?"

"Well, the Bible says you have to pray and then you have to believe it's going to happen. If you have enough faith, you can move mountains. If you don't get what you pray for, then it's your own fault because you didn't have enough faith."

"Osborne, I'd laugh at you if I weren't so busy shuddering at how hard you're going to get sand-bagged one of these days. I haven't been that innocent since I was nine years old."

"Well, Henry, you have to know it in your heart. There are too many Christians praying together. God will not let evil triumph over good."

"And the prayer of the Willingham Righteous will inform God what is evil? And how He should behave?"

Porter recognized the barb of logic hidden in the questions but drew a deep breath and defended his position. "Well, I always get what I pray for. I prayed about my grades, and I've made the Dean's List two quarters in a row. And that included two B's in French, and I thought I was going to flunk that."

"You try praying sometime when you haven't studied or had Tiny coaching you and see how much God cares whether you flunk French or not."

"Well, I'm sure not worried about war. My mother is going to give me a gold wristwatch if I don't smoke until I'm twenty-one, and I promised God that if He kept us out of the war I'd give the gold watch to the poor and never smoke anyhow."

Henry's mouth was a tight hairline. It betokened both exasperation and triumph. He barked, "Aha, accumulated merit and the benevolent patriarch! You Baptists have really managed to create God in your own image and you sure fall down worshipping Him. Flat on your ass."

"Henry, you sound like you don't believe in God. You're not an atheist, are you?"

"Hell, no, Osborne, I'm not stupid enough to be an atheist. I believe in God. It's just that I don't know exactly what to believe all the time, and it's all right with me if I don't have all the answers about Him. I read part of a book called *Sesame and Lilies* by a guy named Ruskin, and one of the essays was advice to young women. He jumped on the Victorian English for their smug assurance about God and wound up saying that the main difference between the little Christian virgin and the little heathen savage is that the former thinks much about God that is wrong and the latter little that is correct."

"I'm not sure I get that."

"If you don't get rid of your childish image of God, which is as full of misconceptions and delusions as Santa Claus, then you'll never be able to see the real God, whatever that is. And the Georgia Baptist Convention is dedicated to keeping the blindfold on."

"That doesn't sound much to me like you believe in God."

"I'm still working on it. It's fascinating how much time man spends thinking about non-essentials. You know 'Fessor Hansford's assistant, Malcolm James? Well, he and I ran into each other a few nights ago and got to talking over a few beers. I had a good time. I was relieved to find out that he has no more illusions about old Hansford's ability as a teacher than I have; James is just working on his Master's because this is a cheap school with a fairly decent reputation, and he doesn't mind teaching on the side till he gets through here. Strictly a stepping-stone, he said. And I said, 'In the final analysis, isn't that the way we should consider every life experience?' He then decided I had some sense and we got to really shooting bull.

"When we got through with the Biology department, we started on politics. Gene Talmadge is gonna run this state from now on unless we get rid of the county unit vote, and I told James there's small chance of that."

Porter shifted his books to the other hip. "I like the county unit system."

"Living where you do, you should. But if we're going to have an oligarchy, you farmers got to do better than Talmadge for the rest of us. Anyhow, we finally got around to religion, and I'm here to tell you that Malcolm James has got a mind and can make you think. He's from Chicago and he's Catholic. At least he used to be. Got an older brother who's a priest. Well, sir, he looks on the entire Old Testament as nothing but Semitic mythology. Claims it's as outdated as Greek or Roman or Norse mythology. He says that it's just a bunch of old family stories the Jews got up, and they try to pass them off as religion. He went to school with a lot of Jews in Chicago, and he says those folks don't really believe anything. Says all that stuff about the chosen people is something their ancestors dreamed up to build their egos and make them feel better about being such born pissants. Says most of them he knows tend to snivel and whine a lot and holler the only reason people don't like them is because they're Jews."

Porter sniffed. "Well, I certainly believe God has Chosen People."

"You should. But here again, don't forget the responsibility that goes with it."

"Well, for Pete's sake, what does Malcolm James the almighty say about the New Testament? About Jesus?"

"You can bet I asked him. I nearly fell out laughing at what he said about the Virgin Birth. Said everybody's all hung up on it, but he privately believes that was just a story Mary made up to sneak by Joseph. And he swallowed it whole and went out and told it. Malcolm says he feels sorry for Mary because he believes she didn't aim for Joseph to tell anybody that. Said no woman in her right mind would want that silly story to get out on her. It was a riot."

Horrified and vulnerable, Porter was nevertheless a little inhibited. "I don't think it's all that funny. That guy's playing with hellfire."

Henry cut his eyes at him as the only acknowledgement that he heard him. "He says Jesus was a real smart Jew who said a lot of things that downtrodden people wanted to believe. Specifically that there is a life after death and better things are coming when you're dead. He said that if the Jews and the Romans had let Him alone and He'd lived to be a senile old man, nobody today would ever have heard of Jesus. They had to go and make a martyr out of Him right at the peak of His popularity, and the whole world loves martyrs and turns them into saints.

"Then here came Paul, he said, who was obviously a paranoid schizophrenic and probably a little queer to boot. At least he sure didn't like women, James says. And Paul whips everybody who had known Christ personally into shape and makes a god out of Jesus. Did you know that the earliest written book in the New Testament was written by Paul, who never even saw Jesus? And it wasn't written until almost thirty years after He died."

Porter drew himself righteously and indignantly upright. "I certainly didn't, and I still don't. But that doesn't make any difference." He then inquired of Henry how Malcolm James managed to deal with the miracles.

Henry said that James got a little flip about them. He looked at Porter and laughed. "He said if the first wine was bad enough and strong enough, then plain water would have tasted pretty good at Cana and would've just kept on getting those lower class Jews drunker. Said Lazarus probably wasn't really dead to start with. He laughed about the loaves and the fishes and said he'd run into some Hunky women in Chicago who cooked so it seemed like that. Did you know that the biological term for virgin birth in a sexual animal is parthenogenesis? He said the real miracle about Christianity is that out of that highly unlikely source has come the best set of rules for man to live by that history has ever known. He says that in nineteen hundred years nobody has been able to improve on it but that very few people have really managed to live by it."

Porter cautiously let out his breath. "Well, it sounds like he's not all bad."

"Oh, he's not bad at all. He's just honest. And brilliant. And also compassionate. We're lucky to have him at Willingham. The thing that really impressed me and set my mind whirring and made me want to tell you about it is what he said about evolution."

"Oh, you mean that man is descended from monkeys?"

"That's not what Darwin said at all, according to Malcolm James. I tell you, that man's smart. He's got me all fired up to do some reading. I want to read *Origin of Species,* some ancient historian named Josephus, and even the Bible. No, he said that if there's

247

anything to the theory of evolution, then it has to be a continuing process and it has to be still going on. Ever so slowly, of course, but it certainly hasn't stopped. He thinks it will be interesting a million years from now to see if there's any difference in what is still called man by then according to whether their forebears worshipped Christ or Confucius, Buddha or Mohammed. Whether they read Paul, the Bhagavad-Gita, or Karl Marx.

"He says the development of man's mind is what may goof up the whole evolutionary process, though. Good or bad, it could interfere with the very gradual changes that characterize evolution as opposed to revolution. Says our minds may jump out ahead of our other capabilities before they can catch up and destroy us. All this made me think about you. You're relatively so unformed and basically so capable that it's going to be interesting to watch how you adapt to environment and how you change."

Porter was insulted to his fundamentalist marrow. He stopped dead in his tracks. "Henry Bean, I don't know when I've heard a statement that offended me more. You remind me of Dr. Huber."

"The French professor? Come off it, Osborne."

"Yes, you do," he shrilled. "Next thing I know you'll be telling me the ass may speak."

"I don't know what you're talking about, but maybe it already has."

"Well, did it ever occur to you that if a person is a strong enough Christian and has enough faith, that it may be the environment that changes instead of the person? I don't care what you and Malcolm James talk about when you're slobbering in your beer; the United States is not going to war. Jesus answers prayer and knows when a sparrow falls and has the hairs on your head numbered."

"I'm gonna watch, Osborne. Hell, I may even take notes."

Within days after this interchange between Porter Osborne and Henry Bean, the entire campus had become obsessed with religion, almost to the exclusion of anything else. It was the topic of conversation from Chichester's to the Co-op, from the Administration Building to the dormitory. Even the *Macon Telegraph* had stories about it. Fundamentalism was the issue, and it split, polarized, and then united Willingham University as no fervent evangelist in chapel had ever been able to do. The most avidly scientific pre-med students, the most loftily cynical journalism majors, the thickest and most intellectually shallow athletes were compelled alike to examine their beliefs and take a stand.

The cataclysm erupted within the student body itself and was precipitated as the fruition, in retrospect, of resentment and rage in the soul of Creed Foxmore. Creed was an ordained Baptist minister of middle years who pastored two churches, lived at home with his wife and children, and attended college as a day student. He was a massive man with shoulders that had developed in youth under two-hundred-pound sacks of fertilizer and now bore with ease the sins of man, particularly those manifest in the frivolous and decadent student body of Willingham. His face was square and solid. Strong pegs of teeth bulged his upper lip into a firmness so masculine it hinted of restrained cruelty. All year he had spent his time between classes accosting fellow students with open Bible in hand. He would stride abruptly up to a boy reading on the Library steps or sipping a Coke in the Co-op and demand, "Are you saved, brother?"

Before his target could do more than look startled, Creed would follow through. "I mean, have you accepted the Lord Jesus Christ as your personal Savior?"

Then he would launch into an evangelical tirade that was impossible to stem or control, an exposition of the Bible that was unbelievably literal, an exhortation to repent before it was too late. Most of his victims were too well-mannered to raise their voices or be rude and would endure the torture until Creed had to go to class or there came an interrupting opportunity to slink away. An occasional independent spirit, annoyed at this intrusion into cherished privacy, would tell Creed Foxmore to mind his own business and shut up. These rejections nourished rather than squelched Foxmore. He countered each repudiation with unbelievable theatrics.

Beating his breast with his empty hand and flourishing his open Bible with the other, he would thunder in delighted martyrdom, "Blessed are ye, when men shall *ree*vile you, and persecute you, and shall say all manner of evil against you, falsely for My sake. *Ree*joice, and be exceeding glad, for great is your *ree*ward in heaven;

for *so* persecuted they the prophets which were before you."

Then he would extend both arms from the shoulders, drop his massive head, cross his feet, and stand momentarily immobile. It was a startling imitation of the Crucifixion and caused students to gawk while they walked widely around him.

Sometimes an idling cynic, usually a freshman Law student, as bored and bemused as a small boy tantalizing a toad on a still, hot afternoon, would deliberately invoke Creed's attention with straight-faced solemnity. "Tell me, preacher, if the world is really round, why does the Bible speak of the four corners of the earth?"

"Brother Foxmore, I'm troubled. If God is all good and all powerful, how do you explain the presence of evil on earth?"

"Answer me this: Can God make a rock so big He can't lift it?"

"Listen, Creed, you can tell me confidentially. Don't you really think the Bible made a mistake in Joshua 10:13 when it says that the sun stood still? Shouldn't they have said the earth stood still? We all know it's the earth that revolves and moves, not the sun. You can trust me; I swear I won't tell a soul what you really think."

The devout butt of these questions would attack the answers with fervor and solemn righteousness, but he usually appeared intellectually impotent in those interchanges. No one on campus took Creed Foxmore very seriously. For the most part, however, he was treated gently.

The head of the Christianity department himself had managed to offend Creed Foxmore to his religiously literal foundations. Dr. George Bozeman had raised the Bible aloft in the opening session of his class on the Old Testament and attracted everyone's gasping attention by declaring, "Young brethren in the household of faith, by no stretch of your imagination can this book be called the Word of God."

Creed Foxmore came so close to fainting that he was unable to thunder out immediate challenge, and by the time he composed himself, Dr. Bozeman already had pointed out chunks of ancient writings, including the Apocrypha, that had been deleted by human compilers and was well into an intensely literate discussion of the contributions of J and P to the Pentateuch.

Creed, too shaken to take notes, was canny enough to realize he had lost his moment and tried to comprehend what he was hearing. He kept flipping in his Bible to the opening titles in the Old Testament and gathered a small satrapy to accost Dr. Bozeman after class.

That gentleman had listened quite calmly, albeit a bit aloofly, and replied in level voice, "You are quite correct, Brother Foxmore. I am implying that Moses did not write the book of Genesis, although its subtitle is indeed the First Book of Moses. In fact, I am proclaiming such as the truth. You will note that in Deuteronomy, which is also called the Fifth Book of Moses, we read of the death of that greatest of all Jewish leaders. Surely, Brother Foxmore, none of you agitated young men would so violate the bounds of common sense as to suggest that even Moses could post-facto chronicle his own death. Sir, it is my duty in this course to lay facts before you, to which end I shall utilize the works of only the most reputable of scholars. Your own personal faith is no responsibility of mine but rests, rather, as a matter of privacy between you and your Creator, Who historically has been very tolerant of idiocy. Good day, sir."

When Creed at the end of the quarter had blustered his outrage at being given a D in the course, Dr. Bozeman had denied *giving* him any grade, pointing out that Creed himself had earned the D. He then cooly referred him for any grievance he had about defects in his intelligence back to the Creator of us all.

Creed began grumbling to his friends and plotting revenge.

The Ministerial Association was the largest group on campus to be recognized as a bona fide organization and get its picture in the annual. It consisted of fifty students who were studying to be Baptist preachers plus one maverick who was going on to a Presbyterian seminary. He was distinguishable from the group only when the Lord's Prayer was recited; he persisted in asking forgiveness for debts rather than trespasses. Creed Foxmore was so voluble in this Association that he forced attention to himself, and with the supporting strength of a few other zealots, one night leveled charges of heresy against Dr. Bozeman and several more faculty members.

At first, none of the other student preachers attached much importance to the proposal. Indeed, the proper and august Ministerial Association attempted to smother the movement in parliamentary procedure, thereby maintaining it within its own confines and reducing its importance to the level of a debate in the Ciceronian

251

Literary Society. The insurgents were incensed. They persisted. They pushed. They finally drew up a formal manifesto that thirteen of the ministerial students were either dumb enough or brave enough to sign, and they went public with it.

It presented detailed complaints against eight members of the faculty, calling their names and spelling out their offenses, decrying the lack of Christian orthodoxy in their teaching. In ringing and formal language worthy of a firebrand at Wittenberg, the document demanded that the Board of Trustees investigate and immediately dismiss the transgressors. The thirteen perpetrators sent copies to the *Willingham Chanticleer,* the *Macon Telegraph,* and the *Christian Index.*

Publicity was instant and demanding. Ministerial students who previously had sat quietly in class or trod the campus in unnoticed mediocrity suddenly were subjected to concentrated scrutiny by their fellow students. Every preacher became conspicuous. Some of them reveled in it, and some of them squirmed. The rebellious group had signed its manifesto "The Holy Thirteen" and rapidly became known on a shocked and retaliatory campus as "The Unholy Thirteen."

From the ranks of The Thirteen, two articulate and positive seniors strode forth as leaders, and the war was begun. One of them, of course, was Creed Foxmore. The other, to the puzzlement of faculty members and students who put their trust in intelligence and assumed that reason, when available, would ride rein on emotion, was a boy named John Birch.

Two disparate personalities became fused by common purpose into one driving force, and the whole was greater than the sum of its parts.

John Birch also was a senior but in contrast to Creed had distinguished himself as a scholar — a master of academic achievement who had become a legend while still a student. The son of missionaries, he had been born in Burma or China or India, or some place, Foxmore assured people, like that. His current home was Macon, and he had so excelled at Willingham that he was a candidate to be a Rhodes scholar. Essentially a loner, he loved tennis. He was aggressively competitive and tolerated his fellow students more readily if they were competent tennis opponents. He spent most of his time either on the courts or in crannies of the Library poring over esoteric books that had not been opened in decades. He was an outstanding member of the debate team and had been for four years. His preparation was so thorough, his mind so quick, his rebuttals so ruthless and scathing, that he had lost not one contest. The debate coach was said to pair him deliberately with the weakest man on the team because Birch could direct and use an inferior partner so that chances of victory actually were enhanced.

He had wiry brown hair with hints of red in it, so thick and lush that it seemed to sprout with uncontrollable vigor from his vibrant brain. His brow bulged just short of hydrocephaly and imparted an elusive hint of the ethereal to his deep-set eyes. His mouth was thick and curving, and his upper canines caused a slight eversion of the mucous surface of his lip. This was most apparent when he spoke or smiled and implied a sensuality that was incongruous in one so rigidly disciplined, so contemptuous of error in his fellows. Everyone on campus took John Birch seriously. He was a force to be reckoned with, and his attack on the members of the faculty showed him to possess cold eyes and a steady hand upon the sword.

Hitler, Chamberlain, and Roosevelt were forgotten in the days of the manifesto, and interest was focused instead on local celebrities. Porter heard it on all sides.

At the fraternity house Clarence Spangler trumpeted, "The formal charge against Professor Twilley says he told his class that Cleopatra was nothing but a common whore. Now, ole Twilley did that all right, but the real reason they're after him is that he told a class with girls in it that the most expressive word in the English language is 'shit.' You know how Twilley spits when he says his S's and glares at you with that one eye. Those namby-pamby ministerial students just ain't got the guts to write 'shit' in that document for the Georgia Baptist Convention. They're really a bunch of cowards."

In the kitchen, Boston Harbor shook his head. "You white Baptists a sight. Preachers come, preachers go, but ain't nobody oughta mess with somebody else's job. You good ole bad boys better

253

hang in there and help those teachers, Sambo. They in trouble."

In the dining hall, Mrs. Raleigh was overheard. "I don't feed Creed nor yet John, so I don't really know them. The way to a man's heart, you know. I always say judge not and don't bite off more, but you also have to respect your elders and do unto others. Those faculty members are certainly tried and true. I am no stranger, myself, to suffering, and it will all come out in the wash and truth will tell."

Tiny Yeomans was belligerent. "I don't know how they got 'Fessor Hansford about not believing in parthenogenesis in humans; I've never heard him talk about anything but bobwhites and soil erosion myself. Besides, what's all the fuss about? The hard part for me about Christianity is that God is Love. If anybody can really and truly believe that, he ought not to have any trouble about a dad-blame virgin having a baby. Big deal!"

Sybil Swygert told all the ADPi girls, "They're going too far when they pick on Dr. Kruger. I had him for physics two quarters, and he's an absolute lamb. The whole department would just collapse if they got him fired. He's absolutely brilliant. And the best-looking man you ever saw. That repulsive Creed Foxmore was in the Co-op waving a list of the generations since Adam that he says proves the world is about three thousand years old. He says Dr. Kruger is anti-Christ because he told a class there was geological proof the earth was formed millions of years ago. Can you imagine? I wanted to slap his smirking jaws."

Mrs. Capulet remarked to Porter, "This entire affair is an absolute outrage, and thank the dear Lord of course that it did not occur while my blessed husband was president. Maligning Montis Wright, however, is an unbelievable atrocity."

Montis Wright, professor of Psychology, was a great, gray man possessed of kindness and soft-spoken control. He was listed for firing because he had assigned some readings from Sigmund Freud to his advanced students. The charges themselves were beyond Creed Foxmore's intellectual grasp, and consequently there was little noise on campus about Dr. Wright.

"I don't mind admitting," Mrs. Capulet continued, "that I work behind the scenes occasionally, and I have talked to my minister at Vineville about this. He's an officer in the Georgia Baptist

Convention and knows all the trustees at Willingham. He's going to apply a little pressure to his friends. He's actually read Sigmund Freud and says if a Christian's faith can be shaken by him, then that person didn't have much faith to start with.

"I tell you, Porter, I know every one of those boys, and twelve of them wouldn't know Sigmund Freud from Adam's off-ox. I am not a complete idiot, and I've noticed the books that Birch boy checks out of the Library. He reads things nobody else ever heard of. He's a born troublemaker and must be a great trial to his parents. He's the one behind this. He's just letting that Foxmore idiot be his cat's-paw. I'm relieved he didn't get me put on the list just for handling some of those books while I was getting them out of the stacks for him. This is as bad as the French Revolution."

Bob Cater turned from the mirror where he had been squeezing a pimple on his chin. "You know they make you take freshman Christianity in this school before you can graduate. Well, there's a bunch of seniors taking it with me, and we've got old Dr. Burn. He's eighty if he's a day. Cutest little old man you ever saw, all dried up and wrinkled. Got that little pot belly sticking out and always wears a vest and a big gold watch chain.

"Somebody asked him one day about evolution — we'd do anything to get away from the journeys of Paul — and he goes to all this trouble to explain it's not incompatible with Christianity. Says the original Hebrew word for 'day' can just as easily be translated 'period of time,' and people that are all torn up about the first chapter of Genesis have to realize we can say God created the world in six periods of time and no one can say how long those periods were. Might have been a million years apiece instead of twenty-four hours.

"Evolution could have been going on all that time, and Adam could have been the finished product, civilized enough, Dr. Burn said, to have religion and also to have the world's first murderer for a son. That pimply-faced freshman from Moultrie that walks like a girl prissed out and told old Creed Foxmore about it, and that's why they've got Dr. Burn up for heresy. They'll never make it stick. He's a saint if I ever saw one."

Porter encountered Mick Jurkiedyk emerging from a weight-lifting session in the gymnasium. "Christamighty, kid, da whole jernt's crazy. Dem fucking preachers trying to fire da teachers, for

Chrissake. If da fucking place was organized wort a shit, da president would just excommunicate da preachers, like in our outfit, and be done wit it. Da loonies in Da Unholy Thirteen ain't got a chance. Ya know why? Dey done stirred up all da fucking country boys against em, and Jesus Christ, are dey gonna get it! Dem country boys from da Sout all get together, ain't nobody stand a fucking chance! Dis worse dan when Sister Margaret Marie jumped on my brudder one time for yelling 'Hail Mary, full of grace, don't let dat ball pass second base.' "

"Do you know any of The Unholy Thirteen personally, Michael?"

"Youse kidding me? None of em on da football team or made Pike, did day? I run into dat old one da udder day at my mailbox. Da fat one wit da Bible. I had a letter from my girlfriend and I was reading it and bumped into him, and ya know what he said to me? 'Are youse saved, brudder?' he says. I jab him in da chest wit one finger and says, 'Listen, cocksucker, I aintcha brudder and don't talk Baptist to me when I hold in my hand a open letter a'ready yet from Miss Noreen Dvonski, who happens to be a refined Cat'olic girl wit sensitive feelings. If youse say anudder word I'll snatch ya fucking tongue out and stuff it down ya fucking troat. Ya got dat, cocksucker?' And, kid, youse know what he did? He held up his arms and crossed his legs. And den he dropped his head and went into a trance. Yeh, a fucking trance! Right dere in da Co-op. Jesus Christ, what a loony!"

The charges against the professors and the demand for a hearing before the church powers fascinated newspapermen. The *Macon Telegraph* ran a headline: "Witch Hunt at Willingham." The student newspaper staff was jubilant, swollen with importance because their *Chanticleer* was noticed by the professionals on the *Telegraph*, who consulted with the student journalists and even gave them reporting assignments. Deacon Chauncey wrote an editorial in the *Chanticleer* with reference to William Jennings Bryan in Tennessee that brought him so much acclaim he dropped pre-Law and declared Journalism as his major. The Kappa Alphas were proud of

256

Deacon.

Walton Hand was a sophomore ministerial student with curly blond hair, blue eyes, and dimples, a combination which made co-eds consider attending vespers until they learned that he was married to his childhood sweetheart. Walton was a transfer student from Norman Park who had been a little diffident about assuming roles of leadership at Willingham. When he witnessed the furious brush fire of campus opinion against the ministerial students, however, and when he realized that publicity in the *Telegraph* destroyed any hope of maintaining the heresy movement as strictly a family scandal, he emerged with quiet authority as the symbol of resistance.

He had about him a sweet solemnity tempered with gentle humor that enabled him to approach anyone. He was possessed of so much ministerial dignity and so habitually wore a double-breasted suit that his appearance on campus without a tie would have been as rakishly improbable as a shirtless football player in Dr. Huber's classroom. Walton reasoned and pled with everyone he met not to judge all preachers by The Holy Thirteen, refraining from condemning them personally but decrying their purpose. He pushed through the Ministerial Association a resolution supporting the beleaguered professors and pointing out that the Association, by a majority of three to one, shared neither the opinions nor the goals of the thirteen non-conforming members. It was a formal document, distinguished primarily by careful dullness, but the *Telegraph* leaped upon it and printed Walton Hand's picture with it.

John Purser, splay-toothed and affectedly weary editor of the *Chanticleer,* was so challenged by Deacon Chauncey's editorial success that he reacted a bit like Saul toward David. He secured his throne, however, with a headline: "Brand the Mavericks!" Under this he printed a large picture of Walton Hand, taken by a stylish photographer in Macon, that showed the subject gazing a little upward with the fervor and sacred backlight of Galahad finally in sight of the Grail. Beneath the article he printed small photographs of The Holy Thirteen with their names typed across their chests. In case the implication they were criminals was too subliminal for some of his readers, the editor ran a simple notice as an announcement in large headline type directly below the gallery of photographs: "Post Office Closed for Holiday." It was an eyecatching example of not printing editorial opinion on the front page, and within a week John Purser had a job with the *Atlanta Constitution* to begin work there as a cub reporter right after graduation.

Dr. Wade Hampton Powell had been president of Willingham so long that his hair was a thick gray thatch and his purposeful stride had geared down to a shuffle. It was a sure and quickfooted shuffle, however, and he had lost none of the regard he enjoyed from the protean Georgia Baptist Convention or from the proprietary mammonites in the business community. Age had dimmed his eye and pinched his bladder but also had confirmed wisdom to be a measure of the impact of experience on intelligence. His mind was as quick and darting as ever.

His consuming passion, now that time had freed him from what Socrates called the Mad Master, was Willingham University and the perpetuation of its brooding benevolence. He had a nose for money and an irresistible candor in asking for it. In addition, he had an unerring judgment about which millionaire would relish a bronze bust and which would be more tempted by an honorary degree. He was particularly ingratiating to those who desired and could afford both. A new dormitory for boys was currently under construction and the funds for the first one for girls securely in hand. Both had been obtained quietly and tastefully through the efforts of Dr. Powell, and he was well content.

Students usually saw him only in chapel, where he beamingly introduced each new speaker as "loyal member of the Georgia Baptist Convention and beloved son of the Institution." Distance, in Dr. Powell's view, contributed to dignity, and he contrived this in subtle ways. Most students were unaware that the considerable respect they afforded their president stemmed partially from having to look up as he presided from the elevated stage at the compulsory chapel sessions.

When The Thirteen desecrated the tranquility of Willingham with their accusations, Dr. Powell's major concern was to preserve Eden rather than destroy the serpent. Wisdom stimulated him to placate the Georgia Baptist Convention and secure the tents of the faithful. Never so remote in an ivory tower nor so removed from the realities of religious politics as to underestimate the effect thirteen dissidents could have on literal-minded congregations across the state, and more chary of losing the reverence of the unlettered than the coins of the educated, he moved with dispatch.

It was rumored that Dr. Powell had summoned the three members of the Christianity department who had been accused of heretical and unorthodox beliefs to his office for a private conference. Speculation on campus was intense about what he would say to them.

Porter Osborne had an overwhelming interest in what would transpire. The bumbling dogma of Creed Foxmore was repugnant to him, but he had only respect for the brain of John Birch. It disturbed him that this brilliant person could repudiate Dr. Burn's reconciliation of science with religion and align himself with the likes of Creed. He could understand the conflict between Birch and Malcolm James but was confused about his own allegiance. In his confusion, he wanted to hear what was going on in higher circles. Porter took an aggressive approach to the problem on the afternoon in question. After lunch he stealthily climbed the huge, thick-leafed old magnolia tree right outside Dr. Powell's office window. He concealed himself with no trouble behind the dark foliage, snuggling his back against the gnarled trunk and sitting on a limb as great in girth as many trees. He could easily hear through the open window desultory conversation between the president and his secretary. He settled there to wait with both thrill and patience. He had fetched along a copy of *Outline of History* by H.G. Wells to help him pass the time, and he began reading. He had no taste at all for plunging into Darwin, but he rather thought that familiarity with Wells would suffice as pleasingly erudite background in the eyes of Henry Bean.

He followed the author's praise of the telescope into his defense of geology and soon became fascinated with that sweeping and simplified discourse on evolution. He became troubled and examined his own heart. He could not honestly deny the evidence of archaeologists and geologists, but it was equally inconceivable that he accept the premise of Malcolm James that the Old Testament was nothing more nor less than Jewish mythology.

He chanced to think of a textbook his sister had brought

259

home from college and that he had perused the previous summer. There was a long and tedious poem by Tennyson that had captured his attention because it had been so heavily underscored in spots by his beloved sister. A line came back to his memory from that poem.

> By faith and faith alone embrace,
> Believing where we cannot prove.

His pulse accelerated. Faith was no problem for a boy who had been Raised Right. Foxmore and Birch had no monopoly on it. His could be as valid as theirs. Porter always had felt much more at home with Faith than he had with Hope and Charity and for some time had held the opinion that Paul was misguided in his assessment of priorities among the three. Why had he not thought of Faith sooner? Another line from Tennyson occurred to him:

> There lives more faith in honest doubt,
> Believe me, than in half the creeds.

He wondered if H.G. Wells had read Alfred, Lord Tennyson. Porter certainly was glad that he had. Now he could believe the anthropologists, the geologists, the scientists, and through his faith was free also to believe the book of Genesis. Down with The Unholy Thirteen — ignorant, misguided bigots! Porter Osborne, Jr., was squarely on the side of the faculty.

A tight bladder compelled him to rise cautiously and circle around the tree where he silently relieved himself against the trunk with no telltale noise or splash. He had barely reseated himself when Dr. Powell ushered his three Christianity professors into his private office and closed the door. Porter listened spellbound as that masterful man, with brusque purpose and no guile at all, explained the facts of life as he saw them. He heard the president suggest that each professor, before leaving his presence, present him with a written confession of faith. With specificity worthy of an instructor in basic composition, he outlined for these Doctors of Divinity and Philosophy the topics of Virgin Birth, the Inspiration of Scriptures, the Atonement, the Transfiguration, and the Resurrection. Porter was impressed.

Dr. Burn finished his assignment in five minutes and tottered off for an afternoon nap. Professor Matthew Roberts had to copy his over because of two misspelled words and took fifteen minutes.

At the end of an hour in the president's office, Dr. Bozeman had wadded up six sheets of paper and was still rubbing the end of the pen against his nose. Porter clutched the magnolia limb and listened intently to Dr. Powell. He hoped they finished before he had to pee again.

"For goodness' sake, George, quit sitting there like a freshman taking a final examination and go ahead. Do it! You know what I must have when I go before the Board of Trustees; so give it to me. The very bricks of the Administration Building are threatened by this situation, and the more quietly I can handle it the better we'll all be. You've served this institution faithfully and lovingly for twenty-five years and turned out some wonderful preachers. Stop scratching your head over your own intellectual integrity and get to writing. I'll tolerate no martyrs in this incident to raise it to any noticeable level of importance."

Dr. Bozeman sighed. "Hamp Powell, I've admired you too long to sabotage your work now, and I know what you mean. I hate to knuckle under to that bunch of fanatics, for they don't have enough brains between them to fill a fifth of a firkin. Now, wouldn't that phrase set old Foxmore slobbering over the Bible?

"You know, Hamp, that Birch boy bothers me. He's brilliant. He's read Freud, Kierkegaard, St. Augustine, Proust; you name it. If he could just come to terms with the fact that the Kingdom of Heaven really is within him, there's no telling what he could do. I fear he's riding his own heart to self-destruction. He wrestles with demons. Oh, well, God knows I did all I could to reach him."

He wrote purposefully for two pages. "There you are, old friend, and you're welcome. It was a real temptation not to expound a bit on what most Baptists *think* they believe about the Atonement. You don't by any chance want my opinion on how many angels will fit on the point of a pin, do you? Lots of luck on your Endowment Fund."

He rose. "One word of counsel, Hamp. Don't let the Board chide those thirteen students or the Administration punish them in any fashion whatsoever. You're absolutely right about the perils

261

inherent in martyrdom. I myself have just tasted the frustration of withholding it from someone who seeks it."

As the president ushered Dr. Bozeman out with an arm across his shoulder, Porter skinned down the magnolia tree and streaked across campus. He realized that he also did not have a monopoly on faith.

Dr. Powell requested no similar testimony from the other professors accused and indeed made little reference to their indictments, thus implying that those charges were of small consequence and only mild annoyance. There was no doubt that Wade Hampton Powell regarded his Christianity department as the heart and guts of Willingham University.

He called an emergency meeting of his Board of Trustees and produced in triumph the three reassuringly orthodox handwritten professions of faith. He requested that a special committee be appointed to investigate the heresy charges and make recommendations back to the Board. He asked that this be done as quickly and quietly as possible.

Mrs. Raleigh prinked her mouth and told Porter, "I tell you one thing, that Dr. Hamp Powell is one more fine Christian gentleman. On top of that, he sure knows which side he's buttered on."

Henry Bean had misgivings. "They're having a closed hearing. Nobody allowed in the room but the accusers, the accused, and witnesses, and they're having it tomorrow. I'm worried about Malcolm James. Different groups of students have circulated petitions supporting all the full professors, but they've left James standing all alone. Those stupid student preachers have him accused of teaching evolution and of being an atheist. He says he's never had any personal contact at all with any of The Thirteen except John Birch. He's played tennis with him and beats him every time. Says the only discussions he's ever had with him were sorta inconsequential stuff about Darwin and Freud. James says he hated to even consider that degree of pettiness, but he thinks the real reason he's on the list is Birch's weak backhand. I think I'll register as a witness for him."

"What in the world do you plan to say?"

"I'll play it by ear."

"If you tell them what he said when he was drinking beer with you, they'll hang him higher than Haman. Especially that part about the Virgin Birth."

"For God's sake, I'm not a Judas. I'll think of something. I'm sure not going to tell them he drank beer. I've got sense enough to know that around here that's as great a sin as blaspheming the Holy Ghost, whatever that is."

"You could ask Creed Foxmore. I bet he could tell you."

"And you could kiss my ass, Osborne. Shut up, will you? This has gotten serious." Porter decided not to bring up H.G. Wells right then. He did not want to distract Henry Bean.

The investigating Committee convened in the small chapel of the Christianity Building at the firm but unpublicized insistence of Dr. Powell. This location of the hearings further emphasized the importance of the three Christianity professors in the accusations. In addition, it gave them the advantage of being interviewed on their home turf, where they could benefit from the security generated by years of familiarity and authority. The chairman immediately announced that they would work without interruption until their assignment was completed and blithely requested that sandwiches be sent in at lunch time if, he said, they were there that late. The testimony of the students, however, was lengthier than anticipated, and the questions of the committee members were sometimes involved.

The hearing lasted from nine in the morning until 11:30 at night, an unforeseen hardship to which the stubborn chairman would not bow. An ongoing problem throughout the ordeal centered around the fact that there was only one commode in the Christianity Building. Three of the committee members were past seventy and subservient to petulant prostates. This necessitated frequent utilization of the single antiquated facility and also demanded an inordinate length of time for equally antiquated performance. The septuagenarians not only missed in repetitive succession some interesting tidbits of testimony but also were under considerable stress as time wore on not to voice unchristian and acrimonious intolerance for each other's common infirmity.

Mrs. Raleigh sent bologna sandwiches and potato salad for

lunch, and when told that supper also would be required, she considered her budget carefully and sent the trustees of Willingham University the standard Sunday night fare of her students. Each received a sack with an apple, a banana, and two packets of crackers — one vanilla and the other peanut butter malted. Inspired by the importance of the occasion, with unexpected largesse she also had Boston Harbor Jones deliver a four-layer cake which she had baked that afternoon and decorated with the school colors — orange and black. The cake was light and moist and would melt in one's mouth. The icing was unique. Around the upper margin was written, "Even so as ye have done it;" across the center was, "Save our teachers;" and curving beneath this was, "Do unto others."

During the temporary diversion of the evening meal, one of the committee members made a silent resolve to canvass his church membership for funds to expand the toilet facilities of the Christianity Building. The chairman, a distinguished jurist accustomed by decades of prosperity to gourmet dining, munched a peanut butter cracker while contemplating the orange and black cake and vowed to himself that, God willing, he would do something about meals for the boys of Willingham.

By mid-afternoon small groups of students were scattered around the building where the hearing was being held. They were quiet and orderly, but their patient presence was proof of interest. They shifted kaleidoscopically around the steps of the Library, the back of the Chapel, the front of the Law Building, and even the lawn behind the Administration Building. Students came and went, drifting from one group to another, quietly swapping anecdotes about favorite professors or relating the latest vagary in the ranks of The Thirteen.

At four o'clock Henry Bean emerged from the hearing and found Porter. "Let's go to the Co-op for a drink. I thought I'd die trying not to laugh before I got out of there. When I left, old Judge Henderson was knocking on the restroom door like a yellowhammer. He's a deacon at Mulberry Baptist and so dignified everybody at the country club automatically gets quiet for a minute when he shows up for Sunday dinner. His own preacher, the Right Reverend High and Exalted Dr. Ezekiel Hammonds, was in the john, and I heard the Judge trying to whisper loud enough to be heard through the door,

264

'Consarn it, Zeke, open up. If you can't pee, let somebody in there who can.' "

"How's Malcolm James coming out?"

"Pretty good, I think. The ones they're really after are the Christianity profs, it looks like to me. The committee ruffled through some papers and asked me if I'd ever heard Mr. James discuss evolution."

"What'd you tell em?"

"I told them I sure had. And then I said he had told me in a private conversation that these were only theories Darwin had advanced, that there was no real scientific proof for any of them, that there were certainly no duplicatable experiments outlined, and that it might be a million years before there was any proof one way or the other. Said James told me it was an interesting theory and nothing else."

"Golly, how'd that sit with them?"

"Well, one of the preachers asked me if I'd ever heard Mr. James make any statement that indicated a conflict between his dedication to science and orthodox Christian beliefs. I tried to remember how you widen your eyes when you talk conservation to 'Fessor Hansford, and I told him that Malcolm James had volunteered to me that Christian codes were the best rules to live by in the history of mankind, and that Mr. James had done more for my Christian faith than any other man at Willingham, including all the illustrious speakers we had in chapel. And that was it. The chairman of that committee is a lawyer, and he said, 'Thank you for coming, Mr. Bean. You may step down.' I'm in a chair not six feet from him and on the same level, and he tells me to 'step down!' Lawyers can really be pompous bastards, but I feel better about James."

"I reckon you do. I've got a colored friend I'd like to have talk to you about the whole truth and the nothing but. You came mighty close to lying, Henry."

"I'd have lied outright if I needed to. I told you how disillusioned I got with the damn communists here in Macon, but I was ready to follow one of their tenets today. Sometimes the end does justify the means. Have you ever watched John Birch's mouth when he talks? That extra flap of mucous membrane turns wrongside out against his upper teeth and looks for all the world like a horse

265

cleaning its ass."

The committee dismissed its witnesses and concluded its hearing near midnight. It announced that it would reconvene the next morning to divulge its findings. At ten o'clock the following day, their chairman called them to order, again banning any outsiders from attendance. The first order of business was sending a message to Mrs. Raleigh that they would need no lunch that day. Then the chairman announced that the plumbing, regrettably, was out of order. There was a sign on the restroom door announcing this catastrophe. Within a rapid hour they had reached unanimity and drafted their findings.

Their recommendations to the Board of Trustees were that no one was culpable, that the professors were innocent of the charges leveled against them, that the thirteen students probably were agitated by some vaguely influential but unnamed outsiders and were themselves misguided and innocent boys, that the best interest of Willingham University would be served by speedily forgetting this investigation and its antecedent events. The committee thanked Mrs. Estelle Raleigh for her gracious and solicitous attention to its gustatory needs, and said that Dr. George Bozeman was to be commended for his unflagging zeal in promulgating Christian doctrine in his department.

The subcommittee of the executive committee of the Board of Trustees of Willingham University, created to investigate charges of heresy and unorthodoxy against certain professors and to recommend action back to the full Board of Trustees, fulfilled its function, disbanded itself, and emerged from the Christianity Building at precisely 11:25.

Dr. Ezekiel Hammond, portly and silver-haired pastor of the most prestigious church in central Georgia, led the hegira. Unaware of the impaired plumbing, he had consumed more coffee that morning than was his custom. He ignored salutations from the students, almost rudely brushed by the reporter from the *Telegraph*, and moved with an alacrity unusual for his age and build down the brick walkway to the Biology Building next door.

As he disappeared through its portal, Sybil Swygert exclaimed, "Isn't he precious? He's going to congratulate 'Fessor Hansford and Malcolm James on being exonerated."

266

Henry Bean murmured, "Purity of heart, Osborne, is to will one thing. The old goat's got to piss."

After lunch Boston Harbor Jones told Porter, "Hoo, sho was a lotta ruckus over much-o-nothing, but I'm glad all them teachers come clear. What you doing climbing through that Christianity window bout daylight with that sign under yo arm, Sambo?"

"Boston, you don't miss a trick, do you? I hung it on the toilet door and messed up the commode. Then I turned off the water to it. If you ever tell on me, I'll probably get expelled."

The campus rapidly settled back to normal, but there was an affinity between the Ministerial Association and the rest of the student body that previously had been absent. Everyone treated the rebellious thirteen with the disinterested formality evinced toward obnoxious third cousins at a family reunion. Porter Osborne confided in Henry Bean. "You know, Henry, the answer to this whole controversy is nothing new. It's age-old. The answer is faith."

"Faith? Faith, Osborne? You're forever prattling about it. Come off that crap."

Porter stood his ground. He had H.G. Wells and Alfred, Lord Tennyson both behind him. "Well, Henry, you know what faith is, don't you?"

"You mighty right I know what faith is. It's believing something you know goddamn well ain't so."

Porter recoiled. "Henry, you have too good a vocabulary to stoop to swearing. I really wish you wouldn't take the Lord's name in vain."

"I'll be damned. I'm still watching, Osborne. Waiting and watching."

Porter postponed H.G. Wells to yet another day and felt that insofar as Tennyson was concerned, he would as soon discuss Kappa Alpha Order with Henry Bean.

He changed the subject. "I'm not sure I understand something you said last week. Just what's the difference between a zealot and a fanatic?"

"Intelligence, Osborne, intelligence. Speaking of which, I ran into James again last night. Said he was grateful and wanted to buy me a beer in absolution for expedient mendacity, which, he said, is only a venal sin and quite common in the upper levels of his church. Said he needed a little penance himself for petty vengeance.

"He invited John Birch to play tennis yesterday and beat him three sets, every game love. When they finished, he shook hands and told Birch he was sorry his Rhodes scholarship had fallen through and asked him what he planned to do now after graduation. Birch looked at him right steady and said the Japanese are desecrating Manchuria and that he may go over there as a missionary to the Chinese. He said, 'After all, James, I can speak the language.' James said he had such an arrogant tone in his voice that he couldn't help shooting back, 'I hope *they* can understand you. I surely don't.' "

The following week Dr. Wade Hampton Powell beamed down from his great height in chapel at the student body. He introduced Dr. George Bozeman as a faithful and ardent laborer in the vineyard of the Lord, beloved son of the institution, pillar of Willingham University, and announced that he would speak on the Transfiguration. The very utterance of the topic produced hooded eyes and an anticipatory somnolence in every listener present.

Dr. Bozeman brought everyone to the edge of the seat with his opening statement. "There is a line in Holy Writ, 'Gray hairs are upon him here and there, and he knoweth it not.' I have no desire whatsoever to place either you or myself in the tedious position of knowing this and not acknowledging it. That would be as deplorable as the fate of the great king of whom it was said, 'Now David was old, and he gat no heat.' Neither do I aspire to emulate Moses, who died on the plain of Moab at age one-hundred-twenty and had it recorded of him, 'His eye was not dim, nor were his natural forces abated.'

"I have served this school for over twenty-five years, and the school in turn has served me well. My students have been both challenging and comforting. They have been stimulating and loving. You are all that a man, a scholar, a teacher, a Christian could ask for. I thank you for the fulfillment you have afforded me. I shall give formal notice of my resignation to our friend, Dr. Powell, and to the Board of Trustees later, but I wanted you students to hear it first from me. After this quarter, I am leaving Willingham University."

268

The silence in the Chapel was complete. In the expectant hush, Dr. Bozeman's words were clear. "I leave with a heart full of gratitude and love, and I hope to continue serving the cause of Christ with voice and pen so long as I shall live. My association with the Administration has been gratifying, and I am most appreciative of all the unswerving confidence bestowed on me by your president and for his unfaltering loyalty under all circumstances.

"My contacts with you young people have afforded me unspeakable joy. Your affection and your responsiveness have been a constant anointing. You will live in my heart forever. Good-bye."

As Dr. Bozeman turned to his seat and President Powell rose to regain the lectern, Sybil Swygert leaped from her numbered seat on the floor of the Chapel and gave a beautiful skirt-flaring twirl in the aisle, her page-boy bob swinging like an aureole around her head. Before President Powell could fill his opened mouth with words, Sybil took over the Chapel. She was not a cheerleader for nothing.

"All together, now, let's hear it for Dr. Bozeman! Hip, hip, hooray! Hip, hip, hooray! Hip, hip, hooray!"

The entire student body rose and, in the sanctified old Chapel of Willingham, clapped, yelled, stamped, and whistled in the most effusive demonstration ever seen therein. Dr. Powell raised his hand for quiet but was ignored. The demonstration was so loud and lengthy that Hamp Powell finally pronounced the benediction and led the faculty off stage. No one heard his closing prayer except the Lord.

That was the day chapel lasted only ten minutes. The Board of Trustees, when it accepted Dr. Bozeman's resignation, voted him a retirement allowance of one hundred dollars monthly for the rest of his life.

Mrs. Raleigh bridled as she primly told Porter, "The Lord's will, and God moves, and man looks on the outside, and judge not and all that, but it does seem to me like the students who stirred up got off scot-free. An unmarried man like Dr. Bozeman will do well on that much money; it's not like he had three children and the widow's mite to raise them on. But no one will ever believe he would of quit right now if it hadn't of been for those holy ones. Oh, I could tell him a thing about hardship if he would just ask. It's not fair for those thirteen not to suffer, though."

She leaned forward in a confidential manner, blinked sparse-lashed eyes, and arched her neck. "Suffering's good for you, Porter. It builds character and tempers your fiber and toughens your steel and prepares you for the evil days to come."

Creed Foxmore, two weeks after the hearing, circulated around the campus as though nothing had happened. He was apparently unaware that any esteem in which he previously had been held was now practically non-existent. He plodded with a deter-mined air of business as usual toward his goal of saving the students of Willingham.

Lila Hadley was a town student who even in her freshman year was already regarded on campus as a cherished eccentric. Daughter of an old and prominent family, she was the repository of so many generations of good manners that she was blissfully secure in her possession of them and consequently could ignore them when she chose. She moved around Willingham like a princess with her mind on higher things. She made average grades but had been known to leave a classroom halfway through a lecture because she suddenly discovered it was not where she was supposed to be. She had pledged ADPi but had to be politely ushered out of a Phi Mu meeting one afternoon. She did much better when she remembered to wear her glasses.

Bob Cater was of the opinion that Lila's glasses were responsi-ble for most of her aura and some of her personality. "Hell, she's not stuck-up. She can't *see*. Those glasses are so thick they make you think you're looking at her eyes through the wrong end of bin-oculars, and they're so heavy I don't know how she can hold them on her nose. She can't see six inches without them and no more than fifteen with them."

Lila was a graduate of Miller High and affected the uniform — at least down to her waist. She always wore a cashmere sweater of proper pastel hue, and she was proportioned to wear it arrestingly. Her hair, when she remembered to remove the bobby pins and comb it, was of the conventional length and curl, and her lipstick was

270

redder and applied more lavishly on her beautifully chiseled lips than any other girl's.

From the waist down, however, Lila was charitably designated a disaster, and Bob Cater may have been correct when he surmised it was because she could not see that far. She always wore at school a brown skirt of indeterminate shape and uneven length that her sorority sisters considered had probably belonged to her mother but that the Phi Mu's asserted was a hand-me-down from the Hadley cook. All the other girls wore saddle oxfords with neatly arranged socks, but Lila appeared in sweat-stiffened moccasins that were always eating up her socks to the point that her heels were bare.

Her unpredictability was one of the most tantalizing facets about Lila. If one chanced on her some morning with her hair rolled up, thick glasses askew, ignoring salutations while she muttered and fretted over finding her proper classroom on time, it was easy to dismiss her as a slovenly and uninteresting frump. If one encountered her on a well-organized day with her sleek blonde hair gently bouncing in rhythm to her stride, even white teeth framed redly by perfect lips, it was impossible to pass her by. If she also chanced to remove her glasses on that day, no male at Willingham could maintain his composure, for without her glasses Lila Hadley had the most irresistibly beautiful face in Macon. Her eyes were deep violet pools in which a boy could surely drown and care not. Even the most experienced of Willingham males were known to yammer incomprehensibly when Lila turned her unshielded gaze upon them, intelligent conversation plummeting to the very lowest of priorities.

Swinging into the Co-op on one of her good days in late spring, left hip balancing her load of books in the same exaggeration of tilt young mothers use to carry a heavy child, Lila was approached by Creed Foxmore. "Are you saved, sister?"

She peered at him carefully through her sight-bestowing prisms.

"I mean, have you accepted the Lord Jesus Christ as your personal Savior?"

Lila with deliberate care placed her books on the window ledge and moved to even closer scrutiny of her interrogator. "Aren't you that horribly silly man who had all those just terrible things to say about Professor Twilley and Dr. Wright? Don't you open your mouth

271

to me again, you slimy old fool, or I'll slap you clean to Texas!"

As the astonished Creed gazed at her in disbelief, she carefully removed her glasses and placed them on her books. "We've heard about people like you in church. You're nothing but a false prophet and don't have any business in this school anyhow."

Creed took a deep breath and looked with disbelief and fading resistance into those beautiful eyes. He discarded any idea of winning this encounter and abandoned the field of battle in his customary manner. He crossed his feet, stretched out his arms, and bowed his head.

"Well, I never," Lila murmured in amazement.

Quick as a striking snake, she stood on tiptoe and kissed Creed Foxmore squarely on his mouth, taking care to smear her painted lips across his cheek and his starched white collar. When the startled Creed reflexively lowered his arms, he was momentarily and quite involuntarily embracing a most active female. Lila shouted at the top of her head-turning voice, "Take your hands off my ... QUIT, FOOL!"

At the same time she reached up with scarlet-tipped, file-sharpened fingernails and raked bleeding gashes down Creed's manly cheeks. Then she screamed. And screamed and screamed. The uproar in the Co-op was tremendous. Everyone converged on the pair, and in the hubbub Creed Foxmore bolted out the door, high-stepping as a frightened horse.

Lila was quickly and easily consoled and directed one of her rescuers, "Hand me my glasses, please."

Creed Foxmore was never seen in the Co-op again and indeed, for some reason not divulged by the Administration, requested and received his diploma in absentia.

Henry Bean told Porter, "Hell, no, Lila Hadley doesn't march to a different drummer, Osborne. I'm not sure she hears a drum.

"If she hears anything, it's tambourines, and nobody can march to them. You can't do anything but dance to tambourines, and the likes of us will never catch the rhythm.

"I just wish she'd tangled with John Birch, too."

e.V. Derrick knocked on Porter's door. "Whatcha doing, Sonny Boy?"

"Studying for finals."

"They're not till next week. You'll forget everything before then. No sense in doing it twice."

"I never forget. I can't stand that unsure feeling of waiting till the last minute and then cramming. Besides, I want to do well in history. That old Englishman who teaches it is a pretty sharp fellow when you get past his talking like he has a mouth full of boiled egg."

"You know you'll make an A."

Porter rocked his chair back on its legs and stretched his arms above his head. "No, I don't. You know what he said the other day about Hitler? He said that in spite of the unfavorable press and regardless of whether we Americans approve of what Hitler's doing and granting that what he's pulled in Austria and Czechoslovakia is deplorable, you can't get around what he's done for Germany."

"And just what does Major Jones-Bethune think Hitler has done for Germany?"

"Well, he's paved all the roads for one thing, which is more than we've done in Georgia, but Major Jones-Bethune says the most remarkable thing is that in less than two decades Germany has come from the very bottom of the heap to be a formidable world power again. The major says this is all the more astounding (you know how he talks) because Hitler, one would have supposed, was an insignificant, opportunistic little chap with no qualities of leadership whatsoever."

"Sonny Boy, I didn't come over here to talk about Hitler and Germany."

"Yeah, I know. But Major Jones-Bethune says they'll never get past the French this time anyway because of something called the Maginot Line. What are you up to?"

E.V. surveyed Porter studiously for several moments and then spoke in overly-solemn tones. "Sonny Boy, have you ever crapped in a shoe box?"

"Have I what? Certainly not. Whatever for?"

"I have this perfectly good shoe box. It's strong and tight. To tell you the truth, it's probably one of the best shoe boxes ever made anywhere. It's a shame to waste it."

"What in the world do you plan to do with it?"

E.V. still did not smile, but his eyes had a lurking twinkle. "I lined it with wax paper and took a dump in it."

"That was a fool thing to do. Why'd you do that?"

"I sort of thought Spangler and Roundtree need a house-warming present. They've moved into a room in that big old two-story house on the park, you know, and we could tell em we're bringing a box of cookies from home."

"E.V., you're crazy. They'd never believe that."

"They would till they got the lid off, and by then the house would sure be plenty warmed."

Porter bent again over his books and said in dismissing tones, "You go ahead with that crazy caper if you want to. I'd rather study."

"But Sonny Boy, I need for you to crap in the box for me."

Walking later across the porch of Nottingham Hall, E.V. amazed Porter by behaving as though they were on the most ordinary of errands. "You wouldn't have studied much anyhow, wondering how ole Spangler and Roundtree were enjoying their present. I'm going to tell em it's a box of cookies Clarence's sister made for them and that she couldn't find them and asked me to deliver it. And I promise not to sing while we walk."

"While ago you said the box wasn't heavy enough, but now I think it's too heavy for just cookies."

"I'll tell em there's different kinds — brownies on the bottom, then ice box cookies, then oatmeal, and then teacakes on top."

"I still don't think they'll believe you for a minute." Porter was worrying about the success of the mission now that he was involved.

E.V. considered for only a moment and calmly responded, "I tell you what we'll do, Sonny Boy. We'll just stop off here at the Libry and have a dress rehearsal. Brother Skip Brannon's working the desk tonight and we'll try the cookies out on him."

"I don't think we ought to do that. He's probably still a little disappointed about not getting elected president of the fraternity."

"Well, that's your fault. This ought to cheer him up."

Porter jerked his head in indignation. "It certainly is not my fault. I voted for him. I still think he's a great guy and should have gotten it."

"That's not what I mean. You and he are probably the only two who did vote for him. Let's tell him his girlfriend sent him the cookies."

"We still ought not to do that. You're not supposed to make any noise in the Library. We might get him in trouble."

"We'll whisper. There's nothing sacred about the Libry. Come on."

"He's not going to believe us."

Skip Brannon looked up with friendly but serious mien at the approach of his two younger fraternity brothers. E.V. placed the shoe box, tantalizing corners of waxed paper showing beneath its lid, in the center of the counter. "We were on our way to the drugstore and Dottie Applewhite asked us if we'd bring this box in to you because she was in a hurry. Said it was something she'd made for you just this afternoon. It's still warm, she said."

"Oh, boy," came back in a coarse whisper. "She makes the best pineapple upside-down cake in the world. If that's what it is, I'll give you fellows a piece."

When he snatched off the lid and gazed at the contents, Skip's skin suddenly resembled green alabaster. His grin froze and he raised disbelieving eyes to Porter's gaze. Porter knew that the reproach in those eyes would live with him forever. When the aroma of the cookies reached Skip, he grabbed his mouth with both hands and fled into the stacks. Porter fled to the outdoors.

E.V. Derrick methodically replaced the lid on the shoe box, tucked it casually under his arm, and tiptoed with exemplary poise

275

through the Library. He nodded in detached politeness at absorbed students who raised disinterested glances to his passage.

Outside, Porter was nervously prancing. "E.V., they will believe us, too. Let's don't go."

"Don't be silly, Sonny Boy. You know Clarence and Slick will remember this experience the rest of their lives. Have you ever thought about the strange power you have over Brother Brannon?"

"I don't know what you're talking about."

"Every time you get around him, he vomits. That's quite a gift, Sonny Boy."

"Oh, you go to hell. I'm sort of sick at my own stomach. Anyhow, I'm not going to Spangler and Roundtree's. I don't want to stand around and hear them call each other 'old lady.' "

"Sure you're going, Sonny Boy. If you're going to be a doctor, you can't be squeamish about things like this shoe box. You have to harden yourself. Besides, lots of roommates call each other 'old lady.' Come on."

When they entered the house where their fraternity brothers had rented a room and started up the stairs to the second floor, Porter spoke to the white-haired lady who appeared in the back of the hall to watch their passage. The more citified E.V. Derrick ignored her. They found Clarence and Slick in a cavernous room with high ceiling, long windows, a fireplace, one double bed, and a study table apiece.

Porter looked around and thought that the two had not really bettered themselves. A carpet with tired threads worn through faded pattern covered most of the floor. Ecru curtains one year past washing lofted turgidly in the breeze from the open windows and smelled of mildew. E.V. placed the offering on a study table with the explanation that Clarence's sister had been unable to find his new dwelling and had asked him to deliver it for her. She was with some other girls and had to get back to Bessie Tift.

Slick Roundtree crowded in, eagerly bending over the table and the box. "God, this is a gift from Heaven! I'm starving to death and didn't have the money to go to the drugstore. Make haste and open it, old lady."

Clarence's laugh boomed out. "Stand back there, old lady. Whose box is this, anyhow? I'll do the honors here.... SON OF A BITCH!"

Both of them leaped in recoil to the center of the room. E.V. and Porter guffawed, slapping their thighs and choking. Slick Roundtree was the first to recover. Beginning with little half-hearted sputters like a Model-T cranking on a cold morning, he soon roared into full-throated laughter and pointed a finger at Clarence. "You sure did the honors all right, old lady. You never told me what a good cook your sister was."

Clarence evinced not the slightest hint of amusement. "Don't call me 'old lady' any more. And don't mention my sister again with the lid off that box."

Suddenly he picked up the open box, holding it gingerly beneath the bottom with a large hand. He grabbed Porter by the shirt front with his other hand and discovered humor in the situation. "You little prick, you've been chapping my ass all year. Now you're fixing to catch it."

His braying laugh filled the room. He pushed Porter backward, holding the shoe box at a threatening angle that gave his victim an all-too-vivid view of its contents. He laughed. E.V. and Slick laughed. Porter's shoulders touched the edge of the mantel and he knew he could back no further. He was cornered. He was dominated. He was doomed.

"Right in your face, Osborne, right in your face is where it's going!"

There was absolutely no doubt in Porter's mind that Clarence was going to consummate his threat. He had nothing to lose. With desperation he kicked Spangler in the shin and simultaneously made a grab for the shoe box. It was not an article any reasonable person would squeeze or tug, and Clarence released it.

Oblivious to the consequences of gravity or centrifugal force, Porter frantically swung the burdened box around his head, its end yielding somewhat but not tearing. "Stand back there, sir, or I'll turn it loose!"

Of a sudden Porter had reversed his role. He was now master of the situation and of the entire room. E. V. and Slick stampeded into the one closet and pulled the door safely shut. Clarence tried to join them, but the shoe box was still circling in Porter's grasp, and his friends would not open the door wide enough to admit him. With a rolling eye, Clarence looked over his shoulder at the incipient missile, gave a bellow, and dived headlong under the bed. Porter was a conqueror surveying an abandoned battlefield.

He gently slowed the shoe box, warped but still intact, and walked to the door. "You can come out of the closet, E.V., and we'll go. Nobody else better move."

At the foot of the stairs, Porter noticed the white-haired lady in the back of the hall again and passed the lidless box to E.V. The lady took a step forward, drew a breath as though to speak, and hastily clamped a handkerchief over her face.

Porter spoke in clear tones to his descending friend. "E.V. Derrick, I don't know why I let you talk me into things. You let them blame me for this and didn't even try to help me."

"It's not my fault. You've been in so much that people automatically blame you if you're around when something happens. And when you think about what you and Spangler were fighting with, there wasn't a man on earth who would have helped you."

He stopped in the front yard. "Sonny Boy, I'm afraid you've ruined my shoe box. What with all that jerking and twirling, it's plumb out of shape. Besides, you left the lid upstairs. Well, I guess we won't ever be able to use it for anything again. No use to save it. Stand back."

He passed the loaded box like a football toward the lighted window above. The heavier contents struck the screen, the shoe box fell away into the shrubbery below, and Porter watched the cookies slide slowly to rest on the window ledge. It was just first dark, and the lightning bugs were winking in the lower darknesses of the porch around the magnolia trees.

"Let's go, E.V. I've got to study that history. If I ever go anywhere with you again, I hope the Good Lord will punish me good."

The following day Boston Harbor Jones stopped him after

278

lunch. "Wait up a minute there, Sambo. I know you got lab and you in a hurry and I won't go into all that bidness bout where you go last night, who you with, and what you do. We skip all that cause I know. I tell you longer I live less I understand you white boys. Ain't no colored alive get in no scrape like you in last night. I believe I rather deal with liquor and straight razors. If I get you through college I gonna be plumb grayheaded. What I gotta tell you is you stay plumb away from Spangler and Roundtree. Don't you go bout they house no more. They after you, Sambo."

"Well, I don't know why. It was all Derrick's idea, and at least I didn't mess up their room. Nothing happened, really."

"Uh huh. At's what you think. Plenty happen when yall leave. Slick come dragging in this morning late to his dishwashing job and Mrs. Raleigh jump him. First off she smile real sweet at him, you know, and twist her neck sorta off to one side like she do and give little speech about 'dillar, a dollar.' Then she turn the smile off and really hoe down on him. Say tardiness next to godliness or some such and then say effen he don't want his job to let her know cause she know plenty what do and some of them prolly more deserving than him anyhow for they candle only burnt on one side. Slick a smart boy, and he just yes-ma'am her real nice and don't talk back, but he cold let me hold it when she gone.

"He say when you and Derrick leave out last night Spangler poke his head out from under the bed like a turkle waking up and say, 'Is they gone?' They hurry out to catch you but run into they landlady and she dress em down good bout effen they cain't have guestes what gentlemen they can't have no guestes atall in her house. They say yessum a heap and go back to study. But Slick say the odor so strong he can't study and he go on to bed.

"He sleep next to the window and he say longer he lay there seem like stouter the smell get. He finely get up and go vomick and Spangler laugh at him and Slick try lay back down again but still can't sleep on account the stink. Then he get mad. He say to Spangler two can play this game. Spangler keep on studying over in the corner, but Slick scratch around in the closet and find hisself a shoe box. Put it in the middle of the floor and hunker down. Say he deliver some cookies his own self up to Nottingham Hall, by God. Then two bad things happen. First off, turnt out Slick's stomach tore up like a calf with the scours, and second, he miss the box.

"Hoo whee, hit was a terrible fix to be in, Slick say. He have to scrub that rug like crazy to git it cleaned up and all time Clarence laughing at him. Slick done heave till he wore out. Finely they both goes to bed and soon as the lights out Slick see how come he ain't been able to lay on his side the bed. Say all them cookies in a wad on the window ledge. Him and Clarence try to get the screen loose to push it off but ole screen nailed in tight.

"They sneak downstairs and Slick git on Clarence's shoulders, he stout as a bull, you know, and reach up with a stick and scrape it off. Then you know what? It fall slap down Clarence's front and he jump back and Slick commence to falling and they both land in they landlady's abelia bushes and break em up bad, and Slick say it was hell! He say doo-doo everwhere. Don't know *what* to tetch. It was everwhere!

"They go back upstairs and wash off real good and then clamb back in bed. Still stink. Slick say he decide close the window but then the room so hot they might nigh smother to death and they both ain't hardly sleep all night, what with heaving and sweating. That's how come he late to dishwashing. And him and Clarence blaming you for all of it and low they catch you round they place again they half kill you."

Porter tried to stop laughing. "Boston, I can't believe all that happened."

"It happen, Sambo. That the most red-eye white boy I ever see. And might nigh the maddest."

"Well, I want you to know I really am innocent this time. It was all Derrick's idea. All I did was help fill up the shoe box."

"Uh huh. I ain't doubt you word, Sambo, but I ain't got the time nor yet the stomach to listen to the particulars. I don't ever want to hear em. You gotta go to lab. I just wanted tell you stay away from them boys' house. As Mrs. Raleigh liable to say, 'A stitch in time is a penny saved.' "

"Boston, I don't think even Mrs. Raleigh would say that, but thanks for the warning. I sure don't need to go back to see those guys anyhow."

"You know, you bout to get right good list places in Macon where you ain't got no bidniss going. Bye, now."

* * * *

Just at dark that evening, E.V. Derrick interrupted Porter's studying again. Bob Cater was in the Library, and Porter had locked the door as precaution against surprise or revenge.

"Hi, E.V. You hear about what all happened last night after we left?"

"Brother Spangler did mention to me that things got a little confused in their room. I'm not real sure they appreciated their housewarming, but then the world seems to be full of ungrateful people. Let's go to the drugstore, Sonny Boy."

"No, sir. I haven't lost anything at the drugstore, and besides, I don't want to run into Spangler and Roundtree until they've had time to cool off. You shouldn't, either."

"Aw, come on, Sonny Boy. Even if we run into them, they can't do anything in the drugstore. And we'll go the long way around through the park so they won't see us from their house. I'm gonna set you up to a Coke because I feel kinda bad about you catching all the blame last night."

"You're gonna buy somebody else a Coke? That's a red-letter event I can't resist. But we're not going to stay and shoot any bull with anybody. I've got to be back here in no more than thirty minutes."

They walked to the far corner of the campus and entered the park by the least-used of its paths.

"It's kinda spooky down here. But doesn't the Administration Building look good from this angle, sticking up in the sky like that? It has one light in it. Look. I guess that's Major Jones-Bethune's apartment."

"Yeah, it is. You ever been in his apartment, Sonny Boy? He ever invite you in for tea?"

"No."

"It's kinda strange. He does his own cooking in there and gives you something called crystallized ginger to eat while he's making the tea. It looks like candy but it's hot as pepper. He has a big box of kitchen matches with a sign he pasted on it that says, 'Don't take two if one will do.' He reads you poetry and the Bible, and the whole place smells like ginger and oatmeal and hard-boiled eggs every time you go. It's sorta crazy."

"Why do you get invited in?"

"I guess he likes me. Seems like he kind of handpicks a favorite student every year, and I'm his favorite German student. Then too, he's a pretty lonesome old fellow and likes some company now and then. I feel sort of sorry for him. Anyhow, it's an easy way to be sure you're gonna get a good German grade."

Porter's tone was virtuous but carefully devoid of accusation. "That's A-K-ing."

"Well, we can't all be geniuses and make A by studying. I need all the help I can get, Sonny Boy. Don't ever go to walk with the Major, though."

"Why?"

"Because he'll walk your legs off. Those English think a five-mile hike is just a brisk little stroll. He's skinny and got those big hairy knees and is always wearing shorts, but he's strong as a mule. He'll wear you out."

There was a rustle of magnolia leaves in the dark. Porter stopped abruptly. "What's that?"

"I don't hear anything, Sonny Boy. We'll cut back across to the drugstore when we get to the middle up here."

From the blackest of the shadows two swift and silent figures leaped out and grabbed Porter. Before he could even yell, he was pummeled to the ground. Slick and Clarence were strong and they were determined. Despite squirming and futile kicking, Porter soon was stripped naked, his clothes and shoes tossed in a dim pile near the edge of the path. Only then did Spangler's teeth flash forth and Roundtree's nervous laugh peal out.

"Gotcha, by God!"

"Yeah, and just wait till we're done with you!"

Porter looked reproachfully at E.V. He was bewildered. "E.V., you set me up, all right, but not to any Coke. Why'd you do this?"

"Well, Sonny Boy, you know we have to try to get along with the president of the fraternity."

"I'll get you, E.V."

"Ah, shut up. You ain't in any position to get anybody. Hand me that brick and that string, old lady."

"You know what we're going to do with this, Brother

Osborne? We've got twenty feet of binder twine tied to this brick. We're going to tie the other end around your nuts and Brother Spangler is going to throw that brick as hard as he can."

Porter relaxed a little. Indignity was still terrible, but his fear ebbed. He had heard of this old hazing trick and knew that a confederate always cut the string just as the brick was tossed. He resolved to be as dignified as he could while standing buck naked in Tatnall Square Park with his arms pinioned behind him. After all, these were his fraternity brothers.

"You fellows don't scare me."

"We don't want to scare you. It's pain we're after. Hold him tight, Slick. The little bastard's nuts are little but his dong you wouldn't believe. I'm gonna tie the string around the whole works."

"OK, Osborne, all set? E.V. will take your clothes back to the dormitory. I'm sure anybody smart as you are won't have any trouble getting home naked. You ready? Here we go! The next shit you smell will be your own."

Spangler arched his left arm and launched the projectile with all the might he could muster. Roundtree released Porter's arms and sprang backward. Porter stood calmly and waited in relaxed confidence for the thud of the separated brick. Instead, the slack in the string suddenly gave way to tautness. Suffering unbearable pain in his groin, he was yanked off his feet. As he groveled and rolled in the gravel of the path, he realized that the scream ringing in the air came from his throat. The mocking laughter growing ever fainter belonged to his fleeing brothers. He retched until he was exhausted.

Later, when he had removed the string and ensured with tender touch that he was still intact, he assessed his plight. It was incomprehensible that he could walk through a lighted park entrance, up a lighted sidewalk, across a lighted porch, and into Nottingham Hall in his birthday suit. The very idea caused a hollow feeling in the pit of his stomach. He moved off the pathway behind some shrubs and chanced to note again the window gleaming from the third floor of the Administration Building. Perhaps he could presume on Major Jones-Bethune's good graces to borrow some clothes or at least an old bathrobe to cover his nakedness. At any rate, the approach between his present position and the Administration Building was comfortably shrouded in darkness.

He slipped furtively from one pocket of shadow to another, dashed across the street at the foot of the old building, and plunged into the blackness at one side of the front door. No one saw him. No one was coming. As soon as the thudding of his heart subsided enough, he could hear the night noises of summertime insects preternaturally early in this Southern city. They really do say 'You-kay-dk,' he thought.

Slipping through the front door, he satisfied himself that no one was astir and that the creaking and groaning he heard were only the natural respirations of century-old timbers. He clung in skulking progress to the wall as he climbed the curving stairway to third floor. Of a sudden he thought of Dr. Huber and was grateful that gentleman could not see him now. On moist bare feet he stole down the hallway to the door of Major Jones-Bethune's apartment. There was no sound from within. Timidly he knocked. There was still no sound from beyond the door. He remembered that Major Jones-Bethune was deaf and rapped harder.

As he raised his fist to pound the third time, the door was suddenly jerked open and the Major towered over Porter like the giant discovering Jack at the top of the beanstalk.

"Here, here, who's there? What? What? Who's knocking me up this hour of the night? What? Dear heavens, lad, where are your clothes? Why in heaven's name are you still wearing your spectacles? What? Come in out of that hall instantly! What?"

"Major, some of the boys pulled a fraternity prank on me and took my clothes off in the park. I was hoping you could lend me something to wear home."

"Dear boy, how terrible for you. Of course. Nothing makes one feel so insecure. What? Here. Put this macintosh on. Poor lad, you're trembling all over. I'll make you a spot of tea. Sit down and tell me what happened. Beastly sense of humor these American schoolboys have. What?"

As Major Jones-Bethune lurched around putting water on a hot plate, Porter had time to note that E.V. had been accurate in his description of the smells. He even discovered the box of matches with the home-lettered epigram on it and almost giggled as he wondered how Mrs. Raleigh and Major Jones-Bethune might get along. When he related the events of the evening to his host, he prudently deleted any reference to the shoe box.

284

"Ah, poor lad. Must have been a terrible shock for you, yes. You're so young, too, for this environment. Quite. Good mind, too. I don't mind your knowing I've been quite impressed with you in European history. Yes. Quite. What?"

"Thank you, Major. I've been impressed with you, too."

"What? Speak up, lad. I'm slightly hard of hearing, don't you know? I'm glad you thought of coming by here tonight. Dreadfully embarrassing to go trotting over campus in one's altogether. Glad you saw my light."

He plucked a book from the shelf. "Do you know this poem by Kipling?

> One man in a thousand, Solomon says,
> Will stick more close than a brother.
> And it's worth while seeking him half your days
> If you find him before the other.
> Nine hundred and ninety-nine depend
> On what the world sees in you,
> But the Thousandth Man will stand your friend
> With the whole round world agin you.
>
> 'Tis neither promise nor prayer nor show
> Will settle the finding for 'ee.
> Nine hundred and ninety-nine of 'em go
> By your looks, or your acts, or your glory.
> But if he finds you and you find him,
> The rest of the world don't matter;
> For the Thousandth Man will sink or swim
> With you in any water.

There's two stanzas more. What? But that's the gist of it. How do you feel about that, young Osborne? Do you think you could be a thousandth man? Eh?"

"Well, Major, I don't rightly know. I don't understand that part about 'the rest of the world don't matter.' It sounds kind of lonely to me."

"Yes, quite. You've no idea at your age exactly how lonely one can be. Even in the midst of an army of men. It's very important

285

when two people find each other as friends that they acknowledge it freely and cling to the relationship. Here, listen to this from the Bible. You've heard of David and Jonathan, haven't you?"

"Oh, yes, sir. David's one of my heroes. I know all about David and Jonathan."

"I daresay you think you do, lad. What? Listen to this. Here is how Jonathan felt toward David. 'Then Jonathan and David made a covenant, because he loved him as his own soul. And Jonathan stripped himself of the robe that was upon him, and gave it to David, and his garments, even to his sword, and his bow, and to his girdle.' What? Isn't that touching, lad? It's remarkable coincidence that I find that verse to read to you while you're wearing my macintosh. And nothing else. What?"

"Yes, sir."

"Now listen to how David felt. He's only this moment stumbled on Jonathan's body after he was slain in battle, don't you know. Have you ever seen a dead man, lad? I have, many of them. Not a pleasant experience at all. War's an ugly business no matter how you cut it. Anyway, here is what David says. 'I am distressed for thee, my brother Jonathan: very pleasant hast thou been unto me: thy love to me was wonderful, passing the love of women.' Now what do you think of that, dear boy? Eh? What?"

The major's thick brows limned a craggy and cadaverous forehead and overhung the most piercing eyes Porter had ever encountered. He squirmed a little in his chair. "I don't know, Major. I've read that before, but I guess I just skipped over it in my mind and didn't pay much attention to it. What do you think of it?"

"Speak up, lad, speak up. Is not this a beautiful example of friendship? A marvelous illustration of the thousandth man? What?"

Porter had politely finished the second cup of hot tea he had ever drunk in his life. He thought of Mrs. Capulet and had no difficulty refusing another. With pretended nonchalance, he rose. "I guess so. I sure appreciate all you've done for me, Major, but I'd better be running on. It's getting late. I'll return your raincoat tomorrow."

Major Jones-Bethune was still ensconced in his arm chair and did not rise. "Come here, boy. Let's see now if those beastly friends of yours caused you any damage to speak of."

"It's all right, sir, it's all right," the diffident Porter protested. But before he could move far enough away, the Major grabbed him.

He pulled the reluctant boy before him and opened the raincoat full length. "My word, boy! Eh? What?"

Porter could not believe what was happening. Suddenly Major Jones-Bethune leaned forward in the chair as though for closer inspection, pressed his forehead against Porter's belly, and planted what unmistakably had to be a kiss right in the pubic hair. For a frozen moment a detached portion of Porter's mind noted that the whiskers scratched and the eyebrows tickled. Then he jumped straight up and backward and gave an involuntary yip. Amid the welter of emotions and impulses that immediately engulfed him, curiosity, of all things, emerged the strongest.

In a tone of wonderment, he spoke. "Major Jones-Bethune, does this mean you're a queer?"

"What? What? Speak up, dear lad. What'd you say?"

Porter obliged him. "I said, ARE YOU A QUEER? I'VE NEVER SEEN ONE BEFORE AND I WAS JUST WONDERING."

The major leaped frantically from the chair to the door, jerked it open, and searched the corridor outside. Satisfied that it was still deserted, he closed the door, reached down with a bony hand and easily pulled Porter to eye level by the front of the trench coat.

"Listen, chap, I've misjudged you completely, it would seem. You're not worth the effort it would take to be your friend, and certainly you're bloody unappreciative and insensitive. I hate that American word *queer*. They say 'puff' in my country. That's bad, too. They're both perversions of perfectly good words, don't you know. But let's get one thing straight, just for the record and for your edification. If there's one thing in the world I enjoy more than kissing pricks, it's thrashing the stuffing out of little smart alecks. What? Jolly good show either way it works out. What?"

He gave the coat a vicious shake and Porter's head bobbed helplessly. "Yes, sir. I didn't mean any harm, Major. I was just curious."

"Curious? What? What? You're not curious; you're a rude and nasty little peasant, that's what you are. For a bloody tuppence I'd bugger you and toss you down the stairwell. What? Who knows you're up here?"

Porter swallowed and lied convincingly. "Only E.V. Derrick, sir. He's the only one. Please turn me loose."

"Derrick, eh? I know Derrick. Fine lad. Somewhat obtuse but a fine lad. What'd Derrick tell you about me? What?"

"Well, he said you were a fine fellow, that you were lonely, and that you were bad to read poetry and the Bible." Porter took a deep breath, tried to straighten his glasses, and gambled. After all, Derrick had it coming. "He also said that you were always trying to play with his deedicle, sir."

Major Jones-Bethune clasped his shining skull in bony hands and sank back into his chair. "That word. Only Derrick says 'deedicle' in the whole world. What? A man is betrayed no matter where he turns. I've found the nine hundred and ninety-nine from Dan to Beersheba, but there is no thousandth man. You're just a child. Get on about your silly business, whatever that may be. And return my mac tomorrow."

Porter began backing toward the door.

"And Osborne, if you see Derrick, you might tell him that at his present level of achievement in German class, it will be miraculous if he musters a passing grade for the quarter. What? As for you, if I ever hear one word of this evening, I shan't be at all responsible for the consequences. You bloody well understand what I'm saying, don't you? What?"

Porter was safely in the corridor, holding the knob of the tall old door in his hand. He looked down the empty hall to the yawning stairwell. With that much open space before him, his confidence rose to the level of his guile. He didn't know what 'bugger' meant but felt this was no time to ask. "Oh, yes, sir. I understand. I do hope myself that Professor Twilley never hears of this. Thanks for the raincoat."

"What? What? Twilley? Out! Out! Begone before I cane you! Out!"

In the shrubbery outside the building once more, Porter stopped his nervous shivering. He felt guilty for a moment about E.V., considered the mouse in the water pitcher, the shoe box, and his entrapment this evening, and absolved himself. He resolved not to relate any of tonight's encounter with Major Jones-Bethune to E.V. He would find out about German soon enough. He thought of a comforting verse of Scripture and murmured it aloud. "Sufficient unto the day is the evil thereof."

He considered his debasement at the hands of Spangler and Roundtree and resolved of a sudden that he would again defend his own front porch. He had no idea yet how he would accomplish it, but some way he would fix them before he went to bed. Boldly he slipped from one shadow to another, the major's raincoat shrouding him almost to his ankles, and approached their rooming house without detection.

As he stole on bare careful feet up the stairs, a tread creaked, but he was in the upper hall before the landlady's testy challenge sounded. "Who's there?"

"E.V. Derrick, ma'am. Spangler's friend from home."

"Well, they went out about an hour ago and haven't come back yet."

"I know it. They're in the drugstore and sent me over to wait for them. I'll just study until they get back."

His heart was racing with excitement, but he had learned that his prey was absent. He entered their room with confidence and closed the door with an excluding click. The lights had been left on, and open books betokened interrupted study and early return. Porter looked around for inspiration. He needed to do something just a little short of arson or mayhem to let his fraternity brothers know that he was unconquered. He regarded the double bed with its snowy chenille spread and its plump pillows. He could short-sheet it, he supposed, but that was such a mild prank he regarded it as girlish.

He walked over to the mantel and happened to notice the fireplace. Never before had there been such thick, soft tendrils of soot. There was a layer at least three inches thick, and it waved and quivered with every disturbing current of air. Porter figured that it must have taken two winters of soft coal to produce such a deposit and he marveled at it. This was just what he needed. "The Lord will provide," he whispered.

Swiftly and neatly he turned down the covers on the bed. Procuring an old teacup from a littered bookshelf, he gingerly scooped out cup after cup of the velvety soot and deposited it carefully all across the lower third of the exposed bottom sheet, taking exquisite pains not to stain his hands or drop one fluffy, telltale morsel on the floor. With a care befitting the most fastidious of chambermaids, he remade the bed, looked around to be sure everything was as he had found it, and departed the room with haste. He prudently crept down the side of the stairs to miss the creaking board and was out the door without arousing the landlady.

He heard Spangler and Roundtree laughing their way up the sidewalk and knelt beneath the thick cover of a camellia-japonica until they passed. By judicious timing and calculated utilization of shadows, he regained Nottingham Hall wearing nothing but the major's raincoat and his own glasses. He was seen by no one. His clothes were neatly stacked by the side of his door. A scrawled, unsigned note protruded from one shoe. "Sonny Boy, I'm sorry."

When his initial drift into sleep was interrupted by the involuntary jerk of his relaxing but not quite trusting muscles, he punched his pillow. "Poor E.V.," he murmured.

For the next few days Porter avoided the fraternity house, kept his room door locked, traveled only in groups, and turned his back on no one. Returning early from a lab final, he found Boston Harbor Jones leaning against a tree with tied apron rolled up over his belly. He was obviously waiting to apprehend Porter. His flattened, half-smoked Bull Durham cigarette had little brown stains where the sealing spittle had dried and charred.

"Comere minute, Sambo. You been voiding me? Glad see you ain't walking spraddle-legged. Lemme shake you hand. You done whup them big boys down. Better'n David and Goliath or Daniel in the lions' den. Spangler, he still 'low he kill you first chancet he git, but Roundtree say for God's sake don't mess wid you no more till finals over. Else they all be done flunk out school and not git no sleep neither. Been three days now and both of em still blacker'n me plumb to they waistes. Done scoured the hide bout off and still ain't come white from wallowing in that sut all night long.

"Landlady tell em they got to move do they have any more company and say for them tell E.V. Derrick do he show up her house air other time she put the police on him. Landlady think E.V. the one lay sut tween her sheets and ruint em and also ruint her bed mattress forevermore, but Slick say him and Spangler know better. Say hit was

290

you. Say they done pull a prank on you and strip you naked and bout pull you balls out and they never dream you show up they house ever again, let alone thout no clothes on. You somepin else, Sambo."

"I did so have on clothes. At least kind of. I had on Major Jones-Bethune's raincoat."

Boston threw his cigarette abruptly away. "Say which?"

"It's terribly embarrassing to try to get around Willingham completely nude. I saw Major Jones-Bethune's light on and I sneaked up there and knocked on his door and borrowed his rain-coat."

"What? What?"

"Well, I did. I couldn't make it across campus the way I was."

"Hoo whee. Middle the night you standing naked as a jaybird at ole Major Jone-Bethume's door? What he say?"

"He said, 'What?' Just like you did a while ago."

"What he do?"

"He loaned me his raincoat and made me drink a cup of hot tea and sent me on. He calls a raincoat a macintosh and hot tea tastes as bad as medicine. Boston, I did go by Slick and Clarence's on my way home, but they can't prove it because nobody saw me; so don't you ever admit it."

"I ain't, but you done stumble up on another place for the ain't-got-no-bidness list. Trouble you, Sambo, you done been Raise Right. Lawd God, you busy, boy. I like Mrs. Raleigh now. I wrack my brain to the bone trying keep up with you. You don't go round that Major Jone-Bethume apartment no more, you hear?"

"Why not, Boston?"

"Cause I say so, that's why. He put on airs, drink hot tea, run around here with that fancy way talking, play tennis in them bloomers old as he is, and take all them long walks, and always got a boy his special friend. But when you get all the hair off that dog, he ain't much."

"What do you mean, Boston?"

"I mean I think he one them funny fellows. I think he plain got the juicy mouth and you stay away from him. I better go before Mrs. Raleigh hunt me up. She done told me twicet already bout them idle hands in the devil's tool shed and I don't wanta hear it again. Be sure and tell me bye before you go home for the summer."

Bob Cater had finished his exams and departed. Porter had the big room to himself that night, and it seemed to have echoes in the corners. When he had finished preparing for his last examination, he sat reflectively for a while and pulled paper into position.

Dear Dad,

Last night of the freshman year! I hope I've made you proud of me. The Dean's List is in the bag again. My history professor told me today after the final that I had made an A in his course. He liked my essay comparing Napoleon with Hitler.

I will be home before this letter reaches you, but I wanted to write to you tonight. I want to thank you for sacrificing so I can go to college. A lot of these boys have to pay their own way. I have tried not to waste your money.

Mother is always saying there is more to college than books. I have decided she is right. I thought I would list some of the things I have learned this year that are not in books. Maybe you and I can talk this summer.

1. Blind people are obnoxious.
2. Fat girls are fractious.
3. Yankees are not all bad.
4. Whores are unpredictable.
5. Preachers are not all good.
6. Some Southern ladies have very short fuses.
7. Queers are not all sissy.
8. Baptists are not always right.
9. Baptists are not always wrong.
10. Professors do not know everything.
11. Fraternities have changed since you were young.
12. All smart people do not go to college.
13. A lot of dumb ones do go to college.

Porter thought awhile, sighed, said, "To hell with it," and tore the letter into pieces. He knelt openly by his bed and said his prayers aloud that evening. He gave an extensive paean of thanksgiving for past and present blessings, a perfunctory supplication for continued peace in America and made no reference at all to personal salvation. That, he already knew, was guaranteed.

That summer on the farm, Porter Osborne, Jr., grew. The ends of his long bones came alive in busy little factories that utilized calcium and hormones to produce rapidly elongating shin and thigh, arm and forearm. His hands were like poorly controlled puppets flapping on flimsy wires, and his feet were forever jockeying with each other for priority of passage. Still he grew.

In the heavy midsummer nights, farm-weary humans tossed in half-sleep without even a covering sheet and the chickens drooped their wings with fluffed-out feathers and held their beaks agape in despairing quest for a current of air. The oily cotton plants grew vigorously in this kind of weather, and so did Porter. Miraculously he grew.

His voice developed unexpected timbre and was forever plunging uncontrollably from thin squeaks to chest-rattling rumbles and back again. He even manifested an occasional crop of pimples. He was well aware of what was happening to him and welcomed the advent of adolescence with exultation, although he was fiercely on guard that no one else notice or comment.

He spent his days plowing with his father's new tractor, dissipating the surges and crests of testosterone in sweat as he tilled the rich, red earth. He also mowed vast expanses of lespedeza, a new cover crop, the advent of which had abolished forevermore the practice of pulling fodder. He marveled at the negation of human labor inherent in machines, applauded the substitution of an easily garnered hay crop for the nutritionally inadequate and painfully acquired harvest of corn leaves, but was still nostalgic for the fast, hot rhythm of harvesting fodder.

*Four hands make a bundle and a bundle hangs on every
third stalk. Keep moving and sweating and even the least
breeze will cool you off, but what's keeping that water
boy? Lord, this stuff itches and stings your neck.*

Calmed by physical weariness, he forsook altogether his bedtime Bible reading and instead memorized the poetry of Kipling and
Service and especially that of Edna St. Vincent Millay, falling asleep
to lyrics or sonnets that he felt were expressly addressed to him. He
dutifully went to Sunday services with his mother and sisters, carefully displaying his fraternity pin on his shirt front and concealing as
best he could the disdain he felt for his childlike country friends and
kin. They had not been exposed to the likes of Creed Foxmore, John
Birch, or the plump preachers of Vineville and consequently were
still deep in the rut of steadfast faith and simple pleasures. Not a
shadow of disbelief had ever floated over their sunny sectarian skies.

Porter was very still and quiet in the church, wanting to create
no waves in this placid backwater of religious certainty. The conversations of Henry Bean and Malcolm James, he felt, would have rent
Peabody Baptist Church asunder, and its deacons would have
screeched unclothed in painful illumination, like unfeathered,
large-eyed birds fallen from a nest. For the first time it was difficult
for him to be comfortable in the House of the Lord and to deal with
the old ways, for certainly he was already much better educated than
anyone else in Peabody. He tolerantly kept his counsel when his
mother praised a sermon about Adam or David or Jezebel.

Their current preacher at Peabody spent the entire summer
in the Old Testament, venturing only twice into texts from the New
Testament. On one of those Sundays he exhorted for forty-five
minutes on the "Unpardonable Sin," leaving everyone in total confusion about definition of this terrible crime against God but setting
gray heads wagging and soliciting bass amens from the benches near
the piano. The other time he wandered all over the book of Revelation, proving that the letters of the Beast spelled Hitler and predict-
ing that the Second Coming was imminent, the implication being
that it might even be as early as a week from next Tuesday. No one
got any dinner that day before one o'clock, and Porter thought his

295

mother's mouth a little tight when she made her farewells on the church ground.

Porter became sated with preaching at Peabody, and when revival came in August, he hugged the tractor like a brother through the morning services and then begged off in the evenings because of exhaustion. It was easy to deal with the temporary pangs of conscience he suffered at the silent pleading in his mother's eyes. He was, after all, faithfully filling and firing the kerosene refrigerator for her every night before he went to bed. A fellow could do only so much for any one person.

He kept assuming that some morning or even late some evening he would have an opportunity to settle into a leisurely conversation with his father, a pleasant hiatus of friendship when talk would flow freely and deep philosophies would be voiced as casually as comments on the weather. They were fraternity brothers, and who else was there in Brewtonton with whom his father could share the ideals of Kappa Alpha Order?

His father's schedule had not changed, however, and on the evenings when Porter managed to keep his eyes open until the car sounded on the gravel in the back yard, his mind would be so dulled that all he could do was note the masculine odor of whiskey combined with tobacco, mutter a respectful good night, and trudge wearily upstairs to bed. By the time his father stirred in the mornings, Porter was bouncing along on the seat of the great Allis-Chalmers, guttural chugging of the motor punctuated by the loud clanging of rocks thrown aside by the earth-biting metal discs, the agrarian tranquility of early day and its lovely rhythms destroyed forevermore by human technology. His father would stop his black Buick on the side of the road, extend an imperiously summoning white-clad arm from the window, and Porter would halt the tractor, throttle it down to a contented snorting, and stumble across the newly-tilled furrows to the roadway, inhaling with renewing joy the faintly musky, somehow saltless fragrance of the freshly turned earth.

Sweat running down his face, wet shirt clinging to his thin torso, he would lean against the car and receive directions for the rest of the day's work. There was no chance of idle companionship with the automobile motor running and the chugging of the waiting tractor calling him from across the field. This was no time to discuss KA, women, or religion. College seemed far away and totally foreign. The important thing was the task at hand, and nurture of one's native soil the only *raison d'être*.

As he remounted the tractor and watched the Buick in slow procession from one sharecropper to the next, Porter realized the similarity of treatment by his father but thought little of it. After all, he shared the blood. He hungered for communication and exchange, but status was never a question. He finally inferred that attainment of manhood involved living by actions, not words, and that it impelled a stoic acceptance of events without much attention to personal feeling and certainly no conversation concerning them.

July ended with thunder and lightning that boomed and crackled until the air sparkled clean and souls were reposed. The storm was accompanied by glistening sheets of rain that half flat-tened the corn, raged in muddy swirls through the ditches, and stood ankle-deep in the cotton middles, transforming the fields for a day into isolated quagmires. Foliage responded with voluptuous growth so lush and dense that the land was filled with promise. The tractor was now used for cutting hay, and Porter marveled anew at the incredible ease with which ancient tasks were accomplished.

Dog Days were upon them, a mysterious block of time each August that loomed with portentous influence over human activity. Porter never discovered how to calculate the beginning and end of Dog Days; they were always heralded and dismissed by the grand-parents. He knew, however, most of the rules. It hardly ever rained during Dog Days unless on the very first day, in which event it would rain every day of the period. One tried not to stump toes, for a cut or scratch would not heal until Dog Days were over. Oddities in weather, peculiar behavior in animals, and previously unexhibited eccen-tricities in humans were all explained away with a shrug and the mysterious mutter, "Dog Days." There was a lifting of spirit as well as a freshness of air when Dog Days were over and the expectant silence of early September wrapped around the farm.

For the first time in his life, Porter went shopping without his mother and purchased a pair of brown and white saddle oxfords and two pairs of wool slacks with pleats in front. Fraternity men at Willingham, he felt, should not wear corduroy. He had grown so much during the summer that his thrifty mother gave a vanquished sigh and produced butter money for him to buy a new suit, stimulating thereby simultaneous guilt and exultation in her son. Summer vacation was over and it was time for him to assume his place in the sophomore class at Willingham University.

At mid-morning on the Sunday of his departure, dressed in his new shoes and slacks, KA pin on his shirt front, Phi Eta Sigma key shiny on his watch chain, Porter stepped into his father's sleeping porch to bid him formal farewell.

"Daddy. Daddy. I hate to wake you up, but we have to leave. I wanted to tell you good-bye."

"Good gracious, boy, what time is it? I didn't mean to sleep so late, but I didn't get to bed until ... Get me a glass of water, will you? ... There, that's better. Well, well. The summer surely has flown by. I kept thinking I'd have a chance to visit with you a little, and here it is time for you to go back."

"Yessir. We've both been busy, I guess."

"Your mother taking you to Macon? Yall drive carefully."

"Yessir. You took me last year."

"I remember. Tell all the KA's hello for me. You made a good record last year and I'm sure you will again. You're running up like a weed, boy. You got a girlfriend?"

"Nosir."

"Well, don't hold yourself to such a tight budget this year. I looked over the cancelled checks and you spent next to nothing last year. I won't go under if you write a check occasionally and take a girl out. You did a lot of work this summer, and I'd have had to pay somebody else to do it."

Porter rubbed a finger idly through a faint film of dust on the bedside table. He felt it was foolish to hope the road ever would be paved. "Thank you, sir. I enjoyed doing it. That tractor's a real experience."

"Well, have a good year. Gimme the KA grip. That's it. I think I'll take another little snooze. Tell the girls to call me for dinner."

"Good-bye, Dad."

* * * *

Porter's advent on campus his sophomore year was without fanfare and seemed unimportant to anyone but himself. His mother deposited him with his baggage on the front porch of the dormitory. Following a farewell — ardent on her part, perfunctory on his — she drove off and left him. Despite his blasé attitude, Porter was inwardly glad that she was a beautiful woman. In case other students might be looking, his mother's appearance could reflect nothing but credit on him. He experienced neither misgiving nor nostalgia. His voice had changed, he was five inches taller than the previous year, and he was considerably more versed in the ways of the world, he thought.

Porter made an especial trip to the kitchen as soon as he piled his bags in his old room at Nottingham Hall and even before he went to the fraternity house.

"Boston! How are you?"

"Lawd God! Who that talk like Sambo but don't look like him? Lemme look at you, boy. You done growed slap outta recognition. You foot bout big as mine. Look like you might be done started shaving, too."

"Bout twice a week, Boston, whether I need it or not. How you been?"

"Fine as frog hair, Sambo. But I a changed man since you see me last. You don't haveta remember you dreams no more. I done quit the bug."

"How come you did that?"

"I bet on credit. Two different times. Oncet for a quarter and nother time for a dollar. Time I be paid the man back I'm out six dollar and eighty cent and done been threatened oncet with a razor. That's enough to make a reasonable man think he running with the wrong crowd."

"Well, I'm proud of you. I thought maybe you'd gotten married and your wife made you quit."

Boston leaned backward from the waist and looked in burlesque toward heaven. "Married? Me? Married? Sambo, I won't never be no married man. You can bet you bottom dollar on that."

"Why do you say that, Boston? What you got against marriage?"

"Nothing against marriage. Sound like a good idea. You find a little gal turn you head plumb around and get you to thumpin so you can't think of nothing else. You call it love, right? OK so far. Then you listen them song on the white man radio — 'Honeymoon, justa crooning in June. Love's tune.' Uh huh. Here you go now. Next you hear about the bungalow. 'Big enough for you, my baby, big enough for two.' Then you go to the moving pictures and set in you section with her head on you arm till you hand plumb go to sleep and hear about 'build a little nest way out in the west and let the rest of the world go by.' Uh huh. Sound good. Come out them movie with blood swishing in you ears and pants full of mo'n you'n handle and you ready. Naw, suh. Not this chicken."

"Why, Boston? There is such a thing as love, you know."

"Uh huh. I ain't dispute that. But they ain't no nest in the west. Ain't real sure there's even a nest at all and I know they ain't no west. Anyhow, not the way they sing about it like a place what's perfect and you don't have to carry you same old self with you when you go there. Naw, Sambo, main reason I don't get married on account I don't want no sister-in-law."

Porter carefully kept inflection out of his voice. "I'm waiting, Boston. You haven't changed."

"Sister-in-laws wreck more marriages than anybody else. Least in my race they do. Them what older'n you be always treat you like a child and try to run you bidness more'n they maw do. The dangerous one, though, is that one what's younger and ain't yet married. She get to looking around and decide her sister so happy it must be on account of you and first thing you know she done talk herself into be in love with you. She want what her sister got, and never-you-mind it ain't legal and how much trouble she stir up. She got to prove herself, and, Lawd God, she got to prove herself with you. And here she come. Ever time you turn around she bugging you till you feel like you slapping flies. She make you feel like you more important than you ever been in you life and you the only one got what it take to make her content. And bout that time you wife come down with the lady sickness and here come little sister moon-eyeing around you and you ain't stout nuf to resist and you bang her.

"Time you do, you sorry. Too late then. It ever bit good as she thought it gonna be and she just can't help but tell her guts. Go running to her best friend and confide in her. Only thing worse'n a sister-in-law is any woman's best friend. Worse'n a highland moccasin. Ole best friend

300

tippy-toe around and spread the news ever so accidental and delicate-like twell she sure it get back to the fambly. Don't just straight out tell it, neither. Got to hide it behind worry. 'Oh, I so worried. I worried my best friend might be pregnant by her own brother-in-law. Tell me bout his wife; I worried bout her. Is she pregnant too?'

"And here come more kinfolks than you ever knowed you had before. Bout three of em got razors in they hand and before you know it you either done cut real bad or else be run slap outta town and little sister and nobody else ever yet miss they first period. All this on account of a gal you hadn't thought enough of to even look at when you was single. Sister-in-laws just ain't worth dying for. Naw, Sambo, it don't make any sense atall for a thinking man like me to get married."

Porter stared in silence for a long moment, and then both of them bowed from the waist toward each other, shook hands, and intoned simultaneously, "Take one to know one."

When their laughter subsided and before their delight waned, Boston counseled his younger friend. "How come you don't see Mrs. Raleigh bout a job? She still shy two workers but time everbody get here she be full up. What it amount to you get you vittles free, and it ain't really all that hard a work. You need somepin to keep you busy, boy, and it won't hurt nothing for you to be where I keep my eye on you three times a day. That might not be enough to keep you plumb out'n trouble, but leastways it's a start. You need something on you mind besides books and girls and them KA's and how much devilment you'n get in. I know you paw pay you way, but you can act needy and pitiful to Mrs. Raleigh and she ain't gonna check on it."

Porter became thoughtful. "You know, Boston, I really ought to do all I can to help my daddy. I had that NYA job last year in the Dean's office and it almost drove me crazy. They had me filing index cards and pamphlets and old magazine articles. You had to put in your hours over there but you could tell it was nothing but made work. On top of that, you had to pretend you were grateful to Roosevelt. I sure don't want to get into anything like that again."

Boston clapped Porter on the shoulder. "You right, boy, you right. My mammy always say something for nothing ain't good for nobody. Folks needs to work for what they get. You needs this job waiting on tables. When you get done here everday, you'll sure God know you done pulled you weight and earned you vittles. Yonder go Mrs. Raleigh now. Go lay it on her good."

Mrs. Raleigh, with vivid recall of the vicissitudes of her own farm life, was easily gulled by Porter's wide-eyed and tremulous recital of drought, boll weevils, Cincinnati-bound blacks, and insufficient fertilizer. When he became overly graphic about a bolt of lightning that had split an ancestral oak and killed three mules and a milk cow sheltering under it, Mrs. Raleigh wiped her eyes with an apron corner.

"Say no more, Porter, say no more. I have heard enough. You do not need to tell me what they smelled like. I am no stranger, myself, to suffering, you know, and I'm glad to do what I can to help you. A friend in need is like a pearl of great price and you can report early tomorrow morning. Come in time to learn your tables and for our opening prayer. I always start a new year by dedicating my staff to Jesus. I often say, 'All things work together,' you know, and 'The Lord won't put more on you.' I only had one vacancy I hadn't filled, and I feel like it's the Lord's will that you asked when you did. We'll just be a silver lining for each other, through the dark cloud shining, you know. See you in the morning."

As he passed Boston Harbor, Porter murmured, "Like taking candy from a baby."

"Hot dog, old kitchen gonna liven up! I'll help you all I can, Sambo. Wanta play a little tune on the old sireen tonight? Just let folks know school done started again?"

"Boston, you remember Mrs. Capulet! I don't want to do anything to get out of her good graces or interrupt her rest. See you tomorrow."

His reception at the KA house that year was one of surprise at the increase in his stature. It then evolved into one of respect for his function as treasurer, a job to which he had been elected at the private command of Brother Theo Montagu. "If a kid from that sort of background can be as stingy with his own money as all of you say he is, then you fellows need him watchdogging Kappa's finances.

302

Your books are in a mess. Get him."

After the election, Brother Montagu addressed Porter. "This is a great honor to be bestowed on anyone so young. It's not calculated to make you popular, but the chapter needs somebody with a sense of thrift and enough backbone to stand up for it. Balance these books and tell the fellows 'no' when they want to spend money they don't have. I'm tired of bailing em out of debt every month or two. These books haven't been balanced in three years."

Within weeks they were. The brothers were reminded and then hounded about back dues accumulated from the previous year. Some of the more defiant and recalcitrant ones stubbornly ignored their debts through the embarrassment of announcements by the treasurer in formal chapter meetings or specific notices on the bulletin board. Even they, however, caved in and paid up when Porter threatened to write their parents. Slick was president and Clarence vice-president, their official titles being Number I and Number II, and Porter discovered early that each would wince if Clarence's title was intoned with enough emphasis and a wrinkled nose.

Slick paid his back dues and cleared his account with such alacrity that the underclassmen speculated Brother Montagu had advanced him the funds. Clarence, rebellious about Porter's new-found and flaunted power, held out to the very end, capitulating only when Porter tacked an eloquent letter to Mr. and Mrs. Spangler on the bulletin board prior to mailing it. The envelope to Clarence's parents was addressed to them in care of the minister of their church, and Porter before dark had in hand the last money owed to the fraternity.

"One of these days, Osborne, don't forget, I'm gonna whip it. You're not as goddamn funny as you think you are."

"Don't take the Lord's name in vain, Spangler; it does not become a Knight of the Order. Thanks for your back dues. Do you realize that we've got a surplus in the treasury of over two hundred and fifty dollars? I thought you'd like to know that, since you're Number II."

Porter did not hesitate to consult Brother Montagu about budget and expenditures, although he carefully avoided his wife except in the protecting formality of a crowd. Porter's father had never in his life bought anything on the installment plan, carefully saving his money and doing without until he could pay for whatever purchase he made. A man's word was his bond but had to be backed by cash in the bank. He would not buy even fertilizer for the crops on credit and regarded people who paid two and a half or three percent interest on borrowed money as financial fools or unwary dilettantes with no thought of the morrow. He thought the buy-now-pay-later philosophy would wreck not only individuals but the national economy. He drove these points home to his children by not-infrequently recounting an anecdote about a neighbor.

"Son, you never knew old man Buonaparte Snead — he died the year after you were born — but he was a real character. His wife had some fancy city cousins who came through in a big black touring car and dropped in to eat supper and spend the night on their way to Florida. Mrs. Snead killed a chicken and cooked a pie and made out the best she could on short notice, and old man Boney listened to em talk about fancy clothes and Atlanta shows all through supper. When he had lighted them up to their rooms, he hollered back up the stairs, 'If yall need anything during the night, just let me know and I'll tell you how to do without it.' "

This had become a popular story in the family, and the children came to use "Just let me know what you need" as a catchphrase to each other signifying that they absolutely were not going to comply with a request. Porter now transplanted it to his college fraternity, and it soon became a signal that the treasurer was not going to budge from his position of cash payment or do without. When Roundtree and Spangler grew petulant and then bellicose about his refusal to authorize twenty-five dollars for a new sofa, the entire fraternity became involved at chapter meeting, and Porter, secure in the backing of the chapter advisor, relished not only the fiscal virtue of his position but the power he now wielded. He stood firm.

Deacon Chauncey brought the brothers to laughter and the matter to a close by announcing, "He keeps telling yall just to let him know what you need, but the message is 'No tickee, no washee.' And he's right, you know. I move we adjourn."

Porter was less successful in rushing for his fraternity. Clarence Spangler had assigned him a freshman to cultivate. "You know Jim

Bazemore, the guy from Conyers who wears glasses? Well, Brother Osborne, we want him. Slick and I were talking to him in the drugstore and invited him to our party. We think he's a real leader and probably the best freshman on campus, and we want him. For some strange reason, he likes you. He's heard a bunch of stories about you and has run into you several times, and he thinks you're sharp. That's the only rushee we're assigning you, and we want you to stick to him like a tick. Hot-box the hell out of him, but get him for KA."

Jim Bazemore was a slim, dark freshman, who was lithely balanced and shaved twice a day. He wore argyle socks with his saddle oxfords and a variety of crew-necked sweaters, none of which was homemade. Porter thought him the picture of suavity and was flattered to think that beneath that polished exterior existed naivete that made him admire a gangling sophomore from the country who in the utmost charity could be called only callow.

He sought out Jim Bazemore frequently, sharing sophisticated observations with him about campus eccentrics or regaling him with scandalously outrageous comments that were as unexpected as they were witty. Porter sparkled and shone, but he never became serious in the other boy's presence until the night Jim knocked on his door and requested advice.

"I hope I'm not interrupting your studying too much, but I'd like to talk to you."

"Certainly not. Come on in. This place is a shambles, but there's small point in fixing it up when everybody's going to be moving to the new dormitory before long anyhow. Sit down."

"Sambo, I want to talk to you about fraternities."

"Why me?"

"Because you're the only fraternity man who's not always telling me how great your group is and making little digs at the others. And because I respect your opinion. You look at things differently from anybody else, and even though you're younger than I am, you seem to get more fun out of life and be more on the right track than most of the guys I've met. You're smart and you clown around a lot, but you've got an honest look in your eyes."

"Gosh, Jim, I'm flattered. What do you want to know?"

"Well, I figure you know me as well or better than anyone at Willingham, and I guess what I want is for you to tell me what fraternity I ought to join. Time's getting close and I need to make up my mind."

Porter very nearly erupted with the obvious and elated invitation to KA, but then he remembered the remark about the honest eyes.

"Tell me, Jim, what fraternity do you like the best?"

"Golly, I like em all, to be real truthful about it. They've all been great to me. But I guess I've sorta narrowed it down to SAE, KA, and Phi Delta Theta."

"OK, you've picked the top three. At least as far as snob appeal goes. There are a lot of boys who would love being in your dilemma."

"And to tell you the truth, Sambo, the real decision for me is between KA and the Thetas. You've been darn nice to me, and I knew I could talk to you."

Porter looked with candor at the well-dressed boy. "You know, you're the one who's going to have to make the decision and live with it. For the rest of your life. There are some good guys in Phi Delt and there are some pricks. And to tell you the truth, the same thing is true of KA. I don't know anything about their initiation ritual, but I would guess the Thetas have some of the same ideals we do and that they fail to live up to them just as frequently. Your fraternity brothers are supposed to be just that. Brothers. You have the chance to pick your college family. Which group of guys do you like the best?"

Jim Bazemore thought a moment and then spoke with some hesitation. "I guess I like more of the Phi Delts than I do the KA's. Especially the guys in my class who already say what they're going to pledge. In fact, most of them say that if you get a bid to Phi Delt, you're a fool to look any further. But I like the KA's, too, and to tell you the truth, Sambo, I'd hate to pledge Phi Delt and lose your friendship. I guess what I'm saying is that you're the best friend I have at Willingham and I want to be in the fraternity you belong to."

An image of his grandmother flashed through Porter's mind. She was known in the community as a dedicated Christian, a Southern lady who had Raised all her children Right, a pillar of the church. By the time Porter knew her, she no longer attended any religious services whatever but used age and position as ploys to remain at home where she saw whoever happened to be her current preacher only as a Sunday afternoon caller. She sat in shawled security and accepted the homage sweetly.

This did not mean she was short on opinions. She was particularly intolerant of people who switched church membership. A body, she said, should pick a church and stick with it for life. People who shopped around because of the personalities of preachers were rootless flibbitygibbets who had peacock brains and were unlikely to advance far in the Kingdom of Heaven. Preachers come and preachers go, she opined, but the church itself is the purpose of religion. A rock is a rock, she was fond of saying, and Christ did not want His followers flopping around from pillar to post simply because they liked this one or did not like that one. Osbornes, she affirmed, stand hitched.

Porter thought of her now and interrupted Jim with alacrity and a degree of acerbity. "Whoa up a minute. You remind me of my grandmother."

"Your grandmother?"

"Yeah. You ought not to like me that much because you don't really know me. I've decided you can't get to know anybody around here until rush is over anyhow, because everybody at Willingham is straining to act nice and pretend to be something he really isn't. Freshmen and upperclassmen. The only ones who aren't putting on airs are the yankee football players in Pike. And the nonfraternity men. And you can't count the preachers cause they always have to act holier than they really are anyway. Say you join KA on account of me and then later I turn out to be less than you thought I was. Or more. You'd hate me and you'd hate KA. And then it'd be too late. Once you're initiated, you're in and you can't get out."

"What are you telling me?"

Porter looked him straight in the eye and spoke slowly. He did not particularly relish this role. "I'm telling you that if the majority of your friends are going to pledge Phi Delta Theta, that's what you ought to pledge. It's hard for me to tell you that because the KA's really want you. I was told to hot-box the hell out of you, and I'll catch it if they ever learn I told you to pledge Phi Delt. But I really think that's what you ought to do. The Phi Delts are good boys, and if that's where the majority of your friends are, that's where you belong. Don't worry about me still being your friend. I've got lots of friends outside of KA. The opposite might be true. *You* may have to give *me* up as a friend. The Phi Delts are a clannish lot, and I don't right

307

offhand know of any of them who have friends who aren't Phi Delt. It's been great knowing you, and I'll see you around."

The next evening Spangler and Roundtree were waiting for him when he returned from his job in the dining hall.

"Osborne, you have gone plumb slap-dab crazy! I thought you were maturing a little and getting a little polish, around the edges at least, and here you go and act like a country fool. We'll never trust you again."

Porter drew back and looked at Clarence. He was genuinely incredulous. "What in the world are you talking about?"

"Me'n Slick ran into Jim Bazemore at the drugstore with a bunch of freshmen that everybody knows are going Phi Delt and most of em we wouldn't have on the Christmas tree anyhow. Slick walked over and told him we hoped to see him around at the house tonight, and you know what he said? He said he appreciated us being nice to him but that he had talked to you last night, and after all the things you said about Phi Delta Theta, he'd definitely made up his mind to pledge with them. Said the KA's were fine fellows but that he didn't think he was as compatible with us as with the Thetas. Said he knew you had been assigned to hot-box him and for us not to think hard of you. We couldn't believe our ears!

"Ain't you ever heard of rebound? The first rule of rushing is that you don't ever, ever come out and say anything against another fraternity. Even if it is the damn Phi Diddly Poo Poos. It makes us look bad and doesn't help pledge anybody! See what you've done? I don't want you talking rush to another living soul. We're making you chairman of the closet committee for the rest of the season."

"Closet committee?"

"Hell, yeah. Every time we have a rush party, we want you locked in the closet."

"Me? In the closet? I thought that's where the rest of you hide while I take the heat."

"Oh, shit! I'd forgotten about that. The basement, then. You understand? From now on you're head of the basement committee and haven't got a damn thing to do with rush. Sign the checks and stay in the basement! You understand? God, Osborne, I knew you were warped but I didn't realize you were stupid!"

As the pair turned away in scorn, Porter resolved to keep his own counsel and felt relief that Jim Bazemore had not been more explicit in his conversation with Slick.

Clarence turned and gave a final comment. "You've just managed to lose us the best damn guy in the freshman class."

Porter thought briefly of Jim Bazemore and then of Mr. Ed Stephens back home and his ringing rebuttal when an oversized antagonist had called him a sumbitch. He instantly emulated him. "That's just one man's opinion, Spangler!"

As he watched the backs of his indignant fraternity brothers receding down the hall, he thought, "What would I do without Brewton County?"

Despite his temporary reputation among his brothers for gaucherie, Porter clung to them for security and really felt quite competent in his role as treasurer of the best fraternity on campus. He had misgivings, however, about his competence in his new courses. He had chosen Professor Twilley for his English Survey class and approached his first encounter with him with a confidence possible only in the conceit of the very innocent. Remembering the comments of the previous year from Professor Huber, he sought an audience with that gentleman late in the afternoon on the day of registration. He mounted the curving, creaking stairs in the Administration Building and knocked on Dr. Huber's door.

"*Entrez.*"

Porter held his shoulders back and entered the room with what he was sure would pass in Dr. Huber's eyes as insouciance.

"*Bonjour, Monsieur le Docteur.*"

"Ah, Porter Osborne! You have grown. *Bienvenue à votre retour à Willingham. Avez-vous donc perdu tout votre français dans l'été, sur votre ferme?*"

Porter could not resist a little mischief. After all, he never had to take another French course as long as he lived.

"Say which?"

The mockingbird flared its wings so vigorously that Dr. Huber's eyes positively bulged for a moment. There was a little flicker of warmth followed by the fleetest of smiles.

"Mr. Osborne. I assumed, most incorrectly I see, that you would by now have quite outgrown and forgotten that odious phrase, especially on these premises and considering the debacle *suivant* your last utterance of it."

"Excuse me, Dr. Huber, but I never forget anything. That's a blessing and a curse, I guess. It's just that I don't believe I'll ever in my life be able to understand spoken French."

"And in that case, Mr. Osborne, what explains your presence here? You know my penchant for speaking only French in this department."

"Yessir, I know. I just wanted to come by and see you. I won't be taking any more French because I'm definitely going into medicine, but the greatest accomplishment I had last year was making B in your course. You really had a profound effect on me and I've thought about you a lot this summer and whether the ass will ever speak or not, and, for Pete's sake, you don't let somebody you like and respect drop out of your life like nothing at all just because you're not going to use them any more. Do you?"

"Forgive me, Mr. Osborne. I keep forgetting what a different young fellow you are. And with what intensity and passion you are different. Mademoiselle Yeomans, I would point out to you in passing, is also enrolled in the Science department and aspires to a major in Chemistry, but she, in addition, is filling her electives with French and directs her energies to at least a minor in that subject."

"Well, good for her. At least in Chemistry she won't have to handle all those pickled animals that are required in the advanced Biology course. Besides, Tiny is so good in French that she ought to go further with it. I'm not going to have time for many electives because I've decided to get double majors in Biology and Chemistry. I'll have most of my required courses out of the way this year when I finish Math and English."

"Ah, yes. And which English professor have you selected for your literature survey?"

"Well, Dr. Huber, I checked around and all the students say that for that particular course there's just no question that Professor

310

Twilley is the best; so I've signed up for him. I'm a little nervous about it, but classes begin tomorrow and I'll soon know if it will work out. We start with Beowulf."

"Hmmm. Ah, yes, Mr. Osborne. I am well aware of the reputation the professor enjoys for that particular course. *En effet,* the man is recognized in academic circles as an authority on Chaucer, as much so as Dr. Minor is on Shelley. Indeed, there is a degree of despair in his department that he is either too lazy or too indifferent to complete his doctorate and publish some of his research and conclusions, thereby acquiring personal recognition and also enhancing the reputation of the Willingham faculty.

"I assure you, Mr. Osborne, that the remarks I made to you last year about Professor Twilley were strictly personal and came from my deep disdain of him as a man. They were not, in any manner of speaking, initiated by the emotions of envy and jealousy that Schopenhauer manifested toward Hegel. No. I have no professional jealousy for Professor Twilley at all. My feelings toward him should detract in your mind nothing from his ability as an English professor. It is simply that I think he is basically uncivilized, I regard him as being less than trustworthy, and, *vraiment,* I think that what might pass for sang-froid in another is, in Professor Twilley, nothing more than a manifestation of deep-rooted meanness.

"I would prefer, Mr. Osborne, I assure you, a visit *comme-ci* than for you to learn well in my course and never seek me out as a person. I have never in twenty years heard of a student calling on the rigid Professor Twilley for a tête-à-tête. I wish you *bonne chance* in your studies. I hope you learn well the English literature. I was just about to treat myself to a little cheese and demitasse. Would you care to join me?"

"Thank you, Dr. Huber, but I've never had a demitasse. I don't drink coffee. I like cheese, though. Could I have just that?"

"*Mais oui,* Mr. Osborne. *Certainement.* It is a very special cheese. One cannot procure it from the grocers in Macon. I have a friend I made while a student in France. An artist, if you will, named Georges Benet, who has enjoyed a modest success as a member of the school of art called Impressionism. He was born in Le Havre and was very *sympathique* in Paris with my nostalgia for Georgia. This cheese is from his home province of Normandy, and every few months he sends me some packed in *le petite boite de bois*. It is called Camembert and is made only in Normandy. See here. You smear a little on the cracker with a knife, *comme ça*, and it is quite delightful. *Voila*."

"Yessir." Porter's nose rolled up as he regarded his tidbit.

"What, Mr. Osborne, you do not like the Camembert? I assure you it is quite a gourmet item."

"It's wrinkled and white and soft on the inside. It's not orange and hard like real cheese, Dr. Huber."

"Yes? So?"

"Can I be perfectly honest with you, Dr. Huber, even if my mama would kill me for being rude?"

"*Mais certainement*, Mr. Osborne."

"This cheese is just too stout for me. It tastes like ammonia and gets all up in your nose like the smell from an old wet baby diaper, and the little bit I got on my finger stinks like toe jam. I thank you kindly, but I just don't think I can eat it, if you'll excuse me, sir."

"*Pas du tout*, Mr. Osborne. You are very graphic in your descriptions, and I must admit that it is an acquired taste and that the cheese may be a little past its prime. But consider this while you are rendering judgment: Have you ever seen the great green hills of Normandy with rivers at their feet and hedgerows dividing the plains? Have you seen the pastures there, so soft and thick with grass, so brightly green they seem to shimmer in counterpoint to the gray and stormy skies? Have you felt either the warm sun or the kissing mist of a light rain as you topped a hill and looked down on Le Havre or Rouen or Cherbourg with their great cathedrals, or better yet, Le Mont St. Michel when you leave Avranche? Have you ever beheld the great spotted kine of this Normandy, all black and white and so gentle that the peasants share their homes with them? Have you heard them moan in the soft twilight as they sway and straddle to the stable with their swollen bags and strutted udders to be relieved of their burden of milk? *Alors*, Mr. Osborne, have you ever visited a humble home for an evening where you smelled just across from your *salle à manger* the natural odors emanating from these *grandes bêtes*? No, you have not.

"I assure you that cheese made from the milk of these cows, if it is true to its origins and therefore to its nature, must of a certainty

312

smell and taste exactly as you have observed. And I say to you, Mr. Osborne, it is good. I cannot permit to pass undefended any disparagement of *les belles vaches,* those beautiful cows. The cheese refreshes my memory of Normandy, where I was happy, or at least content, and I have never offered it to one of my students before. Or to anyone else, *quand j'y pense.*"

"Gosh, Dr. Huber, I'm sorry."

"Il n'y a pas de quoi. You are still young, Mr. Osborne, and if Professor Twilley fulfills his office well, you will sooner or later run across the quotation from Shakespeare: 'There are more things in heaven and earth, Horatio, than are dreamt of in your own philosophy.' Apply it personally, Mr. Osborne, apply it personally."

"Yessir, I will. I guess I better be running. I just wanted to say hello."

"Thank you, Mr. Osborne, for dropping by. Do it again sometime. It is always a stimulus, even a challenge, to visit with you."

"Yessir. *Et la même à vous,* I'm sure. *Au revoir, Monsieur le Docteur.*"

"Au revoir, Monsieur Osborne. Je vous rappellerais que l'âne n'a pas encore parlé."

"Say which?"

"I said, Mr. Osborne, that you should be reminded that the ass has still not spoken."

"Mais oui, mon professeur, mais j'ai encore l'espérance. Where there's a will there's a way, you know."

Porter ran down the stairs to the deserted lavatory adjacent to Dr. Highsmith's classroom, grabbed the bar of black-lined soap, washed the soap, and then scrubbed his hands thoroughly. When he was sure no odor of Camembert lingered, he started across campus to the dormitory. As he considered his conversation with Dr. Huber, he realized that he was still apprehensive about his upcoming association with Professor Twilley. He also realized that there were depths to Dr. Huber that he had not recognized before.

"Golly," he muttered aloud, "the old coot makes me really want to see Normandy some day. He's got a streak of the poet in him under all that dryness. But he's crazy — nothing will ever make me eat that cheese."

Porter did not feel quite so worldly a sophomore, but for once he did not think of Brewton County. It was far away.

XIX **T**he first morning with Professor Twilley was inspiring and not at all intimidating. The man presented each student with a precisely outlined survey of the course. He informed them that there would be a test every two weeks, and the outline had the dates of the tests, the dates of the mid-terms, and the dates of the final examinations for the next two quarters.

There was something about sitting in a sunny classroom in September and looking at what one would be doing all through the winter and on into March that brought to Porter's attention the beauty of a businesslike approach to education. There was no way one could get behind in this man's class. Of course, one would be six months older, but one should be filled with a wealth of information. Porter's desire to learn responded to Professor Twilley's desire to teach, and the boy felt an immediate rapprochement for the man.

His physical affliction was difficult to forget. One was ever conscious of it. The empty socket of his left eye was closed by the flaccid upper lid and it was cleanly approximated to the margin of the lower lid, leaving no rim of redness and no exposure of objectionable tissue. It simply made that side of his face seem smooth and perfectly blank, the more so because he wore steel-rimmed spectacles and his left eye socket gave the impression of a drawn shade behind a window pane. The right eye seemed to be doubly piercing and perceptive to compensate for the absence of the left. No one knew how he had lost his eye or when. Porter felt that Luther Farmer was probably correct, that the eye had offended Professor Twilley and he had, himself, resolutely plucked it out.

Porter had an aunt with a glass eye, and he wondered why in

314

the world Professor Twilley did not avail himself of such cosmetic improvement. Of course, one could tell the aunt's eye, impersonal and non-focusing, was false, but it certainly looked better than Professor Twilley's shockingly blank facade. It was almost as though he sneered at stooping to subterfuge and accepted his affliction as such an integral part of himself that he gave no thought to the effect it might have on others. The onlooker was expected to ignore it as completely as did the possessor. Everyone did. It would have been easier for Porter to do if Professor Twilley had divested himself of the habit of saying "I see," as a conversational response.

Just as English composition the previous year had been Porter's favorite subject, so now English literature became his favorite for the sophomore year, a direct result of the ability and dynamism of Professor Twilley. Nearly all of his students felt the same way. E.V. Derrick was a nonconformist.

"No, Sonny Boy, I don't think this course is just great. It's too full of all those authors and the silly things they wrote a thousand years ago. No, I don't like Chaucer. He's hard to read and that business about Chanticleer and Pertelote puts me to sleep. I never took talking chickens seriously, even when I was reading 'The sky is falling, the sky is falling' in the second grade. Don't talk to me about allegory. I don't want to know what one is. The only reason I'm taking this course is I have to, and I had Professor Twilley last year and he didn't flunk anybody. He's a good old man, but Chaucer doesn't make as much sense as Turkey-lurkey and Foxy-woxy. You make your A. All I want is a C."

A student who shared Porter's enthusiasm for the subject matter as well as for the professor was a newcomer to the campus. She had graduated from Miller High School but had gone to some girls' school in Virginia called Mary Baldwin for her freshman year. She told Porter that it was a very small school, and Porter immediately compared it to Bessie Tift and assumed that her parents had sent her there because they did not have the money to send her to Willingham. He tactfully made no reference to this. Amalita Hunt wore the Miller uniform with subtle modifications of the dress code. Her sweaters were always of muted colors and of the softest texture imaginable. Porter had seen cashmere occasionally, but he had enough acuity to know that it had never before so appropriately graced a human form.

315

Amalita always wore stockings with her saddle oxfords and socks. Her hair was thin, straight, and long, curling just a little upward from her shoulders. She had the smallest, straightest nose imaginable, rather plump cheeks with high cheek bones, and large, slightly protruding blue eyes. Her upper lip was a bow without indentation, reminiscent of a Renoir portrait, and she wore softer-hued lipstick than the other girls. Her teeth were as small and even as baby teeth and perfectly aligned.

Porter perhaps could have withstood these attractions without losing his head, for Willingham was filled with pretty girls, but in addition Amalita had the huskiest, softest voice he had ever heard in his life and was always fragrant with a faintly musky perfume that had to be French. Porter was entranced.

"What is the name of that perfume you wear?" he asked at the end of their first class.

"Toujours moi," she breathed throatily. "Most boys don't notice. I've worn it forever, at least since I was a junior in high school. You're not from Macon, are you?"

Porter was lost. He had thrilled in the last years of high school to Paul Gallico's stories in *The Saturday Evening Post.* They told of the idealized love affair of an American man of provincial background but great education named Hiram Holliday. He adored a lovely young princess named Heidi, from some small royal house of Europe, but felt he could never declare his love because of the disparity in their positions. He was forever helping her out of trouble at great risk to himself, and Gallico contrived marvelous adventure stories from these situations. Her summoning call was always either a note or a telephone call or even a cable that said simply *à moi.* Porter had identified completely with this noble but celibate hero, snatching *The Saturday Evening Post* out of the mailbox every Tuesday before the letter carrier's car was in second gear. He preferred stories of Hiram's exploits to those of Florian Slappey and the "Sons and Daughters of I Shall Arise" or even the marvelous stories of Agatha Christie.

Now he had met an enchanting creature — mysterious, alluring, and obviously aristocratic — who wore perfume called *toujours moi* instead of sending notes that said *à moi.* This was not coincidence. This was fate. Let no one try to reason with him; Porter knew fate

316

when he saw it. He laid his heart at Amalita's feet. She, practical, unaware, and realistic to a degree Porter had never attained, frequently stepped on it. It was a remarkably resilient organ, however, and Porter remained obsessed with the fair Amalita.

Amalita had a friend. Everywhere one saw the one, one saw the other. The friend also was a Macon girl who had just entered Willingham and also had transferred from a girls' school in Virginia. Her name was Sara Belle Steele, and she violated the Miller dress code by having her curly hair bobbed just below her ears. Where Amalita was dignified and a little stately, Sara Belle was ebullient and audibly enthusiastic about everything at her new school. Where Amalita's face might be called her fortune, Sara Belle excelled with a figure that excited masculine comment everywhere she went. Her lithe legs and small waist were unbelievably dominated by large breasts that were as vivacious as their owner. Porter, having great capacity and willingness, also fell in love with her. It was useless to defy fate.

To Porter's question about why they had transferred to Willingham, Amalita was sultrily reflective about distance from home. Sara Belle was explosively direct. "Boys, that's why! Good ole nasty, infuriating, absolutely necessary boys! They don't have a one of the creatures at Sullins. I don't know a thing about them, but I certainly intend to learn. There's more to college than books, I told my father, and he let me transfer.

"You wouldn't believe it now, but I was so painfully shy in high school I was afraid to even look at a boy. The only date I ever had was with the son of a friend of my mother, and he was as shy as I was and went on the date just as much against his will as I did, and we spent the whole evening absolutely *suffering* to get away from each other. The only boy I really know is my little brother, and he's six years younger than me and positively repulsive. Mother and Father think he hung the moon, but he's odious and totally exasperating. I want to learn everything about boys, good old Willingham males. Tell me what you know."

Porter shrugged his shoulders. "Boys are pretty simple. It's girls who are complicated."

"I know they say that's true mentally, but I'm not talking about just their minds."

317

"You mean physically? Well, it's certainly true there. Girls have all those parts, you know, and there's really nothing very fancy about a male."

"Oh, Sambo, you don't understand. There's got to be glamour and mystery and hidden meaning all over the place in these marvelous creatures who have controlled the destiny of the earth since they discovered fire. I want to learn about sex from you! On a purely platonic basis, of course."

"I don't know anywhere to start but way back at the beginning. Sara Belle, I'll let you see mine if you'll let me see yours."

Amalita emitted a delightfully guttural laugh. "Let's go to the drugstore and get out from under Professor Twilley's window. If he happened to overhear this conversation, you'd both be shipped. Sara Belle, I think you've met your match. Sambo's as crazy as you are."

Porter refrained from kicking an empty potted meat can on the edge of the sidewalk. He spoke with reassurance. "Sara Belle, I understand your having an academic interest in a subject without getting personally involved. Some of us KA's went to a brothel last spring and we're all still virgins."

"You did *what*? Tell me all about it. Who were the KA's? What did the girls look like? What happened? Call their names, boy!"

"That's what I'm saying. Nothing happened. Brother Hollingsworth had just got his car and we were all out on the town and just dropped by this house on Oak Street to check it out. The other boys danced with them, and Brother E.V. Derrick even kissed one, but nobody, you know, went any further than that."

Sara Belle gave a delighted snort and an impatient little two-step of glee. "Oh, this is just marvelous! The girls at Sullins would just die if they could see me out here in the coeducational world talking to a real live boy about sex and whorehouses. Oh, I love Willingham!"

"Well, now, Sara Belle, I want you to understand that I'm not the sort of boy who would ever waste his seed in the belly of a whore. I'm still a virgin."

Sara Belle replaced her smile with a scowl. "Gosh, Sambo, you have a strange way of phrasing things. That's enough to give me the active nausea. But just for the record, let it be understood that I made one hundred on the Phi Mu purity test. Listen, I wouldn't even

318

tell my mother when I started menstruating — bothersome condition! I changed panties four or five times a day for the first three times I did it until finally old Daisy, God bless her, went to my mama and said, 'I think Miss Sara Belle's got the lady sickness.' I've never even kissed a boy."

Porter looked at the curl and flare of her beautifully chiseled lips. "Well, I could take care of that any time."

"Oh, Sambo, hush. You'd ruin a perfectly beautiful relationship by getting all personally involved. You're our buddy, our brother. I couldn't possibly kiss you. It'd be incest."

At the drugstore, Amalita ordered a Coke with a paper cup and a lot of ice and, being safely off campus, took a Philip Morris cigarette out of her purse, lit it, and proceeded to inhale the smoke deeply. Porter was a little uncomfortable.

The only women in Brewtonton who smoked were Miss Florida Kitchens and her youngest daughter, who herself was well past thirty. They were both regarded as eccentric, and their ladyhood was definitely suspect — especially that of the daughter. Mrs. Kitchens was a widow woman, her face a palimpsest of wrinkles and liver spots. She was given to genealogical recitations that entrenched her indisputably in the ranks of the gentry. She had not started smoking until her husband died, and she was forgiven the peccadillo as a manifestation of something that had happened in her irrational period of connubial grief.

The daughter, however, was another story. She had started smoking willfully and in cold blood. She was classified as "wild," and most of the missionary ladies automatically lowered their voices when her name was mentioned. The authority on local gentility in Porter's family was the aunt with the glass eye, and whenever he pressed her for details about why India Kitchens was not a lady, the only answer he had ever received was a rolling of the good eye, a tightened lip, and the condemning assertion, "She smokes."

The town boys, who always knew everything, told wild stories about India and her sexual activity, all of them based on the flimsiest of circumstantial evidence and obviously colored by adolescent fantasies. Even they, when challenged for proof, cut off any defense by stating, "She smokes, you know. We've seen that." Porter consequently had departed Brewtonton for the outside world with the embedded conviction that ladies did not smoke and indeed with the unspoken belief that female chastity and cigarette smoking did not coexist.

Now he was confronted with the presence of a girl who was so obviously a lady that not even a boor could question it. The most socially poised and glamorous female he had ever encountered was sitting across from him in Chichester's Drugstore smoking a cigarette as casually as she chewed gum. Before his adoration deepened any further, he felt there was a question that had to be settled, and his bantering conversation with Sara Belle was a perfect opening.

Very casually he leaned back in his iron-backed chair. "Amalita, are you a virgin?"

She was crunching ice between her jaw teeth, but she held her paper cup up and hastily divested herself of the speech-impeding particles. "My word! What a question! Of course I am. Was there ever any doubt?" She held her cigarette between the fingers of the hand that also bore a sapphire encircled with diamonds. The ascending smoke was a steady, unwavering column.

"Of course not. Sara Belle and I had just been cutting up so much we hadn't gotten your views at all. I'm sure you want to marry a virgin, too, don't you?"

"I certainly do not. I'm not like Sara Belle. My mother *has* talked to me." She lowered her voice to an enchanting level of confidentiality. "I asked her about those things men have. You know. And she said they get so big for starting from nothing that you just can't believe it. I asked her how big do they get, and she said sometimes you think they're as big around as a fire plug and as long as a telephone pole. I'm going to be a virgin when I get married, and I sure as hell want my husband to know what he's doing. I don't want any clumsy fool fiddling and fumbling around and learning on me."

Sara Belle's shocked and explosive laughter made acceptable background noise as Porter, with unexpected sang-froid, accepted the demolition of another of his rigid values. He rollicked along with Sara Belle's buffoonery while deep within he acknowledged that people in Brewtonton didn't know everything. Maybe India Kitchens was a virgin after all.

What Porter lacked in social compatibility with Amalita he overcame with scholastic ability. She was genuinely interested in

320

English literature and was gratifyingly impressed when Porter made ninety-eight on the first test. While Porter and Sara Belle established a friendship through clowning and vied with each other to see who could be the most outlandishly comical, Amalita participated in these wild and outrageous conversations primarily as an audience, either laughing with approval or clucking with caution. Sara Belle had only slightly more interest than E.V. Derrick in Chaucer, Shakespeare, or Francis Bacon, being more than content with a solid C. Amalita, however, was perfectly amenable to discussing poetry, philosophy, or development of style and aspired to be an A student. When Porter made one hundred on the second test, Amalita sought him out.

"Now see here, Porter Osborne, you may be a little genius and all that, but you're not fooling me a minute. That test was hard as hell and the next highest grade was eighty-eight. You've got some secret about studying or else an inside track with Professor Twilley. Either way, I want in."

If Delilah had looked sidelong at Samson while drenched in *toujours moi* and had spoken in such a husky voice, that hero not only would have told her everything but would have handed her the scissors. "Amalita, there's really nothing to it. He's the most organized professor I've ever seen. You know how he reviews every time before a test? Listen real carefully. He almost tells us what he's going to ask. It's important sometimes what he *doesn't* mention when he's reviewing, too. He's the easiest man to spot I've ever seen. On top of that, there's a file at the KA house of his exam questions for the last ten years. I make a list every review session and then check the fraternity files, and it's very seldom I add one from there. You make your list next time and I'll make mine, and we'll get together at the Library that night and compare them."

It worked. For more than half an hour Porter was free to inhale *toujours moi* and occasionally be brushed by cashmere or even silky hair while he added to Amalita's list. He offered to go over the answers with her, but she did not have time for that. She had to roll up her hair before she studied. Nevertheless, she performed well on the test next day, achieving a grade in the nineties only four points below Porter's own. They both beamed with pride, and she gave Porter several deliciously enslaving little pats as she thanked him. He felt six feet tall.

321

He rapidly became known in the class as the top student but did not bother to tell his fellows about the formula he had found for anticipating Professor Twilley's questions. That stern and authoritarian gentleman gave no indication that he took any notice of Porter's achievement but handed out papers with majestic indifference. He was accustomed to giving occasional aloof and extremely sibilant homilies on subjects not connected with the current class topic. Since these were always very brief, no one minded the distraction, and since they were invariably cogent and even inspiring, Porter was always enthralled.

"Young people, you frequently hear from those fearful misanthropes around you that the world, as manifested in man, is getting worse and worse. I submit to you that this is a base falsehood. Objective observation from the distance of centuries persuades one convincingly that indeed mankind is slowly but inexorably getting better. Cannibalism has been abolished; no longer do we eat one another. Slavery has been abolished; no longer do we buy and sell each other. The Crusades are behind us; no longer do we put towns to the torch or little children to the sword in the precious name of Jesus.

"Be patient with mankind. It will continue to improve, so slowly perhaps that you will despair of seeing it in so short a span as your own lifetime, but it will improve. Do you know why, young ladies and gentlemen? Because God, Himself, works through man and is manifest in him. Indeed, God has nothing else through which to work except man. We are all that He has, and He will not abandon us nor let us sink into depravity.

"The recent news that Hitler and his hysterical Germans have appropriated Poland is distressing but not cataclysmic. Poland, in its checkered history, has endured much worse and survived. This does not mean, as the columnists would convince you, that we are being plunged into another World War. America has certainly by now learned the value of her geographical removal from Europe and will remain apart from its madness, impregnable to the evil and covetous designs of the little German leader.

"Mankind, young people, is gradually getting better and better. Work in harmony with God's will and not against it. We digress, however. Let us direct our attention to the lesson before us today.

Consider the condition of Egypt when Caesar, and later Marc Antony, arrived. Despite her royal lineage, her wasteful luxury, the glamour that has clung to her through the centuries, are you aware, young people, that Cleopatra was nothing but a common whore?"

The enraptured Porter could not comprehend the Unholy Thirteen or anyone else not enjoying Professor Twilley's class.

E.V. Derrick did not share his sentiment. "Sonny Boy, I've made one F and two D's so far on these tests old One-eye gives, and I need some help. How bout letting me study with you for the next one?"

The new dormitory had not yet been formally dedicated but was already occupied, filled with an influx of students who had abandoned Nottingham Hall. It was a grand and modern new building with a water fountain in the lobby alongside a bust of the Christian gentleman who had given the building to Willingham. Porter was impressed because the floors were all cement overlaid with tiles, even on the second and third floors, and the windows had metal frames that cranked in and out. Fraternity houses had been abolished, and each Greek letter society had been assigned a suite of rooms with its own parlor and bathroom. Porter and E.V. both now lived in the KA suite, although at opposite ends of it.

The living room of the suite was a constant maelstrom of activity, filled with new furniture and Macon students and even a new portrait of Robert E. Lee. The picture was furnished by the National Order and Porter had had to pay for only the frame. There was a record player in the living room, and it was in constant use until late at night, usually playing "Sugar Blues" or something equally as distracting. There was always action in that living room. Someone was either lighting the newspaper while an oblivious brother was reading it, giving a hot foot to a dozing pledge, or just loudly swapping yarns. The KA suite was no place to study. The Library was not available for the conversation necessary in coaching, so Porter repaired with E.V. to the KA chapter room on the top floor of the Administration Building. There, amid the trappings of initiation and the undisturbed dust of at least half a century, he handed his fraternity brother the list of questions he had compiled and patiently helped him with the answers. E.V. made a C on the test on Shakespeare, and Porter promised to help him with mid-terms.

The list of questions that Porter produced for half a quarter of Professor Twilley's lectures numbered one hundred and eighty. Even Amalita groaned when presented with the list. E.V. was indignant and recalcitrant. "Sonny Boy, I can't even learn the questions, let alone the answers."

"E.V. Derrick, you asked me to help you and I'm going to. Sit down, shut up, and write out the answers when I tell them to you. You'll remember it if you write it."

It took more than three hours of concentrated activity, but Porter felt a real sense of accomplishment at bullying E.V. into learning English literature, no matter how transient the accomplishment. On the examination next day, there was only one question that Porter had not foreseen. Professor Twilley included an unexpected query about Piers Plowman but it was an obvious one, and Porter had no difficulty at all.

"Sonny Boy, there wasn't but one question I missed completely. You did such a good job I'm going to have to take you to the drugstore and buy you a Coke. Some day. Maybe."

"You're all heart, Derrick. Control yourself. I don't know whether I can stand all this groveling gratitude. Besides, you already owe me one Coke."

When Professor Twilley handed back the papers, he withheld Porter's and E.V.'s. They looked at each other in wonder and sat through the lecture in some degree of apprehension. At the close of class Professor Twilley, with judicial finality, announced in public, "I shall expect Mr. Derrick and Mr. Osborne to call on me in my office at precisely two o'clock. Be there without fail."

It was not the empty socket he turned upon them, and the classroom emptied in silence.

Sara Belle was less than comforting. "What in the world have you fellows done? For once I'm glad to be a poor, subservient, protected Southern female, just little ole Cuddin Honeysuckle-on-the-vine, batting my eyes and acting as coy as an ADPi at a rush party. I'd rather take my chances at the Last Judgment than face God-almighty Twilley in his office. Let me and Amalita know what happens, Sambo. And don't wet your pants. I've tried that. It never solves anything."

Porter slid the food on his tables and removed the dirty dishes

324

in record time, and he and E.V. walked together to Professor Twilley's office, eschewing anything but inconsequential conversation and avoiding each other's gaze.

"Ah, yes. Osborne and Derrick. Do not bother to seat yourselves. I will come straight to the point. There is a certainty in my mind that you two students cheated on my mid-term examination. The similarity between your papers is too great to be coincidence. From the individual performances of each of you in the past, I would assume that Derrick copied Osborne's paper. You have produced nothing heretofore, Mr. Derrick, that demonstrated even interest, let alone ability, in this course. However, young Osborne, if he did it with your knowledge, then your silence would imply your consent, and you are no less guilty than he.

"Cheating! Cheating! What degradation! What scurrilous depravity! You realize, of course, that this means automatic expulsion from the University. Oh, shame! The only reason I have called you in is that there is one thing I cannot fathom. Mr. Derrick sits two seats in front of Mr. Osborne and one row over, and I cannot imagine how he managed to copy his confederate's paper. I am giving you an opportunity to explain this, and I am striving to keep an open mind. Speak!"

Porter marveled for a detached moment of curiosity that his heart could sink to his knees while it simultaneously thudded so hard in his throat that he could not swallow and could barely breathe. He knew that his face was flaming red. He looked over at Derrick, expecting him to volunteer the explanation. E.V.'s face was a pale chartreuse and he was staring at his own feet.

"I am waiting!"

Porter wondered how Professor Twilley could sound as if he were hissing when there was no "S" in his statement.

The pressure of silence forced him into speech. "Well, sir, we studied together. That's all, I promise you. He didn't copy my paper. We reviewed together, and he knew the answers. I told them to him the night before the test and even had him write them down so he would remember them."

"I see. And how did he know the questions? Really, young Osborne, you take me for a fool. Derrick jumps from D's, F's, and one C to an A-minus on the mid-term. And you provide an explanation that is highly incongruous. The only question out of twenty that he missed completely was the one about Piers Plowman. Come, Osborne, do not compound the sin of cheating by lying."

"Professor Twilley, I'm not lying! You wait right here and I'll go get those questions."

"You have five minutes, Osborne. Produce them. I'll not tolerate anything you fabricate expediently."

Porter ran as fast as he could to his room, snatched his notes from the desk drawer, and raced back to the Chapel Building, completely breathless but grateful for the release of violent physical activity. E.V. Derrick still stood with hanging head, mute and immobile.

"Look at these, Professor Twilley. The questions are in my handwriting, and all the answers are in Derrick's. I couldn't find all his answers cause he was using scrap paper and we threw some of it away, but there's enough there to prove what I'm telling you."

"I see. And where did you say you got all these questions?"

"Out of my head. I made a list every time you reviewed us for a test and then piled them all together and added anything new you mentioned when you reviewed for mid-term." He saw no need to mention the box of old examinations in the KA house.

"I see. This is quite an exhaustive survey of the course, young Osborne. I knew you stared at me all the time, but I had no idea your attention was either this rapt or this productive. It imposes an added burden of care on me that I maintain accuracy when I speak."

He walked to the window, jingled the keys in his pocket abstractedly, and turned his blind side to the two boys. Porter flashed a look of triumph over at E.V. but could not get him to meet his glance. They waited in silence. Finally the oracle spoke.

"You boys may relax about any disciplinary activity. I was correct in my assessment of the relative ability of you two. If you had sat closer to each other in class, this matter would have been turned over to the disciplinary committee with the examination papers as incontrovertible proof of cheating, and this preliminary investigation would not even have occurred. I could not understand how you two could have exchanged information under my careful scrutiny and therefore I called you in. It pays to be thorough, prudent, and above all to respect one's powers of reason and logic. Here are your

326

papers.

"Young Osborne, you are the first student since John Birch to make one hundred on one of my mid-terms. In addition, you are the one, I feel, who made this ninety-three for Derrick. Here is your paper, Derrick. Derrick? Take your paper. I see. Give it to him later, Osborne, will you?"

As Porter turned toward his catatonic friend, Professor Twilley spoke again. "I assume, young Osborne, that you belong to the same fraternity your father did. When I was a student here, it was rumored that Kappa Alpha Order maintained a rather complete file of old examinations. If this be true, their library will be considerably enhanced by the addition of your review questions. Any device to increase learning is acceptable in my opinion.

"There is a quotation from one of the plays we are not studying this year that I always apply personally when I do not understand something: 'There are more things in heaven and earth, Horatio, than are dreamt of in your philosophy.' I am grateful to Shakespeare that the three of us are not embroiled in the brouhaha of expulsion from the university. I regret any inconvenience I may have caused you two. You may go now."

Porter had to lead E.V. out. His mind was filled with complexities he would not sort out for months, but he could not resist reopening the door and thrusting his head back in the office. "Professor Twilley. Osborne men don't cheat. And Osborne men don't lie."

"I see. Be sure you don't ever do the latter about the former, young Osborne. Good-bye."

As they walked across campus, Porter chattered hysterically. "Boy, that was a close call. Aren't we lucky we didn't throw those notes away? That man is tough and he's mean, but thank goodness he's fair to boot. We like to have been in some real hot water. I was surprised at you, E.V. You haven't said a mumbling word since we went in there. I was scared, but I wasn't that scared."

"Scared? Sonny Boy, you ain't ever hated anybody, have you?"

"Why, sure I have. I guess."

"I mean, hated them so bad you planned ways to kill them. Hated them so bad you didn't dare move because if you did you'd kick and gouge and choke and bite. I'm not scared. I'm mad. And I

327

hate that one-eyed bastard like he was the devil. He had no right to do that or say those things. Who does he think he is? God? And now I've got to see him every day for the next two quarters and pretend I respect him."

"Aw, E.V., you can understand how he was suspicious. I was scared and upset at first, but now I think it's kinda funny. Don't worry. We'll study together and both make A's and there won't be a thing he can do but like it."

"Sonny Boy, I don't ever want to study with you again. This is a personal matter between me and ole One-eye now. Whatever I make, I'm going to make on my own. And if I flunk I *will* kill him."

His friend was so intense that Porter fell silent. They moved a full hundred yards before it crossed his mind that in Professor Twilley's eye this also might be an acceptable device to increase learning.

When the boys had been living for a month in the new dormitory, a dedication ceremony was scheduled. The fresh, rank rye grass holding the red clay of the front yard was cut for the first time, and the floors were waxed and polished to an impressive sheen. Since Brother Theo Montagu was the architect, the KA suite was designated as the host area for the visiting dignitaries, and the brothers and pledges cleaned it until it sparkled.

Jo Beth Montagu was to bring her silver service and serve the tea herself. Porter did not ask, but he was sure she would wear a hoop skirt and a ribbon with a cameo on it around her neck. He was particularly curious to see the silver. Theo said it had been in his wife's family for three generations and had been saved from the yankees by a faithful old slave who had hidden it in the well. Slick Roundtree said Theo had bought it at an auction in Birmingham and had gotten a real bargain because it had somebody else's monogram on it. At any rate, it was very valuable, and Porter had never seen a silver service before.

The donor and members of his family would be there, plus President Wade Hampton Powell and as many docile faculty members as he could muster. Attendance was not compulsory. The formal name of the dormitory was Nathan Bedford Forrest Smith Hall, but everyone called it Smith Hall. A bust of the benefactor already was bolted firmly into a niche beside the water fountain in the lobby. Mr. Smith, who was a loyal Georgia Baptist and a beloved son of the institution, had spoken in chapel twice and had been awarded an honorary degree the previous spring with all the rights and privileges thereunto appertaining.

Henry Bean, who seemed to Porter to have become even more fascinatingly cynical over the summer and was taking his Psychology courses seriously, said that the bronze bust was an indication of insecurity. It meant, Henry said, either that Nathan Bedford Forrest Smith was noveau riche and uncomfortable with his money, or else that his dick wasn't as big as his daddy's. Between anticipating the Montagu silver service and speculating on the Smith genitalia, Porter rather looked forward to what might otherwise be a dull dedication.

The night before the ceremony, Porter came in from serving tables, finished his homework, took his bath, and stretched out on his bed waiting for the dormitory to settle down before retiring. E.V. Derrick, returning from a movie and a side trip to the drugstore, entered Porter's room juggling a smoking piece of dry ice between swiftly shifting fingers.

"Hello, Sonny Boy. What you doing in bed so early? You should have gone to the movie with us."

"What you doing with that dry ice? You better be studying English instead of wasting your time on Lana Turner. She doesn't think even as much of you as Professor Twilley does."

"I can read it tomorrow night. The soda jerk gave me this when I got my ice cream cone. It's nothing but cold CO_2. Catch."

He tossed the furry white ice onto Porter's naked chest, where it sizzled for a fleet instant before Porter dashed it frantically against the wall. "Darn it, Derrick! That stuff'll blister you! What's the matter with you?"

"Aw, Sonny Boy, I thought you'd be interested in it. You ever seen it boiling in a glass of cold water? You got any water in here?"

"Derrick, for Pete's sake, I've seen dry ice before. Quit messing around with it and get out of here. It's time to go to bed."

"You ain't got no water, Sonny Boy? Here, look what a little piece of it will do to your bottle of ink."

"Derrick, that's a brand-new bottle of ink. I know you've got better sense than to put that stuff in it. It'll boil over and stain the table."

"Aw, just this tiny little sliver won't hurt. Look at it smoke.... And look at those black bubbles.... Oops. I'm afraid a little did boil over. Have you got a blotter, Sonny Boy?"

Porter, clad only in his drawers, jumped off his bed and began cleaning the puddle of ink. "Derrick, doggone it, you're going to ruin this brand-new furniture. Quit laughing. This is not funny. It's vandalism. And besides, that's a new bottle of ink and it cost me a dime."

"I can't help laughing, Sonny Boy. You look so funny without your clothes on and both your hands so black. You shouldn't be so messy."

Porter grabbed up the bottle, still over three quarters full, and drew his arm back. "We'll see how funny you look when I pour the rest of this ink right over your head."

E.V. took one look at the situation he had created, remembered the night with the shoe box, and bolted out the door. Porter chased him out of the KA suite, down the stairs, through the lobby, and stopped only when E.V. ran through the front door and onto the open campus of Willingham. Frustration gave way to determination, and he hid in the little alcove leading to the ATO suite. He could wait. It wasn't long.

E.V. opened the door, sauntered across the lobby, and stopped warily when Porter jumped out of hiding. "Now, Sonny Boy, don't do anything foolish. It's time for you to be in bed. I can't believe you're being such a poor sport over a little piece of dry ice."

Holding the bottle firmly, no more than four feet from his target, Porter abruptly dashed the ink squarely into E.V. Derrick's face. It was a completely satisfying and isolated moment in Porter's life, no matter how fleeting. He was amazed at how much territory one small bottle of ink could cover when splattered forcibly over one target. Derrick disappeared. A black human form stood before Porter, no vestige of color about it from the level of the knees to the top of its head. When Derrick opened his eyes, they gleamed white in the blackness of his featureless face. Porter made a mental note that this was humorous but was too caught up in the magnitude of the sight to laugh. He and Derrick stood and stared at each other in heavy silence. For a moment Porter thought his fraternity brother would attack him.

The spell was broken by a Phi Delta Theta returning from the Library. "What in the world is going on?"

Without a word, E.V. Derrick turned and mounted the stairs.

The Phi Delt again broke the silence. "My God, Sambo, what have you done?"

Porter looked around. No longer was Nathan Bedford Forrest Smith the focal point of the lobby. On the pristine plaster panel of the wall west of the bronze bust, there was now the unmistakable outline of a human head and torso. The jet black and the dead white vibrated with each other in almost pulsing contrast. The plaster had not been painted, and the ink had immediately soaked into it in permanent bond. The silhouette impelled. It dominated. It caused the Phi Delta Theta, who was a very conscientious person, to squeal, with just a little lisp, "My God! The dedication is tomorrow. Somebody better go get Mr. Mullinax."

Porter gave no thought to the morrow. He hurried up the stairs to the KA suite and joined the festive crowd watching Brother Derrick take a shower. The water running off E.V. was discolored for thirty minutes, and the jeers of the KA's were sweet in Porter's ears.

On his way to class next morning, he had to walk around Mr. Mullinax, who was in the lobby with a painter. The painter was shaking his head, and Mr. Mullinax was smoking his pipe.

"Hit won't do no good. That mess'll bleed through six coats of paint. Yall gonna have to just chip it out and replaster that wall."

"We don't have time. See if you can hang a white sheet over it for that dedication this afternoon. There's gonna be a bunch of upset folks over this."

Porter kept his eyes lowered as he walked past the two men. He was glad that no one but E.V. Derrick and one Phi Delta Theta knew who had defaced that wall.

Porter did not attend the dedication that afternoon because he was too busy in Comparative Anatomy. The class had finished the dogfish and was halfway through the necturus, and Porter was fascinated with the dissection. It was more important, he thought, for a serious student to keep up with his personal studies than to swell the ranks at a rather trivial pseudo-religious ceremony. When he came out of the Biology Building, he encountered Tiny Yeomans.

"Hi, Sambo. How's the kid? You should have been at the

dedication. Swygert and I were coming up from the Co-op and saw the crowd and decided to drop by because we didn't have anything else to do. Boy, are we glad we did! It was a scream, kid! They'd covered that bust of Nathan Bedford Forrest Smith with a sheet and were going to have an unveiling. His little four-year-old grand-daughter was supposed to do it, and the beautiful golden-haired brat got mixed up and grabbed the wrong sheet and gave a big yank, and there was the worst messed up wall you ever saw in your life — some guy silhouetted in black. Looked familiar, Sybil said, but we couldn't figure out who it was. Dr. Powell had to step up himself and uncover the bust, and he was so flustered he ripped the sheet. Gave his usual beloved-son-of-the-institution spiel, but everybody was whispering so hard nobody listened. All we could hear when folks asked who was responsible for that wall was 'Sambo did it.' If you did, kid, you really scored. They'll remember that one as long as there's a Willingham."

Porter's summons to appear before the Discipline Committee was swift in coming and the proceedings brief. By the following afternoon, it was history. It always had a dreamlike quality in Porter's memory, partly induced by the fact that two of the members sat in silence and shadow and seemed to be almost faceless. Porter could not later remember even their names. He never forgot, however, Professor Hiram Augustus Twilley.

It was indeed that gentleman's committee, and he loomed in heroic stature like a Cyclops or an Amos or a combination of the two. Once Porter even thought of Medusa. He hissed and spat as he spoke in level tones of sin and crime and respect for property. For a short while on an early November afternoon, while rain dimmed the campus and brought the leaves off the sugarberry trees in sodden drifts, Porter knew terror.

"Now tell me, Osborne, who threw ink on the new wall in Nathan Bedford Forrest Smith Hall?"

"I did, sir, but —"

"Silence! That is all the information we need. We choose to hear no puling rationale for such heinous conduct. There are some deeds that beggar forgiveness, Osborne, and vandalism is one of them. Wait in the hall. This should not take long."

Porter barely had time before he was called back into the room to plan how he, in the midst of his shame and humiliation, would break the news of his expulsion to his father and request that someone come for him.

"Osborne, you should be expelled. There are two mitigating factors, however, which persuade us to temper justice with mercy. One is your academic record. You are a member of Phi Eta Sigma and consistently on the Dean's List, and you are excelling in English literature this year. The other is your immaturity. I speak not only of your chronological age but of your appearance, which is that of perpetual and naive youth. With your gifts, Osborne, despite your physical appearance, you should be a leader. You are not. You are too easily led and influenced. We feel it perhaps would have been better had you defied family tradition and not joined a fraternity, but it is too late for that consideration.

"We are not going to expel you, Osborne. We are going to isolate you. The entire third floor of Nottingham Hall is vacant. Beginning this evening, you will be its sole occupant. I have called Mrs. Capulet and she has assigned a room to you. You will live in that room, Osborne, for the remainder of this academic year. You will live in that room alone. You are forbidden for the rest of this year even to enter the new dormitory except on official fraternity business. Do you understand?"

"Yes, sir."

"Very well. In addition, you will pay for repairing the wall you defiled. Do you agree to that?"

"Yes, sir."

"Very well. Finally, you will be on probation. This means that any further misconduct on your part serious enough to cause your appearance before this committee will result not in such a hearing as the one this afternoon, but in your automatic expulsion from the campus of Willingham University. Without a hearing. You will be gone. Do you understand this?"

"Yes, sir."

"All right. Be aware that while your banishment to Nottingham Hall and domiciliary solitude is for the remainder of this year only, your term of probation is for the duration of your career at Willingham. Do you understand that?"

334

"Yes, sir."

"Very well. I trust that you will not willfully interrupt that career. You may go, Osborne."

"Thank you, sir."

By bedtime Porter was ensconced in a room on third floor of Nottingham Hall. It was a large room designed and furnished for three students. The two empty beds with mattresses rolled up to expose the springs and the two empty dressers lined against the wall accentuated the loneliness of Porter's freshly-made bed and his crowded dresser top. As he considered his situation and reviewed the events leading to it, he decided that Professor Twilley, although firm, was one of the fairest people he had ever met. He wondered how much the new wall in Smith Hall would cost him, he rehearsed what he would tell his father, and he rejoiced that he was still a student at Willingham. He was so filled with gratitude for that blessing that it never entered his head to feel sorry for himself. In lieu of saying his prayers, he muttered aloud, "I really love that old one-eyed bastard," and immediately fell asleep.

The banning of Porter Osborne probably prevented him from failing a course, although he was unaware of it as a blessing at the time. Shortly after his banishment, he found himself in deeper trouble academically than he had been the previous year in French. The stumbling block this time was Chemistry. The Chemistry professor was a septuagenarian with pate so bald he looked to have been skinned and his rimless glasses glistened like icy twigs catching full sun. He had the reputation of being a devout academician and a demanding scholar with considerable reputation on the national scene for erudition. About three weeks into the quarter, after threatening to flunk any freshman he overheard saying, "The dăta is," instead of "The dāta are," he died in his sleep. It happened right after Porter had resolved to approach him and explain that his high school had not offered Chemistry and that valence was an unfathomable mystery to him.

For three weeks the Chemistry department was without a teacher, and Porter soon grew accustomed to studying only two

335

subjects and having extra time for social affairs. When the new teacher arrived, he was fuzzy-headed and alien and wore glasses thicker than his predecessor's. He had earned his doctorate at the University of Pittsburg but tended to slobber a bit and become mired in unfinished sentences. He assumed that his students had six weeks of beginner's Chemistry behind them and began lecturing on that level. Porter made fifty on the mid-term. With horror he realized that a professor had risen who knew him not, was unaware of his record of academic excellence, and had even mispronounced the word *data* until Tiny Yeomans had corrected him.

Porter reckoned that it would be a pity to escape the Scylla of the Twilley committee and be destroyed by the Charybdis of Inorganic Chemistry. He threw himself into a fury of study involving acid, base, anions, cations, elements, metals, salts, and balanced equations. He was too engrossed to notice that KA seemed not to regret his absence from the parlor of the fraternity suite or that he was becoming ever more isolated from them. After mid-term, the Chemistry professor gave no more tests until the final. Porter, in his lonely room, labored with purpose and apprehension. He had no idea of his class standing, but in the daytime he hid his fears behind outrageous banter with Sara Belle and Amalita.

Those two had pledged Phi Mu, worried little about grades, and were all atwitter about whether they would be invited to the Homecoming dances since they were newcomers to Willingham. All the really cute boys, Sara Belle said, were either pinned or had regular girlfriends, but she wanted to dance and would go even if nobody but Eldridge Dunahoo invited her. This dance was the social highlight of fall quarter, coming on the Saturday night after the football game. Willingham University never would be associated officially with anything so ecclesiastically suspect as dancing, so the dances always were sponsored by Pan-Hellenic Council and held off-campus at the impersonal and nondenominational City Auditorium. Porter could not dance and had a horror of exposing his ignorance in public. For his beloved girlfriends, however, he would expend any effort.

He easily persuaded E.V. Derrick, who seemed to have developed a certain deference toward him since the ink-throwing episode, to invite the fair Amalita. He then put pressure on a fat KA pledge from somewhere in Florida, who was still slightly intimidated by upperclassmen, and Sara Belle had a date. He assured both girls that although they were not being squired by exactly the flowers of KA, the important thing was to be seen at the dance and that their beauty and charm would thenceforth insure forevermore their presence at similar events.

He listened to their chatter about dresses, breathed the *toujours moi,* and somewhat wistfully spent the night of the dance memorizing everything he could find about sodium and potassium and trying to understand why hydrogen had such an affinity for oxygen under one set of circumstances and for chloride under another. He studied hard enough that his final examination was creditable, and he pulled his Chemistry grade up to a D.

When he went home for Christmas with two A's and a D, he did not feel humiliation at falling off the Dean's List but instead had a deep sense of pride at passing Chemistry — never mind how slim the margin. He manfully maintained silence and made no mention of grades to his mother and sisters. After all, they were not paying his way through college. He gauged the time he thought report cards would be sent out and approached his father with an explanation and a semblance of apology.

"Hell, boy, I understand. Don't worry about it. When I was at Willingham, my history professor told me I ought to make a good sailor because I hung around the C's all the time. You'll pull that D up in no time."

"Thanks for understanding, Dad."

"I'm just glad Twilley didn't ship you home for good. By the way, I mailed a check last week for the wall. It wasn't but fifteen dollars. I thought that was pretty reasonable."

"Thanks, Dad."

"How are you making out in that room by yourself? As punishment, that kind of ostracism seems a little cruel and unusual. I feel like maybe you're paying for the sins of your father with Twilley running the show, but if I stepped in it would make it worse. You have to fight this one alone."

"Oh, yes, sir. Don't worry about me. I'm doing fine. It's a great opportunity to study. I was lonesome at first, but now I'm beginning to like it."

337

"Well, don't sit in that room every night. Get out and have a little recreation. Go to the show with your fraternity brothers or something. They haven't banned you from the dances, have they?"

"No, sir, but I don't go. I can't dance."

"Hell, that doesn't make any difference. Nobody can at first. Take a drink and you can."

"Dad, nobody drinks at the dances except the Kappa Sigs and the Pikes and a few of the SAE's. KA's don't drink."

"They used to. What the hell's happened to them? Well, strike that question from the record. Come on and I'll buy you a Coke. It's four o'clock and I've got to see a man about a dog."

Winter quarter at Willingham had none of the exciting antic- ipation that had been generated by the sparkle of autumn. It stretched out in a flat dreariness of gray days, damp skies, and long nights. It was a period of time to be endured, monotonously marked off by dripping trees and countless puddles, so cold and wet there seemed no promise of better times to come. Porter grew restless. The long nights in his room were more than adequate for studying. He knew he was bringing his Chemistry grade up to a B at least, and whenever he could persuade Amalita and Sara Belle to study at the Library he had blissful evenings in their company. What few pranks he pulled were never impulsive and had to be most meticulously planned. He harked back to Mrs. Capulet's advice of the previous year and felt secure. He remembered that she had said if he could fool her, he also would appear innocent in the eye of Professor Twilley, and he was very crafty about any mischief he generated.

He had made up his mind that he was going to the Old South Ball in February. It would be his first dance. This social event was a direct outgrowth of the furor generated by *Gone with the Wind.* The book had focused national attention on Georgia, and most people persuaded themselves that it was all true.

The movie had gulled Georgians into believing its portrayal of antebellum life — even the families who knew better because they still lived on the plantations depicted. They believed in the grandeur of the movie because they needed to believe in it. Margaret Mitchell had neutered Erskine Caldwell. Georgians could hold their noble

338

heads high before the yankees, and all of them did. It was perfectly natural that the KA's across the country (the land below the Mason-Dixon line, of course) should turn this hysteria to their own advantage. They began having Old South Balls, and they were serious about it. It was to become an annual social event for Kappa Alpha Order that was almost what a pilgrimage to Mecca was for a Mohammedan.

Timed to fall on the Saturday nearest to Robert E. Lee's birthday, it was a costume ball at which all participants were expected to appear in dress befitting the Old South. A large percentage of students equated the Old South only with the Confederacy. They revered the gallant, gray-clad soldiers facing death with a swagger in stubborn denial of culture-defeating reality and in mocking challenge of crushing military superiority.

Consequently, most of the KA's had patronized costume agencies in Atlanta and had rented all the Confederate uniforms they could find. The agencies had an adequate supply because of the Atlanta premiere of *Gone with the Wind* and the parties and dances associated with that prestigious event. The fees ran from fifteen dollars for a private's uniform to twice that for a general's. Besides being too thin to wear the smallest size available, Porter was too penurious to spend that much money.

He had a date with Sara Belle, and they discussed costuming with pleasure.

"You know every ADPi who gets invited is going as Scarlett. And they should. They all act like her. Why don't I go as Aunt Pitty-Pat and you go as Gerald O'Hara?"

"You go as Belle Watling and I'll be Jonas Wilkinson."

"Or we could black our faces and I could be Mammy and you a pickaninny. I'd be every bit as good as Hattie McDaniel. 'Umph, umph, umph. Miss Scyarlit, don't you know you cain't show yo bosom fo six o'clock?' And you're already named Sambo."

The last idea appealed to Porter and he encouraged it. As soon as Sara Belle realized he was serious, she speedily reneged. The Willingham co-ed who would deliberately make herself appear ridiculous at the biggest dance of the winter quarter was nonexistent.

Porter did a little superficial research and decided to go as a youthful Sidney Lanier. He could wear the frock coat his father had worn in the ninth grade at Locust Grove Institute. Miss Louvale in Brewtonton had a house full of children, possessed genius with a sewing machine, and could make anything. He wrote her and asked for a pair of white flannel pants with elastic under the insteps, explaining what he wanted and telling her his waist was twenty-four inches. The pants and the coat, complemented by a string tie, would do nicely, he thought, and would cost him less than five dollars, since Miss Louvale would deliver the trousers to his mother who would pay the postage to mail them to Macon.

Sara Belle talked with animation of the black and white lace dress she was having made and assured Porter that her father had been most cordial about lending them his car for the evening. E.V. Derrick asked if he and Amalita could ride with them. Porter agreed, provided E.V. would buy five gallons of gasoline. He began to get so excited over the prospect of the Old South Ball that he buried his misgivings about not being able to dance.

At chapter meeting on Wednesday night before the dance, the secretary went around the room making a date list to be turned in to the social editor of the *Macon Telegraph*. He also inquired about costumes for each brother. Both Spangler and Roundtree were going as confederate generals. Deacon Chauncey was going to wear his tuxedo, put four aces in his sleeve, and go as a Mississippi riverboat gambler. He did not have a date.

When Porter called Sara Belle's name and announced his masquerade as Sidney Lanier, Clarence Spangler laughed loudly and even pointed at Porter. "Sidney Lanier? He was a sissy if ever I heard of one! I don't know how you talked a girl built like Sara Belle into dating you, but you're sure gonna look funny beside her. Why don't you go as Little Lord Fauntleroy?"

Porter withstood the ensuing merriment but resolved to tend to Spangler if he could. He kept his mouth shut and thought about it for two days before he evolved a plan. He had noticed in the short time he had been a resident in the KA suite that Clarence, regularly and invariably, conducted his daily constitutional after supper instead of after breakfast. The bathroom in the new fraternity suite had two showers, three lavatories, three commodes, and one urinal. Anyone who had to visit the toilets after supper always encountered an enthroned Clarence, uninhibited and loudly talking. The commodes were not the ancient brown-seated variety with a pull chain dangling from a tank beneath the ceiling, such as existed in some places in the Administration Building. Neither were they the less antique models with white enameled seats. The toilets in Nathan Bedford Forrest Smith Hall jutted abruptly from the wall with no tank and had shiny black seats with a gap in front, presumably so that thoughtless males who did not remember to lift a seat would at least not wet it. Porter planned carefully.

On the Saturday evening of the dance, while Willingham boys were single-mindedly attacking supper with a zest that obliterated attention to anything else, Porter saw to it that second helpings were on his table before they could be demanded. He sped out the kitchen door, retrieved in darkness the small can and brush he had earlier secreted beneath a ligustrum bush, and swiftly entered the deserted Smith Hall. Very thoroughly and very quickly, he gave each KA commode seat a new, thick, glistening coat of black enamel. He was back at his post in the dining hall without even Mrs. Raleigh realizing he had been absent. While he cleaned away dirty dishes and scrubbed his sector of the dining hall floor, he was wistful at not being able to observe firsthand the results of his effort.

The vicarious enjoyment, however, was almost as sweet and probably safer. E.V. Derrick told him about it when he came to pick him up for the dance. "Sonny Boy, you know how Spangler takes a crap after supper every night? Well, tonight there were three of them went tearing in at the same time. Nervous about getting ready for the Old South ball, I guess. There was Clarence and Slick and that nice pledge from Bainbridge who sings so good. Some of the fellows were already taking their showers and Clarence was yelling about his costume so loud it echoed all over the bathroom, and the showers had everything so foggy I had to keep wiping the mirror where I was shaving. Sonny Boy, you didn't paint those toilet seats, did you?"

"Derrick, what in the world are you talking about? What toilet seats?"

"Deacon and I said it couldn't be you cause you haven't even been over there all day. But somebody did. You know when we found out about it? Roundtree and Spangler were naked when they went to the crapper, and they started back across the hall to get their towels to take showers, and Spangler pointed to Roundtree and says, 'What's

341

that on your ass?' You know what a voice Spangler's got, and every KA in the suite heard him and came out to see.

"And Spangler gets to looking at Roundtree and calling him 'ole black ass' and starts laughing and pointing, and you know how he laughs even louder than he talks. And Roundtree turns around trying to see and finally gets in front of a mirror and starts cussing. And about that time somebody gets a look at Spangler's tail, and it's framed in black, too. Then Roundtree starts laughing and pointing and Spangler starts cussing. Then somebody thinks to check the toilets and the seats have been fresh painted. Your name kept coming up, Sonny Boy. You sure you weren't over there?"

"When do you think I could have been, Derrick? This sounds like I really missed something."

"Well, about that time Pledge Brother Rick decided he better check, and he let down his pants and he was painted, too. It had got his drawers all black, and you know something, Sonny Boy? Charlie Rick's got a lot more hairs on his ass than Clarence and Slick put together."

"Golly, E.V., yall really had a time, didn't you?"

"Everybody got to laughing so hard they were about to be late getting dressed for the dance. Roundtree and Spangler got in the showers and scrubbed and scrubbed, but the best they could do was smear that enamel around. Soap and water wouldn't touch it. Their butts are still framed in black. They said it was worse to get rid of than soot, and your name came up again. They finally went ahead and got dressed in their costumes with all the gold braid on the coats and plumes in their hats, but Deacon Chauncey bout ruined it for them. He saluted and called them 'General Black Ass' and 'General Dirt Butt,' and now everybody's calling them that."

"What about Charlie Rick?"

"Ooh, Sonny Boy, he's in bad shape. He saw what luck Spangler and Roundtree were having with the soap and water and got himself some gasoline. Said he wasn't going anywhere with paint on his tail. He scrubbed so hard he got most of the paint off, but do you know that gasoline blistered him? He wound up in the shower for a long time. He's going to the dance, but he can't sit down, and all the fellows are calling him 'Captain Red.' Sonny Boy, you better get your pants on or we're gonna be late."

Porter had misgivings about his costume. His mother had been late mailing it and Miss Louvale had been close in her measurements. It had arrived only that afternoon, and when Porter got dressed he would have discarded it except that he had nothing else to wear. The coat looked as old as it truly was, and there was a greenish glisten to it and a moth hole in one sleeve, but it would pass. The trousers were the problem. They fit like Porter's own skin and held him as tightly molded as any corset ever devised. They accented the underdevelopment of his muscles and the precocious maturity of other areas. When he stood erect and held his shoulders proudly back as any young Sidney Lanier should, his legs touched each other only at the ankles and knees and left humiliating gaps between the thighs and the calves.

As E.V. Derrick spoke, Porter winced. "You can't go to a dance in your union suit, Sonny Boy. Put your pants on."

"I've got my pants on, Derrick."

There was a pause. "Oh. Well, Sonny Boy, don't you think you ought to wear a jockey strap?"

"I've got on my jockey strap."

There was another slightly longer pause. "You don't happen to have two jockey straps, do you, Sonny Boy?"

Porter wailed, "Oh, E.V., what am I going to do? I look like a damn fool. You'll just have to take Amalita and Sara Belle both and I'll stay here. Tell em I got sick or died or something."

"Oh, Sonny Boy, you're just being sensitive. I was only teasing you. Anybody who can play a joke ought to be able to take a joke. You look great. Come on, let's go. We're going to be late for the grand march if we don't hurry, and that would never do. You're an officer in the fraternity, you know."

Sara Belle had rendered an incomplete description of her dress, although it was, in truth, a manifestation in white satin and black lace of exquisite dressmaking. What she had not mentioned was how it looked on her. It was cut low in front, and her magnificent breasts jutted out and strained against the confining bodice in breathtaking threat of imminent escape. Her cleavage would have put Marie de Medici to shame and would have made Peter Paul Reubens ecstatic. No girl so generously endowed and so exquisitely attired could possibly carry her head with anything less than pride,

343

and Miss Sara Belle was truly a vision. For an instant Porter could only gasp, but he rapidly recovered.

"Laws-a-mussy, Miss Scarlett, you the most beautifullest thing in the whole state of Georgia tonight. From the looks of them things, it must be might nigh on one or two o'clock in the mawning."

"You hush yo mouth, Sidney Lanier, and help me get these damn hoops in the car. Fiddle-de-dee, how you do run on!"

Porter relaxed. He figured that with Sara Belle as his date, no one would ever notice how he was dressed.

Idlewild Country Club was decorated with Confederate flags and hung with crimson and gold crepe paper wherever any could be draped. Sara Belle was an instant and overwhelming success. Porter's fears about dancing abated. He had to stand before her for only a couple of measures, shifting from one foot to the other, before someone broke. And they kept on breaking. Miss Sara Belle Steele was getting what was called a rush. Porter beamed and spent some time observing his first dance.

Because of the girls' hoop skirts, the band was playing mostly slow pieces. The pianist gyrated more than the organist at Vineville Baptist, and the drummer played most of the time in pseudo-rapt abandon with his eyes closed. The saxophonist bowed and bobbed and wagged his instrument from side to side; the clarinetist kept licking his reed and puffing out his cheeks until he became alarmingly red-faced; the bass violinist would occasionally slap his big fiddle and spin it completely around. They all wore tuxedos. Porter was impressed.

It was interesting to watch the various posture patterns of the girls while they were dancing. The ones who were intent on being ladies danced sedately upright while they engaged their partners in conversation and indulged in only occasional lapses of cheek-to-cheek companionship. The more uninhibited girls who had defiantly not worn hoop skirts molded their forms to those of their partners from the knees up and moved with them to the music like one body sporting four legs. They would get themselves talked about in the ADPi and Phi Mu meetings and never get a bid to a sorority.

344

The boys who danced with them would not get talked about but would earn a subliminal, albeit not necessarily accurate, reputation as cocksmen. There were other niggling little idiosyncracies of stance or comportment according to where a girl had been reared or learned to dance, but all of them paled to insignificance in the presence of the Miller High School girls.

They had been invited to the Old South ball in coveys, and they were a beautiful sight to behold. There was apparently a current taboo among them, however, that nice girls did not allow their bodies to touch those of their partners on the dance floor. They might, if they really liked a boy, let the left hand climb up his sleeve and rest on his shoulder or even clasp his neck, but the body itself was sacred and inviolate. The girls enforced this code by the use of their heads. When a boy broke on one of these lovely young creatures, she immediately accepted his waist-encircling right arm and thrust her forehead out to meet his in contact so unyieldingly maintained by stiffened neck muscles that it was impossible to get any closer to her. If a girl caught a boy in this fashion straight on, they wound up looking into each other's eyes like two stalemated game chickens; so most of the girls affected a union of temple with the head cocked a little to one side.

Since it was ludicrous for a girl to stand completely upright with her head butted firmly against that of her partner, this cephalad coupling was complemented by grotesque angling of shoulders, waist, and hips. The Miller girl twisted always to one side as she danced, with the hips as a consequence protruding backward and to the opposite side. This may have compelled a stilted form of balance for her dancing partners, but it presented a marvelous spectacle to the nonparticipants rimming the dance floor. Porter thought that certainly Pattie Lou Mitcham must be the most voluptuously built symbol of chastity currently enrolled at Miller High. The way she was stuck out behind and twisted around was a marvel, but she probably was going to be too sore to attend church the following day.

His superficial attention to the boys on the dance floor caused him to resolve that when he matured and began dancing himself, he would never, ever hold his partner between the shoulder blades or allow his left arm to pump. He knew country when he saw it.

Porter broke on his date several times but gratifyingly never had to spend more than a minute or two rocking from side to side and feverishly forcing conversation before he was in turn tapped on the shoulder. The Phi Delta Thetas all had come dressed as yankee soldiers, and they were thronging around Miss Sara Belle as if they were preparing to take Richmond. She was beaming and enjoying every minute of it. Amalita was getting an equally enthusiastic rush from the SAE's and Kappa Sigs. Porter broke on her after observing the crowd around her, confident that his lack of dancing skill would be safely masked by a brief sojourn with her in his arms. To his discomfort, there came a lull in the fair Amalita's line of swains. He shifted from one foot to the other and back again. He talked. He shifted.

Finally he could stand the growing embarrassment no longer. "Oh, Amalita, I'm sorry. I can't dance a lick and didn't really have any business coming tonight, let alone breaking on you."

Amalita gave a little murmur of inconsequential reassurance. He took a deep breath of *toujours moi*. "Amalita, I'm sure this is awful for you, just standing in one place with me hopping from one foot to the other like this. You deserve better than me. Stand right here and I'll run find one of the KA's to break on you."

Her dainty little right hand closed on his left wrist in an unexpected grip, strong and unyielding. "You'll do no such a damn thing! Have you completely lost your mind, Porter Osborne? I can hear that Clarence Spangler right now if you did that! He'd spread it all over Chichester's Drugstore and then all over Willingham. You're not going to leave me standing like the Statue of Liberty in the middle of this dance floor. The very idea! You stay right where you are." Her throaty voice did not rise, but it had real authority.

"But, Amalita, I know it's humiliating for a beautiful girl like you to be stuck here with a country boy who can't even dance. Would you like to go sit this one out?"

"Hell, no. It's all I can do to stand up and dance with these fool hoops banging around. I sure can't sit. That awful Martha Emma Wilson tried to sit down while ago right over there, and her hoops flew plumb up over her face. She looked like a cancan dancer with her drawers showing, and it couldn't have happened to a better bitch. What I want you to do is relax. You're already keeping time to the music. All you've got to do is slide your feet around like you're drawing boxes with them and turn me around occasionally. And don't step on my toes. If one more football player walks on my feet tonight, I'm going to be limping like I had the infantile paralysis."

"But, Amalita, I can't dance."

"Neither can three-fourths of the boys here. The difference, Sambo, is that you know it. Hold me closer and stay off my toes. And listen to the music."

Porter was immediately transported to the highest pinnacle of the seventh circle of Paradise. He held her closer. With delight. He carefully stayed off her toes. He tried to listen to the music but was sure it was ringing joyfully from within his own heart. Amalita pressed her cheek to his, and he was ecstatic. He turned her to the left. He even ventured a backward step or two. He wondered if she knew about Hiram Holliday. His fantasies multiplied. He felt a delicious pat on his right shoulder and heard a sultry murmur in his ear. "There. You're doing great. I told you I'd teach you, didn't I?" His bliss was boundless.

In surging confidence, Porter pulled his head back and welcomed mischief back to the evening. "But, Amalita, I was afraid to ask. You said you didn't want anybody learning on you."

She gave a little gasp and then a guttural laugh. "You're horrible. You never forget anything, do you? And I never know what's going on in your head. But I sure have an idea what it's about most of the time. Here comes somebody to break. Go dance with Pattie Lou Mitcham and see if you can keep her from breaking her neck or throwing her sacroiliac out of joint."

The six-foot halfback whose eyebrows grew together in a thick straight line across his forehead and who whistled through his nose with every breath tapped him on the shoulder with a heavy forefinger. Amalita gave Porter a little squeeze and slid her half-lidded eyes to meet his gaze. "Enjoyed it," she breathed.

As Porter left the dance floor, he thought of young goats leaping with abandon in spring pastures. It was wonderful to be a Willingham sophomore. It was wonderful to be a fraternity man. It was the ultimate happiness to be a Knight of Kappa Alpha Order. He met Deacon Chauncey in the line around Pattie Lou and spoke with nonchalant camaraderie. "Wonder what the po folks are doing tonight, Deacon."

After the KA's had been introduced with their dates, after Jo Beth Montagu had dramatically sung "The KA Rose" and been dutifully applauded, after the Brothers had lustily rendered "It's a Grand Old Gang," Porter was dreamily revolving in the last dance with Miss Sara Belle. He was really dancing. The tune was "Stardust." He had forgotten how he looked in his costume. He had his forehead glued to that of the most attractive and popular female in Macon. Or maybe the second. His loyalties were divided.

"Law, Mr. Porter Osborne, Jr., suh, yo dancing has certainly improved a sight this evening if you don't mind my saying so, suh."

"Thank you, Miss Sara Belle Steele, ma'am, from the bottom of my heart for your kind and gracious notice. I learned on Amalita. It looked like you were entertaining the whole yankee army this evening, if you'll forgive the comment, ma'am. A poor Georgia poet could hardly get near you for all those blue uniforms."

"Oh, Sambo, it's been a wonderful evening and I do thank you for inviting me. You're the best little ole buddy a girl ever had. I'm dated up solid for the next three weekends."

Porter considered her formidable bosom, still protruding as vigorously and majestically as earlier, and envied the Phi Delta Thetas. His reverie was interrupted by Clarence's swooping and dipping near them with Martha Emma Wilson. This girl was not a Willingham student and Porter was never quite clear where Sara Belle and Amalita had known her, but she drew from them a natural spark of animosity that was lightning-like and almost visible. She was a gracefully proportioned female with perfect teeth and consequently smiled almost constantly. As she whirled on the gold-braided arm of Clarence, she leaned toward Porter and cooed, "Haven't had a chance to speak to you all evening, Sara Belle, but you and Sambo are the talk of the town tonight. Everybody says that when you're facing each other you fit like a jigsaw puzzle."

Porter flinched, but not Sara Belle. She was as imposing and erect as a countess, and her dark eyes flashed. "Well, I declare, if it isn't Martha Emma. I hadn't the slightest idea you were here. Have you been on the dance floor much? I haven't seen you. And I do believe that's General Black you're dancing with. All the Phi Delts have been telling me about him tonight. Yall look after each other, hear?"

As Porter turned her in a careful maneuver, she snorted, "Have you ever in your life seen so many teeth? I bet those two have a hundred and fifty between them. Who would have thought ole Loudmouth Spangler would wind up in a Confederate uniform with his bottom painted black and dancing with ole Martha Enema, the twisted-gut girl from Ty-Ty, Georgia? I'm surprised the enlisted men let her loose from Camp Wheeler for an evening."

Porter was sure Sara Belle spoke so loudly her subjects heard her, but they gave no indication of it. As Clarence and Martha Emma swirled away from them in a froth of blue satin and gray wool, Porter looked over Sara Belle's shoulder and noticed Clarence's supporting right hand in the center of Martha Emma's slender back. All the fingers were curled under except the middle one. It protruded in solitary rigidity, taunting and unmistakably communicative. Porter would have understood a thumb on the nose, but he had never seen this gesture before. He was puzzled, but it never entered his head to be insulted.

XXI **T**he tedium of Porter's nights as the third floor hermit of Nottingham Hall was relieved for the next week or so by his memories of the Old South Ball and his growing relationship with Amalita Hunt and Sara Belle Steele — tolerant friendship on their part, unqualified adoration on his. His days had become a turmoil of activity and passed rapidly.

A larger and larger part of his attention was devoted to Comparative Anatomy. If a student made an A in Professor Hansford's Comparative course, he was assured a place in the Medical College of Georgia at Augusta. The course had begun with dissection of the lowly dogfish and was to culminate in the grand finale of dissecting a mammal. The cat was the animal chosen by Professor Hansford, and each student had to furnish his own. The procurement was pure adventure. Professor Hansford gave a little lecture about the impact of stray cats on the bird population and the possible effect of the proliferation of these feral beasts on the ecology of Macon. The lecture provided a needed nobility of purpose to the quest for laboratory material and checked the misgivings of the tenderhearted. He gave a benign little admonition for his students to capture only stray animals.

"Whatever you boys and girls do, be careful not to bother anyone's pet. Nearly every year I have an upset lady or so jump all over me about their cats disappearing. Of course, all cats look alike when they are skinned and put in formaldehyde, so it's impossible for them to make a positive identification. I always invite them into the basement to inspect the specimens, but that just seems to upset them more, and they're never fully convinced that we haven't kid-

350

napped their kitties. Please remember that you are ambassadors of good will for Willingham and that good public relations with our neighbors depend on you. Great big Persians are popular just now and are never, ever strays. Whatever you do, don't bring a Persian on this campus. Class dismissed."

Armed with crokersacks and sardines, the mighty hunters of Willingham scattered over the western sector of Macon, their chief concession to public relations being to forage after dark whenever possible. They soon learned that a decade of cat prowling had winnowed out almost all the strays in their area and that the few which had survived formed a wary breed, unapproachable by high-pitched, pleading calls and even suspicious of the tantalizing odor of fish. The alley cat of Macon could identify a Willingham student a block away and would immediately become glassy-eyed with caution. Slinking furtively around protecting corners or else scrambling pell-mell over high fences, ferocious and snarling when cornered, the alley cat was a trophy worth bagging, one that separated the men from the boys, the ladies from the ribbon clerks.

The pets of the bourgeois, in contrast, were sitting ducks, playful and trusting, pampered beyond the idea that anyone could do them harm. They answered the enticing calls of sophomores with enthusiastic curiosity — backs arched, tails held rigidly erect, mincing on dainty feet toward their captors and even purring and rubbing against a student's leg in response to a tickled chin or a tidbit of canned fish. They were easy prey, sitting on back doorsteps in the dark, having dug and covered their last sanitary hole of the day in obedience to patient training. They carefully licked their paws or worse while they waited their summons to the nocturnal security of the house.

The trick, however, if one was going to snare a pet, was to do it early in the season. The effect of hearing a lady's voice in the evening calling, "Kitty, kitty, kitty! Here, kitty!" while one sped away with a writhing sack might produce only a callous hardening of conscience in a student, but the lonely and plaintive cry was a tocsin to the ladies of Macon. It told them that it was late winter, that the degenerate boys of Willingham were loose in the land, and that every home-owner in the neighborhood must join again in protective collusion.

Henry Bean grumbled to Porter. "These old biddies have

351

started locking their damn cats up tighter than virgins in a boarding school or nuns in a convent. You'd think they could see the broader picture and be willing to donate a little pussy to the interests of science."

"Henry, don't start me laughing. Grab that one right over there. Nobody's looking."

Walking swiftly away, they heard the call in the night. "Kitty, kitty, kitty! Here, kitty! Come, kitty, kitty, kitty!"

Henry turned his head and answered. "Meow, meow." As they began running, Porter thought how much he admired Henry Bean but how little consideration Professor Twilley would give that fact. He prayed not to get caught.

Conversion of a fresh cat into a finished laboratory specimen was not for the squeamish and required both speed and skill, the former an outgrowth of the latter. If the SPCA existed in Macon, it had not been publicized to the attention of Biology majors at Willingham. The students, under the tutelage of Professor Hansford, nevertheless were very careful not to inflict pain in their animals. Chloroform was the answer.

The cat was placed in a bell jar and quickly anesthetized. Then very smoothly and rapidly the chest was opened down the center, exposing the smooth pink lungs, which promptly collapsed. Between them was the wildly contracting muscular heart. A thick solution of dye containing cornstarch and potassium dichromate was injected through a large-bore needle into the ventricle while the heart gave a few convulsive beats and then was still forever. A wooden plug whittled to size was then inserted into the needle hole to prevent leakage of dye. The cat was cleanly skinned, the abdomen opened to allow penetration of preservative, the jaws wedged open for the same purpose, and a tag with the student's name wired around a foot.

Upon immersion into a crock of pure formaldehyde, all individuality disappeared, and the animal became simply an impersonal, bleached-out laboratory aid, a mammal of the feline genus with well-demarcated muscle groups, glistening white nerves, rubbery viscera, and arteries beautifully outlined with hardened orange dye. The preparation awaited the careful dissection of a serious student and gleamed with the promise of an A.

Porter Osborne had helped Henry Bean, E.V. Derrick, and a couple of other boys prepare their specimens. He had single-handedly done a cat for a girl who could bear neither the sight and odors inherent in the process nor the final tissue-shrinking, eye-watering fumes of formaldehyde. He had delayed his own cat pickling for one simple reason: He wanted the prestige of acquiring a stray cat. Never mind that Bean and Derrick enjoyed reputations for worldly indifference by disobeying Professor Hansford and smuggling in plump and compliant Persians; the aristocrat of cat hunters stalked the wild ones and scorned the softened attitudes of expediency and self-serving ease.

One evening, by patient use of a fish head and a string, Porter enticed and captured a truly reprehensible alley cat, a creature that never had entered a human home, a pure carnivore that had matured on mice and birds and wharf rats and occasional furtive tidbits from midnight garbage cans. It was all Porter could do to get back to campus with the heavy, gyrating sack, its occupant jumping and twisting and emitting yowls of pure rage.

In the bright light, stilled by the chloroform in the bell jar, Porter's cat was obviously female in the last stages of pregnancy. The short span between anesthetization and death allowed no time for speculation or sentimentality, as the dye had to be injected into a living heart. Porter worked rapidly and automatically. When he slit the abdominal wall, there were three bulging uterine pouches. Very quickly and with great curiosity Porter incised one of them and extracted a tiny unit of animal life, fully formed and wet all over, the eyes prominent but sealed in prematurity. As he looked, the kitten gave a weak gasp. Porter began blowing into the little mouth and cupped the body in one hand for warmth, frantically pulling occluding membranes from the head and nose. He was rewarded by a faint mewing and was filled with awe and excitement.

"I've done a Cesarian! I've resuscitated a premature! I wonder if I can make it live!"

He warmed a huck towel and wrapped the baby in it while he attended the final chores on his laboratory specimen. Then he hastened to the dormitory and stayed up half the night dripping warm milk off a match stick into the newborn's mouth. Despite the fashioning of an incubator from a light bulb and a box, it was obvious that he had to find a surrogate mother if this foundling was to survive. He went to breakfast a half hour early the next morning and sought out Boston Harbor Jones.

"Uh huh, Sambo, I understand what you saying. Let me sneak out here and git on the telephone. Lady stay next door to Maw got cats and they having litters ever time you turn around. Whole bunches of em. Place covered up with em. I'm allus stepping on one in the dark and holler hallelujah. Nothing in the world more upsetting than walking long and step on somepin soft that jump up and go spitting and hissing and yowling and clawing right under you feet. Feel like a fool hopping round in the dark and yelling, 'Good Godamighty,' over nothing. I hate cats, but I understand what you looking for and I'll try."

"Now, Boston, it'd be better if her babies are just a day or two old. I want one with real fresh milk."

"Uh huh. My maw say, 'Aint what you want make yo belly poke out. It's what you get.' But I see what I can do. Be back in a minute. You crazy, Sambo, go to all this trouble over a premature kitten. Best it or you either one can ever hope for is it grow up to be a cat."

Within minutes he returned. "We in luck, Sambo. Maw run next door while I helt the phone. Lady say she got a real sweet new mammy with three kittens bout ten days old. Eyes just got open good day fo yestiddy. Maw told her some nice white boy want a wet nurse for his speriment to keep a premature kitten alive what done lost its own mama. She don't tell the lady how that mama cat got lost. Lady say you have to take all three kittens too and give them a good home. Maw say the lady a little jubious on account of what I say to her one time, but she let you have em and wish you well. I git on the bus tereckly and have em for you at dinnertime."

"Gosh, Boston, thanks. I don't know what I'd do without you. What'd you say to your maw's neighbor one time?"

"She ax me how come I despise cats so bad and I look her in the eye and say I ain't got no use for nothing spend least fifty percent its wake-up time licking on its own asshole. Get you tables ready. Sireen gonna blow in a minute."

The idea worked. The mother cat was white, with one blue eye

354

and one brown one, and was extremely placid and friendly. Her three babies stayed glued to her teats, and it was a simple matter for Porter to replace one of them with his orphan and let the natural child stimulate another nipple. The mama cat gave no indication that there was anything unusual about the arrangement. Porter put the family in a box in the corner of his room and prudently positioned a box of sand nearby. The premature suckled and grew stronger.

Three days into the arrangement, Mrs. Capulet stopped him in the hall. "Sambo, there are cats in your room."

"Yes'm, I know."

"Animals are absolutely forbidden in the dormitory. Get rid of them."

"Mrs. Capulet, let me explain. I was having to sacrifice this old alley cat to get a dissection animal and she turned out to be pregnant, and I managed to operate and get one of the little kittens out and make it live. But the only way I can keep it living is to have a wet nurse for it and I need the mama cat, but the woman who loaned her to me made me take the other three kittens, too. As soon as I get the preemie where it can eat on its own, I'll send the others back. They're just on loan. But don't you see how thrilling it will be if I can do a Cesarian on a cat and have the baby survive? I've never heard of this happening before. Not ever. I suspect you're looking at a scientific milestone."

"Stop it, Sambo. The rules specifically say no pets in the dormitory. I'm continually getting rid of stray dogs the football players hide under their beds. Get rid of the cats."

"But, Mrs. Capulet, these aren't pets. They're part of a bona fide scientific experiment. That little kitten's not quite four days old, and you wouldn't want to jeopardize its chance of survival."

"Get rid of the cats."

Two days later she stopped him as he was climbing the steps with a fresh box of sand. "Porter, those cats are still in your room."

"Yes'm."

"Get rid of them."

"Yes'm. I'll do something about them tomorrow."

The next day Porter approached the president's office. He was on very good terms with Dr. Powell's spare and wrinkled secretary, never failing to tell her how nice her hair looked whenever it was obvious she had just renewed the black dye she affected. He always resolutely kept his own gaze steady when her bad eye rolled erratically on an independent course. She was an old maid and a Southern lady, a combination with which Porter's background had made him quite comfortable. He spent ten minutes with her, alternating between teasing compliments and tremulous recitation of his current problem and was rewarded by being ushered into the presence of the president of Willingham University.

Perhaps it was relief at confronting a picayune problem not involving an irate member of the Georgia Baptist Convention, or perhaps it was pleasure in dealing with someone in no position to donate thousands of dollars to Willingham, or perhaps it was even nostalgic identification with the unexpected euphoria adolescents can give to tangential concerns. At any rate, after a sincere and impassioned presentation, Porter left Dr. Powell's office with written permission to harbor a family of cats in his dormitory room so long as his laboratory kitten had need of them. Being accustomed to miracles in his life, he was not unduly surprised at his success, but he noted that Dr. Powell was shaking his head as he called, "Miss Lucy, would you step in here a minute, please?"

Four nights later an unexpected freeze enveloped Macon, and the orphan kitten crawled out from under the warmth of the adult cat. She, unbonded and inattentive, ignored its plight, and Porter awoke to find a cold, stiff corpse. He experienced disappointment but not grief and pragmatically flushed the end of his obstetrical dream down the toilet. Returning to his room, he stood over the box. "Well, Whitey, I guess it's back home for you."

The cat rolled lazily on her back with a lithe and agile grace. Her eyes narrowed lazily, and she kneaded her paws contentedly. Her kittens wavered upright on unsteady legs, slapping at her slowly twisting tail and falling in somersaults over each other. Of a sudden Porter exclaimed, "Be damned if I send you back."

He confided the loss of the premature kitten to no one except Boston Harbor Jones.

"Uh huh, Sambo, I hear what you say bout somepin keep you company in a lonesome room. Cats is cats, but if you done got to like em you can't help it; I don't see no reason for you to get shed of em.

356

When Mrs. Capulet inspect them rooms she ain't counting kittens, and she prolly go the rest of the year without knowing one missing. I say keep em and just be extra careful. You sharp as a rat turd, Sambo, and you'n stay ahead of Mrs. Capulet do you work at it."

Two days later Mrs. Capulet accosted him. "Where's your kitten, Sambo?"

"Ma'am?"

"Don't ma'am me. You know perfectly well that kitten is missing. What happened to it? Did it die?"

"Yes'm."

"Well, I'm sorry. You did quite well, however, to keep it alive for two weeks. Get rid of those others today."

"Ma'am?"

"Sambo! Dr. Powell's letter plainly stated that you could keep that cat and her three kittens only so long as your experimental kitten needed them. If that mother and her babies aren't out of your room tomorrow, I'm going to take some action. I say, a letter from the president of the University! And about a litter of kittens! I never! You don't want Professor Twilley to get word of this, do you?"

"No'm."

"Nor do I. Tomorrow, Sambo."

Porter put the sand box and the family of cats in the spare closet and closed the door when he went to class. Within two days Mrs. Capulet had discovered them. He moved them to his own closet behind his suit and bathrobe. She knew it the very next day. He shifted them to the bottom drawer of one of the empty dressers and got away with it for three days. When he secreted them in the top drawer of the other dresser and Mrs. Capulet found them, he gave up the game. Final examinations were upon him. He had lived precariously long enough and needed none of his attention distracted by trying to outwit Mrs. Capulet any longer. Boston carried Whitey and her babies back to their donor.

"Honor funny, ain't it, Sambo?"

"What you mean?"

"I got honor. Here I sat on the bus carrying that bunch of cats back to live next door to me and torment me, and it'd been slicker'n goose grease just to turn em loose this side town. Neighbor lady don't know you and you don't know her, and I could just told her you

357

took em home with you do she ever ax bout em. Only reason I don't do that is on account of honor. It get in a fella's way, but if you got it you can't help it and you sure can't fight it. You just afflicted with it and that's that. You owe me, Sambo, but we strike it out if I don't never hear no more out'n you bout cats."

Porter finished the quarter by restoring himself to the Dean's List. When he handed in his final examination to Professor Twilley, he received an unexpected accolade in an unbelievably benign tone. "I have enjoyed you as a student in my class, young Osborne. I understand from the housemother that you are well-behaved in your dormitory. I shall follow the rest of your college career with interest."

"Thank you, sir. I want to thank you for moving me back to Nottingham Hall. It's the best thing ever happened to me. I'm going to request the same room next year."

"I see. Good luck, Osborne."

Porter figured that would show Professor Twilley just exactly who really didn't give a damn.

One week later he still missed Whitey and her babies, and he felt a little bitterness toward Mrs. Capulet for their absence. The days were longer, and weather had softened with spring. He was reading the *Macon Telegraph* in the Library one morning after his eight o'clock class when an advertisement opposite the comic page caught his eye.

RACKLEY CAT AND DOG HOSPITAL
50 fifty 50
Cats and Kittens
FREE
to people providing good homes
475 Walnut Street — Telephone 3350

The third time his eye went back to it, he succumbed. It was spring. He had been good too long. Looking around the Library, he noticed Mary Clyde Ballew two tables over. She was Henry Bean's girlfriend and had her own car. It was the ancient family Plymouth her father had given her instead of trading it in when he had to buy a new one,

358

and it afforded Mary Clyde prestige few Willingham girls enjoyed. Porter was a little uncomfortable around her because of a comment with which Henry Bean had silenced a conversation on the importance of virginity one day in the Co-op. Todd Peabody had just uttered the clinching dogma: "Well, nobody wants to marry a girl who'll fuck."

Henry was walking by and heard it. "Well, for God's sake, what idiot wants to marry one who won't?"

Porter had wanted to think this was a rhetorical question and not necessarily an indication of Henry's personal activities. He harbored, nevertheless, just the tiniest doubt about Mary Clyde's purity but had never dared clarify the issue with Henry Bean. Mary Clyde was a sweet and bighearted girl, and Porter had a deep enough affection for her not only to forgive a possible lapse of morality in the name of love but also to feel free to ask a favor of her. He copied down the address and whispered to her, "Mary Clyde, will you drive me down to the Rackley Cat and Dog Hospital?"

"Down on Walnut Street? What do you want to go there for?"

"They've got fifty cats to give away, and I want them."

"Whatever for? You're crazy!"

"I know it. No argument there. Mrs. Capulet's life has been awfully dull lately, and I want to surprise her."

"You want a bus ticket home, boy. That's what you want. Don't you ever tell anybody I helped you."

Porter rounded up some sacks, and by the time he and Mary Clyde arrived at the small frame building with the flashing neon sign, he had not only his plan but their stories complete. He faced the nameless man behind the desk.

"How many do I want? I'll take all fifty of them, sir. My name is Tony Kelly and my dad is superintendent at the Masonic Children's Home. He thought it would be nice for the kids to have some pets, and then too we've had a little trouble with rats around the barn."

"My boy played ball at Lanier High with a Billy Kelly from the Home. He kin to you?"

"Oh, yes, sir. He's my big brother." Porter was not lying. Billy Kelly was indeed a fellow KA, much larger than Porter, and his father was superintendent of the Masonic Home.

"Well, son, we never figured to get rid of all of em this easy. Old lady died in that big two-story house on Elm Street last week, and they just found her two days ago. House was full of cats. They was her life. None of em ever been outdoors. Neighbors said she thought one of them college boys stole a cat from her bout ten years ago, and she ain't let one of hers out the house since. Didn't have no kin; so the police brought the cats over here. Said that house sure did stink. Part old lady and part cat. We ain't managed to give none away yet, and a whole bunch of the least ones died, but we still got thirty-two. You sure your dad wants that many?"

"Oh, yes, sir. See, he even sent the sacks for us to put them in, and he let one of the older girls who has a scholarship to Wesleyan Conservatory borrow his car to come get em. She's waiting outside if you want to talk to her."

"Naw, that's all right. Come on and I'll help you catch em."

Porter had never seen such ugly cats in his life. Generations of inbreeding while confined in their owner's home had concentrated all of their bad features. They were, to an animal, pied and dappled, all brown and yellow and white and gray. Their faces were long and narrow, their eyes were too small and occasionally sat unevenly in their heads. A large number of them had seven toes on each front foot. They were of sizes ranging from half-grown kittens to full-grown cats, and they were lean and hungry. Porter tactfully did not comment on their appearance but lifted a spitting adolescent and dropped it into his sack.

"You sure you want all of em? This is a heap of cats. Police department was paying us five dollars a day to board em and try to farm em out. They won't pay but for a week though, and then Doc Rackley said we'd put em to sleep. Week's up tomorrow, so you done saved their lives. Good thing you brought seven sacks. Some of these fools are really wild. Let's make sure we have the tops tied tight or you'll strew cats all over Macon. The police like to never caught em all in the first place. Said the old lady was smelling pretty stout by the time they found her, and the cats was prowling all over the house and yowling something pitiful."

"I don't think I want to know about that. Let's just get them in the car. All the orphans in Macon are grateful to you, sir."

By the time Porter had sneaked the cats, sack by sack, into his dormitory room and stored them in a closet, Mary Clyde was more excited than he was.

"Sambo, this just may work. I wish I could watch when Mrs. Capulet finds them. You really ought to change your mind. You can get shipped if she reports you to the discipline committee. You can back out any time. I still don't see why you think you have to do this. I never heard of such a thing."

"Mary Clyde, neither did anybody else. It's never been done before. Not in the history of the whole world. That's why I have to do it. Don't you understand? If everything works together, from me thinking about it in the first place right on down to it all meshing together, then I have a responsibility to do it. Otherwise it never would get done because this particular set of circumstances and opportunities never would coincide again. Not ever. And I'd always wonder if it would have worked if I'd just gone ahead with it. All explorers have taken risks. Don't you know that?"

"I don't know anything anymore. Except that I'm glad I know you. I think. Lots of luck."

After lunch Porter hurried to his room, poured enough chloroform in the closet to still the writhing sacks, and hastily placed the groggy cats in one of the empty dressers. He had to use the bottom drawer because it was the largest, and he left a crack large enough for air but too narrow for a cat to squeeze a head through and escape. He aired the room well to remove any hint of chloroform and surveyed the scene. He originally had planned to be safely ensconced in lab when Mother Capulet received her surprise, but he suddenly decided this was too interesting a situation to desert. She would be on her appointed rounds punctually at two, and he decided to wait and watch.

The cats had revived and the noise, though muted, was demanding. Paws kept appearing in the ventilation crack of the dresser drawer, reaching up, reaching down, clawing futilely at open air or varnished wood, withdrawn and replaced, multiple and busy. Porter backed into one of the closets, watched through the slimmest of cracks, and waited.

Mrs. Capulet always was accompanied on her inspection tours by a gangling young mulatto whose wiry frame had not yet attained the mature bulk promised by his huge hands and feet. He carried a cotton-picking basket, into which he emptied the trash cans from each room, and a box, from which he replaced toilet paper in the bathrooms. He was bashful and polite and never had been heard to utter any words except "Yas'm" and "Naw'm." From his hideout in the closet, Porter heard the tap of Mrs. Capulet's heels down the corridor. The slithering noise would be the basket being dragged on the rubber mat. The skeleton key rattled in the lock and his door swung open.

"Julian, get Sambo's trash can and make haste. We're running a little late today."

"Yas'm."

"Look around and be sure that boy doesn't have any more pets in here. I declare, I feel a little sorry for him and I know he's lonesome, but we can't do for one what we can't do for all. Can we?"

"Naw'm."

"My sakes alive, what's that noise! Julian, I do believe he's brought that cat and kittens back and hidden them in that drawer again! When will he ever learn he can't fool me?"

Unheeding and incautious, Mrs. Capulet marched across the room and snatched the bottom drawer open. In sudden release, thirty-two angry, frightened cats erupted into the room, more startling than ten coveys of quail. They scrambled and swarmed and yelled. They swirled and boiled around Mrs. Capulet in frantic confusion. The room was filled with hurtling, scratching balls of fur. The cats began racing faster and faster around the room, hurling themselves in panic halfway up the walls, careening off the tops of dressers. Porter was reminded of the motorcycle show at the Brewton County Fair, where the machines gathered speed and finally mounted the steep sides of a cylindrical wall in ever-increasing dizziness.

Every time Mrs. Capulet tried to move, the cats became more frenzied. They yowled from terror and the sheer excitement of physical release after long imprisonment. Mrs. Capulet tried to get to the door, but the phlegmatic Julian had opened it in prudent self-protection, and the cats began swarming past her now in escape from

362

the room. She stepped on one, and it bounded in spitting contortions higher than her head. As Porter watched the shambles in wonder, Mrs. Capulet raised one hand to her forehead in unbelievably classic gesture and fainted dead away across his bed.

Porter leaped from the closet, the sudden opening of the door catching three cats in mid-flight and slamming them to the center of the room, where they scratched furiously on the planks before racing off toward freedom. He started toward Mrs. Capulet, his heart pounding forcibly in his throat. A hand grabbed him by the shoulder, and he looked up to face Julian.

"You better git outta here, boy, effen you know what good for you. You better git outta here quick. You better be long gone when she come to."

Porter accepted this as sage advice. He looked back, saw a flutter of Mrs. Capulet's eyelids beneath the rimless glasses, and assumed she would be all right.

"Golly, Julian, I think the world of Mrs. Capulet. You look after her and don't let her be too mad at me. I had no idea this was going to happen. I was just trying to pull a little prank."

"You done pull something, all right! Git! It goan take me all day to git them cats out this dormitory. They scattered all over by now."

Porter worried about a number of things that afternoon, chiefly the length of his future at Willingham University and when a summons from Professor Twilley would come. He gained unexpected reassurance at supper time from Boston.

"Sambo, you come here. This minute! What I gonna do with you? I hate cats, I done told you, and here you go last six weeks make me pay more attention to em than the rest of my life put together. I tired of cats, boy, and I hope to the good Lord you done with em forever. You done lucked up again."

"What you talking about, Boston?"

"Either you turn you back while I talking to you, Sambo, or you get that innercent look off you face one. I sick of seeing it. I you friend and I ain't got to put up with that po pitiful face you get whenever you want to. Julian come by to see me while ago. Told me everthing. Say Mrs. Capulet pass out plumb cold on account them cats and then you come out the closet and he run you off to save you hide. Say Mrs. Capulet rouse up and look around awhile, and then she sit up on that bed and all of a sudden start laughing till she cry and git her glasses all steam up.

"She say, 'Julian, that is without a doubt the most mischeevious boy you will ever see. I want you never to mention this episode to anyone. In the first place, no one would believe it, and in the second place, it would tax my powers of organization and description to relate it.' Julian say, 'Naw'm.' She say, 'The poor boy's on probation and this would send him home. I don't want one breath of this to get out.' Julian say, 'Yas'm.' You know how he do.

"Then she up and say, 'Besides, I think it will be a reverse prank on him if we never indicate we know anything about it. He'll always wonder exactly what happened.' Julian say, 'Naw'm,' and she say, 'Well, get your basket and let's finish the other rooms. What *are* you waiting for?'

"Sambo, you ever do anything else to Mrs. Capulet, I gone play like I you paw and frail the piss out you."

"Boston, you don't have to worry. Isn't Mrs. Capulet a perfectly wonderful lady?"

The following week Porter read a story on the third page of the *Macon Telegraph*.

> When Miss Pauline Thorton died recently, it was thought that the last surviving member of a prominent Bibb County family was an eccentric who had died intestate. A will discovered by one of her neighbors, however, has been filed in Probate Court and reveals her to be as civic-minded as her proud lineage would have indicated. The will left all her estate to her cats for their lifetime; any residue was to go to Willingham University when her pets no longer had any need of care.
>
> Police who found Miss Thornton's body reported that there were a number of cats present, which they turned over to a local animal shelter for care. When this reporter interviewed the proprietor of the hospital, the

364

doctor questioned a male employee. He then insisted on placing a telephone call to the Masonic Children's Home before making a statement. Following this, he became noticeably agitated. He acknowledged receiving the cats but stated they were in poor condition because of inbreeding and inattention and a number of them died. When pressed about the whereabouts of any survivors, he admitted that they had been housed for the required length of time and then humanely put to sleep. He assured this reporter that he did not want to discuss the matter further and ended the interview.

Dr. Wade Hampton Powell confirmed that Willingham University is, indeed, the recipient of an unexpected legacy amounting to some two hundred thousand dollars. Dr. Powell told this reporter, "The beloved sons and daughters of this institution are constantly aware of the Hand of Divine Providence intervening in our lives, and we are all humbly grateful for this gift from Miss Thornton. It could not have come at a better time. It will be used for the continued pursuit of our goal of Christian education. It is a miracle."

Porter looked all around the Library. He tilted his chair back and looked at the ceiling. There was no doubt in his mind that he had become an unwitting but magnanimous benefactor of Willingham University. Also he was an anonymous benefactor. He sincerely hoped that the anonymity would remain forever inviolate.

No one but Mary Clyde Ballew knew for certain exactly what had led to this. He would talk to her, but he was sure she wouldn't tell.

He pondered on the improbable power of coincidence in life. He was inclined to think that, all things considered, the Hand of Divine Providence was not paramount in this series of events, but Dr. Powell was welcome to believe anything he liked.

XXII

Spring at Willingham was more beautiful than usual that year, its warmth and fragrance a keen contrast to the dreariness it followed. The rain-soaked earth of middle Georgia was as springy as a giant peat bog, and it pushed tender greenness into the sunny air and loaded it with spicy sweetness. Far away the Germans had invaded France, and for a few weeks everyone breathed cautiously and awaited the devastating carnage that was sure to follow. When the news came that the Maginot Line had been bypassed with an ease that was almost contemptuous and that tanks, trucks, and hordes of strutting Germans filled the boulevards of a surrendered Paris, most of the students at Willingham clucked sympathetically and went about their business.

Henry Bean was enraged. "I've been telling you about those French, haven't I? Chamberlain started all the caving in and now the French have collapsed like wet cardboard! They can't be practical and romantically try to save face at the same time. Divided France indeed! Occupied France and free France! That government at Vichy won't amount to a poot in a whirlwind, and that de Gaulle fellow is just another egotistical opportunist who couldn't lead a platoon into a whorehouse. Just watch. We're gonna have to go save them again. Damn if I want to die for a bunch of folks who are busy trying to save their own skins and then act like we're supposed to save their country. Hitler's got a treaty with those Russians, so they'll stay off his back while he takes England. Just watch. England's next. And I'll bet there are folks in Czechoslovakia who say the English deserve whatever they get. I'm going to double my load and finish this school early. Damn if I want to be caught as an enlisted man when we go to war."

Tiny Yeomans was indignant. "Poor Dr. Huber. He's crushed. I knew how he'd feel so I made a special trip to see him. You know how dignified he is, Sambo, but underneath you can tell he's really wounded. He has lots of friends in France and he's getting letters from them. He told me he'd like to go over there but what could an old academician contribute, he said, 'to the salvation of a glorious civilization that is on the brink of extinction.' He's such a doll. I wish I could get my hands on those Germans and that Hitler! What can you expect from a race of people whose language sounds like they're hiccuping and spitting all the time! Come on, kiddo, let's go get an ice cream Coke."

The ministerial students calmly continued their vespers and were audibly thankful that control of the world and its affairs was securely in the hands of Jesus Christ. Visiting speakers at chapel were fond of using texts like "He will not suffer thy foot to be moved" and "Behold, He who keepeth Israel will neither slumber nor sleep."

Porter listened to everything. He noticed that public opinion about soldiers had reversed itself. Roosevelt's draft had put thousands of nice, hometown boys into uniform all over America. Proper housewives stopped their automobiles now and picked up the hitch-hikers in khaki who suddenly swarmed the roads, whereas scant months previously the same ladies would have pursed their lips at the sight of soldiers and avoided them as mercenary adventurers or thugs in need of discipline. National attention was further focused on them by a popular song on the radio: "Twenty-one dollars a day once a month."

Porter was only peripherally interested in all of this, however. He tended to side with the isolationists and he still believed that God would not let America get into another war. He was too caught up in his own emotional holocaust and transformation to regard events in Europe as more than inconsequential happenings somewhere on the far edge of his awareness. He could not help that Vashti Clemmons chose the month Hitler rolled across France and into Paris to focus her attention on him, but it caused him to forget the French. They would have to look after themselves.

* * * *

Vashti was the daughter of one of the more successful Macon ministers and as such enjoyed a position of some prominence on campus despite certain eccentricities she exhibited. She was older than Porter, but then nearly everyone at Willingham was. It was difficult to decide whether she was a junior or a senior because she was erratic in her grades. If she liked a course, she made an A in it. If it bored her, she sat through it for a quarter, swinging a crossed leg vigorously while gazing out the window, and made an F. None of this perturbed her in the least. She seemed perfectly content with everything about herself and with anything that happened around her. Vashti had poise.

She was unusually tall for a girl, slender and narrow-shouldered with large, heavy breasts. She walked in little mincing, pigeon-toed steps that made her legs look awkward and unused although they were long and beautifully proportioned. One could not imagine Vashti dancing or playing tennis or running. Her gait was reminiscent of a beginner on tommy-walkers. She was one of the few Willingham girls who wore mascara daily; she wore lots of it and also eyebrow pencil drawn to an arched look of incessant surprise. Her mouth was a heavily painted slash across the lower triangle of her face, and she had the most noticeable buck teeth imaginable. They were not large; indeed, one speculated that they still might be her baby teeth, for they were rounded, had spaces between them, and looked like half-formed grains of corn. Although Vashti seemed tranquilly unaware of them, others noticed her teeth with either fascination or embarrassment, for they stuck almost straight out. She could not keep her upper lip pulled over them and most of the time had abandoned any effort toward that goal. They were so nearly horizontal that Porter could not imagine her being able to bite anything with them. On the infrequent occasion when he was around Vashti, he tried not to look at her teeth and consequently always focused on her bosom.

Vashti affected a low voice, even at times whispering some drawn-out words. She breathed deeply and sighed a lot, and when she laughed it sounded like she was either gargling or choking. She swayed around campus with the faraway look of other horizons in her eyes and seemed so overly dramatic when someone spoke to her that many students avoided her. Henry Bean thought her interest-

368

ing.

"Lookit that ole gal not giving a damn what other folks think. She's in a world of her own, thank you, and the rest of us are out of step. She'd remind me of Marie Antoinette if it wasn't for those obscene teeth. I wonder why her old man doesn't get em fixed. They're paying him enough at that church. He's a widower, you know, and every woman in the congregation either has a cousin she wants to marry off to him or else wants to give him advice about raising Vashti."

One Thursday afternoon in early April, Porter was headed rapidly up the walk by the Biology and Christianity buildings. Amalita and Sara Belle had promised to meet him at Chichester's. Amalita had a brand-new convertible her father had given her, and the two girls had promised to take Porter to ride. He had thought it would be more image-building to be picked up at the dormitory, but the three of them had decided that, given the time of day, exposure would be greater at the drugstore. Head down, he almost collided with Vashti when she stepped in front of him.

"Excuse me, Vashti. I didn't see you."

"Hi." She breathed audibly, fixed him with a glittering eye, and almost whispered. "Are you ready?"

"Ready for what, Vashti?"

"Ready to lose it."

"Lose what? What are you talking about?"

"Your cherry, lamb, your cherry. Aren't you about ready to give it up?"

"What do you mean?"

"I mean I'm available, hon."

To Porter, this was an academic discussion on strictly an intellectual plane, but he was nonetheless scandalized.

"Vashti, I can't believe you're saying these things to me, and I know you're not serious."

"Aw, baby. You're so innocent. That's one of the reasons I never make love to anybody but virgins."

"Well, Vashti, you're right on target with that. I've always planned to stay a virgin till I'm married."

"Oh, that's wonderful! It's like the BSU girls who save themselves for one man. I knew you'd be fascinating."

369

"Yeah. Well, Vashti, this is an interesting discussion and everything and you're a real cut-up and I know you're teasing, but I gotta go. I'm meeting somebody. It was nice talking to you."

"Sambo," she breathed, "I'm not teasing. Come here a minute."

She pulled him into the little porch of the Christianity Building, overgrown and shrouded with shrubbery. She took both his hands and placed them on her breasts and then ever so gently let one of her hands slide down his chest and across the front of his trousers. Porter's physiological response was immediate and dispelled any idea that Vashti was teasing. It also precipitously removed the encounter from any academic or intellectual realm. He gave a desperate look around to be sure they were still unobserved, took only the most fleeting notice of the flight of his lofty ideals, and succumbed. His voice was a croak.

"When?"

"There's no time like the present, lamb. Now."

"Where?"

"Well, I hear you live by yourself on third floor in the dormitory. Tell me how to get there and I'll come to your room."

Porter was wary and skeptical. He thought of Shiu Lau Ling, lonely Chinese refugee from the Japanese invasion of Manchuria, who had been brought to Willingham as a student by the Georgia Baptist convention not only to demonstrate to the world the compassion of the university, but also to hold up before the foreign mission field proof that Georgia Christians were truly involved in the labor of the Lord. Shiu Lau spoke only the simplest of English and never progressed to the sophisticated level of stringing two words together, let alone combining noun with verb. He roomed alone directly below Porter, went dutifully to class, and seemed unaware that he was given conditional grades in every course he monitored. People tried to be nice, but it was impossible to communicate with him and most people quit trying.

Porter had detected an unusual odor coming from his room one evening, had knocked on the door and discovered Shiu Lau hunkered down in his drawers over an abject hot plate in the middle of the bare floor. He was stirring a mysterious, steaming mixture that plopped and bubbled thickly.

370

"Hi, Shiu, what you doing?"

"Soup."

"Is that what you have in the pot?"

"Soup."

"Why don't you put the hot plate on the table?"

"Soup."

"What kind of soup is it? Is it some special Chinese soup somebody sent you through the mail?"

"Soup."

"Well, I gotta be going. Thought I'd just drop in and check on you."

"Soup."

Shiu Lau never rose from his squat and never quit stirring, nor did he quit nodding his head and smiling. Porter gave up easily on very few people and later greeted the alien whenever they passed on campus with "Hi, Soupy." Shiu Lau always smiled broadly and nodded repeatedly but gave no indication that he comprehended the sally as an offer of friendship. Two weeks later he vanished from Willingham.

An unsuspecting professor had entered the Christianity Building one afternoon at three and investigated a bumping and groaning he chanced to hear. Under the front bench in Roberts Chapel he discovered Shiu Lau Ling vigorously communicating by semaphoric thrusts and hunches with a short dumpling of a girl who had transferred the previous quarter from Bessie Tift and was indiscreetly overdoing her Christian acceptance of a stranger in our midst. Shiu Lau obviously had overcome the language barrier, but the uncarpeted floor of Roberts Chapel had sent messages as surely as jungle tom-toms. He was confined to his room for the night and shipped off to non-Baptist oblivion at sunup. The girl, with hanging head and swollen eyes, was put on a bus for Valdosta within three hours of discovery. The campus buzzed with titillated righteousness.

Only the voice of Henry Bean was heard in gadfly dissent. "Hell, I think it's terrible. They could have at least let them finish. I've been reading about coitus interruptus and it's not too good for you, even when it's voluntary. They'll both probably have tics and twitches for the rest of their lives."

Porter looked into Vashti's black-rimmed eyes and thought of

371

Mrs. Capulet, Professor Twilley, and the Greyhound station, from which buses departed for many cities besides Valdosta.

"No."

"All right, lamb, you say where. I'm all yours." She gave another lingering stroke down his leg.

"Go to the third floor of the Administration Building and wait for me. I'll get the key to the tower and be with you in three minutes. Nobody'll be there this time of day."

"Ooh, the tower! I've never been there. Oh, I knew you'd be special. Don't be long now. Oops, lamb, I don't mean that literally."

Vashti swayed delicately across the quadrangle while Porter watched, his chest jumping as though to hammer blows. By virtue of being Number VI in his fraternity, he possessed a key to the door of the hidden stairwell leading to the big tower of Willingham University. He had the key in his pocket now but he did not want to be seen walking across campus with Vashti Clemmons — not bent on the mission that was presently consuming him and certainly not in the physical condition in which he found himself. His pants were occupied by a more compelling presence than anything ever generated by his smooching sessions with Mary Martha. It seemed to Porter that it was a separate being and that it was mightier than he. In a corner of his consciousness, he heard Buckalew Tarpley's vaguely reassuring postulate, "A stiff prick has no conscience." Porter tucked the pulsating problem securely under his belt buckle, thanked God again for pleats in front, and sauntered as naturally as he could in Vashti's wake.

Dr. Huber was coming out of the Administration Building with some letters in his hand. He nodded with a formal *"Bonjour, Monsieur Osborne,"* and passed on. Porter met no one else.

He was heading not for the smaller tower of the Administration Building, mountable only by the iron rungs set in its chimneylike interior, but for the larger tower with its commodious platform and white columns high above the trees of Willingham. Access to it was much easier. One had only to get past the locked door and climb the steps to the top floor. There, in one of the dusty back rooms reserved to KA, illumined in grayness by grimy windows recessed in brick walls, a thin and limber ladder stood in the middle of the floor. It tapered to the lofty ceiling and rested against the

372

inner frame of the trapdoor that was the only entrance to the tower. It was not a hinged door but resembled more the snugly fitting lid to a box, covered on its exposed surface by galvanized metal impervious to rain. One stood at the top of the undulating ladder, pushed upward with all one's might to dislodge this cover, and then slid it to one side in order to climb out and stand on the summit of the tower.

Once there with the lid replaced, securely surrounded by the decorative parapet, sunlight and gentle breezes streaming through open spaces, the sounds of earth softened by distance, one could not fail being impressed by both the solitude and beauty of the place. Each was a factor in Porter's choice of rendezvous, but practical safety was uppermost in his mind. He felt that had Shiu Lau Ling known of this tower, Willingham University still would have an oriental weasel at large in its hen house.

Vashti was dubious. "You think I'm going to climb that rickety old wooden ladder? You're crazy. This is the wildest idea I've ever encountered."

"Aw, there's nothing to it, Vashti. Just hold tight with your hands and don't look down. Here, I'll go first."

"You're mighty right you will. I already took my panties off while I was waiting for you."

Porter felt that his belt buckle was in peril of coming loose. He went up the ladder like a ratchet, removed the trapdoor, and called softly down. "Come on up, Vashti. It's beautiful."

Years of dreams were building in his head like cumulus clouds. A breeze stirred Vashti's hair and the thin red ribbon that hung in it. She looked awhile into the distance and seemed unaware of Porter. Finally she turned to him. "I had no idea this place existed. How did you ever manage to find it? It's absolutely gorgeous."

"Nothing but the best, Vashti. Nothing but the best. Stick with me and I'll show you radishes big as diamonds."

"You're a mess, Porter Osborne. I'm glad I spoke to you."

"This trapdoor cover gonna be big enough, Vashti? It's only four feet wide, but if we're on top of it, there's no way anything can interrupt us. Unless it's an airplane or an angel, and I'm not worried about either of them."

Despite himself, Porter's laugh was a little self-conscious.

"Lord, lamb, that'll be easy. You ought to try it in a rumble seat. Long as I have room for these long ole legs, I could do it on a dime. Here, put this on."

She pressed a thin wafer of tinfoil into Porter's hand. The lettering spelled "Sheik." Tearing the package and unrolling the sheath into place was an erogenous experience in itself. It was powdery, and Porter wondered who on earth it had been tailored to fit.

Vashti sank supine onto the trapdoor, her hips at the edge and her legs akimbo. The delicate fresh odor of a new bream bed wafted through the tower. Porter's head whirled and the clouds within it boiled and soared.

"Come on, lamb, what you waiting for?"

A minimum of fumbling informed Porter that the mystic tunnel led in and up, not straight back. Triumphantly he plunged. There was one crash of thunder in his brain, the clouds disappeared, and it was over. His immediate reaction was consternation. Is that all? Is that all? There were no wheels within wheels.

He opened his eyes. A buzzard was sailing by so close his strutted feathers creaked — curved beak rigid and cruel, red eye glinting incuriously. Porter remembered the barnyard fence. That was better than this, he thought. Oh no. Don't let it be. There's got to be more to it than this. He raised his head.

Vashti gave him a little pat. "All done, hon? That was quick. Get off, I'm getting a cramp."

Porter pushed all his feelings to the background. There would be time to deal with them later, when this unusual stranger was not watching. Hastily he divested himself of the protective shield and tucked the stubborn tumescence into his clothes. Looking around, he saw Vashti with a tiny notebook. There was a series of lines and crosshatches in groups of five across the page. With a pencil she deliberately drew another line in the row and restored the pad to her purse. Porter caught himself just before asking, "What's that?" He thought of another of Buckalew Tarpley's axioms — "If you don't want to know the answer, don't ask the question."

Safely down the ladder, in the dimness of the bare room, Vashti stopped his exit.

"That's the most beautiful and romantic and exciting place I ever saw. You want to come back tomorrow?"

374

Porter swallowed only once. He had already sinned The Sin, he supposed, and repetition would not increase punishment. This was an opportunity he was helpless to resist.

"I'll go back right now if you say so."

"Lord, lamb, I bet you would."

She pulled from beneath her sweater a man's pocket watch suspended on a black shoestring around her neck.

"We don't have time. I've got to be across town in fifteen minutes. Be here tomorrow at three?"

"You bet."

"All right. That's settled. Now, let me explain my procedures. I never do it with anybody but virgins. OK? That's so I don't have to worry about disease. I figured out for myself a long time ago that there's no realistic way a virgin can have a venereal disease and that's the reason I don't fool with anybody else. Then, too, they're cute.

"Now, I'll do it with you and nobody but you anytime we can work it out as long as you don't do it with anybody but me. OK? The minute you do it with somebody else, you have to tell me cause that would break the circuit and let disease in. Promise?"

"I promise. How can you tell a guy is a virgin?"

"You can tell. Now, there's another point. We'll keep it secret. I know enough about boys to know you're not going to want to be seen anywhere with me. OK. Now, let me tell you something. I don't want to be seen anywhere with you either. OK? Then let's don't talk about it. Don't you do any bragging to fraternity brothers and I won't tell any giggly secrets to some girl who's supposed to be my best friend. That way nobody'll know but us, and as far as the rest of the world is concerned, we're both still virgins."

"Vashti! I would never tell a soul! Don't you think I've got any honor? I'd die before I'd tell!"

"OK, lamb, OK."

Porter drew a hesitant breath. "Why'd you pick me, Vashti? There are hundreds of virgin boys tearing around Willingham."

"I'll tell you, lamb. Remember the night you gave 'Renascence' at vespers? I love Millay, and I vowed right then that as soon as my current lover branched out and we broke up, I was going to try you."

"You mean, just because I recited poetry?"

"No, lamb, not that. It was the way you recited it, the way you turned the words loose from your mouth. It sounded like you loved the words and respected them. I don't know; it was like I knew you'd never use nasty words to a girl. I am a girl who cannot stand crudity!"

"Oh."

"Bye, lamb. See you tomorrow. Oh, there's one more thing. You buy the rubbers. I only furnish the first one. When we bust up, I expect you to pay me one back."

Porter was so absorbed with attention to the physiology of his newly begun activity that thoughts of morality were pushed to the background. His introduction to sexual intercourse was so far removed from all expectation that he was troubled. After all he had heard, all he had read, all he had fantasized, there simply had to be more to sex than his initial encounter had produced. If not, everybody would not be so conscious of it all the time. Or else ... oh, Lord, suppose there was something wrong with him and he did not have the sensation level of other people. He felt doomed and perverted when he acknowledged that the feeling with Vashti was not as acute and pleasurable as that with masturbation. It never occurred to him to talk to anyone about that; he could hardly bear to think of it.

The following day he went dutifully to buy some rubbers. He decided that discretion forbade the purchase at Chichester's, since it was always thronged with Willingham students, so he caught a bus and went to town. There was a crowded, impersonal, busy drugstore on Cherry Street that he had never entered and where no one could possibly know him. He had heard enough since puberty from other boys to know that this purchase was made directly from the pharmacist, and so he marched with such speed and purpose past the soda fountain and the magazine stand that he almost skidded to a stop before the drug counter. No one was behind it. He felt that his precipitous entrance and abrupt halt were conspicuous and, indeed, there was a sales lady approaching him. He bolted to the sidewalk. He would go to another drugstore. Outside he realized he was not sure where another store was.

He slouched his shoulders, put his hands in his pockets, and made himself saunter back in. He leisurely stopped at the magazine rack and thumbed through a *Colliers;* he picked up an *Esquire* and then idly put it back. He dawdled past the soda fountain and studied with pretended interest the brightly colored cardboard banana splits festooned above the mirror. He ever so casually reached the rear of the store and drifted to an indolent halt in the drug department. The pharmacist was busy on the telephone. A lady with a henna rinse and a hair net materialized from nowhere.

"Can I help you?"

Porter jumped despite all effort. "No'm, I'm just waiting for the doc."

"He's on the phone right now. He'll be with you in a minute."

"Yes'm. I'll wait."

Porter could hear his heart racing. That lady knew what he wanted. Or else she thought he had a disease and was seeking treatment. With studied calmness he reached for a tin of Sayman's Salve. He dropped it with a clatter to the tiled floor. By the time he had replaced it with trembling and fumbling, his face was hot and he was sure everyone in Macon knew he was in this rabbit hole on Cherry Street, cornered and desperate.

"How many you want?' "

The voice was bored and knowing, and the pharmacist had no air of either tolerance or particular interest. His smock had been fresh the previous week.

"Ah, bu, bu, bu, bu, bu, bu, bu, bu! Sir?"

"I said, 'How many you want?'"

"How many what?"

"What'd you come tearing in here for? And then flying out? And then creeping back in like you did? I know what you want and you know what you want and I was trying to save time and help you out. How many you want?"

"Give me a gross."

"Come on, kid, a gross is a hundred and forty-four. Twelve dozen. Relax. You ain't breaking no law. No record either. Relax. How many you want? You'n get the cheap ones three for a quarter."

Porter gathered his dignity.

"I never use anything but Sheiks. Give me a dozen. I have a busy weekend planned."

The pharmacist shrugged, presented Porter with change and a brown sack.

"There y'are. Lotsa luck. Come back to see us."

As Porter gained the haven of the beautiful, noisy, impersonal street, he heard behind him, "C'm'ere a minute, Mabel. You ain't gonna believe this one."

Vashti slipped the big watch on its black cord back beneath her sweater.

"You're a little late, lamb. I was about to give you out. When you're ready to quit me, don't forget to tell me about it. I don't ever wait more'n ten minutes for anybody. I understand bust up, but it annoys me to fool with stood up."

When he left the tower that afternoon, Porter's apprehensions had vanished. Everything had gone much better. He was thrilled beyond his own imagination. The secrets of the universe were open to him. The barnyard fence was nothing. He was eight feet tall and king of the mountain. He tried not to strut or swagger, but when he passed the Library, he gave a running start and leaped in soaring flight over an abelia bush.

For the following week he did well to keep up in class at all. He was obsessed with his daily trips to the tower. He was obsessed with sex. Whenever he thought of Vashti, he had an erection. Whenever he spontaneously had a teen-age erection, he thought of Vashti. If he encountered her on the campus, she gave not the slightest indication that she saw him, and during their mutual activity there was a detachment and reserve about her, an absence of endearments, a lack of kissing or petting that rendered this most intimate of acts an exercise mechanical, a performance private but almost impersonal. Porter was in thrall. It was the mechanics that delighted him. He was enchanted with the status quo and only feared that the frequent traffic might wear down the ancient ladder. He lived for three o'clock.

Although he obediently depended on Vashti's experience and expertise, on one afternoon he ventured to assert his own wishes.

"Sambo, let's take off our clothes before you start."

"You mean all of them? Up here?"

"Sure. Nobody can see us from below unless we go to the edge and wave. This is the most beautiful place in Macon."

"Gosh, Vashti, you take yours off. I'd love that. But I think I'll keep mine on. I look pretty bad naked. The girls have always looked

378

at my scrawny arms and legs and dated somebody else."

"They were looking in the wrong place, hon. Come on."

Porter gaped in wonder at the spectacle before him. Vashti's lovely form was dappled in the spring light, her breasts like fruit at harvest time, her waist a pliant bridge between the plane of ribs and the fluted cup of pelvis brim. She was Venus and Diana and Rita Hayworth and Lana Turner. In the presence of perfection like this, teeth did not matter. Porter stared.

"You like what you see, lamb?"

"Oh, Vashti! You're gorgeous! Would you mind doing me just one little favor?"

"I'll do anything almost. If someone asks me properly. And if I'm in the mood. What you want, lamb?"

"Would you please take off the watch, too?"

A week later, at the foot of the ladder, he received more education.

"Well, lamb, I'll see you next Wednesday at three o'clock."

"What's wrong with tomorrow?"

"Think, lamb. Guess."

"You've found another virgin?"

"No. I haven't looked. How many days between now and Wednesday?"

"Five. Why?"

"What does the female of the species do for five days every lunar cycle, lamb?"

"Oh. See you Wednesday, Vashti."

A man named Petain was prominent at Vichy. De Gaulle left North Africa for England. A story appeared about a castle called Chenonceau that spanned the River Cher with its front door in occupied France and its back door in free France. Hitler bombed England. Churchill thrilled the world on the radio. There were tales of an epic adventure of history at a place called Dunkerque. A Willingham boy emigrated to Canada to join the Eagle Squadron and was volubly admired. Willingham co-eds began dating soldiers — the sorority girls preferring officers. Porter was oblivious to all of it. His life was full.

During the respite occasioned by Vashti's delicate retirement, he did some soul-searching. Despite his assumption that he must be squarely in the hog-wallow of sin, he felt more pride than guilt. Try as he might, he felt no less loved by God than he had before his fall and in exultation decided that Jesus most certainly had been a virgin and therefore was not privy to the nuances of his present condition. If He was not a virgin, how could He possibly have said that thinking about it was the same as doing it? What guilt he felt he assuaged with a letter.

Dear Mother,

Sorry I've been so bad about writing home. Do not worry about me. You would not believe how busy I've been. This place is really hectic.

I want you to know that I have not even had any desire to smoke a cigarette yet. Thanks for the letters. I have to run. See you soon.

My love to everybody,

Sambo

His main burden came in the knowledge that he was a changed person, that he was henceforth and forevermore different, and that no one else knew it or recognized the transformation. He was about to burst to tell somebody. No one at Willingham was acceptable as a confidant. Not Henry Bean or Boston or E.V. Certainly not Amalita or Sara Belle.

It came to him as a revelation. His father, of all people, would understand. Porter had felt that his father had even been a little wary of his son's masculinity, a little disapproving of his sexual inexperience. He would go home and confide in his father. He was certain he would gain support from that direction. He packed for overnight and caught the bus.

On Sunday morning when his mother and sisters left for

380

church, Porter approached the sleeping father.

"Dad. Dad."

"Mmpf."

"I hate to wake you up like this, but I had something to tell you."

"Hello, boy. What time is it?"

"It's ten o'clock. What I had to tell you is sort of personal." His father yawned. His eyes were closed.

"OK. What is it?"

"I'm not a virgin anymore."

"Mmpf."

"Do you understand what I'm saying? I went out and got a piece of pussy."

There was silence. The heavy breathing was suspended. His father opened one watery blue eye.

"How was it?"

"Great, Dad, just great! It started off sort of slow, but it just keeps getting better and better. It's wonderful!"

"That's fine. Congratulations. Did she enjoy it?"

"I don't know. I didn't ask her."

His father turned over and shrugged the cover over his shoulder. "If you have to ask, she didn't. Wake me up when your mother gets in from church and I'll eat dinner with yall."

Heretofore, Porter's concern had been for his own pleasure, his own adjustment, his own apprehension about what was happening in his life. Vashti was strictly a means to an end, a peculiar and unusual girl possessed of a gorgeous body they both were utilizing. The conversation with his father forced him to consider the possibility that perhaps he was not satisfying Vashti, although it did nothing to inform him how to remedy such a situation. Porter would rather have died than bring the subject up again. He worried.

The first thing he considered was that, debasing and humiliating as it would be, his penis might not be large enough. Despite what he had observed of companions in the bathroom and despite the comments about him by Michael Jurkiedyk and others, he had to consider this. He did not see how he could possibly be much bigger than he was, but then he had no real basis for comparison and everyone knew that a real man had to be adequately endowed. He broached the subject with bravado.

"Vashti, maybe my little old goober isn't big enough for you. You'd tell me, wouldn't you?"

"Why, lamb? What could you do about it if it wasn't? All you boys ever think about is size. They ought to let me teach that course called Comparative Anatomy; it'd be over in less than a week."

"I've got enough, haven't I, Vashti?"

He was sure that she would use this opportunity to say that he had more than she had ever encountered before. He wouldn't know whether to believe her or not, but it would be such an appropriate and nice thing to say that she could hardly avoid it.

"Let me tell you one thing, lamb, and you remember it all the rest of your days. It's not what you got that counts; it's how you use it."

"Oh."

He next considered the male axiom he had frequently heard: "Don't put the meat in till the frying pan is hot." He judiciously discarded this as any consideration. After all, Vashti had initiated the relationship, and it was she who made all the rules and all the appointments. Indeed, when he considered it, the only contributions he had been allowed to make were selecting the tower as trysting place and inducing Vashti to include the ugly watch when she disrobed. His efforts to kiss her had always met with a turned cheek and silent evasion. She still gave him a little dismissing pat and made a mark in her special notebook. He decided that the frying pan belonged to Vashti and that although he had access to it, he had no control over it. She was a mystery. But then, weren't women supposed to be?

The quarter grew rapidly older and so did Porter. On an afternoon during the week before finals, Vashti was supine on the trapdoor cover. The dark blue sky of Macon was accented by the gray-limned splendor and glistening billow of a slowly building thunderhead. Porter crouched on his knees at her side, surveying her breeze-kissed body and conscious of the delicious coolness on his own bare skin. He leaned back on his tucked-under toes.

"You know, Vashti, I ran across one of Millay's sonnets last night that reminded me a little bit of us. You want to hear it?"

"You know I do, lamb. I adore Millay, and that's what drew me to you in the first place. Let's hear it. There couldn't be a lovelier setting."

"Well, here's the last part of it:

Your presence and your favours, the full part
That you could give, you now can take away:
What lies between your beauty and my heart
Not even you can trouble or betray.
Mistake me not — unto my inmost core
I do desire your kiss upon my mouth;
They have not craved a cup of water more
That bleach upon the deserts of the south;
Here might you bless me; what you cannot do
Is bow me down, who have been loved by you."

"Oh, God!"

"Vashti, I want to ask you a favor."

"What, Sambo?"

"Let me stick it in naked for a while. Just to to see what it feels like. I promise to take it out and put the rubber on before, you know, anything happens. I promise."

"Lamb, after that sonnet you could do anything. Come on."

Porter had every intention of fulfilling his pledge and conscientiously observed the level of sensation building within him, willing it to be slow. Of a sudden it was beyond any control of his. Vashti gave a little smothered cry, her long legs wrapped tightly about his thin hips, and her arms locked around his shoulders convulsively. Porter felt like he was on a wildly bucking horse, held in too viselike a grip to worry about falling off. With exhilaration he hung on and thrust back. And back. And back. Somewhere, inconsequentially, he was aware that both of them were slippery with sweat. Vashti writhed and arched rigidly upward like a rainbow. When Porter exploded, she raked his back deeply with enameled fingernails. She rocked back and forth with abandon. She sank her teeth into his shoulder. A bolt of lightning rent the sky and thunder rolled in conquering majesty through the heavens. Vashti moaned in helplessness.

"Oh darling, oh darling, oh darling, oh darling, oh darling."

Porter looked around. Vashti's eyes were still closed and were streaming tears. He was terrified.

"Vashti! What happened? What in the world was that?"

She turned abruptly sideways and threw him with a bump onto the floor of the tower. Rain, unblowing and heavy, was falling in steady sheen around them.

Vashti stared impassively at Porter who rested on his buttocks and the heels of his hands, returning her look with bewilderment. Slowly, without moving her gaze, she reached for her purse and withdrew the special little notebook. Porter winced.

With dignity she rose to her splendid height and stepped naked to the parapet. She hurled the notebook overhand into the blanketing rain. Her protruding teeth, in relaxed grimace, made her appear to be smiling. Bemused, she donned her bra and step-ins. She slipped the black shoestring over her head and the watch swung between her breasts. Porter scrambled into his drawers. He wanted out of this tower.

"Vashti," he whispered. "You'll have to help me. I'm bleeding."

There was only swelling and bruising where she had bitten him, but his back was oozing blood in several places, enough to spot the floor. Wordlessly she patted and pressed with his handkerchief, then turned him around, cupped his face between both hands, and kissed him ever so lightly on the lips. He barely felt the prominent teeth. She sighed.

"Sambo, I'm sorry. Your back's a mess, but it'll be all right. Just don't take your shirt off in front of anybody for a week."

"Why in the world did you do that, Vashti? It hurt like hell."

"This is the end, Sambo. Usually I wait for the boy to say it cause it's fun to watch him be embarrassed while he wiggles off what he thinks is a hook, but this time I'm stopping it."

"What do you mean?"

"I mean good-bye. I mean I don't want to see you anymore. I mean that if you speak to me on campus, I'll answer like I can't remember your name."

"Why, Vashti?"

She drew a long breath and looked over his head into the clearing sky. "Because now you're not a virgin any longer, and, really,

384

neither am I. Neither am I."

"That's crazy, Vashti. That's crazy talk."

"Well, good morning, Porter Osborne, Jr.! Come to the party! The whole world is crazy! Didn't you know that? Some of us are just farther out in front of it than others. If you don't stay ahead, the real crazies step on your heels and walk you down till you're lying on your face in the mud. I intend to lead the pack."

"Why, Vashti?"

"Because my name's Vashti, that's why. And because my mama died when I was five and I can barely remember her sometimes. And because my daddy's a preacher and a phony. I can remember him smiling at Mama in front of folks and bragging on her from the pulpit and then fussing at her at home mean enough to make her cry. That's when she'd always rock me and hug me. And then I grew up with him not even speaking to me for weeks on end except to correct me. But when company would come to the parsonage, I got trotted out to play the piano or say a piece and he'd act like I was the greatest thing around till they left.

"My teeth grew in and everybody poked fun at them and I didn't even have any girlfriends, let alone any boyfriends. Oh, I heard them talking about how horrible it would be to kiss ole Vashti Clemmons! And giggling! When I asked Father about getting my teeth fixed, he said he didn't have the money. And the very next month he bought a new car and two new suits and me some new dresses and we moved to a really big church. And then I read about Queen Vashti. That's what did it. Do you know how they treated her and how she reacted? She didn't care what happened! She was fed up! She made her own royal rules. I decided I could be a real queen, too. It's not what you do or what happens to you that makes you a queen. It's how you think inside."

"I don't understand, Vashti."

"Of course you don't. You haven't read the first chapter of Esther. I found out what boys are really interested in instead of kissing, and I decided that I'd make a real impression on them. Except that I'd be *Queen* Vashti. The boys might think they were doing something great, but I've always known I was the one really calling the shots and directing traffic. I've been the queen, and they've been the worker ants. I've been the drill sergeant, and they've been the foot soldiers. Oh, I sing in the choir and I play the piano and I smile in church and act sweet, but I've been keeping a little score card to show Father some time when I was good and ready. Just for his edification, you know. I've been in control of everything every step of the way and I've been laughing behind my fan. But you've ruined it. You've reached me. I'm three years older than you, but you've made me cry. That is not acceptable."

"Vashti, I'm sorry."

"Oh, hush. You probably are, but you don't even understand what you're sorry for. Move that lid and wait up here till I'm gone."

Porter shifted the trapdoor cover and stood up. Vashti paused with one foot on the ledge and held out her palm. "The rubber."

"Whaaat?"

"The rubber, Sambo. Don't you remember? You owe me. I furnished the first one but the deal was that you pay it back when we busted up. Queens do not purchase condoms."

Dumbly Porter withdrew his wallet.

Vashti started down the ladder but paused with her torso still in the tower. "Here's a little poetry for *you*.

Think not for this, however, the poor treason
Of my stout blood against my staggering brain,
I shall remember you with love, or season
My scorn with pity, — let me make it plain:
I find this frenzy insufficient reason
For conversation when we meet again.

Bye now. This really has been a lovely place."

Safely in his room, Porter twisted in front of a mirror until he could see his back. It was crisscrossed with wounds that looked as though he'd been pulled through a briar patch. They stung and throbbed.

"All this," he declared, "is just about enough to turn a fellow against pussy."

Ten days later his back had healed. It was the night before his last final examination and he was well prepared for it. At vespers he approached a short, round girl he had overheard one of the non-fraternity upperclassmen say had round heels. She also had pendulous cheeks and three chins.

"What you doing tonight, Dorothy?"

She was one of the few girls on campus who had to look up at him. She did so with archness and fluttered her eyelids. "Whatever you say, big boy."

"You want to walk over to the football stadium and look at the full moon?"

"What time you want to go and where you want me to meet you? I love full moons."

"Meet me at the corner behind the gym at ten o'clock. You sure you don't mind?"

"My favorite hymn is 'Where He Leads Me, I Will Follow.' I'll be there."

"OK. Bye for now."

"Bye. Think of the last line of the chorus while you're waiting."

Fulfilling a romantic fantasy and feeling like a real man of the world, Porter squeezed through one of the locked iron gates and led the willing girl through the darkened arches. The stadium gaped like a huge mouth, yawning empty and mysterious upward at the moon, the silence so complete that there was ringing in his ears. They both moved softly and spoke in whispers. On the thick grass, already very faintly kissed with dew, sprawled at the fifty-yard line, Porter had little difficulty seducing Dorothy. With only the bright eye of the moon to see him, he kissed and petted. When the last vestige of her clothing lay in a pile, Porter judged that surely the pan must be ready, for it reeked of mullet less than fresh. He rose on his knees and began applying his rubber. Dorothy lay on her back in linking dollops of corpulence, her arms extended above her head.

In affected tone she asked, "Do you see a man in the moon?"

"Why, yes, I've always thought I saw a man in the moon." He moved toward her impatiently.

"Well, I don't. I always see Jesus and Mary. Sort of like on a cameo pin my grandmother passed down to my mother."

Porter fell sideways. Everything about him fell abruptly.

"Excuse me," he muttered.

He gained his feet, buttoned his trousers, and left the stadium as fast as he could. He did not look back. He was sure that Dorothy would be led divinely home in safety. He ran back to the dormitory, his feet unable to keep pace with the turbulent conflicts in his brain. Even more than comfort he needed reassurance. The dormitory was quiet. He put a nickel in the telephone.

"Dr. Clemmons, I hope I didn't wake you up. My name is Porter Osborne and I'm a classmate of your daughter. I know it's late, but I need to talk to her about an exam I'm having tomorrow. Could I please, sir, speak to Vashti? It's terribly important."

"Porter Osborne, you say? It really is quite late, young man. Vashti isn't here."

"Could I reach her somewhere else? She's the only one in the world who might be able to help me with the particular problem I have."

"Vashti left this afternoon to stay with her mother's sister in Atlanta. She's having a little dental work done this summer and may transfer to Agnes Scott next fall. We're discussing it. Do the best you can on your exam. Good night."

Porter felt as heavy and weary as Dr. Clemmon's voice while mounting the stairs to his room. He closed the door and leaned against it.

For the first time in weeks he addressed the Lord directly. "I don't care what anybody else would say, I think I may still be a virgin. Thou knowest, Lord. Have mercy on me. If I really am a sinner, grant me slippuns on this one and I'll be a good boy again. From now on."

Porter remembered his adventure with Vashti as a wild improbability and secreted it in the filing cabinet of memory. When his junior year began, he threw himself into campus activities of all sorts. He was re-elected treasurer of KA. Slick Roundtree, retiring president, confined himself rigidly to his Law School studies and abandoned any interest in the fraternity. Deacon Chauncey said it was because he had been at the top and used KA as much as he could and wasn't interested in anybody but Slick. Porter knew how hard Law School could be and how average Slick's academic background was and tended to doubt Deacon's assessment.

Clarence Spangler was the current Number I in the fraternity and trumpeted around with newly developed seriousness and what Porter regarded as an unwarranted sense of self-importance. Instead of consulting with Porter as treasurer, Clarence issued directives and bellowed in exasperation if they were resisted. The doctrine of "I'll tell you how to do without it" served as nothing more than a goad to him. The newsreels and papers were full of the posturing and belligerent Benito Mussolini, characterized openly as the dictator of Italy. Porter thought that Clarence not only acted like him but had begun to look like him. This observation so amused Amalita and Sara Belle that they passed it on as their original opinion to a group in the drugstore one day when Spangler was loudly holding forth.

Clarence reacted with pique and gradually developed an antagonistic relationship with the two girls that was ongoing and progressively intense. They had daily encounters in the mornings at Chichester's Drugstore, since they all had a vacant third period.

389

Porter's involvement in the feud was minimal and distant since he had a class at the time they all met there, and besides, he hardly ever went to the drugstore anyhow. He heard Clarence's reports of these encounters delivered with noisy bravado in the fraternity suite, and he heard the girls fume and laugh when they took him to ride in Amalita's car in the early afternoons.

Porter rather pitied Clarence. Both girls were smarter, quicker witted, and more popular than their adversary; in addition, they outnumbered him. They were prominent in Phi Mu and kept pointing out to Clarence that this was KA's sister sorority and that consequently they were due deference and respect. They got neither. In defiance, Clarence began extolling the virtues of ADPi, and the feud grew. Both girls were socially very secure on the campus of Willingham. Amalita was dating an SAE football player; Sara Belle was almost pinned to an obsessive-compulsive Phi Delta Theta who was a Law student, played football, and, in addition, enjoyed the lofty position of being a second lieutenant in the Reserves of the United States Marines. He went to summer camp in Quantico, Virginia, every year and had persuaded his brothers to elect Sara Belle Phi Delta Theta sponsor. From their pedestals, the girls made Clarence the butt of jokes, not only in the lodges of Phi Delta Theta and SAE, but also in the Co-op and drugstore.

Porter felt that Spangler was like a sore-headed chicken in a flock of white leghorns — no matter how hard he tried to rally his reserves and win an encounter, the girls always pecked him back. The president of Kappa Alpha Order could not tolerate such cavalier treatment, nor such public ridicule, but like a man struggling in quicksand, he used his own weight against himself. Instead of retiring from the field with what dignity he could muster, Clarence talked faster, laughed louder, strutted harder, and more stubbornly renewed the fray at every opportunity. The girls loved it.

Clarence was dating one of the Phi Mus. She liked him. She liked his Prussian good looks, his extroverted personality, and the fact that he was KA president and a member of Blue Key. She was a pretty girl with a good sense of humor and a high degree of sophistication for Willingham. She was certainly a lady, for she did not smoke. She was a frequent companion of Amalita and Sara Belle, and Porter consequently felt more than a passing degree of loyalty toward her.

In the fraternity suite one evening, rankled and raw from losing another battle of wits to his feminine antagonists, Clarence had nothing short of a temper tantrum. "Those damn broads are driving me crazy!"

Broad was another term introduced from up North — familiarized at Willingham by the mouth of Mick Jurkiedyk. It carried the connotation in Southern ears of coarseness, vulgarity, dulled mentality, and even hinted at indiscriminate sexual activity. It was quite an explosive word, Porter thought. It should not be dropped from the lips of the president in the living room of the Kappa chapter of Kappa Alpha Order. After all, their motto was *Dieu et les dames.* They were expected to revere Southern ladies as deeply as had their medieval counterparts. Nice Southern boys did not refer to any woman as a "broad." He compressed his lips disapprovingly.

"Watch your mouth, Spangler. That's no way to talk about ladies."

"Aw, shut up, you little prissy-britches. What you getting out of it? You get your scrawny little butt wedged in that convertible with them and ride around all the time and gossip with them just like they do. And that's all. You sure ain't cutting any of it. It ain't in you. You're just one of the girls, that's what you are!"

Deacon Chauncey became interested enough to lower his newspaper and sniff. "What broads you talking about, Spangler?"

"Those damn Phi Mu bitches, that's who."

"I thought you were dating a Phi Mu."

"I am, but I'm not talking about Eleanor Woodall. She's the cutest thing in the Phi Mu chapter. I'd like to give her my cherry. She's so sweet I'd love to stick it in some evening and just leave it in all night. Hell, no, I'm talking about that Sara Belle Steele and especially that Amalita Hunt."

As surely as if he had heard *à moi* ringing in the room, Porter felt summoned. "Spangler, you're going too far! If you can't get along with Amalita and Sara Belle, that's your business, but you mustn't foul their names and talk about them behind their backs."

"Yeah? Who's gonna stop me? I'll say what I please and I don't give a damn who hears me! And there's not a blessed thing you can do about it!"

Porter regarded Clarence's face, his muscular chest, his

impressive biceps. He said nothing. Hiram Holliday certainly would handle the situation differently, but Porter Osborne, Jr., was by no means defeated yet. He resolved there was a blessed thing he could do about it. He told the girls.

Word by word, he recounted Clarence's remarks in precious accuracy. The only impediment in his narration was posed by Sara Belle, who still knew very little about the real world and was still dedicated to learning all she could about boys. She was familiar with the term *broad* and only snorted indignantly upon hearing it, but when Porter related the word *cherry,* she interrupted with imperious demand for definition. As Porter taxed his vocabulary to give delicate explanation without sacrificing detail, her eyes widened, her brows drew down with angry comprehension, and then her face broke into mirthful shards.

"That's marvelous! What a ridiculous way to describe male virginity! I think it's hilarious! Oh, Sambo, what would we do without you! And isn't it a riot to think about Clarence having one? Oh, I can't wait to ask him about it in the drugstore tomorrow! He'll die!"

"Wait a minute, Sara Belle. Hold up. You can't do that."

"Why not? I think this is the funniest thing I've heard yet about the old male mystique. Boys are so funny!"

"That's just it, Sara Belle. It's male. And male only. Nice girls don't talk about cherries. It'd make you look bad."

Amalita joined in. "My Lord, Sara Belle, you can't just go around telling everything you know. For pity's sake. Let's drive around to Woodall's house and tell her. I think that's the best way to handle Mr. Spangler."

Eleanor Woodall was quickly divested of any romantic interest in Spangler and became an enthusiastic confederate in avenging herself and her sorority sisters. It was she who walked into the drugstore, marched up to the booth where Spangler was ensconced in loud and lordly leisure, handed him a small, gift-wrapped package, and wordlessly left. Amalita and Sara Belle watched from the adjacent table as Clarence read the card aloud.

" 'This is all you'll get.' What in the world does that mean?"

He tore the ribbon and tissue paper off to reveal a twenty-five cent bottle of bright maraschino cherries, which he displayed in momentary bewilderment to his cronies. In the ensuing bedlam of mirth, Amalita advised him as she and Sara Belle made their gleeful exit, "We also want you to know, Clarence, that Phi Mus are neither broads nor bitches."

Porter interrupted the vituperative tirade that evening in the KA parlor. "But, Clarence, I distinctly heard you say right in this very room that you'd say what you please and you didn't give a damn who heard you."

"You told them! You told them! Now my name's mud with the whole Phi Mu chapter. I ought to kill you."

"Clarence, why don't you just act like a gentleman and quit mentioning these girls when they aren't around?"

"You'll not tell me what to do, pissant! I'll talk about em when I please. That Sara Belle Steele made me want to puke today the way she was laughing."

"Clarence, I'm warning you. Those girls are my dear friends and I can't stand by and let you say things about them any more than you could if somebody were talking about your sister."

"You and your romantic bullshit! What you going to do? Tell em what I say? Well, tell em I said Sara Belle's got such a big mouth her pussy must be humongous. Let me see you tell em that, shitass!"

As Clarence left the room and slammed the door, Porter resolved to do just that. Battle had been joined and this was the only weapon he had. He approached the girls with reservation. What if Sara Belle had never heard this word before? It would be almost beyond his power to explain it. Although nice girls were obliged to have them, he was sure they never had heard them so labeled. If Sara Belle required as much detail for *pussy* as she had for *cherry*, he feared that he would become truly embarrassed. He need not have worried. The reaction was totally satisfying. Amalita immediately laughed. Sara Belle gave a great gasp, scowled ferociously, screamed, and then looked puzzled.

"What in the world does he mean? What an absolutely revolting boy!"

It was obvious that both girls had heard the word before. Sara Belle was upset only about the personal reference. Delightedly scandalized at his own effrontery, giddy with boldness, Porter openly used the term again.

"Sara Belle, I've heard 'Big mouth, big pussy' all my life.

393

Every boy in the world thinks you can look at a woman's mouth and get a good idea of the size of everything else."

Sara Belle and Amalita looked at each other and simultaneously pursed their lips into prim and tight little buttonholes. Sara Belle spoke through hers with difficult speech. "Well, you dooon't say!"

All of them threw back their heads and laughed.

"Let's go tell Woodall, Sara Belle. Come on, Sambo, we'll get you back to Willingham before time for supper."

Porter sat in the back seat and felt comfortably forgotten as his friends chattered mirthfully and instructed Eleanor in their newly discovered lore.

"That's the funniest thing I've ever heard! And the silliest!"

"Think about Martha Enema, the twisted-gut girl from Ty-Ty, Georgia. She must have a whopper! You reckon she's got teeth there, too?"

"And poor Martha Raye! And Carmen Miranda! They're in real trouble."

"And our cook. Law, I bet she could get a shoe in hers, cause her mouth will hold a tea cup full of snuff!"

"And, listen yall, if the mouth has anything to do with it, think what a terrible fix Eleanor Roosevelt is in. Bet she wears teddies, too"

"Yall hush. You should be ashamed."

"Well, what about old Amalita here? Look how small her mouth is. Maybe that's why she's so popular. The boys all believe that saying."

Amalita pursed her lips up again into a tight little rosebud. "Well, girls, I don't mind telling you that some of those old wives' tales are pretty accurate. Eat your hearts out."

Eleanor Woodall remonstrated. "We can't let you get away with that. Down with false doctrine! Let truth shine out! I've got a great big mouth and I don't want anybody to get the wrong impression on account of it. Why, I couldn't accommodate a penny pencil!"

They were all having so much fun — shocking, wicked, witty fun — that Porter was nearly late for his job. The girls let him out at the dining hall and were still bubbly with laughter as they waved good-bye from Amalita's convertible. He was not privy to their later plans and consequently was as surprised as anyone when they mate-

394

rialized. Quite simply, Amalita, Eleanor, and Sara Belle filed into the drugstore the next morning, walked up to Spangler, bunched their mouths into unbelievable little puckers, and spoke tightly in unison.

"Good morning, Clarence Spangler. Good-bye, Clarence Spangler. If you know so much, how come you so dumb?"

Then, maintaining their prunelike posture, without another word they filed out of the drugstore. They were on the sidewalk before Clarence fully comprehended the significance of what had happened. He was about thirty seconds later than Deacon Chauncey, who took it all in, pointed a finger at Clarence and choked with laughter as he explained the charade to the rest of the drugstore crowd.

Within twenty-four hours Clarence could not meet a Phi Mu anywhere on campus whose mouth did not pucker the moment she saw him as though she had been tasting alum. Within forty-eight hours, the ADPi's had taken it up. Clarence, before the week was out, was almost being laughed off campus. The only girls who did not greet him so were the devout members of BSU, whose determination to be Christlike did not allow them even to acknowledge knowing about the shocking premise upon which Clarence's flagellation was based, let alone applying such knowledge.

After a week, Clarence stormed into the KA suite, teeth flashing, swaybacked with battered pride, rattling windows as he spoke. "Who in the hell do these Willingham girls think they are? I've been turned down three times for a date on Saturday night. I'll die before I ask again! Let em suffer! Where's that damn Porter Osborne? It's all his fault! He went and told what I said about Steele having a big pussy, and now every girl on campus is beating me to death with it. It ain't funny anymore! I'm so tired of girls puckering up at me I could puke! To hell with these highfalutin sorority gals! I'm sick of em! One of these days before I die, I hope to be in the position where I can, by God, tell all of em to lie down and shut up and they'll have to do it. I'll figure out some way to do it if it kills me. I despise them! I'll by God show em who's boss! Where's Brother Osborne?"

"Right here, Spangler. Right behind you. But I could hear you at the other end of the hall."

"Let me tell you something, shitass. This ain't funny any more!"

"I already heard you say that. I think it's great that you've come around on that point. I'm sure this means you're not going to mention any girls by name in the KA suite anymore. Thank you. That's all I wanted in the first place."

"Quit putting words into my mouth! Don't ever get the idea you can tell me what to do. I want you to quit acting like some pious, prissy-britches pervert and hiding behind skirts. I'll say anything about those Phi Mu bitches I feel like!"

"OK, Spangler. Long as you don't call them by name."

Clarence went down the hall and slammed the door to his room. Porter settled into an armchair with the newspaper, avoiding eye contact with any of the other brothers. Presently, muted laughter was heard from Clarence's room. Then the door banged open and an invidious voice bellowed down the hall.

"Osborne, you still here? You like poetry. OK. I made up a poem for you.

Sara Belle Steele
Will let you feel.
Amalita Hunt
Will take it in the cunt."

With a scream, Porter abandoned all pretense at poise and leaped into the hall. "You can't say that!"

Clarence stood in his doorway, laughing maniacally. "Got to you, didn't I?" He repeated the doggerel.

Porter reached into the corner and grabbed a baseball and bat. He hurled the ball the length of the hall, straight at Spangler's head. Spangler ducked and laughed. Porter raised the bat and charged. Spangler laughed again, slammed the door, and locked it. From within his room came gusts of laughter and then the profaning verse. Porter beat on the door with the baseball bat and screamed. Clarence laughed and recited again.

In his frenzy, Porter noticed the dents he was making in the door, small concavities in the brown wood like doodlebug dwellings in the dry, thick dust under the church at home. He thought of Professor Twilley and his attitude toward vandalism. Impotently he tossed the bat aside and trudged to his third floor sanctuary in

Nottingham Hall. He went to sleep with the hated verse ringing in his brain. He was sure he would never forget it.

Next day he very calculatedly told the girls what Clarence had said about figuring out some way to make them lie down and shut up, but carefully withheld any reference to the sickening rhyme. In the first place, he could not bring himself to repeat it to a girl, even in the enlightened state they presently occupied. In the second place, he was sure they would be hurt as well as insulted, and if they were as angry as he, they could not possibly be actresses enough to bring off what he had decided was a good way to exact vengeance. Clarence was weary of the tightened mouths. Very well. Porter fancied that the girls on campus were also ready for new material. He was right.

The next morning Amalita, Sara Belle, and Eleanor accosted him individually in his booth, approaching with bobbing head and little shuffling steps.

"Mawning, Boss Clarence, suh."

"Hidy, Mr. Bossman. Can't lie down this mawning."

"Scuse me today, Mr. Boss, my back's sore. I don't feel like lying down and shutting up no time soon."

Then they sat at a table several feet removed and spoke indignantly in tones that carried well.

"Can you imagine any dolt saying such a thing?"

"Who does he think women are? Can you imagine any woman in her right mind ever having anything to do with him?"

"Not if she has one iota of self-respect, I can't. What a jerk!"

Clarence fled, but it was too late. On the sidewalk, girls bobbed their heads and muttered, "Boss." On the paths of Willingham, the same thing occurred. Within a week Spangler could not appear on campus without every co-ed in sight bobbing and ducking as though she had cerebral palsy.

It was not playful activity, either. "Boss" took on a very unpleasant hissing sound when uttered in baleful derision, and the air was full of it. Clarence began avoiding the drugstore. Porter, in prudence, began avoiding the KA suite.

One night he was lying on the bed in his cavernous room in Nottingham when the door burst open. Clarence had just been flayed in serious confrontation before the Library by two ADPi's and a BSU girl. In fury, he accosted his gadfly. He stood over the bed before Porter had a chance to rise and yelled so loud and fast that Porter had little time to reply.

"There you are! Cowering and hiding away from everybody! Well, you should, you little shitass! I've always known you weren't fit to be a KA. We never would have pledged you if it hadn't of been for your daddy. You've ruined me! You've spoiled my whole senior year! You won't come out and fight like a man! OK. That's because there's nothing like a man about you! I can't even say you're a prick, cause that's *part* of a man! You know what you are, Osborne? You're a coward! That's what you are! You're yellow! You're yellow clean through! Yellow to the bone! Yellow!"

He took a deep breath. Porter lay silent and wide-mouthed with surprise.

"Sara Belle Steele will let you feel! Amalita Hunt will take it in the cunt! You're yellow! And that goes for your whole family, too! Even that Uncle Bung! Yellow, yellow, yellow!"

Then he was gone.

For a while Porter lay stunned and disbelieving. His front porch had not only been invaded, it was crumbling under his feet. He had been attacked. His girlfriends had been attacked. His family had been attacked. Especially his family. Why Uncle Bung?

Uncle Bung was the ragtag, inconsequential tail end of Porter's family. He was the ninety-year-old brother of the grandmother and at the age of seventy-seven, after sixty years of marriage, had come to live with the family because he could no longer endure a nagging wife. He was a silver-haired and mustachioed little gnome of a man who twinkled and puttered, never accomplishing anything, but doing it with unfailing good humor. He may not have amounted to much, but he always felt friendly. When any of the children of the family carried guests home, they invariably were captivated by Uncle Bung. He carried on nonsensical and hilarious conversations with them and they never forgot him.

He had regaled Bob Cater. "What you boys saying about dogs, Sambo?"

"We're not talking about dogs, Uncle Bung."

"I could have sworn I heard you say something about dogs. I guess I'm getting a little deaf but I know I heard somebody say something about dogs."

"No, sir. None of us even mentioned dogs."

"Well, I declare. Excuse me. But speaking of dogs, did I ever tell you about the time my old blue-tick hound tried to get that coon off a log in the river?"

When E.V. Derrick had gone home with Porter, Uncle Bung had permanently imprinted himself with his opening greeting to the visitor.

"Uncle Bung, I want you to meet my friend from college. This is E.V. Derrick."

"Pleased to meet you, young man. I ain't so good, now that I've gotten old and stiff. Oops, did I say 'stiff'? What I mean to say is that when I was young and limber — oops, did I say 'limber'?"

Bob and E.V. had made Uncle Bung famous in the ranks of Kappa Alpha even without the anecdotes that Porter contributed during bull sessions. But it was grossly unfair for Clarence to cast slurs on Uncle Bung.

Porter paced his room. He felt humiliated. Violated. He pondered what to do. He knew in his heart that he was a coward. He physically feared Clarence and there was no question about it. The mere thought of a fight with Spangler brought recall of his muscular build and frequent offhand references to Golden Glove accomplishments and sent shudders down his own thin and protuberant spine. But yellow! Being yellow was worse than being just a coward. Porter would have been hard put to delineate the difference, but he felt it in his gut. It was like the difference between being poor and being sorry.

His family yellow? Uncle Bung yellow? If he tolerated this most wounding of insults, he would perpetuate it and be damned by it for the rest of his life. It was better to die, Porter decided, than to live forever with shame. It had come to this. He was terrified but he was prepared to die. He knew what he must do.

It was late when he knocked on Spangler's door, but Spangler was still studying. He did not rise. Porter walked over and stood at his desk.

"Clarence, I've been thinking ever since you left my room.

About a lot of things. You're not going to apologize and I'm not going to apologize. Things have gone too far between us not to be settled any way but physically."

"Is that so?"

"Yes."

"Well, what do you propose to do about it?"

"There's not but one thing to do about it and that's clear. We'll have to fight it out."

"Don't be funny. There's nothing I'd like better, but we'd both get kicked out of school. I'm president of the fraternity and you're Number VI and that wouldn't look good, either. You're not fooling me. You're too smart not to have figured those points, and you know we can't fight. I haven't got any more time for you farting around and being melodramatic."

"I have thought about those points. You respect the fraternity and I respect the fraternity, and we could swear by all the sacred oaths of Kappa Alpha not to tell, and then nobody would know but us."

"Nobody but the whole campus. And I'd whip your ass to a bloody pulp, and since I'm bigger than you are, I'd look like a fool and be a laughing stock. Besides that, where would we go to have a fight?"

"I know a place nobody would ever see us. Or even hear us."

"Where?"

"In the tower next to the meeting room. I've got the key."

"Yeah. That might work. Naw. You don't want to fight. Forget it. Get out of here."

"Clarence, I told you. Things have gone too far. If you don't fight me, then *you're* a coward."

"OK, smartass. You're asking for it. When?"

"Tomorrow afternoon at three o'clock. I'll meet you at the head of the stairwell on third floor."

"You've got a deal."

"Three o'clock."

Porter turned and reached the door.

"Osborne."

"Yes?"

"You ain't fooling me. You're yellow."

Very quietly and gently Porter closed the door.

The next morning in Chemistry class, the professor announced that he had a crisis in his family and would be out of town for the rest of the week but that he would hold an emergency lecture and lab session at two o'clock to avoid interrupting the schedule of his students. Porter listened with dismay, but there was only one thing to do. After all, one more day should make no difference to Spangler. For himself, he enjoyed the prospect of living a little longer.

He found Spangler coming out of the dining hall after lunch. "Clarence, I've got a conflict. Dr. Spitz announced a special Chemistry session I can't miss for this afternoon. Would you mind postponing our appointment?"

Clarence laughed. Loudly. So loudly that two co-eds on their way to the Library turned. They began shuffling and bobbing their heads. If Clarence saw them, he ignored them.

"I knew it. Sure, kid, sure. Forget it. I knew you wouldn't go through with it. Don't worry about it. You can't help it."

Porter's tone became icy. Formal.

"I assure you my goal is not cancellation. Merely deferment. Would the same time and place tomorrow suit you?"

"Sure, kid, sure. But look, I'm a busy man. I'll be in the Biology Building tomorrow at three and I don't have time to keep interrupting my plans to play games with you. Whenever you're ready, just come and get me."

The next day, further removed from the passion of his debasement two nights previously, the memory of the patronizing and taunting tone of this encounter still bolstered Porter's determination. At five minutes before three o'clock, he formally sought out Clarence and walked with strained conversational non sequiturs to the Administration Building. Unlocking the door, he thought fleetingly of Vashti and their meeting in this tower and then Buckalew's voice musingly observing, "If a fellow won't fuck, he won't fight."

Porter felt that from this standpoint he was in much better position than Spangler, but it was of little comfort.

"Where are we going, Brother Osborne?"

Porter led the way across the hall from the ladder into a similar room with bare brick walls, its dust-dimmed windows set close to the filthy floor. Cobwebs hung in tattered streamers in the corners and waved lazily with the current of their entrance.

"This should do nicely, I think." He turned and faced his adversary.

"Well, Brother Osborne, don't you think we ought to take off our shirts?"

Porter had no desire either to expose his own under-developed pectorals or to observe Clarence's beautifully delineated musculature. "Why?"

"This place is pretty nasty. We're liable to get em dirty."

"Oh."

Stripped to the waist, Porter stood uncomfortably facing Clarence. His imagination had not carried him beyond this moment. He had assumed that a Golden Gloves champion would take the initiative and lead the way. Clarence's muscles rippled in the dim light. Porter felt awkward, incongruously in much the same way he did on social occasions when he did not know which fork to use. He shrugged his shoulders helplessly.

"Well?"

"Well? Well, hell! You're the one called this meeting! Start something! If you're not, I'll put on my shirt and go home. I've wasted enough time on you. I knew you didn't want to fight!"

If he had not laughed and his teeth had not flashed, it might have ended there. With no previous expertise but with an unguarded opponent, Porter drew back his fist and struck Clarence as hard as he could in the face. The blow landed squarely in the left eye and was very fleetingly a gratifying sensation to Porter. It was of sufficient force to snap Spangler's head back and to cause him to suck in his breath.

"Well, I'll be damned. You fooled me."

He rushed Porter and grabbed him in a bear hug. He raised

him above his head, like a weight lifter bench-pressing a paltry hundred pounds, and hurled him with a crash against the wall. Porter's world spun dizzily but he felt more weight and pressure than he did pain. He heard the taunting laugh above him and gathered himself off the floor. Again he was lifted and slammed. This was not at all what he had expected. Not from a boxing expert. He dragged himself up and again was hurled down. And again. And again. The air was thick with the disturbed dust. Porter could smell it and taste it. Clarence had stopped laughing. Porter could hear his heavy breathing.

"I'm trying not to hurt you.... Give up.... Call it off."

Give up? thought Porter. This is the day I die, not the day I surrender. Mustering reserves he suspected not, Porter arose again and again. It had become an endurance contest in which his only pride was that of the actuality of enduring. He no longer felt fear, only animal determination.

"Can't believe it. Didn't know you could take this much. Lie down. Stay there. Bout worn out. Quit. You don't, I'll have to hurt you."

Somewhere in his brain, Porter realized that events had worked to his advantage. Clarence, in his sportsmanlike wish not to take undue advantage of an inferior opponent, had exhausted himself. Porter heard the breath coming in great strangling gasps, saw the body gleaming with sweat, beheld the great shoulders drooping with fatigue, and staggered forward with a desperate lunge.

"No more. Quit. Warned you. Can't take. No more."

Porter was tired, too. But Porter was convinced he was going to die. He drew back his fist and passed the second lick of the fight, hitting Clarence in the right side of the face. He slipped and clung to Clarence's shoulder to keep from falling.

"That does it. Warned you. Can't help it."

Dimly, in slow motion, helpless to avert it, indeed almost welcoming it, Porter saw the left fist drawing back and coming toward him. At least I tried, he thought.

When he regained consciousness, Porter Osborne was lying

spread-eagled on his back looking into the dim heights of the dusty room. Clarence Spangler was kneeling by his side desperately fanning him with a shirt. Porter heard him with clarity.

"Oh, my God! Help me, Lord! What am I going to do? I've killed the little son of a bitch."

Porter's blood surged with joy. He lived. Spangler's words in his ear had the lilt of a litany of love. He groaned and tried to rise. His back was hurting unbearably.

"Lie still. It's all over. Thank God you're all right. I never would have hit you so hard but I had to. It was wearing me out to keep throwing you down, and all of a sudden I realized you might last long enough to whip my ass. I had no idea you could take that much. I had to do it. You know that, don't you?"

"It's not over till you say I'm not yellow."

"OK, you ain't yellow. Now it's over."

"Good. I know I'm a coward, but I'm not yellow."

"You ain't a coward. You're the bravest little shitass I ever saw. Or else the most stubborn. Or maybe both. Get up."

Porter moved his eyes around. He had to get it all settled.

"Let me hear you say Uncle Bung's not yellow."

"Hell, I never even saw Uncle Bung. He's not yellow. He's probably the finest thing this side of Santa Claus. Now, get your ass off the floor."

"You're going to have to help me. It hurts to move my legs."

Clarence helped Porter to his feet and then had to support him down the stairs. There was lancinating pain in his back, and he was so stiff he could move only with the difficulty of a robot. Clarence looked at the wreck that was Porter Osborne, looped a supporting arm around him, and said, "You look like hell. What are we going to tell people happened to you?"

Porter surveyed the swollen tissue around Clarence's left eye, the blue and purple color of it.

"Just tell them we were cleaning up the fraternity rooms and I fell down."

"Well, don't forget. We're sure not going to tell anybody we were fighting."

Hobbling across the campus, awkward and crablike, the pair ran into Slick Roundtree.

"What in the hell happened to you two guys? You look like you've been wallowing in a hog pen."

"Oh, we were in the Administration Building trying to clean some of those old filthy rooms."

"How come your shirts are clean and you're so hog-nasty everywhere else?"

"Oh, we took off our shirts to work."

"Well, what in the world happened to Brother Osborne? He's moving like an old man and his face is all bruised and swollen on the right side."

"Oh, he fell down the stairs and hurt his back. That's what made us quit."

"Well, what in the hell happened to you? That's the biggest shiner I ever saw on anybody!"

"What? I've got a black eye? Me? A black eye? It didn't feel like you hit me that hard! You little son of a bitch! I ought to kill you!"

Slick began laughing. He pointed his finger. "The other one's black, too. Just not as bad. Yet. You guys been fighting! That's the funniest thing I ever heard of. You been fighting with little Porter Osborne! And he blacked your eye!"

Slick walked rapidly across campus. His laugh was like music to Porter.

"Clarence, don't pay any attention to him. You've got to help me to my room. I can't walk by myself."

"Why didn't you tell me I had a black eye? We could of made up a different story. Now I'll get laughed off campus."

Porter's tone was earnest. "Clarence, I hadn't even noticed it until Slick did. Why don't we tell that you ran into a door knob?"

"Two of them? Oh, shit!"

Porter had to go to the campus physician in his office downtown.

"The x-rays show you've got a fractured transverse process. There's really no treatment needed. It'll heal eventually by itself."

"What's a transverse process?"

Clarence stopped going by the drugstore and began studying

much more seriously. He was accepted to Medical School for the following year and performed the unusual feat of making straight A's even after his acceptance was securely in hand. So far as Porter knew, he never mentioned any Phi Mus again by name in the confines of the KA suite.

Porter limped for a month. He resolutely stuck to the story that he had fallen down the stairs, taking care to use an exquisite shade of intonation that made everyone know he was lying. He thus managed to achieve a reputation for being a regular fellow who wasn't afraid to fight but who was too noble to talk about it.

He never told Amalita and Sara Belle of the horrible rhyme that had triggered it all, but he basked in their solicitude. When he was officially elected the unofficial sponsor of Phi Mu Sorority, he tried not to smirk, but he felt lifted up.

How he did love those girls.

The story of the fight with Spangler spread over the campus. Embellishments it acquired were illuminating and pointed up to Porter the fallacies probable in any legend. He had adopted the distant and superior attitude that it was a matter not to be discussed, and he made no effort at correction of any inaccuracies ... unless he encountered one he thought unfavorable to himself. In selected circles, Porter even became something of a minor hero. The more he denied there had been a fight at all, the greater his reputation grew.

XXIV

Mrs. Raleigh was concerned. "You poor thing. You can't wait on tables like this. Not in a time of suffering, the which I can truly say I am myself no stranger to. The dishwashing boy has been wanting to transfer out front to wait tables, and I'll just change yall's places. That way you won't lose out on your job. There's more'n one way to skin a problem, I always say. Bless your heart."

"But, Mrs. Raleigh, I won't be able to lift those baskets of dishes till my back's better."

"Now, Sambo, let not thyself be troubled. His eye is on the sparrow, and we are all watching thee, as the saying goes. Boston Harbor says he'll double up and help you until you're able to do it on your own. Now, tell me, how'd you really get hurt?"

"Oh, I fell down some stairs and twisted my back and bruised my chin."

"Well, Mrs. Walthall's next-to-the-baby girl works in Dr. Newton's office, which she is door neighbor to one of my best friends, and she said that you came in his office for x-rays. She said that your back was not broken but that it is fractured and you have to be careful. Then I have my own self seen Clarence Spangler come in to eat with two black eyes, and I was not born yesterday, and those who have ears to hear, I always say. And there is plenty to hear. The twins say that a certain party, who I'll not mention since it seems you are protecting him, had about got too big for his britches anyhow."

"Mrs. Raleigh, this sure is nice of you. I certainly didn't expect it."

"Well, Sambo, you know my heart has always gone out. It seems you are determined not to let your right hand know and that is fine by me, but you just remember that I recognize two plus two when I see it. Also I always say, 'Oh, how the mighty.' Go thank Boston. He's the one who's doubling up."

Boston did, indeed, have to double up. The square dishwasher was a galvanized beast, noisy and demanding. Wire baskets of dirty dishes were lowered into a mechanized cradle which rocked and swished them back and forth through soapy water until they were clean. They then were lifted out and plunged in and out of a scalding bath and allowed to steam dry. The floor in front of the dishwasher was always slippery with sloshed water and wasted powders and constituted a hazard for even the agile. Porter was grateful to his friend.

"Law, Sambo, ain't nothing. Glad to do it. I scared Mrs. Raleigh git on her 'It my Christian duty' hat and fire you. I was wrong, but you can't never tell. One them sho-nuff talk-about-it-all-the-time Christians liable to jump one way same as another. Just can't never really depend on em. You be well fo you know it, and I be glad to have you back here in the kitchen all time anyhow. You really put them two shiners on that big ole Spangler boy?"

Porter looked over his shoulder. "Boston, I don't mind your knowing — I like to got killed. Clarence whipped my ass from here to kingdom come."

"Uh huh. He look like a fool if he didn't, much difference they is in you sizes. Look like a fool now that he done it too. Long as you can scramble around and make it atall, you won that fight, Sambo. I proud of you. Just let it lay now. Don't stir it. It smell worse if you do. Leave Clarence a little room for pride right now and he be you friend for life. He blige to be feeling shamed, and do you run you mouth it just get worse and make him fractious.

"Do you lay low and keep you mouth shut, he sooner or later

408

gonna respect you. Better somebody respect you than like you anyhow. Plus do you respect somebody, it hard as hell not to like em."

Porter's back healed, and he enjoyed the communion of the kitchen as opposed to the compulsive activity of being a waiter. There was not the same pressure of time on the washer of dishes. He did not have to scurry to get food on the table, frantically remove dishes, race the other waiters for desserts, or bang the large oval trays around in haste. The dishwasher boy came in, loaded his plate with food, ate in the kitchen in leisure and solitude, and surveyed the frenzy of activity with detachment. He even granted himself the luxury of chewing his food and perhaps on very rare occasions wheedling an extra dessert from the penurious Mrs. Raleigh. He had nothing to do until the meal was over. He could stand with the cooks and enjoy watching the ritual of Baptist boys eating and Baptist boys serving them and savor the exchange of comments about the peculiarities of each. Boston Harbor and Jesse Lee were veterans. They had seen everything over their years at Willingham, and still they retained freshness in their comments and made him feel special and adopted. Porter delighted them.

"Hoo whee, lookit that ole slew-foot Lamar Watson from Cordele. Way he slop around in them moccasim shoes he wear, wonder he don't fall all over hisself with them big tray fulla dishes. This floor slick back here and he don't never pick up his feet."

"He a sight, Jesse Lee. Sambo, you hear him when the waiters eating day fo yestiddy talk bout last time he went home? Got him a girlfriend, and he say they time a kiss to see just how long can they hold thout breaking it off. Say they went forty-five minutes on one kiss. Had to turn they noses sideways to breath, he say, but didn't never let they lips come loose. For forty-five minutes! Howard Avary say that gal must be bad buck-tooth and they done got hung up like dogs cept at the wrong end, and ole Lamar turn red and say don't talk bout his girl; they both virgins. Ole Howard a plumb mess, you know, don't care what he say, and he pop out and low that must been the worst case of stone ache they ever had in Crisp County. Less'n Lamar tend to hisself on the way home, he say. I bout die laughing.

These white boys somepin else. Lawd have mercy. Virgins, hot nuts, and forty-five minute kisses. I say college education!"

Porter responded with an attitude of tolerant superiority. "Well, don't be surprised at anything these freshmen talk about. Smooching's not a sin and that's probably the first girl he's ever kissed. What bothers me about Lamar is the way he goes around smelling everything."

Jesse Lee wagged his head. "Yeah, Sambo, I know what you mean. I notice that, too. Lean over ever dish we set out, get his ole nose right down close to it, and sniff around like a dog hunting rats. Kinda unsettling and insulting to us cooks."

"Well, it's kinda unsanitary and bad manners, too. The other guys fuss at him about it, but he's so butt-headed he ignores them."

The next day Porter was standing behind Lamar in the line while the waiters and kitchen help served their plates to eat before the siren sounded. A ten-gallon, white enameled pan brimming full of a gray homogenous substance was on the serving counter before them. That was all there was for supper except rolls and ice cream. There was obviously a great deal of mayonnaise in the salad, there were green flecks that promised peas and pickles, and there was presumably meat of some kind. In actuality, it was a new and thrifty dish originated that very afternoon by Mrs. Raleigh. To Porter's knowledge, it was the first time anyone had ever fashioned an amalgam of tuna fish, deviled ham, English peas, and cold mashed potatoes as an entree. After washing the luncheon dishes, he had been witness before he left the kitchen to the eye-rolling exchange between Boston and Jesse Lee as Mrs. Raleigh pulled leftovers from the icebox and lined out the recipe.

Lamar Watson, plate and fork in hand, bent from the waist and peered at the offering. He looked around to be sure Mrs. Raleigh was not within earshot. "What in the world is this crap?"

Porter caught Boston's eye and was immediately filled with evil resolve. "What does it smell like, Lamar?"

Eager as a beagle puppy, Lamar lowered his head and began sniffing audibly, his nose a scant three inches from the surface of the food. Porter swiftly placed a hand on the back of the boy's skull and thrust downward, counting on instant youthful reflex to jerk Lamar's head backward and upward. To his mixed horror and

410

delight, the opposite happened. Lamar's face plunged deep within the salad. It disappeared from sight. For a split second, it was mired so deeply that not even his ears were visible.

Lamar leaped up, swinging a fist violently. His eyes were blinded with mayonnaise, his ears and nostrils were packed with Tuna-ham-potato Surprise, his face was coated heavily, and the front of his hair contained bits of pickle and an occasional pea. It was easy to duck nimbly the swinging arms, but Lamar's roar attracted Mrs. Raleigh. On the second swing, Lamar's feet slipped and he fell, banging down with him to the concrete floor a stack of heavy metal trays. Porter noted that the pan of salad had enough substance to retain the imprint, indelible and unmistakable, of a human head. Fascinated into immobility, he thought, What have I managed to do now?

Mrs. Raleigh spoke like an echo. "What in the world have you managed to do now? Lamar, get up off of that floor this very instant and pick up those trays. I declare, I do not know what in the world or where. Oh, my great stars above, what happened to the Tuna-ham Surprise?"

Lamar was flipping large gobs of it from his ears. "Don't look at me. Porter Osborne pushed me."

"Sambo, what do you know about this? Speak the truth now."

"Well, he was leaning over smelling of it," Porter began.

Boston Harbor gave Jesse Lee a nudge in the ribs, and Jesse Lee spoke. "He sho was that. Lamar was leaning over smelling that ole ham-and-tuna-and-English-pea-sprise, and his feet slip out'n under him and he fell plumb in it. Sambo reach out and grab him by the nap of his neck or else he be done turn that whole pan full of sprise plumb upside-down on the floor. The which it was them ole moccasim shoes done it. They slip on the cement floor and make Lamar stumble in the first place. It stay slick out there. I been telling him bout them ole moccasim shoes and that slippery floor. What you want us to do bout the sprise? Just smooth it over again and let it ride? Or dump it all? Lamar's whole nose and Lawd knows what else done been slap down in it might nigh to the bottom of the pan."

"Oh, Jesse Lee, don't talk about it. You'll give me a headache. Get me that big spoon and I'll scrape away the part he touched, and then the rest will be all right. Oh, waste not, I always say.... There.

411

That looks better. And we didn't lose more than a plateful. A penny saved and what somebody don't know won't hurt anybody. Lamar, you go get cleaned up quick; it's time for the siren. I've been laying off to talk to you about smelling the food anyhow. You've got a bad habit there. All my food is fresh, and there's no use to smell it. Besides the which it doesn't look nice and it's unsanitary, too."

Jesse Lee joined in again. "Uh huh. Sho is, Mrs. Raleigh. Sho is. I been saying that my own self. Hit unsettling, too, hit plumb unsettling."

Against these concerted attitudes, Lamar was too crestfallen to speak out, but he gave Porter a baleful, albeit greasy, glare as he departed to clean himself. Porter did not dare glance at Boston Harbor Jones for fear of Mrs. Raleigh's intercepting and accurately interpreting a look of gratitude, but he was thankful in his heart for such a staunch friend.

Porter recounted the episode to Henry Bean one afternoon in Qualitative Analysis lab.

"My God, Osborne, for once I wish I'd been there when you were wound up. I'm coming over to that dining hall some time just to meet Boston Harbor Jones. He can't be as fabulous as you portray him, but then nobody is. I bet you've broken Lamar Watson from ever smelling food again. I wish you'd put your hot little mind to work on this damn Hyman Goldberg. He's driving me crazy."

"What's wrong with Hyman Goldberg? He won't talk about it, but everybody says he's had a rough time. I kinda like him."

Hyman Goldberg had been at Willingham free of charge for the last two quarters. He was getting his degree in Chemistry and already had a scholarship awaiting him at Baylor for a Master's degree as soon as he finished Willingham. He was older than his fellow students, spoke heavily accented English, and attracted more benevolent patronage than had Shiu Lau Ling. He was a refugee from Austria, and rumor had it that something vague but terrible had happened to his parents and his young wife.

He never smiled except in a nervous, almost apologetic, obviously superficial grimace and scurried around campus as though

412

someone were after him. He studied furiously, took voluminous illegible notes, and went into spasms of frustration and anxiety if a test paper came back with less than a hundred on it. All the other students wore black rubber aprons in Chemistry lab, but Hyman Goldberg wore long, white lab coats with deep pockets. He seemed to feel intellectually superior to his Georgia fellows.

The Baptist Student Union and the regulars at vespers prayed about Hyman a lot. They prayed that Hitler and Goebels would stop confiscating the property of the children of Israel so that they still could live in Germany. Some of the more single-minded prayed that Hyman Goldberg would have his heart touched by the kindness of Willingham students and accept the Lord Jesus Christ as his personal savior, thus averting a fate in the hereafter worse than anything he could possibly have faced had he not departed Austria.

Porter had asked several times why Hitler was so down on the Jews but had never received a satisfactory answer. He was skeptical about any of the German propaganda that occasionally was translated and printed in the papers but was not sufficiently interested in the situation to explore it in depth. After all, it was like the rest of the war — it was happening half a world away and could not affect him, nor could his attention possibly have any effect on the outcome.

He noted that both the Bible and Hitler spoke forthrightly of "Jews," whereas genteel Southerners always said "Jewish people" and often lowered their voices a little. The noun was crude and was to be avoided, no matter how awkward the use of the adjective might be.

His own attitude toward Jews centered around the fact that every time the Living Word of God had a chance, it referred to them as God's Chosen People. This, Porter felt, entitled them to more than a passing degree of respect. Their failure to embrace Christ as the Messiah and to recognize fresh hog meat as a delicacy rendered them also people to be pitied.

Certainly Porter joined the majority of the Willingham students in being solicitous of the persecuted Hyman Goldberg. He deferred to him at every opportunity, as he would to an important and unfamiliar house guest.

Henry Bean was under no such burden. "I tell you what's wrong with Hyman. He's a damn leech, that's what. Always asking,

413

always taking, always grabbing. Never giving. Hell, I'm sorry about his personal misfortunes, whatever they may be, but he's making a damn career out of them. He borrows my books, he borrows my notes, he borrows my clean beakers and Erlenmeyers and then doesn't wash them properly when he returns them. He acts like we're *supposed* to do all this for him. Whatever he wants, he just walks up, says 'please,' and takes it. He says 'please' as imperiously as if he were Caesar and acts like he thinks that one word is all he needs to adjust to us sloppy Americans. On top of that, he has no sense of humor."

"What do you mean?"

"I tried to kid him about his name. I told him we'd call him Maidenhead Goldberg if he had been born a Greek instead of a Jew and his mama had hung that name on him with a little different spelling."

"Henry, you didn't!"

"I certainly did. He looked at me real frosty and said, 'Please?' and I repeated it. Slowly. He huffed up and said 'Dot iss not fonny.' I told him it sure as hell was funny and that he had a language barrier. You know what he did?"

"What?"

"He shrugged his shoulders real deep like I was a child, reached in my cabinet, picked up one of my clean beakers, said 'please,' and started using it in his experiment. That guy is unbelievable. Nobody is going to come in here, tell me in broken English what is or isn't funny, and then treat me like a foot servant."

"Why don't you just tell him you're not going to lend him any more equipment and to leave you alone?"

"That's too simple. He'd just borrow from Tiny Yeomans. I want to get him good. What really pisses me off is that he uses our reagents all the time. Do you know that he hasn't made up any of his own at all? And yesterday he actually shoved me out of the way reaching for my nitric acid bottle."

Porter looked at the wide and commodious shelf above the sinks and the slate desks assigned to him and Henry. It was filled by a row of fifty glass bottles with glass stoppers, all neatly labeled and precisely aligned. They contained the reagents needed for this course in Chemistry and were made up by the students themselves. Qualitative Analysis was primarily a laboratory course in which the professor handed out "unknowns," salts which the student was expected to break down and positively identify by chemical processes outlined in the laboratory manual. The reagents were essential to the process, and their purity became even more important as the course progressed and the chemical unknowns became ever more complex. In making up their reagents, Porter and Henry had combined forces as a matter of expediency. It had been a preparatory experience that was gratifying and made Porter feel like a real chemist. He felt that Henry was justifiably annoyed if his neighbor on the other side was mooching their reagents.

"Henry, I've got it! We'll just change the labels on the reagent bottles and then Hyman won't know what he's using. Of course, he won't be able to identify his unknowns, either, but flunking an unknown will make more impression on him than anything we could say."

"Please? Anything we could *say*? I've already said everything I can think of. Osborne, there's hope for you. I'm really gonna miss you when I go in the Navy next month. Let's change those labels after lab this afternoon. We can keep a secret code in our drawer about what they really are."

"OK. And we won't bother to change the ones on the colored compounds. He can look at copper sulfate and potassium dichronate and tell what they are; so we'll just change labels on the colorless ones. Why are you leaving before spring quarter?"

"I told you I was doubling up and graduating early so I could get a better deal in the service. I don't hanker after any experience at all as an enlisted man. I'm finishing all my degree requirements and going in the Navy at the end of this quarter. I'm going to Midshipman's School at Northwestern University. I know you're fixing to ask 'Where's that?'; so I'll hasten to tell you it's in Chicago. Just the second biggest city in the United States, that's all. I'm a little bit nervous about it, but there's a big war ahead, and they're going to need big boats to haul soldiers to Europe again. And to tell you the truth, Osborne, the Navy will be a safer place to live out the war than the Army."

"Unless you get torpedoed. Don't forget the *Lusitania*. Besides, there's still not going to be a war. Not for us. There's no way the Germans can cross that ocean. We could just put numbers on all

415

the labels and not let Hyman find the list."

"Naw, let's change em and watch him wonder what happened. It'll be good for him to find out he's not infallible and can make a good old plebeian American F."

It worked. Hyman spent hours on a double salt, used up twice the scratch paper he should have, and finally turned in an answer. It was the first zero he had ever met on a personal level. His agitation was increased by the red one hundred shining on the paper that Henry left carelessly and conspicuously on his desk top. Hyman flunked another one and had an arm-waving, wailing conference with the kindly Dr. Spitz. Porter and Henry moved maturely and industriously around the laboratory, so absorbed in their own projects that they could take no notice of this minor event. Tiny Yeomans popped her gum and stared openly while Dr. Spitz went over procedures and the methodical steps in the laboratory manual with Hyman. The frustrated student beat his forehead with a clenched fist and muttered in a strange tongue.

Next day Hyman was in the middle of an experiment, holding a large test tube with the little metal tongs provided. He glanced at his lab manual, perused his neighbor's shelf of reagents, leaned over Henry with a rather impatient "please," and selected the one labeled KOH. Porter was overly busy at his own Bunsen burner, but he watched from the corner of his eye. Hyman unstoppered the reagent bottle, held it up at eye level, and carefully decanted some of the contents into his test tube. There was an immediate "plop," white smoke boiled out of the test tube, and its contents bubbled furiously over the edge. Hyman shrieked, abandoned the mixture into the sink, and went running out of the room to fetch the professor.

Dr. Spitz also wore a long white coat with deep pockets. He kept his hands in them while he listened to Hyman's rapid, practically unintelligible recital, bobbing his fuzzy head in assurance that he comprehended. He informed Hyman that the reaction he described was impossible with the particular unknown he had been assigned if he had followed the procedures correctly. He suggested that Hyman repeat his effort while each of them observed. Porter became even busier. Henry Bean was across the desk with his head down, writing up his experiment. Neither gave any evidence whatsoever of interest in the individual tutelage going on next to them.

416

When Hyman decanted the KOH again, he produced the identical reaction again and gave the identical shriek again. Dr. Spitz also jumped and began his sputtering speech pattern.

"That's strange. Calm down, Goldberg. There's a logical explanation for all of ... Get control of yourself, young ... I do not believe for one moment that you have produced a completely impossible chemical reaction this afternoon in my ... Just relax, Goldberg."

The two long coats converged on Hyman's lab manual. Porter noted that small holes were appearing near the knee on the professor's coat where Hyman had been less than careful with his explosive mixture.

"Step one. Yes. Step two. All right. Here. OK. Yes. Shake vigorously and heat until ... So far, so good. Add KOH. This is where it happened each ... Let me see your KOH, Goldberg."

Hyman produced the borrowed bottle. Dr. Spitz held it up and squinted. He removed the glass stopper and held the bottle gingerly beneath his nose.

"Here's your problem, Goldberg. This bottle has concentrated acetic acid in it, not KOH! Show me the stock bottle you got this ... How did you come to mislabel it?"

Hyman yammered incoherently.

Dr. Spitz continued, "Oh. You didn't. Well, you're supposed ... The laboratory instruction sheet plainly states that each student is responsible for maintaining and replenishing his own ... It says that right here, just after the paragraph stressing the importance of clean, dry glassware, and ... You've been borrowing reagents all quarter from Bean? Relax, Goldberg, just calm down!"

Dr. Spitz turned to confront Henry Bean, but that student had just stepped out to get something from the stock room. Porter met the professor's inquiring gaze with widened eyes and a disclaiming shrug. He did not trust himself to speak.

"Now, don't get excited, Goldberg. I'll let you have another unknown to make up that zero you turned in and ... But I would advise you to spend the necessary time and prepare your own reagents and ... Well, all the other students have. Now remember, Goldberg. Just take it easy. And calm down!"

It took Hyman Goldberg until nearly nine o'clock that evening to prepare his reagent shelf the way it should have been done during the first week of the quarter. Porter knew, for when he left the Library he nearly collided with Hyman, who with lowered head was rushing up the brick walk from the Chemistry Building and muttering under his breath. He ignored Porter's cheerful salutation, and Porter had to stand aside to let him pass.

Hyman occupied his lab space the next day like a sulling bull, moving back and forth in silence and casting occasional black glances at Henry Bean. When Henry finished for the day, locked his cupboard, and prepared to leave, Hyman blocked his way.

"You don't like Chews."

"What do you mean?"

"Vy you do dis ting to me? Vy me? You don't like Chews. Yes?"

"Cut the crap, Goldberg. Anybody as smart as you who always busts a gut going for the high A in Chemistry can't be that stupid about people. I've got nothing against Jews."

"Den vy you trap me? Vy of me do you make the fool in front of Dr. Spitz? Ya. You hate Chews."

Henry put down his books and sighed. "I was in a hurry, but that does it. Sit down, Goldberg. Do you understand 'asshole'? It's assholes I got no use for. What church they go to is their own business. I've known a lot of assholes in my time; in fact I'm sometimes absolutely surrounded by them. As a further fact, you're the first Jewish asshole I've encountered. Do you understand?"

"Please?"

"What I'm saying is, quit hiding behind your Jewishness and face up to your assholeness. Nobody on this campus dislikes you because you're a Jew. You wouldn't even be here if you *weren't* a Jew. The school's sympathy for the Jews and the Georgia Baptist aversion to that Hitler maniac are what brought you here in the first place."

"So? Please."

"So hold up your end. Somebody tries to act nice to you and you act like a damn paranoid rabbit. You're always reaching out clutching and grabbing like you won't get your share or like some of us owe you something. You never even asked me or Osborne if you could borrow our reagents. You acted like we were supposed to do it, so why bother taking notice of us? That's a real asshole, Goldberg, and we wouldn't have let a Baptist get away with it till the water got hot. I don't give a flying damn if you're a Jew or a Hindu. As we Navy

418

boys say, you can shape up or ship out."

"You are saying you vant me to leaf, yes?"

"Hell, no. I'm saying that you need to wake up and start pulling your own weight. This is America and there's room for everybody, but you have to do your part. I personally don't *want* you to do anything. You're a grown man and you can do anything *you* want to. You're not my responsibility. What happens to you is strictly up to you. I'm not going to lose any sleep over it."

Henry slid off the stool facing Hyman and gathered his books again. Hyman made a restraining gesture.

"Don't leaf."

"I have to go. Sorry I blew my top but that crack about not liking Jews hit me wrong. Look, Goldberg. The code to the reagents is in the top of my desk. If you help keep em stocked, you're welcome to use them. Let's go, Osborne."

For a moment, Hyman studied them from beneath puzzled brows with eyes that were flat and black. Porter wondered how he could have missed noting before the manner in which the hairs of his nose bushed out in stiff and glistening puffs.

"Please. *Bitte*. Nobody before haf effer to me like dis been talking. It is great kindness you are making. Ve vill be friends, ya?"

He squared his shoulders, gave a short step forward, snapped his heels with an audible click, and extended his hand.

Henry Bean reddened a little around his neck and responded, "Well, why the hell not? Now, quit saying 'please' every time you turn around; it makes me jumpy. How'd you like to go drink some beer?"

As they walked away from the Chemistry Building, Porter broke the silence. "Golly, that was something else, Henry. You lied about one thing, though. He is, too, your responsibility. After all that, I almost wish I drank beer so I could go with yall tonight."

"There has to be a lot more to him than meets the eye. I've got a month before I leave for the Navy. I'm going to make an American out of that little Jew if it kills me."

Porter's toe hit an uneven brick and he gave a little hop to catch up. He almost missed the next comment as Henry muttered in a musing tone, "Or the son of a bitch may make a Christian out of me. Who knows?"

Porter was so impressed by Henry Bean's encounter with Hyman Goldberg that he related part of it to Boston Harbor Jones at supper while washing dishes.

"That Henry Bean one the best friends you got at Willingham, Sambo. I like to meet him some day. He dead on it. He rough, but life rough, and he dead on it. I don't know no Jews, but what he say apply to us colored just as well. That Hyman got to have some stoutness about him, too, to take all that and face up to more. Let me know how it come out."

The next day Boston was his usual affable self, flashing his cheerful smile with the wide space between the upper teeth like a familiar beacon in the kitchen.

"You going anywheres after supper, Sambo?"

"No, why?"

"You gonna be in you room? With nothing to do?"

"Yeah, why?"

"I got a little favor I wants you to do me. Can I come up'n see you?"

"Sure. I'll be there."

When Boston knocked and entered Porter's room later, he seemed a little ill at ease. He looked about him and then began walking around the room, touching things, picking up a book, straightening a paper.

"Right here where you kept that baby kitten long with that mammy I brought you. Right?"

"That's right, Boston. Right there by the radiator."

"And show me the dresser drawer where you cram all them cats what make Mrs. Capulet fall out and faint away."

"It's that one right there. What can I do for you, Boston?"

Boston reached in his pocket and pulled out a flat spool of black thread. It was stamped "Number Four. Silk." From another pocket he extracted his knife, opened a wafer-thin blade, and cut off a length of the black silk. He offered it to Porter.

"What's this?"

"It's doctor string, that's what. Sew up cuts and things at the

Mercy Room with it."

"Where'd you get it?"

"Got it from my cousin. Viola. You remember the one say she impress with you in that whorehouse on Oak Street you freshman year? That's the one. She got a job now cleaning up in the hospital, and she brought this out'n the Mercy Room. It make good stout fishing line."

"What am I supposed to do with it?"

Boston extended his hand before Porter's face abruptly. The little extra finger with its deformed, almost unborn nail quivered with the movement. "You gonna get this little sucker off'n me."

"I am like hell!"

"Yeah, you is, too, Sambo. Ain't nothing to it. I done tole you my maw took the other'n off when I was born. Told me many a time she tie a string around it and it turn black and shrivel up and drap off. You'n do it."

"Why you want it off? Nobody pays any attention to it after they get to know you."

"The doctor at the induction center do. I got me one them letter say, 'Greetings.' I say, well, Boston Harbor Jones, you time is come. Go down to get my physical. You ain't never had no physical, Sambo. Hoo whee! Them mens strip you plumb nekkid, run a needle in you arm to bleed you, and make you pee in a bottle. They even put on a rubber glove and stick a finger all way up in you ass. That got to be worse'n turn you head to the right and cough. Anytime you see a doctor putting on a rubber glove, you better look out. Nothing good come from it. You can just bet if it bad enough one them doctors need a glove to do it, it might nigh too bad to stand. Got all done with that and then the doctor say can't cept nobody with genital deformities. I say, 'What's wrong with my genitals?' and he say, 'Congenital, man. I talking bout you finger.' Say I ain't qualified for induction United States Army less'n I have surgery."

"What you're telling me is you're 4-F on account of your finger."

"What I'm telling you is what that doctor told me. Oh, he nice and polite and everthing, but what he really saying is they don't want no six-fingered nigger in the U. S. and A. Army. As Mrs. Raleigh say, I ain't born yestiddy and I am no stranger, and I get the message.

421

That's why I want you to tie it off."

"I don't get it, Boston. Lots of fellows would be tickled to death to have that 4-F classification. Especially for nothing worse than that."

"That's part the problem right there, Sambo. You done laid you finger right on it. I was tickled to death myself when I left there. Boston ain't got to go. Ain't got to leave his family. Ain't got to leave his friends. Ain't got to leave his job. I safely 4-F and feel fine as I ever did. I got the world licked."

"Well?"

"Well, then I got shamed of feeling that way. Nobody else gets them 'Greetings' wants to be bothered neither. I feel lucky one minute, shamed the next. Finely I get to the place I feel like I'm a coward if I keep my finger. I feel so bad I ax my ma if she tie a string around it like she done its baby brother twenty-five years ago."

"What'd she say?"

"She say she wouldn't tetch that finger for five hunner dollars. Say if it keep her baby out'n the army, she sorry she mess with the other one. You know how mamas talk. What she finely say is, 'Get outta here; I ain't studying you.' When my ma say she ain't studying somepin, that's the end of it. Case dismissed. So you gotta do it."

"Boston, you have to let me think about this."

"Go right ahead. We got time. I been watching you think for more'n two years now, and it always something you do so fast it make my head swimmified. While you thinking, don't pay no attention to me. I just talking. I talking bout things I been thinking bout myself for a long time. Must have been down underneath. Bout being a Georgia nigger. Bout being a USA nigger."

"Boston, I don't like the way you're saying that. You aren't teasing anymore. You make me uneasy."

"That's part of it, too, Sambo. You remember the first time I ever say 'nigger' in front you? You draw up right prissylike and say you been raised not to use that word. And I told you then that told me a whole lot about you. Remember that? Course you uneasy bout that word. You been taught it ain't 'good taste' to say it. Now, don't look me in the eyeball and say you don't never say it youself when you think ain't none us around. It just ain't 'good taste' to say it do you think any of us can hear it. All you nice white folks uneasy, and I ain't knocking you bout that. Thank God you is."

Porter twisted in his seat but made no effort to answer.

"I uneasy bout it, too. Let me see can I esplain to you what make me uneasy."

"I wish you would."

"Well, it just lately I been uneasy, Sambo. I heard that word all my life. Done got use to it. When I just a little kid I ax my ma what's a nigger. She roll her eyes around at my ontee and say, 'Where you hear that?' My ontee quit rocking her chair and bite off her thread and set real still. I told her Mr. Jerome Murphy tell me I one. All the white folks call him Uncle Rome, and he pull off his hat to em and say 'yassuh' so many times he sound plumb silly. And they give him a dime or a quarter and act like he don't stink, and he say, 'Thankee, boss,' more'n he say 'yassuh.'

"I standing there one day when Mr. Lum Graham come down the street collecting his rents. It close to Christmas, and Mr. Lum done had a dram and he pretty full. Come by Mr. Jerome and say, 'Hidy, Uncle Rome. How you?' And Mr. Jerome snatch that ole greasy hat off and commence bowing and scraping, and Mr. Lum reach in a pocket and say, 'Here a little Christmas for you, Uncle Rome,' and he hand him a five dollar gold piece. That back in the time we still have gold. Mr. Jerome bout turn hisself wrong side outards, and Mr. Lum say, 'You a good old nigger, Uncle Rome. Ain't many left like you,' and soon as he gone Mr. Jerome bite that gold piece with his toofies and then see me watching him. I never forget what he say. 'How come you looking at me with you mouth hanging wide open, you little bastard? You a nigger, too.'

"I told my ma Mr. Jerome say I was a nigger and she say, 'Don't you pay him no nevermind, son. I'll esplain it to you later. Mr. Jerome getting old.' And I say, 'Ma, what's a bastard?' and she jump bout ten feet and say, 'Where you hear that word?' And I say, 'Mr. Jerome, he say I one them, too.' And she fly out the room, say, 'I settle this right now with ole Rome Murphy, that sorry nigger!' "

Porter laughed. "Boston, that's the funniest story I ever heard. But how does that make you uneasy?"

"Cause from that day on I know! They is such a thing! My own ma done call somebody one. And I know I prolly one, too. Down through the years I hear heapa preachers talk about it. Some say ain't

423

no such thing, say it just a figment of white folks' imagination, say we Negroes. Best sermon I ever hear bout it, though, one preacher say, 'What is a nigger?' He say don't let nobody tell you ain't no such thing. Else how come everbody say it? How come us black folks call each other niggers effen they ain't no such thing?

"That make sense, so I prick up my ears and listen. He say do the skin color be what make a man a nigger? Say no, cause some us black as tar and some so light ain't nobody but our own mammies know for sure. Say if they color be what make one, how come white folks always say 'black nigger'? Say that make you think they must be white niggers, too.

"And he getting warm up by then and he yell out, 'Oh, they is such a thing as a nigger, beloved. You want I tell you what a nigger is? A nigger is the devil, oh beloved chirren of God. The devil come amongst us. You can't help being black, cause the good God who created the Heavens and the Earth and the stars that shine above made you black. But you ain't got to be no nigger! Not for nobody! Nigger is the devil! Cast out the devil, you chirren of the living God! Turn you back upon him! Hold God close in you heart, and it don't matter who call you what! Long as *you* know it ain't so! Don't be a black nigger, don't be a white nigger, don't be a yellow nigger, or a red nigger, or a brown nigger. You don't *have* to be a nigger. Be a Christian man! Be a Christian woman! Be a Christian boy or a Christian girl! Born again through the precious blood of Jesus Christ, Who hung on that cross for all men's sins! Born again into the wonderful kingdom of Heaven! Where they is no black or white; they is no rich or po; they is only chirren of God! Where, beloved, they ain't no niggers! Cause they ain't no devil up there!' I always remember that preacher even effen he did get run off for messing with some the young gals in the church. I can't help what he do, but I never forget what he say."

"Boston, this is fascinating, but what's it got to do with your finger?"

"Sambo, I ax you before I come up here did you have plenty of time, and you say 'uh huh.' You ain't got no idea what it feel like to be colored, and I doing my dead-level best to splain to you how I got from where I was to where I is. Which is gonna be why you gonna take my finger off. Can you just be patient a minute and listen?"

424

"Scuse me, Boston. Of course I can."

"Well, I going along all right till Mrs. Roosevelt come along. Now, Sambo, I know you white folks don't like Mrs. Roosevelt. Say she ugly and got buck toofies. Which she has; she has got buck toofies. Course we all know that ain't why yall don't like her, but we too polite to call the real reason. She act like she think colored folks is real people and she got the gumption to say so out loud. Put me to thinking. I decide for my own self what wrong with the colored in Georgia is the plantation system."

"The plantation system? That ended with The War."

"Naw, it didn't. Leastways, Ole Massa still live on. Ole Massa ain't die and never will die. And you know why? Cause the nigger won't let him die, that's why. I see all these colored always want somebody give em somepin, and I see all these Ole Massas act like that's the way they spose to do and haul off and give em a little. Just a little, but still they give it. And that make them feel big and us feel little. That make us be nigger and them be bossman.

"Hardest thing in the world to overcome is gratitude, and Ole Massa know that. Use it all over Georgia like a whip. I ain't knocking it, Sambo. I just telling it like I think it is and I ain't faulting you folks. Now, you got Ole Massa use to giving and ole Nigga use to taking. And guess what happen? All colored folks turn out to be exactly the same."

"What do you mean?"

"I talk about in everbody else's eyes. When you do something bad, all the peoples say, 'Ain't that just like that Sambo?' They don't say, 'What you spect? Ain't he white?' If I do something bad, everbody say, 'Ain't that just like a nigger?' That make my whole race responsible for everthing in the country any other colored do. Make me feel like I got to be extra careful when I go out mongst the white folks so I don't give a bad name to the colored all over. You see what I mean?"

"Yeah. I guess so. You're talking about a loss of individuality because you're colored. I'd never thought of that before."

"Yeah. Well, Sambo, I'm tired of leaning on Ole Massa. I want folks to look at me in my uniform and say, 'He didn't have to do that,' just like they would if you or E.V. or Clarence or Deacon had somepin wrong and got it fixed and enlisted. I want white folks in

Georgia and the USA to know that colored folks loves this country, too, and that we'n sing 'God Bless America' good as Miss Kate Smith. And some of us even better."

"Golly, Boston, you're great. What brought this on so quick?"

"When you told me bout that Henry Bean tell that Jew boy he gotta pull his own weight and they's room for everbody long as they do they part, I decided I been had the devil in me like the old preacher say and that I been acting like a nigger instead of a man. And then I got to studying on what he tell the Jew boy about shape up or ship out, and I decide I gonna do something. Maybe I been hiding behind being colored and I'm tired of it. I gonna break out'n this Macon rut and get away from Ole Massa do it kill me. I sure ain't got to hide hind no little bitty extra finger. Now, will you tie the string?"

Porter reached out and felt his friend's accessory digit. It obviously had no bones in it, and its attaching stem was not large.

"Why not?" he said. Then he studied it a little closer. "Boston, this thing's pretty big. If we just tie it off to let it shrivel up, it's going to stink. Then it might fall off in the food or somewhere else embarrassing. Why don't you let me tie it real tight between two pieces of string and then cut it slap off and be done with it? We can burn a razor blade so we don't have germs, and I don't think it'll get infected. I can hear Mrs. Raleigh right now if you lose a rotten finger in some ham-tater surprise. You wouldn't live to get in the Army."

"Will it hurt effen you cut it, Sambo? I don't mind tie, but I hate the idea of cut."

"Naw. I've watched the interns do blood vessels this way down in the emergency room. I'll tie the string next to the hand extra tight, and I don't think you'll feel a thing."

Within minutes, it was done.

"There it is. What you going to do with this finger, Boston?"

"I ain't thought about that. I don't care. I'm done with it. Flush it down the toilet, I guess. Just don't let no cat get it. I still hates cats."

"Can I have it?"

"What you want with it?"

"Well, I've got Histology next quarter, and we have to make our own slides of mammalian tissue. I'd like to pickle this finger and

426

make slides out of it if you don't care. Nobody else will have a slide like that, for sure and certain. It's a shame to waste a perfectly good finger."

"Law, Sambo, you a sight. Just point up what I say. Nobody won't never look at you an say, 'Ain't that just like a nigger?' Yeah. You'n have my finger. I'm fixing to go to the Army and to college all in the same month. Thanks for helping me, Sambo. I owe you one. Good-night."

"Wait a minute, Boston. 'Shape up or ship out' is Navy talk. Why don't you join the Navy instead of the Army? In the unlikely event we do get in this war, Henry Bean says there's less chance of getting shot there. See you in the morning."

XXV **d**uring his exile in Nottingham Hall, Porter Osborne had been hoarding toilet paper. It had been so easy to procure without detection that it seemed a shame to pass it by, for it required only a quick side-step into an unlocked supply closet while Mrs. Capulet and Julian were making their rounds. He never had taken more than one or two packets at a time, but he had done it frequently and regularly. Porter stashed his booty in a dresser three doors down the hall in a vacant room, the lock to which happened to respond to his own key. The paper, neat and tightly-packed blocks, filled two drawers and was awaiting the propitious moment. Porter had plans.

In early March, just as the trees were breaking their tight, winter buds but before softly unfolding leaves completely hid their branches, there came the time. The skies were clear, the moon was full, and the wind was from the east. This was the night that Porter decided to decorate the grounds of Willingham.

The scheduled meeting on campus next day of the august Georgia Baptist Ministerial Association was not just coincidental in his planning. That powerful body, grave and judgmental, intimidated some members of the administration and invoked respect in most of the student body but did not particularly impress Porter. He rather thought it would be good for that pompous assemblage to discover that the students they affected through their recommendations to the trustees still had a zest for life, a propensity for the unpredictable, an independent and well-defined sense of the ridiculous.

Porter remembered the recommendation two years earlier

428

from the Georgia Baptist Ministerial Association that co-eds never be nearer than three feet to any male student at Willingham. The trustees had not voted this into law, but the possibility had stirred controversy among the students and the memory of it still smoldered in Porter's brain. Very emphatically and very anonymously, he planned to demonstrate to those zealous arbiters of Willingham morals and mores that there was more to college than books.

He gathered in his secret trove of toilet tissue. He had abandoned the embroidered laundry bag his mother had given him on matriculation, the one with the Chinese coolies whose pigtails spelled "Laundry." As manly substitute, he had appropriated a nitrate of soda sack from the farm and had fashioned a drawstring for it from a length of plowline. It was not only durable but unbelievably commodious. When he crammed it full of the brown-wrapped packets, it was heavy and awkward, but it held an impressive store of toilet paper. In fact, it was so heavy that it occurred to Porter he might need help in transporting it. While he studied and waited for Willingham to slumber, he mused upon it. Certainly he wanted no confederate who might blab and focus the vengeful and Cyclopian eye of Professor Twilley. He needed someone strong enough to lug the heavy bag across campus. He thought of Clarence.

Since their fight, the two boys had been mutually polite. Spangler had stopped insulting the girls in the halls of KA, and Porter had stopped being critical of his behavior. They never referred to the fight itself, but each had become considerate and respectful of the other. Porter examined his feelings now.

He really owed Clarence a lot. Clarence could have beat him unmercifully, but he had not. Clarence probably could have humiliated him by turning his bottom up and spanking him, but he had not. He had fought him like a man. Clarence had forced Porter to face his own cowardice and expunge it. Porter realized that he felt much better about himself since the fight. He at least knew that he would fight if he had to and that he could persist even in the valley of death.

He felt self-respect he previously had not enjoyed. He owed this to Spangler. No one else would have done this to him and thereby for him. Hell, Spangler was a great guy and probably would be a good friend. What they needed was the companionship of

429

shared adventure, and time was short for this. Spangler already had been accepted to Medical School and would be leaving Willingham for good in a few months.

At nine o'clock, Porter left his room and went to Smith Hall to solicit Spangler's participation. "Hi, Clarence. Haven't talked to you in awhile."

"Yeah, it's been awhile. What's on your mind?"

"I've got a very special project I need some help with, and I thought about you."

"Why me?"

"Well, you're fixing to leave Willingham and for all I know, you've never been involved in a real super-deluxe prank since you've been here. I thought before you graduate you might really enjoy one. I've got a real humdinger for tonight, and I'd sort of like to share it with you. You know, us doing something together as fraternity brothers. I hate for you to leave college and we haven't done any-thing together since that silly fight, especially now that I've really come around to admiring and respecting you since it's all over."

"Well, by God, Osborne, you may be growing up. A little. What you got in mind?"

At one o'clock in the morning the two fraternity brothers crossed the campus of Willingham, automatically seeking the darkest areas. The brightly glowing moon created a starkly deline-ated landscape, casting impenetrable shadows where none existed in the daytime and forming great pools of blackness around the build-ings. The faces of the boys were a perfect chiaroscuro, and under pressure of the supernatural quiet they automatically spoke in the most muted of whispers.

"I didn't know you could even get in the little tower, let alone climb it."

"You didn't? I found that out the first week I was at Willingham. Let's climb up the fire escape to third floor and get in through the ADPi suite. It's easier than climbing inside all the way from the bottom."

"I sure hope nobody catches us. I've never done anything like this in my life."

"They won't. Come on. I don't think this particular thing has ever been done before in anybody's life."

Clarence carried the heavy sack of toilet paper with ease while Porter stealthily raised the narrow old window into the ADPi bathroom. Removing the board behind the toilet created a draft of air rushing into the hollow brick cylinder before them.

"This is plumb spooky. How in the hell did you ever find it?"

"Somebody showed me. Now, listen. The ladder in this tower's nothing but iron rungs set in the bricks. They're directly opposite from us. Just stand in this hole on the edge and lean all the way across and you'll grab one. Like this. OK. Now hand me the sack and I'll move on up out of your way."

Porter clung to the iron rungs with a locked elbow and carefully slipped the ropes of the sack over his head. "OK. I've got it. Let me move on up and then you start."

"I can't see a thing. It's black as hell in there. We'll really get in trouble if we get caught. I think I'll go back to the dormitory."

"Clarence, I can't believe you said that. Come on. Just lean all the way over and grab a rung. You can't miss."

Clarence nearly did miss, however. He did not lean completely across the cylindrical well as Porter had instructed. Clarence assumed there was a floor in this tower. He stepped confidently out into nothing but thin air. Fortunately he was facing in the right direction, and as he began plummeting three stories straight down in blackness, his clutching hands grabbed a rung. With further fortune, it held.

Porter heard the bumping and kicking and a smothered cry. "What's wrong, Spangler?"

"I fell, that's what's wrong. Why didn't you tell me there wasn't a floor in this place? I just happened to grab this iron rung. And it's about to come out. You're crazy, Osborne."

"I am not. Why'd you think I kept telling you to lean all the way over if there was a floor? For Pete's sake! Some of the rungs are a little loose but they'll hold. I've tested em. There are a couple missing lower down, but they're all in place from here on up. Quit worrying and look straight up and you can see the moonlight. It's bright as day up there. Come on."

431

When they achieved the summit, Clarence was breathing loudly although it was Porter who was burdened with the sack.

"God! You're right about it being pretty up here. You can see for miles. There's the dormitory. And there's Chichester's. And look at downtown. There's the Conservatory, and there's the Auditorium."

Porter straddled the lip of the tower with tightly clinging legs. Clarence remained on the ladder with his elbows locked over the edge.

"Clarence, my idea is to rip the cover off each pack of paper and let the wind blow the little pieces around. Like this."

Porter lofted a pack into the air. The wind caught it with a fluttering sound, and what appeared to be a thousand separate white leaflets scattered in the moonlight above the trees of Willingham. Clarence throttled his usual booming laugh down to a conspiratorial chortle.

"God, that's downright beautiful. Looks like pigeons flying. Gimme some of that paper."

Porter later remembered the ensuing half hour as a happy time. Both boys moved unhurriedly, thrilled and excited by the novelty of a completely new adventure. The combination of wind, moonlight, and snow-white flutter produced an enchantment that encapsulated this moment. Neither boy gave thought to what was happening on the ground. They were so bemused by the bewitching activity that they forgot the goal. They deliberately slowed while opening the last dozen or so packets, like children prolonging the ecstasy of a piece of pie with tiny, savoring bites. Finally the sack was empty. For a moment there was silence.

"God, that was fun! I bet there's a mess on the ground."

"I can't lean far enough over to see. It looks like there's a little caught in the trees, though. We'd better go, I guess."

"Well, you go first and be sure to tell me where we get out at the ADPi toilet."

"I think we'll go all the way to the bottom, since you aren't familiar with it. It's easier climbing down than up, and you might miss your step and fall trying to get off on third floor. I'll tell you when we come to a missing rung. You just stretch a little farther and pick up the next one. There's nothing to it."

432

Once on the bottom, Clarence Spangler delivered a great sigh. "Going up and down that tower is the scariest thing I ever did in my life. You're crazy, Brother Osborne. I mean really! Did you know it?"

"Come on and let's see what it looks like from the bottom."

Stepping out of the building and surveying the result of their work was like getting out of bed in the morning and finding an unexpected snowfall. Even Porter was surprised. Clarence was overwhelmed. The ground from the street to the Christianity Building, from the Administration Building to the Chapel, was totally white. The walkways were lost in the trackless expanse of paper leaflets. Looking up, Porter marveled at the trees. Their branches were laden, especially those in the very top. The magnolias were bedecked in white-tipped tiers like the picture on a calendar. The elms and sugarberries looked as if they were blooming. The easterly breeze spun an occasional white sheet in dipping fall off a branch. The scene was improbable but lovely. Porter thought of Professor Twilley and wondered if he would classify this as vandalism or desecration. He knew beyond doubt that it behooved him to repair to his room without discovery.

"Come on, Clarence. Let's slip around the front and double back up behind the Chemistry Building. We sure don't want to walk across there in all that moonlight."

"God, Osborne, that stuff's knee-deep in some spots! I don't believe we put that much out. Don't you reckon we ought to clean it up?"

"You're the one who's crazy. We couldn't if we wanted to. It's too big a job. Besides, why should we clean it up? We didn't put it down there, did we? Did we, Clarence? I can tell you one thing, you sure don't ever want to go before that discipline committee. Follow me and be very quiet."

On his way to class next morning, Porter sensed excitement on campus. No fewer than six Negro men were busy cleaning up toilet paper. The walks were raked almost clean but the lawns were still thick. Most of the men were busy stabbing paper with pick-up sticks and filling bags with it. One man had a seed fork but the paper

433

kept sliding off it. In the center of the scene, their shoes obliterated by whiteness, stood Mr. Mullinax and President Powell. The former had let his pipe go out, and the latter was forcefully nodding his head and gesticulating with directive sweeps of his arms. Groups of students dawdled on their way to class, not believing the scene before them.

Porter overheard Mr. Mullinax. "I got six more coming in a half an hour, and we'll do the best we can, but they ain't no way we'n get it all up by 9:30. Besides which we can't clear the trees any way you look at it."

Porter waved across at both men but apparently they did not see him, for neither returned his greeting. He wondered if, when the preachers met a little later, some opportunist would refer to the student body of Willingham as being white unto the harvest.

Henry Bean had departed for the Navy, so Porter had to settle for Tiny Yeoman's editorial comments.

"Kiddo! Did you ever see such a mess in your life? With all that extra help they hired this morning, tuition will probably go up. Poor old Dr. Powell. You know he's embarrassed about all the visiting preachers finding this, but I can't help thinking it's more'n halfway funny. I heard one of those colored men say, 'Whoever done this must be dumped it out'n a air-o-plane. I ain't seed such since I was born.' I tell you, kid, if you know anything about this, you better lay low. Don't tell me, don't tell me. Just lay low."

Boston Harbor was at the Great Lakes Training Center in Chicago. Porter missed him terribly and would have relished his response to Mrs. Raleigh's comments.

"No, they don't know who did it. Mr. Mullinax said it must have took about six boys to get that much scattered that far, and sooner or later one of them is bound to let it out for there is no safety in that many. They also can't figure out where it came from. Mrs. Capulet checked her supply closets, and there's no tissue missing at all. Not even from the bathrooms. Well, be sure the truth will find you out, I always say, and to tell it like it flat out is, as bad a thing as it was to do, it looked right pretty before they stirred it all up."

434

Speculation was high about the perpetrators but evidence was nonexistent. Porter waited a discreet day or two and went to Clarence's room. The remembered wildness of that moonlit evening with the wind strewing havoc over Willingham was a bond to cement friendship, he fancied. The added bond of silent and dangerous complicity would lend a maturity to the relationship. He approached Clarence with a grin and a confidence that almost mandated a swagger. He was met, however, with formality and politeness so foreign to anything he had ever witnessed in Spangler before that he was puzzled. There was an aloofness, a cold dignity, a calculated disinterest in the older boy that was most effectively rebuffing, a reserve that was frustratingly impenetrable.

"I'm really too busy to talk, Brother Osborne. I have absolutely no interest in anything that may have transpired between us before. We all commit childish acts occasionally, and the best thing to do is forget them as soon as possible. Close that door on your way out, if you don't mind."

Porter was baffled and more than a little hurt. He shrugged his shoulders and resolved never to show his feelings. If he just had to talk to somebody about the toilet paper, he could always swear E.V. Derrick to secrecy. The only trouble was that E.V. had not been there and consequently could not fully appreciate it. Wistful, feeling very young and raw, he abandoned any idea of closeness with Spangler. The older, bigger boy just did not like him. Porter accepted this with sadness, for he now realized that he liked Spangler a great deal.

Willingham University was in the throes of change. The irresistible force had come to grips with the immovable object. Miss Fanny Burdette had descended from on high the previous fall and was determined to change the Willingham student body. The student body in turn had its heels dug in and was resolved to remain the way it was. Miss Burdette had been hired with the opening of Willingham's first girls' dormitory and the subsequent increase of female students. She was called the Dean of Women, and she took her position more seriously than anything else.

When she was introduced in Chapel, her *curriculum vitae* was recited and her credentials for her new job presented. They may have impressed Dr. Powell and the administration, but the students promptly forgot them, considering them either inconsequential or possibly even fraudulent. This lady in her initial appearance managed to alienate most of the students who were not sleeping in chapel, and she soon awakened those who were. Even the members of the BSU, disciplined in faith and rutted deeply into their religion, who tended to accept unquestioningly the official policies of Willingham, were shocked. There was no way that even the most firmly indoctrinated Baptist could regard Miss Burdette as the will of God or an instrument of the Lord.

She was a massive woman — tall, broad-shouldered, and thickened like a block of granite. Eleanor Woodall said she looked like she was jerked up in front and jacked up behind. She was so heavily corseted that she seemed to be mummified into hard adiposity, and she had to twist a little from side to side when she walked. Her rigidly encased thighs made loud whispers as they squeezed by each other. Porter knew that a gentleman ignored such noises, but he wondered if Dr. Powell, as she made her way past his chair to the lectern, speculated at all on the source of these sounds or the temperature of the source from which they were emitted. Her opening sentences were revealing.

"Young ladies and young gentlemen. Let me assure you that if you are not presently ladies and gentlemen, you will be before you graduate. I have come to bring culture to Willingham."

Silence descended on the Chapel. Precipitously. No cough, no creaking seat, no shuffling shoe, no rustle of paper violated the immediate and total quiet that attuned every ear to Miss Fanny Burdette.

"The poential for culture is here, young people. It is right here on this campus. It is my challenge to take the crude, raw material I find today and refine it tomorrow into a product that this university can be proud of. There is absolutely no reason why the co-ed student body of Willingham cannot become as renowned for its cultured young ladies as Stevens."

Porter was sitting between Amalita and Sara Belle. He heard the one from Sullins give a muffled snort and the one from Mary Baldwin emit a definite hiss. As soon as chapel was over and Miss

436

Burdette had retired to the scantest of applause, Porter exclaimed, "What's Stevens?"

Sara Belle snorted again. "What's Stevens indeed! That's exactly the way I feel! Miss Annie Fanny or old Fanny Annie or whatever you want to call her can be a vulture for culture all she likes, but she can include me out."

Amalita spoke huskily and a little maternally. "Sambo, Stevens is a college that's really got no particular reputation. At least not around Virginia. I believe it's even somewhere in the midwest — that's worse than being a yankee."

"Oh."

"When she says she's going to bring culture to us, it sounds as though there's no culture here to start with. I bet we're going to get little talks about crossing our legs only at the ankles and pushing the soup spoon away from us. And I bet we're going to hear the word *refined* more than any time since my grandmother died."

"The very idea! How does anyone born in Alabama who started off at Huntington have the gall to think she has anything to offer in Macon, Georgia! She'd better not mess with Phi Mu; that's all I've got to say."

Porter was thrilled. Battle had been joined and he heard the drums of war. There is nothing on earth more simultaneously mystifying and entertaining than conflict between females, and Porter relished every moment of it. He had a front-row seat for it and consequently was more caught up in the local fight for changing the Willingham female than in the world-changing clash of nationalistic titans across the ocean. It was infinitely more interesting to observe the thrusts and parries between Amalita Hunt and Miss Fanny Burdette than it was to frustrate oneself with apprehension about what Hitler might be going to do next. Churchill was a hero, all right, but so, by cracky, was Amalita.

Miss Burdette did mess with Phi Mu. She also messed with ADPi. And with the non-sorority girls. And the BSU. No one was safe. She creaked and swayed along the walks of Willingham like a cloud drifting across the sun and with much the same effect. Everywhere she went, joy faded and shadow appeared. Ponderous, dull, and overbearing, she managed to alienate even the good little girls who were too cowed to let her know it. Amalita Hunt was not of that ilk. She had been elected president of Phi Mu recently, and she let Miss Fanny Burdette know in ladylike but certain terms that the Phi Mu's were attending no more teas under her auspices.

Miss Burdette met straightforward resistance with the indifferent dedication of a steamroller, but Amalita refused to be crushed. She was a town student and consequently not subject to some of the pressures Miss Burdette exerted on the dormitory girls. When Miss Burdette tried to avenge herself on Amalita through nit-picking and badgering of the Phi Mu's in the dormitory, Amalita met the challenge by going to no less a figure than Dr. Wade Hampton Powell, who listened but made no comment. The students noted, however, that very shortly thereafter Miss Burdette backed off and began treating the Phi Mu's and Amalita with polite and formal coolness. Apparently Dr. Powell had little palate and no stomach for cat fighting.

Porter loved it. Miss Burdette had replaced Clarence as the center of Sara Belle and Amalita's indignation, and Porter chortled at their fuming summation of current slurs and their extravagant threats of vengeance. This was theater in which he had no involvement whatever as a participant, and he could relax and enjoy it in the role of amused spectator. He had no responsibility for and only passing interest in its outcome.

When spring rolled round, Miss Burdette appeared again in chapel. She wore a pink hat with feathers on it, and her bunched up little overbite twinkled between her fat cheeks as she spoke.

"Young ladies and young gentlemen. Spring is here. To the north our sister school of Vassar has its daisy chain. This year we are going to inaugurate at Willingham a custom that will grow through the years into a tradition even more famous and splendid. We are going to have a May Day celebration, young people. Right here on campus! With a May Pole! And young girls dancing around it! And a Queen of the May elected by the student body! With a beautiful processional before the Queen is crowned! Right up the middle of the quadrangle. Won't that be lovely? And we'll also elect a King of the May as the Queen's escort. We will plan this for Alumni Day when we are assured of a large audience, but we will have the elections next week and begin rehearsals soon afterward. What do you think of this idea?"

438

Amid much sniggering and rolling of eyes, there was a polite drift of applause as light and scattered as blowing mist on an April morn. Miss Burdette beamed as though she had received a standing ovation and lined out further particulars. She and her unidentified committee of student leaders were currently working on a list of six candidates for Queen and six for King of the May. It would appear in the student newspaper in sufficient time for the student body to ponder it before chapel the next week. The unsuccessful candidates for Queen and King automatically would become members of the court — ladies and gentlemen in waiting. There was more than a hint of archness as she dismissed chapel with the exhortation for everyone to return next week to vote for a favorite daughter of Willingham. "And son," she added in conciliatory afterthought as the assembly departed.

Conversation in the drugstore was explosive.

"Vassar? Vassar? First Stevens and now Vassar. Somebody better check that old biddy for a brain tumor."

"I hear there's not a sorority girl on her list for Queen."

"Yeah. Her group of student leaders is made up of the only BSU girls who still speak to her."

"She says the Queen will wear a long white dress and carry red roses and that the King wears white satin knee breeches and a purple cape."

"Vassar? Willingham and Vassar? I still can't get over it! A Maypole at Willingham?"

"The vulture for culture has laid an egg this time."

"Did you hear what Dorothy Parker said about the daisy chain at Vassar? 'If all those young girls were laid end to end, it wouldn't surprise me a bit.'"

"Shut up, Sambo."

When the paper came out with the lists of names, the reaction was Miss Burdette's final undoing. If there was one thing that Southerners took seriously, it was their politics, and Willingham students were no exception. There was a great deal of sputtering at having such a limited choice. There was indignation at the obvious ploy of advancing Miss Burdette's favorites and ignoring her adversaries. There was more than a little resistance to the idea of a May Day celebration at all. Porter capitalized on it.

439

He secured the help of a half dozen confederates, and the night before the election, they canvassed the dormitories. They urged secrecy in cooperation with their plan but they solicited support for Amalita Hunt for Queen of the May. They pointed out the totalitarian approach Miss Burdette had adopted toward a democratic process and assured everyone that selection of Amalita would be a personal affront to this dictator. The older and more callous Law students were delighted. Things needed stirring up in the springtime, and this was more on their level than swallowing goldfish. Porter called on Slick Roundtree.

"Sure, I'll go along with it, Brother Osborne. This is one time I think something is as funny as you do. I'll get as many Law students as I can to chapel tomorrow, too."

"Thanks, Slick. I think this will be a riot."

"Have you seen Spangler?"

"No. I went by his room, but he's gone to a movie."

"Well, I want to tell you something. He finally broke down and told me all about that toilet paper prank yall pulled. Now, I'm not taking sides or anything, but did you know that he thinks you tried to kill him that night?"

"He *what?*"

"He says you gulled him into thinking he was out for a college caper. He was feeling terrible about whipping your ass so bad, and you made him think you really had changed and matured a lot. So he went along with you. And then he says you tricked him into stepping off into a bottomless pit in the Administration Building."

"He's pulling your leg. He knows that was an accident. It never entered my head he could have thought there was a floor in that tower."

"Then it really happened?"

"Sure it did, but there's no way Clarence could have thought I did that on purpose."

"Yes, he does. He says that if he hadn't just happened to catch an old, rickety iron rung, he'd have fallen three stories straight down and be dead as a mackerel."

"That's all true, but he did catch. On top of that, it was after that he went all the way to the top of the tower with me and threw out the toilet paper. It doesn't make sense for him to say he thinks I did

440

that on purpose."

"He says he didn't know what else you might have had planned for him in that tower and that he was on strange territory and was scared to let you know he was suspicious. Said the whole time you were scattering that toilet paper that he hung on to his rung for dear life and kept himself in position so he could push you first if you tried to push him."

"I never in my life heard such a bunch of trash! Spangler can't be serious. This is crazy."

"He's serious all right. And *he* says it's crazy. Says you're a genius but that you're warped. That you've got it in your mind to get even with him for that fight and he doesn't trust you as far as he can see you."

"Why hasn't he confronted me with this?"

"He says it wouldn't do any good. That you'd just look innocent and deny it. He can't prove it and he can't let people know he was throwing toilet paper, him a senior and president of KA. And he sure can't whip your ass again. He's done that. Looks like you've got him by the balls. But he's convinced you tried to kill him."

"Do you believe that, Roundtree?"

"Naw, I really don't. But Spangler does."

Porter slept poorly that night. As he tossed in the bed seeking a position of comfort sufficient to lull him into slumber, his mind ranged from one point of logic to another and gave him no rest at all. He went from incredulity to chagrin. He overcame a sense of injury at being misunderstood and progressed rapidly to consternation. It was a short journey from there to anger, and there is no greater stimulus to insomnia than fury. Finally that subsided, and he considered Clarence's feelings. All he had to do was have a meeting with Clarence and dispel this nonsense. He punched his pillow and slept.

When he awoke, his sense of the ridiculous had taken over and he thought the entire situation humorous. He encountered Clarence on the way to chapel and called him aside.

"Clarence, this is so silly I hate to even bring it up, but Slick says you think I tried to kill you."

Clarence looked all around. His teeth flashed. "Slick told you that? I made him promise not to. I'm gonna kick his butt."

"Well, I told him that it was ridiculous, and I knew all I had to

441

do was talk to you about it."

"Bullshit! I don't want to talk to you about it. If it had worked, I'da been lying at the bottom of that tower till I started stinking. Who knew we were over there besides us? Nobody! So you'd have gotten away with it! All you would have had to do was leave without throwing out the paper and nobody would have ever thought to look for me there. And everybody would have wondered what in the world I was doing there in the first place. Don't try to lie out of it."

"You can't believe that! Let me explain."

"The hell I don't believe it! And I don't want any explanation. I don't want anything to do with you. All I want to do is to lay low and graduate and go on to med school. You can take this one-horse college you've ruined for me and shove it up your ass. But you'll never make me believe you didn't have it in your head to kill me that night."

Porter recognized an ace when he was dealt one. He laughed aloud as he played it. "Clarence, stop and think. Do you seriously believe that if I wanted to kill you you'd be alive today? Think about it."

As Spangler was reduced to silence for the first time in recent memory, Porter turned and hurried into the Chapel. He found his partners in complicity engaged in last-minute recruitment of town students they had heretofore missed. Heads were nodding and smiles were spontaneous. Porter's spirits lifted as he settled into his seat. He was always a little on edge about the outcome of a complicated prank that depended on the intermeshing of variables and individuals, but he felt good about the success of this one.

Miss Burdette came on stage and rapped for order. Her hat today was a beige toque with a single pheasant feather in it.

"Boys and girls! Ladies! Gentlemen! This is the magic hour we have all been waiting for! This is the moment when some fortunate girl will have the signal honor bestowed on her of being elected Queen of the May for the very first time in the history of Willingham University."

The auditorium quieted. Attention focused on her. She reveled in it.

"What an honor it is, young people. This is a proud moment. As the tradition born here today continues through the ages, you

442

may be certain that this will be the most sought-after title on the campus. It holds up before all of her fellows and the alumni of the university a young maiden who is recognized as embodying most completely the ideals of Willingham and of cultured gentlewomen everywhere. This moment is historical.

"Without further ado, we will now proceed to the actual election. Your candidates are all beautifully qualified. Your responsibility is tremendous. You are the ones who make the choice. You are the ones with the burden of deciding who will be your first Queen of the May. Oh, how glad I am that I am not put in the difficult position of choosing among these precious young ladies. You will vote by a show of hands. And here is the first name. Miss Mavis Clark."

The groundwork was adequate. The ranks held. Not a hand went up. Miss Burdette's tone lost any hint of coyness and became very formal.

"Let me see a show of hands of everyone who wants to vote for Mavis Clark for Queen of the May."

The audience was as silent and immovable as if graven in stone. Miss Burdette was obviously nonplussed by Mavis's lack of popularity and just a little embarrassed for her. A good leader does not, however, exhibit emotion in public. With objective calm she continued.

"Miss Elizabeth Fellows. We all call her Betty and love her to pieces. Let me see the hands on Miss Betty Fellows."

The hands of two nervous and browbeaten freshman girls went timidly into the air. Miss Burdette's eyebrows also went up. She carefully said nothing as she made a penciled notation on her election sheet. The student body seemed to breathe in unison.

"Miss Marian Watson. Show of hands, please, for Marian Watson for Queen of the May."

Charles Rick was sitting in the back of the auditorium. He had uninhibitedly proclaimed himself for the last few weeks as a victim of what he called "the hots" for Marian. He punched his neighbor in the ribs, and both of them swung hands vigorously and defiantly upward. Miss Burdette's lips compressed and her disapproving glance managed to convey that Charles Rick was a lout and that Marian Watson was, as a consequence of his endorsement, afflicted with a stigmatizing handicap.

"Jeanne Gard. How many hands for the lovely Miss Jeanne Gard?"

Miss Burdette was more than perplexed. She was becoming nervous. Porter knew she was, or she never would have allowed herself to give what was obviously a tug at her girdle — a futile gesture of crudity that belied her espousement of culture. Her mouth was so compressed one could hardly see any lips at all.

She made an effort at humor. "Well, I believe there has been some politicking going on behind my back. Is the lucky young lady to be Miss Kathryn McFarland? Who is voting for Kathryn today?"

Kathryn was a non-sorority senior who lived on the other side of Macon, and Porter's helpers had not been able to reach all of her friends. Four of them, as puzzled as Miss Burdette, unwittingly voted for their chum. Miss Burdette took a deep breath and a more spraddle-legged stance, the latter limited by her hobbling skirt and the former exaggerated by her constricting brassiere.

"Now I see. You have all put your heads together and decided to elect our last candidate on the list. Very well. It is a superb choice. Let me see the hands for Miss Doris Stewart, our first Willingham Queen of the May."

Not a hand moved. The silence was almost throbbing. Miss Burdette's face was definitely pink. The hat, with no manual assistance at all, had somehow tilted on her head so that the long feather pointed straight up. Her voice cracked and there was a hint of quaver in it.

"I do not understand what is going on, but I do know parliamentary procedure. We have a grand total of only eight students voting so far. Do I hear a nomination from the floor?"

This was the carefully planned moment, the climax to a series of desired but non-guaranteed events. Porter beamed. Deacon Chauncey's hand shot up from across the chapel. He rose to his feet. "Miss Burdette!"

"Yes, Mr. Chauncey."

"Even though it's just barely April, I nominate Miss Amalita Hunt for Queen of the May."

The response was immediate and impressive. A forest of hands shot up. It was impossible to count them. Miss Burdette took an involuntary step backward, placed one hand on her breast, an

444

appendage Porter was certain could be characterized as heaving, and straightened her hat with the other. The student body applauded loudly, and there were several cheers and a few loud whistles to enhance the accolade. Miss Burdette rapped for order. Her face was flaming, but her tone was icy.

"I regard this as basically an antagonistic act on your part, but so be it. Amalita Hunt is duly elected Queen of the May. I do pray that she can bring herself to be a worthy recipient of this honor."

There was a gasp at the effrontery of this statement and a low rumble of dissent from her audience. She continued in an acid voice, spitting sarcasm with every syllable.

"Since it is obvious there has been some secret manipulation, perhaps I would be well-advised to ask you, before I call out any names, if there is a nomination from the floor for King of the May, an elected consort for the unusual Queen you have chosen."

Porter had given no thought at all beyond getting Amalita elected. Who cared who would be King of the May? A thought raced through his mind, and he was impulsively on his feet in a split second. "Miss Burdette!"

"Yes, Porter. Are you involved in this? Do you have a nomination to make?"

"Yes, ma'am. For King of the May of Willingham University, Royal Consort of Her Highness, Queen Amalita the First, I nominate that gallant Knight of Kappa Alpha Order, defender of womanhood, champion of the weak, defender of tradition — Clarence Spangler!"

The eruption of sound was so immediate and so violent that Porter feared the roof would fall. Cheering and laughing students were on their feet in a wild and gleeful ovation. Clarence was elected by the most unanimous acclaim he had ever experienced. His friends hustled him down front, where all he possibly could do was bow and smile and boom an incoherent acceptance. When Miss Burdette departed, hat under her arm and tendrils of hair sweated to her forehead, the melee quieted somewhat. Porter edged up to Clarence.

"You see what I mean, Spangler? It never entered my head to kill you. You mess up as King of the May and Amalita will tend to that for me. Or else Miss Fanny Burdette. Congratulations."

445

The next time Porter received mail, his mother was not the only one writing to him. He had a letter from the Great Lakes Naval Training Center.

XXVI

Dear Sambo,

How are you this leaves me feeling fine and hoping you are the same. Nobody told me how cold I would get in the Navy. They sure aint got no nigger weather up here. (ha!) If I live through my six weeks I will be a seaman. I miss Macon and Mrs. Raleigh and the school. Most of all I miss my mama and you. You ask me one time what homesick was and I told you I had not been to college. (ha!) I still have not been to college but now I'm on a first name base with homesick. Homesick is when you miss your dear mother and your friend and even your old boss lady and you can't explain it to anybody around you. I have trouble explaining some of it to myself. (Ha)

Well so much for me. I am still glad I done it. You know what I mean.

Take care of yourself and stay out of trouble (ha ha). Stay away from Oak Street and Clarence and cats and ham tuna surprize (ha) and leave the shoe boxes alone (ha ha).

None of my buddies up here think you are real. They think I made you up. I didn't, did I, Sambo? (Ha.)

Well I must close. Tell everybody hello and take care of yourself and finish college without me and sometime write to your friend

                                    Boston Harbor Jones

447

Before the week was out, Porter not only posted a letter so voluminous he figured it would take Boston four days to read it but also sent him a package. He chose the contents with care. Included were a tin of tuna fish and one of potted ham that he stole from under Mrs. Raleigh's nose. He taped the message "surprise" on each. He filched a camellia-japonica blossom from near the Administration Building, wrapped the stem in moist toilet tissue and waxed paper, and tucked it carefully into a crevice. He included one of the slides he had just finished making in Histology lab. It was plainly labeled "Human finger. Hero. (Ha!)" He took pains to find a sturdy Buster Brown shoe box to pack it all in and then in addition lettered the lid of the box "Shoes. Shoes? Shoes???? Open at your own risk." Beneath that he printed "To Seaman Jones, from a figment of his imagination."

Porter was no longer enjoying his work in the kitchen. Jesse Lee was his friend, but he was a settled man and a poor substitute for Boston — no repository of confidences and no well-spring of counsel. He had no bounce in his step and no bubble of laughter in his soul. Mrs. Raleigh had complained once too often and a shade more convincingly than true artistry warranted about her work load, and Mr. Mullinax had burdened her with a helper.

The helper was named Mrs. Crockett and she was an intrusion. She bore the title of assistant dietitian, but the highly organized and efficient Mrs. Raleigh in truth had no need of assistance. She was not a lady who easily delegated responsibility or shared chores. She resented her new help. Not only was she contemptuous of having to make work for Mrs. Crockett, but she was envious because the new lady had suffered even more than she. Any sigh or allusion to hardship on Mrs. Raleigh's part was met with a deeper sigh and a taller tale of woe by her new assistant.

Mrs. Crockett was forever tucking an errant wisp of graying hair into the thin bun at the nape of her mole-peppered neck and shifting, with the back of a wrist, her perpetually sliding spectacles back up her diminutive nose to focus her bewildered gaze. She thus implied with silence that Mrs. Raleigh knew little of either suffering

448

or coping. Mrs. Crockett had no story of dealing with the sudden death of a young husband. She had nursed a bedridden mate through six years of a mysterious wasting illness, which, she was careful to emphasize, had not been cancer. It had attacked first his legs, then his arms, and then his powers of speech. He had gone from a hundred and ninety pounds to what Mrs. Crockett bet was less than a hundred and ten, although they had not been able to weigh him. His bank account had plunged from a genteelly described "comfortable" to less than zero before the illness had devoured his material resources as dreadfully as it did his tortured body. The last year of his life, he had been unable to speak and could communicate only by closing his eyes — once for "yes" and twice for "no."

Mrs. Crockett had never left his side. She had tended him like a baby, had laved horrible bed sores, and, as he grew progressively unable to swallow, had patiently wound long ropes of slobber from his throat with rags tied on a stick. She could describe this process so vividly that a listener could see it. One morning at two o'clock she had patiently watched him drown in his own saliva, pronounced it the will of God, and called the doctor. The doctor had patted her hand, called her a brave and devoted women, and assured her again that it was not cancer.

They took up a collection in the church to help pay for the burial, and even though it was a weekday funeral, the crowd was so big it could not fit into the church. The preacher besought the Georgia Baptist Convention to find a job for Mrs. Crockett, who was certainly a worthy Christian woman and had undergone her share of travail.

Mrs. Crockett could trump any ace Mrs. Raleigh attempted to play about suffering. In addition, she inadvertently let Mrs. Raleigh know that for the last two years of Mr. Crockett's life she had gone without any of what she called connubial action at all, and, compounding the horror of the revelation, confided that it was a deprivation most cruel and onerous to her. Mrs. Raleigh could only infer from this that Mrs. Crockett was one of those common people who derived pleasure from that basest of all human activities and undertook, of course in the vaguest of terms, to chide her. Mrs. Crockett had listened, sighed, drawn her own inferences from her employer's

449

remarks, and pushed her glasses back up her nose with her wrist.

Then she had flatly stated, "Well, Mrs. Raleigh, I think everybody will agree with you that it's an animal activity. There's no argument there. But I always figured you just had to turn yourself loose and get right down there with it if you was going to enjoy yourself."

Mrs. Raleigh's level of repugnance plummeted to depths heretofore unimagined, and she developed an immediate sick headache.

Although she had welcomed the bedraggled newcomer with open arms, Mrs. Raleigh, within a week, was trying to avoid any personal conversation with her. Porter watched the head dietitian try in desperation to break her habit of talking about suffering, observed the mounting jealousy between the two women, and settled back to enjoy what he privately dubbed "The War of the Widows." He longed for Boston Harbor Jones.

Mrs. Crockett also had been left with issue, although she had only one to Mrs. Raleigh's three. The child was a boy named Horace, the pride and hope of the declining Crockett clan. Despite his scrawny blue-pimpled body, his timorous scurry of a gait, his sparse and greasy hair, Horace might have amounted to something had he not also been gifted.

Most males can live through and correct the concavity of their chests with dedicated bench pressing. They can surmount callow ugliness with personality and good manners. A gift, however, is a fearsome hurdle to overcome, especially if it be taken too seriously. It sets one apart at a time in one's life when it is vital to blend with the herd. It is especially treacherous if it is only a piddling degree of gift and one mistakes it for the sublime talent that demands total absorption and consumes all one's energies. Horace Crockett was on his way to becoming a concert violinist, and his mother and he subordinated everything else to that goal.

Horace had a job waiting tables but also had to practice every afternoon at the Conservatory, and Mama usually wound up doing his work for him. Mrs. Crockett got Horace excused from physical education because playing ball of any sort was hazardous and might damage one of his spidery fingers. Horace owned white gloves, white tie, and tails, and he wore them on the not infrequent occasions when he was the

450

star of a chapel program, theatrically removing the gloves before he tuned or played his instrument. He never smiled, rarely spoke, and walked around campus as compulsively and unseeing as a wind-up toy.

Deacon Chauncey dubbed him Prufrock Crockett because, Deacon said, he grew old and should wear the bottoms of his trousers rolled. He also said that Horace was sure measuring out his life in coffee spoons and he wondered what women he could muster who would spend much time talking of Michelangelo. Porter also had read Eliot and was impressed with Deacon's summation.

Mrs. Raleigh had not read anything more thought-provoking than *The Christian Index;* she merely had a belly full of Horace. "Mrs. Crockett, I must remind you again, teejous as it is getting to be, that little Horace must be treated like all the other waiters. It is bad enough for you to be waiting tables for him, but when you put back a plate for little Horace you must not give him two pieces of meat! The other waiters see it, and everybody knows we all eat out of the same spoon and, my goodness knows, if every boy had two pieces of meat around here we would soon be bankruptured. A penny saved keeps my head above water."

Mrs. Crockett pushed her glasses up, looked confused and properly cowed, and slipped Horace an extra dessert. Mrs. Raleigh began serving Horace's plate herself when he was late. Mrs. Crockett sighed, talked more frequently of her husband's terminal weeks, and occasionally hinted of his prowess before his illness. When Mrs. Raleigh would leave the kitchen to keep from hearing any of it again, Mrs. Crockett would raid the ice box for extra tidbits for Horace.

Ice cream was Horace's absolute delight. It was stored in the walk-in icebox, and Mrs. Raleigh soon put a lock on it. Mrs. Crockett's hair became more evasive of her bun, and she began talking about Mrs. Raleigh behind her back. None of the waiters reported any of these barbs, but Mrs. Raleigh was too accomplished a Georgia woman not to read sign well when her own front porch was being invaded.

"Now, boys, I know you are wondering why I have called you together this time. Well, in case some of you haven't noticed, things are not like they used to be. Not too long ago in the distant past, we trusted each other completely and were like one big happy family. Now, and I am not naming any names or intending any offense, we are having stealing going on around here. That is all I can call it, is stealing. We all know about waste not, want not, but I want to tell you about steal not, starve not. We are not having any more ice cream sandwiches for the waiters from now on unless I personally count them out. I have the key to the ice cream, and I am the only one who will give it out. Of course, that means extra work for me, but then I am no stranger...." She paused. "I mean, my shoulders are broad and I will do what is necessary. Run along now with a little prayer in your hearts. There is work to be done."

Mrs. Crockett was worse than a protective cow about her pampered Horace. It became a point of somewhat questionable honor for her to pilfer an ice cream sandwich and slip it from beneath her apron into her son's hand, furtively outstretched in cooperative greed. Porter observed this and was annoyed because Horace acted as though it were his due and seemed oblivious to the trouble it was creating among the dining hall personnel. Mrs. Raleigh took to carrying the key constantly on her person and coming back into the kitchen at dessert time to parcel out the ice cream.

Not to be foiled, Mrs. Crockett began asking for the key very early in the meal and then leaving the lock unsnapped. She would return the key to the unsuspecting Mrs. Raleigh, wait until the dietitian was busy out in the dining hall, and then slip into the freezer, purloin the extra goody for her baby, and snap the lock. She did this so cautiously and with such a look of bewildered stupidity that only Porter noticed it and realized what was happening. Mrs. Raleigh daily counted the ice cream and knew what was happening but could not figure out how.

"Young people, I want you to know I was not born yesterday and I was not behind the barn when brains were passed out. We are still missing two, and sometimes three, ice creams every day. I can certainly count and I recognize two plus two when I see it. There is also too much friction going on around here. Hard as it is for me to say it, I want you to know that I have made up my mind and it is like a tree that is planted by the water; it shall not be moved. The very next time I catch anybody in the ice box when I haven't sent him there myself, he is automatically fired. I don't care who that person is. There are no exceptions. Do you understand that, Sambo?"

452

Porter was so stunned at discovering Mrs. Raleigh thought him the culprit he could barely stammer an answer. He had not had an extra dessert since Boston left. Mrs. Crockett put the back of her wrist to her glasses, looked as though she might weep from sheer puzzlement, and wagged her head disapprovingly.

That evening, in righteous indignation and feeling persecuted falsely, Porter put a whole cherry pie under a legustrum bush beside the back door and retrieved it undetected about midnight for a gorging feast in his room. That was the evening three of the waiters and an entire table of football players had to go without dessert, and Quinton Pickett threatened to sue. Mrs. Raleigh had a name for making one pie go a long way and for rarely having waste food to throw away, but Quinton thought this was carrying frugality too far.

It was three nights later before Mrs. Crockett pulled her sleight of hand with the ice box again. She returned the key to Mrs. Raleigh after a legitimate errand but left the lock undone. Even if Porter had not seen the deliveryman, he would have known by her actions that they were having ice cream that night. The dining room seemed in more turmoil than usual. Waiters were running to and fro, and Mrs. Raleigh was absorbed in supervising the interchange between them and the ravenous students.

After a time she came rushing back to the kitchen. "Where is Mrs. Crockett? Little Horace needs some more potatoes for his table. Potatoes are so filling and also nutritious and economical. Where is that woman? I declare, I don't know what things are coming to. Like I always say, if you want something done, you might as well tell them yourself. Horace! Potatoes! And tell your mama I need her out here."

"Has anybody seen Mama?" Horace asked in the kitchen.

Jesse Lee looked around and shook his head.

Porter was eating his own supper out of sight of the dining room crowd and rose to carry his plate to the dishwasher. "Not lately, Horace. What's the matter? You needing your ice cream bad?"

"I don't know what you're talking about. If you see Mama, tell her Mrs. Raleigh wants her. Maybe she went to the restroom."

As the tables were cleared of the serving dishes, Mrs. Raleigh again came rapidly in from the dining room. "Where is that Mrs.

453

Crockett? Has anybody seen Mrs. Crockett? It is time to put out the dessert."

Porter volunteered, "Horace said she'd gone to the restroom, but that was fifteen minutes ago. Do you want me to help you?"

"How much help is a fox in the hen house? Jesse Lee, get that big tray and bring it here while I unlock the icebox. Sambo, you can count out eight to each waiter, but I will count them out to you."

She took the keys from her apron pocket, selected the one for the icebox, and pulled back on the massive handle. The zinc-lined door swung ponderously open and there sat Mrs. Crockett, blinking like an owl in the rush of sudden light after her session in total darkness. She was huddled forlornly on a crate of turnip greens, hugging her shoulders in a futile effort to maintain warmth. Her lips were blue, and she was shaking all over.

"Mrs. Crockett! What in the world! You will ruin that turnip salat mashing it down like that. Here, let me help you. How in the world did you get in there? I swear, as God is my witness, nobody has had the key since you brought it back to me just before the siren blew. Mrs. Crockett, you really are ruining those greens — I will have to ask you to stand up and come out of there."

Mrs. Crockett's glasses steamed over when she stepped into the warm kitchen, and she was shivering so uncontrollably that she would have fallen had Horace not run to her side. Her lower jaw was chattering too rapidly for intelligible reply.

"Sssssuuumbuudy llllllockkkkkked...."

"We know that. We know you wouldn't have had little enough sense to set in there till you're frostbit unless somebody locked you in. But they couldn't have unlocked it in the first place after you returned my key. Unless I have been made a plumb fool of and somebody has a duplicate and that is not possible, for it has never left my pocket except when you borrowed it yourself, Mrs. Crockett. Who knows about this and will be man enough to say so?"

Porter looked around. Boston was not there to wink. He realized that he was bone weary of washing dishes. He also wanted to hear no tearful references to Jesus tonight or the tremulous plea to manifest manhood and accept punishment.

"Mrs. Raleigh, I came by just as the siren went off and saw the icebox lock undone. Just hanging there, and you had to look close to

454

see it was undone. So I snapped it shut. I remembered what you announced about firing anybody who stole ice cream and I know your word is as good as your bondage and that you meant what you said, and I didn't want some innocent boy to be tempted and then punished for something he hadn't been the one doing in the first place. How was I to know Mrs. Crockett was in that icebox?"

Mrs. Crockett spoke, involuntarily telling more than she intended. "Because you saw me. I looked all around before I stepped in, and you was the only one saw me. In fact, you winked at me. I only jumped in for a minute and you slammed that door on me and locked it."

"Sambo, did you know Mrs. Crockett was in the ice box when you locked it?"

Porter thought of Brewton County and the day that old man Tom Falkenberry earned the respect of all his neighbors. He had befriended an elderly recluse in his last years, had brought him into his own home for the last six months of his life and nursed him like a brother until he died. The recluse left nothing but his overalls and a mule. Mr. Falkenberry arranged his burial and was aghast when a nebulous cousin appeared and demanded the mule as the just inheritance of next-of-kin. Mr. Falkenberry resisted and the cousin sued. It was proven on the witness stand that Mr. Falkenberry had been for three years the sole support of the eccentric recluse, and Mr. Falkenberry himself testified that he had been given the mule outright as a token of gratitude. On cross-examination the cousin's attorney persisted with the crucial question, "Do you have it in writing?" After giving beautifully evasive answers for the third time and being admonished by the judge himself to answer the question, Mr. Falkenberry had drawn his shoulders back and delighted the entire courtroom.

"No! The damn mule ain't worth lying for!"

As Porter hesitated and thought about Mr. Falkenberry, Mrs. Raleigh spoke again. "Sambo?"

"Mrs. Raleigh, ice cream ain't worth lying for. I knew it. I've known it every time Mrs. Crockett borrowed your key and then left the door unlocked."

Mrs. Raleigh swung around. "Mrs. Crockett!"

That lady had on a sweater by now and was not shaking at all.

"You can't fire us. We quit. I wouldn't work around this bunch of hooligans for twice the pay, which ain't all that much anyhow. I can get me a job any time I want at Brewton-Parker. I was just putting up with all this because it was easier for Horace not to have to board out while he went to the Conservatory. He's got a scholarship now. In New York City, I'll have you to know. We don't need you any longer. I quit! Right now! You and Porter Osborne can have each other."

"Mrs. Crockett, do not do anything in haste you will be sorry for later. We can work something out. I am sure it is more blessed to forgive than to receive. However! Since you are so determined, I have no choice but to accept your resignation." She turned to face the waiters, gave a deep sigh, and arched her neck.

"I am no stranger to suffering," she intoned, "and there is work to be done and the hour is late. You boys get to your tables."

Porter was cleaning the dishwasher when Mrs. Raleigh approached him. "Sambo, I thank you."

"For what, Mrs. Raleigh?"

"For Mrs. Crockett being gone. She was a fine woman, I know, but she sure had her ways. Too many of them to suit me. I had put up with as much from her and that little Horace as any mortal could be called to bear, and right in my own dining hall with Mr. Mullinax telling me I had to endure. I always say if you can't say anything but something good about anybody, you will never mention little Horace, but then I have not personally heard him play the fiddle. If it hadn't been for you, Mrs. Crockett wouldn't be leaving, and she was driving us crazy and I thank you. Also I feel bad about suspecting you."

"I'm feeling bad about a widow woman losing her job on account of me, and her with a child to support. And what I did was a form of malicious tattling, Mrs. Raleigh. The Crocketts are really sort of pathetic, and I don't feel so good right now."

"Porter Osborne, you hush up. The Lord moves in mysterious ways for Jesus to answer prayer, you know. I had about decided, Lord forgive me, that you were the one deviling me by stealing ice cream even if I couldn't figure out how you were doing it. I had prayed about our problems here. Oh, how I had prayed. I feel like you were led of the Lord to lock that icebox, that He used you to fulfill His purpose on this Earth. Who are you to deny that you are an instru-

456

ment of the Lord? I still say I thank you."

"Well, since you put it that way, Mrs. Raleigh, you're welcome." He retrieved a stray fork and a handful of mushy crumbs from the dishwasher drain. "Mrs. Raleigh."

"Yes, Sambo?"

"Remember that cherry pie that was missing three nights ago?"

"When Quinton Pickett threatened to sue me and have me fired because his table didn't get any? I do, indeed."

"Well, lay not that sin to Mrs. Crockett's charge, Mrs. Raleigh. I took it."

"Sambo! How? I always watch you extra careful when you leave."

"Yes'm, I know. I put it under a bush outside the door and came back later that night and got it."

Mrs. Raleigh's eyes filled with tears. "Porter, I wish you hadn't told me. You know what this means, don't you?"

"Yes'm."

"Oh, I don't see how I can bring myself to do it. You are driving me to an early gray head because I never know one minute what you're going to be doing the next. Still and all, you do liven things up around here, especially with Boston Harbor gone, and I'll miss you bad. Sambo, I do love you and I hate to do it, but you have forced my hand against my will and I guess you don't leave me any recourse. I can't condone stealing, even if the Lord does look on our hearts and us just on the outside. You know I love you, don't you?"

"Yes'm. I love you, too. Mrs. Raleigh, there's a Bible verse that we need right now. It says, 'Be strong and do it.' "

"Sambo, you're fired."

"Thank you, Mrs. Raleigh."

His next letter from Boston was lengthy.

Dear Sambo,

How are you this leaves me feeling fine and hoping you are the same. Thanks for yours of the 20th. Don't feel bad about tattling on Mrs. Crockett and both of you losing your job. If I had been there maybe nobody be fired. But then again maybe everybody be fired. I think a heap, and it is nature for folks to call anything they don't understand the Lord's will. (Ha.) Maybe it is and maybe not, but it will work till we have something better. Do you ever stop to think how much of his living Sambo Osborne does between the rock and the hard place? Some would call that the Lord's will and his name is Boston H. Jones. (Ha.)

I am glad you told me you was not the one who poured gasoline on the maypole and the parade stand and burned them slap to the ground the night before the program. I am not surprize you got the credit for it, though. It sound just like you. Too bad Amalita got mad at Spangler for falling down in his fancy knickers during the march. It ain't safe for women to be mad at you. But then Spangler already knows that. (Ha.) I am like you, I do not think he was the one who burned the pole even if he did stand to gain the most. (Ha.) Check out them DeWitt brothers from Ohio and see where they was when the fire started. Southern nights make yankees wild. (Ha.)

You say Miss Burdette leaving to be a house mother at Auburn. Ain't that in Alabama? Good enough. They have got a lot of good Navy talk up here. You already know about 'shape up or ship out.' They also all the time saying 'now hear this.' The one I like best is 'go piss up a rope.' That means exactly what maw does when she says, 'I ain't studying you.' Wouldn't you like to tell Miss Burdette to go piss up a rope. Course she couldn't do it (Ha) but think how she would look when you told her (Ha). Well, you can't talk like that unless you get in the Navy anyhow. And besides, not to no woman who has already had to move to Alabama. Be sure to keep me up on the news. I pass your letters around up here and all my friends say they glad they safe in the armed forces. (Ha.)

Now I have got some news for you. When I got out of boot camp they sent me to special school, and in two more weeks I will be a steward. That is what they do with the good Colored in the Navy. (Ha.)

Last week I was on a pass in downtown Chicago and guess who I run into at the USO? Henry Bean, that's who. He heard me laughing to some buddies about Sambo and he stop and say there can't be but one and first thing you know we introduced. He is about to be a officer and we can't go nowhere together but we can talk at the USO. He knows how to move around in the Navy and he is going to request I get sent to the same ship he gets on when he is an ensign. Says I may not be his steward but at least we will be on the same boat and can keep a eye out for each other. I told him that makes me feel like I am in college again. (Ha.)

He is a fine fellow. He said to tell you hi. He says he don't write letters but if he did he would write to you. I sure feel good about finding my own officer. Especial this soon in the Navy. Sambo, you remember what I told you about Ole Massa. The night you fix my finger. Well, Ole Massa is everywhere in the world I guess. He sure is in the Navy. Now I have got me one of my very own. And you know what, Sambo? It feels good. Well, I will close for now. Be good and be careful. That is the most I can say to you. And write some more to your friend

Boston H. Jones

Maybe Ole Massa is like God's will. It is something we don't understand and just accept. (Ha.)

XXVII

Settled into farm life early that summer, with Willingham far behind him for three months, Porter was conscious that in Brewton County nothing appeared to have changed. In the midst of all that sameness, he still yearned for communion with his father, and of a sudden one evening he determined to fulfill that hunger. After a wearying day on the tractor, devoid of anything challenging to read, restless in the company of his mother and sisters, he quite simply borrowed his mother's car and drove to town.

He parked in the sandy stretch before the drugstore, passed under the swishing, softly bumping fans, went by the humming ice cream box, and spoke offhandedly to the group around the pool table. With no delay, he strode confidently through the door in the lattice-work partition at the back of the drugstore and there was Porter Osborne, Sr., concluding a conversation with an unshaven man in overalls.

"Don't worry about the twenty. If you breed your bitch to that purebred pointer, I'll take one of the pups. If you don't, I'll get one next time. Sure hope your little girl gets all right, and give your wife my best regards. Why, hello, Sambo. What can I do for you?"

"Not a thing, Dad, not a thing. I was just out driving around and didn't have anything to do. Thought I'd drop by and see how you're getting along."

"I'm glad to see you. Take a seat. I'm just fixing to take a little drink of Four Roses. Can I fix you one?"

"Nosir, thank you. I'm not ready for that yet."

"OK. Just checking. Have a cigarette?"

Porter laughed. "I'm not ready for that either, Dad. I'm going

460

to wait for the gold watch. Don't have but a little more than two years till I get it, so I guess I'll stick it out. What's going on around town?"

His father held his glass up to eye level and squinted through it. "Nothing much. Biscuit Brown blew off another finger playing with dynamite caps this morning, but that's hardly new. He's still got about three to go. Fellow was through here today said there's a rumor around the Capitol that if Talmadge runs for governor next year, this lawyer from Newnan may run against him."

"Well, he won't stand a chance, will he?"

"Can't ever tell. The county unit system favors Talmadge, but he's made a heap of folks mad. Ought to be a good race."

"Reckon they'll ever kill the county unit system? I've got a good friend raised in Macon says it's just a matter of time."

"I sure as hell hope not. It's the only prayer we farmers have for controlling those wild-eyed radicals in Atlanta and keeping true democracy alive in Georgia."

"What's wrong with Atlanta, Dad?"

Mr. Osborne was rotating his glass and studying the amber whirlpool he was creating in it. He raised his eyes. "What's wrong with Atlanta? It's a carpet-bag town! That's one of the things wrong with it. That bunch of yankees and scalawags would run the whole state to suit themselves if they could and not even consider what's good for the little fellow that lives out here in Shakerag or down south on the Okefenokee. Atlanta is no more representative of the state of Georgia than Paris is of France. It's too damn big. County unit holds them down to three legislators in the House and they get only six votes for State offices."

"And we have two."

"That's right. Law says you can't have less than two no matter how small you are. It's a good law."

"Henry Bean says one man's vote in Brewton County equals about three hundred votes in Atlanta."

"He's right. I told you it was a good law. I think I'll have another little drink and then let's go up front to the radio and listen to Walter Winchell. I think those damned Germans are going to invade Russia in spite of all hell."

"That's what started Napoleon's downfall. Maybe this will be the end of Hitler."

461

"Don't count on it, Sambo. Those Germans have fighting bred into them for hundreds of years. I'm worried."

"You don't think we'll get in it, do you?"

Mr. Osborne took a good swallow and licked his lips. "We're already in it. Roosevelt is helping England every way he can. And don't misunderstand me; I'm all for Lend-lease. I just don't think it's enough. We're in the war. We just haven't sent any troops over there yet."

"You don't think we'll do that, do you?"

"We'll be obliged to."

"Why? You don't think the Germans could ever come over here and invade America, do you?"

"They wouldn't have to. If they conquer Russia and don't have to worry about them at their backs, they can take that war machine of theirs into England like Grant through Richmond. If the Germans whip England and set up a bunch of Quislings there, they can control the British Empire and America will be economically forced to accept them. We'd be whipped without ever firing a shot. We're going to have to send our boys over there."

"Well, maybe Hitler *will* invade Russia and then Russia can whip him so bad the Free French can get back in. I just don't believe America is going to get into this war officially, Dad."

His father laid a hand on Porter's shoulder and gave him a gentle push for emphasis. "Look, Sambo. You know what I'd do if I were Hitler? Say I'm going to invade Russia. For a number of reasons. But I've made up my mind and I'm going to invade Russia. OK? Now, I've got this treaty all signed up with the Japanese. OK? Well, I'd just have the Japanese attack Russia on the other side and come at them from all directions. You see why I'm worried?"

"Aw, Dad. Not the Japanese. They've got this crazy Oriental philosophy and can't really comprehend modern machinery. I read a story just a few months ago where they'd stolen plans for a battleship and when they finally launched it, it went right to the bottom of the harbor. And their exports are so good they're all made of celluloid and wind up as prizes in Cracker Jack boxes. The Japanese don't amount to anything."

"There are a lot of them and they already have a foot on the mainland. It's enough to make you worry. Let's go listen to Winchell.

He tells it straight. I've enjoyed visiting with you. Do it again some-time."

Porter did. He went again and again to the back of the drugstore that summer, the den to which his father repaired every evening when he closed his office. The grandmother reigned as a serene Southern matriarch over the house they all occupied, and she had rigidly decreed that no alcohol would ever cross the threshold. Porter's father, bowing to her wishes, observed the letter of this law — although a great deal of alcohol entered her house in his stomach and bloodstream. He stayed at the drugstore every evening until he had a variable number of drinks, but he never left for home with just one or two. Porter's visits to him were pleasurable only according to the progress of the drinking, but he learned a great deal.

Above all, he felt that he and his father finally had established a man to man fellowship that was mutually respecting and gratifying. The drugstore had the charm of being neutral territory that held no personal mementoes or bonds for either of them, a place that Porter could quit as casually as he entered it if things became unpleasant. As a consequence, they rarely did. Their conversations drifted around many subjects and lacked the ponderance of plan or direction, giving them a spontaneity that was appealing.

"By God, I told you they'd invade Russia, didn't I? It scares hell out of me to see the way they're rolling. They've taken off like Moody's goose. The sooner we face up to it and get in it, the better we're going to be. This is World War Two, boy."

"Now, Dad, in reality it's confined to the European continent. I still don't think we'll have to get in it. What's Moody's goose?"

"What? Oh, I don't know. Just another old saying. Means something's fast and uncontrollable, like a goose with the squirts. England needs us; France needs us; the whole world needs us. I never liked the stiff-necked English when I was over there — the men, at least — but God how I admire them now with their backs to the wall. And I was crazy about the French. Don't forget they helped us in our revolution. They're wonderful people. Churchill's a good man to have for an ally, and Roosevelt needs to put his feelings in his pocket and use that big-nosed French sonofabitch to his fullest potential. When do you start med school?"

"Gosh, I don't even apply till this fall; so it'll be the next September. If I get accepted."

His father winked and spoke with offhanded confidence. "Oh, you'll get accepted. They'll give you student deferment till you finish, too, for they'll be needing doctors bad. That means you'll go in as an officer. Doctors are always officers."

"That'll be five years off, Dad. What makes you think I'll have to go?"

"Osbornes always go. It's in our blood. There comes a time when you have to forget your own personal existence. Like I heard Hamp McElroy at a ball game last winter yelling to his boy. The other team was one point ahead and there was one minute left to play, and the whole gym was going crazy. Little Hamp got the ball but wasn't doing anything with it. His daddy was standing by me and kept hollering, 'Shoot, Little Hamp! Shoot! For God's sake, shoot!' And Little Hamp did. From right at midcourt. And we won.

"And Big Hamp turned to me and said, 'Mr. Osborne, there comes a time in life when you just have to jump up in the air, shut your eyes, holler shit, and shoot.' That's sort of the way war gets to be. This country has never had a war without Osborne men. You'll go."

"Oh."

"Sambo, you have no idea how you'll feel until it happens. When you're at war, everybody's caught up in it, and people who should go and don't are really outcasts. We had some prominent folks here in Brewton County who kept their boys out in 1917, and they've been shunned ever since. They couldn't get elected dog catcher."

"Who was it?"

Mr. Osborne's mouth quirked sideways in a hint of mischief. "If they ever run for dog catcher, I'll tell you. There are some things in this world worth dying for, and your name is one them."

"I already know that. Are Osbornes always officers?"

"I don't know, but they should be. Southern men make good officers. I think part of it comes from most of us being farm boys and trained since birth to look after ourselves last. You know. You don't eat until you've fed your livestock. And if your hands get sick or hurt in the

464

night, you get out of bed and look after them. We're born with the kind of responsibility it takes six months to teach city-bred yankees when they get in OCS. Let me fix another little drink over here."

Porter leaned back in his chair and folded his hands behind his head. "I was reading tombstones in the Antioch graveyard one time, and your great-uncle Lum wasn't an officer. Come to think of it, he's the only person I ever heard of who was a private in the Confederate Army. I wasn't sure the South even had them. But his tombstone is bigger than your grandfather's."

"Well, Grandpa was a captain and died in Virginia. Uncle Lum came home and married his brother's widow and lived to be an old man. It's his children who put up the tombstone. I've never heard why he wasn't an officer. He and Pa didn't get along too well. Pa's the one who told me all the family history I know, and he wasn't one to criticize kinfolks."

"You aren't either, Dad, and I didn't mean to be disrespectful myself. I better run. I've got to cut lespedeza tomorrow."

"OK, boy. By the way, didn't you have a date with the little Bankston girl last week?"

"Yessir. Why?"

"Just asking. She's a sweet little girl, fine as she can be. And her father's prosperous, but he couldn't be elected dog catcher. See you soon."

The summer seemed shortened.

"Well, you're going back to school next week. I believe you've grown some this summer. I'm sure you've muscled out. You may wind up being as tall as I am."

"I doubt that, but it doesn't worry me anymore."

"Sambo, I've really enjoyed having you at home. I feel like we've gotten closer than we've ever been before."

"So do I, Dad. There's something I want you to know."

Porter's father became very still and did not look at him. "You in some sort of trouble?"

"I hope not. I just want you to know that if I could have, I'd have voted for Wendell Wilkie. When he ran."

465

"You wouldn't! You would? Well, that's OK, long as he didn't win. Hoover was the last Republican president we had, and we haven't recovered from him yet. You and your mother believe in prayer and I want both of you to pray for Roosevelt to live."

"Why?"

"Because I don't want the vice-president elevated to president! That damn Henry Wallace is communist to the bone, and this country couldn't survive him being president."

"But, Dad, you're pulling hard as you can for the Russians to whip Germany, and there's nothing but communists in Russia."

"That's different. It's like old man Charlie told Hoss Harp when Hunnicut Huddleston came over to his side in the last election. Hoss said, 'Mr. Chollie, you got your arms around Hunnicut now like he was your brother, and yet I been hearing you call him a sumbitch for twenty years.' And old man Charlie said, 'That's right, Hoss, but this year he's our sumbitch.' Right now, Sambo, the Russians are our sumbitches. Definitely the lesser of two evils. We may have to tend to them later, but we need to whip the Germans first. You study hard and get in med school, now. Where do you want to go?"

"Most Willingham boys go to the Medical College over at Augusta, but I don't think there's much need for me to apply there."

"Why not?"

Porter gave a little cough and cleared his throat. "Well, Dad, it's like this. 'Fessor Hansford carries a lot of weight over at Augusta and if he gives you a good recommendation, they say you're sure to get in. But I'm a little leary of what he might say about me right now. I think I'll just apply at Emory and forget Augusta."

"What's wrong between you and Bo-cat Hansford? Your grades fall off?"

"No, sir. I haven't made less than an A in any of his courses. It's just that, well, Dad, I was taking Physiology spring quarter and one of the questions on the final was to draw and label all the parts of your own gender's genitalia. That's because there were two girls in the class. Well, I guess I was sort of bored or something. Anyhow, I drew mine in the, you know, erect position."

His father had been shuffling cards for a new game of solitaire. He froze. "You mean with a hard on? Final examination?"

"Yes, sir. And while I was at it I made it life size. But I labeled everything correctly."

"Life size?"

"Yes, sir."

Porter Osborne, Sr., dealt seven cards face down on the rickety table. Casually he turned the last one face up. "Did it fill the page?"

"Damn near it, Dad."

"Life size. Final examination. I be damned. Well, you can get in Emory with the grades you've got. Don't worry about it." He paused, and the mirth faded from his eyes. "I'm glad you're going to be a doctor."

"You've never said that before."

"Well, I always figured it was your decision. Then, too, I've been a little hesitant because being a doctor is a hard life." He paused. "Strike that word. Demanding life. Especially if you're a country doctor. And there's sure no money in it. Of course, you could specialize and live in Atlanta."

"But, Dad, my wanting to be a doctor in the first place is all tied up with Brewton County. And money sure isn't everything. You could have made more money some place else, too. Why did you come back?"

"What you're saying, Sambo, is that this is home. You can believe real quick that I agree with you. It's just that you need to know it's not always easy to come home. It's something you do because you have to do it. It came to me as a young man while I was teaching school in Virginia. I was in love with this girl — God, she was beautiful — whose father was a prominent lawyer in Washington. Never date an ugly girl, son, for you can't ever tell when you're going to fall in love. She wanted me to study law and join her father's firm. We were walking in the cemetery one Sunday afternoon, and that's when I knew I'd have to come back to Brewton County. Someday. Forever."

"The cemetery?"

The man moved a black nine onto a red ten and turned over another card. "That's right. All of a sudden it hit me that I'd never be able to live happily in a place where I didn't recognize every name on all the tombstones and know which ones were mine."

"I never heard that before, Dad."

467

"Just another way of describing home, son. If you ever get a better definition, line it out for me. Have a good year and keep your nose clean."

Porter Osborne, Jr., strode the campus of Willingham University as a senior. He was tall in confidence and filled with harmony and love. He marveled at his own maturity. Although he never went so far as to feel he was a man, he assured himself that at the very least he was a damned big boy. He registered for the one inconsequential Chemistry course needed to finish his major and also for the Physics demanded of all pre-med applicants. He was through with Biology requirements and cast about for an elective he might take, something edifying but also entertaining.

He rather thought he would like something in the English department, a survey of modern poetry perhaps, but he had a conflict at that hour. The only English courses available were the "Life of Shelley" and the "Complete Works of Lord Byron." He grimaced with distaste and perused the catalog further. He could get a course in French literature under Dr. Huber but did not seriously consider that choice. He finally, quite by chance and in default of anything more interesting, signed up for "Introduction to Philosophy." It spanned two quarters, but he reasoned that he could always change his mind at Christmas.

The senior class comprised the leaders in KA now. He had been elected Number III and E.V. Derrick was Number I. His old freshman roommate, Bob Cater, kindly recipient of universal fondness, was Number II. The fraternity leadership may have lacked some of the loud vivacity it had exhibited under Spangler, but Porter fancied it to be more solid. Derrick had evolved into one of the most dignified seniors imaginable. Porter could hardly reconcile his present demeanor with past escapades. But then, he thought tolerantly, we all grow up.

The fraternity was bigger than ever and enjoyed a most successful rush season that fall. Porter settled comfortably into the fraternity routine, not as passionately involved and as fiercely partisan as he had been his freshman year, but benevolent and almost condescending. KA had done a lot for him, it was said.

Amalita and Sara Belle were glad to see him back in Macon, and he found that he had lost none of his affinity for these girls over the summer. He still regarded them as the most charming and lovely females on earth, and their sisters in Phi Mu were worthy ladies of their enchanted court. He was welcomed in the Phi Mu suite as a mascot, a friend, a champion, a brother. He reveled in it.

Dr. Robert Rudh, recently hired head of the Philosophy Department, within a month turned Porter inside out intellectually. Dr. Rudh was the most unlikely looking college professor one could imagine, and at first meeting Porter wondered if Willingham were once again proving its interest in the downtrodden as it had with Shiu Lau Ling and Hyman Goldberg by reaching out this time to the yankees. Dr. Rudh's Ph.D. was from the University of Chicago.

He was a short little man and immediately brought to mind Miss Clyde Kilgore in Brewtonton. She would have classified him as "pore" and would have said he was as gaunt as a cat that had been eating lizards all summer. He had a little red button of a nose and still endured an active case of acne. He peered myopically through gold-rimmed glasses, but his eyes had a twinkle to them. His teeth had grown persistently in undisciplined clusters, causing him to spray in unpredictable directions when he spoke. Porter's heart sank when he first saw him. Miss Clyde Kilgore also would have said, given her proclivity for flat-footedly mouthing her opinions as law, that Dr. Rudh might not could help being so ugly but he could, by God, have stayed at home. Porter gawked and fought to keep an open mind.

He was swiftly rewarded. Robert Rudh's great intelligence was matched only by his insight into the human condition, his compassion for the participants therein, and his recognition of the robust comedy involved in it all. By the end of one week, he had led the class from Thales and his preoccupation with Earth, Air, Fire, and Water, through the Stoics and Epicureans, into the unsuspected reaches of *The Republic*, with its delighting Myth of the Ring and its demanding Myth of the Cave. Porter thrilled to this introduction of thinkers who had applied an almost algebraic system to thought processes. He was

469

fascinated by Robert Rudh. He had found a new hero. Willingham University had to be the best college in the world.

Why care about money? Why be concerned with prestige? With recognition? What is security? Robert Rudh, in the absence of traditional employment for a Doctor of Philosophy at the conclusion of his thesis and the attainment of his degree, had worked for a year as janitor in a freshman dormitory at Northwestern University in Chicago. He had swept floors, emptied trash cans, and walked with modest anonymity among the arrogant spawn of lawyers and bankers spewed in middle-class snobbery from midwestern high schools.

He regaled his class at Willingham with illustrations involving practical applications of philosophy experienced during that period. He assured them with a dry little grin that he had transferred to Willingham as head of the Philosophy Department because of the deeper challenge, not because the pay was any better. All things are relative, he said — certainly the janitorial pay in Evanston and the professorial salary in Macon. He advanced the theories of many thinkers but espoused none of them.

Porter went wild. He moved from the consideration on one day that this is the best of all possible worlds or else God would have made another one, to the concept another day of the greatest good for the greatest number. He thrilled to the Cartesian stair step of logic upward from *cogito ergo sum,* and agreed with Spinoza's advocacy of harmony with nature. He scanned with curiosity but with little identification the works of Schopenhauer and Nietzsche, said to be Adolf Hitler's favorite mentors. He almost laughed aloud at Dr. Rudh's presentation of the maxim, "Things are not as they are; they are as they seem to me." There, Porter thought, was a philosophy to be reckoned with. He considered that he knew a lot of folks who lived by it, maybe most of them girls.

Doors swung open to rooms of mental treasure heretofore unsuspected, and Robert Rudh was the magnificent wizard with the key. He grew in stature until he became wiser than Solomon, stronger than Samson, saintlier than Schweitzer. Porter was never able to delude himself into thinking him handsome, but he did shift physical beauty considerably lower on the scale for weighing fellow humans. Miss Clyde Kilgore did not know much after all. Dr. Rudh was the best thing to come out of the north since Eli Whitney and

470

Thomas Edison. Porter was glad he had not stayed at home.

His last course in Chemistry was a repetitive discipline involving exact weights, fastidiously clean glassware, and stultifying
tedium. Porter needed the credit and he gave it enough attention to
make an A, but he never let it near his heart. Staying late to catch up
on an experiment one day, he was the last person to leave the
building. It was far enough into fall for an early dusk, the spicy
sweetness of those shorter days tinged with faint melancholy that the
phenomenon of Indian Summer was a fleeting one.

Propped against one of the columns at the head of the steps
sat Tiny Yeomans, her legs extended on the warm cement, their own
weight mashing her calves out to the size of melons. Her gray wool
sweater, donned against the chill of early morning, lay now beside
her. Its stretched thinness hinted at the torque of torso and upper
arms, and it was dotted with little rolled balls that bespoke both age
and frequent wear. Her head was turned away, exhibiting a strutted
jaw and a thickened ear lobe that jutted straight out. Between the
relaxed curl of her dimpled fingers was a slightly soiled envelope.

Tiny was Porter's friend. His buddy. His casual and cheerful
comrade. It was a relationship that had evolved gradually over three
and a half years, and it was one of mutual compromise. Porter had
learned to refrain from touching or patting Tiny and never evinced
the slightest disapproval of her appetite or weight. Tiny, in return,
never took the Lord's name in vain in Porter's presence and had not
derided his size during the time in his life when it was a subject of
derision.

She had helped Porter through freshman French, and he had
helped her with any Biology course that involved animal dissection.
He personally had prepared her Histology slides, and by adding
Genetics, Embryology, Botany, and one a-k course in Conservation,
she was acquiring a minor in Biology. Her electives consistently had
been French, but her major was in Chemistry. It was here that she
and Porter had most frequently encountered each other. Tiny had
indulgently laughed at the pranks Porter pulled at her expense and
had maintained her reputation of being a "good ole girl."

471

Porter had poured water on her head from the second floor laboratory when she went to retrieve her purse that had fallen from the window. He had decanted nitric acid on her socks that she had washed and spread to dry during a lengthy lab session, and then he professed surprise when her toes plunged through them at the end of lab. There was no restroom in the Chemistry Building, and he had borrowed a beaker from her and inserted it beneath his black rubber apron in her unsuspecting presence. He then had replaced it in her cupboard filled with urine. She had always fussed and occasionally cursed, but she had always laughed. Tiny was jolly.

Bustling now toward a rendezvous with Sara Belle and Amalita, Porter greeted Tiny offhandedly in her own jargon. "Hello, kiddo!"

When no voice replied, he stopped halfway down the steps and peered more carefully at her. He saw a tear slide off the end of her squat nose and splotch the concrete pad. It never occurred to him not to involve himself. He reached out a hand toward her, remembered, and withdrew it.

"Tiny, what in the world is the matter? You sick or something?"

The girl raised her head and blew her nose. "Hell, yes, I'm sick. I'm sick at my stomach and I'm sick of the whole lousy world."

"What happened? You were all right an hour ago."

"I went and got my mail, and I'm going to have to drop out of school."

"What? Why?"

"I have this uncle in Manchester who makes a lot of money, and he's been paying my tuition and books. He usually sends me a hundred dollars for each quarter. I didn't hear from him, so I made arrangements with the business office to pay every month on it myself. I thought he'd forgotten about it. I wrote him last week and I just heard from him today, and he's not going to help me anymore."

"Why? Did he lose his job?"

"No. He got married again. Says he has new responsibilities and must utilize all his resources elsewhere now. Hell, I can read between the lines! That new wife, whoever she is, doesn't want him spending money on any poor relations in Macon she doesn't even know. She's cut me off at the trough! I hate the bitch, and I never even heard of her until thirty minutes ago."

"Can't your folks help you?"

"No, they can't. I take that back, Sambo. They *won't* help. They never have."

"What do you mean, Tiny?"

"It's my old man. My mama's a mousy, downtrodden little thing who's scared of her own shadow and especially of the old man. He rules the roost at our house. He says it's a waste of money for girls to get educated because all they're fit for anyhow is marrying, keeping house, and having babies. He thinks I ought to go to work for the phone company like my sisters and give him some money every month."

"Doesn't he have a job?"

"He's got a good job at Bibb Mills. He's a foreman, and they like him. Well, they can have him! He thinks he's been a good father if he lets us finish high school. He really wanted all of us to drop out after the tenth grade like my older sister and start saying, 'Number, please.' Sambo, when I was a sophomore at Miller, he even put his arms around me and rubbed me and told me he knew I was too fat to get married but that 'my old daddy' would always be sweet to me; so why didn't I call the phone company and just forget about being a chemist. Then he kissed me on the mouth and said there was more of me to love than there was of other girls. It made me feel nasty dirty and it made me feel nasty mean, and I haven't said anything but 'yes' or 'no' to him since. He makes me pay twenty dollars a month for room and board."

"Tiny, why don't you move out?"

"Don't think I haven't dreamed about it! First place, I can't afford to. I'm making thirty dollars a month in the afternoons and evenings cooking at the Pig 'n Whistle, and that's the best I've been able to find. And then, too, I'm the last one at home and I'm putting off leaving Mama by herself with him long as I can. She's completely cut off. It's her brother who was helping me, and Pa ran him off last time he came to see us about ten years ago and threatened to whip Mama if she even talked to him on the telephone. He'd have a screaming tizzy fit if he knew Uncle Ben had been helping me, but he, by God, wouldn't whip me! I'm bigger than he is and I'd beat his ass like a drum. Watch the obits, kiddo; I may do it anyhow."

473

Porter felt better to hear Tiny returning to her usual bravado. "Tiny, why don't you just explain this to Mr. Bullard in the business office? He'd work something out. My Lord, we help the Jews and the Chinese. We could sure do something in Home Missions."

The girl gave a sigh and buried her face in her hands. When she raised her head, the little eyes behind the mounding lids were awash with tears. "Because I don't want anyone at Willingham to know. That little girl working in the business office on NYA would spread it all over campus. Oh, hell, Sambo, what's the use? I might as well drop out. You and Sybil Swygert are the only two students on campus who've ever looked at me like a human being anyhow. I don't belong here.

"I've never been invited to a party or social function at Willingham since I've been here. I couldn't have joined a sorority, but it sure as hell would have been nice to get invited to some parties instead of all those sorority dames treating me as if I didn't exist. Big as I am, Sambo, sometimes I feel invisible. They look right through me."

Porter gazed at Tiny while he remembered a conversation with his father that summer. "Now, son, remember your sister starts to college this fall, too. You keep an eye on her. She's brilliant and beautiful, but she's innocent. I wouldn't even be letting her go to a co-ed college if you weren't there to look after her. I don't want her trying to work in the kitchen or anything like you have; it's not becoming for a young lady. You know, Sambo, some people think it's mandatory to get their sons educated and their daughters can take what's left, but I'm the opposite. A boy can work his way through school if he really wants to. I don't care if a one of my girls never draws a paycheck; I'm going to see that they all finish college. If a woman is educated, she's a better wife, a better mother, and she's going to raise better children. Every woman who gets educated improves America and is an investment in the future. I've got Seagram's Seven tonight. Pass me that bottle."

Porter repeated this conversation to Tiny. Most of it.

"God, he's a saint. You're lucky to have him for a father. Where are you going?"

"I'm going across the street and see if Porter Osborne, Sr., will put his money where his mouth is. Don't go away. I'll be right back."

474

He used the pay phone in the lobby of the girls' dormitory. With a little luck, he hoped to catch his father before he left the office, but the timing would be close. He inserted his nickel and spoke to the aloof operator. "This is Porter Osborne, Jr., and I want to call Brewtonton, Georgia, number one-six. I want it to be a collect call, and I'll speak to anyone at that number."

He tried to give her all the information she could need, for he disliked the indifferent arrogance he encountered in the voices of most telephone operators. While he waited, he composed his plea. When his father acknowledged the operator's request, Porter was prepared.

"Hello, Dad. Thanks for accepting my call.... No sir, I'm not in any trouble. I'm doing fine, and so is Janice. I saw her right after lunchtime. Listen, Dad, I'm remembering something you said this summer, and I'm wondering if you'd like to invest a little in the improvement of America, in the future of our country, so to speak.... Well, there's this girl whose parents won't help her at all, and she's managed to get through school to her senior year by working and borrowing money from a uncle. Just a few minutes ago she got a letter that said he's not sending her any more, and she's past due for fifty dollars at the business office. I'm about to have a case of hysterics on my hands and I was wondering if you'd ... No, sir, she's not my sweetheart. She's just a close friend, a good, hardworking girl trying to improve herself and all America. She's even made the Dean's List three or four times. She's ... Yes, sir, I'm absolutely positive she's not pregnant. In fact, I'd stake my life on it.... Yes, sir, I know we can't take on the whole damn country, but this is an exception.... If you'll just help her this one quarter, I'm sure she can work something out, but she's got to have fifty dollars day before yesterday.... You will? ... I can? Gosh, Dad, you're great! This is long distance, so I'd better let you go. Give Mother my love. Thank you! Bye, Dad.... Yessir, I enjoyed this summer, too. Bye.... No, sir, She's not what you'd call pretty, but she maybe could be. Under different circumstances. Bye, now."

He ran back across the street, forgetful of senior dignity. "Tiny, Tiny! He did it! Wipe your weeping eyes, raise your hanging head! Eat, drink, and be merry, for tomorrow nobody dies."

"Sambo, you're the biggest ... You're the craziest nut I ever

475

saw. You could make a dead dog laugh. What are you talking about?"

"My dad said for me just to write you a check for fifty dollars, mark it 'student loan' in the left corner, and sign his name to it. He's great. Said if you didn't pay him back, he'd work it out of my ass on the farm."

"I can't believe it. I feel like Cinderella. What'd your dad think?"

"He thought you were pregnant."

"He what? My God! Why?"

"Because I asked him for fifty dollars for a girl."

"That's crazy! Why'd he let you have it?"

"Because you're not pregnant."

"That's even crazier. You've ruined my good name, Porter Osborne."

"Your name was never even mentioned, Miss Eunice Yeomans, ma'am. You just don't understand Southern patriarchs with only one son to carry on the name. Come on and I'll buy you a Coke."

Tiny wiped her nose and stuffed her handkerchief into a bulging purse. "No, thanks. I was thinking while you were gone that I've been drinking at least ten of those babies a day. That's fifty cents right there even without the ice cream in them. Now figure this. If I give up Cokes, I can pay you back in just one hundred days and not have to worry about your ass on that farm."

Porter laughed. "You don't have to do that, Tiny, I'm going to work anyhow."

"Yes, I do. You don't understand the poor but proud Southern working girl. Besides, it's embarrassing for a girl of my substance to have that scrawny little blob of tissue put up for collateral. It'd ruin my credit rating."

They both laughed. Porter was caught up in the magic of the moment. "Tiny, we're having a fraternity party week after next and I don't have a date yet. How bout going with me?"

There was a long pause. "Why?"

"Because you've never been and because you need to see there's just not all that much to it. You were good in Psychology, and you made A in Sociology when I made only a B. You've built up in your mind something that doesn't really exist, and I think you'd enjoy seeing these people like they really are. And letting them see what a great gal you really are. Come on. I promise I won't get you pregnant."

"You ever see perfectly good collateral just plumb stomped in the ground, kiddo? Don't worry about pregnant. That's my responsibility. Touch me and you die." She took a long breath. "OK, I'll go. But I'll meet you somewhere. I hate to say this, but I don't want you coming to my house."

"Whatever you say, Tiny. We'll have a good time."

"Everybody has a good time with you, kiddo. See you in lab. Wait a minute! What'll I wear?"

"Oh, please wear a dress under your raincoat, Tiny. At least to begin. These fraternity orgies are wild, but we start off slow."

"Oh, kiss my collateral, Sambo Osborne! But thanks for everything."

Porter had more than nagging misgivings about impulsively inviting Tiny to the fraternity party but gallantry forbade any effort on his part to renege. At fraternity meeting on Wednesday night, he could not, however, quell a feeling of defensiveness when the social secretary asked for the names of their dates for the newspaper. When his turn came and he announced Eunice Yeomans, the secretary automatically began writing. Suddenly he stopped.

"Who?"

Brother Harry McDade, a junior, spoke up quickly. "Don't pay any attention to Osborne. He's always pulling pranks. Eunice is ole Tiny's name, and he's just trying to get a rise out of us. Who've you really got a date with, Osborne?"

"I told you. I'm leveling. I've got a date with Tiny."

"Ah, you have not. Cut the crap, Sambo, and tell him your real date so we can get through. That tub of lard ain't ever had a date in her life."

"Well, she has now. She's got a date with me. And I'd appreciate your using a little more respect about ladies. If folks had been nicer to her through the years, she might not be in the fix she's in now."

"Brother Osborne, KA is not a missionary organization."

477

Porter raised his chin and squared his shoulders. "Well, maybe it should be. How could it hurt Kappa Alpha Order to be nice to a girl for just one evening?"

Other brothers spoke up in sequence.

"Outside of being ugly as a mud fence, she's from the wrong side of the tracks. Everybody knows it."

"We're going to have some Lanier seniors at this party that we want to be KA's next year. What would they think?"

"Do you mean what would they think of Tiny or of Brother Osborne for bringing her?"

"I say let him bring her. You don't have to marry every girl you date, and people who don't want to talk to her don't have to. She's just another girl."

"She ain't just another girl, either. She couldn't get in that door over there if she turned sideways. Why, I wouldn't take her to a peter-pulling."

Porter jumped to his feet as President E.V. Derrick's gavel belatedly banged. E.V. spoke first. "Brothers! Brothers! Let's have a little order here. It seems to me this situation is getting out of hand. If you'll just sit down, Brother Osborne, we'll take a calm and orderly vote on this issue."

This assurance only fanned Porter's fury. He was white-faced and thin-lipped. "Vote? Vote, Mr. President? In the United States of America? Vote on who I will or will not take to a party? I never heard of such, and I will not tolerate it. Take her name off the list! She's too good to associate with us. I'm ashamed of Kappa Alpha Order, at least as it is represented at Willingham. And I'd be ashamed to bring this young lady among you. While you're at it, take my name off the list, too. All these years I've been feeling I couldn't quite measure up to KA, but tonight I feel like KA isn't good enough for me! You're not worthy! It's a strange feeling, and I'm leaving."

In the momentary hush, he gained the door. As he grasped the old rattly agate knob, he heard Brother Harry McDade mutter, "And good riddance, too."

A titter went around the room. Goaded beyond endurance, Porter whirled. "I may not ever be back! You can elect another Number III! All of you are ranting bigots!"

He slammed the ancient door so hard that wisps of dust

478

puffed from between the wooden jamb and the plastered wall, and he was gone into the night.

A little before midnight E.V. Derrick knocked and entered his room. The two boys stared at each other a moment in unblinking appraisal. A mischievous smile curled E.V.'s lips, and he sought to manipulate change of mood with buffoonery.

"Sonny Boy, I want you to know I never ranted a bigot in my whole life. I wouldn't even know what one looked like so I could rant it."

Porter was not amused. "Bigots, I should not be at all surprised, look exactly like fraternity men. Everywhere. Knock it off, E.V. I've had a belly full"

"So have I, Sonny Boy. That's why I'm here. I kept the chapter later than we've ever been in a meeting before just to try to iron out this whole problem. I came over here to tell you that we want you back and that we apologize."

"E.V., I'm not ever going back. You don't need to apologize to me, and you sure don't need to apologize to Tiny Yeomans. Lord knows, I hope she never finds out about it. If there's any apologizing, it ought to be to yourselves. No, E.V., I'm through. After I got over being mad tonight, I got to thinking. The reason I invited Tiny in the first place, and don't you ever tell this, was because she was upset about something and said she'd never really belonged at Willingham. I figured out why that remark tore me out of the frame. It's not just because it's the truth; it's because it applies to me, too. Not about Willingham but about the fraternity. I don't belong in it, I never have belonged in it, and I never will belong in it. I've been pretending and the Brothers have been pretending, and I'm tired of it. We've been looking at shadows against the wall of a cave and accepting them as reality."

"There you go, Sonny Boy. Why do you always have to be so much more intense than anybody else? If you're gonna look at it that way, how do you think I feel? I wasn't cut out to be a leader and I don't want to be one, and it never entered my head I'd be president of KA. But people had confidence in me and elected me, and here I am. Saul didn't want to be king of Israel, but he had it to do. There come times in life when you just have to back your ears and do what has to be done whether you like it or not.

479

"You're making my job harder. I should have had sense enough tonight to keep the chapter in order and not ever let things get out of hand like they did. What do you think Theo Montagu is going to say when he finds out my Number III has walked out? He already doesn't like me. Now, Sonny Boy, why don't you just relax and bring Tiny on to the party and forget about being sensitive and noble? And let's all just keep on pretending. It ain't but for a few months longer. If you make up your mind to it, anybody can put up with anything for a month or so."

"E.V., I know I'm not coming to that party. I'm right about Tiny maybe getting embarrassed in front of Harry McDade and some of the others. But there's another reason. While we're being honest and while I'm looking at sunlit reality instead of shadows, I have to admit that I don't want to be seen with Tiny myself. Every time I try to do something that I think is good, or noble, as you put it, it blows up in my face. Like Aristotle says, I haven't learned yet to be the instrument of the unconscious good. I don't guess I'll ever be the person I want to be.

"But I won't be at that party. I'll let you know later about coming back to chapter meeting. After listening to you, I know I'll be back but I'm not sure when. You're a great guy. And a good friend. Thanks for coming by, but get out of here and let's both get some sleep."

Porter could not bring himself to tell Tiny that there had been a change in plans. She was breezy and chatty in Chemistry lab and obviously excited about the party. In his mind, he crafted tales of sudden illness, family deaths, or other catastrophes of similar honor that would release him from his date. He understood for the first time the desperation that had made his great uncle Matthew leave family and homeland and migrate to Texas when Miss Jewel Brewton turned up pregnant. His anguish was compounded by guilt for feeling that way.

The time crawled by and was relieved only by Dr. Rudh's presentation of a minor philosopher who defined pleasure as the absence of pain. Porter felt that an earlier, happier time would have found him lacking in comprehension of this concept. He suffered and he wrestled. He hated Tiny for being fat. He hated her for intruding as a vulnerable human into his consciousness. But he loved her for her determination to finish college and for her ability to dissemble in the face of hardship. He suffered.

Porter was waiting at the head of Cherry Street when Tiny's bus arrived that night. It listed a little when the hand pole and step carried her dismounting weight.

"There you are, kiddo! How's the kid? Way you been moping around all week, ole Tiny wouldn't have been surprised if you'd pulled a no-show tonight. Come on. We can catch the Ingleside bus right across the street."

She was enveloped in a bright blue dress of some shiny material that hung in multiple draping swaths around her. Cascading down her chest was a froth of lace that Porter had heard identified as a jabot. This was the biggest one he had ever seen. Over her shoulders she wore a white shawl with long tassels around the border. Her lips were carmine, and Porter was almost positive she had on mascara.

"Gosh, Tiny, you look nice. That's as pretty a blue as I ever saw."

"Like it, kiddo? It's the only Sunday dress I got, but nobody tonight will have seen it; so it's as good as buying a new one. The wrap is my mama's. Grandma made it for her a hundred years or so ago, but you don't have to tell everything you know. As least not in front of those Macon socialites tonight."

Porter steadfastly tried not to look at Tiny's shoes. Accustomed to her waddling across campus in saddle oxfords or occasionally in shapeless moccasins, he was unprepared for the travesty of style in which she was now shod. Her shoes were dark blue pumps and they were wide. They were squashed-down, wallowed-out wide. Current fashion dictated long spike heels, and Tiny's shoes were fitted with the needlelike supports in compromise with style. The heels were not, however, more than two inches long at best and seemed to Porter to start a third of the way up her instep instead of at the back of her heel. Acknowledging the safety factor involved in reconciling bulk with balance, he was still embarrassed by the appearance of those shoes. He felt such relief they were not going to the fraternity party that he was ashamed. It embarrassed him to be so glad that no one he knew would see him tonight with Tiny. Not in those shoes.

"Tiny, there's been a change of plans."

"What do you mean, kiddo? The party's been moved from Ingleside?"

"No, that's not it. It's that...."

"Don't tell me it's been cancelled. Not after I've bruised myself into this damn girdle."

"No. I decided we weren't going to that party. When you get right down to it, fraternities are childish as they can be, and we've both outgrown that sort of thing. I have reservations at this restaurant in the alley behind the Dempsey. They say it's great. I'm taking you to dinner, Miss Yeomans, and then to the movies. I promise you it'll be worth the girdle. Let's stroll down Cherry Street if you will, fair lady."

He bowed deeply and offered his arm. Tiny accepted it gingerly until they had crossed the street and then dropped it. Porter chattered constantly and gaily, forcing her into occasional replies as she lumbered beside him, the tassels of the shawl adance with every heavy, shifting step.

In the dimness of the candlelit restaurant, Porter leaned across the tablecloth and resolutely kept a conversation going, ignoring the unenthusiastic replies of his companion. Tiny left morsels of untouched food on her plate, but Porter decided this was from the ladylike fetish of not appearing greedy in public. He had never overcome the compulsion to clean his plate, and he saw no reason to forsake it because he was dining in magnificence.

While they were waiting for dessert, a solitary diner from across the low-ceilinged room arose, fished in his pocket for a tip, and departed. When he passed their table, Porter stood up.

"Why Dr. Huber! I didn't know you were in here. I haven't seen you this fall. How are you, sir?"

He stuck out his hand. Dr. Huber accepted it with a dry, impersonal palm and briefly shook it once.

"*Bonsoir, Monsieur Osborne. Comment ça va?*" He turned toward Tiny. "*Ma'amselle Yeomans. Bonsoir.*" He held out a hand to her, and when she raised her own, Dr. Huber quite deftly and naturally

482

pulled it a little higher, bowed formally, and kissed it. Porter gawked.

"Won't you join us, Dr. Huber, for dessert and coffee?"

"Mais non, Monsieur Osborne, merci tout de même. I have finished my repast and am due elsewhere. *Au revoir. C'était un plaisir de vous voir."*

Porter watched him leave the room. "Golly, Tiny, isn't it a small world? Who would have ever thought we'd run into old Dr. Huber in the best restaurant in Macon? I'd athought he'd be holed up somewhere dining on stinky cheese while he graded papers. And, you know, he was right impressive. I never saw anybody kiss a woman's hand before."

"I didn't either."

"What movie you want to see? There's a new one on at the Bibb."

She avoided his glance and spoke with unaccented flatness. "Sambo, I don't want to go to a movie. I want to go home. I can catch a bus just up the block."

"Aw, Tiny, it's not even nine o'clock. I'd planned on taking you to the movie. What's the matter?"

"What is it they say? I've developed a splitting headache. I'm not going to the movie."

"Well, you're not going home by yourself. I'll take you."

"You will not! That was agreed on."

She leaned forward to balance on her feet as Porter slipped her chair away for her. Eagerly he helped her with the improbably tasselled shawl. "Well, at least to your bus stop. It's after dark, and you are my date, you know, and I'm not going to dump you on a downtown bus all by yourself."

"I'm a big girl, you know, and I do it all the time, so that's silly. But let's go."

On the bus Porter sat upright, and Tiny looked out the window. The rumble of the motor provided excuse for a lull in his nervous chattering. Tiny turned to him. Her voice was weary and uncharacteristically soft. "Sambo, I want to thank you again for helping me with that loan. It tided me over, and I think I can get the last two quarters arranged. I'll get you paid back before we graduate. And thanks for the dinner. It sure beat the Pig. Tell me something." She rubbed the back of the seat in front of them with a forefinger and glanced briefly at him. "When did you decide we'd go to dinner instead of to the KA party?"

Porter tried to conceal his involuntary swallow. "Just this afternoon, Tiny. After I left lab. Why?"

"Nothing. Just wondering." She pulled herself to her feet. "Here's my stop. Don't get off."

"I hope you feel better, Tiny. Take a coupla aspirin soon as you get home. I sure enjoyed the evening."

"Yeah. See you around, kiddo. Sometime."

The bus sagged to her descent. Porter rode back to town and then decided to walk through the darkness to Willingham. It was a long trip, but he still had a tightness in his throat when he gained the dormitory.

Tiny did not come to school the next few days. The first day Porter considered with a twinge of guilt that she might be sulking because of the changed plans and the insipid evening they had shared. He struggled with annoyance and dismissed the thought. After three days he was concerned enough to seek out Sybil Swygert and inquire if Tiny was sick, but Sybil knew nothing.

On Saturday, his morning grooming was interrupted by a summons to the telephone. "Porter Osborne? This is Mrs. Vonceil Simmons, head nurse on third floor at the hospital. We have a patient in Room 305 named Eunice Yeomans. She asked me to call you and see if you would drop by to see her sometime today."

"Tiny? I didn't know she was in the hospital."

"She said no one did. That's why she wanted me to call you."

"Gee, I'm sorry. What's the matter? She bust her appendix?"

"Let's just say she was involved in a near-fatal accident, but she's off the critical list this morning. Can I tell her you'll come by today?"

His voice rose with excitement and became more rapid. "You can tell her I'll be there as soon as I get a little breakfast in me. Thanks for calling."

Porter hung up the receiver and decided to forego breakfast. He had never had anyone request his presence from a hospital bed before. The importance of such a mission demanded immediate response. He hurried across campus toward the bus stop on College Street. Passing the Administration Building, he encountered Dr. Huber with a bundle of books under his arm and a furled umbrella in his hand. Porter spoke but did not slow his pace.

The gray, soft-spoken gentleman stopped him. *"Un moment, Monsieur Osborne, s'il vous plaît.* Wait a minute."

"Yes, sir?"

"Miss Yeomans has been absent this week from her class in 'The Works of Molière.' Since she is the only student in that class, her presence is vital. Do you know anything of her whereabouts?"

"Yes, sir. That's where I'm headed now. I just one minute ago found out she's in the hospital. Room 305. She was in a horrible car wreck and wasn't expected to live, and she's only this morning been taken off the critical list. She must have a lot of broken bones and be slung up in traction because she wasn't able to go to the phone herself. She had the nurse call me."

"She sent for you? I had no idea you two had grown so close until I observed you at the restaurant the other evening. You both, I might add, exhibited most exemplary dining habits, although I felt a little disappointed that you were not conversing in French."

"Yes, sir. *C'est la vie,* you know. At least we weren't speaking in chemical equations, either."

"You are ever flip, Mr. Osborne. Miss Yeomans sent for you?"

Something in the man's tone nudged Porter's conscience. He looked into the mockingbird of Dr. Huber's eyes and lied unflinchingly. "Well, the nurse told me that Tiny had first asked her to call you but told her if she couldn't find you to call me. You'll probably get a call when you get to your office."

"That is highly unlikely, Mr. Osborne, since I have no telephone in my office. Will you give Miss Yeomans my regards? And tell her I shall call on her if she has no objections."

"Oh, I'm sure she'd be thrilled to death to see you, Dr. Huber. She's crazy about you. She talks about you all the time. I've got to hurry or I'll have to wait for another bus. Bye."

The elevator operator in the hospital bowed her head in boredom and studied a ragged fingernail. She opened the rattling framework of the door at third floor without ever having responded

485

to Porter's greeting. He stepped around a bucket of soapy water, tiptoed across a freshly wet floor, and found Mrs. Simmons.

"My, you came in a hurry, young man. She'll be glad to see you. Nobody's visited her since she came in except her sister."

"Yes'm. I understand she doesn't have much for a daddy. Is she going to be all right?"

"Oh, yes. We think so anyhow. She's quit hemorrhaging. We've got that part under control, but I was delighted when she asked me to call you."

"Exactly what happened, Mrs. Simmons?"

The nurse's stiff uniform rustled with starch as she walked on squeaking rubber soles down the shiny hall. "I'll let her tell you. I've an idea she wants to talk about it. Eunice? You have a visitor. Don't stay too long, now, young man, and tire her out."

Porter took a lungful of hospital breath. It smelled of alcohol, Lysol, and sweet-scented back rub but was tinged with a flat medicinal odor that gently but unceasingly reminded one of the underlying gravity of this place. Tiny was lying in bed with a blue ribbon in her hair and a bottle of blood hanging above her left arm, its slow drip forecasting that it would be a long time emptying. Porter stood stock-still in wonder.

"Tiny! What in the world? You don't look like you've been in an accident!"

She looked at him with level eyes. "I haven't. It wasn't an accident. I killed myself. On purpose."

Porter approached the bed. "Tiny, that's crazy! You aren't dead. What are you talking about?"

"I'm talking about telling the truth. I've been lying in this bed for almost a week now, tied down to blood transfusions and telling myself I tried to commit suicide. That's a real shocker, kiddo. It puts you in a class unto yourself when you do that, and it makes you different forevermore. This morning about four o'clock, I decided to look at things the way they really are, and I mean I've been doing some thinking. Some soul searching, some real gut-deep thinking.

"The trouble with me is lying. Lying. I've decided I'm through lying. From now on. Absolutely. That's why I sent for you. You're the only person I know I can talk to. The reason for that is not that you're the only one with sense enough to understand — it's that

486

you're the only one who cares enough to listen."

Porter half raised an arm and answered with a small voice. "Thank you, Tiny."

"Thank me, hell! You may hate my guts before I'm through. I've worked through a lot of things and some of them aren't very pretty."

Porter drew a deeper, more comfortable breath. He spoke flippantly. "Well, hang em out there. Beauty is in the eye of the believer, as Mrs. Raleigh would say."

Tiny did not accept the bait of banter. "Well, the thing I'm so excited about right now is that I didn't just *try* to kill myself. I really did it. I killed myself! I think I did it, so as far as I'm concerned, I *did*. Or at least I killed the part of myself I couldn't get along with. I may look the same, but I'm a new person. I've started all over."

Porter felt that he was treading water in a shoreless sea. He kept his tone light. "I've heard the same thing at every revival I ever went to, Tiny. It's called rededication or conversion."

She shifted in the bed toward the arm confined by the blood transfusion and punched her pillow with her free hand. "You're crazy as hell. I may just haul off and slap the living shit out of you if you believe that. Jesus has nothing to do with this. This is mine!

"Those religious freaks embarrass me. None of them ever nearly died. I did! I really thought I was gone! I have no desire to live just because I want to serve the Lord. I want to live because *I,* by God, deserve it. *Me! Eunice Yeomans!* I'm as good as anybody I know and a damn sight better than some! They've got problems, but I've solved mine."

"Tiny, you're really on a tear. I like it. But I sure don't want to get in your way when you're feeling like this. How did you try to ... How did you kill yourself?"

"I swallowed one hundred aspirin tablets. Bayer. Four at a time. They're acetylsalicylic acid, you know, and I swallowed one hundred and then I settled back to die."

"What happened?"

"Well, I had counted on acidosis and coma, but I hadn't figured on gastric irritation. I started vomiting. I couldn't stop. I mean I was stomping and heaving and puking my guts out. I was shaking the whole house. The doctors say I must have torn a blood vessel because I started bleeding like a stuck hog. My sister was spending the night at home and heard me. She came in the bathroom and screamed for Pa. I was covered with cold sweat and about to faint, but I can remember Sis hollered I was vomiting blood and might die. Pa said to shut up and let him get some sleep, and Sis said could she take his car to carry me to the hospital, and that self-centered son of a bitch said no. So Sis pulled me out the door in my nightgown, and we caught the bus.

"In my nightgown, if you can picture that! And Sis in her bobby-pins. I almost filled a dishpan with blood before we got here, and I must have passed out cold getting off the bus. Sis said she ran screaming for help, and the next thing I remember I was in the emergency room with glucose or blood running anywhere they could stick me and interns cussing because I was so fat they couldn't find veins. Don't tell me I didn't die. I did. Now I've done that and I'm through with it. I'll never do it again. Just seeing how upset Sis got made me feel like hell."

Porter wanted to leave but knew that was not an option. His voice was tender. "Tiny, *why* did you do it?"

"I'll tell you why I did it! Don't you ever believe all that crap they feed you in Dr. Wright's Abnormal Psychology course. Suicide is not the end stage of severe depression. At least not for everybody. It sure wasn't for me. I did it because I was mad. I mean I was goddamn mad. I know you don't like for me to say that, but it's not really taking His name in vain. There's no other way to describe how mad I was. I was goddamn mad!"

Porter rested both hands on the end of the bed and did not argue. He could consider this and a lot of other things later. "Why were you mad?"

"Because all of a sudden I decided everybody in the world was lying. The whole world was lying. To *me!* Uncle Ben lied about why he cut off the money. My old man had lived a lie all his life by having children through what is called an act of love and then treating us all like dirt. Ma had lied by not standing up for us, or at least encouraging us behind his back. I had lied to myself by thinking I was going to that fraternity party and have everybody discover that I'm really a pretty good person."

Porter interrupted with deep sincerity. "You are, Tiny. You're

488

a wonderful person."

"You're goddamn right I am. But wait. I'm not finished. I told you I was going to speak only the truth from now on. I was mad because *you* lied to me."

"Me, Tiny?"

"Hell, yes. After I lied to you about having a headache, I asked you when you had decided we wouldn't go to the KA party, and you told me it was just that afternoon. I had already looked at the *Telegraph,* but when I went in the house I checked again. They had the names and dates of every KA going to the party printed in that silly society column. Those names had to go in at least three days ahead of time to get printed. Your name wasn't in there. And mine sure as hell wasn't. You had known for at least that long that we weren't going to that party and you hadn't told me. I got so mad I thought, What the hell's the use? And I took all those aspirin."

"Tiny, I can't stand this. I feel like it's my fault to start with. And then I'm the one who told you to take aspirin when *you* lied about having a headache."

Her reassurance was genuine. "I'm not trying to make you feel bad. You're the only person at Willingham who's ever made me feel good. Don't feel like you were to blame in any way for this. You weren't. But don't you lie to me ever again. Remember, this is the new Eunice Yeomans and I'm not living with anything but the truth. Those superficial, panty-waisted little shitasses didn't think I was good enough to come to their party, did they?"

Porter drew such a deep breath that his chest swelled visibly. "Tiny, I'm going to speak only the truth to you and you'll have to believe it. That wasn't the reason. They sent me word that it would be fine to bring you. I decided that you were *too* good to go to that party. And that's the honest truth. I've had a belly full of fraternities."

"Well, why did you take me to dinner? I saw what that check was. Why didn't you just break the date?"

Porter looked at her levelly. "Tiny, it never occurred to me."

There was a knock, and the door sighed heavily open. Mrs. Vonceil Simmons stood there with a crystal vase containing a bouquet of red roses. Her voice was arch. "Eunice, look what you've got."

"There's some mistake. I don't know anybody who'd send me that kind of flowers."

"There's no mistake. It has your name on it. Here's the card."

It was signed "Huber."

"Well, what do you know?" Tiny looked at the flowers and the card with equal wonder. "There *is* somebody that cares about me. Come to think of it, Sambo, he's always been extra nice to me, too. How'd he know I was here? Count those roses! I believe to my soul there are twenty-four of them! How'd he find out I was in the hospital?"

Porter rose. "I got to be going, Tiny. I ran into Dr. Huber on my way over here and told him you'd been in a near-fatal accident. I never dreamed you'd tried ... you'd killed yourself. That's how he knew."

"That lamb! Those are the first flowers I ever got in my life, let alone red roses. What an angel!"

"Tiny, he said to tell you he was going to call on you if you had no objections, and I told him I was sure you wouldn't because you're crazy about him and talk about him all the time. Which you do, Tiny. You do talk about him a lot. That's at least the hundredth time I've heard you call him a lamb since we took freshman French."

Tiny laughed for the first time since his arrival. Even the air in the room seemed lighter. "I guess I do talk about him a lot, Sambo. And he is a lamb. A kind, smart, sweet, gentle lamb."

"Tiny, there's one little bitty white lie I did tell him. I wouldn't even bother you with it except it might come up and you can cover me. I told him you told the nurse to get him first on the telephone and if she couldn't find him then to call me."

"That is a lie, little buddy. Little fool. It didn't cross my mind. Why'd you do that?"

"Because he had that wistful look about him when he blared those eyes. And who knows? That may be why you got the roses. And those roses are what made you go from 'lamb' to 'angel' in describing him. I've got to run, but I'll be back to see you tomorrow if you want me to."

She smiled at him. It was an honest, forthright smile, and it warmed Porter's heart. "You'd better come. You're the craziest kid I ever saw. But you *better* come. Thanks."

* * * *

Regaining campus at Willingham, Porter found himself battling the power and pull of unendurable emotions. Chief among them was his own feeling of responsibility for what had happened, the overpowering conviction that if he had behaved differently, Tiny would not have done this. He was to blame for it. He saw Dr. Rudh springing along as if on small rubber-ball heels and impulsively followed him into the Christianity Building.

"Dr. Rudh, could I talk with you a minute?"

"Certainly, Porter. I have the whole day."

Thirty minutes later, Porter had finished the story in detail. Dr. Rudh sat in silence across the desk, his fingers slanted like a wigwam. The silence grew. And grew.

Suddenly Porter felt great freshets of tears gushing from him. He flung his head and cushioning arms on the professor's desk and sobbed. He sobbed with abandon. Dr. Rudh was motionless. He made no effort to speak. When Porter finally quit crying, he blew his nose and raised his head. He felt completely drained and very sleepy.

"I'm sorry, Dr. Rudh."

Dr. Rudh's voice was as calm as lake water. "Do not ruin this experience by saying you're sorry, Porter. It is beautiful."

"Beautiful, Dr. Rudh?"

"Yes. I have just been privileged to observe a young man advance in the scant space of an hour from Genesis to Matthew. You came in here with the age-old question of 'Am I my brother's keeper?' with all the guilt and denial inherent in that story, and I have seen you proceed to reinforce the words of Christ Himself."

Porter looked at him in bewilderment. "What words?"

" 'But whereunto shall I liken this generation? It is like unto children sitting in the markets, and calling unto their fellows, and saying, We have piped unto you and ye have not danced; we have mourned unto you, and ye have not lamented.' You have not been guilty of the sin of indifference, Porter. You have both danced and lamented. You are certainly not guilty of uninvolvement. You may be a little unusual, but remember the other words. 'Even so as ye have done it unto the least of these, my brethren, ye have done it unto me.' The only thing I can possibly think of to say to you at this point is, 'Thy sins be forgiven thee; go in peace.' "

Porter submitted to a hiccup without apology. "Dr. Rudh, I sure feel better. Thanks a lot. But the last thing I thought I was going to get from you was a sermon."

"You didn't, Porter. I didn't give you a sermon. You are living one. We all are. I like the way you live yours."

"I thought you'd have some deep philosophy for me."

"I did. You got it. No philosopher has ever lived who improved on Jesus Christ. That's the reason I'm at Willingham. I had an offer at the University of Michigan for twice the money, but it's not a Christian school. I'll be glad to see you again if you like, but good-bye for now."

Porter turned at the door. "What about Tiny? Do you think she'll be all right?"

"Porter, I had a cousin once who kept trying until he finally committed suicide. Everyone who knew him felt responsible for his death. I don't know how she's managed to come this far without a psychiatrist, but Tiny is in great shape. She is taking full responsibility for her actions instead of blaming others, which is a sure sign of maturity. She is absolving everyone close to her, and she has certainly forgiven herself. That's another facet of Christianity. Forgiveness. We have to apply it to ourselves as well as to others. Good-bye."

On Sunday Porter went to the hospital with a large Coke in a paper cup with ice cream in it. Tiny was sitting in a chair, and the roses had opened to voluptuous fullness.

"I brought you something, Tiny."

"Take that thing out of here. I had to give them up because I can't afford them. I've got to pay back my loan shark."

"This is by way of celebration. I'll take it off your bill."

"Thanks, Sambo, but, seriously, I've lost my taste for them. Sit down. I want to tell you something."

"I think you've lost weight, Tiny."

The girl answered with unself-conscious assurance. "I know I have. Can you already tell it?"

"Yeah. Your ear lobes are hanging straight."

"Kiss my ass, you little bastard! *Will* you sit down so I can tell

492

you the most important thing that's ever happened to me? Or ever will."

Porter settled himself on the other chair. "OK. Shoot."

"I'm going to get married."

Porter leaned over and thumped a wet leaf off the toe of his right shoe. "Atta girl! I'm proud of you. I knew you'd come around to thinking men were OK. Someday."

"Always the clown, Osborne. Always the clown. Listen to me. I mean I'm getting married next week. Before I go back to school."

"Aw, Tiny, you told me you were through with lying and you told me I was the first date you ever had, so don't hand me that stuff."

"You *were* my first date, but I had another one yesterday afternoon. And again last night until about three o'clock. Sambo, I'm going to marry John George."

"Who in the hell is John George?"

"Dr. Huber. Dr. John George Huber."

Porter saw that the girl was serious. He gulped. Visibly. "Tiny...."

"I don't want to hear a word you've got to say. You just rest your voice and let me do the talking. He came in here yesterday, and I wound up telling my guts. I mean, I told him everything. I must have talked for three hours straight without a slack. All of it in French, too, not one word of English. Can you believe that? And when I finally finished, do you know what he did? He kind of stretched his eyes like you describe and said 'Miss Yeomans, will you marry me?' I nearly passed out.

"Then he talked for a couple of hours. In French. And you know, Sambo, he came alive. He had a rough childhood, too. His parents died early. His mother was wealthy, but her brothers didn't want to fool with him and sent him off to boarding school, and he's been lonely ever since. We talked and talked, and then he held my hand. And I loved it. He held it forever, it seemed like. And the longer he held it, the better I felt. And we decided that we love each other, and if you laugh, I'll kill you.

"We're getting married right away because John George says I'm not going back into the house with Pa ever again. And he's going to pay my tuition. I don't have to work at the Pig anymore. And when I graduate, we're going to France. We can slip in through Marseille or through Spain, and keep away from the Germans. There's a little town called St. Bertrand de Comminge where he has a good friend we can stay with. It's real close to the Pyrenees, and John George wants to see if he can't help with the French Underground, and I'm so excited I can't stand it. All of a sudden my life has more purpose and more direction and more glamour than I had ever thought possible. Oh, Sambo, he really is a lamb! He likes you; so you be nice to him."

Porter had to broach the question that was now consuming him. "Tiny, don't you think Dr. Huber is too old for you?"

"No! Why don't you ask if I think I'm too young for Dr. Huber? I'm twenty-one and he's fifty — you tell it, you die. Who else has ever paid any attention to me? I'm going to look after him the longest day he lives, and I mean nobody better ever mess with him. I'll bust their eyes out."

"But, Tiny, what about ... you know?"

"Sex? What about it? That's all you guys ever think about. If it happens, great. If it doesn't, great." She giggled. "I bet it does, but you'll never know. That's personal business. I'll tell you this. I've done without for twenty-one years, and I believe I can go another twenty-one with no trouble at all, thank you for your kind concern, sir. There's more to love anyhow, Sambo, than making babies. If John George can love me when I've got an incurable disease, I'll love him no matter what."

Porter jerked his head up. "What incurable disease are you talking about, Tiny? Have you got cancer?"

She laughed. "Hell, no, I've got obesity! I'm fat as a hog and you know it, and I have been all my life. Well, I've decided to face up to that, too, while I'm not lying. It's not glands and I *do* eat all that much, and there's no cure for it. All I can ever hope to do is control it. But, by God, I'm the gal who *can* control it. There are lots of other diseases they don't cure, they just control, and people live normal lives. Like diabetes. And heart failure. And epilepsy.

"I tell you one thing. John George Huber ain't taking no fat wife to France. I want to look good enough so those folks will think he's a pretty sharp guy for landing me and have respect for him. I'm not going over there looking like a mission of mercy. Oh, Sambo, he's marvelous! I didn't know there was anybody that sweet in the whole

494

world! I'd die for him. I've already done it for myself, and now I'd do it for him if I had to."

"Tiny, I'm so happy for you I don't know what to say." He spoke with sudden excitement. "Tiny, you've caught the mockingbird! Congratulations! Wait'll this hits the campus! It's going to cause more talk than the toilet paper! Or the sireen going off! Or the Maypole burning down!"

"Whoa up, Buster! It ain't hitting the campus. The two most invisible people at Willingham are getting married, and you are the only one who knows about it. We announce it after graduation and not before then. Understand? Nobody's ever noticed us before. Why should they start now unless we make spectacles of ourselves? This is our secret! You're the only one in on it, and...."

"I know, I know. I tell it and I die. I'll keep my mouth shut, Tiny, but it'll be hard. This is the most improbable thing that's happened since I've been at Willingham. I never would have dreamed any of this three years ago."

"Nor would I, Monsieur Osborne," the soft voice spoke from the doorway.

Porter whirled to face Dr. Huber. The man did not look as old as he had the day before. He was definitely not as gray. He even had on a red tie. The mockingbird, however, still preened.

"You have had a part in it, and I shall forever be in your debt for it."

"I, sir? I, Dr. Huber?"

"You, Monsieur Osborne. I shall never stoop to that ridiculous *nom de famille* by which Eunice refers to you. Had you not engaged in such artful dissembling yesterday morning when you told me she was seeking me, these events might not have ever transpired."

Porter whirled reproachfully to Tiny. "You told him. That was such a little white lie. You could have let it alone."

"I told you I was through with lying. If I'm not going to lie to myself, I'm certainly not going to lie to the man I love. *Bonjour, mon cher. As-tu bien dormi?*"

Porter suddenly felt like a voyeur. He moved to leave.

"Monsieur Osborne, I realize you have to go, and I will detain you only a moment. I appreciate all you have done for Miss Yeomans.

495

And for me. Standing in the midst of my own personal miracle, I cannot be unmindful of yours. Porter Osborne, you did it. The ass has indeed spoken. And most beautifully."

"*Je vous remercie, Docteur.* This ole ass has had some marvelous tutors. I'll see you around."

"One moment, Mr. Osborne." The eyes flared anew, but there seemed to be more warmth in their depths. "You would please me considerably if you could bring yourself to forego the use of that coy and somewhat kittenish nickname by which you have been in the habit of addressing my fiancee. Her name is Eunice. I find it a beautiful and musical name and one most appropriate for her. Do you think you could do this for an old friend?"

Porter looked at the professor through a shimmer of joyful tears. "Dr. Huber, for the two of you I could do anything! *Au revoir.*"

back in the routine of campus activities, Porter **XXVIII** forced himself not to dwell on Tiny's secret. He welcomed any diversion, and, realizing that the time was appropriate, he secured proper forms and mailed an application to Emory University Medical School for the following fall. He had taken the Medical Aptitude Test and been mystified about what it had to do with medical school.

The test consisted of a map of the Battle of Gettysburg, which all students were instructed to study for fifteen minutes. Then the maps were retrieved, and the students were given questionnaires asking for detailed information about the location of different generals, colonels, majors, and troops. To Porter it had seemed as elementary as memorizing a poem, and he wondered why it contained no reference to Chemistry, Biology, or Physics. He had in preparation rememorized the formula for malachite green and was annoyed at the wasted effort. Maybe med school was not as hard as people said it was.

Professor Twilley stopped him one afternoon on the walkway between the library and the chapel. "Young Osborne, I want to speak with you a moment."

"Yes, sir, Professor Twilley." He went silently on guard like a dog with hackles rising at a presence not yet ominous enough to warrant a growl.

"There is a group here at Willingham called Sigma Mu. This group was formed several years back with complete adherence to all of the requirements and standards of Phi Beta Kappa. It was formed after we were rejected by the national organization of Phi Beta Kappa for a chapter on this campus. It was organized against the day when Phi Beta Kappa will have to give us a charter and then the members of Sigma Mu, past and present, will be inducted into the national fraternity. We have exactly the same standards."

"Yes, sir." Porter began to relax.

"I have been the faculty adviser for Sigma Mu since its inception. The arbiter, one might say, of who gets invited to join. We purposely do not publicize our organization lest we encounter self-debasing pressure from ambitious candidates or bitter disappointment in students who are rejected. It is quite a select group, Osborne, and I am inviting you to join it."

"Me, Professor Twilley? I made a D in my first quarter of Chemistry. Fall grades aren't even in yet — we just finished midterms last week."

"You have the grades, Osborne. You have made more than adequate grade-point atonement for that one academic indiscretion. Insofar as grades are a consideration, you were eligible spring quarter."

Porter's brow wrinkled a little and he spoke slowly. "Spring quarter? Why wasn't I invited then?"

"Because, Osborne, there are considerations other than grades involved in selection for Sigma Mu. Such as character, leadership."

"Oh, I see. Well, Professor Twilley, I certainly mean no disrespect, but what made you change your mind this quarter?"

The one eye transfixed him momentarily and then studied a tree in the distance. "Because, young Osborne, of the regard in which you are held by one of your professors. In my opinion, Willingham University has finally succeeded in hiring a man who has a Ph.D. and is also worthy of being called 'Doctor.' As I might have suspected, when that paragon finally arrived he cared not one whit what he was called but comported himself with the unpretentious grace of a true intellectual aristocrat. I am enjoying him immensely.

"Just last evening we had a discussion about what constitutes true Christian progress. How long does it take a man to grow from the whining question of 'Why me, Lord?' to the mature dedication of 'Why not me, Lord?' One maintains the accent each time, of course, on the word *me*. A one-syllable negative thus separates two entirely

498

different philosophies and also manifests the spiritual depth one has plumbed. He ties this in with 'Many are called, but few are chosen,' and I choose to associate it with 'I came to minister, not to be ministered unto.'

"It was a joy to joust with him. He is a pleasure. At last we have a man on the faculty who can discuss Christianity in depth without getting sidetracked by the irrelevant consideration of Virgin Birth or mired in the nebulous concept of life after death. He sees Christianity as a philosophy by which to live, not as a formula by which to die."

"You're talking about Dr. Rudh, Professor Twilley."

"Exactly, young Osborne. We chanced to mention you last evening also. You would be amazed how often your name crops up in informal gatherings of the faculty. Even though I pointed out to him that he has not known you as long as I nor witnessed as many previously undreamed of phenomena since your advent on this campus, Dr. Rudh is more than defensive; he is agressive in his admiration of you. So much so that I have been forced to reassess my own evaluation of you.

"He is of the opinion that you are no longer caught up in the wonders of the fraternity world, for instance. I find this development fascinating, considering how much it meant to your father and also apparently to you. At any rate, you are perceived in an entirely different light than you were spring quarter. And that is why I am extending you an offer to join Sigma Mu."

Porter wondered why Professor Twilley, of all people, did not perceive the irony of exchanging one exclusionary group for another, but he kept his mouth shut on that point.

"Professor Twilley, I'm so flattered I'm swimmy-headed. It makes me feel like crying to know that Dr. Rudh approves of me, because he's already had as much influence on me as anybody at Willingham. With the possible exception of Dr. Minor. And you. And Mrs. Capulet. And Dr. Huber."

"Huber, Osborne?"

"Yes, sir. Dr. Huber. He's a dark horse around here. He doesn't talk about it, but he practices Christianity, even if you do have to watch fairly close to catch him at it. He's a real man. But I tell you right now, I sure do agree with you about Dr. Rudh. Did yall get around to talking about the forgiveness part of Christianity? That's what got to me."

"I shall look forward to future discussion. I have some ideas of my own about that."

"Yes, sir."

His shoulders squared in posture so habitual it was relaxed, Professor Twilley returned to the subject. "Well, Osborne? Shall I submit your name to Sigma Mu? The initiation fee is ten dollars. You get a scroll and a key for that money."

"And recognition."

"Yes. That, too."

"Well, Professor Twilley, it seems to me that would be a selfish thing to do. My dad has two more children to educate and me to put through med school, and that's ten bucks I don't have to spend."

"I'm sure your father would endorse your spending it."

"Yes, sir. But I'm standing here doing some thinking. Recognition is really the most important thing about Phi Beta Kappa, isn't it? I have a friend in the Navy who used to say it was the pinnacle of intellectual snobbery. Well, that doesn't matter to me anymore. I know I've been anointed, and you know it, and Dr. Rudh knows it."

Porter felt impaled by the Twilley eye but he continued. "And some day I'll tell my daddy. And really and truly, Professor Twilley, I just don't care whether anybody else ever knows it or not. There are probably no more than those four people who would be impressed anyhow."

Professor Twilley cleared his throat. "Did you say anointed, Osborne?"

"Yes, sir. Anointed. There's no way even Miss Burdette could call this being elected."

"I see. Well, what are you going to do?"

Porter relished the moment. He savored it. It was stingingly sweet. "Professor Twilley, you have been famous at Willingham for identifying the most expressive word in the English language; so I'm sure you won't take offense, sir, when I tell you I'm going to refuse Sigma Mu. I'm turning it down because I just plain don't give a shit."

Porter held his breath, but his eyes never wavered. He staunchly met the piercing glare of the one eye of Twilley, resisting the impulse to flick a glance at the empty socket. Suddenly there was

500

a deep coughing intake of breath. Professor Twilley, for the first time in Porter's experience, threw back his head, opened his mouth, and laughed aloud. Porter was transfixed. The sound was mellow and fluting and totally unexpected. It was also brief. Professor Twilley wiped his good eye and dismissed him.

"I see, Osborne. The iconoclast matured. Don't ever say you didn't have this opportunity. You appear to have an unusual facility for grasping the ones you desire. By the way, I assure you that I meant the use of that expressive word you quoted in its literal sense."

Porter winked into the spotlight of the Twilley stare. He managed for it not to be an impudent wink but to imply complicity. "So did I, Professor Twilley. So did I. Thanks for everything."

"Good-bye, Osborne." The head went back again. Porter had never known before that Professor Twilley's jaws were so resplendent with gold.

The following day, at a secret meeting of the senior class, Deacon Chauncey and Porter allied themselves with purpose. Plowing through several nominees, the class voted to dedicate the annual that year to Professor Hiram Augustus Twilley. It was the first time in the history of his service at Willingham that gentleman had been so honored — an honor of great importance to donors and recipient and of complete inconsequence to others. Everyone was surprised. Mrs. Capulet, who had been given that student accolade three times in her career, was mystified. So eloquently persuasive were Deacon and Porter that E.V. Derrick was the only one in the class to cast a dissenting vote.

Deacon wrote the dedication. Porter always felt responsible for the photograph. It was the first one ever published of Professor Twilley that was not a noble profile showing only his good eye. The new studio portrait for the annual was a full-face study. Professor Twilley was faintly smiling. His eye flap looked serene.

The last halcyon week before winter rains chilled middle Georgia was an eruptive one at Willingham. Students were still humming "The Last Time I Saw Paris" as a token of forgiveness and admiration for at least some of the French. The German roll to

501

Leningrad induced support for that city's beleaguered natives. Stories circulated of dogs and rats, and even cats, being eaten in defiant desperation. An emerging respect for Russia raised the hope that this impossible country with its rigid politics might aspire to be something more, after all, than a nation that flunked all its own five-year plans. The British were gallantly enduring and surviving massive air attacks. All of Georgia cheered its heroes and vilified the Germans.

In that contented and isolated atmosphere, the college experience at Willingham was enriched by the advent of Dr. Clarence Jordan. For each of the previous three years, the Baptist Student Union had sponsored Religious Emphasis Week. It had been a time when chapel was held daily and additional services held each evening, with smaller, more personal groups meeting in the afternoons. The sponsors, in the interest of revitalizing flagging interest, had changed the name this year to Christian Focus Week, ignoring the ribald comments this provoked from the more irreverent students and the fact that some people were openly referring to it as Focus Bofus Week. Porter and all the other Raised Right students did not care what anyone called it; they knew a revival when they saw one.

Porter had no intention of attending any of the meetings. He was a senior in college and above such activity. Clarence Jordan, however, changed his attitude. Within twenty-four hours of his stepping onto campus, not only was the student body abuzz but the ministerial hierarchy for miles around was agog. Porter had to go to the meetings just to keep current with Willingham gossip. Not since Salome made her unorthodox request for reward of artistic excellence had religious circles been so convulsively aghast.

Christ may have entered history horizontally, but Clarence Jordan dropped vertically into the Georgia Baptist Convention. He envisioned a Christian commune where all men would live like brothers with common finances and mutually loving support. He planned on purchasing land somewhere in south Georgia for this dream. Land was cheap there, and the climate was mild. Being a Baptist theologian, trained upward in the ranks from early ordination through the Seminary, Clarence Jordan was soliciting funds for this nebulous project without apology.

The crowd at Chichester's was discussing religion as it had not

502

been discussed since John Birch graduated.

"Hell, he's advocating communism! He even had the gall to call it that."

"Relax! What he's preaching is the *true* communism of the early Christian church. Like it says in *Acts*. One common purse and each man takes from it according to his own needs."

"That's communism!"

"That's Christianity. Have you heard Dr. Jordan?"

"Hell, no. I don't want to hear any Reds. It might rub off on me."

"He's not Red. He's a saint. That's not so easy to rub off. Come hear him."

Local ministers descended on Willingham to hear Clarence Jordan for themselves. Their manicured nails and the tightness of their white shirt collars testified to their own self-esteem and to the affluent generosity of their congregations. They questioned and they exhorted. Dr. Jordan met them all with good humor and tolerance. He smiled frequently and not once raised his voice. His answers were uniform.

"But I propose only that which was advocated by our Savior Himself, or by Paul. If you apprehend me in anything else, please be my ministering brothers and call it to my attention. I regard it as your Christian duty."

"Dr. Jordan, how can you stand there and talk about 'true communism' and then deny you are a Marxist?"

"Oh, my brother, I am not a Marxist or any other sort of politician. I am not even a Democrat. I am a Christian. I ponder the words of Christ. Tell me, how do *you* interpret 'Sell all that you have and give it to the poor'?"

Another plump preacher took the floor. "Dr. Jordan, your policies followed to their ultimate conclusion would strip the churches of their budgets and even this great university of its endowment."

"Jesus said, 'Take no thought of the morrow, what you shall eat or what you shall put on.' Do *you* have any quotes he left us about endowments? Luke tells us in his second book that 'The multitude of them that believed were of one heart and one soul; neither said any of them that aught of the things he possessed was his own; but they had all things common.' And a little further on we are told, 'Neither was there any among them that lacked; for as many as there were in possession of lands or houses sold them, and brought the prices of the things that were sold, and laid them down at the Apostles' feet.' And listen to this, Brothers. 'And distribution was made unto every man according as he had need.' Isn't that a marvelous picture of community of worship in Christ? Do you not think that spirit would support the higher education of a participant who deserved it and was endowed by God to receive it?"

Chichester's was lonely as a tomb the rest of the week during chapel period. The most worldly of students attended the debates, the fame of which spread and spread.

"Dr. Jordan, I understand that you suggest taking Negroes into this Utopian community you wish to establish. And on an equal footing with whites. Do you think the sovereign state of Georgia and its good people are ready to see the Southern codes of conduct violated to this extent?"

Dr. Jordan responded with a smile that bespoke tolerance as such an absolute that even his present audience was included. "Brother, do *you* think Georgia and its Southern codes of conduct would condemn the teachings of Christ? Can you show me a single quotation of Jesus that says we should treat a brother differently because of the color of his skin? This revolves around the question of whether we shall serve Mammon or live as children of God."

"Dr. Jordan, your proposals and your theories are so revolutionary that they will strike terror into the hearts of all good white Southern Christians. I fear you tread on dangerous ground."

"My Brother, I teach only what Jesus taught. Are you afraid of Him? A great many of us are, you know. Does He strike terror into your heart?"

"Dr. Jordan, how would you like your daughter or sister to marry a Nigra?"

"Our Master taught that in the Kingdom there is no giving or taking in marriage. What we do on earth is under the direction of our own free will ... tempered, one would hope, by the teachings of Christ."

"What you are advocating here, sir, is perilously close to violating the laws of the land. You would not knowingly endorse an

504

illegal activity, would you?"

"Certainly not, Brother. Christ said that He gave us a new law, written on the hearts of men, instead of graven in stone. Laws change, and so, I firmly believe, do the hearts of men. I know mine did."

Porter stopped by Dr. Rudh's desk one day after class. "What do you think of this Dr. Jordan, sir?"

" 'Some say he is Elias, some John the Baptist. Some say Beelzebub.' I say it's the most classic example of tilting lances with the Pharisees and Sadducees I've ever witnessed. I half expected him to pull out a coin yesterday and ask whose picture was on it. As you say in Georgia, Porter, I think Clarence Jordan is the finest thing since sliced bread."

The last of Porter's reservations vanished. He enthusiastically supported Christian Focus Week and its central figure.

"Where do you propose to establish this commune, Dr. Jordan?"

"Somewhere in southeast Georgia, Brother. Perhaps between Waycross and Dublin. Maybe even in Effingham or Baker County. Wherever we can acquire good farm land at a modest price. This will, of course, be primarily an agrarian community. We have substantial donations already, and we earnestly solicit even the most modest of contributions. No gift is too small."

"And what do you propose to call this place? This most ideal society you propose."

"We have already named it, Brother. It is called *Koinonia,* a Greek word that means fellowship, or to own property communally. We have the name. All we lack is the real estate."

Porter was so beguiled by the concept of Koinonia that he was impelled to contribute to it. He wrote a check on his father's account, signed it "by Sambo," labeled it "for books," cashed it at the Co-op, and presented Dr. Jordan with a twenty-dollar bill. He felt so virtuous that he was not at all dismayed by compounding embezzlement with duplicity. He would be forced to use, for the first time in his life and for the rest of his college career, secondhand or used books. Better that, he thought, than try to explain Greek to his scholarly father when he examined his canceled checks. He felt that his father's sacrifice for religion would be no less effective because it was unwitting. Pleasure, he remembered from Philosophy class, had been defined by one thinker as the absence of pain.

A few days into the next week, the campus was restored to calm and Clarence Jordan was fast becoming a memory. Bored with the chatter at Chichester's, Porter cast around for some way by which he could reaffirm his commitment, could rekindle the warmth he had felt in Clarence Jordan's presence. Service was the answer. There was a small private hospital in town for Negroes only, owned and operated by a Negro physician. It was said to be poorly staffed and poorly equipped. Impulsively Porter caught the bus and went to the doctor's office. After all, he had extensive background in Chemistry and Biology at Willingham University. He might be just the tool the Lord needed to improve the laboratory in this black hospital and make it a credit to the community.

He tapped the bell in the doctor's waiting room. When the nurse appeared, Porter suppressed the thought that her black legs looked funny through her white stockings.

"I'd like to see the doctor, please."

"His appointments is full for this afternoon and he have a early engagement at the hospital. Don't you have a doctor of your own?"

"Oh! I beg your pardon. You thought I was a patient. Heavens, no. I'm a senior at Willingham, and I'm here to do the doctor a favor. Tell him I'll take only a minute. Or I could ride with him to the hospital if he'd rather. I need to inspect it anyhow. He's going to be quite excited at my offer. I'm going to upgrade his laboratory for him."

He was quickly granted an audience. The physician was portly and grizzled but nonetheless imposing. A ring vibrated in winking gold against the blackness of his gnarled fifth finger.

"My name is Porter Osborne. I'm from Willingham University, Doctor." He forsook the teachings of Buckalew Tarpley for those of Clarence Jordan and self-consciously held out his hand. It was inspected suspiciously, fleetingly grasped in a most perfunctory manner, and then released in a manner that smacked of casting

506

aside.

"What you want? Who been complaining about my laboratory? Who sent you?"

"What do you mean, 'Who sent me?'? Nobody did. This is all my idea. I'm here as a volunteer. I have a fairly light schedule this quarter, and I can give you three afternoons a week to work in your lab and help you with it. I'm getting a double major in Biology and Chemistry, and I don't want a penny compensation."

"Who told you I needed any help? Who said I wanted any help? Who sent you round here?"

"Do you know Dr. Clarence Jordan?"

"Never heard of him. What he got to do with my laboratory?"

"Nothing at all. He's a very prominent Baptist minister, and he's the one who inspired me to take this on as a service project. He believes in helping the Colored."

Under the silent gaze of the physician, Porter became unsure. "Maybe you've heard of my father. He's County School Superintendent in Brewton County."

"I never even heard of Brewton County." Contempt gave way to condescension. "Look, boy, I'm a busy man and I got to run. You go on back to your little ole college, and if I ever need you I'll call you. No need you call me; I'll call you. I'n give you a nickel for the bus do you need it."

Walking down the street, Porter felt chagrined and discomfitted. He also felt misunderstood and for some reason just a little threatened.

He kicked a can and muttered, "What do I do now, Dr. Jordan? I have piped unto him and he has not danced."

A sudden thought of Michael Jurkiedyk gave him a surge of confidence. He spoke aloud. "Black cocksucker!"

XXIX

in one of the large old high-ceilinged rooms on the first floor of Nottingham Hall, there lived three seniors in the School of Law. Although they were fraternity men, they disdained those undergraduate social clubs and, in the name of economy, roomed together and took their meals with Mrs. Raleigh. Their joint domicile was on the way to the dining hall, and Porter developed the habit of dropping by to see them on his way to eat.

Following the rift with his own fraternity, he became a regular visitor, the older boys at first tolerating him and then actually becoming his friends. Several inviolable rules were enforced in that lair of post-graduate lords, one of which was that no conversation could interrupt study until five minutes before supper time. Members of the Law School were all serious students, or they did not remain students for long. If Porter entered their room while the taboo on speech was still in effect, he sat quietly and waited.

The friendship between those three roommates was an unusual relationship that Porter had not encountered before. They were all masters of the fast quip and the humorous slash, and Porter never heard them indulge in any serious exchange unless it pertained to examinations, wills, torts, or schedules. All personal repartee between them was brittle and witty with never a lapse into anything other than bright superficiality. They included Porter in their salvos of friendly insults. Each of them, however, on the infrequent occasions when alone with him, became considerate, interested, and concerned. He felt like a baby brother who is treated like a big boy in private.

Only one of those self-assured students had been Raised

Right. James Eulenfeld was the son of a retired Baptist preacher. He had been observed and admired through an upward-spiraling succession of pulpits in Georgia until his father had reached the summit of a dedicated career and been appointed editor of *The Christian Index*. James was serious and filled with dignity, mindful of public scrutiny and its importance, careful of reputation and appearance. He still went to church every Sunday, and he had never been called anything but "James" in his life. One had the feeling that he would never commit an impetuous or frivolous act, and it was foreordained among his peers that he would be a judge. He enjoyed a measure of limited notoriety by stoutly maintaining that he had never masturbated. Opinion was about equally divided between those who thought him an outright liar and those who upheld him as a bastion of unblemished virtue. After all, since James was engaged to be married and his father was a preacher, it could be true.

Rabbit Gosnell had collected three stepfathers by the time he entered Willingham University but knew a lot more about women that he did about men. He was comfortable with girls to a degree none of his friends possessed. He slept till noon every Sunday and had less use for church than he had for preachers, which wasn't much. He was overly precise of speech and had more than a touch of priss about him. His gender orientation might have been suspect had he not been notorious for having seduced Dottie Bay Smith.

Dottie Bay was an ADPi who had dated yankee football players until Camp Wheeler became active, and then she drove a succession of northern lieutenants crazy. Dottie Bay was a beauty with a reputation for being a prick tease. It was she who got tight and revealed her seduction at the hands of Rabbit; he only smirked and refused to deny it had happened. It made his name.

"Yall know that little ole Rabbit Gosnell? That Phi Delt who goes to Law School? The one that walks and talks like a pansy? Well, he is something else, I'm here to tell you. Before I broke up with Big Al, I was dating him one night and was waiting in the car while he changed clothes and called his mama long-distance in Akron. That's in Ohio. And along comes little Rabbit and says, 'Hidy, how you?' And he just as natural-like eases in the front seat with me, and the first thing you know he's telling me about his mama's Oriental rugs and what kind of curtains are on his widows at home. And before you know it he's up my dress slick as greased lightning. Never quit talking and never acted like he was doing anything out of the ordinary. I got the feeling it wouldn't have been ladylike to notice what he was doing. When he was done, I never will forget what he said. 'I had no idea it was this late,' he said. 'Time really flies when you're having fun. I enjoyed talking to you.'

"Talking to me! Can you imagine that? Talking to me! And I didn't even have a date with him! He met Big Al on the front porch of the dormitory and said, 'Hidy, how you?' cool as a cucumber. I don't know why we call him little Rabbit, either. I tell you, if a girl's not safe with a sissy, she just can't trust anybody."

When Porter heard this legend and attempted to get Rabbit to confirm it, he was only minimally successful.

"Dottie Bay's got what the women in my mama's bridge club call peacock brains. Hell, Sambo, she's downright stupid. She's got a beautiful face and body, though, and gals like that need a good fucking now and then. Just to keep em from putting on airs.

"I tell you a gal who got my goat, Sambo, and that was that ole tall Vashti Clemmons. Do you remember her? The one with the gorgeous body and the buck teeth she could have gnawed an apple through a knot-hole with? We had a pledge brother for a very short while named Jimmy Dewberry who got drunk and told me that's where he lost his cherry. Which was a lie, cause after Jimmy flunked out, I tried to put the make on Vashti and she frailed the living hell out of me. She always walked around like she was holding a marsh-mallow in the crack of her ass and was afraid she'd mash it, but I always had the hots for her."

Porter stretched and gave Gosnell a very casual glance. "Oh yes, I remember Vashti, now that you mention her."

Marshmallow? The very idea!

He injected just a touch of tolerant scorn into his voice. "Rabbit, you were crazy ever to think you could do anything there. Everybody on campus knew she was a nice girl."

Rabbitt Gosnell did not believe for one minute that James Eulenfeld had never masturbated. He said it was against nature for him not to have, and besides, everybody knew what liars preachers' kids were.

Ed Sturgis was the member of the triumvirate who really held them together. He had not been Raised Right, either. He had no mother, two stepmothers, and had been reared an Episcopalian. In addition, he was from Alabama. Rabbit said he had never seen anything good come out of Alabama except the highway from Phenix City, and James said they even had a statue of a heathen god outside Birmingham. To this Ed retorted that at least they didn't have so many Baptists in Alabama they had to index them, and that Alabama had once been part of Georgia until it had the good sense to change it.

"Go beat ya meat, Eulenfeld," he said, and to Rabbit, "Better get your silk stockings on, Sis; it's time for supper."

It was fast company in that room, and Porter loved it. Ed Sturgis was so tall that he automatically ducked going through doorways, but even so his arms, legs, and neck were disproportionately long for his body. There was a fury to his intelligence, a compassion in his sharp humor, a loneliness in his searching eyes that set him apart. Porter had been mightily impressed with *Look Homeward, Angel,* and there was something about Ed that embodied Eugene Gant. He feared Ed's scorn but felt warmed by his derisive and cuttingly humorous sallies. Ed had a hunger for knowledge that matched Porter's own and a three-year head start on him. It was as challenging for Porter to keep up with him intellectually as it was to match his giant strides when they occasionally walked together.

Ed Sturgis challenged and stimulated Porter Osborne and only rarely made him feel patronized. "Kid, you been rattling on about communes and 'true communism' for two, three weeks now. You ever read *Das Kapital?*"

"Just the title. That was enough to scare me off."

"You ever see a communist? You know what a cell is?"

"It's a unit of life with its own wall and a nucleus, individually distinct and capable of reproducing itself."

"God, kid. What a narrow education you're getting in this crummy town. You wanta go to a communist meeting?"

"By myself? Where? Do I have to join? Do I need to take any money? Is it dangerous?"

"Meet me in front of the Law Building right after supper, and I'll take you with me. We'll walk to town."

"Then that answers one question. I won't need any money."

511

"Don't wear anything red, either. That's a myth."

The wind was not unduly cold, but it was strong enough to swing the nearly bare November limbs in jerking dance across the street lights of Macon. The two students plunged through one tunnel of wind-swept, light-shattered darkness after another, their mood as wild as the weather.

"Will there be any bombs there?"

"No bombs, kid. Just a few daggers and a straight razor here and there."

"Do communists stink? Do they shave?"

"Only when they fart, kid. And they shave occasionally. In spots."

"Where's this meeting going to be?"

"Let's just say it ain't at the Auditorium."

"Where?"

"It's a secret. I'll have to blindfold you and lead you backward three or four blocks before we get there."

"Aw, be serious, Ed. I'm already about half scared and feel like I don't have any business there. Is it true that Karl Marx says religion is the soporific of the masses?"

"Now where'd you hear that?"

"I forgot. Some bull session. Do communists believe in God?"

"Do you?"

"Me? You talking to me?"

"Who the hell else could I be talking to? I don't see anybody else for two blocks."

"Sure, I believe in God. You mighty right I do."

"All the time?"

"Yes, all the time. Every minute of the day."

"Why?"

Porter gave a fast hop to catch up. He did not want to sound young and ignorant before Ed, but this was beyond flippancy. "Why? What kind of question is that? Because I can't help it. He's there. All the time. All around. I've sat down and deliberately tried to believe there's no God. To pretend He doesn't exist. It's impossible. It's like trying to pretend there's no earth. Or stars, or moon, or sun, or trees. There's got to be a focal point, a reason that keeps the whole world from flying apart."

"You believe that strong, huh?"

"Yes, I do. I'd go crazy if I thought there were no God. Nothing would make sense. Or have any meaning. Or be beautiful."

"What about sin?"

"Aw, come on, Ed. We ain't talking about sin. We're talking about God. Sin's His problem. It makes my head swim. And we're talking about communists. Will there be any Russians there tonight?"

"Old Ivan Bittatitsoff may show up, but I ain't looking for any grand duchess in disguise."

"Aw, Ed, be serious. Are you a communist?"

"No."

"Then why do you go to their meetings?"

"I like new ideas, kid. And new people."

"Will the communists like me, Ed?"

"Probably not. Most of them are non-fraternity men, I think."

"Aw, crap. Ed, do *you* believe in God? ... Ed?"

"I heard you. Sometimes, kid. I think He's a real pisser, but sometimes I do. In spite of myself."

He increased his stride and pace, and Porter had to trot. Conversation became impossible. They traversed Cherry Street, Walnut, Mulberry. They hastened through darkened alleys Porter had never known existed. They went through the depot, for no reason at all that he could discover. They tramped by darkened, monolithic warehouses, brooding and vaguely threatening. They turned sharp corners into gusting roads of wind, and they turned others to be lulled by quiet backwaters of stillness. At the end of an hour and a half, Porter was completely out of breath.

"Ed, where is that damn meeting? I'm completely lost if you're worrying about me ever finding the place again."

"The meeting's been canceled, kid."

"How do you know? We haven't spoken to a living soul. And I haven't seen any sign posted anywhere. When did you decide the meeting was canceled?"

"Oh, about an hour ago, kid."

"You decided I was too young to go, didn't you? Too green."

"Nah. You green, kid? A sophisticated KA outcast like you? Don't you believe it. I just decided I didn't want to go. I've learned all

I want to from that bunch."

"Well, why have you walked my ass off?"

"I love wild weather and wild nights. And walking in rain and wind. And you're a good walker. Let's go down to the river."

On the bridge with their backs turned to the stinging gusts of fine mist, they leaned on the balustrade and studied the water below. The muddy Ocmulgee was transformed tonight into an inky torrent, its surface riffled by the wind of early winter. The river was mysterious, filled with a purpose of its own. Ed looked at Porter.

"Amalita Hunt says you know a lot of poetry."

"She does?"

"Let me hear you recite one that fits this moment and this place."

"I only recite poetry for girls. Fellows think you're a sissy if you recite a poem."

"Oh, bullshit, Osborne. Don't you know one?"

"Sure. What about this? It's called 'God's World.' " Porter began the poem with all the feeling he could muster.

"Oh, world, I cannot hold thee close enough!
Thy winds, thy wide grey skies!
Thy mists, that roll and rise!
Thy woods, this autumn day, that ache and sag
And all but cry with colour! That gaunt crag
To crush! To lift the lean of that black bluff!
World, World, I cannot get thee close enough!"

"OK. That's good. That's Millay. Right? Well, I've got you beat. In spades. Let me give you this. This is a man's poem.

I ride the great black horses of my heart
With reins of steel across their flying hair;
So slow are they to halt, so swift to start,
The stormy-breasted stallions of despair.
Dark as the night and fretful as the air,
Fleeter than hounds that go with bellies thinned —
My wrists of all their strength have none to spare
When those black hunters lean against the wind.

What if the sudden thunder of their feet
Wakes like a dream some farmer from his rest?
Dreams had I too, farmer, before these fleet
Steeds of the night had broken from their nest.
Their weary flanks are green and white with foam.
Sleep, brother, sleep; I bring my horses home."

There was a long stretch of silence. An infrequent automobile made patterns in the night with its headlights. Below them, during occasional respite from the fiercely blowing wind, the whisper of the river could be heard. It spoke to Porter of unswerving purpose, its deep progress serenely unmarred by the bluster of wind and noise. It was steady beneath the tumultuous events that occurred in the blustering air above; it betokened response to challenge and undeterred resolution.

Porter compared the river to his own life. He thought of many things that had happened since he came to Willingham, but the undeterred flow of the current below promised constancy and continuity. The river carried Vashti. And Tiny. And Amalita. And maybe Mrs. Capulet. The horses of his heart, like the wild night around him, were as stormy-breasted as any he knew, but the whisper of the river promised he could tame them. Maybe. He felt comforted.

"Gosh, Ed, that's beautiful. Thanks. Who wrote it?"

"A guy named Robert Nathan. About ten years ago."

"When did you learn it?"

"About a hundred years or so ago, kid."

There was a pause. Porter had a new thought and spoke with excitement. "Ed, you know this is a crazy feeling, but that river is meaningful. It seems so quiet but it's really important. More so than all the fury going on above it. It makes you think the sleep after the ride is better than the dreams on the horses. Ed, maybe this is Alph, the Sacred River!"

"That does it. Time to go! Christamighty, kid. That's just the Ocmulgee, and there ain't no caverns measureless to man down there. It's headed for South Georgia and not some sunless sea. I'm about to freeze. Let's see if you can keep up on the way back to Willingham."

* * * *

Within the next few days, Porter received an invitation for an interview at Emory. He had an appointment in the Anatomy Building at two o'clock on Wednesday before Thanksgiving. His friends from Law School took notice of the upcoming event.

"Well, I guess you'll be above us after such a prestigious adventure."

"Hurry and get your M.D. so I can sue you. I need the money."

"You going to a real live med school? Bring me back a little morphine, kid. I've always wanted to try some."

Porter made inquiries, but no one at Willingham had any information about how interviews were conducted at Emory Medical School. He decided there was nothing to study in preparation and consoled himself with sporadic little prayers on the early bus to Atlanta. At Five Points he caught a street car labeled "Emory-Druid Hills," aware that he was all alone in a very big city. He thrilled to the rocking motion, the rattle and clang of the unyielding conveyance, vibrations from the iron wheels and tracks causing a faint shimmer to his vision. He imagined he was ensconced within the carapace of a great iron grasshopper and felt far removed from the familiarity of Macon and Willingham. Atlanta was grand, but the homes of Druid Hills were both grand and beautiful. At his stop, Porter asked directions from a student hurrying along to his holiday, and he arrived for the appointment thirty minutes early.

Everything at Emory University was built of pink and white marble squares and roofed with terra-cotta tiles, enough to impress someone of more experience than a farm boy from Brewton County. Porter found the Anatomy Building, twin to another marble rectangle facing it that was labeled Physiology. These two buildings comprised the medical school at Emory University. In toto. The rest of it, he learned later, consisted of the sprawling brick piles of Grady Memorial Hospital in downtown Atlanta, its facilities for blacks connected with those for whites only by a tunnel beneath the street.

He found the office he sought and was greeted by a young woman with a black pageboy bob. "Oh, yes. You're Porter Osborne?

516

We're expecting you. My name's Peg Rogers. I'm the secretary and general flunky around this place. I mean, I really have a job trying to keep things going around here and all these people in line. I'm sorry there are no students to show you around, but everybody's gone for Thanksgiving."

Porter studied her and decided that her superb figure more than compensated for the row of tiny black hairs, faint but obvious, on her upper lip. "That's all right. I'm a little early. I hope that's no inconvenience. I can wait outside if you like."

"Oh, no. I believe Dr. House was supposed to meet with you, but he's not here right now. Let me check and see if somebody else can see you. If you come to Emory, you'll find out I look after my boys. I love all the med students, but the freshmen are closest to me. I love to go to their dances."

As she passed, Porter pretended to be unaware of her brown wool skirt and matching cashmere sweater. The sleeves were pushed halfway up her arms. He wondered if he stood in the presence of a fabled Atlanta Pink. Maybe he finally had met one. Not bad, he thought, as he watched the active skirt disappear up the stairs, but she couldn't hold a candle to Sybil Swygert.

She called to him moments later. "Come on up. Everybody's glad you're early. You're helping all of us's schedules. Somebody's going to see you right now. Over there. Just go to the end of the hall and turn left. It's the office sort of behind everything. The one with the door open."

She gave him a brief smile, brightly red and white, and a little pat on his shoulder. "Good luck."

He was acutely conscious of the odor on second floor. It was demanding. It hung in the corridor. Heavy. Still. Thick. He recognized the stinging staleness of formaldehyde from his days with the cats of Willingham, but there was a mysterious sweetness intermingled here that was cloying, and one automatically knew it would permeate clothing and cling to hair. It smells almost greasy, he thought, but that's silly. Dr. Minor would get me for mixing metaphors; odors can't be greasy. He peered around the open door and knocked on the wall.

Porter had seen some offices in his day and some of them had been impressively cluttered, but he had never seen one like this.

What he assumed must be a desk was against the left wall, totally obscured and mounded over with books, papers, and stained lab coats. All along the right wall, higher than waist level, extended a shelf, obviously added at the whim of its owner. Its surface was obliterated by more books and papers. On one corner of the shelf stood a hot plate, a coffee pot, and a half-empty bottle of buttermilk, its long glass neck mapped with tapering rivulets like a sand spit drying after a rain. Scattered the length of the shelf were several bones, varnished and presumably human. They had little numbers painted in strategic spots with India ink. Occasionally the margin of a soiled plate showed from beneath the litter. In the window ledge above the shelf, a grinning skull lay askew, sharing space with two cracked coffee mugs. This, thought Porter, is not an office; it's a den, a warren, a cave. This is Emory?

Its resident did nothing to soften the impression. He sat on a tall stool facing the door, grinning incessantly with the widest set of false teeth Porter had ever seen. He flaunted a thatch of iron-gray hair bursting haphazardly in untrained defiance, as thick and coarse as a doormat. His heavy brows pushed back against steel-rimmed spectacles. He had a gray mustache, close-trimmed as privet hedge, just as dense and thick, but it ended on either side before it reached the edges of the grinning teeth. Although he wore a necktie and a long white laboratory coat, Porter felt sure he was a slave. It was obvious that whoever ran the place never permitted this creature, whatever his nefarious duties, to leave this particular room. Porter was positive that if he allowed his glance to stray, he would discover leg irons with a loose chain shackling the man to the radiator.

He steadfastly looked into eyes of chalcedony and matched the grin with one of his own. "Hello, sir. I'm Porter Osborne. From Willingham."

The voice was unexpectedly soft. Almost silky. "Hello, Osborne. I'm Dr. Blinco. Have a seat and tell me about yourself."

The only available seat was another stool near the window ledge. Porter clambered up, trying to avoid the tilted grin of the skull and also not be mesmerized by the wide, bright grin of Dr. Blinco. It is difficult to perch atop a stool in anything but total relaxation, and Porter settled comfortably there. "What do you want to know, sir?"

"Oh, what your favorite subjects are, why you want to be a

doctor, are there any doctors in your family, why you made a D your first quarter of chemistry. Things like that."

Dr. Blinco was a very attentive listener with no compulsion whatever to interrupt, and Porter chattered busily away.

"What do you think of Emory, Osborne?"

"Well, it's a lot bigger than Willingham, sir, and they sure have a lot of marble around here. My philosophy professor says it's not buildings that make a good school, though, but the interaction between good students and dedicated teachers."

"What do you think of the war, Osborne?"

"Well, I guess you'd have to say I'm in favor of it. I'm sure the British and Russians will wind up beating the Germans, especially with us sending them supplies, but I wish they'd hurry and do it. A lot of people think we're going to get in the war, but I don't."

"Why not?"

"Well, first of all, it's a European fracas. My father thinks the Germans are going to talk the Japanese into invading Russia from the other side, but I don't. Russians historically defeat anybody who invades them just by letting them wear themselves out. After all, Napoleon was stronger for his day than Hitler is now. Then, too, we have a professor at Willingham who says that down through history things have been gradually getting better and that the will of God for good slowly prevails. If the United States got in this war, things would suddenly get a whole lot worse, and I can't see the first thing good about it. It would be Armageddon."

"This professor must be a pretty strong personality. What does he teach?"

"English."

"I see. What will you do if the United States does get in the war?"

"Oh, I'll go, Dr. Blinco. Osbornes always jump up and go. Usually as officers."

"What are your hobbies, Osborne?"

"Sir?"

"Your hobbies. What are they?"

Porter thought for a moment. "Well, I guess I don't have any, sir. I don't build things or collect stamps or play any sport. I don't have any hobbies."

"What do you do for fun? For relaxation?"

"Well, I like to read. And I like to watch a lot, I guess."

"Watch what?"

"Everything, Dr. Blinco. Trees, fields, birds, anything around me. But now that you bring it up, mostly people. I like to watch them and try to figure out where they came from and what they're liable to do and how much they're lying when they talk and how much they know about things and how they managed to know more than I do and things like that. People are more entertaining than anything in the world. And more complicated. You can learn a lot just watching them."

"Well, Osborne, I guess we can let you go now. Thanks for coming by. We'll let you hear something soon. Do you have any questions before you leave?"

"Just one, sir. What is that odor?"

"What odor?"

"Sir?"

"Osborne, I have no sense of smell. Some say that's caused by prolonged exposure to formaldehyde over the years, others from a case of flu I had. At any rate, I have smelled nothing for years. Perhaps you are still smelling the liver and onions I cooked for my lunch. Miss Rogers complains occasionally when I do that. Do you have any other questions?"

"No, sir."

"In that case, you may go. We'll be in touch with you."

"Thank you, Dr. Blinco. I've surely enjoyed meeting you. You tell Dr. House that you make a good ambassador of Emory in his absence and he should be proud of you."

"Dr. House?"

"Yes, sir. Miss Rogers said he was supposed to meet me but had been detained."

"Good-bye, Osborne."

"Good-bye, Dr. Blinco. I'm sorry about your nose."

Porter stopped briefly at the first floor office and thanked Peg Rogers.

"How'd it go?"

"Just fine. Tell me, did you go to Washington Seminary? Or maybe NAPS?"

520

"Heavens, no. I'm from a little town in North Carolina."

"Oh. Well, you fooled me. Tell Dr. House I'm sorry I missed him. Hope I see you next fall."

On the front steps he was accosted by a nervous blond youth with reddened face. "You pre-med? You just have an interview?"

"Yes. How did you know?"

"The word's out that this is the first day of interviewing and they're only asking high priority students. I'm so nervous I could die. Where you from? I haven't seen you around Emory."

"I'm from Willingham. There's nothing for you to be nervous about. I didn't get asked any questions about science at all. It wasn't anything you could have prepared for. It was sort of like visiting with an uncle who hadn't seen you since you were a little boy. You from Emory?"

"Yeah. Four years. Straight A's, ATO, Glee Club, Phi Beta Kappa, ODK. The works. And I'm scared to death."

"Relax. There's nothing to be scared of. What does ODK mean?"

"Well, in the college it means you're BMOC, but from where I stand now it doesn't mean a damn thing. I feel like I'm going in the cage with a tiger."

"Naw. A walrus, maybe. Or even a great horned owl. But not a tiger. And it isn't a cage; it's a lair. Dr. House isn't here this afternoon, and a Dr. Blinco is doing his interviews for him."

The boy's face turned crimson, and his eyes flashed. "Dr. Blinco? You're kidding me! Oh, my God! I'll turn to jelly!"

"Naw you won't. He's the nicest, kindest old fellow you'll ever run across. Sort of like Heidi's grandfather."

"You're not from Emory. You don't know! Dr. House is a lab assistant. Dr. Blinco is head of the department and he eats freshman med students alive! He flunks half the class every year. He has a heart of stone. Why, they even say he cooks his own lunch every day right up there next to all those dead bodies. Can you imagine anybody eating around those cadavers? Oh, my God! Thanks for talking to me. Let me go find a restroom."

Porter caught his bus for Brewtonton, and by the time he met his father at the drugstore to begin his Thanksgiving holidays, he was reflective. "You know, Dad, I may apply to Medical College of

Georgia after all. Like a lady at school says it, 'You always need two things on your bow.' "

"She says what? You know, son, you may be right about those Russians. If they can just have the guts to hang on at Leningrad, maybe the Krauts will be whipped."

At school on the Monday after Thanksgiving, Porter Osborne, Jr., received official notification that he had been accepted by the Emory University School of Medicine as a freshman student for the class beginning in September. His heart soared. His spirit sang. His assessment of character had been vindicated, never mind his poor grasp of protocol. Right does triumph over wrong. Virtue may be its own reward, but it also has lovely fringe benefits.

All day he found himself humming "Jesus Answers Prayer." With beautiful nonchalance, stifling a yawn, he tossed his letter of acceptance on Ed Sturgis's desk at supper time. The enthusiastic congratulations of his friends, peppered with sardonic and sarcastic comments, made sweet music in his ears. There was no doubt now that he would be a doctor.

Later that week, he received another letter that made his happiness complete.

Dear Sambo,

How are you this leaves me feeling fine and hoping you are the same. Sit down and rest your feet because this will be a long letter. My fingers will be tired before I finish and so will your but. (Ha.) If you got one yet. (Ha.) I have not wrote in a long time and I will catch you up. A lot has happened to your friend.

I am in Hawaii at a place call Pearl plus my middle name. The U.S. Navy is the best thing going. I have told my mama I am going to be regular Navy and stay in for thirty years. I hope most of it will be right here in Hawaii. Your friend and my friend, Henry Bean, Lt. j.g., got me on the same boat with him. It is the USS Arizona and it is too big to make you believe and got as many folks on it as all of Macon. The chief steward likes me and I am going up he says.

Sambo, this navy is something else. It's full of

yankees so we have not got any niggers. Plenty of coons, jigaboos, jungle bunnies, and spades but no niggers, nigras or darkies. (Ha.) Colored do good in the mess. That's what they call the food on the boat but I say they don't know what mess is if they have not work for Mrs. Raleigh. (Ha.)

Sambo, one of the reasons I am going to stay in the Navy is that I lied to you one time. I told you there was not no West and there was not no nest. You remember that? Well, there is. Sambo, I am in love. It did not take but one movie and two dates before I was crooning in June sweet tune honeymoon and all of that. She was too. Now we talking about that bungalow big enough for two, my baby, big enough for three.

Sambo, her name is Osaki. I call her Sook. She is a Jap, but she says if I don't call her that she won't call me Coon. Then I call her Sook of the South Wind or else Sugar-Sook and she calls me Boston-baby Harbor-honey. Sometimes if I talk smart alex, she call me Mr. Bones Jones and tell me to shut up. We have a lot of fun. She comes almost up to my shoulder but not quite. She is clean and lean like winter woods.

She says she is going to squinch all my children's eyes and I say I am going to frizz all her children's hair and maybe thick they lips. Course she does not know it but I might give one or two of them a extra finger. If you get to Hawaii and see squinch-eyed, frizzy-headed, thick-lip children just follow them home. They will be mine. Sook wants a dozen. Sambo, she is a only child. I told her I like that because I am still right about sister-in-laws, and she said the reason she a only child is her daddy died young and she ain't going to let me off that easy.

We laugh a lot. I have taught her about grits but she have not yet taught me raw fish. I have told her if the Japs would fry their fish their eyes would not squinch. (Ha.)

I might as well tell it all. Sambo, we are getting married. In her church. She has turned into a Presbyterian but her mama has not. Henry Bean, Lt. j.g., is going to stand up with me and my mess steward has promised a cake four feet tall. The wedding will be on the next first Sunday and I will be a changed man. But I will always be your loving friend.

Boston Harbor Jones

P.S. Be sure to write. Sook wants to meet you but we will most likely not ever come to Macon because she would not even be a Jap there.

Tell Mrs. Raleigh my news. The Captain ask who made the hush puppies and the chief steward sent me out from the galley to meet him and he ask my name and where did I learn to cook. I told him in college, sir, and he bragged a plumb sight and said they was the best he ever had eat and he would not forget my name. Of course most people do not ever forget my name but I did not tell him that. It is a good sign when the Captain has your name tied up with good cooking. What if I get a stripe out of Mrs. Raleigh's hush puppies? I would say it is a small world and Mrs. Raleigh would likely say it is a good seed coming home to roost.(Ha.)

Sambo, I am the happiest man in the world. Take care of yourself.

Boston Harbor Jones.

P.S. again. Sook does not like cats.

Porter would have liked to share the letter with Ed Sturgis but did not care to read it in front of all three of his new friends. He was of no mind to hear Boston ridiculed, and he consequently kept it to himself.

James Eulenfeld invited him to ride to Columbus and back on the next Sunday. "Come on and go with me. I'm going to eat with my girlfriend's folks. She's got to leave right after Sunday dinner to go

524

back to Sophie Newcomb, and it's my last chance to see her before Christmas. It's a two-hour drive over there, and I could sure use some company."

"You ought to go, Sambo. James wants to show off how rich he's going to be after he's married."

"Yeah, kid. Rabbit and I can't go, and somebody needs to keep James from sneaking over to Phenix City and catching the clap. Look after him."

Porter enjoyed the ride. James was not as audacious as Rabbit nor as unpredictable and challenging as Ed, but he was steady and sincere. He also must have been a little nervous, for he smoked one Chesterfield after another.

"Sambo, you'll like Hazel. Don't pay any attention to Gosnell and Sturgis about how rich she is. She's a beautiful girl and the sweetest one in the whole world. You'll see. Her father is a little intimidating at first, but he's basically a nice guy. Tell me more about med school."

"There's not all that much to tell. I was surprised to get accepted so fast, and I'm a little scared of going. But then I've always been scared whenever I made a change in my life. I was scared of high school when I graduated from the seventh grade, and I was sure scared of college when I came to Willingham. And now that's about over, and I'm convinced it's the best school in the whole world. Things will work out."

"Sure they will. You'll be a good doctor. And on top of that, you'll get student deferment for four more years. Surely by that time the war will be over and you won't ever have to be drafted."

Sunday dinner with Hazel's family was a rather formal occasion and Porter was on guard about table manners and grammar. Hazel was indeed a lovely person, and he made a mental note to advise Rabbit and Ed that she would be the catch of the year even if she were as impoverished as a goose girl. He visited superficially with her parents for half an hour while she and James made private farewells, after which the two boys took a polite departure.

"I know that couldn't have been a lot of fun for you. Come on

525

and I'll set you up to a movie. I hate Sunday afternoons in Macon, and I don't want to get back there before dark."

When they turned the corner and parked, Porter goggled at the line of men winding down the block. "Golly, James, have you ever seen so many soldiers in your life? We'll never get in that theater."

"Sure we will. They're from Fort Benning and have a Sunday pass. Come on. The line's moving fast."

There was only a scattering of civilians at the movie. The audience was primarily a sea of khaki, uniforms sharply pressed, shoes gleaming, caps tucked neatly under webbed belts. They sat through the newsreel, the latest "Our Gang" short, and settled comfortably into their seats as the MGM lion roared from within its laurel wreath. In the midst of the credits for the feature attraction, the overhead lights came on and the projector flickered and died. A man in a business suit walked to the center of the stage, diminutive in his surroundings but commanding. He raised both hands aloft to silence the protests that had arisen.

"I have been asked to make an important announcement. Quiet, please! I have been asked to make an important announcement! Please! All soldiers in this theater are asked to return immediately to their base! Please! Quiet! All soldiers are to return immediately to Fort Benning. By order of the Commander! The United States has been attacked by enemy war planes and we are at war! The Japanese have just bombed Pearl Harbor!"

A stampede ensued. Soldiers were yelling and cursing and shoving each other in a frantic exodus from the theater. Porter was stunned into immobility. James Eulenfeld leaped to his feet. "Come on, Osborne. Let's get out of here!"

"Why, James? We're not soldiers. We can wait and watch the movie."

"Are you crazy? Let's go!"

They pushed their way through the milling, excited throng on the sidewalk and reached the car. Porter was silent, trying to comprehend what was happening.

James Eulenfeld was babbling. "We're in it! Oh, God, this is terrible! Turn on the radio, Osborne. Where *is* Pearl Harbor, anyhow? Get some news!"

An excited announcer was speaking as rapidly as the man

who had described the burning of the Graf Zeppelin. The Navy was in shambles. The Air Force had been destroyed on the ground. Pearl Harbor was a mass of smoke and flames and explosions. Porter remembered the invasion from Mars a few years earlier and insanely hoped that Orson Welles was loose again.

In the torrent of despairing news, one item caught his ear and seared his consciousness. The U.S.S. Arizona was sunk with nearly all hands on board. His ears roared, his head spun, and he heard nothing else as he struggled to suck air into his chest. He fought to keep from fainting. James reached over and snapped the radio off.

"I can't stand it, Osborne! There go all my plans! I can't get married now! I'll have to go in the Army, and with my luck I'll get killed and never get to marry Hazel and join her daddy's law firm. Why did this have to happen to me? Why don't you pray, Osborne? You're a big one for prayer. You better pray like you've never prayed before."

Porter took a deep breath. "James, I may never pray again in my whole life. What good does it do?"

"Oh, my God! Look at that, will you!" A black cat was slinking across the highway in front of them. With a screech of brakes and a precarious lurch, James spun the automobile in a U-turn. "Damn if I'm going to let that sucker cross my path! We'll find another way out of town. Talk about bad luck! That's all it would take to finish me off."

"James, you're not that superstitious. I'd rather take my chances with a black cat than an automobile wreck. Slow down!"

"Oh, you can sit there and be calm all you want to. You're going to med school! You'll be safe and sound and secure. Lawyers are a dime a dozen and they'll draft me right away. I'm not ready to die! Turn the radio back on and let's find out where Pearl Harbor is. I never heard of it."

"James, I know where Pearl Harbor is. It's in Hawaii."

"Hawaii? What the hell are we doing way out there? Let the Japs have Hawaii. It's not worth dying for."

Porter heard his own voice coming softly from a great distance. "It is, too. There are some people there that I'd die for. Right now."

"You can talk! You won't be going! You'll be in medical school without any interruption in your life at all. Doing exactly what you've been wanting to do all along! I wish I had that option."

"Eulenfeld, you're crazy! Be quiet a minute, will you?"

There was a moment of silence.

Dry-eyed and numb, Porter Osborne, Jr., lifted his chin and squared his shoulders.

"Just fuck it! To hell with med school. It doesn't matter anymore. Give me a goddamned cigarette!"